Traditional Japanese Literature

ABRIDGED EDITION

TRANSLATIONS FROM THE ASIAN CLASSICS

Also by Haruo Shirane

The Bridge of Dreams: A Poetics of The Tale of Genji
Traces of Dreams: Landscape, Cultural Memory, and the Poetry of Bashō
Inventing the Classics: Modernity, National Identity, and Japanese Literature
Early Modern Japanese Literature: An Anthology, 1600–1900
Classical Japanese: A Grammar
Traditional Japanese Literature: An Anthology, Beginnings to 1600
Classical Japanese Reader and Essential Dictionary
Envisioning The Tale of Genji: *Media, Gender, and Cultural Production*
Japan and the Culture of the Four Seasons: Nature, Literature, and the Arts

Traditional Japanese Literature

ABRIDGED EDITION

AN ANTHOLOGY, BEGINNINGS TO 1600

Edited by Haruo Shirane

TRANSLATORS

Sonja Arntzen, Robert Borgen, Karen Brazell, Steven Carter,
Anthony H. Chambers, Anne Commons, Lewis Cook, Torquil Duthie,
Michael Emmerich, Thomas Harper, Mack Horton, Donald Keene,
Laurence Kominz, Herschel Miller, Douglas E. Mills, Jean Moore,
Ivan Morris, Kyoko Nakamura, Jamie Newhard, Donald Philippi,
Edward G. Seidensticker, Haruo Shirane, Virginia Skord,
Jack Stoneman, Royall Tyler, Marian Ury, and Burton Watson

COLUMBIA UNIVERSITY PRESS

NEW YORK

Columbia University Press wishes to express its appreciation for assistance given by the
Pushkin Fund toward the cost of publishing this book.

Columbia University Press
Publishers Since 1893
New York   Chichester, West Sussex
cup.columbia.edu

Library of Congress Cataloging-in-Publication Data
Traditional Japanese literature, abridged edition : an anthology, beginnings
to 1600 / edited by Haruo Shirane.—Abridged ed.
p. cm.—(Translations from the Asian classics)
Includes bibliographical references and index.
ISBN 978-0-231-15730-8 (cloth : acid-free paper)
ISBN 978-0-231-15731-5 (pbk. : acid-free paper)
ISBN 978-0-231-50453-9 (ebook)
1. Japanese literature—To 1600—Translations into English.
I. Shirane, Haruo, 1951–
PL782.E1T733 2012
895.6'08—dc23
2011047618

Columbia University Press books are printed on permanent and durable acid-free paper.
This book is printed on paper with recycled content.

Printed in the United States of America

c 10 9 8 7 6 5 4 3 2 1
p 10 9 8 7 6 5 4 3 2 1

COVER IMAGE: Attributed to Tosa Mitsuyoshi (1539–1613), detail from *Genji monogatari: Kochō*
(*Butterflies*), Momoyama period (1573–1615). Six-panel folding screen: ink, color, and gold on
gilded paper. (By permission of the Mary and Jackson Burke Foundation)

CONTENTS

2. The Heian Period   66

The Emergence of Kana Literature   68

The Rise of Women's Writing   69

Late Heian Kana Histories and Anecdotal Literature   71

Keikai   72

Record of Miraculous Events in Japan (Nihon ryōiki)   72

On the Death Penalty in This Life for an Evil Son Who Tried
to Kill His Mother out of Love for His Wife   73

On the Immediate Reward of Being Saved by Crabs for Saving
the Lives of Crabs and a Frog   75

On Receiving the Immediate Penalty of Violent Death for Collecting
Debts by Force and with High Interest   76

Ono no Komachi   78

Selected Poems   79

Sugawara no Michizane   83

Children   84

Speaking of My Children   85

Career   85

Through the Snow to Morning Duties   85

Professorial Difficulties   86

Exile   87

Seeing the Plum Blossoms When Sentenced to Exile   87

Autumn Night, the Fifteenth Day of the Ninth Month   88

In Exile, Spring Snow   88

Kokinshū (Collection of Ancient and Modern Poems)   89

The Kana Preface   92

Spring   92

Summer   97

Autumn   98

Travel   104

Love   105

ACKNOWLEDGMENTS

This abridged edition of *Traditional Japanese Literature: An Anthology, Beginnings to 1600*, is the companion volume to the abridged *Early Modern Japanese Literature: An Anthology, 1600–1900*. Like the *Early Modern* volume, this one was organized and written with several objectives. First was the need to select representative texts and subtexts to present a broader and more complex view of Japanese literature without sacrificing the familiar texts. Throughout the book, in the introductions to each text, in the special introductions to genres and periods, and in the notes and commentaries, I have provided sociohistorical, religious, cultural, and literary contexts.

Most of the texts here have been translated for the first time, and many of the familiar texts have been retranslated specifically for this anthology. I strongly believe in the need for multiple translators, who can bring different voices to the texts. The quality and accuracy of the translations, the notes, and commentary are, of course, my responsibility, and unless otherwise noted, the introductions and commentary were written by me.

I am indebted to the many scholars from North America and Japan who aided me in countless ways. I owe special thanks to Lewis Cook, who helped with the seemingly endless editing and corrections. I am grateful to Sonja Arntzen, Steven Carter, Wiebke Deneke, James Dobbins, Fujii Sadakazu, Mack Horton, Hyōdo Hiromi, Ii Haruki, Imai Masaharu, Kawahira Hitoshi, Donald Keene, Komine Yasuaki, Lawrence Kominz, Kōnoshi Takamitsu, David Lurie, Matsuoka

Shinpei, Okuda Isao, Edward Seidensticker, Shinada Yoshikazu, Tomi Suzuki, Mari Takamatsu, Paul Varley, Burton Watson, Michael Watson, and Yamanaka Reiko. My special thanks to Anne Commons, Torquil Duthie, Linda Feng, Naomi Fukumori, Marco Gottardo, Satoko Naito, Jamie Newhard, Saeko Shibayama, Jack Stoneman, and Akiko Takeuchi. I want to thank the editorial director of Columbia University Press, Jennifer Crewe, who initiated the project, and Irene Pavitt, who did a great job for me at the press.

HISTORICAL PERIODS AND KEY TERMS

HISTORICAL PERIODS

Ancient (to 784)

Jōmon	10,000–300 B.C.E.
Yayoi	300 B.C.E.–300 C.E.
Tomb	300–552
Asuka	552–710
Jinshin war	672
Nara	710–784

Heian (794–1185)

Heian	794–1185

Medieval (1185–1600)

Kamakura	1183–1333
Fall of the Heike	1185
Jōkyū rebellion	1221
Kenmu restoration	1333–1336

Northern and Southern Courts (Nanboku-chō)	1336–1392
Muromachi	1392–1573
Ōnin war	1467–1477
Warring States (Sengoku)	1467–1573
Azuchi–Momoyama	1573–1598
Battle of Sekigahara	1600

Early Modern and Modern (1600–Present)

Edo (Tokugawa)	1600–1867
Meiji	1868–1912

KEY TERMS AND GENRES

Japanese	*English*
chōka	long poem
engi-mono	story of temple-shrine origins
fudoki	provincial gazetteer
gunki-mono	warrior tale
haikai	popular linked verse
hōgo	vernacular Buddhist literature
imayō	modern-style song
jōruri	puppet theater
kagami-mono	vernacular history (mirror piece)
kanbun	Chinese prose (written by Japanese)
kangaku	Chinese studies
kanshi	Chinese poetry (written by Japanese)
katari-mono	orally recited narrative
kayō	song
kikōbun	travel literature
kodai kayō	ancient song
kouta	little song
kyōgen	comic theater
monogatari	vernacular tale
nō	nō drama
norito	prayer to the gods
otogi-zōshi	Muromachi tale
renga	classical linked verse
sarugaku	comic mime and skits
sekkyōbushi	sermon ballad
setsuwa	anecdote

tanka	short poem (thirty-one syllables), same as *waka*
uta-awase	poetry match
uta-monogatari	poem tale
utamakura	place with poetic associations
waka	classical poem (thirty-one syllables)
wasan	Buddhist hymns in Japanese
zuihitsu	essay, pensée, miscellany

RANKS, TITLES, AND OFFICES

Japanese	*English*
sesshō	regent
kanpaku	regent (for adult emperor)
daijō daijin	prime minister
sadaijin	minister of the left
udaijin	minister of the right
naidaijin	palace minister
daijōkan	council of state
naka no kanpaku	middle regent
nyōgo	high imperial consort
kōi	lesser imperial consort
chūgū	empress
dainagon	senior counselor
chūnagon	middle counselor
shōnagon	junior counselor
sangi	consultant
taishō (daishō)	major captain
chūjō	middle captain
shōshō	lesser captain
kami	governor
kugyō	senior noble
tenjōbito	courtier (literally, "hall person")
daiben	major controller
chūben	middle controller
shōben	lesser controller
jige	gentlemen of low rank
zuryō	provincial governor

JAPANESE NAMES AND JAPANESE PRONUNCIATION

All Japanese names are given in the normal Japanese order, surname first. Up through the Kamakura period, the surname and the first name often were linked by the attributive particle *no*, as in Fujiwara *no* Shunzei. Fujiwara is the surname and Shunzei the given name. In addition, premodern writers are often referred to by their given name. Thus, one would say "a poem by Shunzei." Each syllable in Japanese is distinct, with no accent, and each vowel sounds similar to that in Italian. Vowels with macrons (long mark) over them are held twice as long as the unmarked vowels.

ABBREVIATIONS OF MODERNS SERIAL EDITIONS

CZS	*Chūsei zenke no shisō*, vol. 16 of *Nihon shisō taikei* (Tokyo: Iwanami shoten, 1972)
KNKB	*Kanshō Nihon koten bungaku*, 35 vols. (Tokyo: Kadokawa shoten,. 1977–1978)
NKBT	*Nihon koten bungaku taikei*, 102 vols. (Tokyo: Iwanami shoten, 1957–1968)
NKBZ	*Nihon koten bungaku zenshū*, 60 vols. (Tokyo: Shōgakukan, 1970–1976)
SNKBT	*Shin Nihon koten bungaku taikei* (Tokyo: Iwanami shoten, 1989–)
SNKBZ	*Shin Nihon koten bungaku zenshū* (Tokyo: Shōgakukan, 1994–)
SNKS	*Shin Nihon koten shūsei*, 79 vols. (Tokyo: Shinchōsha, 1976–1989)

Citations are followed by an abbreviation of the series title, the volume number, and the page. For example, NKBZ 51:525 refers to page 525 of volume 51 of *Nihon koten bungaku zenshū*.

Traditional Japanese Literature

ABRIDGED EDITION

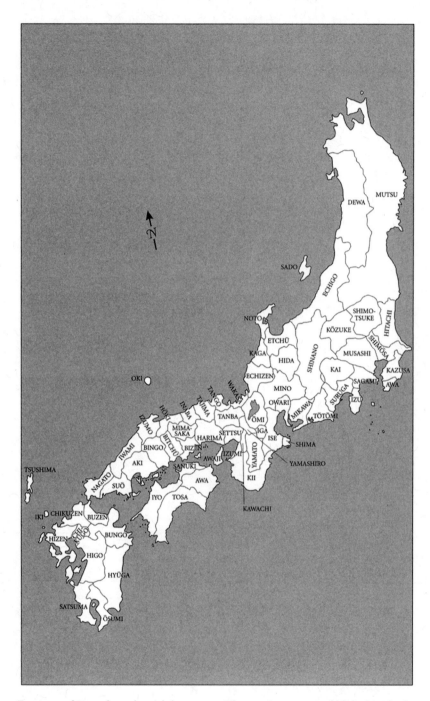

Provinces of Japan from the eighth century. (The provinces were established in the late seventh and eighth centuries, and it now is standard practice to use retrospectively the same names for the regions that they later represented.)

INTRODUCTION

In this anthology, each chapter or period (Ancient, Heian, Kamakura, and Muromachi) begins with a brief historical overview of the major political, social, and economic changes, followed by shorter introductions to authors and genres, and then brief introductions to specific texts. Whenever possible, the texts are grouped by genre. But because some of the genres (such as *waka*, *monogatari*, *setsuwa*, and warrior tales) span many centuries, they are arranged not by genre but chronologically, across various periods. Readers are thus urged to read by both genre and period. The following introduction highlights some of the recurrent issues spanning these different historical periods and genres.

LANGUAGE AND WRITING

The oldest extant literary and historical texts in Japan date back to the beginning of the eighth century. The *Kojiki* (*Record of Ancient Matters*, 712) and *Nihon shoki* (*Chronicles of Japan*, 720) were written in order to legitimize the new state order by providing an account of how the world came into being and by tracing the origins of the emperor to the age of the gods. Anthologies of Japanese poetry began to be compiled in the late seventh century, and the *Man'yōshū* (*Collection of Myriad Leaves*), an encyclopedic collection of poetry, was compiled

throughout the eighth century. Although a long tradition of songs existed before the *Man'yōshū*, it was only after the Chinese system of graphs was imported
and adapted to record Japanese words that written literature came into being. In
fact, Chinese became the official language of government and religion, and the
most esteemed literary genres in the eight century were, as in China, histories,
religious-philosophical writings, and poetry. Whereas the *Kojiki* and *Nihon shoki*
are written almost entirely in Chinese, the *Man'yōshū* uses Chinese graphs pho-
netically to record poetry composed in Japanese. With the notable exception of
folk songs adapted in the *Man'yōshū*, the literature of the early period was written
by the nobility, particularly those close to the emperor and the imperial court,
which held the reins of power through both the Nara and the Heian periods.

A major turning point in the history of Japanese literature came in the late
ninth century with the emergence of *kana*, the native phonetic syllabary, which
led to the first great flowering of vernacular literature, including the *Kokinshū*
(*Collection of Ancient and Modern Poems*, ca. 905); *The Tales of Ise*; *Kagerō Diary* by the Mother of Michitsuna; Sei Shōnagon's *Pillow Book*; Murasaki Shikibu's *The Tale of Genji*; and *Sarashina Diary* by the Daughter of Takasue. The high
quality of this vernacular literature, much of it by women writers of the middle
level of the aristocracy, was one reason why this period was later (in the medieval period) canonized as the "classical period," becoming the linguistic model
for written Japanese for the next thousand years.

The main element of literary continuity between the ancient period and the
Heian period is Japanese poetry, the thirty-one-syllable *waka* or *uta*, which was
composed extensively in the seventh and eighth centuries and became even
more important in the tenth and eleventh centuries. Indeed, in Heian aristocratic society it was impossible to function, in either public or private, without
the ability to compose waka. Furthermore, a significant number of literary diaries (*nikki*) and poem tales (*uta monogatari*) in the Heian period grew out of
private collections of poems that had been exchanged between the author and
his or her acquaintances. The Kana Preface to the *Kokinshū*, the first imperial
collection of waka, reminds its readers that giving voice to one's feelings through
poetry is an inevitable response to expèriences of seasonal changes and human
events. Much of the kana literature by women, which blossomed in the mid-
Heian period, is highly lyrical, with stress on emotions and private thoughts,
often encapsulated in the waka that emerge at climactic moments in the narrative. *The Tale of Genji*, with more than eight hundred poems, is a good example
of this phenomenon.

POWER AND COURTSHIP

From its beginning at the imperial court, Japanese poetry, which became the
central genre in the premodern period, had both a public, political role, often

in the ritual affirmation of power, and a private, social role, as an intimate form of dialogue and the primary vehicle for courtship between the sexes. Although most of the poems in the *Kokinshū* were drawn from private exchanges and collections, the anthology was commissioned by the emperor and served as a whole to enhance the cultural authority and aura of the throne. The private, dialogic function of poetry, which resulted in the Heian literary diaries, should thus be distinguished from its ritualistic, public functions in the form of anthologies.

The early chronicles, such as the *Nihon shoki* and *Kojiki*, which were commissioned by the Yamato court in the early eighth century at a critical period in nation-state building, and the first two volumes of the *Man'yōshū* affirmed the power and authority of the head of the Yamato clan, which became the imperial household. By contrast, the vernacular *monogatari* in the tenth and eleventh centuries represent alternative voices, of those left out of power. The function of literary culture in the Heian period, particularly after the tenth and eleventh centuries, is very different from that of the ancient period. The center of political power had shifted from sovereigns to regents, from the throne to commoner clans (primarily the Fujiwara), who controlled the throne through marital politics. In the sixth and seventh centuries, the emperor ruled directly and administered through the *daijōkan* (state ministries), but starting in the Heian period, a division gradually formed between the imperial palace and the state ministries. New power also devolved to the provincial governors, over whom the state ministries had increasingly less control.

The Heian vernacular monogatari came from the hands of the provincial governor class (who had economic stability but were one step removed from the upper echelons of power) and, as a consequence, is a much more private genre than the early chronicles and court poetry (such as Hitomaro's *chōka*, or long poems) found in the first two volumes of the *Man'yōshū*. The Heian monogatari continued to deal with the nobility and the emperor, and in that sense they maintained the aristocratic, court culture of the Nara period. But in contrast to the *Kojiki* and *Nihon shoki* and the early volumes of the *Man'yōshū*, which enforce the authority, power, and divinity of the sovereign and his or her surrogates, the protagonists of the monogatari violate the sociopolitical order and relativize the authority of the throne. The protagonists of *The Tales of Ise* and *The Tale of Genji* belong to clans (the Ariwara and the Genji) that were ousted. Instead of affirming the dominant clan (the northern branch of the Fujiwara), *The Tales of Ise*, for example, reveals deep sympathy for those (such as the clan of Ariwara Narihira, the protagonist) who have been defeated by or fallen into the shadow of the Fujiwara.

One consequence of being at a slight remove from the center of power is that the Heian monogatari offer an alternative voice. *The Tale of Genji*, for example, glorifies court culture and the position of the emperor who stood at its center, harking back to a time, a century earlier, when the sovereign had direct power, as opposed to the regency system, in which the emperor was a puppet of his

Fujiwara relatives. At the same time, however, *The Tale of Genji*, which depicts an illegitimate son on the throne, seriously undermines the myth of direct and unbroken descent from the gods that became so important in later, twentieth-century pre–World War II discourse. The sympathy for the political losers and the expression of alternative voices are a major feature of the monogatari genre and continue into the medieval period with, for example, *The Tales of the Heike*, a warrior tale that portrays the fall of the house of the Heike (Taira), and the *Clear Mirror* (*Masukagami*), one of the four historical "mirrors" or chronicles of political leaders, which looks back nostalgically to the exiled emperors GoToba and GoDaigo at a time when the imperial court was on the verge of extinction. Other monogatari and historical chronicles, however, glorify those who achieved power. *A Tale of Flowering Fortunes* (*Eiga monogatari*) and *The Great Mirror* (*Ōkagami*), both written in the late Heian period, portray the life and political rise of Fujiwara no Michinaga, the most powerful regent in the Heian period.

LOSS AND INTEGRATION

Cultural forms and rituals provide a general model for social behavior, one that also takes into account possible threats and dangers. The evil-stepmother tale, which was the fundamental paradigm of the monogatari in the tenth century, is one such model of loss and reintegration. The oppressive evil stepmother represents a trial that the unprotected stepdaughter must endure and overcome if she is to become an adult member of the community. The heroine overcomes this threat, the evil characters are punished and driven out, and the cultural norms and values are articulated and reinforced. The exile of the young noble, another familiar plot pattern in both early-Nara-period myths and the Heian monogatari, is the male version of the evil-stepmother tale. A young god or aristocrat who has committed a transgression or sin undergoes a severe trial in a distant and hostile land. In the process, the young man proves his mettle, meets a woman, and acquires the power necessary to become a leader and hero. A good example is the myth of "The Luck of the Sea and the Luck of the Mountain," one of the key stories in the eighth-century *Kojiki*. In *The Tale of Genji*, the hero likewise commits a sin (having a secret son by Fujitsubo, the consort of his father, the emperor). He is exiled to Suma, where he meets a woman who eventually bears his only daughter, a key to his subsequent political success. The exile thereby functions as a means of atonement and a ritualistic coming of age.

SOCIALITY

One of the primary functions of culture is the cultivation of "sociality," the capacity for complex social behavior. Sociality is marked by the ability to be mutually responsive, to read the minds of others, and to be able to understand such notions as politeness and rudeness. Sociality includes knowing how to greet, part, and attend to the "face" of the other. Sociality of this type assumes that the community finds it valuable to invest time and energy not only in mastering the basic social rules but also in appreciating innovative variations and changes, which require judgment and imagination and distinguish between the novice and the sophisticate. Heian aristocratic vernacular texts frequently had this role of developing, embodying, and transmitting sociality. At the lower social end, one of the obvious purposes of anecdotal collections such as the *Tales of Times Now Past* (*Konjaku monogatari shū*) was to teach commoners how to behave, what to do (act filial, pay respect to Buddhist priests, and so on), and what not to do (not steal, lie, murder, and so on) by revealing the consequences of certain actions. More sophisticated examples are *The Pillow Book* (*Makura no sōshi*) and *The Tale of Genji* (*Genji monogatari*), which are concerned with sociality at the highest levels of aristocratic society. Much of *The Pillow Book* is concerned with aesthetics, not as some objective standard of beauty, but as part of sociality, as the fine appreciation of the nuances of social response and interaction. The same is true in the first part of *The Tale of Genji*, in which superior social ability becomes an admired quality of the hero and heroines. The humor often derives from those characters (such as Suetsumuhana, the red-nosed lady) who unwittingly fail to understand those complex rules of behavior.

Literary texts explore the complex nature of sociality and offer a wider range of possibilities and perspectives than could normally be experienced firsthand. This particular cultural function can be found in a range of Heian genres, from vernacular literary diaries (such as *Tosa Diary*, *Kagerō Diary*, and *Sarashina Diary*) to poem tales (such as *The Tales of Ise*), which often focus on the ability to compose waka, one of the key aspects of aristocratic sociality. Some of the women's diaries may in fact have been written for the authors' daughters as a way of showing them how to both survive and function properly in society. (To judge these texts solely on modern "literary" grounds—according to modern standards of structural unity, plot, and character development or for their mimetic or expressive qualities—would thus miss one of their main cultural functions.)

CONDENSATION AND INTERTEXTUALITY

Many traditional Japanese literary and aesthetic forms, particularly those that stress brevity, condensation, and overtones, assume an intimate audience. The paring down of form and expression occurs in a wide variety of forms: poetry, nō drama, landscape gardening, bonsai, tea ceremony, and ink painting, to mention only the most obvious. Historically, Japanese poetry evolved from the *chōka* (literally, "long poem"), which is found in the early *Man'yōshū*; to the thirty-one-syllable waka, the central form of the *Kokinshū* and the Heian period; to linked verse in the medieval period; and, finally, in the Tokugawa (or Edo) period, to the seventeen-syllable *hokku*, later called *haiku*, probably the shortest poetic form in world literature.

A similar condensation of form can be found in nō drama. As it evolved under Zeami (1363?–1443?), the greatest nō playwright, nō was a drama of elegance, restraint, and suggestion. Human actions were reduced to the bare essentials, to highly symbolic movements such as tilting the mask to express joy or sweeping the hand to represent weeping. In A *Mirror Held to the Flower* (*Kakyō*), Zeami writes that "if what the actor feels in the heart is ten, what appears in movement should be seven." He stresses that the point at which physical movement becomes minute and then finally stops is the point of greatest intensity. The physical and visual restrictions—the fixed mask, the slow body movement, the almost complete absence of props or scenery—create a drama that must occur as much in the mind of the audience as on the stage.

In *Essays in Idleness* (*Tsurezuregusa*, 1329–1333), often considered the ultimate compendium of Heian court aesthetics, the aristocrat-priest Kenkō argues that what is not stated, cannot be seen by the eyes, and is incomplete in expression is more moving, alluring, and memorable than what is directly presented. Since ancient times, the Japanese have prized the social capacity for indirection and suggestion. Poetry was recognized for its overtones, connotations, and subtle allegory and metaphor rather than for what it actually stated. In large part, this particular literary and social mode depends on a close bond between the composer and reader, with their common body of cultural knowledge, which was absorbed through literary texts.

ATTACHMENT AND DETACHMENT

The three primary ideological centers in the premodern period were Buddhism, Confucianism, and native beliefs that were later called Shinto. Buddhism and Confucianism were imported from the continent in the ancient period. Buddhism stressed issues of individual salvation, suffering, and protection from various dangers. Confucianism became the guide for ethical behavior and social and political relations, based largely on the model of the family and filial piety. Finally, the local folk beliefs focused on fertility, nature, ancestral worship, purification, and pollution. Dramatic conflict in Japanese literary texts often derives from the interaction among these different ideologies. Much of Japanese literature from the Nara through the medieval era stands in a larger Buddhist context that regards excessive attachments—especially family bonds and the deep emotions of love—as a serious deterrent to individual salvation, particularly in a world in which all things are viewed as impermanent. Each individual is bound to a cycle of life and death, to a world of suffering and illusory attachment, until he or she achieves salvation.

By the mid-Heian period, the Japanese believed that strong attachments, particularly at the point of death, would impede the soul's progress to the next world, which, it was hoped, would be the Pure Land, or Western Paradise. In a typical nō play by Zeami, the protagonist is caught in one of the lower realms— often as a wandering ghost or a person suffering in hell—as a result of some deep attachment or resentment. For the warrior, the attachment is often the bitterness or ignominy of defeat; for women, jealousy or the failure of love; and for old men, the impotence of age. In Zeami's "dream plays," such as the warrior play *Atsumori*, in which the protagonist appears in the dream of the traveling monk (the *waki*), the protagonist cathartically reenacts or recounts the source of his attachment to the dreaming priest, who offers prayers for his salvation and spiritual release.

Except for didactic literature composed by Buddhist priests, Heian vernacular fiction and women's diaries such as *The Tale of Genji* and *Sarashina Diary* usually take a highly ambivalent view of Buddhist ideals, focusing on the difficulty of attaining detachment in a world of passion and natural beauty. Indeed, at the heart of Japanese aristocratic literature, particularly from the mid-Heian period onward, lies the conflict between Buddhistic aspirations of selflessness (which eventually merged with samurai ideals in the medieval period) and the sensual, aesthetic, and emotional orientation of early native beliefs. In *An Account of a Ten-Foot-Square Hut* (*Hōjōki*, thirteenth century), the waka poet Kamo no Chōmei, confronted with the world of suffering and impermanence— natural disasters, famine, the destruction of the capital—retreats to a small hut outside the capital. In the process of preparing for rebirth in the Pure Land, however, he becomes attached to the tranquillity and pleasures of his rustic retreat and thereupon fears that his attachment to nature and to writing will hinder his salvation.

Conflict tends to be internalized in Japanese vernacular literature, often creating a highly psychological or lyrical work. In Zeami's nō dramas, for example, the characters usually have no substantial external conflict. Instead, the climax occurs when the protagonist is freed of his or her internal attachment or is reconciled to himself or herself, not when the opposition, if there is any, is vanquished. When the influence of Buddhism abated in the Tokugawa period (a secular age of urban growth, capitalism, and commerce, dominated by urban commoners), more secular plot paradigms became prominent, such as the conflict between human desire or love (*ninjō*) and social duty or obligation (*giri*), which lies at the heart of Chikamatsu Mon'zaemon's puppet plays (*jōruri*). Even so, the ultimate focus of the literature and drama tends to be on the intense emotions, generated by or in conflict with the irreconcilable pressures of society and social responsibility (supported by Confucian ethics). Although dramatic conflict exists, the primary objective of drama is not always the pursuit and development of dramatic conflict to its logical consequences.

Although sometimes possessing elaborate and complex plot structures, vernacular prose fiction often is concerned with the elaboration of a particular mood or emotion and tends to be fragmentary and episodic. For example, in vernacular fiction, the poetic diary, and drama (nō, jōruri), it is no accident that one of the most popular scenes is the parting: a poetic topos that can be traced back to the poetry of the *Man'yōshū*. *The Tale of Genji* is highlighted by a series of partings, which culminate in the climactic parting: the death of the heroine. The same can be said of *The Tales of the Heike*, a complex and detailed military epic that repeatedly focuses on the terrible partings that war forces on human beings. The closeness of traditional social ties—between parent and child, lord and retainer, husband and wife, individual and group—make the parting an emotionally explosive situation, which is often presented in highly poetic language.

PERFORMANCE AND NARRATION

The primary vernacular genres in the Heian period were the thirty-one-syllable poem (*waka*) and related forms, particularly poetic diaries (*nikki*) and vernacular tales (*monogatari*). The poetic orientation of Heian vernacular literature, however, should not obscure the fact that Japanese vernacular literature also was rooted in a narrative tradition that often imported texts from the continent and was presented orally to the audience. This narrative, storytelling literature, which came to fore in the late Heian and medieval periods when commoner culture began to surface, included a wide assortment of myths, legends, anecdotes (*setsuwa*), and folktales, often about strange, supernatural, or divine events. This narrative tradition, which drew on anecdotes from China and India, became particularly prominent in the late Heian period, when Buddhist priests used for didactic purposes popular stories that they recorded and rewrote to preach to a largely illiterate audience. The *Konjaku monogatari shū*, which was compiled in the late Heian period, is the most famous example of a collection of such anecdotes. This storytelling tradition also appears in the form of extended epic-like narratives like *The Tales of the Heike*, composed around the thirteenth or fourteenth century, which was memorized and chanted to the accompaniment of the *biwa* (lute) by blind minstrel-priests.

One major consequence of this narrative, storytelling tradition is that Japanese vernacular fiction tends to have a strong narrational voice: a narrator(s) describes and comments on the action from a subjective point of view. The conventions of oral storytelling are evident in almost all Japanese prose fiction, including highly sophisticated, stream-of-consciousness narratives like *The Tale of Genji*. In narrational genres like *The Tales of the Heike*, nō drama, and *sekkyōbushi* (sermon ballads), this type of narrational voice flows over the action, dialogue, and scenery. First- and third-person narrations overlap. In nō, for example, the dialogue alternates with descriptive passages narrated by both the chorus and the protagonist. The position of the narrator is most prominent in jōruri, in which the chanter (*gidayū*), on a dais separate from the puppet stage, performs both the puppet dialogue and the narration.

This double structure—action enveloped in descriptive narration—lends itself to extremely powerful lyric tragedy, in which the tone is elegant, poetic, and uplifting even when the subject matter or situation is unpleasant and sorrowful. The love suicide plays by Chikamatsu, the greatest jōruri playwright, are one example. The climactic travel scene (*michiyuki*)—a subcategory of the parting topos—is one of tragedy and pathos: the lovers, who are traveling to the place of their death, have resolved to be united in death rather than live under their present circumstances. The overriding narration is chanted to music and interwoven with allusions to poetic places and classical poetry. The narration consequently elevates the character even as he or she dies. The same can be said of climactic scenes in *The Tale of Genji* or in the final chapter of *The Tales of the Heike*, when Kenreimon'in reflects on the destruction of her clan. In most of these scenes, the poetic descriptions of nature and seasons, so central to Japanese poetry, suggest that death is not an end but a return to nature.

The lyrical character of Japanese vernacular literature also derives from a fusion of genres and media that in European literature are generally thought of as being intrinsically separate. Except for some folk literature (*setsuwa*), it is hard to find a work of premodern Japanese prose literature that does not include poetry. Since the Renaissance, European theater has generally been split into three basic forms—drama, opera, and ballet—whereas traditional Japanese theater has combined these elements (acting, music, and dance) in each of the major dramatic forms: nō drama, *kyōgen* (comic drama), jōruri (puppet theater), and kabuki. Of these, only kyōgen does not depend on music. One of the central principles of nō and jōruri is the *jo/ha/kyū* (introduction, development, and finale), which regulates the tempo of the play, particularly in relationship to dance and song. This multimedia quality often makes the drama more performative than mimetic; instead of emphasizing the represented world, the work calls attention to itself as a performative medium.

Chapter 1

THE ANCIENT PERIOD

THE BEGINNINGS OF JAPANESE LITERATURE

Chinese writing was first brought to the Japanese archipelago around the first century C.E. For many centuries, however, the use of writing was largely limited to inscriptions on stone and metal (mirrors, swords), thereby serving a primarily symbolic function. It was not until the seventh century that Chinese writing began to be used widely for administrative, religious, and commercial purposes. The oldest extant literary and historical texts date from the beginning of the eighth century. The *Kojiki (Record of Ancient Matters,* 712) and *Nihon shoki (Chronicles of Japan,* 720) were written in order to legitimize the new state order by providing an account of how the world came into being and by tracing the origins of the emperor to the age of the gods. In 713, an imperial order was issued to record the origins of the names of various places and products, and the result was the *fudoki,* or provincial gazetteers, which included reports by provincial governors from five different provinces: Hitachi, Harima (present-day Hyōgo Prefecture), Izumo, Bungo, and Hizen (the last two are in Kyushu). Anthologies of Japanese poetry began to be compiled in the late seventh century, and the *Man'yōshū (Collection of Myriad Leaves),* an encyclopedic collection of poetry, was compiled throughout the eighth century. An anthology of Chinese poetry, the *Kaifūsō,* was completed in 751.

Before the late seventh century, songs and narratives were transmitted orally in a variety of ways, sometimes as part of tales and at other times as part of festivals and rituals. Traces of these oral narratives (*katari*) survive in the myths and stories of the *Kojiki* and *Nihon shoki*, albeit in a different form. Ancient poems (*uta*) of courtship and praise for the ruler also survive in these two texts and in the *Man'yōshū*. The fudoki contain examples of courtship songs known as *utagaki* (literally, "fence songs") or *kagai*, which were sung to the accompaniment of song and dance.

The need to make Chinese writing accessible to non-Chinese speakers led scribes in the Yamato court from the archipelago and the continent to devise methods of reading Chinese script in Japanese. This process gave rise to the development of new hybrid styles of writing that required a knowledge of both the Chinese script and the Japanese language. For instance, in contrast to the *Nihon shoki*, which is written almost entirely in orthodox classical Chinese, the *Kojiki*, which places more emphasis on the spoken word and claims to be a record of oral transmissions, uses Chinese characters arranged with both Chinese and Japanese syntax, with the addition, for clarity, of some characters representing phonetic syllables. In the *Man'yōshū*, poems are written in a variety of ways, ranging from a style close to orthodox classical Chinese to one using Chinese characters as phonetic syllables. All these works, however, were read in the aristocratic Japanese dialect of the Yamato nobility.

Under the influence of Chinese literature, genres of Japanese poetry (*uta*) such as *sōmon* (exchange poems) and *banka* (laments) developed, and the myth-histories of the Yamato court were divided into emperor reigns (as in the Chinese dynastic histories) and chronologized according to the Chinese cosmological calendar (in the case of the *Nihon shoki*). These early written texts were compiled as the products of a court culture that would rival that of the Chinese court. As such, they were primarily literate texts. However, while writing represented a new medium that could be transmitted as a material object, it also created a new type of oral culture in which the written text was used as the base and cue for oral and public performance.

Major Events in the Seventh and Eighth Centuries

622	Death of Prince Shōtoku (b. 574)
645	Taika Reforms
667	Move of the capital to Ōmi
671	Death of Emperor Tenchi (r. 662–671)
672	Jinshin war
686	Death of Emperor Tenmu (r. 672–686)
701	Taihō Code
702	Death of Empress Jitō (r. 687–696)
710	Move of the capital to Nara (Heijō)

712   Completion of the *Kojiki*
713   Order to compile the fudoki
720   Completion of the *Nihon shoki*
731   Death of Ōtomo no Tabito (665–731)
733   Death of Yamanoue no Okura (660?–733)
746   Compilation of the *Man'yōshū*, vols. 1–16?
751   Compilation of *Kaifūsō*
784   Move of the capital from Nara to Nagaoka
785   Death of Ōtomo no Yakamochi (717?–785), final compiler of the
        Man'yōshū
794   Move of the capital to Heian (Kyoto)

KOJIKI
(RECORD OF ANCIENT MATTERS, 712)

According to its preface, the *Kojiki* (*Record of Ancient Matters*) was commissioned by Emperor Tenmu (r. 672–686) and was completed and presented to Empress Genmei (r. 707–715) in 712 by a scribe named Ō no Yasumaro. It is a mythology and history in three volumes, starting with the creation of Japan in the age of the gods and the descent to earth of the ancestor of the imperial family through the reign of the legendary first sovereign, Emperor Jinmu, and successive rulers up to the reign of the thirty-third sovereign, Empress Suiko (r. 592–618).

The key concept of the creation myth, which describes the origin of Japan but not of the universe, is *musuhi*, or "creating force," a spontaneous power through which the gods come into existence. After seven generations of gods are created by this force, the last generation, a male and a female god called Izanagi[1] and Izanami, create the islands of Japan. This creation begins with the present-day Shikoku (Tosa, Iyo, Sanuki, Awa), then moves west to Kyushu (Tsukushi), and finally to Honshū. Izanagi and Izanami also give birth to the gods of various natural phenomena, including the gods of the sea and rivers, of the mountains and plains, of the wind, and finally of fire, who causes the death of the female deity Izanami. The male deity Izanagi then gives birth by himself to the central figure in the *Kojiki* mythology, the Sun Goddess Amaterasu. It is Amaterasu's descendant, the god Ninigi, who comes down from heaven to earth and becomes the ancestor of the Yamato emperors.

The *Kojiki* is a bricolage of various myths woven together into a story of the divine ancestry of the Yamato emperors. According to the *Kojiki* cosmology, the earth is dependent on heaven, and the Yamato emperors, as the descendants of

---

1. In the ancient period, the correct pronunciation of the male god's name was "Izanaki," but in modern times the customary reading is "Izanagi."

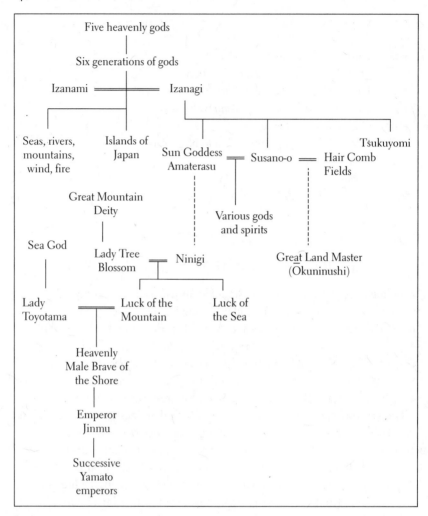

Genealogy of the Gods

the heavenly gods, are entitled to rule the earth. Although some of the myths contained in the *Kojiki* may date from long before the eighth century, their primary function in the narrative was to legitimate the world order of the early-eighth-century Japanese state. Within the various mythical accounts are explanations of the origin of place-names, of the hierarchical relationships between different clans, and of ritual ceremonies.

One key feature of the *Kojiki* is the importance it places on the power of speech. For example, conquests are often described in terms of a verbal pledging of subjection. In the *Kojiki* the word for "subdue" (*kotomuku*) means literally "to make (someone) speak his subjection." The magical power of words is also emphasized in the story of Luck of the Mountain and Luck of the Sea, as well as in the tragic end of Prince Yamato Takeru.

Key Japanese Names and Places

Takama-no-hara	Plain of High Heaven
Ashihara no kuni	Central Land of the Reed Plains
Izanagi	He Who Invites God
Izanami	She Who Invites God
Amaterasu	Great Heaven-Shining Goddess
Tsukuyomi	Moon God (Moon-Counting God)
Susano-o	Ferocious Virulent Male God
Ho-deri	Fire-Shine, Luck of the Sea
Ho-ori	Fire-Fade, Luck of the Mountain
Ōkuni-nushi	Great Land Master
Ninigi	(descendant of Amaterasu)

Book 1

THE BEGINNING

When heaven and earth first appeared, there came into existence in the Plain of High Heaven a deity named Lord Midst-of-Heaven God; then High Creative Force God; and then Divine Creative Force God. All these three deities came into existence as single deities, and their forms were not visible. Next, when the land was young, resembling floating oil and drifting like jellyfish, a thing sprouted forth like reed shoots, and from this there came into existence a deity named Splendid Reed Shoot God and then Eternally Standing Heaven God. These two deities also came into existence as single deities, and their forms were not visible. The five deities in the preceding section are the Separate Heavenly Deities.

Next there came into existence Eternally Standing Land God and then Abundant Clouds Field God. These two deities also came into existence as single deities, and their forms were not visible. Next there came into existence Clay Male God and then his spouse, Silt Female God. Next, Emergent Form God and then his spouse, Living Form God. Next, Great Male Organ God and then his spouse, Great Female Organ God. Next, Ample Face God and then his spouse, Awe-Inspiring God. Next, Izanagi, He Who Invites God, and then his spouse, Izanami, She Who Invites God. The deities in the preceding section, from Eternally Standing Land God through Izanami, are known collectively as the Seven Generations of the Age of the Gods. . . .

SOLIDIFYING THE LAND

At this time the heavenly deities, acting jointly, commanded the two deities Izanagi and Izanami: "Complete and solidify this drifting land." Giving them the Heavenly Jeweled Spear, they entrusted the mission to them. Thereupon, the two deities stood on the Heavenly Floating Bridge and, lowering the jeweled spear, stirred, churning the brine with a resonating sound, and when they lifted it up, the brine dripping down from the tip of the spear piled up and became an island. This was Onogoro, Self-Congealing Island.

Descending from the heavens to this island, they erected a heavenly pillar and a spacious palace. At this time Izanagi asked his spouse Izanami, "How is your body formed?" She replied, "My body, formed though it be formed, has one place that is formed insufficiently." Then Izanagi said, "My body, formed though it be formed, has one place that is formed to excess. Therefore I would like to take that place in my body that is formed to excess and insert it into that place in your body that is formed insufficiently and give birth to the land. How would this be?" Izanami replied, "This would be good." Then Izanagi said, "Then let us, you and me, walk in a circle around this heavenly pillar and meet and have conjugal intercourse."

Having thus agreed, Izanagi then said, "You walk around from the right, and I will walk around from the left and meet you." After having agreed to this, they circled around. Then Izanami said first, "O, how good a lad!" after which Izanagi said, "O, how good a maiden!" After each had finished speaking, Izanagi said to his spouse, "It is not proper that the woman speak first."

Nevertheless, they commenced procreation and gave birth to a leech-child. They placed this child into a boat made of reeds and floated it away. Next, they gave birth to an island of foam. This also is not reckoned as one of their children. Then the two deities consulted together and said, "The children that we have just borne are not good. It is best to report this matter to the heavenly deities." Then they ascended together and sought the will of the heavenly deities. The heavenly deities thereupon performed a grand divination and said, "Because the woman spoke first, the outcome was not good. Descend once more and say it again." Then they descended again and walked once more in a circle around the heavenly pillar as before.

Then Izanagi said first, "O, how good a maiden!" Afterward, his spouse Izanami said, "O, how good a lad!" After they had finished saying this, they were united and bore, as a child, Awaji Island.

Next they bore the double island of Iyo. This island has one body and four countenances, each with a separate name. Thus, the land of Iyo is named Darling Woman; the land of Sanuki is named Grain Spirit Possessed Man; the land of Awa is called Great Food Woman; and the land of Tosa is called Fierce Spirit Possessed Man. Next they bore the triple island of Oki. . . .

When they finished giving birth to countries, they began giving birth to deities anew. . . . Then they gave birth to the Swift Burning Fire Deity. As a result of giving birth to this child, Izanami's genitals were burned, and she lay down sick. In her vomit there came into existence the Metal Mountain God. Next, in her feces, there came into existence the Clay Earth God and the Clay Earth Goddess. Next, in her urine, there came into existence the Goddess of Irrigation and the God of Agricultural Creation. The child of this deity was the Goddess of Food. Thus, at last, Izanami, because she had given birth to the fire deity, divinely passed away.

A grieving Izanagi buries his spouse and kills the fire deity, whose birth caused Izanami's death. Still grieving, Izanagi decides to visit Izanami in the land of Yomi.

VISIT TO THE LAND OF YOMI

At this time, Izanagi, wishing to meet again his spouse Izanami, went after her to the land of Yomi. When she came out of the door of the hall to greet him, Izanagi said, "O, my beloved spouse, the lands that you and I were making have not yet been completed. You must come back."

Then Izanami replied, saying, "How I regret that you did not come sooner. I have eaten at the hearth of Yomi. But, O, my beloved husband, how honored I am that you have come here! Therefore I will go and discuss for a while with the deities of Yomi my desire to return. Pray do not look at me." Thus saying, she went back into the hall, but she was gone so long that Izanagi could no longer wait. So he broke off one of the large end-teeth of the comb he was wearing in his left hair bunch, lit a fire, and entered the hall to look. Maggots squirmed and rolled; on her head sat Great Thunder; on her breast sat Fire Thunder; on her belly sat Black Thunder; on her genitals sat Crack Thunder; on her left hand sat Young Thunder; on her right hand sat Earth Thunder; on her left foot sat Sounding Thunder; and on her right foot sat Reclining Thunder. All together, eight thunder deities were there.

Upon seeing this, Izanagi became afraid and turned and fled. Then his spouse Izanami said, "He has shamed me." Right away she dispatched the hags of Yomi to pursue him. Then Izanagi undid the black vine securing his hair and flung it down. Immediately it bore grapes. While the hags were picking the grapes and eating them, he fled. Still they pursued him. Next Izanagi pulled out the comb he was wearing in his right hair bunch and flung it down. Immediately bamboo shoots sprouted forth. While the hags were pulling the bamboo shoots and eating them, he fled. Later, Izanami dispatched the eight thunder deities and a horde of warriors of Yomi to pursue him. Then Izanagi unsheathed the ten-hands-long sword that he wore at his side and waved it behind him as he fled. The pursuit continued. When Izanagi reached the foot of the Steep Pass of Yomi, he took three peaches that were at the foot of the pass and ambushed his pursuers. They all turned and fled. Then Izanagi said to the peaches, "Just as you have saved me, if in the Central Land of the Reed Plains, any of the race of mortal men should fall into painful straits and suffer in anguish, please save them also." Saying this, he bestowed on the peaches the name Oho-kamu-zu-mi, Great Divine Spirit God.

Finally, his spouse Izanami herself came in pursuit of him. Then Izanagi picked up an enormous boulder, requiring the strength of a thousand men to move, and blocked the Steep Pass of Yomi. They stood facing each other, one on each side of the boulder, and broke their troth. At this time, Izanami said, "O, my beloved husband, if you do thus, I will each day strangle to death one thousand of the populace of your land." To this Izanagi said, "O, my beloved spouse, if you do thus, I will each day build fifteen hundred birthing huts." This is the reason why one thousand people inevitably die and fifteen hundred people inevitably are born every day. Therefore, the deity Izanami is also called the Great Deity of Yomi. Also, because she joined in the pursuit, she is called the Great Deity Who Lays the Road. The boulder that closed the Steep Pass of Yomi is called the Great Deity Who Repels Enemies on the Road. It is also called the Great Deity Who Blocks the Door of Yomi. This Steep Pass of Yomi is said to be now the Ifuya Pass in the land of Izumo.

At this point Izanagi said, "I have been to a most unpleasant land, a horrible, unclean land. Therefore I shall purify myself." Arriving at the plain of Awaki by the river mouth of Tachibana in Himuka in Tsukushi, he purified and exorcised himself.

When he flung down his stick, there came into existence a deity named Cane in the Road Bend.

As Izanagi cleanses himself, many deities are born.

Then when he washed his left eye, there came into existence a deity named Amaterasu, the Great Heaven Shining Goddess. Next, when he washed his right eye, there came into existence a deity named Tsukuyomi, the Moon-Counting God. Next, when he washed his nose, there came into existence a deity named Susano-o, Ferocious Virulent Male God.

The fourteen deities in the preceding section, from the Many Afflictions Spirit through Susano-o, are deities born from bathing his body.

At this time Izanagi, rejoicing greatly, said, "I have borne child after child, and finally in the last bearing I have obtained three noble children." Then he removed his necklace, shaking the beads on the string so that they jingled, and, giving it to the deity Amaterasu, he entrusted her with a mission, saying: "You shall rule the Plain of High Heaven." . . .

Next he said to the deity Tsukuyomi, entrusting him with this mission: "You shall rule the realms of night."

Next he said to the deity Susano-o, entrusting him with this mission: "You shall rule the ocean."

Although Susano-o is given the rule of the ocean, he weeps and howls for his mother and neglects the realm entrusted to him. Angered by Susano-o's disobedience, Izanagi expels Susano-o.

SUSANO-O AND AMATERASU

At the time, Susano-o said, "In that case, before I go I will take my leave of the Great Deity Amaterasu." When he ascended to the heavens, all the mountains and rivers roared, and all the land trembled. Amaterasu heard this, was startled, and said, "It is certainly not with any good intentions that my brother is coming up. He must wish to usurp my lands." So, undoing her hair, she wrapped it in hair bunches. She wrapped long strings of myriad *magatama* beads[2] in the hair bunches on the left and right of her head, on the vine securing her hair, as well as on her left and right arms. On her back she bore a thousand-arrow quiver; at her side she strapped a five-hundred-arrow quiver and also put on a magnificent bamboo arm-cover. Shaking the upper tip of her bow, stamping her legs up to her very thighs into the hard earth, and kicking the earth about as if it were light snow, she let out a tremendous war cry and stamped her feet with fury. Thus waiting for him, she asked, "Why have you come?"

Then Susano-o replied, "I have no evil intentions. It is merely that the Great Deity Izanagi divinely inquired about my weeping and howling, so I said that I was weeping because I wished to go to the land of my mother. Then the Great Deity said, 'You may not live in this land' and expelled me with a divine expulsion. Whereupon I came up intending to take leave upon my departure. I have no other intentions." Then Amaterasu said, "If that is so, how am I to know that your intentions are pure and clear?" Then Susano-o replied, "Let us swear oaths and bear children."

Then they each stood on opposite sides of the Serene River of Heaven and swore their oaths. At this time, Amaterasu first asked for the ten-hands-long sword that Susano-o wore at his side. Breaking the sword in three pieces, she rinsed them in the heavenly well, the jewel-like ringing resonating clearly, chewed them to pieces, and spat them out. In the misty spray there came into existence a deity named Lady Mist, also named Lady of Oki Island. Next, Lady of Ichiki Island, also named Lady Sayori. Next, Lady Gushing Water.

Susano-o, asking for the long strand of myriad magatama beads wrapped on Amaterasu's left hair bunch, rinsed them in the heavenly well, the jewels' ringing

---

2. *Magatama* are curved beads, usually with a hole bored through them in order to use in a necklace, made of semiprecious stones.

resonating clearly, chewed them to pieces, and spat them out. In the misty spray there came into existence a deity named Truly-I-Have-Won Victorious-Virulent-Spirit-Heavenly-Majestic-Grain-Force. Again, he asked for the beads wrapped on her right hair bunch, chewed them to pieces, and spat them out. In the misty spray there came into existence a deity named Heavenly Grain Spirit. Again, he asked for the beads wrapped on the vine securing her hair, chewed them to pieces, and spat them out. In the misty spray there came into existence a deity named Heavenly Male Child. Again, he asked for the beads wrapped on her left arm, chewed them to pieces, and spat them out. In the misty spray there came into existence a deity named Vibrant Male Child. Again, he asked for the beads wrapped on her right arm, chewed them to pieces, and spat them out. In the misty spray there came into existence a deity named Wondrous Spirit of Kumano. All together there were five deities.

At this time, Amaterasu said to Susano-o, "The latter-born five male children came into existence from my possessions and are therefore naturally my children. The firstborn three female children came into existence from your possessions and are therefore your children." Thus, she determined the allotment of the offspring. . . .

Then Susano-o said to Amaterasu, "It was because my intentions were pure and clear that in the children I begot I obtained graceful maidens. By this it is obvious that I have won." Thus saying, he raged with victory, breaking down the ridges of Amaterasu's rice paddies and filling up the ditches. Also he defecated and strewed his feces about in the hall where the first fruits were tasted. Even though he did this, Amaterasu did not reprove him but said, "What appears to be feces must be what my brother has vomited and strewn about while drunk. Also, as to his breaking down the ridges of the rice paddies and filling up the ditches, my brother must have done so because he felt land was being wasted." Even though she spoke this way, hoping for a remedy, his misdeeds did not cease but became even more flagrant. When Amaterasu was inside the sacred weaving hall, seeing to the weaving of the divine garments, he opened a hole in the roof of the weaving hall and dropped into it the heavenly dappled horse, which he had skinned backward. The heavenly weaving maiden, shocked at the sight, struck her genitals against the shuttle and died.

Now Amaterasu, seeing this, became afraid, and opening the door of the Heavenly Rock-Cave, went in and shut herself inside. Then the Plain of High Heaven was completely dark, and the Central Land of the Reed Plains was entirely dark. Because of this, constant night reigned, and the cries of the myriad deities filled the air like flies in the summer, and all manners of calamities arose.

Then the eight hundred myriad deities assembled in a divine assembly on the banks of the Serene River of Heaven. They called upon the deity Profound Thinker, child of the deity High Creative Force, to think. They gathered together the long-crying birds of Tokoyo, the Everlasting Realm, and caused them to cry. They took the heavenly hard rock from the upper streams of the

Serene River of Heaven, took iron from the Fragrant Mountain of Heaven, sought the smith Heavenly Mara, and commissioned Stone-Cutting Woman to make a mirror. They commissioned Forefather of Jewel Workers to make long strings of myriad magatama beads. They summoned Heavenly Koyane and Futo-tama, the Magnificent Jewel God, to remove whole the shoulder bone of a male deer of the Fragrant Mountain of Heaven and take heavenly *hahaka* wood from the Fragrant Mountain of Heaven and perform divination. They uprooted by the very roots the flourishing *masakaki* tree of the Fragrant Mountain of Heaven. To the upper branches they affixed long strings of myriad magatama beads; in the middle branches they hung a mirror many spans wide; and in the lower branches they suspended white strips of *nikite* cloth and blue strips of *nikite* cloth. Magnificent Jewel carried these various objects as solemn offerings; Heavenly Koyane intoned a solemn liturgy; the deity Heavenly Powerful-Handed Male stood concealed beside the door; and Uzume, the Heavenly Woman-with-Hair-Piece Goddess, bound up her sleeves with a cord of the heavenly *hikage* vine, tied around her head a head band of the heavenly *masaki* vine, and bound together bundles of *sasa* leaves to hold in her hands. Overturning a bucket before the door of the Heavenly Rock-Cave, she stamped thunderously and, becoming divinely possessed, exposed her breasts and pushed her skirt band down to her genitals. Then the Plain of High Heaven shook as the eight hundred myriad deities laughed at once.

At this time, Amaterasu, thinking this strange, opened a crack in the door of the Heavenly Rock-Cave and said from within, "Because I have shut myself in, I thought that the Plain of High Heaven would be dark and the Central Land of the Reed Plains would be completely dark. Why is it that Uzume, Heavenly Woman-with-Hair-Piece, sings and dances and all the eight hundred myriad deities laugh?"

Then Uzume, Heavenly Woman-with-Hair-Piece, said, "We rejoice and dance because there is here a deity superior to you." While she was saying this, Heavenly Koyane and Magnificent Jewel brought out the mirror and showed it to Amaterasu. Then Amaterasu, thinking this more and more strange, gradually came out of the door and approached the mirror. Then the deity Heavenly Powerful-Handed Male, who had hidden himself, grasped her hand and pulled her out. Immediately Magnificent Jewel extended a sacred rope behind her, and said, "You may not go back behind this." When Amaterasu came forth, the Plain of High Heaven and the Central Land of the Reed Plains naturally became light. At this time the eight hundred myriad deities deliberated together and imposed on Susano-o a fine of a thousand platters of restitutive goods. In addition, they cut off his beard and the nails of his hands and feet, had him exorcised, and expelled him with a divine expulsion.

SUSANO-O SLAYS THE EIGHT-TAILED SERPENT

Therefore Susano-o was expelled and descended to the upper reaches of the Hi River in the land of Izumo, to a place called Torikami. At that time a chopstick came flowing down the river. Thinking that there were people upstream, Susano-o set out in search of them. He came upon an old man and an old woman, with a maiden between them, crying. He asked them, "Who are you?" The old man replied, "I am a child of an earthly deity, the Great Deity of the Mountains. My name is Rubbing Feet; my wife's name is Rubbing Hands; and our daughter's name is Hair Comb Fields."

Susano-o asked further, "Why are you crying?"

Rubbing Feet replied, "We originally had eight daughters, but the eight-tailed serpent of Koshi has come every year and eaten them. We are crying because it is now time for him to come again." Susano-o asked, "What is his appearance?" Rubbing Feet replied, "His eyes are like red ground cherries, and his body has eight heads and eight tails. On his body grow moss and cypress and cryptomeria trees. His length is such that he spans eight valleys and eight mountain peaks. If you look at his belly, you see that blood is oozing out all over it."

Then Susano-o said to the old man, "Will you give me your daughter?" Rubbing Feet answered, "Awed as I am, I do not know your name." Susano-o replied, "I am the brother of the great deity Amaterasu and have just descended from heaven." Then Rubbing Feet and Rubbing Hand said, "If that is so, we reverently present her to you."

Then Susano-o transformed the maiden into a hair comb, which he put in his hair. He said to Rubbing Feet and Rubbing Hand, "Distill thick wine of eightfold brewings, build a fence, and make eight doors in the fence. At each door, set up eight woven platforms, and on each of these platforms place a wine barrel. Fill each barrel with the thick wine of eightfold brewings, and wait."

They made the preparations as he had instructed, and as they waited, the eight-tailed serpent came indeed, as the old man had said. Putting one head into each of the barrels, the serpent drank the wine, then becoming drunk, he lay down and slept. Then Susano-o unsheathed the ten-hands-long sword that he was wearing at his side and hacked the serpent to pieces. The Hi River ran with blood. When he cut the serpent's middle tail, the blade of his sword chipped. Thinking this strange, he thrust deeper with the stump of his sword, until a great sharp sword appeared. He took out this sword and, thinking it an extraordinary thing, presented it to the great deity Amaterasu. This is the sword Kusanagi, Grass Feller.

Thereupon Susano-o sought a place in the land of Izumo to build his palace. Arriving at Suga he said, "Coming here, my heart is refreshed [sugashi]," and in that place he built his palace and dwelled. Therefore that place is still called Suga. When this great deity first built the palace of Suga, clouds rose from that place. He composed a song, which said:

yakumo tatsu	In eight-cloud-rising
Izumo yaegaki	Izumo an eightfold fence
tsumagomi ni	to enclose my wife
yaegaki tsukuru	an eightfold fence I build,
sono yaegaki o	and, oh, that eightfold fence!

Then he summoned Rubbing Feet and said, "Be the headman of my palace." He also bestowed upon him the name Palace-Master of Inada, Deity of Suga with Manifold Spiritual Powers. Then he commenced procreation with Hair Comb Fields. . . .

LUCK OF THE SEA AND LUCK OF THE MOUNTAIN

Thereupon Fire-Shine Lord, as Luck of the Sea, hunted the wide-finned and the narrow-finned fish, and Fire-Fade Lord, as Luck of the Mountain, hunted the coarse-furred and the soft-furred game. Then Luck of the Mountain said to his elder brother Luck of the Sea, "Let us exchange our luck." Although he repeated this request three times, his elder brother refused. Finally, however, he was able to get his brother to consent to the exchange. Then, when Luck of the Mountain was fishing with the luck of the sea, he was unable to catch even a single fish, and he lost his fishhook in the sea.

Then his elder brother Luck of the Sea asked to have the fishhook back, saying, "The luck of the mountain is your own luck-luck, the luck of the sea is my own luck-luck, let us now give each back his own luck." Then the younger brother Luck of the Mountain replied, "When I fished with your fishhook, I caught not a single fish, and I finally lost it in the sea." However, his elder brother stubbornly insisted. Even when the younger brother broke up a ten-hands-long sword and made it into five hundred hooks as compensation, he would not accept them. Again, he made a thousand hooks as compensation, but he still would not accept them, saying, "I still want my original hook."

Then when the younger brother was weeping and lamenting by the seashore, the Tide Path God came and asked, "Why are you weeping and lamenting, He Who Is High as the Sun in the Sky?" Luck of the Mountain replied, "I borrowed my elder brother's fishhook, and I lost it. Since he asked for his hook, I repaid him with many hooks, but he will not receive them, saying, 'I still want my original hook.' That is why I am weeping and lamenting."

Then the Tide Path God said, "I will give you good counsel." He then made a small boat of closely woven bamboo, put Luck of the Mountain into this boat, and instructed, "When I push this boat free, continue to sail for a little while. Then there will be a very good path of tide in the sea. Continue going on this path, and you will come to a palace made as if with the scales of fish, the palace of Watatsumi, the sea god. When you reach the gate of this deity, there will be a luxuriant *katsura* tree next to a well at its side. If you climb to the top of this tree, the daughter of the sea deity will see you and will give you counsel."

Thereupon Luck of the Mountain went as he was instructed, and everything was exactly as he had been told. He climbed up the katsura tree and waited. Then the serving maid of Toyotama, Lady Precious Soul, daughter of the sea god, brought out a fine jar to draw water, at which time she noticed a light in the well. Looking up, she saw a lovely young man. She thought this exceedingly strange. At this point Luck of the Mountain, seeing the serving maid, asked her to give him some water. The maid drew water, put it into the fine jar, and offered it to him. Then, instead of drinking the water, he unfastened a jewel from his neck, put it into his mouth, and spat it into the fine jar. Thereupon the jewel stuck fast to the jar, and the maid could not remove it. Therefore she presented it to Lady Toyotama with the jewel attached inside.

Seeing this jewel, she asked the maid, "Is there perhaps someone outside the gate?" The maid replied, "There is a person in the katsura tree next to the well. He is an exceedingly lovely young man, much nobler than our master. He asked for water, and when I offered water to him, he did not drink but spat this jewel into the jar. Since I was unable to remove it, I brought it with the jewel attached inside to present to you." Then Lady Toyotama, thinking this strange, went outside to take a look. Quite taken at the sight, they gazed at each other.

To her father she said, "There is a noble person at our gate." Then the sea god went out himself to take a look and said, "This is He Who Is High as the Sun in the Sky, son of He Who Is High as the Sun in Heaven." Then he brought him inside, spread out eightfold layers of sealskin carpets, then spread out eightfold layers of silk carpets above them, seated Luck of the Mountain on top of these, set out a hundred tables laden with gifts, prepared a banquet, and gave him his daughter Toyotama in marriage. Therefore he lived in this land for three years.

At this time, Luck of the Mountain remembered the things of the past and sighed deeply. Toyotama heard this sigh and said to her father, "In the three years he has lived here, he has never sighed, yet last night he sighed deeply. What could be the reason?" Then her father, the great god, asked his son-in-law, "According to what my daughter said this morning, in the three years that you have lived here, you have never sighed, yet last night you sighed deeply. What is the reason? Also, what is the reason for your coming here?" Then Luck of the Mountain told the great god in detail about how his elder brother demanded the fishhook that had been lost.

Thereupon, the sea deity summoned together all the large and small fish of the sea and asked them whether any fish had taken the fishhook. Then the myriad fish said, "Recently the sea bream has complained that a bone is caught in its throat and it cannot eat anything. Certainly this fish has taken it." At this time they looked in the sea bream's throat and found the fishhook. Therefore they took it out, washed it, and presented it to Luck of the Mountain. At this time the great sea god Watatsumi instructed, "When you give this hook to your elder brother, you should say, 'This hook is a gloomy hook, an uneasy hook, a poor hook, a dull hook.' So saying, hand it to him behind your back. Then if your elder brother makes rice paddies on high ground, make yours on low ground. If your elder brother makes rice paddies on low ground, make yours on high ground. If you do this, since I control the water, within three years your brother will be poverty stricken. If he becomes bitter and angry and attacks you, take the tide-raising pearl and cause him to drown. If he pleads for mercy, take the tide-ebbing pearl and cause him to live. So cause him anguish and suffering." Saying so, the sea god gave Luck of the Mountain the tide-raising pearl and the tide-ebbing pearl.

Then he summoned together all the crocodiles and asked, "Now, He Who Is High as the Sun in the Sky, son of He Who Is High as the Sun in Heaven, is about to journey to the upper land. Which one of you will escort him and return to report, in how many days?" Then each of them answered, numbering the days in accordance with their length. Among them, the one-length crocodile said, "I will escort him and return in one day." Then the sea god said to the one-length crocodile, "In that case, escort him. Do not give him cause for fright while crossing the sea." Thus, the sea god put Luck of the Mountain on the crocodile's neck and sent him off. As had been promised, the crocodile escorted him home in a day. When the crocodile was about to start back, Luck of the Mountain removed the dagger he had been wearing and fastened it around the crocodile's neck before sending it off. Therefore this one-length crocodile is now called the God Who Holds a Dagger.

Then Luck of the Mountain returned the hook to his brother exactly as he had been instructed by the sea deity. From that time onward, his elder brother became poorer and poorer. His disposition became more violent, and he came to attack Luck of the Mountain. Whenever he was attacked, Luck of the Mountain took out the tide-raising pearl and caused his elder brother to drown. Then when the elder brother pleaded for mercy, he took out the tide-ebbing pearl and saved him. So he caused his elder brother anguish and suffering. At the time the elder brother prostrated himself and said, "From now on, I shall serve you day and night as your guard." Thus, to this day the elder brother's descendants (the Hayato) still serve the emperor by performing these drowning motions.

At this time, the daughter of the sea god, Toyotama, came forth and said: "I have been with child for some time, and now the time of my delivery is near. I thought that it would not be fitting for the child of the heavenly deities to be born in the ocean. Therefore I have come forth." Then, by the edge of the beach, a parturition hut was built, thatched with cormorant feathers. But before the parturition hut had been completely thatched, the urgency of her womb became unendurable, and she entered into the parturition hut. As she was about to be delivered of her child, she said to her husband: "All persons of other lands, when they bear their young, revert to the form of their original land and give birth. Therefore I too am going to revert to my original form and give birth. Pray do not look at me!"

Then thinking her words strange, he watched in secret as she was about to give birth; she turned into a giant crocodile and went crawling and slithering around. Seeing this, he was astonished and ran away. Then Toyotama, learning that he had been watching, felt extremely shamed and, leaving behind the child she had borne, said: "I had always intended to go back and forth across the pathways of the sea; however, now that my form has been seen, I am exceedingly ashamed." Then, closing the sea border, she went back into the sea. For this reason, the child whom she bore is called Heavenly Male Brave of the Shore.

Nevertheless, although she was angry with him for having looked at her, she was still unable to subdue her yearning and sent her younger sister Lady Tamayori to nurse the child, entrusting her with a song, which said:

akadama wa	Beautiful are red jewels;
o sae hikaredo	even their cord seems to sparkle.
shiratama no	But I prefer pearls
kimi ga yosoishi	for the awesome beauty
toutoku arikeri	of your pearl-like form.

Then her husband replied with the song:

oki tsu tori	As long as I have life,
kamo doku shima ni	I shall never forget
waga ineshi	my beloved, with whom I slept
imo wa wasureji	on an island where wild ducks,
yo no kotogoto ni	birds of the offing, came to land.

Luck of the Mountain dwelled in the palace of Takachi-ho for 580 years. His tomb is west of Mount Takachi-ho.

After this, Heavenly Male Brave of the Shore takes his aunt Lady Tamayori as his wife, and she gives birth to three children: the eldest crosses over to the Eternal Land (Tokoyo); the second enters the ocean to follow his mother; and the third (Kamu Yamato Iware Hiko no Mikoto, Divine Yamato Iware Male Lord) becomes the first emperor of Yamato, Jinmu. From here on, the Kojiki is divided into chapters of the succeeding imperial reigns.

YAMATO THE BRAVE

Emperor Keikō (traditional dates 71–130 C.E.) ruled from the Hishiro Palace at Makimuku (today Nara Prefecture). By his various consorts and concubines, he had eighty children; second and third among them were Prince Ō-usu (Big Mortar) and his younger brother Prince O-usu (Little Mortar). Prince O-usu became Yamato Takeru no Mikoto, or Prince Yamato the Brave. His story is unique in the *Kojiki* because even though he is only a prince (the emperor's son), the text treats him as if he were an emperor (his wife is styled as "empress"). His exploits against the "braves" of other lands (Kumaso, Izumo) appear to be an allegory for the Yamato clan's military expansion. Although Prince Yamato's almost supernatural might leads him to conquer and kill the gods of various lands, he meets a tragic end when he misspeaks a charm against a wild boar, who turns out to be the god of Mount Ibuki, and loses his power.

The emperor said to Prince Little Mortar: "Why does your elder brother not come to the morning and evening meals? Take it upon yourself to teach and admonish him." After this had been said, five days passed, but he still did not come. The emperor then asked Prince Little Mortar: "Why has your elder brother not come for such a long time? Is it perhaps that you have not yet admonished him?" He replied: "I have already entreated him." "In what manner did you entreat him?" He replied: "Early in the morning when he went into the privy, I waited and captured him, grasped him and crushed him, then pulled off his limbs and, wrapping them in a straw mat, threw them away."

At this, the emperor was terrified at the fearless, wild disposition of this prince and said: "Toward the west, there are two mighty men called the Kumaso Braves. They are unsubmissive, disrespectful people. Therefore go and kill them." Thus saying, he dispatched him. At this time, he was still a youth wearing his hair up on his forehead. Then Prince Little Mortar received from his aunt Princess Yamato an upper garment and a skirt and, with a small sword in his bosom, set out.

When he arrived at the house of the Kumaso Braves, he found that the home was surrounded by three rows of warriors and that they were building a pit dwelling and were inside it. At the time there was a great deal of noise about the coming feast to celebrate the new pit dwelling, and food was being prepared. Walking around the vicinity, he waited for the day of the feast. When that day arrived, he combed his hair down in the manner of a young girl's and put on the upper garment and the skirt of his aunt. Completely taking on a young girl's appearance, he mingled with the women and went into the dwelling.

Then the two Kumaso Braves, the elder and the younger, looked with admiration at this maiden and had her sit between them as the festivities continued. Then, when the feast was at its height, Prince Little Mortar took his sword from his bosom and, seizing the older Kumaso's collar, stabbed him clear through the chest. Then the younger Kumaso, seeing this, was afraid and ran out. Pursuing him to the foot of the stairs leading out of the pit dwelling, he seized him by the back, took the sword, and stabbed him clear through from the rear.

Then, the Kumaso Brave said: "Do not move the sword. I have something to say." The prince gave him a respite while holding him down. When asked, "Who are you, my lord?" the prince replied "I am the son of Emperor Oho-tarashi-hiko-oshiro-wake, who dwells in the palace of Hishiro and rules the Land of the Eight Islands; and my name is Prince Yamato-oguna. Hearing that you Kumaso Braves were unsubmissive and disrespectful, he dispatched me to kill you."

Then the Kumaso Brave said: "Indeed this must be true. For in the west there are no brave, mighty men besides us. But in the great land of Yamato there is a man exceeding the two of us in bravery! Because of this I will present you with a name. May you be known from now on as Prince Yamato the Brave." After he had finished saying this, the prince killed him, slicing him up like a ripe melon.

From that time, he was called Yamato Takeru, Yamato the Brave, to praise his name. Then as he returned, he subdued and pacified all the mountain deities, river deities, and deities of the sea straits.

At that time Yamato Takeru entered the land of Izumo. Intending to kill the Izumo Brave, he pledged friendship with him on his arrival. Then he secretly made an imitation sword of *ichii* wood, which he wore at his side. They bathed together in the Hi River. At this time, Yamato Takeru came out of the river first and put on the sword that the Izumo Brave had worn, saying: "Let us exchange swords!" Then the Izumo Brave came out of the river and put on the imitation sword that Yamato Takeru had worn. Whereupon Yamato Takeru invited him, saying: "Come, let us cross swords!" As they were unsheathing their swords, the Izumo Brave was unable to unsheathe the imitation sword. Then Yamato Takeru, unsheathing his sword, struck and killed the Izumo Brave. Then he made a song, saying:

yatsumesasu	The many-clouds-rising
Izumo-take ga	Izumo Brave
hakeru tachi	wears a sword
tsuzura sawa maki	with many vines wrapped around it,
sami nashi ni aware	but no blade inside, alas!

Thus, having swept away and pacified his foes, he went up and reported on his mission.

Then the emperor once again commanded Yamato Takeru: "Subdue and pacify the unruly deities and the unsubmissive people of the twelve regions to the east!" He dispatched together with him the ancestor of the Omi of Kibi, whose name was Mi-suki-tomo-mimi-take-hiko, and bestowed on him a giant spear of *hihiragi* wood. Thus, when he received the command and set out, he went to the shrine of the Great Deity of Ise and worshiped at the court of the deity.

Then he said to his aunt Princess Yamato: "Is it because the emperor wishes me to die soon? Why did he dispatch me to attack the evil people of the west? Then when I came back up, why did he dispatch me once more after only a short while, without giving me troops, to subdue the evil people of the twelve regions to the east? In view of all this, he must cause me to die soon." He lamented and wept.

On his departure, Princess Yamato gave him the sword Kusanagi, Grass Feller. She also gave him a bag and said: "Should there be an emergency, open this bag." Afterward, he arrived in the land of Owari and went into the house of Princess Miyazu, the ancestress of the governor of Owari. Although he wanted to marry her, he decided to marry her on his return. Thus promising, he proceeded to the eastern lands and subdued and pacified all the unruly deities and unsubmissive people of the mountains and rivers.

At that time, when he arrived in the land of Sagamu, the governor of that land deceived him, saying: "In this plain there is a great pond. In the pond there lives a deity who is an extremely unruly deity." Then when he went into the plain in order to see that deity, the governor set fire to the plain. Realizing that he had been deceived, he opened the bag given him by his aunt Princess Yamato, looked inside, and found a fire-striking implement.

Then, first he mowed away the grass with his sword; then he lit a fire with the fire-striking implement and set a counterfire to keep the fire away. Then he went back out and killed the governor and all of his clan. Then he set fire to them and burned them. Today the place is therefore called Yakizu, Burning Ford.

From there he proceeded to cross the sea of Hashiri-mizu, Running Water. Just then the deity of the crossing stirred up the waves so that the boat went adrift and could not move forward. Then his empress, whose name was Princess Oto-tachibana, said: "I will go into the sea in your stead, O prince. You, O prince, must complete the mission entrusted to you and return to report on it." When she was about to go into the sea, they took many layers of sedge mats, many layers of skin carpets, and many layers of silk carpets and spread them out on top of the waves, and she went down onto them. At this time the rough waves of themselves became calm, and the boat was able to move forward. Then the empress sang this song:

sanesashi	O you, my lord, alas—
Sagamu no ono ni	you who once, standing among the flames
moyuru hi no	of the burning fire, spoke my name
honaka ni tachite	on the mountain-surrounded
toishi kimi wamo	Plain of Sagamu!

Seven days later, the empress's comb was washed ashore. Taking this comb, they made her tomb and placed it inside.

From there he proceeded and subdued all of the unruly Emishi and pacified the unruly deities of the mountains and rivers. Then on his way back to the capital, he arrived at the foot of the pass of Ashigara, and just as he was eating his travel rations, the deity of the pass, assuming the form of a white deer, came and stood there. Then he took a piece of *hiru* plant left over from his meal and struck the deer. It hit the deer's eye and killed him.

Then he climbed up the pass and, grieving, sighed three times: "My wife, alas!" Therefore the name of the land is Azuma. Then he proceeded overland from that land to Kai. While he was there at the palace of Sakaori, he sang this song:

> *Niibari*   How many nights have we slept
> *Tsukuba o sugite*   since passing Niibari
> *ikuyo ka netsuru*   and Tsukuba?

Then the old man tending the fire sang this song to continue his song:

> *kaga nabete*   The number of days is, all together,
> *yo ni wa kokonoyo*   of nights, nine,
> *hi ni wa tooka o*   and of days, ten.

Then he rewarded the old man and made him the governor of the land of Azuma.

From that land he crossed over to the land of Shinano. There he subdued the deity of the Shinano pass and returned to the land of Owari. He entered the dwelling of Princess Miyazu with whom he had previously made a promise of marriage. At that time, when presenting his food, Princess Miyazu brought the great wine cup and presented it to him. But Princess Miyazu had menstrual blood staining the hem of her cloak. Noticing the menstrual blood, he sang this song:

> Across the heavenly Kagu Mountain
> the long-necked swan flies like a sharp sickle.
> Your arm slender and delicate like the bird's neck—
> although I wish to clasp it in my embrace,
> although I desire to sleep with you,
> on the hem of the cloak you are wearing
> the moon has risen.

Then Princess Miyazu sang this song in reply:

> O high-shining Sun Prince,
> O my great lord ruling in peace!
> as the years one by one pass by,
> the moons also one by one elapse.
> It is no wonder that while waiting in vain for you,
> on the cloak I am wearing the moon should rise.

Then they were conjugally united, and he, leaving his sword Kusanagi at Princess Miyazu's dwelling, went to take the deity of Mount Ibuki.

At this time he said, "I will take the deity of this mountain with my bare hands," and went up the mountain. Then on the mountain he met a white boar the size of a cow. Thereupon he spoke a charm, saying: "This is the deity's messenger, which is here transformed into a white boar. I will not kill it now but will kill it when I come back," and went up.

At this time the deity of the mountain caused a violent hailstorm and dazed Yamato Takeru. It was not the deity's messenger that had been transformed into the white boar but the deity itself. He was dazed because he had spoken a charm to it.[3]

Then he came back down the mountain; his mind awoke somewhat as he rested at the spring of Tama-kura-be. For that reason it is called Isame, Spring of Coming to the Senses. From there he set out, and arriving on the plain of Tagi, he said: "I had always thought in my heart of flying through the skies, but now my legs cannot walk; they have become wobbly." For this reason that place is called Tagi, or Totter.

From there he proceeded a little farther and, because of his extreme fatigue, walked along slowly, using a staff. For this reason that place is called Walking-Stick Pass. When he arrived at the foot of the single pine on the Cape of Otsu, he found that a sword that he had left behind when he had eaten there had not disappeared but was still there. Then he sang this song:

> Directly across from Owari,
> on the Cape Otsu you stand,
> O lone pine—O my brother!—
> O lone pine, were you a man,
> I would give you a sword to wear,
> I would dress you with clothes,
> O lone pine—O my brother!—

Proceeding from there, when he arrived at the village of Mie, he again said: "My legs are like a threefold curve, and I am extremely tired." For this reason that place is called Mie, or Threefold.

From there he proceeded to the plain of Nobo, where he sang this song recalling his homeland:

> Yamato is the highest part of the land;
> the mountains are green partitions, lying layer upon layer.
> Nestled among the mountains,
> how beautiful is Yamato!

---

3. The charm was supposed to make Prince Yamato Takeru's words come true (that is, that he would indeed return and kill the boar). But it goes awry because the words spoken in the charm are mistaken: the boar is not the messenger but the god himself. It is the misspeaking of the charm that causes Prince Yamato to lose his power.

Again he sang:

> Let those whose life is secure
> take from Mount Heguri of the rush matting
> leaves of great oak and wear them in their hair
> —O my lads!—

These are "songs of yearning for the homeland." Again he sang:

> From the direction
> of my beloved home
> the clouds are rising.

This is a "half song." By this time his illness had become critical. Then he sang this song:

> Next to the maiden's
> sleeping place
> I left the saber, the sword—
> alas, that sword!

Immediately after he had sung the songs, he died. Then couriers were sent to the emperor.

At this time his empresses and children who were in Yamato came down to the plain of Nobo and constructed his tomb. Then, crawling around the neighboring rice paddies, they sang while weeping:

> The vines of the *tokoro*
> crawl around
> among the rice stems,
> the rice stems in the rice paddies
> bordering on the tomb.

At this time he was transformed into a giant white bird and, soaring through the skies, flew away toward the beach. Then the wives and children, although their feet had been cut by the stumps of the bamboo reeds, forgot the pain and ran after the bird, weeping. At this time they sang this song:

> Moving with difficulty, up to our waists
> in the field of low bamboo stalks,
> we cannot go through the skies—
> but alas, must go by foot!

Again, when they waded into the sea and moved through the waves with difficulty, they sang:

> Going by sea, waist deep in the water,
> we move forward with difficulty;
> like plants growing by a large river,
> we drift aimlessly in the ocean currents.

Again, when the bird had flown to the rocky shores, they sang:

> The plover of the beach
> does not go by the beaches,
> but follows along the rocky shores.

These four songs were sung at his funeral. For this reason, even today these songs are sung at the funeral of an emperor. From that land the bird flew away and stopped at Shiki in the land of Kōchi. For this reason they built his tomb at that place and enshrined him there. This tomb is called the White Bird Tomb. But from that place the bird again soared through the heavens and flew away. During the entire time that Yamato Takeru went about subduing the country, the ancestor of the Atae of the Kume, whose name was Nana-tsuka-hagi, served in his company as his food server.

[Adapted from a translation by Donald Philippi]

MAN'YŌSHŪ
(COLLECTION OF MYRIAD LEAVES, CA. 785)

The Man'yōshū (Collection of Myriad Leaves), Japan's oldest anthology of poetry, consists of twenty volumes containing more than 4,500 poems (uta), most of which were composed between the mid-seventh and the mid-eighth century. The Man'yōshū appears to have been edited in several stages by different people over seventy or eighty years. The first half of volume 1 was probably compiled at the beginning of the eighth century, and the first sixteen volumes had been written by 744. The finished product was probably completed between 770 and 785.

The three main poetic categories of the Man'yōshū are zōka, sōmon, and banka. Zōka eventually came to mean "miscellaneous poems," but originally it may have meant something like "public poems." Sōmon literally means "exchanges" and includes poems about love as well as (but to a far lesser extent) interpersonal and family relationships. Banka literally means "coffin-pulling songs" and originally referred to poems that were recited at the site of the temporary burial of emperors and princes. When this ritual practice was replaced by cremation at the end of the seventh century, the category of *banka* came to refer to poems about death in a more general sense. The terms *banka* and *zōka* are poetic categories in the *Wen xuan* (*Monzen*), a noted Chinese anthology of poetry. *Sōmon* was not a poetic category in China but existed as a poetic term meaning "exchange."

The two main poetic forms of the *Man'yōshū* are the *tanka* (short poem) and the *chōka* (long poem). When a tanka is placed after a chōka, it is sometimes referred to as a *hanka* (envoy). The tanka consists of five metric units, or *ku* (measures), in a 5/7/5/7/7 syllable pattern. The chōka, which can be of various lengths, alternates between measures of five and seven syllables, closing with three measures usually in a 5/7/7 syllable pattern. Some of the early chōka in the *Man'yōshū*, however, follow a short-measure/long-measure pattern, without strict syllable measures. Most of the poems in the *Man'yōshū* are tanka, with the chōka form tending to be composed by specialized poets on specific themes. Two other forms are the *sedōka* (head-turning poem), with a pattern of 5/7/7/5/7/7, of which there are sixty-two examples, and the *bussokuseki-ka* (Buddhist stone poem), with a pattern of 5/7/5/7/7/7, of which there is only one poem in the anthology.

The main rhetorical figures of the poetry of the *Man'yōshū* are the *makura-kotoba* (pillow word), the *jokotoba* (preface phrase), and the *tsuiku* (binary measures). Makurakotoba, usually consisting of five syllables, are formulaic epithets that modify a specific word. In many cases, they are used before place-names, but they also modify words like "palace," "gods," "life," and other terms of special significance. Some makurakotoba are words of praise, others are simply descriptive, and many have obscure meanings and origins. One function of pillow words appears to have been rhythmic, producing a 5–7/5–7–7 rhythm in the tanka and a 5–7/5–7/5–7 rhythm in the chōka, since the pillow word (5) and the modified phrase (7) must be read together as a unit. Originally they may have lent a sacred significance to the words they modified. Some may also be references to legends, particularly those modifying place-names. In Kakinomoto no Hitomaro's poems, though, pillow words tend to have specific meanings and are usually translated as adjectives or as adjectival phrases.

The *jokotoba* (preface phrase) usually consists of two or three measures and introduces the main topic of the poem or a particular section of a long poem. In general, the jokotoba is connected to the poem's main statement through a pun, in which case it often has no direct connection to the meaning of the poem, or through metaphoric association (for instance, "the river passes away [like] my love [passed away]"). In contrast to makurakotoba, jokotoba are not formulaic epithets and often are unique to a particular poem. They can be considered metaphorical or punning introductions to the main statement of the poem. Because of the difficulty of translating puns, most preface phrases are translated with an explanatory word such as "like" or "as."

Tsuiku (binary measures) are a rhetorical technique of Chinese origin most often used in chōka. The most common tsuiku establish some kind of spatial or temporal framework, such as day/night, morning/evening, spring/autumn, land/ sea, and heaven/earth. Many of them are formulaic phrases used in a variety of contexts.

The *Man'yōshū* is generally divided into four historical periods. The first period covers the poetry produced before the Jinshin war (672). The second period begins after the Jinshin war and ends with the capital's move to Nara (710). The third period contains poetry produced from 710 to the somewhat arbitrary date of 733 (the date of the poet Yamanoue no Okura's death). The fourth period continues to 759, the date of the last poem in the *Man'yōshū*.

The *Man'yōshū* is a vast anthology that includes poems composed over more than a century and compiled over some seventy-five years. The *Man'yōshū* probably began to be compiled in and around the court in the second period. In the third period, with the move of the capital to Nara and the expansion of the ritsuryō state, poetic circles also were formed outside the capital when courtiers were sent to the provinces as governors. By the fourth period, the compilation of the *Man'yōshū* appears to have become mainly a private enterprise by Ōtomo no Yakamochi (d. 785) and his circle in Etchū Province.

The *Man'yōshū* is written entirely in Chinese characters, which were used in two main ways: as *kun*, or Japanese readings (reading the graph for "house" as *ihe*), and as *on*, or one-unit Sino-Japanese readings (reading the graph for "house" as *ke*). In addition, the kun readings could have a semantic value or could have been used also for their sound. The other possibilities include the reading of characters by semantic association, such as writing the character for "winter" but reading it as "cold."

The *Man'yōshū* was a cultural production of the aristocracy, and therefore emperors and high-ranking aristocrats are well represented. But with the exception of the Ōtomo clan poets (Tabito, Lady Sakanoue, Yakamochi), most of the major poets of the *Man'yōshū* seem to have been lower-ranking aristocrats, such as Hitomaro, Akahito, Okura, and Mushimaro. Many of these lower-ranking poets may have had collections of their own, as can be deduced by references in the *Man'yōshū* to the *Hitomaro Collection*, the *Mushimaro Collection*, and *Yamanoue no Okura's Forest of Classified Poetry*, to cite just a few examples. The *Man'yōshū* was, in a sense, a collection of collections.

In regard to the *Man'yōshū* as a whole, it is clear that *uta* (poetry) was a very versatile practice: it was used as a mythical-historical narrative, as an expression of mourning, and as entertainment at banquets; to describe the political order; to tell tales and legends, for both real and fictional social interaction and correspondence; and to mark public occasions at court. In addition, and perhaps most important, poetry was something to be collected and classified in encyclopedic fashion. The *Man'yōshū* thus was compiled not only as a definitive guide to poetic practice but also as a monument of poetic knowledge.

[Introduction by Torquil Duthie]

FIRST PERIOD

With the exception of poems attributed to early emperors like Nintoku (r. 313–399) and Yūryaku (r. 456–479), the first period of the *Man'yōshū* covers the reigns of Jomei (r. 629–641), his wife Kōgyoku (r. 642–645), Kōgyoku's brother Kōtoku (r. 645–654), Kōgyoku's reaccession as Saimei (r. 655–661), and Jomei's son Tenchi (r. 662–671). It has been argued that the first compilers of the *Man'yōshū* looked back to Jomei as the founder of a line of rulers to which their own court belonged. This would explain why Kōtoku's reign is not mentioned in the *Man'yōshū*, since Kōtoku was Jomei's brother-in-law and therefore not part of Jomei's line. In addition, scholars have speculated that for the early-eighth-century compilers, Jomei's reign marked the transition from what was perceived as the "ancient" period to the "modern" period. This is supported by the fact that the *Kojiki* begins with the age of the gods and tells the story of the sovereigns up to Suiko (r. 593–628), the empress who preceded Jomei. The corpus of poetry of the *Man'yōshū's* first period is very small and includes, in addition to a number of poems attributed to various "ancient" and "modern" emperors of Yamato, poetry by women of the imperial family, such as Lady Nukata.

EMPEROR YŪRYAKU

The first poem in the anthology is attributed to Emperor Yūryaku (r. 456–479). The name Yūryaku is a posthumous name from the Nara period, but in the *Man'yōshū* his name is given as "the Heavenly Sovereign Ōhatsuse Wakatakeru." Yūryaku/Wakatakeru is given particular importance in the *Kojiki*, where he is described as a great lover. Accordingly, it is fitting that the first half of the poem is a courtship song. The speaker calls out to the girl picking herbs (a rite of spring associated with fertility and courtship) and asks her to identify her house (family) and her home, the equivalent to proposing marriage. In the second half of the poem, however, this "suitor" describes himself in solemn terms as the ruler of Yamato.

Given the choice of diction and grammar of the poem, scholars agree that it cannot possibly date from Wakatakeru's reign in the fifth century but instead is probably a later adaptation of an old courtship song. The choice of this poem to begin the anthology was perhaps based on its combination of the themes of courtship and power (two main themes of *Man'yōshū* poetry), as well as on the supposed authorship of a model lover and ruler of the ancient age like Wakatakeru/Yūryaku.

Your Basket, with Your Lovely Basket

1:1

A poem by the Heavenly Sovereign.

komo yo mikomochi
fukushimo yo mibukushimochi
kono oka ni na tsumasu ko
ie norase na norasane

Your basket, with your lovely basket,
your trowel, with your lovely trowel,
girl, you who pick herbs on this hill,
speak of your house. Speak of your
name.

soramitsu Yamato no kuni wa

In the Land of Yamato, seen from
the sky,[4]

oshinabete ware koso ore
shikinabete ware koso imase
ware kosoba norame
ie o mo na o mo

it is I who conquer and reign,
it is I who conquer and rule.
Let it be me who speaks
of my house and my name.

EMPEROR JOMEI

The second poem in the *Man'yōshū* is attributed to Emperor Jomei (r. 629–641). It usually is read as a poem describing a "land-looking" (*kuni-mi*) ritual in which the lord would climb a mountain to look over the land and affirm its prosperity as well as his own power over it. In the *Nihon shoki*, in an entry in the chapter dedicated to the ancient emperor Nintoku (313–399), the sovereign is described as climbing a mountain. When he finds no smoke rising from the hearths of his people, he exempts the whole realm from taxes for three years and allows his palace to fall into disrepair for the sake of his subjects. Jomei's poem, however, seems to represent the opposite scenario, as smoke is rising (indicating that his subjects are prosperous) and birds are flying over the sea (indicating plentiful fish): Jomei is thus celebrating, or perhaps "praying" for, Yamato as a bountiful and prosperous land.

The place-name Yamato has two meanings. The first is the province of Yamato (present-day Nara), where Mount Kagu is located and the capital was situated. The second meaning is the "land of Yamato" in the last phrase of the poem, which refers to the whole of "Japan." Mount Kagu is one of the so-called three mountains of Yamato, together with Mount Unebi and Mount Miminashi, which were in the vicinity of the Asuka capital. A legend in the *Kojiki* describes how Mount Kagu fell to the earth from heaven, and it is probably

---

4. "Seen from the sky" (*sora mitsu*) is a pillow word for the place-name Yamato.

due to this that the name of the mountain is almost always preceded by the epithet "of heaven."

Climbing Mount Kagu and Looking upon the Land

1:2

The Heavenly Sovereign, a poem at the time of climbing Mount Kagu and looking upon the land.

Yamato ni wa murayama ari to	In Yamato, amid a ring of hills,
toriyorou ame no Kaguyama	stands Mount Kagu of Heaven,
noboritachi kunimi o sureba	and when I climb up to look on the land,
kunihara wa keburi tachitatsu	from the plain of the land, smoke rises and rises,
unahara wa kamame tachitatsu	from the plain of the sea, birds rise and rise;
umashi kuni so akizushima	a splendid land, the dragonfly island,
Yamato no kuni wa	the land of Yamato.

LADY NUKATA

Little is known about Lady Nukata (Nukata no Ōkimi, b. ca. 638, active until 690s). Judging by her title, she was a descendant of a previous emperor (the title "Ōkimi" was used by descendants of emperors up to the fifth generation). She had a relationship with Prince Ōama (later Emperor Tenmu, r. 672–686), by whom she had a daughter (Princess Tōchi), but then appears to have entered the service of Ōama's elder brother, Emperor Tenchi (r. 662–671). Many of Lady Nukata's poems in the *Man'yōshū* are attributed also to Empress Saimei (r. 655–661), indicating that she composed poems on the empress's behalf, perhaps in the role of a medium or priestess.

On Spring and Autumn

The following is one of the most famous poems in the *Man'yōshū*. The emphasis on spring and autumn (versus summer and winter) was originally due to the importance of these seasons in the agricultural year. As Nukata's poem illustrates, spring and autumn are seasons of transition and change, a seasonal theme that in the later poetry of the *Kokinshū* (*Collection of Ancient and Modern Poems*, ca. 905) developed into an aesthetic of impermanence.

1:16

When the Heavenly Sovereign commanded the great minister of the center, Fujiwara no Asomi,[5] to compare the charms of the myriad flowers of the spring hills with the beauty of the thousand leaves of the autumn hills, Lady Nukata expressed her judgment with a poem.

fuyugomori haru sarikureba	When spring arrives, emerging from winter,[6]
nakazarishi tori mo kinakinu	where nothing sang, the birds now sing,
sakazarishi hana mo sakeredo	where nothing blossomed, flowers blossom,
yama oshimi irite mo torazu	yet the hills are so lush, that nothing can be picked,
kusabukami torite mo mizu	and the grass is so deep that nothing can be seen.
akiyama no ko no ha o mite wa	But in the autumn hills I can see the tree leaves
momichi oba torite so shinofu	and pick the yellow ones with wonder
aoki oba okite so nageku	while I leave the green ones with longing:
soko shi urameshi	and that is my only regret,
akiyama so are wa	as I choose the autumn hills.

[Introductions and translations by Torquil Duthie]

SECOND PERIOD

The second period of the *Man'yōshū*, from the time of the Jinshin war (672) up to the capital's move to Nara (710), covers the reigns of Tenmu (672–686), Jitō (687–696), Monmu (697–707), and Genmei (707–715). Until Tenmu's reign, it had been the custom for each succeeding ruler to construct a new palace on a new site in the area of Asuka (the southern part of the Nara basin). But starting in Tenmu's reign, the court showed greater interest in constructing a permanent palace within a surrounding capital city on the model of Chinese cities, such as the Tang capitals of Chang'an and Luoyang, designed in accordance with principles of cosmology and geomancy. The first of such attempts was the capital of Fujiwara (also in the southern part of the Nara basin), to which the court of Tenmu's consort and successor Empress Jitō moved in 694. This first "permanent" capital lasted only until 710, when the court of Jitō's daughter-in-law Genmei moved the capital north of Fujiwara to Heijō (Nara).

---

5. Fujiwara no Kamatari. At this time, though, he would have been known as Nakatomi Kamatari, since the name Fujiwara was given to him on his deathbed by Emperor Tenchi. This suggests that the heading of the poem dates from later than the poem's original composition.

6. "Emerging from winter" (*fuyugomori*) is a pillow word for "spring" (*haru*).

The building of these Chinese-style capitals was part of an effort to establish a Chinese-style state, along with elaborate penal and administrative codes (ritsuryō), hierarchical systems of rank, the codification of state rituals, and the production of state mythologies, histories, and official poetry collections. It was while the capital was at Fujiwara that the *Man'yōshū* began to be compiled.

The outstanding poet of the second period is Kakinomoto no Hitomaro, who composed a number of chōka commemorating important occasions at court, such as journeys by members of the royalty and the deaths of princes, as well as more private poems.

KAKINOMOTO NO HITOMARO

Kakinomoto no Hitomaro (active late seventh century) is regarded as the greatest poet in the *Man'yōshū*. His dates are unknown, and there are no extant references to him besides the prose headnotes to his poems. For this reason, he is thought to have been a courtier with a rank too low to merit mention in the official histories, the *Nihon shoki* and the *Shoku Nihongi* (ca. 797). Most of the poems "composed by Hitomaro" are chōka accompanied by envoys in the tanka form, the earliest of which can be dated to the year 689. Thus, even though Hitomaro may have been active during Tenmu's reign, it was during Jitō's reign that he played a major role. His poems are often divided into two types: "public poems" in honor of the sovereign and members of the ruling family and "private poems" such as those on the death of his wife.

Hitomaro's poetry is a clear departure from that of his predecessors. His chōka are much longer and more elaborate, and his use of pillow words (*makurakotoba*), preface phrases (*jokotoba*), and paired measures (*tsuiku*) is more complex. He composed many *banka* (laments) on the deaths of princes of the imperial family and was responsible for the poetic deification of Emperor Tenmu and Empress Jitō. In addition, his poetry is characterized by the use of metaphors and comparisons that occur nowhere else. The most famous example is the analogy between swaying seaweed and a woman lying down, in the poem on the death of his wife.

Not long after his death, the persona of Hitomaro became the subject of legend, and in the Kana Preface to the *Kokinshū*, he is described as "the sage of poetry."

The Lament for Prince Kusakabe

The following is the earliest poem by Hitomaro that can be dated. The heading states that it was composed "at the time of the temporary burial palace of the Sovereign Prince Peer of the Sun," which refers to Tenmu's son and heir, Prince Kusakabe. According to

By the mid-eleventh century, Kakinomoto no Hitomaro had become the "patron saint of poets" (*uta no hijiri*) and was worshiped as a god. This hanging scroll, possibly produced in the Kamakura period, is traditionally attributed to Fujiwara no Nobuzane (1176–1269?), a court painter best known for his realistic style of portraiture. The inscription is by Nakamikado Nobuhide (1469–1531). (By permission of the Kyoto National Museum)

the *Nihon shoki*, Kusakabe died in 689, after Tenmu had died (686) but before he had officially succeeded his father. Temporary burial palaces were buildings in which the bodies of rulers and princes were placed for an indefinite period of mourning before their final cremation and interment. In the case of Emperor Tenmu, the period of temporary burial and rites lasted for more than two years, during which time Tenmu's wife, Jitō, and their son Kusakabe appear to have been in charge of the court. Although Kusakabe was designated to succeed his father, he died only six months after Tenmu's burial. In the following year, Tenmu's wife, Jitō, was officially installed as empress.

Hitomaro's poem begins with a mythological narrative of how sovereignty over heaven and earth was initially divided. This account differs from the more familiar mythology of the *Kojiki* and the various creation myths recorded in the *Nihon shoki*. In Hitomaro's account, the first god-ruler of the "land of rice and reed plains" was Tenmu himself, who was sent down from heaven to rule. Within this framework Kusakabe becomes not just the heir to the ruler but also the heir to a "heavenly lord," and thus his death acquires mythological significance.

1:167–169

At the time of the temporary burial palace of the Sovereign Prince. Peer of the Sun, a poem composed by Kakinomoto no Hitomaro, with short poems.

ametsuchi no hajime no toki	In the beginning of heaven and earth
hisakata no ama no kawara ni	on the riverbanks of celestial heaven,
yaoyorozu chiyorozu kami no	the eight hundred myriad, thousand
	myriad gods,
kamutsudoi tsudoi imashite	when in divine assembly they assembled
kamu wakachi wakachishi toki ni	and in divine decision they decided
amaterasu hirume no mikoto	that the heaven-shining sun-woman
	sovereign
ame oba shirashimesu to	would reign and rule in heaven
ashihara no mizuho no kuni o	and that in the land of rice and reed plains,
ametsuchi no yoriai no kiwami	until heaven and earth came to a close,
shirashimesu kami no mikoto to	the divine sovereign was to reign and rule,
amakumo no yaekaki wakete	they opened the eightfold heavenly clouds
kamu kudashi imasematsurishi	and in divine descent sent down
takaterasu hi no miko wa	the high-shining sun prince,[7]
Asuka no Kiyomi no miya ni	who in the palace of Kiyomi in Asuka,[8]

---

7. The "high-shining sun prince" (*takaterasu hi no miko*) was Emperor Tenmu's title. The poem suggests that in heaven Tenmu was known as the "divine sovereign" (*kami no mikoto*), and on earth (the "land of rice and reed plains") he was revealed as the "high-shining sun prince."

8. Tenmu's palace, also known as Kiyomihara.

kamu nagara futoshikimashite	being divine, firmly ruled and decreed
sumeroki no shikimasu kuni to	that the land would be ruled by the heavenly lords,[9]
ama no hara iwato o hiraki	then opened the stone gates to the heavenly plain,
kamu agari agariimashinu	and in divine ascent has ascended.
waga ōkimi miko no mikoto no	Our great lord the sovereign prince,[10]
ame no shita shirashimesu yo wa	the realm he is to reign and rule beneath heaven,
haruhana no tōtoku aramu to	may it flourish nobly like the spring blossoms,
mochizuki no tatawashikemu to	may it wax great like the full moon,
ame no shita yomo no hito no	thus the people of the four corners beneath heaven
ōbune no omoitanomite	hope for his reign as if for a great ship[11]
amatsumizu augite matsu ni	and wait in awe as for water from heaven
ikasama ni omohoshimese ka	—but what designs are in his mind?—[12]
tsure mo naki Mayumi no oka ni	on Mayumi Hill, where he has no destiny,[13]
miyabashira futoshiki imashi	he firmly builds the palace pillars,
miaraka o takashirimashite	he raises high the sacred hall[14]
asakoto ni mikoto towasanu	and does not speak his morning words.[15]
hitsuki no maneku narinure	Now many days and months have passed
soko yue ni miko no miyahito	and that is why the prince's courtiers
yukue shirazu mo	do not know where to go.
hanka nishū	Two Envoys
hisakata no ame miru gotoku	As though looking up at celestial heaven
augi mishi miko no mikado no	we looked up in awe at the prince's palace
aremaku oshi mo	and now we grieve at its abandonment.

---

9. By the descendants of the first "heavenly lord" who came down to earth—that is, Tenmu himself.

10. Tenmu's son and chosen successor, Prince Kusakabe, referred to in the headnote as the Sovereign Prince Peer of the Sun (Hinami no miko no mikoto).

11. "As if for a great ship" (*ōbune no*) is a pillow word for "hope" (*omoitanomu*).

12. In Prince Kusakabe's mind.

13. That is, his destiny was to accede to the throne.

14. "Firmly builds the palace pillars, . . . raises high the sacred hall" is a formulaic expression normally used to describe accession to the throne. In this case, however, since what Kusakabe is building is his own temporary burial palace, the purpose of the expression is to describe Kusakabe's death euphemistically as "accession" to the other world.

15. That is, he does not give the palace courtiers their morning commands.

akanesasu hi wa teraseredo   Although the striking red sun shines,
nubatama no yo wataru tsuki no   the moon[16] crosses the black jewel night
kakuraku oshi mo   and we grieve at its concealment.

In another text, the second poem is the envoy to a poem from the time of the temporary burial palace of another sovereign prince.[17]

The Yoshino Praise Poems

According to the *Nihon shoki*, Empress Jitō made thirty-one visits to the Yoshino Palace between 689 and 696, the year of her abdication, an average of three or four times a year. Yoshino, located about ten miles south of the Asuka capital, was a site of great symbolic importance for the Jitō court because of its association with Jitō's husband and predecessor, Tenmu, who had established his headquarters at Yoshino before the Jinshin war. Thus Yoshino was seen as the origin of the current political order. Yoshino also seems to have been associated with a Daoist cult of immortality, which may have been a factor in Tenmu's choice of this site.

As the *Man'yōshū* compilers speculate in the endnote, the poems probably date from the time around Jitō's official accession to the throne. The two chōka have an almost identical structure, the first describing the empress's rule over the human world and the second, her rule over the divine world. Both poems are characterized by the presence of binary measures (*tsuiku*) with spatial and temporal motifs. In the first chōka, the empress is described as building the "palace pillars," and the courtiers cross the river to the palace in the morning and in the evening (suggesting that they are at her service all day long). The chōka ends with the mountain that "commands the heights" and the river that "flows unceasingly." Both are metaphors praising the palace. In the envoy, the courtiers' pledge to "return to see [Yoshino] flow unceasingly" is a reference to a poem by Emperor Tenmu, in which he commands his descendants to "look well on Yoshino."

In the second chōka, the empress again "raises high the high halls" and climbs to the top of the palace to "look on the land," just as Jomei climbed Mount Kagu in *Man'yōshū* 1:2. Here the mountain gods are said to present offerings in the spring and in the autumn (indicating that they are at her service all year round), and the river gods send cormorants to the "upper shoals" and cast nets across the "lower shoals" to present food to her. This pairing of "mountain and river" is influenced by Chinese precedent, in which it stands as a metaphor for the entire realm. The climax of the chōka describes Empress Jitō as a god who rules over the lesser gods of the mountains

---

16. The "moon" is Prince Kusakabe, and the "sun" probably refers to Empress Jitō.

17. Probably Prince Takechi, who died in 696 and for whom Hitomaro also wrote a long banka, which also has been translated here.

and rivers and defines her reign as "the age of a god." Empress Jitō is thus presented as an absolute ruler, reigning over people, gods, space, and time.

1:36–39

At the time of the Heavenly Sovereign[18] going to the Yoshino palace, poems composed by Kakinomoto no Hitomaro.

yasumishishi waga ōkimi no	Our great lord of the eight corners,
kikoshiosu ame no shita ni	she who commands and rules all beneath heaven,
kuni wa shi mo sawa ni aredomo	although her lands are indeed many,
yamakawa no kiyoki kafuchi to	for the clear pools of its mountain river
mikokoro o Yoshino no kuni no	her heart is drawn to the land of Yoshino,[19]
hana jirau Akizu no nohe ni	and on the Akizu plains, where flowers scatter
miyabashira futoshikimashite	she firmly builds the palace pillars
momoshiki no ōmiyahito wa	and thus the courtiers of the glorious palace
funa namete asakawa wataru	line up the boats to cross the morning river
funa gioi yūkawa wataru	and race the boats to cross the evening river.
kono kawa no tayuru koto naku	This river that flows unceasingly,
kono yama no iya takashirasu	this mountain that commands the heights,
mina sosogu tagi no miyako wa	the glorious palace by the surging water,
miredo akanu kamo	we never tire to see.
hanka	Envoy
miredo akanu	We never tire to see
Yoshino no kawa no tokoname no	the eternal bed of the Yoshino River
tayuru koto naku mata kaerimimu	may we return to see it flow unceasingly.[20]

---

18. Empress Jitō (r. 687–697)

19. There is a play on words here between the place-name Yoshino and *yoshi* (good) and *yosu* (draw).

20. "Flow unceasingly" refers to both the river and the speaker's pledge to return.

yasumishishi waga ōkimi	Our great lord who reigns in peace,
kamu nagara kamu sabisesu to	being divine, acts divinely,
Yoshinogawa tagitsu kafuchi ni	and by the rapids of Yoshino River
takadono o takashirimashite	raises high the high halls,
noboritachi kunimi o seseba	and when she climbs up to look on the land,
tatanaharu aokakiyama no	from the green and manifold mountains
yamatsumi no matsuru mitsuki to	the mountain gods present their offerings,
haru he wa hana kazashimochi	bringing her blossoms in the spring
aki tateba momichi kazaseri	and yellow leaves when autumn comes,
yukisou kawa no kami mo	and the running river gods too
ōmike ni tsukaematsuru to	make their offerings for the sacred meal,
kamitsuse ni ukawa o tachi	sending cormorants to the upper shoals
shimotsuse ni sade sashiwatasu	and casting nets in the lower shoals.
yamakawa mo yorite tsukauru	Such is this glorious age of a god
kami no miyo kamo	whom both mountain and river come to serve.
hanka	Envoy
yamakawa mo yorite tsukauru	Being a god
kamu nagara	whom both mountain and river come to serve
tagitsu kafuchi ni funade	in the rapids she sets her boat to sail.
sesu kamo	

In reference to the preceding, the *Nihon shoki* states, "In the New Year of the third year of the reign (689), the Heavenly Sovereign went to the palace of Yoshino. In the eighth month the Heavenly Sovereign went to the palace of Yoshino. In the second month of the fourth year of the reign (690), the Heavenly Sovereign went to the palace of Yoshino. In the fifth month, the Heavenly Sovereign went to the palace of Yoshino. In the New Year of the fifth year of the reign (691), the Heavenly Sovereign went to the palace of Yoshino. In the fourth month, the Heavenly Sovereign went to the palace of Yoshino." It is not clearly known in which month (Hitomaro) was in attendance and the poems were composed.

The Lament for Prince Takechi

The following is the second of Hitomaro's "poems on temporary burial" and is the longest poem in the *Man'yōshū*. Prince Takechi died in the year 696 at the age of forty-three. For the last six years of his life, he was Empress's Jitō's chancellor (*daijō daijin*). Although in principle Takechi's mother was of too low a rank for him to become emperor, in the heading to the poem he is styled as "the sovereign Prince" (*miko no mikoto*), indicating that he does appear to have been, at least temporarily, the next in line to the throne. He was the highest in rank of Emperor Tenmu's surviving sons, since both Prince Kusakabe and Prince Ōtsu had died. The *Nihon shoki* suggests that by granting him larger fiefs, Empress Jitō made him far more powerful than any of the other princes. Takechi's death was therefore of immense significance to the entire court.

The poem begins by describing the Jinshin war and Tenmu's command to subdue the "unruly peoples" and the "defiant lands," which refer to the forces of Emperor Tenchi's son Prince Ōtomo and the allies of the Ōmi court. Takechi receives Tenmu's command, and the first half of the poem is a mythical narrative of the war, resulting in Tenmu's unchallenged rule of the "land of rice and reed plains" (a mythical name for Japan). The *Nihon shoki* also cites Takechi's central role in the war. The second half of the poem begins by mentioning Takechi's role as chancellor and describes his death in tragic terms similar to that of Prince Kusakabe, Takechi's "building" his own palace of temporary burial, and the courtiers' bereavement and confusion at his death.

2:199–201

At the time of the temporary burial palace of the sovereign Prince Takechi, a poem composed by Kakinomoto no Hitomaro, with short poems.

kakemaku mo yuyushiki kamo	Too sacred to utter aloud,
iwamaku mo aya ni kashikomi	too awesome even to speak of,
Asuka no Makami no hara ni	he[21] who in Asuka on the Makami plains
hisakata no amatsu mikado o	established in awesome splendor
kashikoku mo sadametamaite	the celestial heavenly palace
kamu sabu to iwagakurimasu	and now hides divinely in the rocks,
yasumishishi waga ōkimi no	our great lord of the eight corners,[22]
kikoshimesu sotomo no kuni no	in the northern lands he commands and rules,
maki tatsu Fuwayama koete	crossed Mount Fuwa of the evergreen trees,[23]
koma tsurugi Wazami ga hara no	and on the plain of Wazami of the Korean swords[24]
karimiya ni amoriimashite	descended from heaven[25] to his temporary palace:

---

21. Emperor Tenmu.
22. "Of the eight corners" (*yasumishishi*) is a pillow word for "our great lord" (*waga ōkimi*).
23. "Of the evergreen trees" (*maki tatsu*) is a pillow word for Fuwa.
24. "Of the Korean swords" (*komatsurugi*) is a pillow word for Wazami.
25. "Descended from heaven" (*amoriimashite*) suggests that Tenmu is a heavenly god.

ame no shita osametamai	let us conquer all beneath heaven
osu kuni o sadametamau to	and bring peace and rule to the lands,
tori ga naku azuma no kuni no	let us summon the glorious troops
miikusa o meshitamaite	from the Eastern Lands where birds cry
chihayaburu hito o yawase to	to vanquish the unruly peoples
matsurowanu kuni o osame to	and conquer the defiant lands.
miko nagara maketamaeba	Thus by the sun prince[26] appointed to the task,
ōmimi ni tachi torihakashi	to his[27] glorious body he girded his sword,
ōmite ni yumi torimotashi	in his glorious hand he grasped his bow,
miikusa o adomoitamai	and as he called the troops into battle,
totonouru tsuzumi no oto wa	the sound of the summoning drums
ikazuchi no koe to kiku made	was like the booming voice of thunder
fukinaseru kuda no oto mo	and the sound of the blowing horns,
ata mitaru tora ga hoyuru to	like the roar of a hunting tiger,
morohito no obiyuru made ni	terrified the enemy multitudes.
sasagetaru hata no maneki wa	The rippling of the hoisted banners
fuyugomori ham sarikureba	wafting and waving in the wind
nogoto ni tsukite aru hi no	was like the fires that alight on the plains
kaze no muta nabikau gotoku	when spring arrives, emerging from winter,[28]
torimoteru yuwazu no sawaki	and the resounding of the bowstrings
miyuki furu fuyu no hayashi ni	was so awesome to hear
tsumuji kamo ima kiwataru to	it felt like a whirlwind was blowing
omou made kiki no kashikoku	through the snow in a winter forest;
hikihanatsu ya no shigekeku	and the swarm of arrows that flew
ōyuki no midarete kitare	came scattering down like a snowstorm,
matsurowazu tachimukaishi mo	and the defiant as they stood,
tsuyushimo no kenaba kenu beku	like the dew and the frost destined to perish,
yuku tori no arasou hashi ni	like flying birds were fighting to the last,
Watarai no itsuki no miya yu	when from the sacred shrine of Watarai[29]
kamikaze ni ifukimatowashi	a divine wind suddenly blew forth,
amakumo o hi no me mo miezu	the heavenly clouds concealed the sun,
tokoyami ni ōhitamaite	and they were covered by an eternal darkness.

---

26. The [High-Shining Sun] Prince—that is, Emperor Tenmu.

27. This refers to Prince Takechi, who is "appointed to the task" of conquering the realm by his father Tenmu (the "sun prince").

28. "Emerging from winter" (*fuyugomori*) is a pillow word for "spring" (*haru*).

29. The Ise Shrine.

sadameteshi mizuho no kuni o	Thus was conquered the land of rice and reed plains,
kamu nagara futoshikimashite	which being divine, he[30] firmly ruled,
yasumishishi waga ōkimi no	and our great lord of the eight corners,[31]
ame no shita ōshitamaeba	since he governed[32] the realm beneath heaven,
yorozu yo ni shika shi mo aramu to	we thought it would be for a myriad ages,
yūhana no sakayuru toki ni	but just at the time of the flourishing blossoms,
waga ōkimi miko no mikado o	the glorious halls of our great lord the prince
kamumiya ni yosoimatsurite	we decorate as his divine palace
tsukaishishi mikado no hito mo	and the people who served his glorious halls,
shirotae no asagoromo kite	wearing long robes of fine white hemp,
Haniyasu no mikado no hara ni	on the plain of the Halls of Haniyasu,
akanesasu hi no kotogoto	every single striking red day,[33]
shishijimono iwaifushitsutsu	like wild beasts lie prostrated,
nubatama no yūhe ni itareba	and when the gem-black evenings come,[34]
ōtono o furisake mitsutsu	look up to the glorious palace
uzura nasu iwaimotohori	and crawl around like quail:
samoraedo samoraieneba	they[35] would serve, but there is no one to serve,
harutori no samayoinureba	and wailing like spring birds
nageki mo imada suginu ni	their sorrow does not pass,
omoi mo imada tsukineba	their pain is not exhausted,
koto saeku Kudara no hara yu	as on the plain of chattering Kudara[36]
kamu haburi haburiimashite	in divine burial they bury him,
asa mo yoshi Kinoe no miya o	and Kinoe palace, fair in the morning,[37]
tokomiya to takaku shitatete	as his eternal palace he[38] builds high

30. Tenmu.

31. Takechi.

32. Takechi, the chancellor during Empress Jitō's reign.

33. "Striking red" (*akanesasu*) is a pillow word for "day" or "sun" (*hi*).

34. "Gem-black" (*nubatama no*) is a pillow word for "evening" (*yū*) or, more commonly, "night" (*yo*).

35. The courtiers.

36. One of the Korean kingdoms. "Chattering" (*koto saeku*) is a pillow word that probably refers to the foreign languages of the Korea Peninsula.

37. "Fair in the morning" (*asa mo yoshi*) is a pillow word for Kinoe.

38. This refers to Prince Takechi, who, like Prince Kusakabe in *Man'yōshū* 1:167, is described as building his own palace of temporary burial, his "eternal palace."

kamu nagara shizumarimashinu
shikaredomo wa ga ōkimi no
yorozu yo to omohoshimeshite
tsukurashishi Kaguyama no miya
yorozu yo ni sugimu to omoe ya
ame no goto furisake mitsutsu
tamadasuki kakete shinowamu

kashikoku ari to mo

tanka nishū

hisakata no ame shirashinuru
kimi yue ni
hitsuki mo shirazu koiwataru
     kamo

Haniyasu no ike no tsutsumi no
komorinu no yukue o shira ni
toneri wa matou

and being divine, rests there in peace.
And yet the palace of Mount Kagu,[39]
which our lord built to stand
for a myriad ages, who can doubt
that it will outlast a myriad ages?
As we look up at it, as if to heaven,
with cords of gems let us mourn him
     in sorrow,
though we be full of awe.

Two Short Poems

He has left to rule the celestial heavens,
our lord for whom we grieve
with no regard for the days and
     the months.

In the enclosed marsh of Haniyasu Lake
the courtiers are lost
and do not know which way to go.

Poems on Passing the Ruined Capital of Ōmi

The date that the following sequence of poems was composed is unknown. The occasion is a journey on which the travelers pass by the ruined capital of Ōmi. In 668, Emperor Tenchi (r. 662–671) moved the capital from its historical location in Asuka (in the province of Yamato) to the province of Ōmi (on Lake Biwa). This was an unprecedented move. According to the *Nihon shoki*, Tenchi had named his brother Prince Ōama his successor, but shortly before he died Tenchi appears to have changed his mind and transferred the succession to his son Prince Ōtomo. After Tenchi's death, a conflict known as the Jinshin war broke out between the forces of Ōtomo, who was based in the Ōmi capital, and Ōama, who was based in Yoshino, close to the old Asuka capital in Yamato. Ōama won the war and moved the capital back to Asuka, reigning as Emperor Tenmu. Tenmu was then succeeded by his wife (Tenchi's daughter), Empress Jitō. Thus, for the Jitō court, for which Hitomaro was writing, the Ōmi capital was a problematic topic. On the one hand, the present court was the product of a war that had been waged on the Ōmi capital. On the other, the Jitō court had many ties with the Ōmi court, not the least of which was the fact that the Ōmi emperor, Tenchi, was the current sovereign's father.

---

39. The palace of Mount Kagu seems to have been Takechi's dwelling in life.

Hitomaro's poem on the Ōmi capital has often been read as an attempt to ritually pacify the spirits of the dead courtiers of the Ōmi capital. Many of the poem's expressions also appear in elegies (banka), suggesting that the poem is a lament on the ruins. By definition, the capital was the center of the realm, situated directly beneath "heaven." According to the poem, the present capital and all capitals (except Ōmi) were in Asuka in Yamato Province. Thus it follows that from the Yamato-centered point of view, Ōmi was "a barbarous place, far from heaven," and yet it was from Ōmi that Tenchi "reigned and ruled all beneath heaven." In other words, during Tenchi's reign, Ōmi was the center of the realm.

1:29–31

Passing by the ruined capital of Ōmi, poems composed by Kakinomoto no Hitomaro.

tamadasuki Unebi no yama no	Since the glorious age of the Kashiwara
Kashihara no hijiri no miyo yu	sun-ruler,[40] by Mount Unebi of the cords of gems,[41]
aremashishi kami no kotogoto	each and every of the gods that have appeared[42]
tsuga no ki no iya tsugitsugi ni	like the winding spruce one after the next,
ame no shita shirashimeshishi o	have reigned and ruled all beneath heaven,
sora ni mitsu Yamato o okite	but to leave Yamato, so full of heaven,
ao ni yoshi Narayama o koe	and cross the Nara hills, so rich in green,[43]
ikasama ni omohoshimese ka	—what designs were in his mind,[44]
amazakaru hina ni wa aredo	that in a barbarous place, far from heaven,[45]
iwabashiru Ōmi no kuni ni	in the land of Ōmi of the racing rocks,[46]
sasanami no Ōtsu no miya ni	in the palace of Ōtsu of the lively waves,[47]

40. According to the *Kojiki* and the *Nihon shoki*, the legendary first emperor, known as Emperor Jinmu, reigned from the palace of Kashiwara.

41. "Cords of gems" is a pillow word for Unebi. Unebi is one of the Three Mountains of Yamato (the other two being Mount Kagu and Mount Miminashi), which were in the vicinity of the Asuka capital.

42. Each and every one of the successive sovereigns.

43. "Rich in green" is a pillow word for Nara.

44. In Emperor Tenchi's mind.

45. "Far from heaven" is a pillow word for "barbarous." Anywhere far from the capital was also "far from heaven."

46. "Of the racing rocks" is a pillow word for Ōmi.

47. "Of the lively waves" (*sananami no*) is a pillow word for Ōtsu and other place-names in Ōmi. It also is a place-name itself.

ame no shita shirashimeshikemu	he[48] reigned and ruled all beneath heaven?
sumeroki no kami no mikoto no	The heavenly lord, divine sovereign,
ōmiya wa koko to kikedomo	though we have heard here was his glorious palace,
ōtono wa koko to iedomo	though it is said here were his glorious halls,
harukusa no shigeku oitaru	now all is overgrown by the spring grass,
kasumi tachi haruhi no kireru	and clouded by the haze of the spring sun,
momoshiki no ōmiyadokoro	as we look at the site of the glorious palace
mireba kanashi mo	we are filled with sadness.
hanka	Envoys
Sasanami no Shiga no Karasaki	O Kara Cape of Shiga in Sasanami,
sakiku aredo	though you are unchanged,
ōmiyahito no fune machikanetsu	in vain we wait for the courtiers' boats.
Sasanami no Shiga no ōwada	O Shore of Shiga in Sasanami,
yodomu to mo	though your waters are still,[49]
mukashi no hito ni mata	how could we meet the people of
awame ya mo	the past?

Poems on Parting from His Wife in Iwami

The poetic category of *sōmon* (exchanges) includes mostly short poems (*tanka*), with the following renowned exception of two chōka with tanka by Hitomaro. Although the poems have often been regarded as autobiographical, recent scholarship suggests that the male protagonist, the "I," was probably meant as a fictional figure with whom the courtiers traveling from the provinces to the capital could identify. The heading of the poem, which names Hitomaro himself as the protagonist, was likely a later addition by the compilers of volume 2, who fictionalized and romanticized Hitomaro's life.

One of the most curious aspects of the first chōka is its long introduction. The first half of the poem seems to be an extended preface phrase that introduces the woman by means of a pun on the seaweed drawing to the shore and the girl drawing close to the man in sleep. This metaphor of seaweed swaying for a woman lying down or making love is unique to Hitomaro.

---

48. Emperor Tenchi.

49. Flowing water is a metaphor for time passing. "Though your waters are still" has the connotation of "although time does not seem to pass."

2:131–137

Kakinomoto no Hitomaro, on parting from his wife in the land of Iwami and traveling up to the capital, two poems with short poems.

Iwami no umi Tsuno no urami o	In the sea of Iwami[50] is Tsuno Bay,
ura nashi to hito koso mirame	which people may see as having no coves,
kata nashi to hito koso mirame	and people may see as having no inlets,
yoshieyashi ura wa naku to mo	but yet, all the same, though it has no coves,
yoshieyashi kata wa naku to mo	and yet, all the same, though it has no inlets,
isanatori umihe o sashite	toward the shore of that whale-hunting sea,[51]
Watazu no ariso no ue ni	and onto the barren beach of Watazu,
kaaoku ouru tamamo okitsumo	may the green gem weed and the open seaweed
asa hafuru kaze koso yoseme	be drawn by the morning wings of the wind,
yū hafuru nami koso kiyore	be drawn by the evening wings of the waves:
nami no muta kayori kakuyoru	and so by the waves drawn back and drawn forth,[52]
tama mo nasu yorineshi imo o	like gem weed, my girl drew to me in sleep,
tsuyushimo no okiteshi kureba	and since I left her, like the dew and the frost,[53]
kono michi no yasokumagoto ni	though a myriad times I turn to look back
yorozu tabi kaerimi suredo	on each of the eighty bends of this road,
iya tō ni sato wa sakarinu	farther and farther I've come from her village,
iya taka ni yama mo koekinu	and higher and higher I've crossed the hills.
natsukusa no omoishinaete	As I think of my girl, wilting with sorrow

---

50. Iwami was a province on the Japan Sea coast, on the west side of present-day Shimane Prefecture.

51. "Whale-hunting" (*isanatori*) is a pillow word for "sea" (*umi*).

52. The first half of the poem is an extended preface phrase introducing "my girl."

53. "Like the dew and the frost" (*tsuyushimo no*) is a pillow word for "leave" (*oku*) and implies "since I left her, like the dew and the frost are left on the ground."

shinofuramu imo ga kado mimu	like the summer grass, I wish I could see her gate:
nabike kono yama	Let these hills move aside!
hanka nishū	Two Envoys
Iwami no ya	In Iwami,
Takatsuno yama no	through the trees on the hill
ko no ma yori	of Takatsuno,
waga furu sode o imo mitsuramu ka	can my girl see me as I wave my sleeves?
sasa no ha wa	Though the *sasa*[54] leaves
miyama mo soya ni midaru to mo	may rustle and scatter on the hills,
are wa imo omou	I think of my girl from whom I
wakarekinureba	have parted.
Tsuno sawau Iwami no umi no	In Tsuno Bay[55] in the sea of Iwami,
koto saeku Kara no saki naru	on Kara Cape of the chattering voices,[56]
ikuri ni so fukamiru ouru	on the seabed the deep seaweed grows,
ariso ni so tamamo wa ouru	and on the barren beach the gem weed grows,
tamamo nasu nabikineshi ko o	and the girl who like gem weed slept beside me,
fukamiru no fukamete omoedo	like the deep seaweed was deep in my thoughts,
saneshi yo wa ikuda mo arazu	yet few were the nights that we slept together
hautsuta no wakareshikureba	before I left her like a parting vine,
kimo mukau kokoro o itami	with a heavy heart, my courage failing,[57]
omoitsutsu kaerimi suredo	and as I yearn now, turning to look back
ōbune no Watari no yama no	from Mount Watari, as if from a great ship,[58]

---

54. A type of short bamboo.

55. "In Tsuno Bay" is a translation of an obscure pillow word, *tsuno sawau*.

56. Kara appears to be a place on the coast of Iwami; it also was used to refer to the Korea Peninsula. The pillow word "of the chattering voices" (*koto saeku*) probably refers to the foreign languages spoken in Korea.

57. "Courage failing" is a conjectural translation of the pillow word *kimo mukau*, which literally means "facing the liver." *Kimo mukau* tends to appear in instances when the heart is described as weak.

58. "As if from a great ship" is a pillow word for the name Watari, which means "crossing."

momichiba no chiri no magai ni	through the yellow leaves as they scatter
imo ga sode saya ni mo miezu	I cannot see my girl waving her sleeves,
tsumagomoru Yakami no yama no	and over the wife-hiding Mount Yakami,[59]
kumoma yori watarau tsuki no	the moon now crosses through the clouds,
oshikedomo kakuraikureba	and as it passes, regrettably, out of sight
amazutau irihi sashinure	the heaven-sent sun[60] has already set,
masurao to omoeru ware mo	and though I had thought I was a brave man,
shikitae no koromo no sode wa	the sleeves of my robe of fine quilted cloth
tōrite nurenu	are drenched with tears.
hanka nishū	Two Envoys
aokoma ga agaki o hayami	So fast is the gallop of my gray horse
kumoi ni so	that I have left behind
imo no atari o sugite kinikeru	the village of my girl beyond the clouds.
akiyama ni otsuru momichiba	Yellow leaves, falling on the autumn hill,
shimashiku wa na chiri magai so	stop scattering for just a while
imo no atari mimu	so I may see the village of my girl.

Poems on the Death of His Wife

In addition to composing elegies (*banka*) in honor of members of the imperial family, Hitomaro composed a set of two poems on the death of his wife, the first of which is translated here. It is not known whether the poem is autobiographical or fictional. The opening suggests that the relationship is secret or forbidden and that the two lovers find it hard to meet. Then the "messenger" (through whom they correspond) comes to tell the protagonist that his wife has died. The death is described in a series of natural metaphors of passing (the sun setting, the autumn leaves) that are characteristic of Hitomaro. In the second half of the poem, the protagonist goes to the Karu market, not in search of the woman herself, but of her spirit. And yet, since he cannot hear the cries of the birds on Unebi Mountain (the dead were thought to manifest themselves as birds shortly after death) and she does not appear to him in the faces of passersby, he can do nothing but call her name and wave his sleeves (a ritual to summon the spirits of the dead back to life).

---

59. "Wife-hiding" is a pillow word for *ya* (house/hut), modifying the place-name Yakami. The pillow word also implies that the wife ("my girl") is hidden behind the mountains and the speaker cannot see her.

60. "Heaven-sent" (*ametsutau*) is a pillow word for sun (*hi*).

2:207–209

Kakinomoto no Hitomaro, after his wife died, crying tears of blood in his grief, composed two poems, with short poems.

ama tobu ya Karu no michi wa	On the road to Karu, that soars in heaven,[61]
wagimoko ga sato ni shi areba	was the village where my girl lived,
nemokoro ni mimaku hoshikedo	and I wanted to visit her with all my heart,
yamazu ikaba hitome o ōmi	but if I went too often, too many would see,
maneku ikaba hito shirinu bemi	and if I went many times, too many would know,
sanekazura nochi mo awamu to	so we parted like vines that meet again
ōbune no omoitanomite	or so I hoped, as if for a great ship,[62]
tamakagiru iwagakifuchi no	and to a pool surrounded by gem-gleaming[63] rocks
komori nomi koitsutsu aru ni	I retreated, but as I longed for her,
wataru hi no kurenuru ga goto	like the sky-crossing sun sets in the evening,
terutsuki no kumogakuru goto	like the light of the moon is obscured by the clouds,
okitsumo no nabikishi imo wa	my girl, who like the deep seaweed had slept beside me,
momichiba no sugite iniki to	had passed away like the autumn leaves,
tamazusa no tsukai no ieba	so, said the messenger of the catalpa gem,[64]
azusayumi oto ni kikite	and as I heard his voice like a catalpa bow,[65]
iwamu sube semu sube shira ni	I knew not what to say or what to do,
oto nomi o kikite arieneba	but since I could not bear to hear the words,
aga kouru chie no hitoe mo	and thinking there must be a way to find solace
nagusamoru kokoro mo ari ya to	for just a single part of my thousandfold longing,
wagimoko ga yamazu idemishi	I went where my girl always used to go,

---

61. "That soars in heaven" (*ama tobu ya*) is a pillow word for Karu, which means "light."

62. "Great ship" (*ōbune no*) is a pillow word for "hope" (*omoitanomu*).

63. Here, "gem gleaming" (*tamakagiru*) is a pillow word for "rock" (*iwa*).

64. "Catalpa gem" (*tamazusa*) is a pillow word for "messenger" (*tsukai*).

65. "Catalpa bow" (*azusayumi*) is a pillow word for "sound" or "voice" (*oto*).

Karu no ichi ni waga tachikikeba	to Karu Market, and stood there and listened,
tamadasuki Unebi no yama ni	but on Mount Unebi of the cords of gems
naku tori no oto mo kikoezu	I could not hear the voices of the birds,
tamahoko no michiyukibito no	and of the people walking on the road
hitori dani niteshi yukaneba	not a single one resembled my girl,
sube o nami imo ga na yobite	and all I could do was call out her name
sode so furitsuru	as I waved my sleeves.
tanka nishū	Two Short Poems
akiyama no momichiba o shigemi	I search for my girl who has lost her way
matoinuru imo o motomemu	in the thick yellow leaves of the autumn hill
yamaji shirazu mo	but do not know the mountain path.
momichiba no chiriyuku nae ni	As the yellow leaves scatter and fall,
tamazusa no tsukai o mireba	when I see a messenger of the catalpa gem[66]
aishi hi omohoyu	I think of the days when we met.

The Lament for Princess Asuka

The following lament for Princess Asuka is, in addition to being Hitomaro's last datable poem, the third of Hitomaro's three "laments of temporary interment" (*hinkyū banka*), the other two being for Prince Kusakabe and Prince Takechi. Whereas both Kusakabe and Takechi were successors to the throne at the time of their deaths, there is nothing to indicate that Princess Asuka was a figure of particular importance. She was a daughter of Emperor Tenchi and Lady Tachibana. According to the *Shoku Nihongi* (ca. 797), she died in 700. The poem has none of the political-mythical content of the laments for Kusakabe and Takechi and is more reminiscent of love exchanges and personal laments. The poem mentions Princess Asuka's husband (her "magnificent lord"), who is not identified. Scholars have speculated that he was Tenmu's second son, Prince Osakabe (d. 705).

The poem is an interesting mix of Hitomaro's public and private poetry. The voice of the poem grieves as a courtier of Princess Asuka but also describes her husband's grief at her death. The binary measures that were used in the Yoshino poems to express the absoluteness of Empress Jitō's power are used here to describe the absoluteness of Asuka's splendor and the husband's grief.

---

66. This refers to seeing any messenger between two lovers.

2:196–198

At the time of the temporary burial palace of Princess Asuka, a poem by Kakinomoto no Hitomaro, with short poems.

tobutori no Asuka no kawa no	On the Asuka River, where the birds fly,[67]
kamitsuse ni ishibashi watashi	in the upper shoals there is a bridge of stone,
shimotsuse ni uchihashi watasu	and in the lower shoals a bridge of wood.
ishibashi ni oinabikeru	The gem weed that grows on the bridge of stone,
tamamo mo zo tayureba ouru	though it may wither, will grow back again.
uchihashi ni oi o oreru	The stream weed that grows on the bridge of wood,
kawamo mo zo karureba hayuru	though it may dry, will spring forth again.
nani shi ka mo waga ōkimi no	So for what reason then, has my great lady,
tataseba tamamo no mokoro	who was like gem weed when she stood,
koyaseba kawamo no gotoku	and like stream weed when she lay down
nabikaishi yoroshiki kimi ga	by the side of her magnificent lord,
asamiya o wasuretamau ya	why has she forgotten his morning palace?
yūmiya o somukitamau ya	and why does she forsake his evening palace?
utsusomi to omoishi toki ni	When we thought she was of this world,
haruhe ni wa hana orikazashi	her lord would bring her flowers in spring
akitateba momichiba kazashi	and yellow leaves when autumn came,
shikitae no sode tazusawari	and holding her hand beneath quilted sleeves
kagami nasu miredo mo akazu	he never tired to see her, radiant like a mirror,[68]
mochizuki no iya mezurashimi	and sometimes with her lord, who thought
omohoshishi kimi to tokidoki	she was fairer than the full moon,
idemashite asobitamaishi	she would go out on pleasure visits
mike mukau Kinoe no miya oto	to Kinoe palace, where feasts were held,[69]

---

67. "Where the birds fly" (*tobu tori no*) is a pillow word for Asuka. In fact, Asuka (the place) was customarily written with the characters for "fly" and "bird." In this poem, however, "Asuka" is written with the same characters as those of Princess Asuka's name.

68. "Like a mirror" (*kagami nasu*) is a pillow word for "see" (*miru*).

69. "Where feasts were held" (*mike mukau*) is a pillow word for the place-name Kinoe.

tokomiya to sadametamaite

but now she makes that her eternal palace

ajisawau mekoto mo taenu
shikare kamo aya ni kanashimi
nuedori no katakoizuma
asadori no kayowasu kimi ga

and her words and eyes are no more.
And that is why, in his terrible sadness,
like the tiger thrush longing for its mate,
her lord goes to visit her with the morning birds,

natsukusa no omoishinaete
yūtsuzu no kayuki kakuyuki
ōbune no tayutau mireba
nagusamoru kokoro mo arazu
soko yue ni semu sube shire ya
oto nomi mo na nomi taezu
ametsuchi no iya tōnagaku
shinoi ikamu mina ni kakaseru

wilting in sorrow like the summer grass,
going back and forth like the evening star,
and as we see him reel like a great ship,
we have no way to give him solace
and do not know what we can do
but let the sound of her name extend
as far and as long as heaven and earth
and let us mourn by that which shares her name,

Asukagawa yorozu yo made ni
hashikiyashi waga ōkimi no

the Asuka River, and for a myriad ages
may we remember our great and beloved lady

katami ni koko o

here by her memento.

tanka nishū

Two Short Poems

Asukagawa shigarami watashi
sekamaseba nagaruru mizu mo
nodo ni ka aramashi

If we had placed branches to stop its flow,
across the Asuka River,
the running waters would have become still.

Asukagawa asu dani mimu to
omoe ya mo
waga ōkimi no mina wasuresenu

River of Tomorrow, and though tomorrow
we will not see her
we will not forget our great lady's name.

[Introductions and translations by Torquil Duthie]

THIRD PERIOD

The third period, beginning with the capital's move to Nara in 710 and ending with Yamanoue no Okura's death in 733, is when the majority of the poems of the *Man'yōshū* were composed. It includes the reigns of Genmei (707–715), Genshō (715–723), and Shōmu (724–749). With the establishment of a Chinese-style legal (ritsuryō) state, poetic circles appeared in the provinces, formed by middle-rank courtiers who were sent out from the capital as provincial governors. The most notable example of this was the poetic circle at Dazaifu (in

Kyushu) headed by Ōtomo no Tabito and Yamanoue no Okura. Volume 5 of the *Man'yōshū* is devoted entirely to the poetry of Dazaifu and is thought to have been compiled by Okura and Tabito.

YAMABE NO AKAHITO

Yamabe no Akahito was active between 724 and 736, but his exact dates are unknown. Like Hitomaro, there are no references to him except in the prose headnotes to his poems, and for this reason he is thought to have been of low rank. The date of his earliest poem in the *Man'yōshū*, on Mount Fuji (translated here), is usually estimated to have been between 720 and 724, and the date of his last poem is 736. Akahito is thought to have been at the forefront of a revival of court poetry during Shōmu's reign. One of Akahito's signature characteristics is his description of landscape. For this reason, it is often said that Hitomaro was a poet of sound and Akahito was a poet of images.

On Looking at Mount Fuji

The following poem is the first mention of Mount Fuji in the *Man'yōshū*. The poem opens by announcing Mount Fuji's mythical origins in language that is reminiscent of the opening phrases of the *Kojiki*. Then the mountain's power is described in both spatial terms and temporal terms. The poem closes with an exhortation to transmit the glory of Mount Fuji to future generations.

3:317–318

A poem by Yamabe no Akahito on looking at Mount Fuji, with one envoy.

ametsuchi no	Since the heavens
wakareshi toki yu	and earth were parted,
kamu sabite	it has stood, godlike,
takaku tōtoki	lofty and noble,
Suruga naru	the high peak of Fuji
Fuji no takane o	in Suruga;
ama no hara	when I look up to see it
furisake mireba	in heaven's high plain,
wataru hi no	hidden is the light
kage mo kakurai	of the sky-crossing sun,
teru tsuki no	invisible the glow
hikari mo miezu	of the shining moon;

shirakumo mo	even the white clouds
iyuki habakari	fear to move over it,
tokijiku so	and for all time
yuki wa furikeru	the snows are falling;
kataritsugi	let us tell about it,
iitsugi yukamu	and pass on the word
Fuji no takane wa	of Fuji's high peak.

hanka	Envoy

Tago no ura yu	Going out on Tago Bay,
uchiidete mireba	when I look
mashiro ni so	it is pure white;
Fuji no takane ni	on the high peak of Fuji
yuki wa furikeru	snow is falling.

[Introduction by Torquil Duthie and translation by Anne Commons]

YAMANOUE NO OKURA

Perhaps because of his low rank, nothing is known about the first half of Yamanoue no Okura's life (660?–733?). In 701, however, at the age of forty-two, he was selected to go on an embassy to the Tang court in China, where he spent seven years. In 721 he was appointed as one of Emperor Shōmu's tutors, and in 726 (at the age of sixty-seven), probably as a reward for a lifetime of service to the court, he was appointed governor of Chikuzen, in northern Tsukushi (present-day Kyushu), where he organized a poetic circle with the Dazaifu commander, Ōtomo no Tabito, another major *Man'yōshū* poet. Volume 5 of the *Man'yōshū*, which is thought to have been compiled by Okura, is dedicated to the poetry of this circle in Tsukushi. Okura is one of the *Man'yōshū*'s most idiosyncratic poets. He took almost all the topics of his poems from Chinese texts, and many of his poems include long prefaces in Chinese. His poetry has a strong philosophical content (Buddhist, Confucianist, Daoist), and his choice of themes, such as old age or love for one's children, was often unusual.

Dialogue with the Impoverished

Okura's "Dialogue with the Impoverished" is perhaps his best known poem and clearly shows his unique place in the *Man'yōshū*. The structure of the poem is unconventional, with two chōka in the form of a dialogue, capped by a hanka (envoy).

Although the theme of poverty also is found in Chinese poetry composed in Japan, its use in a Japanese poem was unique to Okura. The poem has long been interpreted as a dialogue between a poor man and an even poorer man. But the first speaker may not be truly poor but merely frustrated in his ambition for higher rank and glory, looking at poverty as an outsider, as someone who feels he has had a taste of suffering. The second chōka begins with "Heaven and earth."

5:892–893

Dialogue with the Impoverished, with a short poem.

kaze majiri	On nights the wind
ame furu yo no	mingles with the falling rain,
ame majiri	nights the rain
yuki furu yo wa	mingles with the falling snow,
sube mo naku	nothing can be done
samuku shiareba	against the bitter cold,
katashio o	and so I nibble
toritsuzu shiroi	a lump of rock salt
kasuyuzake	and sip the lees
uchisusuroite	of saké in hot water,
shiwabukai	clear my throat,
hana bishi bishi ni	sniff, sniff back my running nose,
shika to aranu	and stroke my whiskers,
hige kakinadete	barely even a beard,
are o okite	as I say with pride,
hito wa araji to	"Aside from me alone,
hokoroedo	no man is worthy," and yet
samuku shiareba	against the bitter cold
asabusama	I pull my hempen
hikikagafuri	quilt tight around me
nuno kataginu	and pile on
ari no kotogoto	every single cloth vest
kisoedomo	that I own, but still
samuki yo sura o	the night is cold as ever.
ware yori mo	And what of those
mazushiki hito no	less fortunate than I?
chichi haha wa	Your father and mother
uekoyuramu	must be starving in the cold.
mekodomo wa	Your wife and children
kou kou naku ramu	must be crying out "food, food."
kono toki wa	At times like these,
ika ni shitsutsu ka	how do you ever manage
na ga yo wa wataru	to make your way through life?

ametsuchi wa	Heaven and earth
hiroshi to iedo	are said to be so vast,
a ga tame wa	but for me
saku ya narinuru	have they constricted so?
hitsuki wa	The sun and moon
akashi to iedo	are said to be so bright,
a ga tame wa	but for me
teri ya tamawanu	do they fail to shine?
hito mina ka	Are all men thus,
a nomi ya shikaru	or is it only so for me?
wakuraba ni	Lucky to be born
hito to wa aru o	in the world of men, and yet . . .
hitonami ni	I work and toil
are mo tsukuru o	as all men do, and yet . . .
wata mo naki	my cloth vest,
nuno kataginu no	without even any padding,
miru no goto	dangles off my body
wawake sagareru	like tattered strands of seaweed,
kakafu nomi	scraps of cloth
kata ni uchikake	wrapped around my shoulders.
fuseio no	In my crumbling
mageio no uchi ni	broken down little hut,
hita tsuchi ni	I spread out straw
wara toki shikite	for bedding on the bare earth.
chichi haha wa	Father and mother
makura no kata ni	are there beside my pillow,
mekodomo wa	wife and children
ato no kata ni	are there at my feet,
kakumi ite	all huddled together
re e samayoi	whimpering with grief.
kamado ni wa	In the stove,
hoke fukitatezu	there is no sign of flame.
koshiki ni wa	In the pot,
kumo no su kakite	a spider has spun its web.
iikashiku	We have forgotten even
koto mo wasurete	what it is to cook rice,
nuedori no	and our helpless cries
nodoyoi oru ni	are weak as the voice of thrushes.
itonokite	Then, worse yet,
mijikaki mono o	"trimming the ends of a thing
hashi kiru to	already too short,"
ieru ga gotoku	as the saying goes,

shimoto toru	there comes the voice
sato osa ga koe wa	of the headman with his whip,
neyado made	reaching into my bedroom
kitachi yobainu	to call me out to him.
kaku bakari	Is this all?
subenaki mono ka	Is this helplessness all there is
yo no naka no michi	of our path through this life?

hanka	Envoy

yo no naka o	We may believe
ushi to yasashi to	that grief and shame are all
omoedomo	there is of the world,
tobitachikanetsu	but because we are not birds
tori ni shi araneba	we cannot simply fly away.

Presented with deep humility by Yamanoue no Okura.

On Thinking of Children

"On Thinking of Children" is the second of three poems presented together by Okura in the Kama district of Chikuzen in 728. Okura begins the preface with two passages from Buddhist scripture. The first passage emphasizes the unconditional love of Shakyamuni for all living creatures by comparing it with his love for Rahula, the son born to him before he renounced all worldly attachments. Okura, however, interprets this as an expression of Shakyamuni's personal love for his child. In the second quotation, "love" refers to desire as a worldly attachment. If there is no greater love than that for one's child, then that love is the greatest obstacle to achieving enlightenment.

5:802–803

On Thinking of Children (with preface).

Shakyamuni, the Thus-Come Buddha, with his golden mouth preached, "I care for all living creatures as for my son Rahula." He also preached, "Of love, none surpasses that for one's child." If even the wisest of holy sages had a heart filled with love for his child, who among us mere mortal beings[70] could not help but love his child?

uri hameba	Eating melons,
kodomo omōyu	I remember my children.

---

70. Literally, "the green grass of the world."

kuri hameba	Eating chestnuts,
mashite shinowayu	I miss them all the more.
izuku yori	From what source
kitarishi mono zo	do these visions come to me?
manakai ni	Before my eyes
motona kakarite	they uselessly taunt me,
yasui shi isanu	not letting me sleep in peace.

hanka	Envoy

shirogane mo	Not silver,
kugane mo tama mo	or gold, or precious jewels,
nani semu ni	could ever match
masareru takara	the far greater treasure
ko ni shikame ya mo	that is one's own child.

Poem on Departing a Banquet

3:337

Poem by Yamanoue no Okura on Departing a Banquet.

Okurara wa	And now Okura
ima wa makaramu	really must be departing.
ko nakuramu	My children must be
sore sono haha mo	crying, and their mother too
wa o matsuramu so	must await my return.

[Introduction and translations by Jeremy Robinson]

Chapter 2

THE HEIAN PERIOD

The Heian period refers to the four hundred years from the end of the eighth century to the end of the twelfth century, when the center of political power was located in Heian-kyō, or the Heian capital (today known as Kyoto), from which the period takes its name. The political beginning of the Heian period can be traced to 781, when Emperor Kanmu (r. 781–806) ascended the throne. In 784, he moved the capital from Heijō (Nara) to Nagaoka and then in 794 to Heian-kyō. The end of the Heian period is usually considered to be 1185, when the Taira (Heike) clan was demolished and Minamoto no Yoritomo (1147–1199), the new military leader, established the *shugo/jitō* system and the Kamakura *bakufu* (military government) in eastern Japan.

The Heian period can be divided again, both politically and culturally, into three periods: early, middle, and late Heian. The first of these periods extended from the establishment of the Heian capital to the early tenth century through the reign of Emperor Daigo (r. 897–930); the second period lasted from Daigō's reign to the second half of the eleventh century, the reign of Emperor GoSanjō (r. 1068–1072); and the third period stretched from the latter half of the eleventh century to the establishment of the Kamakura bakufu. The first of these two periods, when the ritsuryō state system continued to function, at least in name, is sometimes regarded as the latter part of the ancient period, and the third period, when the *insei*, or cloistered emperor system, emerged, as the beginning of the medieval period.

At the end of the eighth century the powerful aristocratic families that had been at the center of the ritsuryō state during the Nara period were gradually replaced by new aristocratic clans. By the mid-ninth century, the ranks of the nobility (*kugyō*) were dominated by the Fujiwara and Minamoto (Genji) clans. Within them, the northern branch of the Fujiwara eventually prevailed, and in the mid-Heian period, beginning in the latter half of the tenth century, they controlled the throne through the regent (*sekkan*) system, in which a Fujiwara regent ruled in place of a child emperor. By marrying their daughters to emperors, the Fujiwara became the uncles and grandfathers of future emperors, thereby placing them in the position to be the regents who ruled in place of the child emperor.

The northern branch of the Fujiwara came to the fore first with Fujiwara no Fuyutsugu (775–826). His son Yoshifusa became the regent (*sesshō*), a title he was officially given in 866 when Emperor Seiwa (r. 858–876) came to the throne at the young age of nine. During the Kanpyō era (889–898), Emperor Uda (r. 887–897), with the aid of Sugawara no Michizane (845–903), who became a major literary figure, managed to hold off the Fujiwara. Uda's son Emperor Daigo (r. 897–930), with the assistance of the minister of the left, Fujiwara no Tokihira, and Sugawara no Michizane, similarly attempted to return to direct imperial rule. Although this imperial restoration by Uda and Daigo ultimately failed, the Uda/Daigo reigns—often referred to as the Engi (901–923) era—were subsequently considered to be a golden age of direct imperial rule and cultural efflorescence. Emperor Daigo ordered the compilation of the *Kokinshū* (*Collection of Ancient and Modern Poems*, ca. 905), the first imperial anthology of native poetry (the thirty-one-syllable *waka*).

Even though the system of public land ownership gradually fell apart, the ritsuryō state system—with its apparatus of ranks, ministries, and university—continued to operate, at least in name, throughout the Heian period and supported a court-based state system, which emerged at the beginning of the tenth century. One of the major characteristics of this court-based state was the concentration of power in the hands of the provincial governors (*zuryō*). During the regency period, the nobility in the capital focused most of their attention on court rituals and little on the actual administration of the provinces. Consequently, the central government in the capital, while making the appointments and receiving tributes from the provinces, gradually lost direct administrative control of them, which resulted in increasing chaos there. In 939 two rebellions took place—one led by Taira no Masakado (d. 940) and the other by Fujiwara no Sumitomo—both of which were subdued. Meanwhile, the provincial governors, exploiting their positions as state appointees, gathered more and more wealth and power.

Emperor Daigo and his successor, Emperor Murakami (r. 946–967), managed to avoid Fujiwara regents, but their imperial successors were not so successful. In 967, with the accession of Emperor Reizei, Fujiwara no Saneyori became regent, leading to the institutionalization of the Fujiwara regency, which peaked between 995 and 1027, when Fujiwara no Michinaga (966–1027), the most powerful and successful regent, held sway. Michinaga's eldest daughter, Shōshi, became the empress and consort of Emperor Ichijō (r. 986–1011) and gave birth to two subsequent emperors: GoIchijō and GoSuzaku. Murasaki Shikibu probably wrote much of *The Tale of Genji* while serving as a lady-in-waiting to Empress Shōshi, while Sei Shōnagon, the author of *The Pillow Book*, was a lady-in-waiting to Empress Teishi, a consort of Emperor Ichijō and Shōshi's rival.

In the last half of the eleventh century, with the accession of Emperor GoSanjō (r. 1068–1072)—a sovereign who, for the first time in 170 years (since Emperor Uda's reign), did not have Fujiwara maternal relatives—the power of the Fujiwara regency suddenly declined. The retired emperor, Shirakawa (r. 1072–1086, 1053–1129), who relinquished the throne in 1086, established the retired or cloistered emperor (*insei*) system, in which the cloistered emperor controlled the emperor and held political power. Retired Emperor Shirakawa, who took religious vows in 1096, thus held control for forty-three years through three imperial reigns.

During the Heian period, the system of public land ownership established by the ritsuryō system gradually broke down, and by the third period, in the eleventh and twelfth centuries, it was replaced by a system of private estates (*shōen*), which became the foundation for a new, village-based society. The samurai, most of whom grew up in these villages, gained military strength, and by the latter half of the twelfth century the Taira (Heike), a military lineage, came into conflict with the cloistered emperors, who until then had controlled the throne. The Taira lineage took over the reins of the court government until they were, in turn, toppled by the Minamoto (Genji), a military lineage based in the east, in Kamakura, thereby bringing an end to the Heian period and ushering in the medieval period.

THE EMERGENCE OF KANA LITERATURE

The first period of the Heian era lasted for just over a hundred years, from 794, when the capital was moved to Heian, to the first half of the tenth century. It was a time marked by the continued prominence of Chinese-based literature and culture and the gradual introduction of native vernacular and cultural forms, particularly the court-based vernacular literature written in *kana*, the native syllabary, which flourished from the tenth century onward. An example of the Chinese-based literature is the *Record of Miraculous Events in Japan* (*Nihon ryōiki*, ca. 822) by the priest Keikai, which was written in Chinese and gives both a Buddhist and a commoner's view of the world. Continuing this tradition was the most important writer in the early Heian period, Sugawara no Michizane (845–903), a statesman known for his writings in both Chinese poetry (*kanshi*) and Chinese prose (*kanbun*). Michizane, who rose to the pinnacle of power before abruptly falling, wrote on topics (student days, professional career, intellectual world, exile) that differed significantly from those found in the later kana writing by women.

The rise in popularity of kana in the late ninth century, particularly in the form of *waka*, thirty-one-syllable Japanese poems, gave birth to a variety of vernacular literature in the tenth century. Waka became integral to the everyday life of the aristocracy, functioning as a form of elevated dialogue and the primary means of communication between the sexes, who usually were physically segregated from each other. These poems also became an important part of public life, particularly at banquets where the composition of poetry in Japanese or Chinese was required. They often were collected, in either large anthologies, like the *Man'yōshū* and the *Kokinshū*, or smaller private collections of the works of a single poet. The first imperial waka anthology, the *Kokinshū*, established the model for Japanese poetry and became the foundation (in both diction and thematic content) for subsequent court literature.

The private waka collections, which included exchanges between the poet and his or her acquaintances, also led to a variety of new genres: (1) poetic travel diaries, such as the *Tosa Diary* by Ki no Tsurayuki; (2) confessional, semiautobiographical poetic diaries by women, like the *Kagerō Diary* by Mother of Michitsuna and the *Sarashina Diary* by Daughter of Takasue; and (3) poem tales (*uta-monogatari*) centering on the poetry of a particular poet, of which the most famous example is *The Tales of Ise*, initially based on the poetry of Ariwara no Narihira (825–880), the implicit protagonist. In short, the early tenth century marked the beginning of both vernacular poetry and vernacular fiction, the latter represented by *The Tale of the Bamboo Cutter* (*Taketori monogatari*, ca. 909) and *The Tales of Ise* (*Ise monogatari*, ca. 947). Not accidentally, the Engi era (901–923) was also the time when the native leaders of poetry in Chinese and of Chinese studies (*kangaku*)—such as Sugawara no Michizane and Ki no Haseo (845–912)—died, yielding the literary spotlight to Japanese poetry.

The second major period of Heian literature, from the latter half of the tenth century through the first half of the eleventh century, can be said to start with the *Kagerō Diary*, by Mother of Michitsuna, written in the 970s and marking the beginning of major prose writings by women. The peak of this period comes with the reign of Emperor Ichijō (986–1011), during which *The Pillow Book, The Tale of Genji*, and the *Diary of Izumi Shikibu* were written. Although there were important women writers in the ancient period such as Lady Nukata, Lady Sakanoue, and Lady Kasa, all poets represented in the *Man'yōshū*, they did not have the productivity and quality of those in the mid-Heian period.

THE RISE OF WOMEN'S WRITING

One of the striking characteristics of the emergence of Japanese vernacular literature was the central role played by women writers who were either at or closely associated with the imperial court in the late tenth and early eleventh centuries, such as Murasaki Shikibu, Sei Shōnagon, Mother of Michitsuna, Izumi Shikibu, and Daughter of Takasue. One reason for the prominent role of aristocratic women at this time is the writing system. Kana, the vernacular syllabary, became prominent in the early tenth century, enabling the Japanese to write more easily in their own language. Until then, writing had been in Chinese (as in the *Kojiki* and *Nihon shoki*) or had used Chinese characters to transcribe the native Japanese language (as in the *Man'yōshū*). Despite the emergence of a native syllabary, the male nobility continued to write in Chinese, which remained the more prestigious language and the language of government, scholarship, and religion. By contrast, aristocratic women, who were generally relegated to a nonpublic sphere, adopted the native syllabary as their first language and used it to write diaries, memoirs, poetry, and fiction. One consequence was that women's writing had an internal, psychological dimension that was rarely found even in men's kana writing, which, in any case, remained secondary to their work in Chinese.

The second reason for the development of women's writing was the political, social, and cultural importance of the ladies-in-waiting at the imperial court. The leading Fujiwara families poured their resources into the residences, cultural activities, and entourages of their daughters, who competed for the attention of the emperor. Indeed, the ladies-in-waiting to these Fujiwara daughters wrote much of the vernacular literature of the mid-Heian period. They were the daughters of provincial governors, the mid-level aristocrats, who were frequently in unstable political and economic positions. Having failed to rise in the court hierarchy, many of these provincial governors went to the provinces to make a living and so had an outsider's perspective on court life. One consequence was that the literature written by women at court paid homage to the powerful Fujiwara patrons (as in *The Pillow Book* and *Murasaki Shikibu's Diary*) while also expressing deep disillusionment with court life (as in the *Sarashina Diary*) and with the marital customs that supported this sociopolitical system (as in the *Kagerō Diary*). Part of the complexity of *The Tale of Genji*, in fact, comes from this conflicting view of court culture and power.

The thirty-one-syllable classical poem (waka) emerged as the most important vernacular (kana) genre. Occasions and topics for these poems ranged from the seasons to love to miscellaneous topics such as celebration, mourning, separation, and travel, which form separate chapters in the *Kokinshū*. Poems were composed for public functions, at poetry contests (*uta-awase*) and poetry parties, and for illustrated screens (*byōbu uta*), which were commissioned by the royalty and the powerful Fujiwara families. Waka functioned privately as a social medium for greetings, courtship, and farewell, as well as a means of self-reflection. Poets also edited private collections, of either their own poetry or that of a poet like Ariwara no Narihira or Ono no Komachi. These private poetry collections could take the form of a travel diary, as in the *Tosa Diary*, one of the first diaries written in kana. Private poetry collections could also lead to confessional autobiographies like the *Kagerō Diary*, which probably began as a private collection of poems by Mother of Michitsuna. Private collections of poetry also gave rise to the poem tale, which contained anecdotes about poems that were compiled to create a biographical narrative like *The Tales of Ise*, itself based on the poems and legends surrounding Ariwara no Narihira.

In Murasaki Shikibu's day, as in previous centuries, men wrote prose in Chinese, the official language of religion and government. In the tenth century, therefore, vernacular prose, particularly literary diaries, belonged to women to the extent that, in the *Tosa Diary*, the leading male poet of the day, Ki no Tsurayuki, assumes the persona of a woman in writing a literary diary in Japanese. Male scholars, however, were the first to write vernacular tales, or *monogatari*, although they did so anonymously, for such writing was considered a lowly activity directed only at women and children. These early vernacular tales, which began with *The Tale of the Bamboo Cutter* (ca. 909), tend to be highly romantic, fantastical, and dominated by folkloric elements. Women, by contrast, tended to write highly personal, confessional literature based on their private lives and centered on their own poetry. The author of the *Kagerō Diary*, the first major literary diary by a woman, wrote out of a profound dissatisfaction with contemporary monogatari, which, in her view, were "just so much fantasy." Murasaki Shikibu was able to combine both traditions. *The Tale of Genji* carries on the earlier monogatari tradition in its larger plot and in its amorous hero, who echoes the earlier Narihira in *The Tales of Ise*. But in its style, details, psychological insight, and portrayal of the dilemmas faced by women in aristocratic society, *The Tale of Genji* remains firmly rooted in the women's writing tradition.

LATE HEIAN KANA HISTORIES AND ANECDOTAL LITERATURE

With the decline of the northern branch of the Fujiwara lineage and the Fujiwara regency in the late eleventh century, a new historical literature in kana emerged. The first major example is *A Tale of Flowering Fortunes* (*Eiga monogatari*, ca. 1092), a historical tale attributed to a woman, which looks back at Fujiwara no Michinaga (966–1027), who brought the Fujiwara regency to its peak. *A Tale of Flowering Fortunes* was quickly followed by the "mirror pieces" (*kagami mono*), a series of historical chronicles written in Japanese, beginning with *The Great Mirror* (*Ōkagami*, late eleventh century), which also recounts Michinaga's achievements.

The late Heian period was also marked by the emergence of anecdote (*setsuwa*) collections, the first of which was the massive *Collection of Tales of Times Now Past* (*Konjaku monogatari shū*, ca. 1120), that reflect the heavy influence of Pure Land Buddhism, incorporate stories of rebirth in the Pure Land, and depict the life of commoners in the provinces. *Tales of Times Now Past*, which continues the tradition of the *Nihon ryōiki*, looks forward to the many setsuwa collections of the medieval period and reveals the widening social and religious interest of the aristocracy and priesthood. In contrast to the *Nihon ryōiki*, which was written in Chinese, *Tales of Times Now Past* was written in a mixed style that merged kana with the *kanbun kundoku* (a Japanese style of reading Chinese prose) style. This new *wakan* (Japanese–Chinese) mixed style, with its rhythmical base, eventually produced military narratives (*gunki-mono*) like *The Tales of the Heike*, which became a hallmark of early medieval literature. Another product of the late Heian period was the *Treasured Selections of Superb Songs* (*Ryōjin hishō*, ca. 1179), a collection of folk songs (*kayō*), which might be considered the poetic equivalent of *Tales of Times Now Past* in reflecting Pure Land Buddhism and commoner life.

KEIKAI

Keikai (otherwise known as Kyōkai, late eighth–early ninth century), the compiler of the *Record of Miraculous Events in Japan* (*Nihon ryōiki*), was a *shidosō*, or private priest, as opposed to a publicly recognized and certified priest ordained by the ritsuryō state. (The ritsuryō state attempted to keep a tight control on the priesthood and cracked down on private priests, who took vows without official permission, often as a way to avoid taxation and service.) Keikai's own accounts of himself in the *Nihon ryōiki* state that in 787 he realized that his current poverty and secular life were the result of evil deeds in a previous life and so he decided to become a priest. Keikai was probably born in the latter half of the Nara period, around 757 to 764, and lived into the early Heian period.

RECORD OF MIRACULOUS EVENTS IN JAPAN
(*NIHON RYŌIKI*, CA. 822)

During Keikai's time, during the reigns of Emperor Kanmu and his son Emperor Saga (r. 809–823), the country was rocked by considerable social disorder, famine, and plagues. It was a particularly hard time for the farmers, many of whom fled from their home villages. Some of these refugees were absorbed into local temples and private estates, and others became private priests. Unlike the official priests in the capital who had aristocratic origins, these private priests attracted a more plebian constituency, and for them the *Record of Miraculous Events in Japan* functioned as a kind of handbook of sermons. In this regard, the *Nihon ryōiki* differs significantly from the elite literature being produced at this time, such as *Kaifūsō* (751) and *Bunka shūreishū* (818), two noted collections of Chinese poetry and refined Chinese prose written by aristocrats. Instead, the *Nihon ryōiki* is written in a rough unorthodox style of Chinese-style prose that depicts the underside of society and the reality of everyday commoner life.

The *Nihon ryōiki*, often considered to be Japan's first *setsuwa* (anecdote or folk story) collection, bears the signs of earlier oral storytelling. Although 80 percent of the stories take place in the Yamato area, the place-names come from almost every part of the country, from Michinoku (northeast Honshū) to Higo (in Kyushu), strongly suggesting that the private priest would preach at a certain village, gather stories, and then use them at another village, as a storyteller would. In the process, local folk stories and anecdotes became Buddhist parables. Whereas the *Nihon shoki* and *Kojiki* combined many of the local and provincial myths and legends into a larger state mythology, Buddhism similarly began to absorb local folk stories, converting them to its own use and producing the kinds of Buddhist anecdotes found in the *Nihon ryōiki*. As a consequence, the interest of a number of the stories in the *Nihon ryōiki* is not in the Buddhistic message, which is usually found at the end, but in the story itself, which often was erotic or violent.

As he notes in the introduction, Keikai arranged these stories in such a way as to demonstrate the Buddhist principle of karmic causality, in which the rewards and retribution for past actions are directly manifested in this world. This principle is embodied in the full title, *Record of Miraculous Cases of Manifest Rewards and Retribution for Good and Evil in Japan* (*Nihonkoku genpō zen'aku ryōi-ki*). The stories generally are one of two types: those in which good deeds are rewarded and those in which evil deeds are punished. Other stories demonstrate the miraculous powers of Buddha, the bodhisattvas, sutras, and Buddhist icons.

In the *Kojiki* and *Nihon shoki*, the underworld (Yomi) is a place marked by pollution where bodies decompose. By contrast, in the *Nihon ryōiki*, we suddenly are confronted with a terrifying Buddhist hell where past actions are severely punished. In the ancient period, sin was often the result of transgressing the communal order, usually agricultural violations or pollutions, but in the *Nihon ryōiki*, sin takes on new meaning as a moral and social violation, with the individual responsible for his or her own actions. In the early chronicles, disease was something cured by communal means, by purification and cleansing, but later, disease, which figures prominently in the *Nihon ryōiki*, became the punishment for sin, the result of previous karma.

On the Death Penalty in This Life for an Evil Son Who Tried to Kill His Mother out of Love for His Wife (2:3)

Killing a parent was one of the eight crimes under ritsuryō codes. In Buddhism it was considered one of the five heinous sins, for which one would go to hell. Similar stories appear in the *Collection of Tales of Times Now Past* (20:33) and in volume 7 of the *Collection of Treasures of the Buddhist Law* (*Hōbutsushū*).

Kishi no Ōmaro came from the village of Kamo, Tama District, Musashi Province.[1] Ōmaro's mother was Kusakabe no Matoji.[2] During the reign of Emperor Shōmu, Ōmaro was appointed a frontier soldier[3] at Tsukushi by Ōtomo[4] (name unknown) and had to spend three years there. His mother accompanied him and lived with him while his wife stayed behind to take care of the house.

Out of love for his wife who had been left behind, Ōmaro came up with the wicked idea of killing his mother and returning home to his wife, claiming exemption from duty on the pretext of mourning.[5] Because his mother's mind was set on doing good, he said to her, "In the eastern mountain, there will be a great meeting for a week of lectures on the Lotus Sutra. Would you like to go to hear them?"

His mother, deceived, was eager to go, and, devoutly purifying herself in a hot bath, accompanied her son to the mountain. Then he looked at her fiercely, as though with the eyes of a bull, and commanded, "You, kneel down on the ground!" Gazing at his face, she said, "Why are you talking like that? Have you been possessed by a fiend?" But her son drew a sword to kill her. Kneeling down in front of her son, she said to him, "We plant a tree in order to get its fruit and to take shelter in its shade.[6] We bring up children in order to get their help and to depend on them. What on earth has driven you so crazy? I feel as though the tree I have been depending on has suddenly ceased to protect me from the rain." But he would not listen to her, so she sorrowfully took off her clothes, put them in three piles, knelt down, and told him her last wish: "Will you wrap up these clothes for me? One pile goes to you, my eldest son, one to my second son, and one to my third son."

When the wicked son stepped forward to cut off his mother's head, the earth opened up to swallow him. At that moment his mother grabbed her falling son by the hair and appealed to heaven, wailing, "My child has been possessed by a spirit and has been driven to commit such an evil deed. He is out of his mind. I beg you to forgive his sin." Despite all her efforts to pull him up by the hair, he fell. The merciful mother brought his hair back home to hold funeral rites and put it in a box in front of an image of Buddha and asked monks to chant scriptures.

---

1. Tama is in present-day Tokyo.

2. Kusakabe is a family name, and Matoji is a given name.

3. *Sekimori*, or soldiers sent to Tsukushi (Kyushu) to defend the country from a possible invasion by foreign troops from Korea or China. Their tour of duty was three years, and they were not allowed to bring any family members.

4. The Ōtomo clan was traditionally in charge of military matters and served the emperors as imperial guards.

5. The mourning period for parents was one year, during which people were exempted from any labor duties.

6. From the *Daihatsu nehan-gyō*, vol. 21, one of the central texts of the Buddhist canon.

How great was the mother's compassion! So great that she loved an evil son and did good on his behalf. Indeed, we know that an unfilial sin is punished immediately and that an evil deed never avoids a penalty.

On the Immediate Reward of Being Saved by Crabs for Saving the Lives of Crabs and a Frog (2:12)

A similar story appears in the *Record of Miraculous Powers of the Lotus Sutra in Japan* (*Honchō hokke genki*), but without Gyōki's name, at a different place (Kuse), and ending with a reference to the Kanimata-dera (Crab Temple), indicating that it was an *engi*, or story, about the origins of a temple. A similar story also is found in the *Collection of Tales of Times Now Past* (16:16) and the *Collection of Things Written and Heard in Past and Present* (*Kokon chomonju*) (20:682).

In Kii District, Yamashiro Province,[7] there lived a woman whose name is unknown. She was born with a compassionate heart and believed in the law of karmic causation, so she never took a life, observing the five precepts[8] and the ten virtues.[9]

During the reign of Emperor Shōmu, some young cowherders in her village caught eight crabs in a mountain brook and were about to roast and eat them. She saw this and begged them, "Will you please be good enough to give them to me?" They would not listen to her, insisting, "We will roast and eat them." Repeating her earnest request, she removed her robe to pay for the crabs. Eventually they gave them to her. She invited a Buddhist master to give a blessing and released them.

Later, she was in the mountain and saw a large snake swallowing a big toad. She implored the large snake, "Please set this frog free for my sake, and I will give you many offerings." The snake did not respond. Then she collected more offerings and prayed, "I will consecrate you as a god. Please give the frog to me." Without answering, the snake continued to swallow the toad. Again she pleaded, "I will become your wife in exchange for this toad. I beg you to release it to me." Raising its head high, the snake listened, staring at her, and disgorged the toad. The woman made a promise to the snake, saying, "Come to me in seven days."

She told her parents in detail about the whole episode. They despaired, asking, "Why on earth did you, our only child, make a promise you cannot fulfill?"

At that time the most venerable Gyōki was staying at Fukaosa Temple in Kii District. She went and told him what had happened. When he heard her story, he said, "What an incredible story! Just keep believing in the Three Treasures."[10]

---

7. Present-day Kyoto area.

8. Not to steal, not to kill, not to commit adultery, not to lie, and not to drink alcohol.

9. Not to kill, not to steal, not to commit adultery, not to lie, not to use immoral language, not to slander, not to equivocate, not to covet, not to give way to anger, and not to hold false views.

10. Buddha, Buddhist law, and Buddhist priests.

With these instructions she went home, and on the evening of the appointed day, she closed up the house, prepared herself for the ordeal, and made various vows with renewed faith in the Three Treasures. The snake came, crawled around and around the house, knocked on the walls with its tail, climbed onto the top of the roof, tore a hole in the thatch of the roof with its fangs, and dropped in front of her. She heard only the noise of scuffling, jumping, and biting. The next morning she found that the eight crabs had assembled and had cut the snake into shreds. She then learned that the released crabs had come to repay her kindness to them.

Even an insect that has no means of attaining enlightenment returns a favor. How can a man ever forget a kindness he has received? From this time on, people in Yamashiro Province have honored big crabs in the mountain streams and, if they are caught, set them free in order to do good.

On Receiving the Immediate Penalty of Violent Death for Collecting Debts by Force and with High Interest (3:26)

Several stories in the *Nihon ryōiki* (for example, 1:10) are about people stealing from others and, after dying, turning into a cow to be used for labor. This story differs in that the sinner becomes a cow in this life.

Mahito Hiromushime of the Tanaka lineage was the wife of Agatanushi Miyate of the Oya lineage, who was of the junior sixth rank, upper grade, and a governor of Miki District, Sanuki Province.[11] She gave birth to eight children and was very rich. Among her possessions were cattle, slaves, money and rice,[12] and fields. But she lacked faith and was so greedy that she would never give anything away. She used to make a great profit by selling rice wine diluted with water. On the day when she made loans, she used a small measuring cup, whereas on the day she collected, she used a big measuring cup. When she lent rice, she used a lightweight scale, but when she collected it, she used a heavyweight scale. She showed no mercy in forcibly collecting interest, which was sometimes ten times and sometimes a hundred times as much as the original loan. She was strict in collecting debts, never being generous. Because of this, many people worried a great deal and abandoned their homes to escape from her, going to other provinces. Never was there anyone so greedy.

On the first of the Sixth Month in 776, Hiromushime took to her bed and stayed there for many days. On the twentieth of the Seventh Month she called her husband and eight sons to her bedside and told them about the dream she had had.

---

11. In present-day Kagawa Prefecture.
12. Lent with interest.

"I was summoned to King Yama's palace[13] and was told of my three sins. The first one was using too much of the property of the Three Treasures and not repaying it; the second was making great profits by selling diluted rice wine; and the third was using two kinds of measuring cups and scales, giving only seven-tenths for a loan but collecting twelve-tenths for a debt. 'I summoned you because of these sins. I just want to show you that you should receive a penalty in this life,' he said."

The woman died on the same day that she related the dream. For seven days, her husband and sons did not have her cremated but called thirty-two monks and lay brothers to pray to Buddha for her for nine days. On the evening of the seventh day the woman was restored to life and opened the lid of the coffin. When they came to look at her, the stench was indescribable. Above the waist her body had turned into an ox with four-inch horns on her forehead, and her two hands had become hooves, with the nails cracked like the insteps of an ox hoof. Below the waist her body had a human form. The woman did not like rice but preferred grass and, after eating, ruminated. She did not wear any clothes but lay in her filth. Streams of people from the east and west hurried to gather and look at her in wonder. In shame, grief, and pity, her husband and children prostrated themselves on the ground, making numerous vows. In order to atone for her sins, they offered various treasures to the Miki-dera Temple, and seventy oxen, thirty horses, fifty acres of fields, and four thousand rice bundles to the Tōdai-ji. They wrote off all debts. At the end of five days, after the provincial and district magistrates had seen her and were about to send a report to the central government, she died. All the witnesses in that district and province grieved and worried about her.

Being unreasonable and unrighteous, the woman did not know the law of karmic retribution, but we know that this was an immediate penalty for unreasonable deeds and unrighteous deeds. Since the immediate penalty comes as surely as this, how much more certain will be the penalty in a future life.[14]

One scripture says: "Those who don't repay their debts will atone for them, by being reborn as a horse or an ox."[15] The debtor is compared with a slave, the creditor with a master. The former is like a pheasant, the latter a hawk. If you make a loan, don't use excessive force to collect the debt, for if you are unreasonable, you will be reborn as a horse or an ox and made to work by your debtor.

[Adapted from a translation by Kyoko Nakamura]

---

13. The king of hell (Yama).

14. The narrator is distinguishing between karmic retribution in this life and karmic retribution in the next life. The results of both good and evil deeds are manifested in either of these two ways.

15. A summary of a passage from the *Jōjitsu-ron*, a Buddhist treatise.

ONO NO KOMACHI

Little is known about the life of Ono no Komachi (fl. ca. 850), one of the most prominent early female waka poets, but her poetry and stories about her life have attracted popular and scholarly attention for centuries. The poems most reliably attributed to her are the eighteen attributed to her in the early-tenth-century *Kokinshū*, the first and most prestigious of the imperial waka anthologies. Komachi is praised in the *Kokinshū* by its chief compiler, Ki no Tsurayuki, as one of the six outstanding poets of "recent times" (who are known collectively as the Rokkasen, or Six Poetic Immortals).[16] She also is included in another grouping of notable poets, the Sanjūrokkasen, or Thirty-six Poetic Immortals, identified by the influential critic Fujiwara no Kintō (966–1041) as the greatest poets of the ancient and early Heian periods. In his Kana Preface to the *Kokinshū*, Tsurayuki comments, "Ono no Komachi is of the same lineage of Princess Sotoori of old. [Her poetry] is moving but not strong, resembling a beautiful woman afflicted by illness."[17] Tsurayuki was probably comparing the style of Komachi's poetry with that of Princess Sotoori, two of whose poems appear in the *Nihon shoki*.[18] Princess Sotoori's best-known characteristic— although she later was canonized as a deity of waka—was her radiant beauty. Subsequent interpretations of Tsurayuki's comments as referring to the physical appearance rather than the poetic skill of Komachi and Princess Sotoori became the basis of the legends about Komachi.

These legends foreground Komachi's amorousness, beauty, and fickleness, and their origins can be found in these comments by Tsurayuki and in Komachi's poems—for example, no. 554, in which the poet is overwhelmed by longing; no. 113, in which she laments the fading of her beauty; and no. 623, in which she rejects a persistent suitor. The nō play *Stupa Komachi (Sotoba Komachi)*, translated later in this anthology, is one of the best-known dramatic treatments of Komachi and the medieval legends about her. In addition to her appearance as a character in nō plays and medieval prose narratives, interest in Komachi is evident in the compilation of the *Komachi Poetry Collection (Komachishū)* by unknown editors. Most of the 117 poems in the longest version of this collection are apocryphal, but their attribution to her reveals the ongoing fascination with Komachi legends. The poems most reliably attributed to Komachi, however, are those found in the *Kokinshū*, among which are those translated here.

---

16. The other five poets thus praised by Tsurayuki in the Kana Preface to the *Kokinshū* are Ariwara no Narihira, Bishop Henjō, Monk Kisen, Fun'ya no Yasuhide, and Ōtomo no Kuronushi. "Recent times" here refers to the mid- to late ninth century, a few decades before the *Kokinshū* was compiled.

17. Based on the text in *Kokinwakashū*, SNKBT 5.

18. One of Princess Sotoori's *Nihon shoki* poems also appears in the *Kokinshū* (no. 1110).

SELECTED POEMS

The poems by Komachi in the *Kokinshū* are mostly love poems, reflecting the prevailing trend in Heian and later classical poetry toward the depiction of dissatisfaction and discord in love. All the love poems in the *Kokinshū* are arranged in narrative order, describing the progress of love from beginning to end, and Komachi's poems are given here in the order in which they appear in the *Kokinshū*. Dreams are a major image in classical love poetry and feature prominently in Komachi's works. She describes the world of dreams as an alternative—often preferable—reality in which the social restrictions of the waking world might be overcome. Yet even this dream world is not a perfect escape from the constraints of waking life, and Komachi's dream poems, set within the larger narrative arc of the *Kokinshū* love poems, reveal a gradual disillusionment with dreams as a venue for love. Indeed, the dream imagery in Komachi's poetry can be seen as one manifestation of her larger concern with the tenuous boundaries between illusion and reality, as seen, for instance, in no. 797, which questions the misleading nature of appearances. Both the perception of appearances as deceptive—in a world that is itself barely distinguishable from dreams—and concern with the passage of time are ultimately rooted in Buddhist teachings on the illusoriness of the phenomenal world. The concept of impermanence informs the preeminent Heian aesthetic ideal, seen in the *Kokinshū* and elsewhere, of *mono no aware*, often translated as "the pathos of things," according to which beauty is enhanced by its very ephemerality.

Komachi's poetry is noted for its rhetorical complexity and makes extensive use of pivot words (*kakekotoba*), a kind of pun characteristic of *Kokinshū* poetry. This technique allows the poet to compress multiple layers of meaning within the brief bounds of the waka form. Komachi's poems also frequently feature word associations (*engo*), images conventionally linked in classical waka; that is, one such image suggests others associated with it, evoking resonances in the reader's mind and, as with pivot words, intensifying the meaning without exceeding the prescribed length of the poem.

113

hana no iro wa	The color of the flowers
utsuri ni keri na	has faded—in vain
itazura ni	I grow old in this world,
waga mi yo ni furu	lost in thought
nagame seshi ma ni	as the long rain falls.[19]

---

19. This is one of Komachi's best-known poems and is included in Fujiwara no Teika's exemplary collection *One Hundred Poets, One Hundred Poems* (*Hyakunin isshu*). "The color of the flowers" is usually taken to refer also to the poet's physical beauty. *Furu* is a pivot word meaning

552

omoitsutsu	Longing for him
nureba ya hito no	I fell asleep—
mietsuramu	is that why he appeared?
yume to shiriseba	Had I known it was a dream
samezaramashi o	I would never have awakened.[20]

553

utatane ni	Since seeing in my sleep
koishiki hito o	the one whom I love,
miteshi yori	it's these things
yume chō mono o	called dreams
tanomi someteki	I've learned to trust.[21]

554

ito semete	In desperation,
koishiki toki wa	pressed hard by longing,
mubatama no	this berry-black night
yoru no koromo o	I wear my robes
kaeshite zo kiru	turned inside out.[22]

623

mirume naki	Is it because
waga mi o ura to	he does not know
shiraneba ya	there is no seaweed in this bay

---

both "[rain] falls" and "[time] passes," and *nagame* is another pivot word meaning "long rains" and "to gaze while deep in thought."

20. This is the first poem of the second book of love poetry in the *Kokinshū* and the first of a sequence of three dream poems (nos. 552–554) by Komachi. It starts with a rhetorical question: the poet's thoughts of her lover as she fell asleep caused him to appear in her dreams. The closeness of her dream to waking reality is evident in the poet's failure to realize she was dreaming. Her confusion calls into question the very distinction between the real and the illusory.

21. After further encounters with her lover, the poet not only recognizes that their meetings are taking place in her dreams but also identifies dreams as the superior venue for love. It is dreams, rather than the waking world, on which she has come to rely.

22. Dreams are again a motif in this poem, although they are not explicitly mentioned. It was popularly believed at the time that turning back one's sleeves would ensure that one dreamed of one's lover. Here the poet turns not just her sleeves but her entire robe inside out in her eagerness to meet her lover in her dreams. *Mubatama no* (berry-black) is an epithet (*makura-kotoba*, or "pillow word") for words imaging night and blackness (here, for *yoru no koromo*, literally, "night robe"). The *mubatama* is the round, black fruit of the *hyōgi* plant.

karenade ama no	that the fisherman comes so often,
ashi tayuku kuru	his legs growing weary?[23]

656

utsutsu ni wa	In the waking world
sa mo koso arame	perhaps it must be so,
yume ni sae	but even in my dreams
hitome o moru to	to see him hide from others' eyes
miru ga wabishisa	is misery itself.[24]

657

kagiri naki	In boundless desire
omoi no mama ni	lit by the fire of love
yoru mo komu	this night at least
yumeji o sae ni	may you tread the path of dreams
hito wa togameji	and no one blame us.[25]

---

23. This poem appears in the *Kokinshū* directly after a poem by Ariwara no Narihira: "Wetter even than the mornings I made my way home through the low bamboo—how soaked are my sleeves those nights I came but could not meet you." The juxtaposition of these poems in the *Kokinshū* became the basis of their adaptation in *The Tales of Ise* (sec. 25) as an exchange between the protagonist and "an amorous woman," thus linking two idealized exemplars of Heian courtly love: Narihira and Komachi. Komachi's poem begins with the word *mirume*, a pivot word meaning both "seaweed" and "a chance to meet," followed in the second phrase by *ura*, meaning both "bay" and "miserable." The literal meaning of *mirume naki ura* is thus "bay with no seaweed," and the parallel figurative meaning of *mirume naki waga mi o ura* is "I who am miserable and will not meet you." Komachi's unfortunate suitor is cast as a fisherman who does not seem to realize that his journeys will go unrewarded. *Ama* (fisherman), *ura* (bay), and *mirume* (seaweed) are associated words (*engo*).

24. This is the first of another sequence of dream poems by Komachi (*Kokinshū*, nos. 656–658) in the third book of love poetry. Whereas the earlier set of dream poems (nos. 552–554) presents dreams as an alternative world in which lovers have the opportunity to meet, these later poems show an increasing awareness of the limitations of that world, and the intrusion of less welcome aspects of the waking world. In this poem the poet's expectations are confounded: the dream world has become as restrictive as the real world. Even in dreams, the poet's lover must conceal their relationship from others.

25. The main image here is *yumeji* (the path of dreams), along which the poet's lover will, she hopes, travel to her, his way lit by the flame of her desire. The beliefs underlying dream imagery in classical love poetry held that the intensity of one's feelings for one's lover could induce him to appear in one's dream or could cause one to appear in his dreams. The (*hi*) of *omoi* (desire) is a pivot word with *hi* (fire), imaging the strength of the poet's feelings and a contrast with the dark of night. Anxieties about the censure of society make their presence felt, however, with the poet's hoping that at least her lover's travels on the path of dreams will not be condemned by others. (The implication is that an encounter with her lover in waking life *would* invite blame.)

658

yumeji ni wa	On the path of dreams
ashi mo yasumezu	my feet never rest
kayoedomo	as I run to see you,
utsutsu ni hitome	though it's not worth a glimpse
mishigoto wa arazu	of your waking self.[26]

797

iro miede	What fades away
utsurou mono wa	its color unseen
yo no naka no	is the flower
hito no kokoro no	of the heart
hana ni zo arikeru	of those of this world.[27]

938

When Fun'ya no Yasuhide became the third-ranked official of Mikawa Province and invited me to come sightseeing in the provinces, this was my reply:

wabinureba	Lonely and forlorn
mi o ukikusa no	as a drifting weed:
ne o taete	should flowing waters
sasou mizu araba	beckon
inamu to zo omou	I think I'd follow.[28]

[Translated by Anne Commons]

---

26. This poem reads almost as a response to the previous one. Although the poet is traveling frequently on the path of dreams, she also is becoming disillusioned with dreams as a substitute for the waking world. In *Kokinshū*, no. 553, it was dreams on which the poet had started to rely as a means of meeting her lover. Now, however, she realizes that the many dream encounters she has with him are not the equal of even a single glimpse of him in real life.

27. This poem appears in the fifth and final book of love in the *Kokinshū*, which contains eighty-two poems on the failures and deceptions of love. In this context, we may read the poem as a comment on the fickleness of one person's heart, a former lover who has lost interest in the poet, and on the unreliability of human feelings in the world at large, in which nothing is as it seems.

28. The headnote identifies this poem as a response to one by another prominent poet of the early Heian period, Fun'ya no Yasuhide, a contemporary of Komachi who also is identified in the *Kokinshū* as one of the Six Poetic Immortals. The *uki* of *ukigusa* is a pivot word meaning both "floating" (of the waterweed) and "miserable" (the poet). The poet compares her unhappy self (*mi*) to the floating weed: both are adrift at the mercy of their surroundings. The "flowing waters" represent the message from Yasuhide. The poet implies that like a weed drifting on the water, she would journey to the provinces in response to his invitation. This poem appears in a book of the *Kokinshū* that includes many poems about the uncertainties and disappointments of life in the mundane world.

SUGAWARA NO MICHIZANE

The early Heian period was marked by the heavy influence of Chinese culture and Chinese literature, with Chinese the written language of the court and the emperors sponsoring imperial anthologies of the best examples of Chinese poetry by Japanese poets. Sugawara no Michizane's grandfather, who had visited China as a diplomat, established a family tradition of Sinological scholarship. Signs of change, however, began to appear in the middle of the ninth century with a revival of interest in waka and the emergence of the Fujiwara regency. The rise of the Fujiwara signaled the weakening of Sinified administrative institutions and the new enthusiasm for vernacular literature eventually led to a partial decline in enthusiasm for literature written in Chinese.

Writing in Chinese required mastery of both classical Chinese and the vast body of lore alluded to in Chinese literature. Having been born into a scholarly family, Sugawara no Michizane (845–903) received extensive training in Chinese, and his career resembled that of Chinese literati officials. After studying at the state university, he passed a civil service examination and held a series of posts until 877, when he was made a professor of literature, making him a dominant figure among court intellectuals. Nine years later, he was appointed governor of Sanuki (now Kagawa Prefecture) in Shikoku. Although he objected to his rustication, Michizane wrote some of his most interesting poetry in the province. Perhaps the novelty of the setting inspired a more imaginative approach to his art, or perhaps he simply had more time to write. After his return to the capital in 890, the new emperor promoted him to high office as a counterbalance to the Fujiwaras' power, arousing the enmity of Michizane's rivals, both political and academic. As a result, he was slandered and, in 901, exiled to Kyushu, where he died two years later, still protesting his innocence.

The following years were marked by the untimely deaths of some of Michizane's former rivals, most conspicuously in 930, when lightning struck the palace and killed four of them. Michizane was posthumously pardoned, promoted, and deified as Tenjin (Heavenly Deity). Shrines were built to worship Tenjin, the oldest being at the site of his grave in Kyushu and another, built in 947, at Kitano, just north of the capital. Although people originally had feared Tenjin's wrath, by 986 the court literati were presenting poems to Kitano Shrine and describing Tenjin as "the progenitor of literature, the lord of poetry." Reverence for Tenjin spread, and today, shrines dedicated to him are among the most numerous in Japan. They often were centers of literary activity, although in recent years Tenjin has come to be worshiped as a patron of all trying to pass university examinations.

Michizane may have been deified to placate his angry ghost, but his poetry, particularly that written in Chinese, continues to find an audience for its literary qualities. Michizane excelled at composition in Chinese at a time when it was first beginning to lose its monopoly on literary and cultural prestige and to be eclipsed by waka. In contrast to the brevity of waka and its relatively narrow

Formal robe (*sokutai*) for noblemen and emperor.

range of topics, Chinese poetry allowed more detailed exposition and favored some topics excluded from waka, as seen in the following examples.

Michizane's works in Chinese are preserved in two anthologies. The first is *Kanke bunsō*, roughly translated as *Literary Drafts of the Sugawara Family*. Michizane himself compiled and presented this anthology to the emperor in 900, along with the now-lost works of his father and grandfather. *Kanke bunsō* begins with six books of poetry arranged chronologically, followed by another six books of prose, subdivided by genre. Shortly before his death, Michizane sent the poems he had written in exile to a disciple in the capital, who compiled them into a second anthology, *Kanke kōshū (The Later Collection of the Sugawara Family)*. Examples of Michizane's waka are preserved in several imperial anthologies. The following selections from Michizane's writings are grouped by topic, which have been arranged to leave some of the poems in their original chronological order. The headings to the individual poems were written by Michizane himself.

CHILDREN

Children were not a central concern of waka. By contrast, following the conventions of Chinese poetry, Michizane wrote affectionately about his children but barely mentions his wife and says nothing of the concubines he must have had if we are to believe the claim that he fathered twenty-three children. In addition to the examples translated here, both dating from his years in Sanuki, Michizane composed a poem recalling a son who had died in childhood and another to comfort the children who had accompanied him into exile.[29]

---

29. Burton Watson translated other poems about Michizane's children in *Japanese Literature in Chinese: Poetry and Prose in Chinese by Japanese Writers of the Early Period* (New York: Columbia University Press, 1975), 1:90–91, 113.

Speaking of My Children

This poem was written in 888 when Michizane, then forty-four, was governor of Sanuki. In this example, the disparaging remarks about his children and the elegiac tone might be read as clichés, but the concerns expressed may have been real. Michizane was certainly far from home, and the Sugawara held only middling status among court aristocrats. Their success was based on the literary skills of Michizane and his immediate forebears.

260

My sons are foolish, my daughters ugly: such is their nature.
The proper times to celebrate their adulthood have slipped by.
Flowers that bloom on a winter tree lack crimson hue.
Birds raised in a dark valley are slow to take wing.
My family has no property; it must rely on me.
My profession is literature, but who shall inherit it?
Such thoughts are as pointless as lamenting old age,
yet when I speak of my children so far away, I feel sad.

CAREER

Whereas the vernacular literature leaves the impression that Heian courtiers devoted most of their time to romance and poetry, Michizane's writing in Chinese reminds us that most poets had official careers as well. During his years in high office, virtually all Michizane's poetry consisted of the formal verse needed for court ceremonies; presumably he did not have time for the more personal poems that require fewer footnotes for modern readers. The third poem in this section is a waka from this period, included here to illustrate the type of occasion requiring poetry from a high official. It also demonstrates how waka adapted a poetic technique, a metaphor in the form of feigned confusion, found in Chinese poetry, as in the first poem.

Through the Snow to Morning Duties

This poem was written in 876 when Michizane was the deputy assistant minister of popular affairs. The court offices held morning and evening rites, and Michizane is reporting for the former.

73

Wind-sent tolling of palace bell: I hear the sound of dawn,[30]
encouraging me on my way through powdery snow.
Matching my status, I wear a fur coat three feet long;
just right to warm my mouth, two drafts of wine.
I wonder if it could be floss my groom is clutching,
and am startled to see my tired horse trod drifting clouds.[31]
In my office, not a moment's rest:
puffing on my hand a thousand times, I keep drafting documents.[32]

Professorial Difficulties

Written in 882, five years after Michizane was appointed professor of literature, this poem suggests that students at the court university took a serious interest in advancing their career, if not necessarily their studies.

87

My family is not one of generals.
As Confucian scholars we earn our keep.
My revered grandfather attained the third rank.
My kind father's office was high court noble.[33]
Well, they knew the power of learning
and wished to bequeath it for their descendants' glory.
The day I was promoted to advanced student,[34]
I resolved to master the craft of my forefathers.
The year I became a professor,

---

30. Literally, he hears "the morning clepsydra." In this poem, Michizane plays with perceptions in a manner that, adopted from Chinese models, became characteristic of the waka of his day. In this case, instead of seeing the dawn, he hears it, as measured by the clock and sounded by the bell.

31. Pretending to confuse snow with floss or clouds, Michizane again is using a Chinese technique, a form of metaphor, that became common in waka.

32. Michizane breathes on his hands to warm them as he drafts official documents, which would have been written in Chinese, Michizane's specialty.

33. Michizane's grandfather Kiyokimi (770–843) had served as professor of literature and in 839 was awarded the exalted third rank. Michizane's father, Koreyoshi (812–880), after also serving as professor of literature, became a high-ranking noble (kugyō) in 872 when he was given the office of consultant (sangi), placing him among the highest officials in the land.

34. Shūsai or tokugōshō, sometimes translated as "advanced students of literature," were specially selected students who prepared for the civil service examination. Michizane was given this title at the unusually young age of twenty-three.

happily, the lecture hall was rebuilt.
When everyone rushed to congratulate me,
my father alone expressed concern.
Why did he express concern?
"Alas, you are an only child," he said;
"the office of professor is not mean,
the salary of a professor is not small.
Once I too held this post
and learned to fear people's feelings."
Having heard this kind admonition,
I proceeded with care as if walking on ice.
In the fourth year,[35] the council met
and ordered me to lecture the students.
But after teaching only three days,
my ears heard slanderous voices.
This year, evaluating students for advancement,
the decisions were absolutely clear.
But the first student dropped for lack of talent,
denounced me, and begged unearned promotion.
In my teaching, I did not make mistakes.
My selections for advancement were fair.
How true was my father's advice
when he warned me before all this occurred.

EXILE

Just as Michizane's public career resembled that of the Chinese scholar officials
whose writings he so admired, exile also was a fate shared with some of China's
greatest poets. In his last years, Michizane joined them in lamenting his misfortunes and protesting his innocence. The poetry he wrote in Kyushu alludes to both
the specific circumstances of his exile and the appropriate Chinese exemplars.

Seeing the Plum Blossoms When Sentenced to Exile

This is Michizane's best-known poem written in Japanese. He is said to have particularly admired plum blossoms (*ume*), and, according to legend, the tree in his garden
was so touched by this poem that it flew to be with him at his place of exile.

---

35. The fourth year of the Gangyō era (880), three years after Michizane had been named
professor of literature. Normally there were two professors of literature, and at the time of his
appointment, his former civil service examiner was the other one. Apparently, Michizane did
not begin giving formal lectures until after the senior professor had died in 879.

SHŪISHŪ, NO. 1006

kochi fukaba	When the east wind blows,
nioi okoseyo	send me your fragrance,
ume no hana	plum blossoms:
aruji nashi tote	although your master is gone,
haru o wasuruna	do not forget the spring.

Autumn Night, the Fifteenth Day of the Ninth Month

As in so many of the poems he wrote in exile, Michizane protests his innocence while complaining of his personal hardships.

485

My complexion a withered yellow, topped by white frost,
worse still, I am banished over a thousand *ri* from home.[36]
Once ensnared in the trappings of glory,
now I am an exile, imprisoned amid rustic weeds.
The moon, shining like a mirror, exposes no crime.
The wind, blowing with swordlike force, cannot end my protests.
Looking or listening, both make me shiver.
This year's autumn is my own personal autumn.

In Exile, Spring Snow

This is Michizane's last poem. In it, he discovers some flowers in Dazaifu, the plum blossoms he is said to have so admired. He died on the twenty-fifth day of the Second Month, 903, probably not long after writing this. According to the lunar calendar, spring usually began in February, and so "spring snow" was not, in fact, uncommon. Perhaps still more common were poems pretending that the plum blossoms of that month were snow.

514

Filling the town, overflowing the district, so many plum blossoms.
Wind rustling them in the sunlight, the first flowers of the year!

---

36. In earlier times, a *ri* had been approximately 1770 feet, but around Michizane's day an alternative "great *li*" of approximately 2.5 miles also was used. In literary works, phrases such as "a thousand *ri*" were commonly used to mean simply "a great distance."

They stick to the feet of the geese, just like pieces of cloth.[37]
They dot the heads of crows: perhaps I will return home.[38]

[Introduction and translations by Robert Borgen]

KOKINSHŪ
(COLLECTION OF ANCIENT AND MODERN
POEMS, CA. 905)

The *Kokin wakashū* (*Collection of Ancient and Modern Poems*), informally known as *Kokinshū*, is an anthology of 1,111 Japanese poems (in the most widely circulated editions) compiled and edited in the early tenth century. The collection begins with a *kana* (Japanese) preface and, in some editions, concludes with a postface in Chinese. The Kana Preface, opening with the famous words "Japanese poetry takes as its seed the human heart," was long regarded as a model of classical prose and, line for line, is undoubtedly the most heavily commented secular prose text of the Japanese tradition. The poems are divided into twenty scrolls or books (*maki*), each of whose titles refers to a conventional poetic topic (the seasons, love, parting, mourning, miscellaneous or "mixed" topics) or to a genre ("acrostic" poems, "mixed" or miscellaneous forms, poems of the "Bureau of Song"). Most of the poems (all but nine, in fact) are in the form of waka (thirty-one-syllable Japanese poem), the canonical form of Japanese poetry from the eighth until the late nineteenth century.

The *Kokinshū*'s poems can be roughly divided into three periods, which also reflect certain broad stylistic differences: anonymous poems of the early to mid-ninth century or before; those of the age of the Six Poetic Immortals, the mid-ninth century; and poems by the editors and their contemporaries, from the late ninth and early tenth centuries. Well over half the poems are attributed to nearly 130 known poets, mostly of the late ninth century. Of the approximately 450 anonymous poems, many are believed to derive from folk songs, although some Heian and medieval commentaries assert, plausibly enough, that the editors deliberately identified as anonymous certain poems by those of the highest social rank, others by persons of very low status, some of those by the compilers themselves, and poems that touched on various taboos.

The waka is defined prosodically as a poem of thirty-one syllables grouped according to a pattern of five *ku*, or measures, of, respectively, 5, 7, 5, 7, and 7 syllables, each of which is also required to be grammatically independent in

---

37. In the Han dynasty, Su Wu was a captive of barbarians for nineteen years. He attached to a goose's leg a message written on a piece of cloth. The emperor shot the goose, learned of Su Wu's misfortune, and sent troops to rescue him.

38. Prince Dan of Yan, held hostage by the king of Qin, was told he could return home when crows' heads turned white and horses grew horns. When that happened in response to his prayers, he was allowed to go home.

that the phrasal breaks in syntax regularly coincide with the divisions between successive measures. At a higher level of organization, the first three measures were traditionally called the *kami-no-ku* (upper measure) and the last two, the *shimo-no-ku* (lower measure). Although this was a purely quantitative distinction, it reflects a tendency (increasingly evident after the late twelfth century) to place a strong syntactic break after the third measure and less often after the first, resulting in what is called a 7/5 rhythm (as opposed to the alternative, a 5/7 rhythm in which breaks occur after a seven-syllable measure). The 7/5 rhythm is a characteristic distinguishing the later poetry of the *Kokinshū* from that of the eighth-century anthology *Man'yōshū* and much oral poetry, including many of the early anonymous poems of the *Kokinshū*, which favor breaks after the second and fourth measures. By the time of the early-thirteenth-century anthology *Shinkokinshū*, the 7/5 rhythm had become established as the waka's dominant rhythm.

A majority of the poems in the *Kokinshū* can be parsed syntactically as a single compound sentence or as two simple sentences. In the latter case, these often are in a relation between question and answer, enigma or dilemma and (often inadequate) solution, or a generalization followed by a restrictive condition. Exceptions abound, and some of the anthology's most memorable poems can be read as lyrical observations of how things are. But it is safe to say that a questioning or plaintive mood prevails, with the poet asking why things must be as they are or why experience does not better agree with either reason or imagination. This prevailing mood has earned the *Kokinshū* (or, more precisely, the middle- and later-period poems usually taken to typify the anthology) a reputation for ironic wit and ratiocination that in turn has, in a favorable interpretation, been read as evidence of a sophisticated awareness of the discrepancies between language and reality or, in a less sympathetic reading, as indulgence in sophistry or sheer wordplay.

Along a somewhat different axis, later scholars and critics have debated whether this interrogative mood reflects the ironic affirmation of a recently acquired technical facility of poetic expression; a sense of nostalgic resignation, even of despair, perhaps inspired by the dissemination of Buddhist doctrine; the increasing political hegemony of the Fujiwara lineage; or some combination of these. It is up to the reader to decide, but even though individual poems do display a fairly wide range of tonal variation, few, especially those in the seasonal and love books (which together make up more than two-thirds of the collection) are completely free of irony, and only a rather small minority of the *Kokinshū*'s poems can be counted as celebratory or "pastoral" without qualification.

The immense prestige of the *Kokinshū* as the unrivaled canon of classical waka, especially after its recanonization in the late twelfth century, meant that it largely determined the range of acceptable variations on a given poetic motif as well as the rules of decorum governing the choices of diction and topics.

Some of the most influential poets of the late twelfth century (including Shun-zei, Saigyō, and Kamo no Chōmei, as well as Teika) asserted that the *Kokinshū's* poetry represented the whole range of acceptable styles for serious poetry.

Most, though not all, of the *haikai* poetry in the *Kokinshū* is gathered in a subsection of book 19, "Mixed Forms," suggesting that although prosodically identical with waka, haikai was regarded as a distinct genre. This book apparently was thus classified on the basis of its unorthodox (colloquial or archaic) diction as well as its obtrusive irony or wit (to the editors of the *Kokinshū*, the term *haikai* seems to have meant "discordant" or "dissonant" as well perhaps as "comic"). If we regard haikai as marking the lower bound of decorum, then its antithesis, *yūgen* (mystery and depth), represented, at least for medieval readers, the surpassing ideal that few poems in fact achieved.

One quality of the *Kokinshū* that helped define its authority as the paradigm against which subsequent imperial anthologies (there were twenty) were measured and on which they were modeled and that may account for the number of years apparently spent compiling the anthology is the manifest care its editors applied to the structural arrangement of individual poems in sequences within each book, most conspicuously in the sequences of seasonal and travel poems. These many arrangements include temporal progression through the seasons and through the stages of a courtly love affair, subsequences of topical images with subtle variations in treatment, alternation of anonymous (older) poems with those by contemporary (new or modern) authors and of rhythmic forms (poems with a caesura after the second versus those with one after the third measure), patterns in which strongly original poems are set off by more conventional verses, and so forth. Medieval exegetes were very attentive to these principles of arrangement, which they identified as *budate* (structure of the book or section) and *shidai* (sequence) and regarded as more pertinent than satisfactorily interpreting individual poems in the context of the anthology.

One consequence of the editors' concern with arranging the poems into larger, aesthetically tangible patterns was that they omitted some of the finest poems at their disposal (most of which were eventually used by later anthologists) but included many that have never since been esteemed very highly. The *Kokinshū* sufficiently mapped the world of courtly poetic topoi such that (supplemented by the two later imperially commissioned anthologies, the *Gosenshū* and the *Shūishū*) it was regarded for centuries as an indispensable guide for aspiring poets. But it was evidently not meant to be a treasury of all (and only) the best poetry of its age, and it has rarely been regarded as such. Instead, thanks to the care with which it was arranged, the *Kokinshū* is an eminently readable anthology, which may have contributed as much to its endurance as the excellence of its finest poems.

The Kana Preface

The Kana Preface to the *Kokinshū*, by Ki no Tsurayuki, foremost among the editors of the anthology, was among the earliest statements of Japanese poetics and by far the most influential. The passage translated here is an assertion of the universal value of poetry and of waka in particular.

The songs of Japan take the human heart as their seed and flourish as myriad leaves of words.[39] As long as they are alive to this world, the cares and deeds of men and women are endless, so they speak of things they hear and see, giving words to the feelings in their hearts. Hearing the cries of the warbler among the blossoms or the calls of the frog that lives in the waters, how can we doubt that every living creature sings its song? Not using force, it moves heaven and earth, makes even the unseen spirits and gods feel pity, smoothes the bonds between man and woman, and consoles the hearts of fierce warriors—such a thing is poetry.

Spring 1

1

Composed on a day when spring arrived within the old year.

toshi no uchi ni	Spring has come
haru wa kinikeri	before the year's turning:
hitotose o	should I speak now
kozo to ya iwamu	of the old year
kotoshi to ya iwamu	or call this the new year?[40]

Ariwara no Motokata[41]

---

39. "Songs" is a translation of the word *uta*, which literally means "song" but was also used to refer to Japanese poetry, as opposed to Chinese (which was called *shi*). Tsurayuki, the author of the Kana Preface, plays on both senses of the word throughout this passage. The metaphor "leaves of words" depends on a conventional pun, linked here to the metaphor of the heart (*kokoro*, or "heart/mind") as a seed.

40. The poem plays on a discrepancy between the official lunar and the unofficial solar calendars. Risshun, the first day of spring by the solar calendar, always occurs on February 4 or 5 (by the Gregorian calendar). In the lunar calendar, the new year begins on the day of the new moon, variably between January 21 and February 19. Hence about once every two years, the (solar) first day of spring preceded the (lunar) New Year's Day. The theme of "time out of joint" is pervasive in early classical waka, often (see *Kokinshū*, nos. 2 and 3) hinging on a contrast between convention and perception. Some medieval exegetes interpreted this poem as a compact allegory of the chiasmus of "old" and "new," alluding to the *Kokinshū* editors' apparent program of thoughtfully intercalating old (late eighth and early to mid-ninth century) poems with new (late ninth to early tenth century).

41. Dates unknown. Motokata was a grandson of Narihira, but little is known about his career. He is the author of fourteen poems in the *Kokinshū*.

2

Composed on "the first day of spring."

sode hijite	Waters I cupped my
musubishi mizu no	hands to drink, wetting
kooreru o	my sleeves, still frozen:
haru tatsu kyou no	might this first day of
kaze ya tokuramu	spring's wind thaw them?[42]

Ki no Tsurayuki[43]

3

Topic unknown.

harugasumi	Where are the promised
tateru ya izuko	mists of spring?
Miyoshino no	In Yoshino, fair hills
Yoshino no yama ni	of Yoshino, snow
yuki wa furitsutsu	falling still.[44]

Anonymous[45]

---

42. The topic calls for the "Anticipation of Spring," never soon enough. The theme is an implied contrast between the calendar, which has announced the arrival of spring and its warm breezes, and the conceit of sleeves wet with water from the previous year's summer that are still frozen with winter's cold. Although the promise of spring remains unfulfilled, by taking the compass of three successive seasons, the poet affirms his faith in the calendar.

43. His dates are thought to be around 870 to 945. Despite his relatively humble social status, Tsurayuki was, in his later years, among the most highly respected poets of his age. One of four poets commissioned to compile the *Kokinshū*, he was effectively its editor in chief, and the collection closely conforms to his tastes. As the author of the Kana Preface to the anthology, the single most canonical statement of the principles of native Japanese poetry, his influence on the tradition was immense and remained unquestioned until the end of the nineteenth century. As a poet, he was a consummate technician as well as the author of many of the most memorably lyrical poems in the anthology.

44. The topic is "Lingering Snow." The sequence has established the arrival, by the calendar, of spring. Yoshino, with mountains among the deepest in the Yamato region and the vicinity of the capital, was a poetic place-name (*utamakura*) noted for both heavy snowfall and cherry blossoms. The poet complains (complaint is among the most common moods of *Kokinshū* poetry) that despite the official arrival of spring, the mists (much less the flowers) of spring have yet to appear.

45. "Anonymous" poems are those for which the editors did not have a reliable attribution—in most cases, poems of the late eighth or early ninth century circulated orally—or for which they had reasons not to identify the author in a collection commissioned by the emperor and subject to his approval.

35

Topic unknown.

ume no hana	I lingered only a moment
tachiyoru bakari	beneath the plum blossoms
arishi yori	and now I am
hito no togamuru	blamed for my
ka ni zo shiminuru	scented sleeves.[46]

Anonymous

Spring 2

69

Topic unknown.

harugasumi	On hills where mists of spring
tanabiku yama no	trail, glowing faintly,
sakurabana	do the flowers' fading
utsurowamu to ya	colors foretell
iro kawariyuku	their fall?[47]

Anonymous

70

Topic unknown.

mate to iu ni	If saying "stay!"
chirade shi tomaru	would stop their
mono naraba	falling, could I hold

---

46. In the context of its presumed source, the personal collection of Fujiwara no Kanesuke (d. 933), this is a love poem sent to a woman facetiously complaining that incense, redolent of apricot (or plum) blossoms, burned to scent her robes, has infused his own, and that their relationship has thus been discovered by members of his household. That his complaint is facetious is attested by the evidence that he sent this poem to the woman (who knows better) by way of stating his intention not to be dissuaded. The editors signal their intentions to reread this as a seasonal poem on the topic "Plum Blossoms," not as a love poem, by listing it as anonymous.

47. Mist and cherry blossoms are the preeminent images of spring. The placement of this poem at the beginning of the second book of spring asserts that the imminent fading of the blossoms, perhaps showing through a screen of (faint pink, by Chinese poetic convention) mist, marks the passage beyond the midpoint of the season and thus appropriately opens the second movement of spring. This is the first of a sequence of twenty-one poems on the topic "Falling Cherry Blossoms." (Concerning the importance of topical sequences in the *Kokinshū*, see n. 63.)

nani o sakura ni	these blossoms
omoimasamashi	more dear?[48]

Anonymous

71

Topic unknown.

nokori naku	It's their falling without regret
chiru zo medetaki	I admire—
sakurabana	Cherry blossoms:
arite yo no naka	a world of sadness
hate no ukereba	if they'd stayed.[49]

Anonymous

72

Topic unknown.

kono sato ni	I seem bound to sleep
tabine shinu beshi	in this village tonight:
sakurabana	led astray by falling
chiri no magai ni	blossoms, I've forgotten
ieji wasurete	my way home.[50]

Anonymous

73

Topic unknown.

utsusemi no	Are they not like
yo ni mo nitaru ka	this fleeting world?

---

48. It is because the blossoms are bound to fall so soon that they are so admired (see *Kokinshū*, no. 71). If one could command them, with a word, to last, their fragile beauty would be diminished. In an earlier context (presumably the late eighth or early ninth century), the anonymous poet's intention may have been, instead, to suggest that if only the blossoms would stay, on demand, nothing could surpass their beauty. Such a reading, though grammatically less plausible, is accepted by some medieval and modern commentators.

49. This is a statement of what became the normative aesthetic and ethos of the cherry blossom as a symbol of the fragility of beauty (and the beauty of fragility): it is better to die early than to linger in this world and suffer the consequences, among them an awareness of the vanity of human aspirations and of the futility of living on.

50. Entranced by clouds of falling blossoms, a traveler has lost track of the way home and is resigned to spending the night in an unfamiliar village.

hanazakura	Cherry blossoms:
saku no mishi ma ni	no sooner do they flower
katsu chirinikeri	than they fall.[51]

Anonymous

103

From the empress's poetry contest in the Kanpyō era.

kasumi tatsu	The hills where
haru no yamabe wa	spring mists rise are distant,
tookeredo	yet the wind comes,
fukikuru kaze wa	bringing the
hana no ka zo suru	blossoms' scent.[52]

Ariwara no Motokata

104

Composed when looking at fading blossoms.

hana mireba	When I gaze on
kokoro sae ni zo	fading blossoms
utsurikeru	this heart, too, would fade with them:
iro ni wa ideji	may my feelings not be seen
hito mo koso shire	lest others come to know.[53]

Ōshikōchi no Mitsune[54]

---

51. In ninth-century usage and later, the phrase *utsusemi no yo* (this fleeting world), with its image of the discarded shell of a cicada, refers to this world of (human) existence as empty and insubstantial *or* as mutable and ephemeral. The force of the simile in this poem draws on the second sense.

52. A long sequence (forty-one poems) on the topic "Cherry Blossoms Blooming and Falling," extending from the latter part of the first book of spring through the beginning of the second book, is followed by two shorter sequences on the topics "Blossoming Flowers" and "Falling Flowers." These are poems on late spring flowers. This poem concludes the sequence on "Blossoming Flowers."

53. This is the first in the sequence of poems on the topic "Falling Flowers." The speaker seems to fear acquiring a reputation for extreme sensitivity, a quality in which Heian poets took some pride.

54. Late ninth to early tenth century. The author of sixty poems in the *Kokinshū*, one of the compilers of the anthology, and, along with Tsurayuki, a master of compositional technique.

105

Topic unknown.

uguisu no	To each meadow where
naku nobe goto ni	the warbler cries
kite mireba	I come and see
utsurou hana ni	the wind blow
kaze zo fukikeru	fading flowers.[55]

Anonymous

Summer

135

Topic unknown.

wa ga yado no	Wisteria flowers
ike no fujinami	blossom in waves
sakinikeri	on my garden pond:
yamahototogisu	will the mountain cuckoo
itsu ka kinakamu	come, then, and sing?[56]

Anonymous

Some say that the preceding poem was composed by Kakinomoto no Hitomaro.[57]

152

Topic unknown.

yayoya mate	Wait, cuckoo,
yamahototogisu	take my message

---

55. Under the topic "Falling Flowers," this is the first of a subsequence of six verses on "Warblers Lamenting the Blossoms." The speaker, viewing the flowers in the meadows where trees are in bloom, finds that in each meadow, warblers are crying and the wind is blowing petals from the boughs and thus infers the relation between the two events. The sense is not that the speaker was drawn by the warblers' cries to seek their cause.

56. The topic is "Early Summer." The flowers of the garden are mirrored in the surface of the pond, their reflection perhaps superimposed on waves raised by an early summer breeze. The mountain cuckoo (*hototogisu*) is the dominant image of the brief book of summer in the *Kokinshū*, appearing in twenty-five of the thirty-four poems and associated, in the *Kokinshū* and after, with the Fifth and Sixth Months of the lunar calendar. Summer begins in the Fourth Month, and the cuckoo has not yet begun to sing. Wisteria blossoms are a late spring/early summer image.

57. The most notable poet of the *Man'yōshū*.

> *kotozutemu*   to the mountains:
> *ware yo no naka ni*   I, too, have learned
> *sumiwabinu to yo*   to weary of this world.[58]

Mikuni no Machi[59]

Autumn 1

172

Topic unknown.

> *kinou koso*   Only yesterday
> *sanae torishika*   seedlings were planted:
> *itsu no ma ni*   so soon, now,
> *inaba soyogite*   ears of grain tremble
> *akikaze no fuku*   as the autumn wind blows.[60]

Anonymous

176

Topic unknown.

> *koikoite*   Longing and longing
> *au yo wa koyoi*   tonight at last we meet:
> *Ama no kawa*   may the mist rise thick
> *kiri tachiwatari*   on the River of Heaven
> *akezu mo aranamu* and keep the day from dawning.[61]

Anonymous

---

58. The cuckoo was thought to act, like various birds in many traditional cultures, as a messenger between this and other worlds. The intended recipient of the message here may be one who has entered the afterworld, since the cuckoo was also believed to be an intermediary between the living and the dead, or a recluse who has departed from this mundane world to practice austerities in the mountains, the proper abode of the mountain cuckoo (*yama-hototogisu*) addressed in the poem.

59. A member of the Ki family, empress to Ninmyō and sister of Ki no Aritsune. Dates uncertain.

60. The implied topic is "Autumn Wind." One prevalent theme of early autumn poems, those of the opening of the first book of autumn in the *Kokinshū* and others later in the classical tradition, is surprise at how quickly and stealthily the season arrives. Surprise is registered here by hyperbole: only a day ago, so it seems, the rice seedlings were planted, yet today they are ready for harvesting. The word *soyogite* (tremble) is a weak onomatopoeia of susurration.

61. The topic is Tanabata, Festival of the Herdsman and the Weaver, lovers who were transformed into the stars Altair and Vega in the Milky Way (River of Heaven) and condemned to meet only one night in the year, the seventh of the seventh lunar month. Autumn mist (*kiri*), a

222

Topic unknown.

hagi no tsuyu	Should I pluck the drops of dew
tama ni nukamu to	to thread as jewels
toreba kenu	they'd vanish:
yoshi mimu hito wa	best see them as they are,
eda nagara miyo	set on boughs of clover.[62]

Anonymous

Some say that the preceding poem was composed by the Nara emperor.

223

Topic unknown.

orite miba	If I were to bend a bough
ochizo shinu beki	to pluck it
akihagi no	they must surely scatter:
eda mo tawawa ni	trembling drops of dew
okeru shiratsuyu	on autumn bush clover.[63]

Anonymous

Autumn 2

256

On seeing autumn leaves on Otowa Mountain while visiting Ishiyama.

akikaze no	From that first day
fukinishi hi yori	the winds of autumn sounded,

---

strongly seasonal image, is the counterpart of spring mist or haze (*kasumi*). The implied speaker may be either of the two stars or both.

62. The *mitate* (visual metaphor) of dewdrops as evanescent jewels is a familiar one. Dew is closely associated with the bush clover (*hagi*), a distinctive autumn flower.

63. Sequences (*shidai*) of poems on the same topic, composed of subtle variations in thematic treatment, are the building blocks that make the *Kokinshū* a coherent and readable text rather than a simple collection of poems arranged topically. Medieval commentators devoted considerable attention to the editors' composition of such sequences (prominent in the seasonal and love books), which come into view only when one poem is read as a response to a preceding poem or series of poems. In this instance, the reader is invited to reread no. 222 against no. 223 and weigh the differences between a conceit and a more literal treatment of the same topic: gemlike droplets of dew on leaves or petals of bush clover.

Otowayama   the tips of trees on
mine no kozue mo   Otowa Mountain's peak
irozukinikeri   were turning color.[64]

Ki no Tsurayuki

257

Composed for a poetry contest at the house of Prince
Koresada.

shiratsuyu no   White dew
iro wa hitotsu o   all of a single color:
ika ni shite   how then does it dye
aki no ko no ha o   the leaves of autumn
chiji ni somuramu a thousand different shades?[65]

Fujiwara no Toshiyuki[66]

258

Composed for a poetry contest at the house of Prince
Koresada.

aki no yo no   As the dew of autumn's night
tsuyu o ba tsuyu to settles in place,
oki nagara   will the falling tears
kari no namida ya of wild geese
nobe o somuramu dye the fields yet deeper?[67]

Mibu no Tadamine[68]

---

64. The name Otowa Mountain, a pillow word, makes a pun on the word *oto*, meaning "sound." This is the eighth of a series of nineteen poems on the topic "Autumn Leaves," which opens the second book of autumn. Brightly colored autumn leaves is also the dominant image of the latter part of the season, appearing in more than half the poems in the book. The poem suggests, retrospectively, the idea of nature anticipating the calendar (compare no. 3 and many other spring poems in which the season is perceived as falling behind the calendar).

65. The theory underlying this and the following poems is that dewdrops (together with frost and raindrops of cold autumn showers) are the cause of the coloration of leaves. "White dew" is often a near synonym for "dew," but the specific association of autumn with the color white (following Chinese theories of the "five elements") is exploited here to underscore the paradox. The "thousand different shades" is conventional hyperbole. The primary colors of autumn foliage in classical poetry were red, yellow, and rust.

66. Died early tenth century. Noted for his poems for illustrated standing screens (*byōbu-uta*).

67. Again the theory that dew causes the leaves to change color is invoked. The conceit is that because the wild geese, flying south in autumn, cry, they must shed tears and that since tears are a poetic homologue of dew, those (figurative) tears might combine forces with the dew to intensify the coloration of the grasses of the fields.

68. Late ninth to early tenth century. One of four poets ordered to compile the *Kokinshū*.

259

Topic unknown.

aki no tsuyu	Surely the autumn dew
iroiro koto ni	must have its varied ways
okeba koso	to turn the mountain's leaves
yama no ko no ha no	so many shades
chigusa narurame	of color.[69]

Anonymous

266

Composed for a poetry contest at the house of Prince Koresada.

akigiri wa	Let no autumn mist
kesa wa tachi ni so	rise this morning,
Saoyama no	that I might at least from afar
hahaso no momiji	see the colored leaves
yoso nite mo mimu	of the oaks of Mount Sao.[70]

Anonymous

274

Composed on a figure of a person waiting, beside chrysanthemum blossoms, for another person.

hana mitsutsu	Looking at flowers,
hito matsu toki wa	waiting for my love
shirotae no	I took the blossoms

---

69. This poem, a variation on the theme of *Kokinshū*, no. 257, also is a tentative response to that poem's question: it must be something in the way that dew settles on the leaves that accounts for its varied effects: leaves of differing colors.

70. This is the penultimate poem in the sequence of nineteen poems on the topic "Colored Autumn Leaves" (*momiji*), which opens the second book of autumn. This sequence is followed by thirteen poems on "Chrysanthemum Flowers," but the topic of *momiji* is then resumed under the rubric "Falling Leaves" (*rakuyō*) in a twenty-five-poem sequence that extends to nearly the end of the book. A parallel is thus established between the sequential arrangement of poems on the topic "Cherry Blossoms" in the two books of spring and these on "Autumn Leaves."

sode ka to nomi zo   for the white
ayamatarekeru   sleeve of his gown.[71]

                                              Ki no Tomonori[72]

284

Topic unknown.

Tatsutagawa   Tatsuta River is
momijiba nagaru   flush with red leaves:
Kamunabi no   autumn showers must be
Mimuro no yama ni   falling on Mimuro Mountain
shigure furu rashi   in Kamunabi.[73]

                                              Anonymous

A variant text reads "Asuka River is flush with red leaves . . ."

289

Topic unknown.

aki no tsuki   Does the autumn moon
yamabe sayaka ni   cast its light so starkly
teraseru wa   on the mountain's edge
otsuru momiji no   that we may count
kazu o miyo to ka   each colored leaf that falls?[74]

                                              Anonymous

---

71. An allusion to a verse by the Chinese poet Tao Qian (d. 427), cited by early Kamakura commentators, may have been intended here, but as the *renga* poet Sōgi and his teacher Tō no Tsuneyori asserted, recognition of the allusion adds nothing to an understanding of the poem in the *Kokinshū* context. The "figure" mentioned in the headnote is most likely a model placed on a tray of sand representing, in miniature, a landscape.

72. Of the same lineage as Tsurayuki, he was another of the four poets ordered to compile the *Kokinshū*. He died early in the tenth century, before the collection was completed.

73. *Mimuro*, a noun meaning "sacred grove" or "dwelling place of the gods," became the name of a mountainous area that was the site of Tatsuta Shrine, above the Tatsuta River. Kamunabi (mountains "where gods dwell") refers to the same area, noted for its autumn leaves. The poet speculates on the unseen cause of a very visible (and desirable) effect: a brocade of red and yellow leaves covering the Tatsuta River, downstream from Mimuro.

74. The speaker asks why the autumn moon casts its light so starkly (*sayaka*) and proposes an answer: that the moon's intention is to intensify our perception of the falling of leaves and thus of the passage of the season toward winter. It is not "fallen leaves" but "leaves (now) falling" that the speaker sees so clearly.

290

Topic unknown.

fuku kaze no	The gusting wind
iro no chigusa ni	shows itself
mietsuru wa	in a cloak of many colors:
aki no ko no ha no	a scattering of
chireba narikeri	autumn leaves.[75]

Anonymous

291

Topic unknown.

shimo no tate	Warp of frost, weft of dew,
tsuyu no nuki koso	these must be weak indeed:
yowakarashi	no sooner are they woven than
yama no nishiki no	the mountain's brocades
oreba katsu chiru	scatter in shreds.[76]

Sekio[77]

297

Composed during a visit to the northern hills to pick autumn leaves.

mini hito mo	They must fall
nakute chirinuru	with no one to see them:
okuyama no	red leaves of autumn
momiji wa yoru no	deep in the mountains
nishiki narikeri	like brocades worn by night.[78]

Ki no Tsurayuki

---

75. A familiar *mitate* (visual metaphor), autumn leaves seen as a cloak of brocade, dresses another well-worn trope, the wind making itself visible, to create something new. Many of the "new" poems in the *Kokinshū*, those of the late ninth and early tenth centuries, are based on permutations and recombinations of rhetorical precedents rather than on the invention of unfamiliar conceits.

76. Frost and dew are taken to be the agents causing the autumn leaves to turn (see *Kokinshū*, no. 257) and weaving from them a multicolored brocade. "Scatter" (*chiru*) refers to the falling of the leaves.

77. Dates are 805 to 853. A noted calligrapher and musician.

78. The poem alludes to a passage in the biography of Xiang Yu in the *Han shu*—"to achieve wealth and glory, and not return to one's native village, is like wearing brocades by night"—which became proverbial for an advantage put to no use.

305

Composed and presented in response to an imperial command
for a folding screen at Teiji-in depicting a person standing beneath falling autumn leaves, beside a halted horse, about to ford
a river.

tachitomari	Let me pause to watch
mite o wataramu	before I cross:
momijiba wa	though they fall like rain
ame to furu tomo	the red leaves
mizu wa masaraji	will not swell the river's waters.[79]

Ōshikōchi no Mitsune

306

Composed for a poetry contest at the house of Prince Koresada.

yamada moru	The dew that settles
aki no kariio ni	on a makeshift hut
oku tsuyu wa	in this mountain field:
inaoosedori no	tears shed by the
namida narikeri	rice-bearing bird.[80]

Mibu no Tadamine

Travel

409

Topic unknown.

honobono to	Into the mist, glowing with dawn,
Akashi no ura no	across the Bay of Akashi
asagiri ni	a boat carries my thoughts

---

79. This is the last of a sequence of twenty-five poems on the topic "Falling Leaves" and one of
three poems in that sequence that were composed for screen paintings (*byōbu-uta*). As medieval
commentators noted in regard to such poems in the *Kokinshū*, the poet was generally expected to
assume the point of view of a figure in the painting when composing a poem like this one.

80. The topic is "Autumn Fields." For a similar confusion of dew with the tears of birds, see
Kokinshū, no. 258. In this poem, the dew on the hut or its roof is a *mitate* for such tears. The "rice-
bearing bird" (*inaoose-dori*), whose identity was debated in early commentaries, became one of the
"Three Birds" of the "Secret Teachings of the *Kokinshū*," a knowledge of which was requisite to
formal recognition as a waka poet throughout most of the medieval and early Tokugawa periods.

shimagakure yuku	into hiding,
fune o shi zo omou	islands beyond.[81]

Anonymous

Some say that the preceding poem was composed by Kakinomoto no Hitomaro.

Love 2

571

From the empress's poetry contest in the Kanpyō era.

koishiki ni	If in despair of love -
wabite tamashii	my soul should wander,
madoinaba	am I to be remembered
munashiki kara no	as one who left
na ni ya nokoramu	a corpse in vain?[82]

Anonymous

572

From the empress's poetry contest in the Kanpyō era.

kimi kouru	If not for the tears
namida shi naku wa	my loved one makes me shed,
karakoromo	this fine Chinese robe would be
mune no atari wa	singed round the breast
iro moenamashi	with the colors of passion.[83]

Ki no Tsurayuki

---

81. Passage into Akashi Bay meant crossing the official gateway at Settsu Province from the inner to the outer provinces, and the implied topic is border crossing. This is one of the most often quoted and allegorically glossed poems of the *Kokinshū* and became one of a core of poems treated as having profoundly esoteric meanings within the "Secret Teachings of the *Kokinshū*." Its reputation was enhanced, certainly, by the attribution to Hitomaro, venerated as one of the deities of the Way of poetry. One Nijō school commentary suggests that the poem, generally regarded as an allegory of the death of Prince Takechi, was deliberately placed by the editors in the book of travel rather than the book of mourning in order to free it from taboos attached to poems of mourning.

82. The speaker asks whether despair at unrequited love might cause his soul to depart from his body, leaving a reputation for having lived for nothing more than vain affection. In this context, the auxiliary particle of causation, *kara*, imposes an indecorous pun on the noun *kara*, meaning "empty shell" or "corpse."

83. The topic, as in the previous poem, is "Unrequited Love" and extends the familiar conceit that tears can quench the flames of longing. In *Kokinshū* love poetry, the passion of unrequited love typically leads to resentment and tears of blood. This appears to be an exception.

Love 3

635

Topic unknown.

aki no yo mo
na nomi narikeri
au to ieba
koto zo to mo naku
akenuru mono o

Autumn nights, long
only in name:
let's meet, we say,
yet dawn comes to part us
before we've begun.[84]

Ono no Komachi[85]

636

Topic unknown.

nagashi to mo
omoi zo hatenu
mukashi yori
au hito kara no
aki no yo nareba

For me, not long
enough at all:
autumn nights have always
taken their measure
from the depths of one's love.[86]

Ōshikōchi no Mitsune

637

Topic unknown.

shinonome no
hogara hogara to
akeyukeba
ono ga kinuginu
naru zo kanashiki

Just as the morning sky
is brightening to dawn,
how sad that we must
sort our robes
and part.[87]

Anonymous

---

84. In the vocabulary of classical poetry, which (as in this case) tends to conform to the calendar, autumn nights are longer than those of summer. Not long enough for love, however: the complaint is that the reality fails to live up to the name.

85. Active mid-ninth century. Almost nothing certain is known about Komachi except that she was indisputably the greatest female poet of her age. Some of her poems are among the most erotic in the classical tradition, and she set new standards for technical facility with the use of *kakekotoba* (pivot words and puns). See the section on Ono no Komachi.

86. Mitsune is quoted here as seconding Komachi's judgment in the previous poem and emphasizes that the length of an autumn night is entirely relative.

87. From the "night" of the previous, poems, the time advances to morning (*shinonome* refers to the moments just before dawn), and the topic here and in the following series of poems is

638

Topic unknown.

akenu tote	Dawn has come—
ima wa no kokoro	I resign myself to parting:
tsuku kara ni	why then must thoughts
nado iishiranu	I can't find words for
omoi souramu	cling to my heart?[88]

Fujiwara no Kunitsune

639

From the empress's poetry contest in the Kanpyō era.

akenu tote	Dawn has come—
kaeru michi ni wa	on the path home from love
kokitarete	I am drenched:
ame mo namida mo	rainfall swelling
furisohochitsutsu	my falling tears.[89]

Fujiwara no Toshiyuki

640

Topic unknown.

shinonome no	I begin to cry
wakare o oshimi	regret for our parting
ware zo mazu	even before the rooster
tori yori saki ni	crows the break
nakihajimetsuru	of dawn.[90]

Utsuku

"Parting at Dawn" (*kinuginu*). *Kinuginu* (literally, "robes," with the sense of "these robes and those") refers to the custom of lovers sharing the clothes they were dressed in for use as bedding for the night, then separating their respective robes in the morning before parting.

88. This and the following two poems continue the theme "Parting at Dawn," which extends through a sequence of about twelve verses.

89. The confusion of tears and rainfall was a cliché, but the poet renews it with the use of uncommon diction, *kokitarete* (drenched), and a pivot word making both rain and tears the subjects of the same verb, *furisohochi* (literally, "to fall and soak through").

90. The arrival of dawn, conventionally announced by the crowing of a rooster, means that the lover who has been visiting for the night must depart, all too early. Anticipating the bird's cry as well as her own, the speaker contrasts the implacability of time (and of convention) with the depth of her feelings.

645

When Narihira visited the province of Ise, he met, secretly, the person who was serving as the high priestess. The next morning, before he was able to find a way to send her a message, this poem was delivered from the woman.

kimi ga koshi	Did you come to me?
ware ya yukikemu	Did I visit you?
omooezu	I cannot know.
yume ka utsutsu ka	Dream? Reality?
nete ka samete ka	Was I asleep or awake?

Anonymous

646

Reply.

kakikurasu	I wandered, too,
kokoro no yami ni	in heart-blinding darkness:
madoiniki	was it dream
yume utsutsu to wa	or reality?
yohito sadame yo	Let others decide.

Ariwara no Narihira[91]

Love 5

797

Topic unknown.

iro miede	Not changing color
utsurou mono wa	yet fading all the same:
yo no naka no	such is the flower of
hito no kokoro no	the heart of one in
hana ni zo arikeru	this world of love.

---

91. Ariwara no Narihira (825–880) was a descendant of the imperial family. He had an unsuccessful political career but enjoyed great esteem as a poet and a reputation as an erotic adept. Many of his poems encompass a measure of ironic reflection which invites comparison with those of Ono no Komachi, a close contemporary. For more on Narihira as a legend and poet, see the section on *The Tales of Ise*.

In an equally plausible reading of the ambiguous verb *miete*, the same poem might be translated as

iro miete	All too visibly
utsurou mono wa	its color fades:
yo no naka no	the flower of the heart
hito no kokoro no	of one passing through
hana ni zo arikeru	this world of love.[92]

Ono no Komachi

Mourning

832

Composed after the Horikawa chancellor died and his remains were interred near Mount Fukakusa.

Fukakusa no	If cherry trees indeed
nobe no sakura shi	have feelings, may those
kokoro araba	of the fields of Fukakusa
kotoshi bakari wa	this year, at least,
sumizome ni sake	shroud themselves in black blossoms.[93]

Kamutsuke no Mineo

---

92. The wording of the poem offers two logically opposed readings, depending on whether the verb "to be visible" is interpreted affirmatively (*miete*) or negatively (*miede*), a question the script in which the *Kokinshū* was recorded leaves undecided. A majority of commentators, medieval and modern, have preferred the direct irony of the negative reading reflected in the first of the two translations. Others have argued in favor of the more subtly ironic affirmative reading. A small minority suggest that the *miete/miede* crux is to be taken as a pun (*kakekotoba*), inviting the reader to suspend judgment between the two contrary readings and entertain the possibility that both may be accepted at once.

93. The belief that cherry trees are animate and sentient beings, invoked frequently in classical waka (and in nō drama), likely drew force from folk-religious cults of cherry trees as local deities and further support from syncretic Tendai doctrines of the universal Buddha-mind. The apostrophe in this poem, addressed to the cherry trees, can thus be taken literally. This does not diminish the extremity of the conceit of black blossoms, meant to convey the burden of the speaker's grief.

Miscellaneous Topics 2

947

Topic unknown.

izuku ni ka	Where might I find
yo o ba itowamu	distaste for this world?
kokoro koso	In pastures and hills alike
no ni mo yama ni mo	my heart yearns
madoubera nare	to stray.[94]

Sosei[95]

981

Topic unknown.

iza koko ni	So be it, let me
waga yo wa henamu	live out my life
Sugawara ya	here in Sugawara Fushimi,
Fushimi no sato no	lest my old home go
aremaku mo oshi	sadly to ruin.[96]

Anonymous

982

Topic unknown.

waga io wa	My house is
Miwa no yamamoto	at the foot of Miwa Mountain:

---

94. The poems gathered in the two books of miscellaneous topics are indeed diverse. A few, at the beginning of the first book, are celebratory, but most dwell on themes of disappointment, mortality, and loss. The speaker complains of a double bind: the imperative to flee the corruptive influences of civilization and seek detachment in the purity of the pastoral is undermined by the (eminently civilized) delights of nature, which prove to be no less a distraction from the path to ascetic withdrawal.

95. Active late ninth century. A master of the decorous irony taken to characterize the poetry of his age, Sosei was esteemed by contemporaries as a poet and courtier-cleric and is regarded as one of the leading poets of his age.

96. This and the following three poems, on the topic "Dwellings," were treated in the medieval esoteric teachings as densely allegorical poems uttered by deities or immortals and framed as lessons based on syncretic Shinto-Buddhist and protonativist doctrine. In the sequence here, the poems were understood, on one level, as lamenting the moral corruption of society (suggested by the anticipated ruin of "my old home") that has forced the gods and their Buddhist avatars to manifest themselves in the world and set things right.

koishiku wa	should fondness call,
toburaikimase	please visit the gate
sugi tateru kado	where cedars stand.

Anonymous

983

Topic unknown.

waga io wa	Dwelling to the east
miyako no tatsumi	and south of the capital,
shika zo sumu	in Uji Hills I live:
yo o ujiyama to	some say I've forsaken
hito wa iu nari	their sad world.

Monk Kisen[97]

Miscellaneous Forms (haikai)

1015

Topic unknown.

mutsugoto mo	Words and acts
mada tsukinaku ni	of love yet undone
akenumeri	and now, too soon, it's dawn:
izura wa aki no	what of those "long
nagashi chou yo wa	autumn nights"?[98]

Ōshikōchi no Mitsune

1038

Topic unknown.

omou chou	If only I could creep
hito no kokoro no	into each corner

---

97. One of the six "immortals" (*kasen*) singled out in the preface to the *Kokinshū* to exemplify the major traditions of waka. This is the only poem in this collection attributed to him, and almost nothing is known about his career.

98. This was likely meant as a parody of Komachi's poem on the same topic (*Kokinshū*, no. 635). Poets of the late Heian era and after were puzzled by the term *haikai* (by which the editors of the *Kokinshū* probably meant "dissonant" poems using archaic or colloquial diction, or obtrusive, vaguely grotesque conceits), with good reason, since a fair number of poems not placed in the haikai section are similar to poems like this one. What marks this poem as haikai is the somewhat colloquial diction, not the topic or its treatment.

kuma goto ni	of the heart of the one
tachikakuretsutsu	who says she loves me
miru yoshi mo ga na	and keep watch.[99]

Anonymous
[Introduction and translations by Lewis Cook]

THE BIRTH OF VERNACULAR PROSE FICTION

The *monogatari*, or vernacular tale, emerged in the latter half of the ninth century together with the kana syllabary. The earliest extant example is *The Tale of the Bamboo Cutter* (*Taketori monogatari*, ca. 909), considered in *The Tale of Genji* to be the ancestor of the monogatari. The monogatari, which originally meant "desultory conversation," can be traced back to the early chronicles (*Kojiki, Nihon shoki*) and the provincial gazetteers (*fudoki*)—with their myths, histories, and clan legends—as well as to the practice of oral storytelling, which led to anecdotal (*setsuwa*) literature. The most important development in the birth of the monogatari, however, was the use of kana, which allowed for complex psychological description and eventually resulted in *The Tale of Genji*, now considered by many to be the world's first psychological novel.

The Tale of the Bamboo Cutter begins with the set phrase *ima wa mukashi* (now it was long ago) and ends with *to zo iitsutaetaru* (and so it has been passed on), thus preserving, at least in outline, the traditional storytelling conventions found in setsuwa. But in contrast to setsuwa, which claimed to tell the truth, monogatari are admittedly fictional. They may be based on historical events, but they do not purport to be faithful to history. Nonetheless, as noted in the famous defense of fiction in the "Fireflies" (Hotaru) chapter of *The Tale of Genji*, monogatari were often more accurate than the highly regarded historical chronicles in their depiction of people's personal lives, emotions, and thoughts. Unlike such setsuwa collections as the *Nihon ryōiki* and the later *Konjaku monogatari shū*, which often were written to educate the audience in the Buddhist way, the Heian monogatari had no overt didactic purpose.

Monogatari are generally aristocratic in content, depicting the lives of the nobility at court and in the capital. They were written for and by the aristocracy,

---

99. This could just as well be "the one who says he loves me." It is not the diction so much as the conceit that marks this poem as haikai. The premise is that promises of love invite suspicion and, too often, lead to resentment. The phrase "poems of resentment" (*urami no uta*) became a synonym for "poems of love" (*koi no uta*) early in the classical waka tradition. For a somewhat more decorous variation on the same conceit, compare the poem in section 15 of *The Tales of Ise*: "I long to find a path to the depths of Mount Shinobu that I might fathom the secrets of another's heart." "Shinobu," reputedly the name of a mountain in what is now Fukushima Prefecture and a poetic place-name (*utamakura*), is also a verb meaning "to endure," "conceal," "long for," and "remember."

probably by middle-rank scholar nobles who had considerable exposure to both Japanese poetry and Chinese fiction. Today, monogatari are divided into two major types: the "fabricated tale" (*tsukuri monogatari*), represented by *The Tale of the Bamboo Cutter*, *The Tale of Ochikubo* (*Ochikubo monogatari*), and *The Tale of the Hollow Tree* (*Utsubo monogatari*), and the "poem tale" (*uta-monogatari*), epitomized by *The Tales of Ise* (*Ise monogatari*), *The Tales of Yamato* (*Yamato monogatari*), and *The Tales of Heichū* (*Heichū monogatari*). Fabricated tales describe fantastic and miraculous events, often involving a journey to an "other world." In contrast, poem tales are stories about poetry and tend to be about love, the four seasons, and nature, the central topics of waka. Both types generally revolve around the topic of love, particularly the private relationships between men and women. *The Tale of Genji*, written in the early eleventh century and considered the best of the Heian monogatari, skillfully combines both types of monogatari with the women's tradition of diary writing.

In the tenth century, when monogatari first flourished, the aristocracy did not consider them serious literature, regarding them as a genre written for women and children. (The most important literature was the historical chronicles and poetry, and the most prestigious writing system was Chinese.) As the preface to the *Illustration of the Three Jewels* (*Sanbōe-kotoba*, 984) reveals, the Buddhist clergy had an even more negative view of monogatari, condemning them as fiction and lies. One consequence is that we do not know the names of the authors of any of the monogatari written before *The Tale of Genji*. By the early thirteenth century, however, *The Tales of Ise*, *The Tale of Genji*, and *The Tale of Sagoromo* had achieved—at least among the leading poets of the day, such as Fujiwara no Shunzei and Fujiwara no Teika—canonical status, not as fiction, but as guides to and narratives of the thirty-one-syllable waka, the most prestigious of the vernacular genres.

THE TALE OF THE BAMBOO CUTTER (TAKETORI MONOGATARI, CA. 909)

The Tale of the Bamboo Cutter (*Taketori monogatari*), referred to in *The Tale of Genji* as the "parent of the monogatari," was written around 909. It can be divided into four sections: (1) the story of the poor woodcutter who becomes rich as a result of a miraculous birth; (2) the stories of the five suitors, each of whom unsuccessfully courts the shining princess; (3) the courtship of the shining princess by the emperor; and (4) the return of the shining princess to the moon.

The Tale of the Bamboo Cutter drew heavily on existing legends and folktales, particularly in regard to the story of the bamboo cutter, his discovery of the shining princess, and her return to the moon. In the feathered robe (*hagoromo*) legend, which appears in the earlier provincial gazetteers (*Suruga fudoki* and *Ōmi fudoki*), a heavenly lady descends to earth and her feathered robe is taken away, preventing her from returning to heaven. She then recovers the robe, which has celestial power, and returns to heaven. *The Tale of the Bamboo Cutter* also is a story of the origins of words and place-names (such as that of Mount Fuji), a convention found as early as in the fudoki in the ancient period.

Whereas the outer sections of *The Tale of the Bamboo Cutter* are a mixture of various folktales and legends, the inner section, the courtship by the five aristocratic suitors, appears to be a newer addition. Here the author uses satire to reveal the greed, duplicity, pretense, excessive attachment, and materialism of the different suitors, to expose their excessive belief in the power of calculation. The first three of the five suitor stories form a distinct group, whose characters are summarized quickly, and their deception fails. All the suitors are of the highest rank: elite aristocrats—prince, minister of the right (*udaijin*), major counselor (*dainagon*), middle counselor (*chūnagon*)—but none of them acts like a refined, elegant aristocrat. The author was probably a middle-rank scholar-aristocrat who stood at a critical distance from those in power at the time.

In the courtship section, the princess is heartless, disgusted with her suitors, but in the last section, she becomes a human figure: emotional, pensive, and melancholy, emotionally attached to her earthly parents. The narrative thus establishes a contrast between the beautiful, clean moon, where immortals live and there are no melancholy thoughts, and the dirty, polluted world, where people suffer and die. The moon also suggests the Western Paradise (*jōdo*) found in Pure Land Buddhism. This association is reinforced by the descent of the "moon" people, which resembles the *raigō* (heavenly descent) in Pure Land paintings, in which the spirits of the dead are met by a group of heavenly beings who descend on clouds.

Even though the earth is a place of exile and punishment for the princess, she becomes attached to it and finds value in human emotions and the human heart. Her celestial robe represents the divide between the two worlds, and significantly, the princess resists putting it on. The emperor also refuses to drink the elixir left him by the princess, complaining, "What use is it, this elixir of immortality, if one cannot have love?" In short, the human world, a world of pathos, is juxtaposed with and comes into conflict with the world of the moon, which is associated with a Buddhistic world of detachment and no suffering.

The Bamboo Cutter

Many years ago there lived a man they called the Old Bamboo Cutter. Every day he would make his way into the fields and mountains to gather bamboo, which he fashioned into all manner of wares. His name was Sanuki no Miyakko. One day he noticed among the bamboos a stalk that glowed at the base. He thought this was very strange, and going over to have a look, saw that a light was shining inside the hollow stem. He examined it, and there he found a most lovely little girl about three inches tall. The old man said, "I have discovered you because you were here, among these bamboos I watch over every morning and evening. It must be you are meant to be my child."

He took the little girl in his hands and brought her back home. There he gave the child into the keeping of his old wife, for her to rear. The girl was incomparably beautiful, but still so small they put her in a little basket, the better to care for her.

It often happened afterward that when the Old Bamboo Cutter gathered bamboo he would find a stalk crammed with gold from joint to joint, and in this way he gradually became very rich.

The child shot up under their loving care. Before three months had passed she stood tall as a grown woman, and her parents decided to celebrate her coming of age. Her hair was combed up and they dressed her in trailing skirts. The greatest pains were lavished on her upbringing—they never even allowed her to leave her curtained chamber. This child had a purity of features quite without equal anywhere in the world, and the house was filled with a light that left no corner dark. If ever the old man felt in poor spirits or was in pain, just to look at the child would make the pain stop. All anger too would melt away.

For a long time afterward the old man went on gathering bamboo, and he became a person of great importance. Now that the girl had attained her full height, a diviner from Mimurodo, Inbe no Akita by name, was summoned to bestow a woman's name on her. Akita called her Nayotake no Kaguya-hime, the Shining Princess of the Supple Bamboo. The feast given on the occasion of her name-giving was graced by diversions of every kind and lasted three days. Men and women alike were invited and grandly entertained.

The Suitors

Every man in the realm, whether high or low of rank, could think of nothing but of how much he wanted to win Kaguya-hime, or at least to see her. Just to hear the rumors about her made men wild with love. But it was not easy for those who perched on the fence nearby or lurked around her house, or even for those inside, to catch a glimpse of the girl. Unable to sleep peacefully at night, they would go out into the darkness and poke holes in the fence, attempting in this foolish way to get a peep at her. It was from this time that courting a woman came to be known as "night-crawling."

But all their prowling around the place, where no one showed the least interest in them, was in vain. Even when they made so bold as to address the members of the household, no answer was forthcoming. Many a young noble, refusing to leave the vicinity, spent his nights and days without budging from his post. Suitors of shallower affections decided eventually that this fruitless courtship was a waste of time and ceased their visits.

Five among them, men renowned as connoisseurs of beauty, persisted in their suit. Their attentions never flagged, and they came courting night and day. These were Prince Ishizukuri, Prince Kuramochi, the minister of the right Abe no Miushi, the major counselor Ōtomo no Miyuki, and the middle counselor Isonokami no Marotari. Whenever these men heard of any woman who was even moderately good-looking, and the country certainly had many such, they burned to see her; and when they heard about Kaguya-hime they wanted so badly to meet her that they gave up all nourishment and spent their time in brooding. They would go to her house and wander aimlessly about, even though nothing was likely to come of it. They wrote her letters that she did not even deign to answer; they penned odes bewailing their plight. Though they knew it was in vain, they pursued their courtship, undaunted by hindrances, whether the falling snows and the ice of mid-winter or the blazing sun and the thunderbolts of the summer.

One day they called the Bamboo Cutter to them, and each in turn got down on his knees and rubbed his hands, imploring the old man, "Please give me your daughter!"

But the old man replied, "The child was not of my begetting, and she is not obliged to obey my wishes." And so the days and the months went by.

Confronted by this situation, the gentlemen returned to their houses, where, lost in despondent thoughts, they prayed and offered petitions to the gods, either to fulfill their love or else to let them forget Kaguya-hime. But, however they tried, they could not put her from their minds. Despite what the old man had said, they could not believe that he would allow the girl to remain unwedded, and this thought gave them hope.

The old man, observing their ardor, said to Kaguya-hime, "My precious child, I realize you are a divinity in human form, but I have spared no efforts to raise you into such a great, fine lady. Will you not listen to what an old man has to say?"

Kaguya-hime replied, "What request could you make of me to which I would not consent? You say I am a divinity in human form, but I know nothing of that. I think of you and you alone as my father."

"Oh, how happy you make me!" exclaimed the old man. "I am now over seventy, and I do not know if my end may not come today or tomorrow. In this world it is customary for men and women to marry and for their families then to flourish. Why do you refuse to be wedded?"

Kaguya-hime said, "How could I possibly do such a thing?"

The old man replied, "You are a transformed being, it is true, but you have a woman's body. As long as I am alive, you may, if you choose, remain unmarried, but one day you will be left alone. These gentlemen have been coming here faithfully for months and even years. Listen carefully to what they have to say, and choose one of them as your husband."

"All I can think is that I should certainly regret it if, in spite of my unattractive looks, I married a man without being sure of the depth of his feelings, and he later proved fickle. No matter how distinguished a man he may be, I wouldn't be willing to marry him unless I were sure he was sincere," said Kaguya-hime.

"That's exactly what I myself think," answered the old man. "Now, what must a man's feelings be before you are willing to marry him? All these gentlemen have certainly shown unusual devotion."

Kaguya-hime said, "Shall I tell you the depth of sentiments I require? I am not asking for anything extraordinary. All five men seem to be equally affectionate. How can I tell which of them is the most deserving? If one of the five will show me some special thing I wish to see, I will know his affections are the noblest, and I shall become his wife. Please tell this to the gentlemen if they come again."

"An excellent solution," the old man said approvingly.

Toward sunset the suitors gathered as usual. One played a flute, another sang a song, the third sang from score, and the others whistled and beat time with their fans. The old man appeared while this concert was still in progress. He said, "Your visits during all these months and years have done my humble house too great an honor. I am quite overwhelmed. I have told Kaguya-hime that my life is now so uncertain I do not know whether today or tomorrow may not be my last day, and I have suggested to her that she consider carefully and choose one of you gentlemen as her husband. She insists, however, on being sure of the depth of your feelings, and that is only proper. She says she will marry whichever of you proves his superiority by showing her some special thing she wishes to see. This is a fine plan, for none of you will then resent her choice." The five men all agreed that it was indeed an excellent suggestion, and the old man went back into the house to report what had happened.

Kaguya-hime declared, "I should like Prince Ishizukuri to obtain for me from India the stone begging-bowl of the Buddha. Prince Kuramochi is to go to the mountain in the Eastern Sea called Horai and fetch me a branch of the tree that grows there, with roots of silver and trunk of gold, whose fruits are pearls. The next gentleman is to bring me a robe made of the fur of Chinese fire-rats. I ask Otomo, the major counselor, please to fetch me the jewel that shines five colors, found in a dragon's neck. And Isonokami, the middle counselor, should present me with a swallow's easy-delivery charm."

The old man said, "These are indeed difficult tasks. The gifts you ask for are not to be found anywhere in Japan. How shall I break the news of such difficult assignments?"

"What is so difficult about them?" asked Kaguya-hime.

"I'll tell them, at any rate," said the old man and went outside. When he had related what was expected of them, the princes and nobles exclaimed, "Why doesn't she simply say, 'Stay away from my house!'?" They all left in disgust.

The Stone Begging-Bowl of the Buddha

Nevertheless, Prince Ishizukuri felt as though his life would not be worth living unless he married the girl, and he reflected, "Is there anything I would not do for her, even if it meant traveling to India to find what she wants?" He realized, however, being a prudent man, how unlikely he was to find the one and only begging-bowl, even if he journeyed all eight thousand leagues to India. He left word with Kaguya-hime that he was departing that day for India in search of the begging-bowl and remained away for three years. At a mountain temple in Tochi district of the province of Yamato he obtained a bowl that had stood before the image of Binzuru and was pitch-black with soot. He put the bowl in a brocade bag, fastened it to a spray of artificial flowers, and carried it to Kaguyahime's house. When he presented the bowl, she looked it over suspiciously. Inside she found a note and opened it: "I have worn out my spirits on the roads over sea and mountains; in quest of the stone bowl my tears of blood have flowed."

Kaguya-hime examined the bowl to see if it gave off a light, but there was not so much as a firefly's glimmer. She returned the bowl with the verse, "I hoped that at least the sparkle of the fallen dew would linger within—why did you fetch this bowl from the Mountain of Darkness?"

The Prince threw away the bowl at the gate and replied with this verse, "When it encountered the Mountain of Brightness it lost its light perhaps; I discard the bowl, but shamelessly cling to my hopes." He sent this into the house, but Kaguya-hime no longer deigned to answer. When he discovered she would not even listen to his pleas, he departed, at a loss for words. Because he persisted in his suit even after throwing away the bowl, people have ever since spoken of surprise at a shameless action as being bowled over.

Prince Kuramochi and Ōtomo no Miyuki, the major counselor, are equally unsuccessful in obtaining the treasures assigned to them.

The Easy-Delivery Charm of the Swallows

The middle counselor Isonokami no Marotari gave orders to the men in his employ to report if any swallows were building nests. "Yes, sir," they said. "But why do you need this information?" He answered, "I intend to get the easy-delivery charm that a swallow carries."

The men said variously, "I've killed many swallows in my time, but I've never seen anything of that description in a swallow's belly." "How do you suppose a swallow manages to pull out the charm just when it's about to give birth?" "It keeps the charm hidden, and if any man gets a glimpse of it, it disappears."

Still another man said, "Swallows are building nests in all the holes along the eaves of the Palace Kitchen. If you send some dependable men there and set up perches from which they can observe the swallows, there are so many swallows that one of them is sure to be giving birth. That will give your men the chance to grab the charm."

The middle counselor was delighted. "How perfectly extraordinary!" he said, "I had never noticed! Thank you for a most promising suggestion." He ordered twenty dependable men to the spot, and stationed them on lookout perches built for their task. From his mansion he sent a steady stream of messengers asking if the men had successfully obtained the easy-delivery charm.

The swallows, terrified by all the people climbing up to the roof, did not return to their nests. When the middle counselor learned of this, he was at a loss what to do now. Just at this point an old man named Kuratsumaro who worked in the Palace Kitchen was heard to remark, "I have a plan for His Excellency if he wishes to get a swallow's easy-delivery charm." He was at once ushered into the presence of the middle counselor and seated directly before him.

Kuratsumaro said, "You are using clumsy methods to get the charm, and you'll never succeed in that way. The twenty men on their lookout perches are making such a racket that the swallows are much too frightened to come close. You should tear down the perches and dismiss all the men. One man only, a dependable man, should be kept in readiness inside an open-work basket that has a rope attached to it. As soon as a swallow starts to lay an egg, the man in the basket should be hoisted up with the rope. Then he can quickly grab the charm. That is your best plan."

"An excellent plan indeed," said the middle counselor. The perches were dismantled and the men all returned to the palace. The counselor asked Kuratsumaro, "How will we know when the swallow is about to give birth, so the man can be hoisted up in time?"

Kuratsumaro answered, "When a swallow is about to give birth it raises its tail and circles around seven times. As it is completing its seventh turn you should hoist the basket immediately and the man can snatch the charm."

The counselor was overjoyed to hear Kuratsumaro's words. "How wonderful to have my prayers granted!" he exclaimed. "And to think you're not even in my service!" He removed his cloak and offered it to the old man. "Come tonight to the Palace Kitchen," he said, dismissing him.

When it grew dark the middle counselor went to the Kitchen. He observed that swallows were indeed building nests and circling the place with lifted tails, exactly as Kuratsumaro had described. A man was put in a basket and hoisted up, but when he put his hand into the swallow's nest he called down, "There's nothing here!"

"That's because you aren't searching in the proper way!" the counselor angrily retorted. "Is there nobody competent here? I'll have to go up there myself." He climbed into the basket and was hoisted up. He peered into a nest and saw a swallow with its tail lifted circling about furiously. He at once stretched out his arm and felt in the nest. His fingers touched something flat. "I've got it! Lower me now; I've done it myself!" he cried. His men gathered round, but in their eagerness to lower him quickly they pulled too hard, and the rope snapped. The middle counselor plunged down, landing on his back atop a kitchen cauldron.

His men rushed to him in consternation and lifted him in their arms. He lay motionless, showing the whites of his eyes. The men drew some water and got him to swallow a little. At length he regained consciousness, and they lowered him by the hands and feet from the top of the cauldron. When they at last felt they could ask him how he was, he answered in a faint voice, "My head seems a little clearer, but I can't move my legs. But I am happy anyway that I managed to get the easy-delivery charm. Light a torch and bring it here. I want to see what the charm looks like." He raised his head and opened his hand only to discover he was clenching some old droppings the swallows had left. "Alas," he cried, "it was all to no avail!" Ever since that time people have said a project that goes contrary to expectations "lacks charm."

When the middle counselor realized he had failed to obtain the charm, his spirits took a decided turn for the worse. His men laid him inside the lid of a Chinese chest and carried him home. He could not be placed inside his carriage because his back had been broken.

The middle counselor attempted to keep people from learning he had been injured because of a childish escapade. Under the strain of this worry he became all the weaker. It bothered him more that people might hear of his fiasco and mock him than that he had failed to secure the charm. His anxiety grew worse each day, until he felt in the end it would be preferable to die of illness in a normal manner than lose his reputation.

Kaguya-hime, hearing of his unfortunate condition, sent a poem of inquiry: "The years pass, but the waves do not return to the pines of Suminoe, where I wait in vain; you have failed to find the charm, I am told, is it true?"

He asked that her poem be read to him. Then he lifted his head very feebly, barely able to write in great pain while someone else held the paper: "My efforts were in vain, and now I am about to die in despair; but will you not save my life?" With these words he expired. Kaguya-hime was rather touched.

From this time something slightly pleasurable has been said to have a modicum of charm.

The Imperial Hunt

The emperor, learning of Kaguya-hime's unrivaled beauty, said to a maid of honor, Nakatomi no Fusako by name, "Please go and discover for me what kind of woman Kaguya-hime is, this beauty who has brought so many men to ruin and refuses to marry."

Fusako, obedient to his command, departed. When she arrived at the Bamboo Cutter's house the old woman deferentially showed her in. The maid of honor said, "I have been ordered by His Majesty to ascertain whether Kaguyahime is as beautiful as people say. That is why I am here now."

"I shall tell her," said the old woman and went inside. "Please," she urged Kaguya-hime, "Hurry out and meet the emperor's messenger."

Kaguya-hime replied, "How can I appear before her when I am not in the least attractive?"

"Don't talk nonsense! Do you dare to show such disrespect to someone sent here by the emperor?"

"It doesn't make me feel especially grateful to think the emperor might wish to summon me," answered Kaguya-hime. She showed no sign of relenting and meeting the lady. The old woman had always considered Kaguya-hime as being no different from a child she had borne herself, but when the girl spoke so coldly, it much embarrassed her, and she could not reprimand Kaguya-hime as she would have liked.

The old woman returned to the maid of honor and said, "I must apologize, but the girl is terribly obstinate and refuses to see you."

The maid of honor said, "I was ordered by His Majesty to verify her appearance without fail. How can I return to the palace without seeing her? Do you think it proper for anyone living in this country to be allowed to disobey a royal command? Please do not let her act so unreasonably!" She intended these words to shame Kaguya-hime, but when the latter was informed, she refused all the more vehemently to comply. "If I am disobeying a royal command, let them execute me without delay," she declared.

The maid of honor returned to the palace and reported what had happened. The emperor listened and said merely, "You can see she's quite capable of causing the deaths of a great many men." He seemed to have given up all thought of summoning Kaguya-hime into his service, but he still had his heart set on her, and refused to accept defeat at her hands. He sent for the old man and stated, "I want this Kaguya-hime you have at your place. Word has reached me of the beauty of her face and figure, and I sent my messenger to look her over, but she returned unsuccessful, unable to obtain so much as a glimpse of the girl. Did you bring her up to be so disrespectful?"

The old man humbly replied, "The girl absolutely refuses to serve at court. I am quite at a loss what to do about her. But I'll go back home and report Your Majesty's command."

The emperor asked, "Why should a child you have raised with your own hands refuse to do what you wish? If you present the girl for service here, you can be quite sure I will reward you with court rank."

The old man returned home, overjoyed. He related this conversation to Kaguya-hime, concluding, "That was what the emperor told me. Are you still unwilling to serve him?"

Kaguya-hime answered, "I absolutely refuse to serve at the court. If you force me, I'll simply disappear. It may win you a court rank, but it will mean my death."

"Never do such a dreadful thing!" cried the old man. "What use would position or rank be to me if I couldn't behold my child? But why are you so reluctant to serve at the court? Would it really kill you?"

"If you still think I am lying, send me into service at the court and see if I don't die. Many men have showed me most unusual affection, but all of them in vain. If I obey the emperor's wishes, no sooner than he expresses them, I shall feel ashamed how people will consider my coldness to those other men."

The old man replied, "I don't care about anyone else. The only thing that disturbs me is the danger to your life. I'll report that you are still unwilling to serve." He went to the palace and informed the emperor, "In humble obedience to Your Majesty's command, I attempted to persuade the child to enter your service, but she told me that if I forced her to serve in the palace, it would surely cause her death. This child was not born of my body. I found her long ago in the mountains. That is why her ways are not like those of ordinary people."

The emperor commented, "She must be a transformed being. There's no hope, then, of having her serve me, but at least I should like somehow to get a glimpse of her."

"I wonder how this could be arranged," said the old man.

The emperor said, "I understand, Miyakkomaro, your house is near the mountains. How would it be if, under pretext of staging an imperial hunt, I stopped by for a look at her?"

"That is an excellent plan," said the old man. "If Your Majesty should happen to call at a time when she does not expect a visitor, you can probably see her." The emperor at once set a date for the hunt.

During the course of the hunt the emperor entered Kaguya-hime's house and saw there a woman so lovely she shed a radiance around her. He thought, this must be Kaguya-hime, and approached. She fled into the adjoining room, but the emperor caught her by the sleeve. She covered her face, but his first glimpse was enough to convince him that she was a peerless beauty. "I won't let you go!" he cried. But when he attempted to take her away with him, Kaguyahime declared, "If I had been born on earth I would have served you. But if you try to force me to go with you, you will find you cannot."

The emperor said, "Why can't I? I'll take you with me!" He summoned his palanquin, but at that instant Kaguya-hime suddenly dissolved into a shadow. The emperor realized to his dismay and disappointment that she was indeed no ordinary mortal. He said, "I shall not insist any longer that you come with me. But please return to your former shape. Just one look at you and I shall go." Kaguya-hime resumed her original appearance.

The emperor was still too entranced with Kaguya-hime's beauty to stifle his feelings, and he displayed his pleasure with the old man for having brought about the meeting. Miyakkomaro, for his part, tendered a splendid banquet for the emperor's officers. The emperor was bitterly disappointed to return to the palace without Kaguya-hime, and as he left the Bamboo Cutter's house he felt as though his soul remained behind. After he had entered his palanquin he sent this verse to Kaguya-hime: "As I go back to the palace my spirits lag; I turn back, I hesitate, because of Kaguya-hime, who defies me and remains behind."

To this she wrote in reply, "How could one who has lived her life in a house overgrown with weeds dare to look upon a jeweled palace?"

The emperor felt there was less reason than ever to leave when he saw this poem, but since he could not spend the night with Kaguya-hime, he had no choice but to return. When he saw again the palace ladies who usually waited on him they seemed unworthy even to appear in Kaguya-hime's presence. Indeed, the very ladies he had always considered more beautiful than other women, when compared to Kaguya-hime, seemed scarcely worthy of the name of human beings. He ceased visiting his consorts, finding no pleasure in their company. He wrote letters only to Kaguya-hime, and her answers were by no means un-kind. He used also to send her poems attached to flowers or branches that struck him as especially attractive.

The Celestial Robe of Feathers

They passed some three years in this way, each consoling the other. At the beginning of the next spring Kaguya-hime seemed more pensive than usual as she watched the moon rise in all its splendor. Someone nearby admonished her, "People should avoid staring the moon in the face." But when no one was around, Kaguya-hime would often gaze at the moon and weep bitterly. At the time of the full moon of the Seventh Month she sat outside, seemingly lost in thought. Her maidservants informed the Bamboo Cutter: "Kaguya-hime has always looked with deep emotion at the moon, but she has seemed rather strange of late. She must be terribly upset over something. Please keep an eye on her."

The old man asked Kaguya-hime, "What makes you look so pensively at the moon?"

She answered, "When I look at the moon the world seems lonely and sad. What else would there be to worry me?"

He went over to Kaguya-hime and looked at her face. She definitely appeared melancholy. He asked, "My dear one, what are you thinking of? What worries you?"

"I am not worried about anything. But everything seems so depressing."

"You shouldn't look at the moon," the old man said. "Whenever you do, you always seem so upset."

"How could I go on living if I didn't look at the moon?" Each night, as the moon rose, she would sit outside, immersed in thought. On dark moonless nights she seemed to emerge from her reverie, but with the reappearance of the moon she would sometimes sigh and weep. Her maids whispered to one another, "There really does seem to be something disturbing her," but no one, not even her parents, knew what it was.

One moonlit night toward the middle of the Eighth Month Kaguya-hime, sitting outside, suddenly burst into a flood of tears. She now wept without caring whether or not people saw. Her parents, noticing this, asked in alarm what was troubling her. Kaguya-hime answered, still weeping, "I have intended to tell you for a long time, but I was so sure I would make you unhappy that I have kept silent all this while. But I can be silent no more. I will tell you everything. I am not a creature of this world. I came from the Palace of the Moon to this world because of an obligation incurred in a former life. Now the time has come when I must return. On the night of the full moon people from my old country will come for me, and I will have no choice but to go. I was heartbroken to think how unhappy this news would make you, and that is why I have been grieving ever since this spring." She wept copiously.

The old man cried, "What's that you say? I found you in a stick of bamboo when you were no bigger than a poppy seed, and I have brought you up until now you stand as tall as I. Who is going to take my child away? Do you think I'll let them?" He added, "If they do, it will kill me." His distraught weeping was really unbearable to behold.

Kaguya-hime said, "I have a father and mother who live in the City of the Moon. When I came here from my country I said it would be just for a short while, but already I have spent many years in this land. I have tarried among you, without thinking of my parents on the moon, and I have become accustomed to your ways. Now that I am about to return I feel no great joy, but only a terrible sadness. And yet though it is not by my choice, I must go." They both wept uncontrollably. Her maids, who had been in her service for years, thought how unspeakable parting would be, and how much they would miss her noble and lively disposition, to which they had grown so familiar. They refused all nourishment and grieved no less than the others.

When the emperor learned what had occurred, he sent a messenger to the Bamboo Cutter's house. The old man went out to receive him, weeping profusely. His beard had turned white from sorrow, his back was bent, and his eyes were swollen. He was just fifty this year, but his troubles seemed to have aged him suddenly. The imperial messenger transmitted the emperor's words: "I am informed that you have been afflicted by a grave misfortune—is it true?"

The Bamboo Cutter, weeping, answered the message, "On the night of the full moon men are coming from the City of the Moon to fetch Kaguya-hime. I am deeply honored by His Majesty's kind enquiry, and beg him to send soldiers here on that night, to catch anyone who may arrive from the moon."

The messenger departed and, after reporting to the emperor on the old man's condition, repeated his request. The emperor said, "If I, who had but a single glimpse of Kaguya-hime, cannot put her from my thoughts, what must it be like for her parents, who are used to seeing her day and night, to lose her?"

On the fifteenth, the day of the full moon, the emperor issued orders to the different guards headquarters, and, designating as his official envoy the junior commandant of the Palace Guards, Takano no Okuni, sent a force of some two thousand men from the Six Headquarters to the Bamboo Cutter's house. No sooner did they arrive than a thousand men posted themselves on the wall and a thousand on the roof. Together with the numerous members of the household they formed a defense that left no openings. The defenders were equipped with bows and arrows, and inside the main house the womenfolk were stationed, guarding it.

The old woman sat in the strong-room of the house, holding Kaguya-hime in her arms. The old man, having tightly barred the door, stood on guard at the entrance. He declared, "Do you think anybody, even if he comes from the moon, is going to break through our defenses?" He called to the roof, "Shoot to kill if you see anything flying in the sky, no matter how small!"

The guards answered, "With defenses as strong as ours we're sure we can shoot down even a mosquito. We'll expose its body as a warning to the others." Their words greatly reassured the old man.

Kaguya-hime said, "No matter how you lock me up and try to guard me, you won't be able to resist the men from the moon. You won't be able to use your weapons on them. Even if you shut me up in this room, when they come everything will open before them. Resist them though you may, when they come even the bravest man will lose heart."

"If anyone comes after you, I'll tear out his eyes with my long nails," cried the old man. "I'll grab him by the hair and throw him to ground. I'll put him to shame by exposing his behind for all the officers to see!" He shouted with anger.

"Don't talk in such a loud voice," cautioned Kaguya-hime. "It would be shocking if the men on the roof heard you. I am very sorry to leave you without ever having expressed my gratitude for all your kindnesses. It makes me sad to think that fate did not permit us to remain together for long, and I must soon depart. Surely you know it will not be easy for me to leave without ever having shown in the least my devotion to you, my parents. When I have gone outside and have sat looking at the moon I have always begged for just one more year with you, but my wish was refused. That was what made me so unhappy. It breaks my heart to leave you after bringing you such grief. The people of the moon are extremely beautiful, and they never grow old. Nor have they any worries. Yet, I am not at all happy to be returning. I know I shall miss you and keep wishing I could be looking after you when you are old and helpless." She spoke in tears.

"Don't talk of such heartrending things!" the old man exclaimed. "No matter how beautiful those people may be, I won't let them stand in my way." His tone was bitter.

By now the evening had passed. About midnight the area of the house was suddenly illuminated by a light more dazzling than that of high noon, a light as brilliant as ten full moons put together, so bright one could see the pores of a man's skin. Then down from the heavens men came riding on clouds, and arrayed themselves at a height some five feet above the ground. The guards inside and outside the house, seemingly victims of some supernatural spell, quite lost their will to resist. At length they plucked up their courage and tried to ready their bows and arrows, but the strength had gone from their hands, and their bodies were limp. Some valiant men among them, with a great effort, tried to shoot their bows, but the arrows glanced off harmlessly in all directions. Unable to fight boldly, like soldiers, they could only watch, stupefied.

Words cannot describe the beauty of the raiment worn by the men who hovered in the air. With them they had brought a flying chariot covered by a parasol of gauzy silk. One among them, apparently their king, called out, "Miyakkomaro, come here!" The old man, who had assumed such an air of defiance, prostrated himself before the stranger, feeling as if he were in a drunken stupor. The king said, "You childish old man! We sent the young lady down into the world for a short while, in return for some trifling good deeds you had performed, and for many years we have bestowed riches on you, until you are now like a different man. Kaguya-hime was obliged to live for a time in such humble surroundings because of a sin she had committed in the past. The term of her punishment is over, and we have come, as you can see, to escort her home. No matter how you weep and wail, old man, you cannot detain her. Send her forth at once!"

"I have been watching over Kaguya-hime for more than twenty years," the old man answered. "You speak of her having come down into this world for 'a short while.' It makes me wonder if you are not talking about some other Kaguya-hime living in a different place." He added, "Besides, the Kaguya-hime I have here is suffering from a serious illness and cannot leave her room."

No answer met his words. Instead, the king guided the flying chariot to the roof, where he called out, "Kaguya-hime! Why have you lingered such a long time in this filthy place?" The door of the strong room flew open, and the lattice-work shutters opened of their own accord. The old woman had been clutching Kaguya-hime in her arms, but now the girl freed herself and stepped outside. The old woman, unable to restrain her, could only look up to heaven and weep.

Kaguya-hime approached the Bamboo Cutter, who lay prostrate, weeping in his bewilderment. "It is not by my own inclination that I leave you now," she said. "Please at least watch as I ascend into the sky."

"How can I watch you go when it makes me so sad? You are abandoning me to go up to Heaven, not caring what may happen to me. Take me with you!" He threw himself down, weeping.

Kaguya-hime was at a loss what to do. She said, "Before I go I shall write a letter for you. If ever you long for me, take out the letter and read it." In tears she wrote these words: "Had I but been born in this world I should have stayed with you and never caused you any grief. To leave this world and part from you is quite contrary to my wishes. Please think of this cloak, that I leave with you, as a memento of me. On nights when the moon shines in the sky, gaze at it well. Now that I am about to forsake you, I feel as though I must fall from the sky, pulled back to this world by my longing for you."

Some of the celestial beings had brought boxes with them. One contained a robe of feathers, another the elixir of immortality. "Please take some of the elixir in this jar," said a celestial being to Kaguya-hime. "You must be feeling unwell after the things you have had to eat in this dirty place." He offered her the elixir and Kaguya-hime tasted a little. Then, thinking she might leave a little as a re-membrance of herself, she started to wrap some of the elixir in the cloak she had discarded, when a celestial being prevented her. He took the robe of feathers from its box and attempted to throw it over her shoulders, but Kaguya-hime cried out. "Wait just a moment! They say that once you put on this robe your heart changes, and there are still a few words I must say." She wrote another letter.

The celestial beings called impatiently, "It's late!"

"Don't talk so unreasonably!" exclaimed Kaguya-hime. With perfect seren-ity she gave the letter to someone for delivery to the emperor. She showed no signs of agitation. The letter said: "Although you graciously deigned to send many people to detain me here, my escorts have come and will not be denied. Now they will take me with them, to my bitter regret and sorrow. I am sure you must find it quite incomprehensible, but it weighs heaviest on my heart that you may consider my stubborn refusal to obey your commands an act of disrespect." To the above she added the verse: "Now that the moment has come to put on the robe of feathers, how longingly I recall my lord!" Kaguya-hime attached to the letter some elixir of immortality from the jar and, summoning the com-mander of the guards, directed him to offer it to the emperor. A celestial being took the gift from her hands and passed it to the commander. No sooner had the commander accepted the elixir than the celestial being put the robe of feathers on Kaguya-hime. At once she lost all recollection of the pity and grief she had felt for the old man. No cares afflict anyone who once puts on this robe, and Kaguya-hime, in all tranquillity, climbed into her chariot and ascended into the sky, accompanied by a retinue of a hundred celestial beings.

The old man and woman shed bitter tears, but to no avail. When her letter was read to them, they cried, "Why should we cling to our lives? For whose sake? All is useless now." They refused to take medicine, and never left their sick-beds again.

The commander returned to the palace with his men. He reported in detail the reasons why he and his men had failed with their weapons to prevent Kaguya-hime from departing. He also presented the jar of elixir with the letter attached. The emperor felt much distressed when he opened the letter and read Kaguya-hime's words. He refused all nourishment, and permitted no entertain-ments in his presence.

Later, the emperor summoned his ministers and great nobles and asked them which mountain was closest to Heaven. One man replied, "The mountain in the province of Suruga. It is near both to the capital and to Heaven." The emperor thereupon wrote the poem: "What use is it, this elixir of immortality, to one who floats in tears because he cannot meet her again?"

He gave the poem and the jar containing the elixir to a messenger with the command that he take them to the summit of the mountain in Suruga. He directed that the letter and the jar be placed side by side, set on fire, and allowed to be consumed in the flames. The men, obeying this command, climbed the mountain, taking with them a great many soldiers. Ever since they burned the elixir of immortality on the summit, people have called the mountain by the name Fuji, meaning immortal. Even now the smoke is still said to rise into the clouds.

[Translated by Donald Keene]

THE TALES OF ISE (ISE MONOGATARI, CA. 947)

In its most familiar versions, The Tales of Ise (Ise monogatari) is a collection of 125 uta-gatari (or uta-monogatari, literally, "poem tale") presented as episodes in the life of Ariwara no Narihira (825–880), a nobleman celebrated as the greatest male poet of his age. Within a decade or so of his death, Narihira had become the legendary hero of early Heian court society, idealized for sacrificing political favor, fortune, and propriety for love and poetry. The legend of Narihira flourished for centuries and ensured The Tales of Ise a place—equaled only by the Kokinshū, The Tale of Genji, and One Hundred Poets, One Hundred Poems (Hyakkunin-isshu)—among the most widely read and quoted classics of Japanese literature.

Classical Japanese poetry often was anthologized, either in large collections of works by many poets, like the Man'yōshū or the Kokinshū or, usually, in smaller personal collections of works by a single poet. These personal collections in turn gave rise to a variety of genres: (1) poetic travel diaries like the Tosa Diary by Ki no Tsurayuki; (2) confessional, semiautobiographical poetic diaries by women like the Kagerō Diary by Mother of Michitsuna and the Sarashina Diary by Daughter of Takasue; and (3) collections of poem tales focused on the life or work of a particular poet, the most famous example of which is The Tales of Ise. Its earliest versions are based on the poetry of Narihira, the implicit protagonist of The Tales of Ise. Because classical poems (waka) were short and often social in nature, they invited questions of when, where, and for whom or for what purposes they were composed. One consequence was the creation of stories about the poems. The combination of Narihira's skill as a poet—he is known for his extensive use of parallelism and rhythm—and his fame as a lover made him the object of many poetic legends. Other poem tales appearing around this time were *The Tales of Yamato (Yamato monogatari*, ca. 951) and *The Tales of Heichū (Heichū monogatari*, ca. 965).

The original core of *The Tales of Ise* was most likely an early version of Narihira's personal collection of waka. Later editors expanded it by adding poems from the *Kokinshū* ascribed to Narihira, many with long headnotes (*kotobagaki*). Later additions to *The Tales of Ise* included anonymous poems from the *Kokinshū* and the *Gosenshū* (951) attributed to the protagonist. (Fewer than one-quarter of the more than two hundred poems in the 125-section texts of *The Tales of Ise* are believed to have been written by Narihira himself.)

The prose, which has been reduced to the bare essentials, typically supplies a fictionalized historical context or dramatic circumstances, and the poetry reveals the thoughts and emotions of the characters and brings the narrative to a climax, a sophisticated narrative technique that foreshadows *The Tale of Genji*.

Even though each of the 125 sections of *The Tales of Ise* is essentially autonomous, they are arranged in a partially biographical sequence, beginning with the protagonist's youth and progressing from his transgressions in the capital, his exile to the east (sec. 9), his return to the capital, and, finally, his death (sec. 125). Significantly, Narihira violates social convention, engaging in forbidden love in unexpected places and violating the prerogatives of the throne (sec. 69) or subtly mocking the fortunes of the dominant Fujiwara lineage (sec. 101). The inevitable consequences for himself and his lovers become the impetus for poetry of profound feeling and resignation to separation, disappointment, and sorrow, composed with an elegance of diction and rhetorical subtlety that seem to overcome every form of loss or defeat.

Among other things, *The Tales of Ise* demonstrated the proper protocols and occasions for the social uses of poetry, a necessary part of an aristocrat's education and social training, and became a familiar source for poetic diction, themes, and allusive variation. By the late Heian period, it had become one of the three most influential texts in the kana tradition (along with the *Kokinshū* and *The Tale of Genji*), and it served as a handbook for waka poets throughout the rest of the medieval period. *The Tales of Ise* also provided literary topoi and precedents for later writers—including Murasaki Shikibu, whose hero Genji shares many of the features of the fictionalized Narihira—as well as for painters and dramatists. The noted nō play *Sumida River* is based on "Journey to the Eastern Provinces" (sec. 7, 8, 9, and after) in *The Tales of Ise*. After being canonized by Fujiwara no Teika and other poets in the thirteenth century, *The Tales of Ise* became the object of extensive commentary and, in certain early strains of this tradition, was either read as history (biography of Narihira) or allegorized as an esoteric religious text.

Journey to the Eastern Provinces (9)

In the past there was a man. Having made up his mind that his position was worthless, he thought that he should live in the east rather than in the capital, and he set out to find a province where he could reside. He went with an old friend or two. Since none of them knew the way, they wandered about. They arrived at a place called Eight Bridges in Mikawa Province. The place is called Eight Bridges because the rivers in which the water flows branch like a spider's legs and were spanned by eight bridges. They dismounted in the shade of a tree at the edge of the marsh there and ate dried rice. In the marsh, irises [*kakitsub-ata*] were blooming beautifully. Seeing them, one of the party said, "Compose a poem on the subject of travel, using the five syllables *ka-ki-tsu-ba-ta* to begin each of its five phrases."

karagoromo	Since I have a wife
kitsutsu narenishi	familiar to me as the hem
tsuma shi areba	of a well-worn robe,
harubaru kinuru	I think sadly of how far
tabi o shi zo omou	I have traveled on this journey.[100]

When he composed this, all of them shed tears on their dried rice until it swelled with the moisture.

Moving on, they came to the province of Suruga. When they arrived at Mount Utsu, they were troubled to find that the road they planned to take was very dark and narrow, with dense growth of creepers and maples. As they were thinking what unexpected and difficult experiences they were having, they met with a pilgrim. "What are you doing on such a road as this?" he asked them, and the man recognized him as someone he knew. He wrote a letter and asked the pilgrim to take it to the lady he had left in the capital.

Suruga naru	Near Mount Utsu
Utsu no yamabe ni	in Suruga
utsutsu ni mo	I can meet you
yume ni mo hito ni	neither in reality
awanu narikeri	nor in my dreams.[101]

---

100. Narihira, *Kokinshū*, no. 410. In addition to meeting the condition proposed by his traveling companion, the poem contains several puns that could not be incorporated in the translation. *Kitsutsu* means both "coming" and "wearing"; *narenishi* is both "accustomed to" and "grown fond of"; *tsuma* is both "wife" and "hem"; *haru* means "to full [cloth]"; and *harubaru* means "far."

101. The name Mount Utsu suggests the word for "reality" (*utsutsu*), and the first two lines of the poem are a preface leading to the word. At the time, people believed that someone who was thinking of them would appear in their dreams. The man's failure to meet his beloved even in his dreams implies that the woman is not thinking of him.

The Eight Bridges in Mikawa Province. (From the Sagabon edition, early seventeenth century)

When they came to Mount Fuji, they saw that it was very white with falling snow even on the last day of the Fifth Month.[102]

> *toki shiranu*   The peak of Mount Fuji
> *yama wa Fuji no ne* is oblivious to time.
> *itsu to te ka*   What season does it take this to be
> *ka no ko madara ni* that the falling snow
> *yuki no fururamu*   should dapple it like a fawn?

If we compare this mountain with those here in the capital, it is twenty times the height of Mount Hiei, and its shape is like a cone of sand used for making salt.[103]

Continuing on as before, they came to a very large river between Musashi and Shimotsufusa provinces. It is called the Sumida River. As they stood in a group on the edge of the river and thought of home, lamenting together how very far they had come, the ferryman said, "Hurry up and get in the boat. It's getting dark." About to board the boat and cross the river, they all felt forlorn, for there was not one of them who did not have someone he loved in the capital. Just then they saw a white bird with a red bill and legs, about the size of a snipe, cavorting in the water and eating fish. Since this is not a bird one sees in the capital, none of them recognized it. When they asked the ferryman what it was, he said, "Why, that's a capital bird." Hearing this, the man composed a poem:

---

102. That is, in summer.
103. The meaning of the word *shiojiri*, translated here as "cone of sand," is disputed.

na ni shi owaba	If you are true to your name
iza koto towamu	then I shall ask:
miyakodori	O capital bird,
waga omou hito no	is the one I love
ari ya nashi ya to	alive or dead?[104]

Everyone in the boat burst into tears.

The Imperial Huntsman (69)

In the past there was a man. When he was dispatched to Ise Province as an imperial huntsman,[105] the mother of the high priestess of the Ise Shrine[106] told her daughter to treat him better than she would the usual messengers. Since these were her mother's instructions, she took very good care of him. In the morning she saw him off on his hunting, and when he returned in the evenings she had him stay in her own lodgings. In this way, she treated him well.

On the night of the second day, the man said quite passionately that he wanted to meet her privately. The woman, too, was not ill-disposed toward their meeting. However, since there were many prying eyes, they were unable to meet. Since the man was the chief huntsman, he was lodged not far from the woman's own sleeping quarters. At the first hour of the rat,[107] when everyone had gone to sleep, she came to him. For his part, he had been unable to sleep and was lying down looking out into the night when he saw her standing there in the dim moonlight with a little girl in front of her. The man was overjoyed and led her into his chamber. She stayed until the third hour of the ox,[108] but they had hardly had time to do much at all when the woman returned to her rooms. The man, deeply saddened, could not sleep. In the morning he was impatient to hear from her, but it would not have been proper for him to send her a note, and he was waiting in distress when shortly after dawn, the following poem came from the woman, with no further message:

kimi ya koshi	Did you come to me?
ware wa yukiken	Did I go to you?
omōezu	I cannot tell.
yume ka utsutsu ka	A dream, or reality?
nete ka samete ka	Was I asleep, or awake?

---

104. The implication is that a "capital bird" should know what is going on in the capital.

105. "Imperial huntsmen" were sent by the emperor to nearby provinces both to bring back game and to investigate the affairs of the provincial governments.

106. The high priestess was an unmarried princess chosen at the beginning of a new emperor's reign to serve at the Inner Shrine at Ise, dedicated to the Sun Goddess Amaterasu.

107. Between 11:00 and 11:30 P.M.

108. Between 2:00 and 2:30 A.M.

Weeping piteously, the man composed this:

kakikurasu	I have wandered
kokoro no yami ni	in the darkness
madoiniki	of my heart.
yume utsutsu to wa	Let us decide tonight:
koyoi sadame yo	dream or reality.

After sending this to her, he went out hunting. He rode through the fields but was distracted by thoughts of meeting her that night, soon after the others went to sleep. But the governor of the province, who also oversaw affairs at the shrine, had heard that an imperial huntsman was visiting. He kept the man drinking through the night, and the pair was quite unable to meet. Since he had to move on to Owari Province the next day, the man wept tears of blood,[109] unbeknownst to anyone, but still they could not meet. When dawn was breaking, a poem came from the woman, written on the saucer of a cup of parting. He took it up, and read:

kachibito no	Since ours is a bond
wataredo nurenu	shallow as waters that do not wet
e ni shi areba	the hem of a traveler's robes . . .

She had written this much, leaving the poem incomplete. Using charcoal from a pine torch, he wrote the last lines on the saucer:

mata Ausaka no	again I will cross
seki wa koenamu	the Gate of Meeting.

At daybreak he crossed into Owari Province.

The woman served as high priestess of Ise during the reign of Emperor Seiwa. She was the daughter of Emperor Montoku and the sister of Prince Koretaka.

Nagisa-no-in (82)

In the past, there was a prince known as Prince Koretaka. He had a palace at a place called Minase, on the far side of Yamazaki. Every year when the cherry blossoms were in full bloom, he went to that palace. On those occasions he always took along a person who was the director of the right imperial stables.[110] It was long ago and I have forgotten his name.

---

109. "Tears of blood" is a conventional metaphor for extreme grief.
110. A post held by Narihira.

Not enthusiastic about hunting, they just drank saké continuously and turned to composing poems in Japanese. The cherry blossoms at the Nagisa residence in Katano, where they often hunted, were especially beautiful. They dismounted under the trees, and breaking off blossoms to decorate themselves, everyone, of high, middle, and low rank, composed poems. The director of the stables composed this:

> *yo no naka ni*   If only this world
> *taete sakura no*   were without cherry blossoms
> *nakariseba*   then would our hearts
> *haru no kokoro wa*   be at ease
> *nodokekaramashi*   in springtime.

Another person composed this:

> *chireba koso*   It is because they fall soon
> *itodo sakura wa*   that the cherry blossoms
> *medetakere*   are so admired.
> *ukiyo ni nani ka*   What can stay long
> *hisashikarubeki*   in this fleeting world?

When they left the trees to return to Minase, it already was dark. The prince's attendants came from the fields with servants bringing the saké. Seeking out a good place to drink it, they came to a place called Amanokawa.[111] The director of the stables gave the prince a cup of saké. The prince said, "When you hand me the cup, compose a poem on coming to the banks of Amanokawa after hunting at Katano." The director of the stables composed this and handed it to him:

> *karikurashi*   I've spent the day hunting
> *tanabata tsume ni*   and now will seek lodging
> *yado karamu*   from the Weaver Maid
> *Ama no kawara ni*   for I have come
> *ware wa kinikeri*   to the River of Heaven.

The prince recited this over and over but could not come up with a response. Ki no Aritsune[112] was attending the prince. He responded:

> *hitotose ni*   She who waits patiently
> *hitotabi kimasu*   for a lord who comes

---

111. Literally, "river of heaven."
112. Ki no Aritsune (816–877) was Koretaka's uncle and Narihira's father-in-law.

kimi mateba	but once a year
yado kasu hito mo	will not, I am sure,
araji to zo omou	lodge any other[113]

They went back to Minase, and the prince entered his palace. They drank and conversed until deep in the night, and then the prince prepared to sleep, somewhat drunk. As the moon of the eleventh day of the month[114] began to sink behind the mountains, the director of the stables composed this:

akanaku ni	How can the moon
madaki no tsuki no	hide itself
kakururu ka	before we are satisfied?
yama no ha nigete	I wish the mountain rim would flee
irezu mo aranamu	so the moon might stay in view.

In place of the prince, Ki no Aritsune replied:

oshinabete	I wish the peaks
mine mo taira ni	one and all
narinanamu	might be leveled:
yama no ha naku wa	if there were no mountain rims
tsuki mo iraji o	the moon would not hide.

In the Shade of Wisteria Blooms (101)

In the past, there was a commander of the left guards called Ariwara no Yukihira. Hearing that there was a batch of good wine at his house, some people who were at court visited, among them the middle controller of the left, Fujiwara no Masachika, who served as guest of honor for the day.

Since Yukihira was a man of sensibility, he had placed flowers in a vase. Among the flowers was a striking and unusual bough of wisteria extending more than three feet in length. Those present composed poems with that as their topic.

Just when they were finished, a brother of the host,[115] hearing that Yukihira was entertaining guests, came to join them. They cornered him and demanded

---

113. These poems refer to the legendary Herdsman (the star Altair) and his wife, the Weaver Maid (the star Vega), who were separated by the River of Heaven (the Milky Way) and able to meet only once a year, on the seventh day of the Seventh Month (celebrated as the Tanabata Festival).

114. A waxing moon, about halfway between quarter and full.

115. Narihira was Yukihira's half brother.

he compose a poem. Claiming he knew nothing of poetry he declined,[116] but when they insisted, he made this:

> saku hana no   How many they are
> shita ni kakururu   who take refuge in the shade
> hito o oomi   of wisteria that are
> arishi ni masaru   greater now than
> fuji no kage kamo   ever before![117]

When someone asked, "Why did you compose a poem like that?"[118] he replied, "I was thinking of the chancellor's glorious ascent and the great successes of the Fujiwara clan." No one could find fault with his answer.[119]

Rain Test (107)

In the past, there was a man of some distinction. Someone called Fujiwara no Toshiyuki, who was a private secretary,[120] began to pursue a girl of the man's household. The girl, however, was very young, knew little of writing, had no command of diction, and could hardly compose a poem. The man prepared a draft of a poem and had her write it out and send it off. The recipient was quite dazzled.[121] He composed this in reply:

> tsurezure no   Helpless to meet you,
> nagame ni masaru   I can only gaze on these
> namidagawa   endless rains,

---

116. Narihira was the most celebrated male poet of the age. The claim here that he knows nothing about poetry may be taken as a ploy of modesty or an expression of distaste for having to compose a "banquet" poem on a set topic for the entertainment of officials of the Fujiwara lineage, his own lineage's historical enemies. The irony of his denial sharpens that of the following poem.

117. The poem can be read allegorically as a sarcastic comment on the usurpation of imperial authority by the Fujiwara lineage—of which the *fuji* (wisteria) blossom was an emblem—at the expense of Narihira's own Ariwara lineage, whose name is suggested in the phrase *arishi*, meaning "as things were" (translated here as ". . . ever before"). It can also be taken, in a more naive but still allegorical reading, as praise for the largesse of the Fujiwara hegemons.

118. The question is posed by one of the Fujiwara guests and calls attention to the ambiguity of the poem, which is far more sophisticated than was expected of a conventional banquet poem.

119. To find fault with the poem, reading it as veiled sarcasm despite the poet's claim that he simply meant to praise the Fujiwara lineage's success, would cast doubt on the loyalties of the critic rather than the poet.

120. This post, in the Ministry of Central Affairs, called for expertise in drafting official documents, and in fact Toshiyuki was one of the most acclaimed calligraphers of his time.

121. Toshiyuki assumes that it was the girl's poem and not that of her employer, Narihira.

> *sode nomi hichite*   a river of tears
> *au yoshi mo nashi*   drenching my sleeves.

In reply the man wrote, again on the girl's behalf:

> *asami koso*   How shallow
> *sode wa hitsurame*   a river of tears
> *namidagawa*   that wets only your sleeves:
> *mi sae nagaru to*   when I hear you are drowning
> *kikaba tanomu*   I'll trust the depths of your love.

On receiving this, Toshiyuki[122] was so overwhelmed that he rolled it up and to this day is said to keep it in his letter box.

Toshiyuki sent a letter to the woman. This was some time after he had won her consent. "I'm afraid it may rain. If I am fortunate, the rain won't fall."[123] As before, the girl's employer composed a poem on her behalf and had it delivered:

> *kazukazu ni*   It is not for me
> *omoi omowazu*   to ask if I matter
> *toigatami*   or not to you:
> *mi o shiru zo*   rain like falling tears
> *ame wa masareru*   will tell.

On receiving this, he left both raincoat and hat behind and rushed blindly to her, drenched in rain and tears.

Deep Grasses (123)

In the past, there was a man. He must have grown weary of a woman who lived in Fukakusa, since he sent her this poem:

> *toshi o hete*   If I leave this village
> *sumikoshi sato o*   my home all these years
> *idete inaba*   will it become
> *itodo fukakusa*   a moor
> *no to ya narinamu*   of ever deeper grasses?

---

122. The text has "the man," which refers here and later not to Narihira but to Toshiyuki. The word signals clearly that Toshiyuki is or will soon become the girl's lover.

123. Rainfall was one of many familiar excuses men used to avoid visiting a wife or lover at night. Toshiyuki suggests that he is hoping to visit her tonight, but only if rain does not fall.

The woman replied:

> no to naraba   If it becomes a moor
> uzura to narite   I will become a quail
> nakioramu   and cry.
> kari ni dani ya wa   Would you then come back,
> kimi wa kozaramu   even for a while, as a hunter?

Moved by her reply, the man gave up the thought of leaving her.

The Road All Must Travel (125)

In the past, a man fell ill and felt that he would soon die.

> tsui ni yuku   I had heard
> michi to wa kanete   there is a path
> kikishikado   that all must follow
> kinō kyō to wa   but didn't think yesterday
> omowazarishi o   that I'd be going today ... [124]

[Introduction and translations by Jamie Newhard and Lewis Cook]

SEI SHŌNAGON

Sei Shōnagon (b. 965?) was the daughter of Kiyohara no Motosuke, a noted waka poet and one of the editors of the *Gosenshū*, the second imperial waka anthology. (The Sei in Sei Shōnagon's name comes from the Sino-Japanese reading for the Kiyo in Kiyohara.) Around 981, Sei Shōnagon married Tachibana no Norimitsu, the first son of the noted Tachibana family, but after she bore him a child the next year, they were separated.

In 990 Fujiwara no Kaneie, the husband of the author of the *Kagerō Diary*, stepped down from his position as regent (*kanpaku*) and gave it to his son Fuji-wara no Michitaka, who was referred to as middle regent (*naka no kanpaku*). Michitaka married his daughter Teishi to Emperor Ichijō (r. 986–1011) in 990, and she soon became a high consort (*nyōgo*) and then empress (*chūgū*). Sei Shōnagon became a lady-in-waiting to Teishi in 993, the year that Michitaka became prime

---

124. An alternative, less piquant interpretation of the last two lines would read: "but I never thought it might be yesterday or today." This is the interpretation that most modern scholars and many premodern commentaries prefer and is grammatically simpler. A late-sixteenth-century commentary by Hosokawa Yūsai, for example, states indignantly of the reading taken as the basis of our translation that it is "very improper" (or "impudent" [*ooki ni kitanashi*]), implying that it violates the aesthetic of imprecision associated with postclassical ideals of elegance.

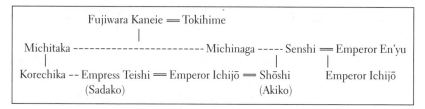

Political context for Sei Shōnagon

minister (*daijō daijin*). In 994 Korechika, Michitaka's eldest son and the apparent heir to the regency, became palace minister (*naidaijin*). In 995 Michitaka died in an epidemic, and in the following year Korechika was exiled in a move engineered by Michitaka's younger brother and rival Michinaga, and Teishi was forced to leave the imperial palace. Sei Shōnagon continued to serve Teishi until Teishi's death in childbirth in 1000. In the meantime, in 999, Shōshi, Michinaga's daughter and Murasaki Shikibu's mistress, became the chief consort to Emperor Ichijō, marking Michinaga's ascent to the pinnacle of power.

THE PILLOW BOOK (MAKURA NO SŌSHI, CA. 1000)

The Pillow Book, which was finished after the demise of Teishi's salon, focuses mainly on the years 993 and 994, when the Michitaka family and Teishi were at the height of their glory, leaving unmentioned the subsequent tragedy. Almost all the major works by women of this time were written by women in Empress Shōshi's salon: Murasaki Shikibu, Izumi Shikibu, and Akazome'emon. Only Sei Shōnagon's *Pillow Book* represents the rival salon of Empress Teishi. Like many other diaries by court women, *The Pillow Book* can be seen as a memorial to the author's patron, specifically, an homage to the Naka no Kanpaku family and a literary prayer to the spirit of the deceased empress Teishi. One of the few indirect references to the sad circumstances that befell Teishi's family is "The Cat Who Lived in the Palace," about the cruel punishment, sudden exile, and ignominious return of the dog Okinamaro, who, like Korechika, secretly returned to the capital and later was pardoned.

The three hundred discrete sections of *The Pillow Book* can be divided into three different types—lists, essay, and diary—that sometimes overlap. The list sections consist of noun sections (*mono wa*), which describe particular categories of things like "Flowering Trees," "Birds," and "Insects" and tend to focus on nature or poetic topics, and adjectival sections (*monozukushi*), which describe a particular state, such as "Depressing Things," and contain interesting lists and often are (particularly in the case of negative adjectives) humorous and witty. The diary sections, such as "The Sliding Screen in the Back of the Hall," describe specific events and figures in history, particularly those related to Empress Teishi and her immediate family.

The essay sections sometimes focus on a specific season or month, but unlike the diary sections, they bear no historical dates. The textual variants of *The Pillow Book* treat these three section types differently. The Maeda and Sakai variants separate them into three large groups. By contrast, the Nōin variant and the Sankan variant, which is translated here and has become the canonical version, mix the different types of sections. The end result is that *The Pillow Book* appears ahistorical; events are not presented in chronological order but instead move back and forth in time, with no particular development or climax, creating a sense of a world suspended in time, a mode perhaps suitable for a paean to Teishi's family.

Another category, which overlaps with the others and resembles anecdotal literature, is the "stories heard" (*kikigaki*)—that is, stories heard from one's master or mistress—which provided knowledge and models of cultivation. Indeed, much of *The Pillow Book* is about aristocratic women's education, especially the need for aesthetic awareness as well as erudition, allusiveness, and extreme refinement in communication. Sei Shōnagon shows a particular concern for delicacy and harmony, for the proper combination of object, sense, and circumstance, usually a fusion of human and natural worlds. Incongruity and disharmony, by contrast, become the butt of humor and of Sei Shōnagon's sharp wit. *The Pillow Book* is often read as a personal record of accomplishments, with a number of the sections about incidents that display the author's talent. Indeed, much of the interest of *The Pillow Book* has been in the strong character and personality of Sei Shōnagon.

The Pillow Book is noted for its distinctive prose style: its rhythmic, quick-moving, compressed, and varied sentences, often set up in alternating couplets. Although the typical Japanese sentence ends with the predicate, the phrases and sentences in *The Pillow Book* often end with nouns or eliminate the exclamatory and connective particles so characteristic of Heian women's literature. The compact, forceful, bright, witty style stands in contrast to the soft, meandering style found in *The Tale of Genji* and other works by Heian women. Indeed, the adjectival sections in particular have a *haikai-esque* (comic linked verse) quality, marked by witty, unexpected juxtaposition.

The Pillow Book is now considered one of the twin pillars of Heian vernacular court literature, but unlike the *Kokinshū*, *The Tales of Ise*, and *The Tale of Genji*, which had been canonized by the thirteen century, *The Pillow Book* was not a required text for waka poets (perhaps because it contained relatively little poetry) and was relatively neglected in the Heian and medieval periods. But *The Pillow Book* became popular with the new commoner audience in the Tokugawa (Edo) period and was widely read for its style, humor, and interesting lists. By the modern period, *The Pillow Book* was treated as an exemplar of the *zuihitsu* (meanderings of the brush) or miscellany genre, centered on personal observations and musings. Since then, it has been regarded in modern literary histories as the generic predecessor of *An Account of a Ten-Foot-Square Hut* (*Hōjōki*) and *Essays in Idleness* (*Tsurezuregusa*).

In Spring It Is the Dawn (1)

In spring it is the dawn that is most beautiful. As the light creeps over the hills, their outlines are dyed a faint red, and wisps of purplish cloud trail over them.

In summer the nights. Not only when the moon shines but on dark nights, too, as the fireflies flit to and fro, and even when it rains, how beautiful it is!

In autumn the evenings, when the glittering sun sinks close to the edge of the hills and the crows fly back to their nests in threes and fours and twos; more charming still is a file of wild geese, like specks in the distant sky. When the sun has set, one's heart is moved by the sound of the wind and the hum of the insects.

In winter the early mornings. It is beautiful indeed when snow has fallen during the night, but splendid too when the ground is white with frost; or even when there is no snow or frost, but it is simply very cold and the attendants hurry from room to room stirring up the fires and bringing charcoal, how well this fits the season's mood! But as noon approaches and the cold wears off, no one bothers to keep the braziers alight, and soon nothing remains but piles of white ashes.

The Cat Who Lived in the Palace (8)

The cat who lived in the palace had been awarded the headdress of nobility[125] and was called Lady Myōbu. She was a very pretty cat, and His Majesty saw to it that she was treated with the greatest care.

One day she wandered onto the veranda, and Lady Uma, the nurse in charge of her, called out, "Oh, you naughty thing! Please come inside at once." But the cat paid no attention and went on basking sleepily in the sun. Intending to give her a scare, the nurse called for the dog, Okinamaro.

"Okinamaro, where are you?" she cried. "Come here and bite Lady Myōbu!" The foolish Okinamaro, believing that the nurse was in earnest, rushed at the cat, who, startled and terrified, ran behind the blind in the imperial dining room, where the emperor happened to be sitting. Greatly surprised, His Majesty picked up the cat and held her in his arms. He summoned his gentlemen-in-waiting. When Tadataka, the chamberlain,[126] appeared, His Majesty ordered that Okinamaro be chastised and banished to Dog Island. All the attendants started to chase the dog amid great confusion. His Majesty also reproached Lady Uma. "We shall have to find a new nurse for our cat," he told her. "I no longer

---

125. Originally given by the emperor to nobility of the fifth rank and above. The cap was small, round, and black with a protuberance sticking up in the back and a wide, stiff ribbon hanging down the back.

126. One of the officials in the emperor's private office, which was in charge of matters relating to the emperor and his palace.

feel I can count on you to look after her." Lady Uma bowed; thereafter she no longer appeared in the emperor's presence.

The imperial guards quickly succeeded in catching Okinamaro and drove him out of the palace grounds. Poor dog! He used to swagger about so happily. Recently, on the third day of the Third Month,[127] when the controller first secretary paraded him through the palace grounds, Okinamaro was adorned with garlands of willow leaves, peach blossoms on his head, and cherry blossoms around his body. How could the dog have imagined that this would be his fate? We all felt sorry for him. "When Her Majesty was having her meals," recalled one of the ladies-in-waiting, "Okinamaro always used to be in attendance and sit across from us. How I miss him!"

It was about noon, a few days after Okinamaro's banishment, that we heard a dog howling fearfully. How could any dog possibly cry so long? All the other dogs rushed out in excitement to see what was happening. Meanwhile, a woman who served as a cleaner in the palace latrines ran up to us. "It's terrible," she said. "Two of the chamberlains are flogging a dog. They'll surely kill him. He's being punished for having come back after he was banished. It's Tadataka and Sanefusa who are beating him." Obviously the victim was Okinamaro. I was absolutely wretched and sent a servant to ask the men to stop, but just then the howling finally ceased. "He's dead," one of the servants informed me. "They've thrown his body outside the gate."

That evening, while we were sitting in the palace bemoaning Okinamaro's fate, a wretched-looking dog walked in; he was trembling all over, and his body was fearfully swollen.

"Oh dear," said one of the ladies-in-waiting. "Can this be Okinamaro? We haven't seen any other dog like him recently, have we?"

We called to him by name, but the dog did not respond. Some of us insisted that it was Okinamaro; others that it was not. "Please send for Lady Ukon," said the empress, hearing our discussion. "She will certainly be able to tell." We immediately went to Ukon's room and told her she was wanted on an urgent matter.

"Is this Okinamaro?" the empress asked her, pointing to the dog.

"Well," said Ukon, "it certainly looks like him, but I cannot believe that this loathsome creature is really our Okinamaro. When I called Okinamaro, he always used to come to me, wagging his tail. But this dog does not react at all. No, it cannot be the same one. And besides, wasn't Okinamaro beaten to death and his body thrown away? How could any dog be alive after being flogged by two strong men?" Hearing this, Her Majesty was very unhappy.

When it got dark, we gave the dog something to eat, but he refused it, and we finally decided that this could not be Okinamaro.

---

127. A festival day marked by banquets held beside garden streams and by ritual purification. It was also known as the Peach Festival (Momo no sekku).

On the following morning I went to attend the empress while her hair was being dressed and she was performing her ablutions. I was holding up the mirror for her when the dog we had seen on the previous evening slunk into the room and crouched next to one of the pillars. "Poor Okinamaro!" I said. "He had such a dreadful beating yesterday. How sad to think he is dead! I wonder what body he has been born into this time. Oh, how he must have suffered!"

At that moment the dog lying by the pillar started to shake and tremble and shed a flood of tears. It was astounding. So this really was Okinamaro! On the previous night it was to avoid betraying himself that he had refused to answer to his name. We were immensely moved and pleased. "Well, well, Okinamaro!" I said, putting down the mirror. The dog stretched himself flat on the floor and yelped loudly, so that the empress beamed with delight. All the ladies gathered round, and Her Majesty summoned Lady Ukon. When the empress explained what had happened, everyone talked and laughed with great excitement.

The news reached His Majesty, and he too came to the empress's room. "It's amazing," he said with a smile. "To think that even a dog has such deep feelings!" When the emperor's ladies-in-waiting heard the story, they too came along in a great crowd. "Okinamaro!" we called, and this time the dog rose and limped about the room with his swollen face. "He must have a meal prepared for him," I said. "Yes," said the empress, laughing happily, "now that Okinamaro has finally told us who he is."

The chamberlain, Tadataka, was informed, and he hurried along from the Table Room.[128] "Is it really true?" he asked. "Please let me see for myself." I sent a maid to him with the following reply: "Alas, I am afraid that this is not the same dog after all." "Well," answered Tadataka, "whatever you say, I shall sooner or later have occasion to see the animal. You won't be able to hide him from me indefinitely."

Before long, Okinamaro was granted an imperial pardon and returned to his former happy state. Yet even now, when I remember how he whimpered and trembled in response to our sympathy, it strikes me as a strange and moving scene; when people talk to me about it, I start crying myself.

The Sliding Screen in the Back of the Hall (11)

The sliding screen in the back of the hall in the northeast corner of Seiryō Palace is decorated with paintings of the stormy sea and of the terrifying creatures with long arms and long legs that live there.[129] When the doors of the empress's

---

128. A room with a large table adjoining the imperial dining room.

129. According to traditional Chinese beliefs, the northeast was the unlucky direction. The sliding screen "protected" this room from the northern veranda of the palace by scaring away any evil spirits that might be lurking in the vicinity.

room were open, we could always see this screen. One day we were sitting in the room, laughing at the paintings and remarking how unpleasant they were. By the balustrade of the veranda stood a large celadon vase, full of magnificent cherry branches; some of them were as much as five feet long, and their blossoms overflowed to the very foot of the railing. Toward noon the major counselor, Fujiwara no Korechika,[130] arrived. He was dressed in a cherry-color court cloak, sufficiently worn to have lost its stiffness, a white underrobe, and loose trousers of dark purple; from beneath the cloak shone the pattern of another robe of dark red damask. Since His Majesty was present, Korechika knelt on the narrow wooden platform in front of the door and reported to him on official matters.

A group of ladies-in-waiting was seated behind the bamboo blinds. Their cherry-color Chinese jackets hung loosely over their shoulders with the collars pulled back; they wore robes of wisteria, golden yellow, and other colors, many of which showed beneath the blind covering the half shutter. Presently the noise of the attendants' feet told us that dinner was about to be served in the Daytime Chamber, and we heard cries of "Make way. Make way."

The bright, serene day delighted me. When the chamberlains had brought all the dishes into the chamber, they came to announce that dinner was ready, and His Majesty left by the middle door. After accompanying the emperor, Korechika returned to his previous place on the veranda beside the cherry blossoms. The empress pushed aside her curtain of state and came forward as far as the threshold. We were overwhelmed by the whole delightful scene. It was then that Korechika slowly intoned the words of the old poem,

> The days and the months flow by,
> but Mount Mimoro lasts forever.[131]

Deeply impressed, I wished that all this might indeed continue for a thousand years.

As soon as the ladies serving in the Daytime Chamber had called for the gentlemen-in-waiting to remove the trays, His Majesty returned to the empress's room. Then he told me to rub some ink on the inkstone. Dazzled, I felt that I should never be able to take my eyes off his radiant countenance. Next he folded a piece of white paper. "I should like each of you," he said, "to copy down on this paper the first ancient poem that comes into your head."

"How am I going to manage this?" I asked Korechika, who was still out on the veranda.

"Write your poem quickly," he said, "and show it to His Majesty. We men must not interfere in this." Ordering an attendant to take the emperor's inkstone

---

130. Korechika, the elder brother of the empress, who was appointed to major counselor in 992.
131. From the *Man'yōshū*.

to each of the women in the room, he told us to make haste. "Write down any poem you happen to remember," he said. "The Naniwazu[132] or whatever else you can think of."

For some reason I was overcome with timidity; I blushed and had no idea what to do. Some of the other women managed to put down poems about the spring, the blossoms, and such suitable subjects; then they handed me the paper and said, "Now it's your turn." Picking up the brush, I wrote the poem that goes,

> The years have passed
> and age has come my way.
> Yet I need only look at this fair flower
> for all my cares to melt away.

I altered the third line, however, to read, "Yet I need only look upon my lord."[133]

When he had finished reading, the emperor said, "I asked you to write these poems because I wanted to find out how quick you really were.

"A few years ago," he continued, "Emperor En'yū ordered all his courtiers to write poems in a notebook. Some excused themselves on the grounds that their handwriting was poor; but the emperor insisted, saying that he did not care in the slightest about their handwriting or even whether their poems were suitable for the season. So they all had to swallow their embarrassment and produce something for the occasion. Among them was His Excellency, our present chancellor, who was then middle captain of the third rank. He wrote down the old poem,

> Like the sea that beats
> upon the shores of Izumo
> as the tide sweeps in,
> deeper it grows and deeper—
> the love I bear for you.

"But he changed the last line to read, 'The love I bear my lord!,' and the emperor was full of praise."

When I heard His Majesty tell this story, I was so overcome that I felt myself perspiring. It occurred to me that no younger woman would have been able to use my poem, and I felt very lucky. This sort of test can be a terrible ordeal: it often happens that people who usually write fluently are so overawed that they actually make mistakes in their characters.

---

132. A famous poem attributed to the Korean scholar Wani and later to Emperor Nintoku. Children in the Heian period were taught the poem for writing practice.

133. Fujiwara no Yoshifusa, *Kokinshū*, no. 52.

Next the empress placed a notebook of *Kokinshū* poems in front of her and started reading out the first three lines of each one, asking us to supply the remainder. Among them were several famous poems that we had in our minds day and night; yet for some strange reason we were often unable to fill in the missing lines. Lady Saishō, for example, could manage only ten, which hardly qualified her as knowing her *Kokinshū*. Some of the other women, even less successful, could remember only about half a dozen poems. They would have done better to tell the empress quite simply that they had forgotten the lines; instead they came out with great lamentations like "Oh dear, how could we have done so badly in answering the questions that Your Majesty was pleased to put to us?"—all of which I found rather absurd.

When no one could complete a particular poem, the empress continued reading to the end. This produced further wails from the women: "Oh, we all knew that one! How could we be so stupid?"

"Those of you," said the empress, "who had taken the trouble to copy out the *Kokinshū* several times would have been able to complete every single poem I have read. In the reign of Emperor Murakami there was a woman at court known as the Imperial Lady of Sen'yō Palace. She was the daughter of the minister of the left who lived in the Smaller Palace of the First Ward, and of course you all have heard of her. When she was still a young girl, her father gave her this advice: 'First you must study penmanship. Next you must learn to play the seven-string zither better than anyone else. And also you must memorize all the poems in the twenty volumes of the *Kokinshū*.'

"Emperor Murakami," continued Her Majesty, "had heard this story and remembered it years later when the girl had grown up and become an imperial consort. Once, on a day of abstinence,[134] he came into her room, hiding a notebook of *Kokinshū* poems in the folds of his robe. He surprised her by seating himself behind a curtain of state; then, opening the book, he asked, 'Tell me the verse written by such-and-such a poet, in such-and-such a year and on such-and-such an occasion.' The lady understood what was afoot and that it was all in fun, yet the possibility of making a mistake or forgetting one of the poems must have worried her greatly. Before beginning the test, the emperor had summoned a couple of ladies-in-waiting who were particularly adept in poetry and told them to mark each incorrect reply by a *go* stone. What a splendid scene it must have been! You know, I really envy anyone who attended that emperor even as a lady-in-waiting.

"Well," Her Majesty went on, "he then began questioning her. She answered without any hesitation, just giving a few words or phrases to show that she knew

---

134. One of the frequent inauspicious days determined by the masters of divination, when, according to current superstition, it was essential to stay indoors and, as much as possible, to abstain from all activities, including eating, sexual intercourse, and even such seemingly innocuous acts as reading a letter.

each poem. And never once did she make a mistake. After a time the emperor began to resent the lady's flawless memory and decided to stop as soon as he detected any error or vagueness in her replies. Yet, after he had gone through ten books of the *Kokinshū*, he had still not caught her out. At this stage he declared that it would be useless to continue. Marking where he had left off, he went to bed. What a triumph for the lady!

"He slept for some time. On waking, he decided that he must have a final verdict and that if he waited until the following day to examine her on the other ten volumes, she might use the time to refresh her memory. So he would have to settle the matter that very night. Ordering his attendants to bring up the bedroom lamp, he resumed his questions. By the time he had finished all twenty volumes, the night was well advanced; and still the lady had not made a mistake.

"During all this time His Excellency, the lady's father, was in a state of great agitation. As soon as he was informed that the emperor was testing his daughter, he sent his attendants to various temples to arrange for special recitations of the scriptures. Then he turned in the direction of the imperial palace and spent a long time in prayer. Such enthusiasm for poetry is really rather moving."

The emperor, who had been listening to the whole story, was much impressed. "How can he possibly have read so many poems?" he remarked when Her Majesty had finished. "I doubt whether I could get through three or four volumes. But of course things have changed. In the old days even people of humble station had a taste for the arts and were interested in elegant pastimes. Such a story would hardly be possible nowadays, would it?"

The ladies in attendance on Her Majesty and the emperor's own ladies-in-waiting who had been admitted into Her Majesty's presence began chatting eagerly, and as I listened I felt that my cares had really "melted away."

Depressing Things (13)

A dog howling in the daytime. A wickerwork fishnet in spring.[135] A red plum-blossom dress[136] in the Third or Fourth Month. A lying-in room when the baby has died. A cold, empty brazier. An ox driver who hates his oxen. A scholar whose wife has one girl child after another.[137]

---

135. These nets were designed for catching whitebait during the winter.

136. Dresses of this color were worn only during the First Month or early spring.

137. Scholarly activities, like most other specialized occupations, tended to run in families, and they were not considered suitable for girls.

One has gone to a friend's house to avoid an unlucky direction,[138] but nothing is done to entertain one; if this should happen at the time of a seasonal change, it is still more depressing.

A letter arrives from the provinces, but no gift accompanies it. It would be bad enough if such a letter reached one in the provinces from someone in the capital; but then at least it would have interesting news about goings-on in society, and that would be a consolation.

One has written a letter, taking pains to make it as attractive as possible, and now one impatiently awaits the reply. "Surely the messenger should be back by now," one thinks. Just then he returns; but in his hand he carries not a reply but one's own letter, still twisted or knotted[139] as it was sent, but now so dirty and crumpled that even the ink mark on the outside has disappeared. "Not at home," announces the messenger, or else, "They said they were observing a day of abstinence and would not accept it." Oh, how depressing!

Again, one has sent one's carriage to fetch someone who had said he would definitely pay one a visit on that day. Finally it returns with a great clatter, and the servants hurry out with cries of "Here they come!" But next one hears the carriage being pulled into the coach house, and the unfastened shafts clatter to the ground. "What does this mean?" one asks. "The person was not at home," replies the driver, "and will not be coming." So saying, he leads the ox back to its stall, leaving the carriage in the coach house.

With much bustle and excitement a young man has moved into the house of a certain family as the daughter's husband. One day he fails to come home, and it turns out that some high-ranking court lady has taken him as her lover. How depressing! "Will he eventually tire of the woman and come back to us?" his wife's family wonder ruefully.

The nurse who is looking after a baby leaves the house, saying that she will be back soon. Soon the child starts crying for her. One tries to comfort it with games and other diversions and even sends a message to the nurse telling her to return immediately. Then comes her reply: "I am afraid that I cannot be back this evening." This is not only depressing; it is no less than hateful. Yet how much more distressed must be the young man who has sent a messenger to fetch a lady friend and who awaits her arrival in vain!

It is quite late at night and a woman has been expecting a visitor. Hearing finally a stealthy tapping, she sends her maid to open the gate and lies waiting excit-

---

138. When a master of divination informed someone that a certain direction was "blocked" by one of the invisible, moving deities central to Heian superstition, he or she might circumvent the danger by first proceeding in a different direction. Then after stopping on the way at an intermediate place and staying there at least until midnight, that person would continue to the intended destination.

139. The two main types of formal letters were "knotted" and "twisted." Both were folded lengthwise into a narrow strip; but whereas the knotted kind was knotted in the middle or at one end, the twisted kind was twisted at both ends and tended to be narrower.

edly. But the name announced by the maid is that of someone with whom she has absolutely no connection. Of all the depressing things, this is by far the worst.

With a look of complete self-confidence on his face an exorcist prepares to expel an evil spirit from his patient. Handing his mace, rosary, and other paraphernalia to the medium who is assisting him, he begins to recite his spells in the special shrill tone that he forces from his throat on such occasions. For all the exorcist's efforts, the spirit gives no sign of leaving, and the Guardian Demon fails to take possession of the medium.[140] The relations and friends of the patient, who are gathered in the room praying, find this rather unfortunate. After he has recited his incantations for the length of an entire watch,[141] the exorcist is worn out. "The Guardian Demon is completely inactive," he tells his medium. "You may leave." Then, as he takes back his rosary, he adds, "Well, well, it hasn't worked!" He passes his hand over his forehead, then yawns deeply (he of all people!), and leans back against a pillar for a nap.

Most depressing is the household of some hopeful candidate who fails to receive a post during the period of official appointments. Hearing that the gentleman was bound to be successful, several people have gathered in his house for the occasion; among them are a number of retainers who served him in the past but who since then have either been engaged elsewhere or moved to some remote province. Now they all are eager to accompany their former master on his visit to the shrines and temples, and their carriages pass to and fro in the courtyard. Indoors there is a great commotion as the hangers-on help themselves to food and drink. Yet the dawn of the last day of the appointments arrives, and still no one has knocked at the gate. The people in the house are nervous and prick up their ears.

Presently they hear the shouts of forerunners and realize that the high dignitaries are leaving the palace. Some of the servants were sent to the palace on the previous evening to hear the news and have been waiting all night, trembling with cold; now they come trudging back listlessly. The attendants who have remained faithfully in the gentleman's service year after year cannot bring themselves to ask what has happened. His former retainers, however, are not so diffident. "Tell us," they say, "what appointment did His Excellency receive?" "Indeed," murmur the servants, "His Excellency was governor of such-and-such a province." Everyone was counting on his receiving a new appointment and is desolated by this failure. On the following day the people who had crowded

---

140. The aim of the exorcist was to transfer the evil spirit from the afflicted person to the medium, usually a young girl or a woman, and to force it to declare itself. The exorcist used various spells and incantations to make the Guardian Demon of Buddhism take possession of the medium. When he was successful, the medium would tremble, scream, have convulsions, faint, or behave as if in a hypnotic trance. The spirit would then declare itself through her mouth. The final step was to drive the spirit out of the medium.

141. One watch was the equivalent of two hours.

into the house begin to slink away in twos and threes. The old attendants, however, cannot leave so easily. They walk restlessly about the house, counting on their fingers the provincial appointments that will become available in the following year. Pathetic and depressing in the extreme!

One has sent a friend a verse that turned out fairly well. How depressing when there is no reply poem! Even in the case of love poems, people should at least answer that they were moved at receiving the message or something of the sort; otherwise they will cause the keenest disappointment.

Someone who lives in a bustling, fashionable household receives a message from an elderly person who is behind the times and has very little to do; the poem, of course, is old-fashioned and dull. How depressing!

One needs a particularly beautiful fan for some special occasion and instructs an artist, in whose talents one has full confidence, to decorate one with an appropriate painting. When the day comes and the fan is delivered, one is shocked to see how badly it has been painted. Oh, the dreariness of it!

A messenger arrives with a present at a house where a child has been born or where someone is about to leave on a journey. How depressing for him if he gets no reward! People should always reward a messenger, though he may bring only herbal balls or hare sticks.[142] If he expects nothing, he will be particularly pleased to be rewarded. On the other hand, what a terrible letdown if he arrives with a self-important look on his face, his heart pounding in anticipation of a generous reward, only to have his hopes dashed!

A man has moved in as a son-in-law; yet even now, after some five years of marriage, the lying-in room has remained as quiet as on the day of his arrival.

An elderly couple who have several grown-up children, and who may even have some grandchildren crawling about the house, are taking a nap in the daytime. The children who see them in this state are overcome by a forlorn feeling, and for other people it is all very depressing.

To take a hot bath when one has just woken is not only depressing; it actually puts one in a bad humor.

Persistent rain on the last day of the year.

One has been observing a period of fast but neglects it for just one day—most depressing.

A white underrobe in the Eighth Month.[143]

A wet nurse who has run out of milk.

---

142. Herbal balls: during the Iris Festival (Tango no sekku) on the fifth day of the Fifth Month, various kinds of herbs were bound into balls and put into round cotton or silk bags, which were decorated with irises and other plants, as well as with long, five-color cords. They were then hung on pillars, curtains, and the like to protect the inhabitants of the house from illness and other misfortunes. Hare-sticks, three-inch sticks with long, colored tassels, were hung on pillars in the palace and in the houses of the nobility to keep away evil spirits.

143. A white underrobe was normally worn only in the summer months; the Eighth Month was the second month of autumn.

Hateful Things (14)

One is in a hurry to leave, but one's visitor keeps chattering away. If it is someone of no importance, one can get rid of him by saying, "You must tell me all
about it next time"; but should it be the sort of visitor whose presence commands one's best behavior, the situation is hateful indeed.

One finds that a hair has got caught in the stone on which one is rubbing
one's inkstick, or again that gravel is lodged in the inkstick, making a nasty,
grating sound.

Someone has suddenly fallen ill, and one summons the exorcist. Since he is
not at home, one has to send messengers to look for him. After one has had a
long fretful wait, the exorcist finally arrives, and with a sigh of relief one asks
him to start his incantations. But perhaps he has been exorcising too many evil
spirits recently; for hardly has he installed himself and begun praying when his
voice becomes drowsy. Oh, how hateful!

A man who has nothing in particular to recommend him discusses all sorts
of subjects at random as though he knows everything.

An elderly person warms the palms of his hands over a brazier and stretches
out the wrinkles. No young man would dream of behaving in such a fashion;
old people can really be quite shameless. I have seen some dreary old creatures
actually resting their feet on the brazier and rubbing them against the edge while
they speak. These are the kinds of people who, when visiting someone's house,
first use their fans to wipe away the dust from the mat and, when they finally sit
on it, cannot stay still but are forever spreading out the front of their hunting
costume[144] or even tucking it up under their knees. One might suppose that
such behavior was restricted to people of humble station, but I have observed it
in quite well-bred people, including a senior secretary of the fifth rank in the
Ministry of Ceremonial and a former governor of Suruga.

I hate the sight of men in their cups who shout, poke their fingers in their
mouths, stroke their beards, and pass on the wine to their neighbors with great
cries of "Have some more! Drink up!" They tremble, shake their heads, twist
their faces, and gesticulate like children who are singing, "We're off to see the
governor." I have seen really well-bred people behave like this and I find it most
distasteful.

To envy others and to complain about one's own lot; to speak badly about
people; to be inquisitive about the most trivial matters and to resent and abuse
people for not telling one, or, if one does manage to worm out some facts, to
inform everyone in the most detailed fashion as if one had known all from the
beginning—oh, how hateful!

One is just about to be told some interesting piece of news when a baby starts
crying.

---

144. Men's informal outdoor costume, originally worn for hunting.

A flight of crows circle about with loud caws.

An admirer has come on a clandestine visit, but a dog catches sight of him and starts barking. One feels like killing the beast.

One has been foolish enough to invite a man to spend the night in an unsuitable place—and then he starts snoring.

A gentleman has visited one secretly. Although he is wearing a tall, lacquered hat,[145] he nevertheless wants no one to see him. He is so flurried, in fact, that upon leaving he bangs into something with his hat. Most hateful! It is annoying too when he lifts up the Iyo blind[146] that hangs at the entrance of the room, then lets it fall with a great rattle. If it is a head blind, things are still worse, for, being more solid, it makes a terrible noise when it is dropped. There is no excuse for such carelessness. Even a head blind does not make any noise if one lifts it up gently on entering and leaving the room; the same applies to sliding doors. If one's movements are rough, even a paper door will bend and resonate when opened; but if one lifts the door a little while pushing it, there need be no sound.

One has gone to bed and is about to doze off when a mosquito appears, announcing himself in a reedy voice. One can actually feel the wind made by his wings, and slight though it is, one finds it hateful in the extreme.

A carriage passes with a nasty, creaking noise. Annoying to think that the passengers may not even be aware of this! If I am traveling in someone's carriage and I hear it creaking, I dislike not only the noise but also the owner of the carriage.

One is in the middle of a story when someone butts in and tries to show that he is the only clever person in the room. Such a person is hateful, and so, indeed, is anyone, child or adult, who tries to push himself forward.

One is telling a story about old times when someone breaks in with a little detail that he happens to know, implying that one's own version is inaccurate—disgusting behavior!

Very hateful is a mouse that scurries all over the place.

Some children have called at one's house. One makes a great fuss of them and gives them toys to play with. The children become accustomed to this treatment and start to come regularly, forcing their way into one's inner rooms and scattering one's furnishings and possessions. Hateful!

A certain gentleman whom one does not want to see visits one at home or in the palace, and one pretends to be asleep. But a maid comes to tell one and shakes one awake, with a look on her face that says, "What a sleepyhead!" Very hateful.

---

145. A black, lacquered headdress worn by men on the top of the head and secured by a mauve silk cord that was fastened under the chin.

146. An Iyo blind is a rough type of reed blind manufactured in the province of Iyo on the Inland Sea. A head blind is a more elegant type of blind whose top and edges were decorated with strips of silk. It also had thin strips of bamboo along the edges and was therefore heavier than ordinary blinds.

A newcomer pushes ahead of the other members in a group; with a knowing look, this person starts laying down the law and forcing advice on everyone—most hateful.

A man with whom one is having an affair keeps singing the praises of some woman he used to know. Even if it is a thing of the past, this can be very annoying. How much more so if he is still seeing the woman! (Yet sometimes I find that it is not as unpleasant as all that.)

A person who recites a spell himself after sneezing.[147] In fact I detest anyone who sneezes, except the master of the house.

Fleas, too, are very hateful. When they dance about under someone's clothes, they really seem to be lifting them up.

The sound of dogs when they bark for a long time in chorus is ominous and hateful.

I cannot stand people who leave without closing the panel behind them.

How I detest the husbands of nursemaids! It is not so bad if the child in the maid's charge is a girl, because then the man will keep his distance. But, if it is a boy, he will behave as though he were the father. Never letting the boy out of his sight, he insists on managing everything. He regards the other attendants in the house as less than human, and if anyone tries to scold the child, he slanders him to the master. Despite this disgraceful behavior, no one dare accuse the husband; so he strides about the house with a proud, self-important look, giving all the orders.

I hate people whose letters show that they lack respect for worldly civilities, whether by discourtesy in the phrasing or extreme politeness to someone who does not deserve it. This sort of thing is, of course, most odious if the letter is for oneself, but it is bad enough even if it is addressed to someone else.

As a matter of fact, most people are too casual, not only in their letters, but in their direct conversation. Sometimes I am quite disgusted at noting how little decorum people observe when talking to each other. It is particularly unpleasant to hear some foolish man or woman omit the proper marks of respect when addressing a person of quality; and when servants fail to use honorific forms of speech in referring to their masters, it is very bad indeed. No less odious, however, are those masters who, in addressing their servants, use such phrases as "When you were good enough to do such-and-such" or "As you so kindly remarked." No doubt there are some masters who, in describing their own actions to a servant, say, "I presumed to do so-and-so"!

Sometimes a person who is utterly devoid of charm will try to create a good impression by using very elegant language, yet he succeeds only in being ridiculous. No doubt he believes this refined language to be just what the occasion demands, but when it goes so far that everyone bursts out laughing, surely something must be wrong.

---

147. Sneezing was a bad omen, and it was normal to counteract its effects by reciting some auspicious formula, such as wishing long life to the person who had sneezed.

It is most improper to address high-ranking courtiers, imperial advisers, and the like simply by using their names without any titles or marks of respect; but such mistakes are fortunately rare.

If one refers to the maid who is in attendance on some lady-in-waiting as "Madam" or "that lady," she will be surprised, delighted, and lavish in her praise.

When speaking to young noblemen and courtiers of high rank, one should always (unless their majesties are present) refer to them by their official posts. Incidentally, I have been very shocked to hear important people use the word "I" while conversing in their majesties' presence.[148] Such a breach of etiquette is really distressing, and I fail to see why people cannot avoid it.

A man who has nothing in particular to recommend him but who speaks in an affected tone and poses as being elegant.

An inkstone with such a hard, smooth surface that the stick glides over it without leaving any deposit of ink.

Ladies-in-waiting who want to know everything that is going on.

Sometimes one greatly dislikes a person for no particular reason—and then that person goes and does something hateful.

A gentleman who travels alone in his carriage to see a procession or some other spectacle. What sort of a man is he? Even though he may not be a person of the greatest quality, surely he should have taken along a few of the many young men who are anxious to see the sights. But no, there he sits by himself (one can see his silhouette through the blinds), with a proud look on his face, keeping all his impressions to himself.

A lover who is leaving at dawn announces that he has to find his fan and his paper.[149] "I know I put them somewhere last night," he says. Since it is pitch dark, he gropes about the room, bumping into the furniture and muttering, "Strange! Where on earth can they be?" Finally he discovers the objects. He thrusts the paper into the breast of his robe with a great rustling sound; then he snaps open his fan and busily fans away with it. Only now is he ready to take his leave. What charmless behavior! "Hateful" is an understatement.

Equally disagreeable is the man who, when leaving in the middle of the night, takes care to fasten the cord of his headdress. This is quite unnecessary; he could perfectly well put it gently on his head without tying the cord. And why must he spend time adjusting his cloak or hunting costume? Does he really think someone may see him at this time of night and criticize him for not being impeccably dressed?

A good lover will behave as elegantly at dawn as at any other time. He drags himself out of bed with a look of dismay on his face. The lady urges him on:

---

148. Etiquette demanded that in the presence of the emperor or empress, one referred to oneself by one's name rather than by the first-person singular.

149. Elegant colored paper that gentlemen carried in the folds of their clothes.

"Come, my friend, it's getting light. You don't want anyone to find you here."
He gives a deep sigh, as if to say that the night has not been nearly long enough
and that it is agony to leave. Once up, he does not instantly pull on his trousers.
Instead he comes close to the lady and whispers whatever was left unsaid during
the night. Even when he is dressed, he still lingers, vaguely pretending to be
fastening his sash.

Presently he raises the lattice, and the two lovers stand together by the side
door while he tells her how he dreads the coming day, which will keep them
apart; then he slips away. The lady watches him go, and this moment of parting
will remain among her most charming memories.

Indeed, one's attachment to a man depends largely on the elegance of his
leave-taking. When he jumps out of bed, scurries about the room, tightly fas-
tens his trouser sash, rolls up the sleeves of his court cloak, overrobe, or hunting
costume, stuffs his belongings into the breast of his robe, and then briskly se-
cures the outer sash—one really begins to hate him.

Rare Things (47)

A son-in-law who is praised by his father-in-law; a young bride who is loved by
her mother-in-law.

A silver tweezer that is good at plucking out the hair.

A servant who does not speak badly about his master.

A person who is in no way eccentric or imperfect, who is superior in both
mind and body, and who remains flawless all his life.

People who live together and still manage to behave with reserve toward
each other. However much these people may try to hide their weaknesses, they
usually fail.

To avoid getting ink stains on the notebook into which one is copying stories,
poems, or the like. If it is a very fine notebook, one takes the greatest care not to
make a blot; yet somehow one never seems to succeed.

When people, whether they be men or women or priests, have promised
each other eternal friendship, it is rare for them to stay on good terms until
the end.

A servant who is pleasant to his master.

One has given some silk to the fuller, and when he sends it back, it is so beautiful that one cries out in admiration.

Embarrassing Things (63)

While entertaining a visitor, one hears some servants chatting without any restraint in one of the back rooms. It is embarrassing to know that one's visitor can
overhear. But how to stop them?

A man whom one loves gets drunk and keeps repeating himself.

To have spoken about someone not knowing that he could overhear. This is embarrassing even if it is a servant or some other completely insignificant person.

To hear one's servants making merry. This is equally annoying if one is on a journey and staying in cramped quarters or at home and hears the servants in a neighboring room.

Parents, convinced that their ugly child is adorable, pet him and repeat the things he has said, imitating his voice.

An ignoramus who in the presence of some learned person puts on a knowing air and converses about men of old.

A man recites his own poems (not especially good ones) and tells one about the praise they have received—most embarrassing.

Lying awake at night, one says something to one's companion, who simply goes on sleeping.

In the presence of a skilled musician, someone plays a zither just for his own pleasure and without tuning it.

A son-in-law who has long since stopped visiting his wife runs into his father-in-law in a public place.

Things That Give a Hot Feeling (78)

The hunting costume of the head of a guards escort.
A patchwork surplice.
The captain in attendance at the imperial games.
An extremely fat person with a lot of hair.
A zither bag.
A holy teacher performing a rite of incantation at noon in the Sixth or Seventh Month. Or at the same time of the year a coppersmith working in his foundry.

Things That Have Lost Their Power (80)

A large boat that is high and dry in a creek at ebb tide.
A woman who has taken off her false locks to comb the short hair that remains.
A large tree that has been blown down in a gale and lies on its side with its roots in the air.
The retreating figure of a sumo wrestler who has been defeated in a match.[150]
A man of no importance reprimanding an attendant.

---

150. Sumo-wrestling tournaments usually took place in the imperial palace every year at the end of the Seventh Month, with skilled fighters being specially recruited from the provinces.

An old man who removes his hat, uncovering his scanty topknot.

A woman, who is angry with her husband about some trifling matter, leaves home and goes somewhere to hide. She is certain that he will rush about looking for her; but he does nothing of the kind and shows the most infuriating indifference. Since she cannot stay away forever, she swallows her pride and returns.

Awkward Things (81)

One has gone to a house and asked to see someone; but the wrong person appears, thinking that it is he who is wanted; this is especially awkward if one has brought a present.

One has allowed oneself to speak badly about someone without really intending to do so; a young child who has overheard it all goes and repeats what one has said in front of the person in question.

Someone sobs out a pathetic story. One is deeply moved; but it so happens that not a single tear comes to one's eyes—most awkward. Although one makes one's face look as if one is going to cry, it is no use: not a single tear will come. Yet there are times when, having heard something happy, one feels the tears streaming out.

Adorable Things (99)

The face of a child drawn on a melon.[151]

A baby sparrow that comes hopping up when one imitates the squeak of a mouse; or again, when one has tied it with a thread round its leg and its parents bring insects or worms and pop them in its mouth—delightful!

A baby of two or so is crawling rapidly along the ground. With his sharp eyes he catches sight of a tiny object and, picking it up with his pretty little fingers, takes it to show to a grown-up person.

A child, whose hair has been cut like a nun's,[152] is examining something; the hair falls over his eyes, but instead of brushing it away he holds his head to the side. The pretty white cords of his trouser skirt are tied round his shoulders, and this too is most adorable.

A young palace page, who is still quite small, walks by in ceremonial costume.

One picks up a pretty baby and holds him for a while in one's arms; while one is fondling him, he clings to one's neck and then falls asleep.

The objects used during the Display of Dolls.

---

151. Drawing faces on melons was a popular pastime, especially for women and children.
152. That is, cut at shoulder length.

One picks up a tiny lotus leaf that is floating on a pond and examines it. Not only lotus leaves, but little hollyhock flowers, and indeed all small things, are most adorable.

An extremely plump baby, who is about a year old and has lovely white skin, comes crawling toward one, dressed in a long gauze robe of violet with the sleeves tucked up.

A little boy of about eight who reads aloud from a book in his childish voice.

Pretty, white chicks who are still not fully fledged and look as if their clothes are too short for them; cheeping loudly, they follow one on their long legs or walk close to the mother hen.

Duck eggs.

An urn containing the relics of some holy person.

Wild pinks.

Pleasing Things (148)

Finding a large number of tales that one has not read before. Or acquiring the second volume of a tale whose first volume one has enjoyed. But often it is a disappointment.

Someone has torn up a letter and thrown it away. Picking up the pieces, one finds that many of them can be fitted together.

One has had an upsetting dream and wonders what it can mean. In great anxiety one consults a dream interpreter, who informs one that it has no special significance.

A person of quality is holding forth about something in the past or about a recent event that is being widely discussed. Several people are gathered round him, but it is oneself that he keeps looking at as he talks.

A person who is very dear to one has fallen ill. One is miserably worried about him even if he lives in the capital and far more so if he is in some remote part of the country. What a pleasure to be told that he has recovered!

I am most pleased when I hear someone I love being praised or being mentioned approvingly by an important person.

A poem that someone has composed for a special occasion or written to another person in reply is widely praised and copied by people in their notebooks. Although this is something that has never yet happened to me, I can imagine how pleasing it must be.

A person with whom one is not especially intimate refers to an old poem or story that is unfamiliar. Then one hears it being mentioned by someone else and one has the pleasure of recognizing it. Still later, when one comes across it in a book, one thinks, "Ah, this is it!" and feels delighted with the person who first brought it up.

I feel very pleased when I have acquired some Michinoku paper or some white, decorated paper or even plain paper if it is nice and white.

A person in whose company one feels awkward asks one to supply the opening or closing line of a poem. If one happens to recall it, one is very pleased. Yet often on such occasions one completely forgets something that one would normally know.

I look for an object that I need at once, and I find it. Or again, there is a book that I must see immediately; I turn everything upside down, and there it is. What a joy!

When one is competing in an object match[153] (it does not matter what kind), how can one help being pleased at winning?

I greatly enjoy taking in someone who is pleased with himself and who has a self-confident look, especially if he is a man. It is amusing to observe him as he alertly waits for my next repartee; but it is also interesting if he tries to put me off my guard by adopting an air of calm indifference as if there were not a thought in his head.

I realize that it is very sinful of me, but I cannot help being pleased when someone I dislike has a bad experience.

It is a great pleasure when the ornamental comb that one has ordered turns out to be pretty.

I am more pleased when something nice happens to a person I love than when it happens to myself.

Entering the empress's room and finding that ladies-in-waiting are crowded round her in a tight group, I go next to a pillar that is some distance from where she is sitting. What a delight it is when Her Majesty summons me to her side so that all the others have to make way!

One Day, When the Snow Lay Thick on the Ground (157)

One day, when the snow lay thick on the ground and it was so cold that all the lattices had been closed, I and the other ladies were sitting with Her Majesty, chatting and poking the embers in the brazier.

"Tell me, Shōnagon," said the empress, "how is the snow on Mount Xianglu?"[154]

I told the maid to raise one of the lattices and then rolled up the blind all the way. Her Majesty smiled. I was not alone in recognizing the Chinese poem she had quoted; in fact all the ladies knew the lines and had even rewritten them in Japanese. Yet no one but me had managed to think of it instantly.

---

153. Literally, "comparison of objects": a game played by two teams, left and right. Among the "objects" used in these games were flowers, roots, seashells, birds, insects, fans, and paintings.

154. The empress is referring to some famous lines in a poem by Bo Juyi: "The sun has risen in the sky, but I idly lie in bed. In my small tower-room the layers of quilts protect me from the cold. Leaning on my pillow, I wait to hear Yiai's temple bell. Pushing aside the blinds, I gaze upon the snow of Xianglu peak . . ."

"Yes indeed," people said when they heard the story. "She was born to serve an empress like ours."

This Book (185)

It is getting so dark that I can scarcely go on writing, and my brush is all worn out. Yet I should like to add a few things before I end.

I wrote these notes at home when I had a good deal of time to myself and thought no one would notice what I was doing. Everything that I have seen and felt is included. Since much of it might appear malicious and even harmful to other people, I was careful to keep my book hidden. But now it has become public, which is the last thing I expected.

One day Lord Korechika, the minister of the center, brought the empress a bundle of notebooks. "What shall we do with them?" Her Majesty asked me. "The emperor has already made arrangements for copying the 'Records of the Historian.'"[155]

"Let me make them into a pillow,"[156] I said.

"Very well," said Her Majesty. "You may have them."

I now had a vast quantity of paper at my disposal, and I set about filling the notebooks with odd facts, stories from the past, and all sorts of other things, often including the most trivial material. On the whole I concentrated on things and people that I found charming and splendid; my notes also are full of poems and observations about trees and plants, birds and insects. I was sure that when people saw my book they would say, "It's even worse than I expected. Now one can really tell what she is like." After all, it is written entirely for my own amusement and I put things down exactly as they came to me. How could my casual jottings possibly bear comparison with the many impressive books that exist in our time? Readers have declared, however, that I can be proud of my work. This has surprised me greatly; yet I suppose it is not so strange that people should like it, for, as will be gathered from these notes of mine, I am the sort of person who approves of what others abhor and detests the things they like.

Whatever people may think of my book, I still regret that it ever came to light.

[Adapted from a translation by Ivan Morris]

---

155. The Chinese historical work *Shi ji* (J. *Shiki*).

156. A pillow book, a term referring to a collection of notebooks kept in some accessible but relatively private place and in which the author would from time to time record impressions, daily events, poems, letters, stories, ideas, descriptions of people, and the like.

MURASAKI SHIKIBU

Murasaki Shikibu (d. ca. 1014) belonged to the northern branch of the Fujiwara lineage, the same branch that produced the regents. In fact, both sides of her family can be traced back to Fujiwara no Fuyutsugu (775–826), whose son Yoshi-fusa became the first regent (*sesshō*). Murasaki Shikibu's family line, however, subsequently declined and by her grandfather's generation had settled at the provincial governor, or *zuryō*, level. Murasaki Shikibu's father, Fujiwara no Tametoki (d. 1029), although eventually appointed governor of Echizen and then Echigo, had an undistinguished career as a bureaucrat. He was able, however, to make a name for himself as a scholar of Chinese literature and a poet.

Murasaki Shikibu was probably born sometime between 970 and 978, and in 996 she accompanied her father to his new post as provincial governor in Echizen, on the coast of the Japan Sea. A year or two later, she returned to the capital to marry Fujiwara no Nobutaka, a mid-level aristocrat who was old enough to be her father. She had a daughter named Kenshi, probably in 999, and Nobutaka died a couple of years later, in 1001. It is generally believed that Murasaki Shikibu started writing *The Tale of Genji* (*Genji monogatari*) after her husband's death, perhaps in response to the sorrow it caused her, and it was probably the reputation of the early chapters that resulted in her being summoned to the imperial court around 1005 or 1006. She became a lady-in-waiting (*nyōbō*) to Empress Shōshi, the chief consort of Emperor Ichijō and the eldest daughter of Fujiwara no Michinaga (966–1027), who had become regent. At least half of *Murasaki Shikibu's Diary* (*Murasaki Shikibu nikki*) is devoted to a long-awaited event in Michinaga's career—the birth of a son to Empress Shōshi in 1008—which would make Michinaga the grandfather of a future emperor.

Murasaki Shikibu was the sobriquet given to the author of *The Tale of Genji* when she was a lady-in-waiting at the imperial court and is not her actual name, which is not known. The name Shikibu probably comes from her father's position in the Shikibu-shō (Ministry of Ceremonial), and Murasaki may refer to the lavender color of the flower of her clan (Fujiwara, or Wisteria Fields), or it may have been borrowed from the name of the heroine of *The Tale of Genji*.

THE TALE OF GENJI (GENJI MONOGATARI)

The title of *The Tale of Genji* comes from the surname of the hero (the son of the emperor reigning at the beginning of the narrative), whose life and relationships with various women are described in the first forty-one chapters. *The Tale of Genji* is generally divided into three parts. The first part, consisting of thirty-three chapters, follows Genji's career from his birth through his exile and triumphant return to his rise to the pinnacle of society, focusing equally, if not more, on the fate of the various women with whom he becomes involved. The second part, chapters 34 to 41, from "New Herbs" (Wakana) to "The Wizard" (Maboroshi), explores the darkness that gathers over Genji's private life and that of his great love Murasaki, who eventually succumbs and dies, and ends with Genji's own death. The third part, the thirteen chapters following Genji's death, is concerned primarily with the affairs of Kaoru, Genji's putative son, and the three sisters (Ōigimi, Nakanokimi, and Ukifune) with whom Kaoru becomes involved. In the third part, the focus of the book shifts dramatically from the capital and court to the countryside and from a society concerned with refinement, elegance, and the various arts to an other-worldly, ascetic perspective—a shift that anticipates the movement of mid-Heian court culture toward the eremetic, religious literature of the medieval period.

The Tale of Genji both follows and works against the plot convention of the Heian monogatari in which the heroine, whose family has declined or disappeared, is discovered and loved by an illustrious noble. This association of love and inferior social status appears in the opening line of *Genji* and extends to the last relationship between Kaoru and Ukifune. In the opening chapter, the reigning emperor, like all Heian emperors, is expected to devote himself to his principal consort (the Kokiden lady), the lady with the highest rank, and yet he dotes on a woman of considerably lower status, a social and political violation that eventually results in the woman's death. Like the protagonist of *The Tales of Ise*, Genji pursues love where it is forbidden and most unlikely to be found or attained. In "Lavender" (Wakamurasaki), chapter 5, Genji discovers the young Murasaki, who has lost her mother and is in danger of losing her only guardian until Genji takes her into his home.

In Murasaki Shikibu's day, it would have been unheard of for a man of Genji's high rank to take a girl of Murasaki's low position into his own residence and marry her. In the upper levels of Heian aristocratic society, the man usually lived in his wife's residence, in either her parents' house or a dwelling nearby (as Genji does with Aoi, his principal wife). The prospective groom had high stakes in the marriage, for the bride's family provided not only a residence but other forms of support as well. When Genji takes into his house a girl (like the young Murasaki) with no backing or social support, he thus is openly flouting the conventions of marriage as they were known to Murasaki Shikibu's audience. In the monogatari tradition, however, this action becomes a sign of excessive, romantic love.

Some of the other sequences—involving Yūgao, the Akashi lady, Ōigimi, and Ukifune—start on a similar note. All these women come from upper- or middle-rank aristocratic families (much like that of the author herself) that have, for various reasons, fallen into social obscurity and must struggle to survive. The appearance of the highborn hero implies, at least for the attendants surrounding the woman, an opportunity for social redemption. Nonetheless, Murasaki Shikibu, much like her female predecessor, the author of the *Kagerō Diary*, concentrates on the difficulties that the woman subsequently encounters, in either dealing with the man or failing to make the social transition between her own social background and that of the highborn hero. The woman may, for example, be torn between pride and material need or between emotional dependence and a desire to be more independent, or she may feel abandoned and betrayed—all conflicts explored in *The Tale of Genji*. In classical Japanese poetry, such as that by Ono no Komachi, love has a similar fate: it is never about happiness or the blissful union of souls. Instead, it dwells on unfulfilled hopes, regretful partings, fears of abandonment, and lingering resentment.

The Tale of Genji is remarkable for how well it absorbs the psychological dimension of the *Kagerō Diary* and the social romance of the early monogatari into a deeply psychological narrative revolving around distinctive characters. Despite closely resembling the modern psychological novel, *The Tale of Genji* was not conceived and written as a single work and then distributed to a mass audience, as novels are today. Instead, it was issued in very short installments, chapter by chapter or sequence by sequence, to an extremely circumscribed, aristocratic audience over an extended period of time.

As a result, *The Tale of Genji* can be read and appreciated as Murasaki Shikibu's oeuvre, or corpus, as a closely interrelated series of texts that can be read either individually or as a whole and that is the product of an author whose attitudes, interests, and techniques evolved significantly with time and experience. For example, the reader of the Ukifune narrative can appreciate this sequence both independently and as an integral part of the previous narrative. *Genji* can also be understood as a kind of multiple bildungsroman in which a character is developed through time and experience not only in the life of a single hero or heroine but also over different generations, with two or more characters. Genji, for example, attains an awareness of death, mutability, and the illusory nature of the world through repeated suffering. By contrast, Kaoru, his putative son, begins his life, or rather his narrative, with a profound grasp and acceptance of these darker aspects of life. In the second part, in the "New Herbs" chapters, Murasaki has long assumed that she can monopolize Genji's affections and act as his principal wife. But Genji's unexpected marriage to the Third Princess (Onna san no miya) crushes these assumptions, causing Murasaki to fall mortally ill. In the last ten chapters, the Uji sequence, Ōigimi never suffers in the way that Murasaki does, but she quickly becomes similarly aware of the inconstancy of men, love, and marriage and rejects Kaoru, even though he appears to be an ideal companion.

Murasaki Shikibu probably first wrote a short sequence of chapters, perhaps beginning with "Lavender," and then, in response to her readers' demand, wrote a sequel or another related series of chapters, and so forth. Certain sequences, particularly the Broom Tree sequence (chapters 2–4, 6) and its sequels (chapters 15 and 16), which appear to have been inserted later, focus on women of the middle and lower aristocracy, as opposed to the main chapters of the first part, which deal with Fujitsubo and other upper-rank women related to the throne.

The Tamakazura sequence (chapters 22–31), which is a sequel to the Broom Tree sequence, may be an expansion of an earlier chapter no longer extant. The only chapters whose authorship has been questioned are the three chapters following the death of Genji. The following selections are from the third part, after Genji's death, beginning with "The Lady at the Bridge" (chap. 45) and the story of the Eighth Prince, his daughters, and Kaoru.

Main Characters

AKASHI EMPRESS: Consort and later empress of the emperor reigning at the end of the tale. Mother of numerous princes and princesses, including Prince Niou.

BENNOKIMI: daughter of Kashiwagi's wet nurse, and later attendant to the Eighth Prince and the Uji princesses. Confidante of Kaoru.

CAPTAIN: former son-in-law of Ono nun. Unsuccessfully courts Ukifune.

EIGHTH PRINCE: eighth son of the first emperor to appear in the tale. Genji's half brother. Father of Ōigimi, Nakanokimi, and Ukifune. Ostracized by court society for his part in Kokiden's plot to supplant the crown prince (the future Reizei emperor). Retreats to Uji, where he raises Ōigimi and Nakanokimi and devotes himself to Buddhism.

EMPEROR: The fourth and last emperor in the tale, ascending to the throne after the Reizei emperor. Father of Niou.

GENJI: son of the first emperor by the Kiritsubo lady and the protagonist of the first and second parts.

JIJŪ: attendant to Ukifune.

KAORU: thought by the world to be Genji's son by the Third Princess but really Kashiwagi's son. Befriends the Eighth Prince and falls in love with his daughter Ōigimi but fails to make her his wife. Subsequently pursues his other daughters, Nakanokimi and Ukifune. Marries the Second Princess.

KASHIWAGI: eldest son of Tō no Chūjō. Falls in love and has an illicit affair with the Third Princess. Later dies a painful death. Father of Kaoru.

KOJIJŪ: attendant to the Third Princess and helps Kashiwagi's secret affair with the Third Princess.

MURASAKI: Genji's great love. Daughter of Prince Hyōbu by a low-ranking wife, and niece of Fujitsubo.

NAKANOKIMI: second Uji princess, daughter of the Eighth Prince. Marries Niou and is installed by him at Nijō mansion. Bears him a son.

NIOU, PRINCE: beloved third son of the last emperor and the Akashi empress. Looked after by Murasaki until her death. Marries Nakanokimi and later Rokunokimi. Pursues Ukifune.

ŌIGIMI: eldest daughter of the Eighth Prince. Loved by Kaoru but refuses to marry him.

ONO NUN: sister of the bishop of Yokawa. Takes care of Ukifune after her disappearance from Uji and attempts to marry her to the captain, her former son-in-law.

REIZEI EMPEROR: thought to be the son of the first emperor and Fujitsubo but actually Genji's son.

ROKUNOKIMI: sixth daughter of Yūgiri. Becomes Niou's principal wife.

SECOND PRINCESS: Second daughter of the fourth and last emperor. Principal wife of Kaoru.

TŌ NO CHŪJŌ: son of the Minister of the Left and brother of Aoi. Genji's chief male companion in his youth. Son-in-law of the Minister of the Right. Father of Kashiwagi.

TOKIKATA: Niou's retainer.

UKIFUNE: unrecognized daughter of the Eighth Prince by an attendant. Half sister of Ōigimi and Nakanokimi. Raised in the East. Pursued by Kaoru and Niou. Tries to commit suicide but is saved by the bishop of Yokawa and taken to a convent at Ono, where she becomes a nun.

UKON: attendant to Ukifune.

YOKAWA, BISHOP OF: high priest of Yokawa and brother of Ono nun. Discovers Ukifune, looks after her, and gives her the tonsure.

YŪGIRI: son of Genji by Aoi. Becomes the most powerful figure at court after Genji's death. Marries his daughter Rokunokimi to Niou.

The Lady at the Bridge

There was in those years a prince of the blood, an old man, left behind by the times. His mother was of the finest lineage. There had once been talk of seeking a favored position for him; but there were disturbances and a new alignment of forces,[157] at the end of which his prospects were in ruins. His supporters, embittered by this turn of events, were less than steadfast: they made their various excuses and left him. And so in his public life and in his private, he was quite alone, blocked at every turn. His wife, the daughter of a former minister, had fits of bleakest depression at the thought of her parents and their plans for her, now of course in ruins. Her consolation was that she and her husband were close as husbands and wives seldom are. Their confidence in each other was complete.

But here too there was a shadow: the years went by and they had no children. If only there were a pretty little child to break the loneliness and boredom, the prince would think—and sometimes give voice to his thoughts. And then, surprisingly, a very pretty daughter was in fact born to them. She was the delight of

---

157. The reference is to the accession of the Reizei emperor after Genji's return from exile.

their lives. Years passed, and there were signs that the princess was again with child. The prince hoped that this time he would be favored with a son, but again the child was a daughter. Though the birth was easy enough, the princess fell desperately ill soon afterward, and was dead before many days had passed. The prince was numb with grief. The vulgar world had long had no place for him, he said, and frequently it had seemed quite unbearable; and the bond that had held him to it had been the beauty and the gentleness of his wife. How could he go on alone? And there were his daughters. How could he, alone, rear them in a manner that would not be a scandal?—for he was not, after all, a commoner. His conclusion was that he must take the tonsure. Yet he hesitated. Once he was gone, there would be no one to see to the safety of his daughters.

So the years went by. The princesses grew up, each with her own grace and beauty. It was difficult to find fault with them, they gave him what pleasure he had. The passing years offered him no opportunity to carry out his resolve.

The serving women muttered to themselves that the younger girl's very birth had been a mistake, and were not as diligent as they might have been in caring for her. With the prince it was a different matter. His wife, scarcely in control of her senses, had been especially tormented by thoughts of this new babe. She had left behind a single request: "Think of her as a keepsake, and be good to her."

The prince himself was not without resentment at the child, that her birth should so swiftly have severed their bond from a former life, his and his princess's.

"But such was the bond that it was," he said. "And she worried about the girl to the very end."

The result was that if anything he doted upon the child to excess. One almost sensed in her fragile beauty a sinister omen.

The older girl was comely and of a gentle disposition, elegant in face and in manner, with a suggestion behind the elegance of hidden depths. In quiet grace, indeed, she was the superior of the two. And so the prince favored each as each in her special way demanded. There were numerous matters which he was not able to order as he wished, however, and his household only grew sadder and lonelier as time went by. His attendants, unable to bear the uncertainty of their prospects, took their leave one and two at a time. In the confusion surrounding the birth of the younger girl, there had not been time to select a really suitable nurse for her. No more dedicated than one would have expected in the circumstances, the nurse first chosen abandoned her ward when the girl was still an infant. Thereafter the prince himself took charge of her upbringing.

Years pass, and the prince refuses to marry again, despite the urging of the people around him. He spends much of his time in religious observances but cannot bring himself to renounce the world. His daughters are his principal companions. As they grow up, he notices that although both are quiet and reserved, the elder, Ōigimi, tends to be moody, and the younger, Nakanokimi, possesses a certain shy gaiety.

He was the Eighth Prince, a younger brother of the shining Genji. During the years when the Reizei emperor was crown prince, the mother of the reigning emperor had sought in that conspiratorial way of hers to have the Eighth Prince named crown prince, replacing Reizei. The world seemed hers to rule as she wished, and the Eighth Prince was very much at the center of it. Unfortunately his success irritated the opposing faction. The day came when Genji and presently Yūgiri had the upper hand, and he was without supporters. He had over the years become an ascetic in any case, and he now resigned himself to living the life of the sage and hermit.

There came yet another disaster. As if fate had not been unkind enough already, his mansion was destroyed by fire. Having no other suitable house in the city, he moved to Uji, some miles to the southeast, where he happened to own a tastefully appointed mountain villa. He had renounced the world, it was true, and yet leaving the capital was a painful wrench indeed. With fishing weirs near at hand to heighten the roar of the river, the situation at Uji was hardly favorable to quiet study. But what must be must be. With the flowering trees of spring and the leaves of autumn and the flow of the river to bring repose, he lost himself more than ever in solitary meditation. There was one thought even so that never left his mind: how much better it would be, even in these remote mountains, if his wife were with him!

> "She who was with me, the roof above are smoke.
> And why must I alone remain behind?"

So much was the past still with him that life scarcely seemed worth living.

Mountain upon mountain separated his dwelling from the larger world. Rough people of the lower classes, woodcutters and the like, sometimes came by to do chores for him.[158] There were no other callers. The gloom continued day after day, as stubborn and clinging as "the morning mist on the peaks."[159]

There happened to be in those Uji mountains an abbot,[160] a most saintly man. Though famous for his learning, he seldom took part in public rites. He heard in the course of time that there was a prince living nearby, a man who was teaching himself the mysteries of the Good Law. Thinking this a most admirable undertaking, he made bold to visit the prince, who upon subsequent interviews was led deeper into the texts he had studied over the years. The

---

158. There is possibly a suggestion that their manner was more familiar than their station should have allowed.

159. Anonymous, *Kokinshū*, no. 935: "My gloomy thoughts run on and on, unbroken as the morning mist on the peaks the wild geese pass."

160. *Ajari* (Skr. *acarya*). In general, any monk of sufficient learning to act as a preceptor; and in the Shingon and Tendai sects a specific clerical rank.

prince became more immediately aware of what was meant by the transience and uselessness of the material world.

"In spirit," he confessed, quite one with the holy man, "I have perhaps found my place upon the lotus of the clear pond; but I have not yet made my last farewells to the world because I cannot bring myself to leave my daughters behind."

The abbot was an intimate of the Reizei emperor and had been his preceptor as well. One day, visiting the city, he called upon the Reizei emperor to answer any questions that might have come to him since their last meeting.

"Your honored brother," he said, bringing the Eighth Prince into the conversation, "has pursued his studies so diligently that he has been favored with the most remarkable insights. Only a bond from a former life can account for such dedication. Indeed, the depth of his understanding makes me want to call him a saint who has not yet left the world."

"He has not taken the tonsure? But I remember now—the young people do call him 'the saint who is still one of us.'"

Kaoru chanced to be present at the interview. He listened intently. No one knew better than he the futility of this world, and yet he passed useless days, his devotions hardly so frequent or intense as to attract public notice. The heart of a man who, though still in this world, was in all other respects a saint—to what might it be likened?

The abbot continued: "He has long wanted to cut his last ties with the world, but a trifling matter made it difficult for him to carry out his resolve. Now he has two motherless children whom he cannot bring himself to leave behind. They are the burden he must bear."[161]

The abbot himself had not entirely given up the pleasures of the world: he had a good ear for music. "And when their highnesses deign to play a duet," he said, "they bid fair to outdo the music of the river, and put one in mind of the blessed musicians above."

The Reizei emperor smiled at this rather fusty way of stating the matter. "You would not expect girls who have had a saint for their principal companion to have such accomplishments. How pleasant to know about them—and what an uncommonly good father he must be! I am sure that the thought of having to leave them is pure torment. It is always possible that I will live longer than he, and if I do perhaps I may ask to be given responsibility for them."

He was himself the tenth son of the family, younger than his brother at Uji. There was the example of the Suzaku emperor, who had left his young daughter in Genji's charge. Something similar might be arranged, he thought. He would have companions to relieve the monotony of his days.

---

161. The abbot here uses an unusual verb form that apparently gives his speech a somewhat stilted or archaic flavor.

Kaoru was less interested in the daughters than in the father. Quite entranced with what he had heard, he longed to see for himself that figure so wrapped in the serenity of religion.

"I have every intention of calling on him and asking him to be my master," he said as the abbot left. "Might I ask you to find out, unobtrusively, of course, how he would greet the possibility?"

"And tell him, please," said the Reizei emperor, "that I have been much affected by your description of his holy retreat." And he wrote down a verse to be delivered to the Eighth Prince.

"Wearily, my soul goes off to your mountains,
and cloud upon circling cloud holds my person back?"

With the royal messenger in the lead, the abbot set off for Uji, thinking to visit the Eighth Prince on his way back to the monastery. The prince so seldom heard from anyone that he was overjoyed at these tidings. He ordered wine for his guests and side dishes peculiar to the region.

This was the poem he sent back to his brother:

"I am not as free as I seem. From the gloom of the world
I retreat only briefly to the Hill of Gloom."[162]

He declined to call himself one of the truly enlightened. The vulgar world still called up regrets and resentments, thought the Reizei emperor, much moved.[163]

The abbot also spoke of Kaoru, who, he said, was of a strongly religious bent. "He asked me most earnestly to tell you about him: to tell you that he has longed since childhood to give himself up to study of the scriptures; that he has been kept busy with inconsequential affairs, public and private, and has been unable to leave the world; that since these affairs are trivial in any case and no one could call his career a brilliant one, he could hardly expect people to notice if he were to lock himself up in prayers and meditation; that he has had an unfortunate way of letting himself be distracted. And when he had entrusted me with all this, he added that, having heard through me of your own revered person, he could not take his mind from you, and was determined to be your pupil."

"When there has been a great misfortune," said the prince, "when the whole world seems hostile—that is when most people come to think it a flimsy facade, and wish to have no more of it. I can only marvel that a young man for whom

---

162. The poem contains a common pun on Uji, which suggests gloom. There also is a reference to a poem by Kisen, *Kokinshū*, no. 983: "In a hut to the south and east of the capital I dwell; the place is known as the Hill of the World of Gloom."

163. The Reizei emperor seems to think that the Eighth Prince's poem refers to the rivalry over the succession.

everything lies ahead, who has had everything his way, should start thinking of other worlds. In my own case, it often seems to me, the powers deliberately arranged matters to give my mind such a turn, and so I came to religion as if it were the natural thing. I have managed to find a certain amount of peace, I suppose; but when I think of the short time I have left and of how slowly my preparations creep forward, I know that what I have learned comes to nothing and that in the end it will still be nothing. No, I am afraid I would be a scandalously bad teacher. Let him think of me as a fellow seeker after truth, a very humble one."

Kaoru and the prince exchanged letters and presently Kaoru paid his first visit.

It was an even sadder place than the abbot's description had led him to expect. The house itself was like a grass hut put up for a few days' shelter, and as for the furnishings, everything even remotely suggesting luxury had been dispensed with. There were mountain villages that had their own quiet charm; but here the tumult of the waters and the wailing of the wind must make it impossible to have a moment free of sad thoughts. He could see why a man on the way to enlightenment might seek out such a place as a means of cutting his ties with the world. But what of the daughters? Did they not have the usual fondness for delicate, ladylike things?

A sliding partition seemed to separate the chapel from their rooms. A youth of more amorous inclinations would have approached and made himself known, curious to see what his reception would be. Kaoru was not above feeling a certain excitement at being so near; but a show of interest would have betrayed his whole purpose, which was to be free of just such thoughts, here in distant mountains. The smallest hint of frivolity would have denied the reason for the visit.

Deeply moved by the saintly figure before him, he offered the warmest avowals of friendship. His visits were frequent thereafter. Nowhere did he find evidence of shallowness in the discourses to which he was treated; nor was there a suggestion of pompousness in the prince's explanations of the scriptures and of his profoundly significant reasons, even though he had stopped short of taking the tonsure, for living in the mountains.

The world was full of saintly and learned men, but the stiff, forbidding bishops and patriarchs[164] who were such repositories of virtue had little time of their own, and he found it far from easy to approach them with his questions. Then there were lesser disciples of the Buddha. They were to be admired for observing the discipline, it was true; but they tended to be vulgar and obsequious in their manner and rustic in their speech, and they could be familiar to the point of rudeness. Since Kaoru was busy with official duties in the daytime, it was in the quiet of the evening, in the intimacy of his private chambers, that he liked to have company. Such people would not do.

---

164. Sōzu, Sōjō.

Now he had found a man who combined great elegance with a reticence that certainly was not obsequious, and who, even when he was discussing the Good Law, was adept at bringing plain, familiar similes into his discourse. He was not, perhaps, among the completely enlightened, but people of birth and culture have their own insights into the nature of things. After repeated visits Kaoru came to feel that he wanted to be always at the prince's side, and he would be overtaken by intense longing when official duties kept him away for a time.

Impressed by Kaoru's devotion, the Reizei emperor sent messages; and so the Uji house, silent and forgotten by the world, came to have visitors again. Sometimes the Reizei emperor sent lavish gifts and supplies. In pleasant matters having to do with the seasons and the festivals and in practical matters as well, Kaoru missed no chance to be of service.

Three years went by. It was the end of autumn, and the time had come for the quarterly reading of the scriptures.[165] The roar of the fish weirs was more than a man could bear, said the Eighth Prince as he set off for the abbot's monastery, there to spend a week in retreat.

The princesses were lonelier than ever. It had been weighing on Kaoru's mind that too much time had passed since his last visit. One night as a late moon was coming over the hills he set out for Uji, his guard as unobtrusive as possible, his caparison of the simplest. He could go on horseback and did not have to worry about a boat, since the prince's villa was on the near side of the Uji River. As he came into the mountains the mist was so heavy and the underbrush so thick that he could hardly make out the path; and as he pushed his way through thickets the rough wind would throw showers of dew upon him from a turmoil of falling leaves. He was very cold, and, though he had no one to blame but himself, he had to admit that he was also very wet. This was not the sort of journey he was accustomed to. It was sobering and at the same time exciting.

> "From leaves that cannot withstand the mountain wind
> the dew is falling. My tears fall yet more freely."

He forbade his outrunners to raise their usual cries, for the woodcutters in these mountains could be troublesome. Brushing through a wattle fence, crossing a rivulet that meandered down from nowhere, he tried as best he could to silence the hoofs of his colt. But he could not keep that extraordinary fragrance from wandering off on the wind, and more than one family awoke in surprise at "the scent of an unknown master."[166]

---

165. There was no fixed time for this. The meaning is that winter is coming, and if he does not hurry he will have missed the autumn observances. Autumn (see the next sentence) was the fishing season.

166. Sosei, *Kokinshū*, no. 241: "Purple trousers—left behind by whom?—give sweetly forth the scent of an unknown master."

As he drew near the Uji house, he could hear the plucking of he did not know what instrument, unimaginably still and lonely. He had heard from the abbot that the prince liked to practice with his daughters, but somehow had not found occasion to hear that famous koto. This would be his chance. Making his way into the grounds, he knew that he had been listening to a lute, tuned to the ōjiki mode.[167] There was nothing unusual about the melody. Perhaps the strangeness of the setting had made it seem different. The sound was cool and clean, especially when a string was plucked from beneath. The lute fell silent and there were a few quiet strokes on a koto. He would have liked to listen on, but he was challenged by a man with a somewhat threatening manner, one of the guards, it would seem.

The man immediately recognized him and explained that, for certain reasons, the prince had gone into seclusion in a mountain monastery. He would be informed immediately of the visit.

"Please do not bother," said Kaoru. "It would be a pity to interrupt his retreat when it will be over soon in any case. But do tell the ladies that I have arrived, sodden as you see me, and must go back with my mission unaccomplished; and if they are sorry for me that will be my reward."

The rough face broke into a smile. "They will be informed."

But as he turned to depart, Kaoru called him back. "No, wait a minute. For years I have been fascinated by stories I have heard of their playing, and this is my chance. Will there be somewhere that I might hide and listen for a while? If I were to rush in on them they would of course stop, and that would be the last thing I would want."

His face and manner were such as to quell even the most untamed of rustics. "This is how it is. They are at it morning and night when there is no one around to hear. But let someone come from the city even if he is in rags, and they won't let you have a twang of it. No one's supposed to know they even exist. That's how His Highness wants it."

Kaoru smiled. "Now there is an odd sort of secret for you. The whole world knows that two specimens of the rarest beauty are hidden here. But come. Show me the way. I have all the best intentions. That is the way I am, I assure you." His manner was grave and courteous. "It is hard to believe that they can be less than perfect."

"Suppose they find out, sir. I might be in trouble."

Nonetheless he led Kaoru to a secluded wing fenced off by wattled bamboo and the guards to the west veranda, where he saw to their needs as best he could.

A gate seemed to lead to the princesses' rooms. Kaoru pushed it open a little. The blind had been half raised to give a view of the moon, more beautiful for the mist. A young girl, tiny and delicate, her soft robe somewhat rumpled, sat shivering at the veranda. With her was an older woman similarly dressed. The

---

167. Or ōshiki. The tonic is A.

princesses were farther inside. Half hidden by a pillar, one had a lute before her and sat toying with the plectrum.[168] Just then the moon burst forth in all its brilliance.

"Well, now," she said. "This does quite as well as a fan for bringing out the moon." The upraised face was bright and lively.

The other, leaning against an armrest, had a koto before her. "I have heard that you summon the sun with one of those objects,[169] but you seem to have ideas of your own on how to use it." She was smiling, a melancholy, contemplative sort of smile.

"I may be asking too much, I admit, but you have to admit that lutes and moons are related."[170]

It was a charming scene, utterly unlike what Kaoru had imagined from afar. He had often enough heard the young women of his household reading from old romances. They were always coming upon such scenes, and he had thought them the most unadulterated nonsense. And here, hidden away from the world, was a scene as affecting as any in a romance. He was dangerously near losing control of himself. The mist had deepened until he could barely make out the figures of the princesses. Summon it forth again, he whispered—but a woman had come from within to tell them of the caller. The blind was lowered and everyone withdrew to the rear of the house. There was nothing confused, nothing disorderly about the withdrawal, so calm and quiet that he caught not even a rustling of silk. Elegance and grace could at times push admiration to the point of envy.

He slipped out and sent someone back to the city for a carriage.

"I was sorry to find the prince away," he said to the man who had been so helpful, "but I have drawn some consolation from what you have been so good as to let me see. Might I ask you to tell them that I am here, and to add that I am thoroughly drenched?"

The ladies were in an agony of embarrassment. They had not dreamed that anyone would be looking in at them—and had he even overheard that silly conversation? Now that they thought of it, there had been a peculiar fragrance on the wind; but the hour was late and they had not paid much attention. Could anything be more embarrassing? Impatient at the woman assigned to deliver his message—she did not seem to have the experience for the task—Kaoru decided that there was a time for boldness and a time for reserve; and the mist was in his favor. He advanced to the blind that had been raised earlier and knelt deferentially before it. The countrified maids had not the first notion of what to say to

168. This is a much debated passage. We have been told that the older sister is a master of the lute; the younger, of the koto. But the description of the girl with the plectrum seems to fit the younger girl better.

169. This is obviously an allusion, but it has not been traced.

170. There are three sound holes on the face of a biwa lute, two known as half moons, the other as the full or "hidden" moon.

him. Indeed they seemed incapable of so ordinary a courtesy as inviting him to sit down.

"You must see how uncomfortable I am," he said quietly. "I have come over steep mountains. You cannot believe, surely, that a man with improper intentions would have gone to the trouble. This is not the reward I expected. But I take some comfort in the thought that if I submit to the drenching time after time your ladies may come to understand."

They were young and incapable of a proper answer. They seemed to wither and crumple. It was taking a great deal of time to summon a more experienced woman from the inner chambers. The prolonged silence, Ōigimi feared, might make it seem that they were being coy.

"We know nothing, nothing. How can we pretend otherwise?" It was an elegantly modulated voice, but so soft that he could scarcely make it out.

"One of the more trying mannerisms of this world, I have always thought, is for people who know its cruelties to pretend that they do not. Even you are guilty of the fault, which I find more annoying than I can tell you. Your honored father has gained deep insights into the nature of things. You have lived here with him. I should have thought that you would have gained similar insights, and that they might now demonstrate their worth by making you see the intensity of my feelings and the difficulty with which I contain them. You cannot believe, surely, that I am the usual sort of adventurer. I fear that I am of a rather inflexible nature and refuse to wander in that direction even when others try to lead me. These facts are general knowledge and will perhaps have reached your ears. If I had your permission to tell you of my silent days, if I could hope to have you come forward and seek some relief from your solitude—I cannot describe the pleasure it would give me."

Ōigimi, too shy to answer, deferred to an older woman who had at length been brought from her room.

There was nothing reticent about her. "Oh no! You've left him out there all by himself! Bring him in this minute. I simply do not understand young people." The princesses must have found this as trying as the silence. "You see how it is, sir. His Highness has decided to live as if he did not belong to the human race. No one comes calling these days, not even people you'd think would never forget what they owe him. And here you are, good enough to come and see us. I may be stupid and insensitive, but I know when to be grateful. So do my ladies. But they are so shy."

Kaoru was somewhat taken aback. Yet the woman's manner suggested considerable polish and experience, and her voice was not unpleasant.

"I had been feeling rather unhappy," he said, "and your words cheer me enormously. It is good to be told that they understand."

He had come inside. Through the curtains, the old woman could make him out in the dawn light. It was as she had been told: he had discarded every pretense of finery and come in rough travel garb, and he was drenched. A most extraordinary fragrance—it hardly seemed of this world—filled the air.

"I would not want you to think me forward," she said, and there were tears in her voice; "but I have hoped over the years that the day might come when I could tell you a little, the smallest bit, of a sad story of long ago." Her voice was trembling. "In among my other prayers I have put a prayer that the day might come, and now it seems that the prayer has been answered. How I have longed for this moment! But see what is happening. I am all choked up before I have come to the first word."

He had heard, and it had been his experience, that old people weep easily. This, however, was no ordinary display of feeling.

"I have fought my way here so many times and not known that a perceptive lady like yourself was in residence. Come, this is your chance. Do not leave anything out."

"This is my chance, and there may not be another. When you are my age you can't be sure that you will last the night. Well, let me talk. Let me tell you that this old hag is still among the living. I have heard somewhere that Kojijū, the one who waited upon your revered mother—I have heard that she is dead. So it goes. Most of the people I was fond of are dead, the people who were young when I was young. And after I had outlived them all, certain family ties[171] brought me back from the far provinces, and I have been in the service of my ladies these five or six years. None of this, I am sure, will have come to your attention. But you may have heard of the young gentleman who was a guards captain when he died. I am told that his brother is now a major counselor.[172] It hardly seems possible that we have had time to dry our tears, and yet I count on my fingers and I see that there really have been years enough for you to be the fine young gentleman you are. They seem like a dream, all those years.

"My mother was his nurse. I was privileged myself to wait upon him. I did not matter, of course, but he sometimes told me secrets he kept from others, let slip things he could not keep to himself. And as he lay dying he called me to his side and left a will, I suppose you might call it. There were things in it I knew I must tell you of someday. But no more. You will ask why, having said this much, I do not go on. Well, there may after all be another chance and I can tell you everything. These youngsters are of the opinion that I have said too much already, and they are right." She was a loquacious old person obviously, but now she fell silent.

It was like a story in a dream, like the unprompted recital of a medium in a trance. It was too odd—and at the same time it touched upon events of which he had long wanted to know more. But this was not the time. She was right. Too many eyes were watching. And it would not do to surrender on the spot and waste a whole night on an ancient story.

---

171. The old woman, Bennokimi, is a first cousin of Kojijū and of the Eighth Prince's deceased wife.

172. Kashiwagi was a guards captain, and his brother is Kōbai.

"I do not understand everything you have said, I fear, and yet your talk of old times does call up fond thoughts. I shall come again and ask you to tell me the rest of the story. You see how I am dressed, and if the mist clears before I leave I will disgrace myself in front of the ladies. I would like to stay longer but do not see how I can."

As he stood up to leave, the bell of the monastery sounded in the distance. The mist was heavy. The sadness of these lives poured in upon him, of the isolation enforced by heavy mountain mists. They were lives into which the whole gamut of sorrows had entered, he thought, and he thought too that he understood why they preferred to live in seclusion.

"How very sad.

> "In the dawn I cannot see the path I took
> to find Oyama of the Pines in mist."

He turned away, and yet hesitated. Even ladies who saw the great gentlemen of the capital every day would have found him remarkable, and he quite dazzled these rustic maids. Ōigimi, knowing that it would be too much to ask one of them to deliver it for her, offered a reply, her voice soft and shy as before, and with a hint of a sigh in it.

> "Our mountain path, enshrouded whatever the season,
> is now closed off by the deeper mist of autumn."

The scene itself need not have detained him, but these evidences of loneliness made him reluctant to leave. Presently, uncomfortable at the thought of being seen in broad daylight, he went to the west veranda, where a place had been prepared for him, and looked out over the river.

"To have spoken so few words and to have had so few in return," he said as he left the princesses' wing of the house, "makes it certain that I shall have much to think about. Perhaps when we are better acquainted I can tell you of it. In the meantime, I shall say only that if you think me no different from most young men, and you do seem to, then your judgment in such matters is not what I would have hoped it to be."

His men had become expert at presiding over the weirs. "Listen to all the shouting," said one of them. "And they don't seem to be exactly boasting over what they've caught. The fish[173] are not cooperating."

Strange, battered little boats, piled high with brush and wattles, made their way up and down the river, each boatman pursuing his own sad, small livelihood at the uncertain mercy of the waters. "It is the same with all of us," thought Kaoru to himself. "Am I to boast that I am safe from the flood, calm and secure in a jeweled mansion?"

---

173. *Hiuo* (literally, "ice fish"). The young of the *ayu* (sweet fish).

After his return to the city, Kaoru sends a note to Ōigimi in which he expresses the hope that he might appear before the princesses more freely in the future. The Eighth Prince, seeing the letter, chides Ōigimi for her treatment of the serious young man—he is no trifler, and the Eighth Prince has already hinted to him that he would like him to take care of the princesses after his own death. Kaoru tells his friend Niou, who has a reputation for amorousness and is "always mooning about the possibility of finding a great beauty lost away in the mountains," about the princesses. Niou is interested.

Kaoru makes another visit to Uji near the beginning of the Tenth Month. He hints to the prince that he would like to hear another sample of the princesses' music, but they refuse to accommodate him. Again, the prince mentions his concern about what will become of them when he is gone, and Kaoru renews his promise to look out for them.

When the prince had withdrawn for matins, Kaoru summoned the old woman. Her name was Bennokimi, and the Eighth Prince had her in constant attendance upon his daughters. Though in her late fifties, she was still favored with the graces of a considerably younger woman. Her tears flowing liberally, she told him of what an unhappy life "the young captain," Kashiwagi, had led, of how he had fallen ill and presently wasted away to nothing.

It would have been a very affecting tale of long ago even if it had been about a stranger. Haunted and bewildered through the years, longing to know the facts of his birth, Kaoru had prayed that he might one day have a clear explanation. Was it in answer to his prayers that now, without warning, there had come a chance to hear of these old matters, as if in a sad dream? He too was in tears.

"It is hard to believe—and I must admit that it is a little alarming too—that someone who remembers those days should still be with us. I suppose people have been spreading the news to the world—and I have had not a whisper of it."

"No one knew except Kojijū and myself. Neither of us breathed a word to anyone. As you can see, I do not matter; but it was my honor to be always with him, and I began to guess what was happening. Then sometimes—not often, of course—when his feelings were too much for him, one or the other of us would be entrusted with a message. I do not think it would be proper to go into the details. As he lay dying, he left the testament I have spoken of. I have had it with me all these years—I am no one, and where was I to leave it? I have not been as diligent with my prayers as I might have been, but I have asked the Blessed One for a chance to let you know of it; and now I think I have a sign that he is here with us. But the testament: I must show it to you. How can I burn it now? I have not known from one day to the next when I might die, and I have worried about letting it fall into other hands. When you began to visit His Highness I felt somewhat better again. There might be a chance to speak to you. I was not merely praying for the impossible, and so I decided that I must keep what he had left with me. Some power stronger than we has brought us together." Weeping openly now, she told of the illicit affair and of his birth, as the details came back to her.

"In the confusion after the young master's death, my mother too fell ill and died; and so I wore double mourning. A not very nice man who had had his eye on me took advantage of it all and led me off to the West Country, and I lost all touch with the city. He too died, and after ten years and more I was back in the city again, back from a different world. I have for a very long time had the honor to be acquainted indirectly with the sister of my young master, the lady who is a consort of the Reizei emperor, and it would have been natural for me to go into her service. But there were those old complications, and there were other reasons too. Because of the relationship on my father's side of the family[174] I have been familiar with His Highness's household since I was a child, and at my age I am no longer up to facing the world. And so I have become the rotted stump you see,[175] buried away in the mountains. When did Kojijū die? I wonder. There aren't many left of the ones who were young when I was young. The last of them all; it isn't easy to be the last one, but here I am."

Another dawn was breaking.

"We do not seem to have come to the end of this old story of yours," said Kaoru. "Go on with it, please, when we have found a more comfortable place and no one is listening. I do remember Kojijū slightly. I must have been four or five when she came down with consumption and died, rather suddenly. I am most grateful to you. If it hadn't been for you I would have carried the sin[176] to my grave."

The old woman handed him a cloth pouch in which several mildewed bits of paper had been rolled into a tight ball.

"Take these and destroy them. When the young master knew he was dying, he got them together and gave them to me. I told myself I would give them to Kojijū when next I saw her and ask her to be sure that they got to her lady. I never saw her again. And so I had my personal sorrow and the other too, the knowledge that I had not done my duty."

With an attempt at casualness, he put the papers away. He was deeply troubled. Had she told him this unsolicited story, as is the way with the old, because it seemed to her an interesting piece of gossip? She had assured him over and over again that no one else had heard it, and yet—could he really believe her?

After a light breakfast he took his leave of the prince. "Yesterday was a holiday because the emperor was in retreat, but today he will be with us again. And then I must call on the Reizei princess, who is not well, and there will be other things to keep me busy. But I will come again soon, before the autumn leaves have fallen."

"For me, your visits are a light to dispel in some measure the shadows of these mountains."

---

174. Her father was the uncle of the Eighth Prince's wife.

175. Kengei, *Kokinshū*, no. 875: "The form is a rotted stump, in mountains deep; you can, if you try, make the heart come back to life."

176. The sin of not having properly honored his real father.

Back in the city, Kaoru took out the pouch the old woman had given him. The heavy Chinese brocade bore the inscription "For My Lady."[177] It was tied with a delicate thread and sealed with Kashiwagi's name. Trembling, Kaoru opened it. Inside were multi-hued bits of paper, on which, among other things, were five or six answers by his mother to notes from Kashiwagi.

And, on five or six sheets of thick white paper, apparently in Kashiwagi's own hand, like the strange tracks of some bird, was a longer letter: "I am very ill, indeed I am dying. It is impossible to get so much as a note to you, and my longing to see you only increases. Another thing adds to the sorrow: the news that you have withdrawn from the world.

> "Sad are you, who have turned away from the world,
> but sadder still my soul, taking leave of you.

"I have heard with strange pleasure of the birth of the child. We need not worry about him, for he will be reared in security. And yet—

> "Had we but life, we could watch it, ever taller,
> the seedling pine unseen among the rocks."

The writing, fevered and in disarray, went to the very edge of the paper. The letter was addressed to Kojijū.

The pouch had become a dwelling place for worms and smelled strongly of mildew; and yet the writing, in such compromising detail, was as clear as if it had been set down the day before. It would have been a disaster if the letter had fallen into the hands of outsiders, he thought, half in sorrow and half in alarm. He was so haunted by this strange affair, stranger than any the future could possibly bring, that he could not persuade himself to set out for court. Instead he went to visit his mother. Youthful and serene, she had a sutra in her hand, which she put shyly out of sight upon his arrival. He must keep the secret to himself, he thought. It would be cruel to let her know of his own new knowledge. His mind jumped from detail to detail of the story he had heard.

Beneath the Oak

In the Second Month of the following year, Niou goes on a pilgrimage to Hatsuse and stops at Uji, hoping to have an opportunity to pay a call on the princesses, but the size of his entourage prevents him from getting away. Kaoru, who is with him, delivers a note

---

177. It bears the character for "up" or "over" (*ue*). There are several theories as to what it might mean, of which this seems the most credible.

on his behalf. The Eighth Prince urges his daughters to reply, albeit cautiously and casu-
ally, so as not to excite him, and thus Niou begins a correspondence with Nakanokimi,
though he is never sure which of the princesses is responsible for the letters he receives.
At this point, Ōigimi is twenty-five and Nakanokimi is twenty-three.

The prince has reached an age that corresponds to a dangerous year and wishes to
renounce the world but continues to worry about his daughters. In the autumn, Kaoru
visits Uji and promises again to look after the princesses. The Eighth Prince indicates that
he suspects his death is near and speaks to his daughters.

With the deepening of autumn, the prince's gloom also deepened. Concluding that he must withdraw to some quiet refuge where nothing would upset his
devotions, he left behind various admonitions.

"Parting is the way of the world. It cannot be avoided: but the grief is easier
to bear when you have a companion to share it with. I must leave it to your
imagination—for I cannot tell you—how hard it is for me to go off without you,
knowing that you are alone. But it would not do to wander lost in the next world
because of ties with this one. Even while I have been here with you, I have as
good as run away from the world; and it is not for me to say how it should be
when I am gone. But please remember that I am not the only one. You have
your mother to think of too. Please do nothing that might reflect on her name.
Men who are not worthy of you will try to lure you out of these mountains, but
you are not to yield to their blandishments. Resign yourselves to the fact that
it was not meant to be—that you are different from other people and were
meant to be alone—and live out your lives here at Uji. Once you have made up
your minds to it, the years will go smoothly by. It is good for a woman, even
more than for a man, to be away from the world and its slanders."

The princesses were beyond thinking about the future. It was beyond them,
indeed, to think how they would live if they were to survive their father by so
much as a day. These gloomy and ominous instructions left them in the cruel-
est uncertainty. He had in effect renounced the world already, but for them, so
long beside him, to be informed thus suddenly of a final parting—it was not
from intentional cruelty that he had done it, of course, and yet in such cases a
certain resentment is inevitable.

On the evening before his departure he inspected the premises with unusual care, walking here, stopping there. He had thought of this Uji villa as
the most temporary of dwellings, and so the years had gone by. Everything about
him suggesting freedom from worldly taints, he turned to his devotions, and
thoughts of the future slipped in among them from time to time. His daughters
were so very much alone—how could they possibly manage after his death?

He summoned the older women of the household.

"Do what you can for them, as a last favor to me. The world does not pay much
attention when an ordinary house goes to ruin. It happens every day. I don't suppose people pay so very much attention when it happens to one like ours. But if

fate seems to have decided that the collapse is final, a man does feel ashamed, and wonders how he can face his ancestors. Sadness, loneliness—they are what life brings. But when a house is kept in a manner that becomes its rank, the appearances it maintains, the feelings it has for itself, bring their own consolation. Everyone wants luxury and excitement; but you must never, even if everything fails—you must never, I beg of you, let them make unsuitable marriages."

As the moonlight faded in the dawn, he went to take leave of his daughters. "Do not be lonely when I am gone. Be happy, find ways to occupy yourselves. One does not get everything in this world. Do not fret over what has to be."

He looked back and looked back again as he started up the path to the monastery.

The girls were lonely indeed, despite these admonitions. What would the one do if the other were to go away? The world offers no security in any case; and what could they possibly do for themselves if they were separated? Smiling over this small matter, sighing over that rather more troublesome detail, they had always been together.

It was the morning of the day when the prince's meditations were to end. He would be coming home. But in the evening a message came instead: "I have been indisposed since this morning. A cold, perhaps—whatever it is, I am having it looked after. I long more than ever to see you."

The princesses were in consternation. How serious would it be? They hastened to send quilted winter garments. Two and three days passed, and there was no sign of improvement. A messenger came back. The ailment was not of a striking nature, he reported. The prince was generally indisposed. If there should be even the slightest improvement he would brave the discomfort and return home.

The abbot, in constant attendance, sought to sever the last ties with this world. "It may seem like the commonest sort of ailment," he said, "but it could be your last. Why must you go on worrying about your daughters? Each of us has his own destiny, and it does no good to worry about others." He said that the prince was not to leave the temple under any circumstances.

It was about the twentieth of the Eighth Month, a time when the autumn skies are conducive to melancholy in any case. For the princesses, lost in their own sad thoughts, there was no release from the morning and evening mists. The moon was bright in the early-morning sky, the surface of the river was clear and luminous. The shutters facing the mountain were raised. As the princesses gazed out, the sound of the monastery bell came down to them faintly—and, they said, another dawn was upon them.

But then came a messenger, blinded with tears. The prince had died in the night.

Not for a moment had the princesses stopped thinking of him; but this was too much of a shock, it left them dazed. At such times tears refuse to come. Prostrate, they could only wait for the shock to pass. A death is sad when, as is the commoner case, the survivors have a chance to make proper farewells. For the princesses, who did not have their father with them, the sense of loss was even more intense. Their laments would not have seemed excessive if they had wailed to the very heavens. Reluctant to accept the thought of surviving their father by a day, they asked what they were to do now. But he had gone a road that all must take, and weeping did nothing to change that cruel fact.

As had been promised over the years, the abbot arranged for the funeral. The princesses sent word that they would like to see their father again, even in death. And what would be accomplished? replied the holy man. He had trained their father to acceptance of the fact that he would not see them again, and now it was their turn. They must train their hearts to a freedom from binding regrets. As he told of their father's days in the monastery, they found his wisdom somewhat distasteful.

It had long been their father's most fervent wish to take the tonsure, but in the absence of someone to look after his daughters he had been unable to turn his back on them. Day after day, so long as he had lived, this inability had been at the same time the solace of a sad life and the bond that tied him to a world he wished to leave. Neither to him who had now gone the inevitable road nor to them who must remain behind had fulfillment come.

Kaoru and Niou send notes to the princesses, expressing their condolences. Nakanokimi is too distressed to reply. Ōigimi, reflecting on Niou's sophistication, is fearful and permits no response to him. Thinking of her father's last instructions, she resolves to live out her life as a spinster. She replies freely to Kaoru's earnest letters but remains reserved when he visits, somewhat to his annoyance.

Things become even lonelier for the princesses with the coming of winter, and Kaoru calls again, urging Ōigimi to accept Niou as a suitor for Nakanokimi. Genji's son Yūgiri, now minister of the right, hopes to arrange a match between Niou and his daughter Rokunokimi, but Niou does not seem interested. In the summer, Kaoru has an opportunity to spy on the princesses through a small hole in a partition, which further whets his interest.

Trefoil Knots

Kaoru visits Uji again in the fall to assist with the memorial services on the anniversary of the Eighth Prince's death. He indicates to Ōigimi his interest in her and attempts to persuade her to be more friendly. She rebuffs him, citing her father again, but hopes Kaoru will help arrange something for Nakanokimi.

He summoned Bennokimi.

"It was thoughts of the next life that first brought me here; and then, in those last sad days, he left a request with me. He asked me to look after his daughters in whatever way seemed best. I have tried; and now it comes as something of a surprise that they should be disregarding their own father's wishes. Do you understand it any better than I do? I am being pushed to the conclusion that he had hopes for them which they do not share. I know you will have heard about me, what an odd person I am, not much interested in the sort of things that seem to interest everyone else. And now, finally, I have found someone who does interest me, and I am inclined to believe that fate has had a hand in the matter; and I gather that the gossips already have us married. Well, if that is the case—I know it will seem out of place for me to say so—other things being equal, we might as well do as the prince wished us to, and indeed as everyone else does. It would not be the first case the world has seen of a princess married to a commoner.

"And I have spoken more than once about my friend Niou to your other lady. She simply refuses to believe me when I tell her she needn't worry about the sort of husband he is likely to make. I wonder if someone might just possibly be working to turn her against her father's wishes. You must tell me everything you know."

His remarks were punctuated by many a brooding sigh.

There is a kind of cheeky domestic who, in such situations, assumes a knowing manner and encourages a man in what he wants to believe. Bennokimi was not such a one. She thought the match ideal, but she could not say so.

"My ladies are different from others I have served. Perhaps they were born different. They have never been much interested in the usual sort of thing. We who have been in their service—even while their father was alive, we really had no tree to run to for shelter. Most of the other women decided fairly soon that there was no point in wasting their lives in the mountains, and they went away, wherever their family ties led them. Even people whose families had been close to the prince's for years and years—they were not having an easy time of it, and most of them gave up and went away. And now that he is gone it is even worse. We wonder from one minute to the next who will be left. The ones who have stayed are always grumbling, and I am sure that my ladies are often hurt by the things they say. Back in the days when the prince was still with us, they say, well, he had his old-fashioned notions, and they had to be respected for what they were. My ladies were, after all, royal princesses, he was always saying, and there came a point at which a suitor had to be considered beneath them, and that was that; and so they stayed single. But now they are worse than single, they are completely alone in the world, and it would take a very cruel person to find fault if they were to do what everyone else does. And really, could anyone expect them to go through their lives as they are now? Even the monks who wander around gnawing pine needles—even they have their different ways of doing things, without forgetting the Good Law. They cannot deny life itself, after all. I am just telling you what these women say. The older of my ladies refuses to listen to a word of it, at least as it has to do with her; but I gather she does hope that something can be found for her sister, some way to live an ordinary, respectable life. She has watched you climb over these mountains year after year and she knows that not many people would have assumed responsibility as if it were the most natural thing in the world. I really do think that she is ready to talk of the details, and all that matters is what you have in mind yourself. As for Prince Niou, she does not seem to think his letters serious enough to bother answering."

"I have told you of her father's last request. I was much moved by it, and I have vowed to go on seeing them. You might think that, from my point of view, either of your ladies would do as well as the other, and I really am very flattered that she should have such confidence in me. But you know, even a man who doesn't have much use for the things that excite most people will find himself drawn to a lady, and when that happens he does not suddenly go running after another—though that would not be too difficult, I suppose, for the victim of a casual infatuation.

"But no. If only she would stop retreating and putting up walls between us. If only I could have her here in front of me, to talk to about the little things that come and go. If so much did not have to be kept back.

"I am all by myself, and I always have been. I have no brother near enough my own age to talk to about the amusing things and the sad things that happen. You will say that I have a sister, but the things I really want to talk about are always an impossible jumble, and an empress is hardly the person to go to with them. You will think of my mother. It is true that she looks young enough to be my sister, but after all she is my mother. All the others seem so haughty and so far away. They quite intimidate me. And so I am by myself. The smallest little flirtation leaves me dumb and paralyzed; and when it seems that the time has come to show my feelings to someone I really care for, I am not up to the smallest gesture. I may be hurt, I may be furious, and there I stand like a post, knowing perfectly well how ridiculous I am.

"But let us talk of Niou. Don't you suppose that problem could be left to me? I promise that I will do no one any harm."

It would be far better than this lonely life, thought the old woman, wishing she could tell him to go ahead. But they were both so touchy. She thought it best to keep her own counsel.

Kaoru whiled away the time, thinking that he would like to stay the night and perhaps have the quiet talk of which he had spoken. For Ōigimi the situation was next to intolerable. Though he had made it known only by indirection, his resentment seemed to be rising to an alarming pitch. The most trivial answer was almost more than she could muster. If only he would stay away from that one subject! In everything else he was a man of the most remarkable sympathy, a fact that only added to her agitation. She had someone open the doors to the chapel and stir the lamps, and withdrew behind a blind and a screen. There were also lights outside the chapel. He had them taken away—they were very unsettling, he said, for they revealed him in shameful disorder—and lay down near the screen. She had fruit and sweets brought to him, arranged in a tasteful yet casual manner. His men were offered wine and very tempting side dishes. They withdrew to a corridor, leaving the two alone for what they assumed would be a quiet, intimate conversation.

She was in great agitation, but in her manner there was something poignantly appealing that delighted and—a pity that it should have been so—excited him. To be so near, separated from her only by a screen, and to let the time go by with no perceptible sign that the goal was near—it was altogether too stupid. Yet he managed an appearance of calm as he talked on of this amusing event and that melancholy one. There was much to interest her in what he said, but from behind her blinds she called to her women to come nearer. No doubt thinking that chaperones would be out of place, they pretended not to hear, and indeed withdrew yet further as they lay down to rest. There was no one to replenish the lamps before the holy images. Again she called out softly, and no one answered.

"I am not feeling at all well," she said finally, starting for an anteroom. "I think a little sleep might do me good. I hope you sleep well."

"Don't you suppose a man who has fought his way over mountains might feel even worse? But that's all right. Just having you here is enough. Don't go off and leave me."

He quietly pushed the screen aside. She was in precipitous flight through the door beyond.

"So this is what you mean by a friendly talk," she said angrily as he caught at her sleeve. Far from turning him away, her anger added to the fascination. "It is not at all what I would have expected."

"You seem determined not to understand what I mean by friendliness, and so I thought I would show you. Not what you would have expected—and what, may I ask, did you expect? Stop trembling. You have nothing to be afraid of. I am prepared to take my vow before the Blessed One here. I have done everything to avoid upsetting you. No one in the world can have dreamed what an eccentric affair this is. But I am an eccentric and a fool myself, and will no doubt continue to be so."

He stroked the hair that flowed in the wavering light. The softness and the luster were all that he could have asked for. Suppose someone with more active inclinations were to come upon this lonely, unprotected house—there would be nothing to keep him from having his way. Had the visitor been anyone but himself, matters would by now have come to a showdown. His own want of decision suddenly revolted him. Yet here she was, weeping and wringing her hands, quite beside herself. He would have to wait until consent came of its own accord. Distressed at her distress, he sought to comfort her as best he could.

"I have allowed an almost indecent familiarity, and I have had no idea of what was going through your mind; and I may say that you have not shown a great deal of consideration, forcing me to display myself in these unbecoming colors. But I am at fault too. I am not up to what has to be done, and I am sorry for us both." It was too humiliating, that the lamplight should have caught her in somber, shabby gray.

"Yes, I have been inconsiderate, and I am ashamed and sorry. They give you a good excuse, those robes of mourning. But don't you think you might just possibly be making too much of them? You have seen something of me over the years, and I doubt if mourning gives you a right to act as if we had just been introduced. It is clever of you but not altogether convincing."

He told her of the many things he had found it so hard to keep to himself, beginning with that glimpse of the two princesses in the autumn dawn. She was in an agony of embarrassment. So he had had this store of secrets all along, and had managed to feign openness and indifference!

He now pulled a low curtain between them and the altar and lay down beside her. The smell of the holy incense, the particularly strong scent of anise, stabbed at his conscience, for he was more susceptible in matters of belief than most people. He told himself that it would be ill considered in the extreme, now of all times, when she was in mourning, to succumb to temptation; and he would be going against his own wishes if he failed to control himself. He must wait until she had come out of mourning. Then, difficult though she was, there would surely be some slight easing of the tensions.

Autumn nights are sad in the most ordinary of places. How much sadder in wailing mountain tempests, with the calls of insects sounding through the hedges. As he talked on of life's uncertain turns, she occasionally essayed an answer. He was touched and pleased. Her women, who had spread their bedclothes not far away, sensed that a happy arrangement had been struck up and withdrew to inner apartments. She thought of her father's admonitions. Strange and awful things can happen, she saw, to a lady who lives too long. It was as if she were adding her tears to the rushing torrent outside.

The dawn came on, bringing an end to nothing. His men were coughing and clearing their throats, there was a neighing of horses—everything made him think of descriptions he had read of nights on the road. He slid back the door to the east, where dawn was in the sky, and the two of them looked out at the shifting colors. She had come out toward the veranda. The dew on the ferns at the shallow eaves was beginning to catch the light. They would have made a very striking pair, had anyone been there to see them.

"Do you know what I would like? To be as we are now. To look out at the flowers and the moon, and be with you. To spend our days together, talking of things that do not matter."

His manner was so unassertive that her fears had finally left her. "And do you know what I would like? A little privacy. Here I am quite exposed, and a screen might bring us closer."

The sky was red, there was a whirring of wings close by as flocks of birds left their roosts. As if from deep in the night, the matin bells came to them faintly.

"Please go," she said with great earnestness. "It is almost daylight, and I do not want you to see me."

"You can't be telling me to push my way back through the morning mists? What would that suggest to people? No, make it look, if you will, as if we were among the proper married couples of the world, and we can go on being the curiosities we in fact seem to be. I promise you that I will do nothing to upset you; but perhaps I might trouble you to imagine, just a little, how genuine my feelings are."

"If what you say is true," she replied, her agitation growing as it became evident that he was in no hurry to leave, "then I am sure you will have your way in the future. But please, this morning, let me have my way." She had to admit that there was little she could do.

"So you really are going to send me off into the dawn? Knowing that it is 'new to me,'[178] and that I am sure to lose my way?"

The crowing of a cock was like a summons back to the city.

> "The things by which one knows the mountain village
> are brought together in these voices of dawn."

She replied:

> "Deserted mountain depths where no birds sing,
> I would have thought. But sorrow has come to visit."

Seeing her as far as the door to the inner apartments, he returned by the way he had come the evening before, and lay down; but he was not able to sleep. The memories and regrets were too strong. Had his emotions earlier been toward her as they were now, he would not have been as passive over the months. The prospect of going back to the city was too dreary to face.

Ōigimi, in agony at the thought of what her women would have made of it all, found sleep as elusive. A very harsh trial it was, going through life with no one to turn to; and as if that huge uncertainty were not enough, there were these women with all their impossible suggestions. They as good as formed a queue, coming to her with proposals that had nothing to recommend them but the expediency of the moment; and if in a fit of inattention she were to accede to one of them, she would have shame and humiliation to look forward to. Kaoru did not at all displease her. The Eighth Prince had said more than once that if Kaoru should be inclined to ask her hand, he would not disapprove. But no. She wanted to go on as she was. It was her sister, now in the full bloom of youth,

---

178. Probably an allusion.

who must live a normal life. If the prince's thoughts in the matter could be applied to her sister, she herself would do everything she could by way of support. But who was to be her own support? She had only Kaoru, and, strangely, things might have been easier had she found herself in superficial dalliance with an ordinary man. They had known each other for rather a long time, and she might have been tempted to let him have his way. His obvious superiority and his aloofness, coupled with a very low view of herself, had left her prey to shyness. In timid retreat, it seemed, she would end her days.

Ōigimi tries to keep Kaoru at arm's length and even considers offering Nakanokimi as a substitute for herself. One evening Kaoru, with the assistance of the princesses' attendants, intrudes again behind their screens. In a panic, Ōigimi slips out and leaves the sleeping Nakanokimi behind. Kaoru is aware that he is with the other girl but spends the night beside her anyway—he finds her rather attractive. Nakanokimi believes, incorrectly, that her sister had allowed this to happen deliberately and refuses to speak to her. Kaoru decides to resolve the situation by bringing Niou to Nakanokimi at last. Niou is more than willing. Niou sneaks in to Nakanokimi's side, much as Kaoru had done, while Kaoru spends another chaste night with Ōigimi, who is aghast at Kaoru's subterfuge. The young men leave Uji, and Ōigimi convinces Nakanokimi that she had no part in the men's plan. Niou returns each of the next two nights, thus sealing his marriage with Nakanokimi. The younger sister is won over by his charm. Because of his position and the scrutiny his activities receive in the capital, however, he is unable to visit as much as he would like thereafter. His mother and father, the empress and emperor, disapprove of his nocturnal wanderings. They force him to reside in the palace and to marry Yūgiri's daughter Rokunokimi. Niou's heart remains with Nakanokimi, but the princesses are greatly dismayed by rumors of his impending marriage combined with his failure to visit Uji. Kaoru makes plans to bring Ōigimi to the capital, but feeling responsible for leaving her sister prey to Niou's apparent defection, she stops eating and begins wasting away. Kaoru is very concerned and commissions services for her recovery, but to no avail.

He seldom left Ōigimi's bedside, and his presence was a comfort to the women of the house. The wind was so high that Nakanokimi was having trouble with her curtains. When she withdrew to the inner rooms the ugly old women followed in some confusion. Kaoru came nearer and spoke to Ōigimi. There were tears in his voice.

"And how are you feeling? I have lost myself in prayers, and I fear they have done no good at all. It is too much, that you will not even let me hear your voice. You are not to leave me."

Though barely conscious, she was still careful to hide her face. "There are many things I would like to say to you, if I could only get back a little of my strength. But I am afraid—I am sorry—that I must die."

Tears were painfully near. He must not show any sign of despair—but soon he was sobbing audibly. What store of sins had he brought with him from previous lives, he wondered, that, loving her so, he had been rewarded with sorrow and sorrow only, and that he now must say goodbye? If he could find a flaw in her, he might resign himself to what must be. She became the more sadly beautiful the longer he gazed at her, and the more difficult to relinquish. Though her hands and arms were as thin as shadows, the fair skin was still smooth. The bedclothes had been pushed aside. In soft white robes, she was so fragile a figure that one might have taken her for a doll whose voluminous clothes hid the absence of a body. Her hair, not so thick as to be a nuisance, flowed down over her pillow, the luster as it had always been. Must such beauty pass, quite leave this world? The thought was not to be endured. She had not taken care of herself in her long illness, and yet she was far more beautiful than the sort of maiden who, not for a moment unaware that someone might be looking at her, is forever primping and preening. The longer he looked at her, the greater was the anguish.

"If you leave me, I doubt that I will stay on very long myself. I do not expect to survive you, and if by some chance I do, I will wander off into the mountains. The one thing that troubles me is the thought of leaving your sister behind."

He wanted somehow to coax an answer from her. At the mention of her sister, she drew aside her sleeve to reveal a little of her face.

"I am sorry that I have been so out of things. I may have seemed rude in not doing as you have wished. I must die, apparently, and my one hope has been that you might think of her as you have thought of me. I have hinted as much, and had persuaded myself that I could go in peace if you would respect this one wish. My one unsatisfied wish, still tying me to the world."

"There are people who walk under clouds of their own, and I seem to be one of them. No one else, absolutely no one else, has stirred a spark of love in me, and so I have not been able to follow your wishes. I am sorry now; but please do not worry about your sister."

She was in greater distress as the hours went by. He summoned the abbot and others and had incantations read by well-known healers. He lost himself in prayers. Was it to push a man toward renunciation of the world that the Blessed One sent such afflictions? She seemed to be vanishing, fading away like a flower. No longer caring what sort of spectacle he might make, he wanted to shout out his resentment at his own helplessness. Only half in possession of her senses, Nakanokimi sensed that the last moment had come. She clung to the corpse until that forceful old woman, among others, pulled her away. She was only inviting further misfortunes, they said.

Was it a dream? Kaoru had somehow not accepted the possibility that things would come to this pass. Turning up the light, he brought it to the dead lady's face. She lay as if sleeping, her face still hidden by a sleeve, as beautiful as ever. If only he could go on gazing at her as at the shell of a locust. The women combed her hair preparatory to having it cut, and the fragrance that came from it, sad and mysterious, was that of the living girl. He wanted to find a flaw, something to make her seem merely ordinary. If the Blessed One meant by all this to bring renunciation and resignation, then let him present something repellent, to drive away the regrets. So he prayed; but no relief was forthcoming. Well, he said presently, nothing was left but to commit the body to flames, and so he set about the sad duty of making the funeral arrangements. He walked unsteadily beside the body, scarcely feeling the ground beneath his feet. In a daze, he made his way back to the house. Even the last rites had been faltering, insubstantial; very little smoke had risen from the pyre.

Kaoru remains in Uji for some time, lost in grief. Niou receives permission from his mother to bring Nakanokimi to the capital and to install her in the Nijō mansion (which he had inherited from Genji and Murasaki). She moves in the Second Month of the following year. Kaoru wishes he could make Nakanokimi a substitute for her sister and berates himself for having let Niou have her. Niou settles down happily with Nakanokimi, who eventually bears him a son. Plans are made for Kaoru to marry the Second Princess, a daughter of the reigning emperor and half sister of Niou, but he is unenthusiastic about the match, still longing for Ōigimi, and makes advances toward Nakanokimi, who is rather distressed by the finalization of Niou's marriage to Yūgiri's daughter Rokunokimi. Nakanokimi manages to distract Kaoru by telling him about a half sister whom she has just met, the result of the Eighth Prince's affair with one of his attendants. The girl, Ukifune, was never recognized by her father and had been living in the eastern provinces with her mother and stepfather, the governor of Hitachi. Told that she greatly resembles Ōigimi, Kaoru is intrigued. He catches a glimpse of her at the Uji bridge, on her way back from a pilgrimage to Hatsuse and, struck by her similarity to the princesses, resolves to have her.

A Boat upon the Waters

Ukifune's boorish stepfather becomes angered by her mother's partiality to the girl over his own children and disrupts her impending marriage to a guards lieutenant. The mother asks Nakanokimi to take the girl in, and Nakanokimi allows her to hide in the west wing of her house. The girl is shy and somewhat countrified, but Nakanokimi is much moved by her resemblance to Ōigimi. The women of the household attempt to keep her presence there secret from Niou, but the incorrigible prince discovers her and makes advances to her. Nakanokimi's women manage to thwart him, but Ukifune's mother is horrified and moves the girl secretly to another residence. With the assistance of Bennokimi, Kaoru whisks Ukifune off to Uji and leaves her there while he prepares a house for her in the capital.

Niou has been unable to forget the girl, and tries desperately to find out who she is. Eventually he succeeds in intercepting a letter from Ukifune to Nakanokimi and learns that Kaoru has a lady hidden at Uji. He sneaks off to Uji and gains admittance to the girl by pretending to be Kaoru. He notes Ukifune's resemblance to Nakanokimi but is unable to discover her identity. Smitten, he spends two nights with her.

Kaoru, meanwhile, having a brief respite from his duties, set off in his usual quiet way for Uji. He went first to pay his respects and offer a prayer at the monastery. In the evening, after distributing gifts to the monks whom he had put to invoking the holy name, he went on to the Uji villa. Though incognito might have been appropriate, he had made no attempt to hide his rank. In informal but careful court dress, he was the embodiment of calm nobility. How could she possibly receive him? thought Ukifune, in near panic. The very skies seemed to reproach her. The dashing figure of his rival came back to her. Could she see him[179] again? Niou had said that she had every chance of driving all his other ladies away and capturing his affections for herself alone. She had heard that he was ill and had sharply curtailed his affairs, and that his house echoed with services for his recovery. How hurt he would be when he learned of this visit! Kaoru was very different. He had an air as of unsounded depths and a quiet, meditative dignity. He used few words as he apologized for his remissness and he said almost nothing that suggested loneliness and deprivation. Yet he did say, choosing his words most carefully, that he had wanted to see her, and his controlled earnestness moved her more than any number of passionate avowals could have. He was very handsome; but that aside, she was sure that he would be a more reliable support, over long years, than Niou. It would be a great loss if he were to catch word of the strange turn her affections had taken. Niou's improbable behavior had left its mark, and she had to thank him for it; but he was altogether too impetuous. She could expect nothing of an enduring nature from him. She would be very sad indeed if Kaoru were to fling her away in anger.

She was a sad little figure, lost in the turmoil of her thoughts. She had matured, acquired new composure, over the months. No doubt, in the boredom of country life, she had had time for meditation.

"The house I am building is almost finished." His tone was more intimate and affectionate than usual. "I went to see it the other day. The waters are gentle, as different as they can be from this wild river, and the garden has all the flowers of the city. It is very near my Sanjō place. Nothing need keep us from seeing each other every day. I'd like to move you there in the spring, I think, if you don't mind."

Niou could scarcely have known of his friend's plans when, in a letter the day before, he had spoken of finding a quiet place for her. She was very sorry, but she should not yield further, she knew, to his advances. And yet his image did keep floating before her eyes. What a wretched predicament to be in!

"Life was much easier and much pleasanter," said Kaoru, "back in the days when you were not quite so given to tears. Has someone been talking about me? Would a person in my position come over such a long and difficult road if he had less than the best intentions?"

---

179. The antecedent could be either Kaoru or Niou.

He went to the veranda railing and sat gazing at the new moon. They were both lost in thoughts, he of the past, of days and people now gone, she of the future and her growing troubles. The scene was perfection: the hills were veiled in a mist, and crested herons had gathered at a point along the frozen strand. Far down the river, where the Uji bridge cut its dim arc, faggot-laden boats were weaving in and out. All the details peculiar to the place were brought together. When he looked out upon the scene it was always as if events of old were fresh before his eyes. Even had he been with someone for whom he cared nothing, the air of Uji would have brought on strange feelings of intimacy. How much more so in the company of a not unworthy substitute for Ōigimi. Ukifune was gaining all the while in assurance and discernment, in her awareness of how city people behaved, and she was more beautiful each time he saw her. At a loss to console her, for it seemed that her tears were about to spill over, he offered a poem:

> "No need to grieve. The Uji bridge stands firm.
> They too stand firm, the promises I have made you.

"I am sure that you know what I mean."
She replied:

> "The bridge has gaps, one crosses gingerly.
> Can one be sure it will not rot away?"

He found it more difficult than ever to leave her. But people talked, and he would have his fill of her company once he had moved her to the city. He left at dawn. These evidences of improvement added to the sorrow of parting.

Toward the middle of the Second Month the court assembled to compose Chinese poetry. Both Niou and Kaoru were present. The music was appropriate to the season, and Niou was in fine voice as he sang "A Branch of Plum."[180] Yes, he was the most accomplished of them all, everyone said. His one failing, not an easy one to forgive, was a tendency to lose himself in amorous dalliance of an unworthy sort.

It began to snow and a wind had come up. The festivities were quickly halted and everyone withdrew to Niou's rooms, where a light repast was served. Kaoru was called out to receive a message. The snow, now deeper, was dimly lit by the stars. The fragrance which he sent back into the room made one think how uselessly "the darkness of the spring night" was laboring to blot it out.[181]

---

180. *Saibara* is a type of popular song.

181. Oshikōchi no Mitsune, *Kokinshū*, no. 41: "The darkness of the spring nights may hide their colors, but can the scent of the plum blossoms be hidden too?"

"Does she await me?"[182] he said to himself, able somehow to infuse even such tiny, disjointed fragments of poetry with sudden life.

Of all the poems he could have picked, thought Niou. His heart racing, he pretended to be asleep. Clearly his friend's feelings for Ukifune passed the ordinary. He had hoped that the lady at the bridge had spread her cloak for him alone, and it was sad and annoying that Kaoru should have similar hopes. Drawn to such a man, could the girl possibly shift her affections to a trifler like himself?

The next day, with snow drifted high outside, the courtiers appeared in the imperial presence to read their poems. Niou was very handsome, indeed at his youthful best. Kaoru, perhaps because he was two or three years older, seemed the calmer and more mature of the two, the model of the personable, cultivated young aristocrat. Everyone agreed that the emperor could not have found a better son-in-law. He had unusual literary abilities and a good head for practical matters as well. Their poems read, the courtiers withdrew. The assembly was loud in proclaiming the superiority of Niou's, but he was not pleased. How easygoing they were, he said to himself, how fortunate to have room in their heads for such trivia.

Some days later, unsettled still at Kaoru's behavior that snowy evening, Niou made elaborate excuses and set out for Uji. In the capital only traces of snow remained, as if awaiting a companion,[183] but in the mountains the drifts were gradually deeper. The road was even more difficult than he had remembered it. His men were near tears from apprehension and fatigue. The secretary who had been his guide to Uji was also vice-minister of rites. Both positions carried heavy responsibilities, and it was ridiculous to see him hitching up his trousers like any ordinary foot soldier.

The people at Uji had been warned, but were sure that he would not brave the snow. Then, late in the night, word was brought in to Ukon of his arrival. So he really was fond of her, thought Ukifune. Ukon's worries—how would it all end? she had been asking herself—dropped away, at least for the night. There was no way of turning him back, and she concluded that someone else must now be made a partner in the conspiracy. She chose the woman Jijū, who was another of Ukifune's special favorites, and who could be trusted not to talk.

"It is most improper, I know," said Ukon, "but we must stand together and keep it from the others."

They led him inside. The perfume from his wet robes, flooding into the deepest corners of the hall, could have been troublesome; but they told everyone, convincingly enough, that their visitor was Kaoru. To go back before dawn would be worse than not to have come at all; yet someone was certain to spy

---

182. Anonymous, *Kokinshū*, no. 689: "Cloak spread for lonely sleep, does she await me, the lady at the Uji Bridge tonight?"

183. Ki no Tsurayuki, *Gosenshū*, no. 472: "Black was my hair, and now it is white and whiter, like snows that wait for their comrades to return."

him out in the morning light. He had therefore asked Tokikata to have a certain house beyond the river made ready. Tokikata, who had gone on ahead to see to the arrangements, returned late in the night and reported that everything was in the best of order. Ukon too was wondering how he meant to keep the escapade a secret. She had been awakened from deep slumber and she was trembling like a child lost in the snow.

Without a word, he took Ukifune up in his arms and carried her off. Jijū followed after and Ukon was left to watch the house. Soon they were aboard one of the boats that had seemed so fragile out on the river. As they rowed into the stream, she clung to Niou, frightened as an exile to some hopelessly distant shore. He was delighted. The moon in the early-morning sky shone cloudless upon the waters. They were at the Islet of the Oranges,[184] said the boatman, pulling up at a large rock over which evergreens trailed long branches.

"See," said Niou, "they are fragile pines, no more, but their green is so rich and deep that it lasts a thousand years.

> "A thousand years may pass, it will not waver,
> this vow I make in the lee of the Islet of Oranges."

What a very strange place to be, thought the girl.

> "The colors remain, here on the Islet of Oranges.
> But where go I, a boat upon the waters?"

The time was right, and so was the girl, and so was her poem: for him, at least, things could not have been more pleasingly arranged.

They reached the far bank of the river. An attendant helped him ashore, the girl still in his arms. No one else was to touch her, he insisted.

The custodian of the house was wondering what sort of woman could have produced such an uncourtly uproar. It was a temporary house, rough and unfinished, which Tokikata's uncle, the governor of Inaba, had put up on one of his manors. Crude plaited screens such as Niou had not seen before offered almost no resistance to the wind. There were patches of snow at the fence, clouds had come up, bringing new flurries of snow, and icicles glistened at the eaves. In the daylight the girl seemed even prettier than by candlelight. Niou was dressed simply, against the rigors of the journey. A fragile little figure sat huddled before him, for he had slipped off her outer robe. And so here she was, she said to herself, not even properly dressed, before a royal prince. There was nothing, nothing at all, to protect her from his gaze. She was wearing five or six white singlets, somewhat rumpled, soft and lustrous to the hems of the sleeves and skirts, more

---

184. Tachibana no Kojima.

pleasing, he thought, than any number of colors piled one upon another. He seldom saw women with whom he kept constant company in quite such informal dress. He was enchanted.

And so Jijū too (a pretty young woman) was witness to the scene. Who might she be? Niou had asked when he saw her climbing uninvited into the boat. She must not be told his name. Jijū, for her part, was dazzled. She had not been in the company of such a fine gentleman before.

The custodian made a great fuss over Tokikata, thinking him to be the leader of the party. Tokikata, who had appropriated the next room for himself, was in good form. He made an amusing game of evading the questions the custodian kept putting in reverent tones.

"There have been bad omens, very bad, and I must stay away from the city for a while. No one is to see me."

And so Niou and Ukifune passed pleasant hours with no fear of being observed. No doubt, thought Niou, once more in the clutches of jealousy, she was equally amiable when she received Kaoru. He let it be known that Kaoru had taken the emperor's own daughter for his bride and seemed devoted to her. He declined (let us say out of charity) to mention the snatch of poetry he had overheard that snowy evening.

"You seem to be cock of the walk," he said when Tokikata came with towels and refreshments. "But keep out of sight while you're about it. Someone might want to imitate you."

Jijū, a susceptible young lady, was having such a good time. She spent the whole day with Tokikata.

Looking toward the city over the drifting snow, Niou saw forests emerging from and sinking back into the clouds. The mountain above caught the evening glow as in a mirror. He described, with some embroidering, the horror of last night's journey. A crude rustic inkstone having been brought to him, he set down a poem as if in practice:

> "I pushed through snowy peaks, past icy shores,
> dauntless all the way—O daunting one!

"It is true, of course, that I had a horse at Kohata."[185]
In her answering poem she ventured an objection:[186]

> "The snow that blows to the shore remains there, frozen.
> Yet worse my fate: I am caught, dissolve in midair."

---

185. *Man'yōshū*, no. 2425, from the *Hitomaro Collection*: "A horse I might have had, to cross Kohata. But love would not let me wait. I have come on foot."

186. Unclear. Perhaps she inks out his poem or, immediately after having written it, her own.

This image of fading in midair rather annoyed him. Yes, she was being difficult, she had to agree, tearing the paper to bits. He was always charming, and he was quite irresistible when he was trying to please.

He had said that he would be in retreat for two days. Each unhurried hour seemed to bring new intimacy. The clever Ukon contrived pretexts for sending over fresh clothes. Jijū smoothed her mistress's hair and helped her into a robe of deep purple and a cloak of figured magenta lined also with magenta—an unexceptionable combination. Taking up Jijū's apron,[187] he had Ukifune try it on as she ladled water for him. Yes, his sister the First Princess would be very pleased to take such a girl into her service. Her ladies-in-waiting were numerous and wellborn, but he could think of none among them capable of putting the girl to shame.

But let us not look in too closely upon their dalliance.

He told her again and again how he wanted to hide her away, and he tried to extract unreasonable promises from her. "You are not to see him, understand, until everything is arranged."

That was too much to ask of her. She shed a few silent tears. He, for his part, was almost strangled with jealousy. Even now she was unable to forget Kaoru! He talked on and on, now weeping, now reproaching her.

Late in the night, again in a warm embrace, they started back across the river.

"I doubt if the man to whom you seem to give the top ranking can be expected to treat you as well. You will know what I mean, I trust."

It was true, she thought, nodding. He was delighted.

Ukon opened the side door and the girl went in, and he was left feeling utterly desolate.

As usual after such expeditions, he returned to Nijō. His appetite quite left him and he grew paler and thinner by the day, to the consternation of the whole court. In the stir that ensued he was unable to get a decent letter off to Uji.

That officious nurse of Ukifune's had been with her daughter, who was in confinement; but now that she was back Ukifune was scarcely able to glance at such letters as did come. Her mother hated having her off in the wilderness, but consoled herself with the thought that Kaoru would make a dependable patron and guardian. The indications were that he would soon, albeit in secret, move her to a place near his Sanjō mansion. Then they would be able to look the world square in the face! The mother began seeking out accomplished serving women and pretty little girls and sending them off to her daughter. All this was as it should be, Ukifune knew; yet the image of the dashing, impetuous Niou, now reproaching her, now wheedling and cajoling, insisted upon coming back.

---

187. *Shibira* is an overgarment of some kind. He is treating her like an underling to see how she might perform in the service of his sister.

When she dozed off for a moment, there he would be in her dreams. How much easier for everyone if he would go away!

The rains continued, day after day. Chafing at his inability to travel that mountain road, Niou thought how constricting was "the cocoon one's parents weave about one"[188]—and that was scarcely a kind way to characterize the concern his royal parents felt for him. He sent off a long letter in which he set down his thoughts as they came to him.

> "I gaze your way in search of the clouds above you.
> I see but darkness, so dreary these days of rain."

His hand was if anything more interesting the less care he took with it. She was still young and rather flighty, and these avowals of love set up increasingly strong tremors in response. Yet she could not forget the other gentleman, a gentleman of undoubted depth and nobility, perhaps because it was he who had first made her feel wanted. Where would she turn if he were to hear of this sordid affair and abandon her? And her mother, who lived for the day when he would give her a home, would certainly be upset, and very angry too. Prince Niou, judging from his letters, burned with impatience; but she had heard a great deal about his volatility and feared that his fondness for her was a matter of the passing moment. Supposing he were indeed to hide her away and number her among his enduring loves—how could she then face Nakanokimi, her own sister? The world kept no secrets, as his success in searching her out after that strange, fleeting encounter in the dusk had demonstrated. Kaoru might bring her into the city, but was it possible that his rival would fail to seek her out there too? And if Kaoru were to turn against her, she knew that she would have herself to blame.

Both men make plans to bring Ukifune to the capital. Eventually Kaoru learns that Niou has been writing to Ukifune, and he hints to her that he knows. Ukifune is in an agony of indecision. Although excited by Niou's ardor, she feels she owes allegiance to Kaoru. Eventually Niou, frustrated that she has stopped writing to him, rushes off to Uji and attempts to see her. Her women refuse to admit him.

Ashamed of her swollen eyes, she was late in arising the next morning. She put her dress in a semblance of order and took up a sutra. Let my sin be light, she prayed, for going ahead of my mother. She took out the sketch Niou had made for her, and there he was beside her again, handsome, confident, courtly. The sorrow was more intense, she was sure, than if she had seen him the night before. And she was sad too for the other gentleman, the one who had vowed

---

188. Kakinomoto no Hitomaro, *Shūishū*, no. 895: "How tight the cocoon one's parents weave about one. Its prisoner, I may not see my love."

unshakable fidelity, who had said that they would go off to some place of quiet retirement. To be laughed at, called a shallow, frivolous little wench, would be worse than to die and bring sorrow to such an estimable gentleman.

> "If in torment I cast myself away,
> my sullied name will drift on after me."

She longed to see her mother again, and even her ill-favored brothers and sisters, who were seldom on her mind. And she thought of Nakanokimi. Suddenly, indeed, the people she would like to see once more seemed to form in troops and battalions. Her women, caught up in preparations for the move, dyeing new robes and the like, would pass by with this and that remark, but she paid no attention. She sat up through the night, ill and half distraught, wondering how she might steal into the darkness unobserved. Looking out over the river in the morning, she felt nearer death than a lamb on its way to the slaughter.

A note came from Niou, telling once more of his unhappiness. Not wishing to compromise herself at this very late date, she sent back only a poem:

> "Should I leave no trace behind in this gloomy world,
> what target then would you have for your complaints?"

She wanted also to tell Kaoru of her last hours; but the two men were very close friends and the thought of their comparing notes revolted her. It would be better to speak openly of her decision to neither.

A letter came from her mother: "I had a most ominous dream of you last night, and am having scriptures read in several temples. Perhaps because I had trouble getting back to sleep, I have been napping today, and I have had another dream, equally frightening. I waste no time, therefore, in getting off this letter. Do be careful. You are so far away from all of us, the wife of the gentleman who visits you is a disturbingly strong-minded lady, and it worries me terribly that I should have had such a dream at a time when you are not well. I really am very worried. I would like to visit you, but your sister goes on having a difficult time of it. We wonder if she might be in the clutches of some evil spirit, and I have the strictest orders from the governor not to leave the house for a moment. Have scriptures read in your monastery there, please, if you will."

With the letter were offerings of cloth and a request to the abbot that sutras be read. How sad, thought the girl, that her mother should go to such trouble when it was already too late. She composed her answer while the messenger was off at the monastery. Though there was a great deal that she would have liked to say, she set down only this poem:

> "We shall think of meeting in another world
> and not confuse ourselves with dreams of this."

She lay listening to the monastery bells as they rang an accompaniment to the sutras, and wrote down another poem, this one at the end of the list that had come back from the monastery of the sutras to be read:

> "Join my sobs to the fading toll of the bell,
> to let her know that the end of my life has come."

The messenger had decided not to return that night. She tied her last poem to a tree in the garden.

"Here I am having palpitations," said Nurse, "and she says she's been having bad dreams. Tell the guards to be extra careful. Why will you not have something to eat? Come, a cup of this nice gruel."

Do please be quiet, Ukifune was thinking. The woman was still alert and perceptive enough, but she was old and hideously wrinkled. Yet another one who should have been allowed to die first—and where would she go now? Ukifune wanted to offer at least a hint of what was about to happen, but she knew that the old woman would shoot bolt upright and begin shrieking to the heavens.

"When you let your worries get the best of you," sighed Ukon, asking to lie down near her mistress, "they say your soul sometimes leaves your body and goes wandering. I imagine that's why she has these dreams. Please, my lady, I ask you again: make up your mind one way or the other, and call it fate, whatever happens."

The girl lay in silence, her soft sleeve pressed to her face.

Ukifune disappears, and the Uji house is in chaos. The women discover her note to her mother and realize what she has done. They inform everyone that she died in the night and hold a hasty funeral for her. Kaoru, Niou, and the girl's mother all grieve.

At Writing Practice

The bishop of Yokawa, on Mount Hiei, a holy and learned man, had a mother some eighty years old and a sister in her fifties. In fulfillment of a vow made long ago, they had been on a pilgrimage to Hatsuse. The bishop's favorite disciple had been with them. Having finished their prayers and offered up images and scriptures, they were climbing the Nara Slope on the return journey when the old woman was taken ill. She was in such discomfort that they could not ask her to go on. What were they to do? An acquaintance had a house at Uji, and it was decided to stop there for a day or two. When the old woman failed to improve, word was sent to the bishop. He had determined to remain in his mountain retreat until the end of the year, not even venturing down to the city, but. there seemed a danger that his mother, of such an age that she could go at any time, might die on the journey. He hurried to her side. He himself and certain of his disciples whose ministrations had on other occasions been successful set about prayers and incantations—though one might have told them, and they would not have denied it, that she had lived a long enough life already.

The Uji acquaintance was troubled. "I have plans for a pilgrimage to Mitake, and for a week now I have been fasting and otherwise getting ready. Can I risk having a very old and ailing lady in the house?"

The bishop understood, and the house was in any case small and shabby. They would proceed back toward Hiei by easy stages. Then it was discovered that the stars were against them, and that plan too had to be abandoned. The bishop remembered the Uji villa of the late Suzaku emperor. It would be in the vicinity, and he knew the steward. He sent to ask whether they might use it for a day or two.

The messenger came back to report that the steward and his family had left for Hatsuse the day before.

The caretaker, a most unkempt old man, came with him. "Yes, if it suits your convenience, do please come immediately. The main hall is vacant. Pilgrims are always using it."

"Splendid." The bishop sent someone to make an inspection. "It is a public building, you might say, but it should be quiet enough."

The caretaker, used to guests, had simple accommodations ready.

The bishop went first. The house was badly run-down and even a little frightening. He ordered sutras read. The disciple who had been to Hatsuse and another of comparable rank had lesser clerics, to whom such tasks came naturally, prepare torches. For no very good reason, they wandered around to the unfrequented rear of the main hall. Under a grove of some description, a bleak, forbidding place, they saw an expanse of white. What could it possibly be? They brought their torches nearer and made out a seated human figure.

"A fox? They do sometimes take human shapes, filthy creatures. If we don't make it come out I don't know who else will." One of the lesser monks stepped forward.

"Careful, careful," said another. "We can be sure it's up to no good." Not letting his eyes wander for an instant from the thing, he made motions with his hands toward exorcising it.

The bishop's favored disciple was sure that his hair would have been standing on end if he had had any. The bold torchbearer, however, advanced resolutely upon the figure. It was a girl with long, lustrous hair. Leaning against the thick and very gnarled root of a tree, she was weeping bitterly.

"Why, this is strange. Maybe we should tell the bishop."

"Very strange indeed," said another, running off to report the discovery.

"People are always talking about foxes in human form," said the bishop, "but do you know I have never seen one?" He came out for a look.

All the available domestics were at work in the kitchen and elsewhere, seeing to the needs of the unexpected guests. These postern regions were deserted save for the half-dozen men watching the thing. No change was to be detected in it. The hours passed, the night seemed endless. Daylight would tell them whether or not it was human, thought the bishop, silently going over appropriate spells, and seeking to quell whatever force it might be with mystic hand motions.

Presently he reached a conclusion. "It is human. It is no monstrous apparition. Go ask her who she is and why she is here. Don't be afraid. She is no ghost—though possibly a corpse thrown away hereabouts has come back to life."

"A corpse thrown away at the Suzaku emperor's own villa? No, Your Reverence. At the very least it is someone a fox spirit or a wood spirit or something of the sort has coaxed away from home and then abandoned. The place will be contaminated, and for our purposes the timing could hardly be worse."

Someone called for the caretaker, and the summons echoed menacingly across the empty grounds. He came running out, a somewhat ludicrous figure with his cap perched high on his head.

"Do you have any young women living here? Look at this, if you will."

"Ah, yes. The foxes are at it again. Strange things are always turning up under this tree. Two years or so ago, in the fall it would have been, a little boy, maybe two years old, he lived up the road. They dragged him off and left him right here at the foot of this tree. It happens all the time." He did not seem in the least upset.

"Had the child been killed?"

"Oh, no. He's still alive, I'd imagine. Foxes are always after people, but they never do anything really bad." His manner suggested that such occurrences were indeed commonplace. The emergency domestic arrangements seemed to weigh more heavily on his mind.

"Suppose we watch for a while," said the bishop, "and see whether or not we observe foxes at work."

He ordered the brave torchbearer to approach and challenge the strange figure.

"Who are you? Tell us who you are. Devil, fox, god, wood spirit? Don't think you can hold out against His Reverence. He won't be cheated. Who are you? Come on, now, tell us who you are."

He tugged at a sleeve. The girl pressed it to her face and wept all the more bitterly.

"Come on, now. The sensible thing would be to tell us." He tugged more assertively, though he rather hoped he would not be permitted a view of the face. It might prove to be the hideous mask of the eyeless, noseless she-devil[189] he had heard about. But he must give no one reason to doubt his mettle. The figure lay face in arms, sobbing audibly now.

---

189. *Meoni* has been taken by some commentators to mean not "she-devil" but the homophonous "eye-devil." According to medieval commentaries, an eyeless and noseless monster lived on Mount Hiei, to which the brave torchbearer has come.

"Whatever it is, it's not the sort of thing you see just every day." He peered down at the figure. "But we're in for a storm.[190] She'll die if we leave her out in it, that's for sure. Let's move her in under the fence."

"She has all the proper limbs," said the bishop, "and every detail suggests that she is human. We cannot leave her to die before our eyes. It is sad when the fish that swim in the lake or the stag that bays in the hills must die for want of help. Life is fleeting. We must cherish what we have of it, even so little as a day or two. She may have fallen into the clutches of some minor god or devil, or been driven from home, a victim of foul conspiracy. It may be her fate to die an unkind death. But such, even such, are they whom the Blessed One will save. Let us have a try at medicines and seek to revive her. If we fail, we shall still have done our best."

He had the torchbearer carry her inside.

"Consider what you are doing, sir," objected one of the disciples. "Your honored mother is dangerously ill and this will do her no good."

"We do not know what it is," replied another, "but we cannot leave it here for the rain to pound to death."

It would be best not to let the servants know. The girl was put to bed in a remote and untenanted part of the hall.

The old nun's carriage was brought up, amid chatter about the stubbornness of her affliction.

"And how is the other?" asked the bishop when the excitement had somewhat subsided.

"She seems to have lost her very last ounce of strength—sometimes we wonder if she is still breathing—and she has not said a word. Something has robbed her of her faculties."

"What is this?" asked the younger nun, the bishop's sister.

"Not in my upward of six decades have I seen anything so odd." And the bishop described it.

"I had a dream at Hatsuse." The nun was in tears. "What is she like? Do let me see her."

"Yes, by all means. You will find her over beyond the east door."

The nun hurried off. No one was with the girl, who was young and pretty and indefinably elegant. The white damask over her scarlet trousers gave off a subtle perfume.

"My child, my child. I wept for you, and you have come back to me."

She had some women carry the girl to an inner room. Not having witnessed the earlier events, they performed the task equably.

The girl looked up through half-closed eyes.

---

190. There is mention in the preceding chapter of a heavy rain on the day after Ukifune's disappearance.

She did not seem to understand. The nun forced medicine upon her, but she seemed on the point of fading away.

They must not let her die after she had been through so much. The nun called for the monk who had shown himself to be the most capable in such matters. "I am afraid that she is not far from death. Let her have all your best spells and prayers."

"I was right in the first place," he grumbled. "He should have let well enough alone." But he commenced reading the sutra for propitiating the local gods.

"How is she?" The bishop looked in. "Find out what it is that has been at her. Drive it away, drive it away."

"She will not live, sir, I am sure of it. And when she dies we'll be in for a retreat we could perfectly well have avoided. She seems to be of good rank, and we can't just run away from the corpse. A bother, that is what I call it."

"You do talk a great deal," said the nun. "But you are not to tell anyone. If you do you can expect an even worse bother." She had almost forgotten her mother in the struggle to save the girl. Yes, she was a stranger, nothing to them, if they would have it so; but she was a very pretty stranger. Everyone who saw her joined in prayers that she be spared. Occasionally she would open her eyes, and there would be tears in them.

"What am I to do? The Blessed One has brought you in place of the child I have wept for, I am sure of it, and if you go too, I shall have to weep again. Something from another life has brought us together. I know that too. Speak to me. Please. Say something, anything."

"I have been thrown out. I have nowhere to go." The girl barely managed a whisper. "Don't let anyone see me. Take me out when it gets dark and throw me back in the river."

"She has spoken to me! But what a terrible thing to say. Why must you say such things? And why were you out there all by yourself?"

The girl did not answer. The nun examined her for wounds, but found none. Such a pretty little thing—but there was a certain apprehension mingled with the pity and sorrow. Might a strange apparition have been dispatched to tempt her, to challenge her calm?

The party remained in seclusion for two days, during which prayers and incantations went on without pause. Everyone was asking who this unusual person might be.

Certain farmers in the neighborhood who had once been in the service of the bishop came to pay their respects.

"There has been a big commotion over at the prince's place," one of them remarked by way of apology. "The General of the Right was seeing the prince's daughter, and then all of a sudden she died, of no sickness at all that anyone could see. We couldn't come yesterday evening when we heard Your Reverence was here. We had to help with the funeral."

So that was it. Some demon had abducted the Eighth Prince's daughter. It scarcely seemed to the bishop that he had been looking at a live human being. There was something sinister about the girl, as if she might at any moment dissolve into thin air.

"The fire last night hardly seemed big enough for a funeral."

"No, it wasn't much to look at. They made it as small as they could." The visitors had been asked to remain outside lest they communicate the defilement.

"But who might it be? The prince's daughter, you say—but the princess the general was fond of has been dead for some years. He has another princess now, and he is not the sort to go out looking for new wives."

The old nun was better and the stars no longer blocked the way. Everything that had happened made them want to leave these inhospitable precincts as soon as possible.

"But the young lady is still very weak," someone objected. "Do you really think she can travel?"

They had two carriages. The old nun and two others were in the first and the girl was in the second, with an attendant.[191] They moved at an easy pace with frequent stops. The nuns were from Ono, at the west foot of Mount Hiei. It was very late when they arrived, so exhausted that they regretted not having spent another night along the way. The bishop helped his mother out. With many pauses, the younger nun led the girl into the nunnery. It was a sore trial to have lived so long, the old nun, near collapse, was no doubt saying to herself. The bishop waited until she had recovered somewhat and made his way back up the mountain. Because it had not been proper company for a cleric to find himself in, he kept the story to himself. The younger nun, his sister, also enjoined silence, and was very uneasy lest someone come inquiring after the girl. Why should they have found her all alone in such an unlikely place? Had a malicious stepmother taken advantage of an illness in the course of a pilgrimage, perhaps, and left her by the wayside? "Throw me back in the river," she had said, and there had been not a word from her since. The nun was deeply troubled. She did so want to see the girl restored to health, but the girl did not seem up to the smallest effort in her own behalf. Perhaps it was, after all, a hopeless case—but the very thought of giving up brought a new access of sorrow. Secretly requesting the presence of the disciple who had offered up the first prayers, the nun told of her dream at Hatsuse and asked that ritual fires be lighted.

And so the Fourth and Fifth months passed. Concluding sadly that her labors had been useless, the nun sent off a pleading letter to her brother: "May I ask that you come down and see what you can do for her? I tell myself that if she had been fated to die she would not have lived this long; and yet whatever has taken possession of her refuses to be dislodged. I would not dream, my sainted brother, of asking that you set foot in the city; but surely it will do you no harm to come this far."

---

191. The commentators are agreed that the bishop's sister is in the second carriage.

All very curious, thought the bishop. The girl seemed destined to live—in that matter he had to agree with his sister. And what then would have happened if they had left her at Uji? All that could be affirmed was that a legacy from former lives had dictated a certain course of events. He must do what he could, and if then she died, he could only conclude that her destiny had worked itself out.

Overjoyed to see him, the nun told of all that happened over the months. "A long illness generally shows itself on a person's face; but she is as fresh and pretty as ever she was." She was weeping copiously. "So very many times she has seemed on the point of death, and still she has lived on."

"You are right." He looked down at the girl. "She is very pretty indeed. I did think all along that there was something unusual about her. Well, let's see what we can do. She brought a store of grace with her from other lives, we can be sure of that. I wonder what miscalculation might have reduced her to this. Has anything come to you that might offer a clue?"

"She has not said a word. Our Lady of Hatsuse brought her to me."

"Everything has its cause. Something in another life brought her to you."

Still deeply perplexed, he began his prayers. He had imposed upon himself so strict a regimen that he refused to emerge from the mountains even on royal command, and it would not do to be found in ministrations for which there was no very compelling reason.

He told his disciples of his doubts. "You must say nothing to anyone. I am a dissolute monk who has broken his vows over and over again, but not once have I sullied myself with a woman. Ah, well. Some people reveal their predilections when they are past sixty, and if I prove to be one of them, I shall call it fate."

"Oh, consider for a moment, Your Reverence." His disciples were more upset than he was. "Think what harm you would be doing the Good Law if you were to let ignorant oafs spread rumors."

Steeling himself for the trials ahead, the bishop committed himself silently to vows extreme even for him. He must not fail. All through the night he was lost in spells and incantations, and at dawn the malign spirit in possession of the girl transferred itself to a medium.

Assisted now by his favorite disciple, the bishop tried all manner of spells toward identifying the source of the trouble; and finally the spirit, hidden for so long, was forced to announce itself.

"You think it is this I have come for?" it shouted. "No, no. I was once a monk myself, and I obeyed all the rules; but I took away a grudge that kept me tied to the world, and I wandered here and wandered there, and found a house full of beautiful girls. One of them died, and this one wanted to die too. She said so, every day and every night. I saw my chance and took hold of her one dark night when she was alone. But Our Lady of Hatsuse was on her side through it all, and now I have lost out to His Reverence. I shall leave you."[192]

---

192. It is not that the possession caused Ukifune's unhappiness but that the unhappiness gave the possessing spirit its opportunity.

"Who is that addressing us?"

But the medium was tiring rapidly and no more information was forthcoming.

The girl was now resting comfortably. Though not yet fully conscious, she looked up and saw ugly, twisted old people, none of whom she recognized. She was assailed by intense loneliness, like a castaway on a foreign shore. Vague, ill-formed images floated up from the past, but she could not remember where she had lived or who she was. She had reached the end of the way, and she had flung herself in—but where was she now? She thought and thought, and was aware of terrible sorrows. Everyone had been asleep, she had opened the corner doors and gone out. The wind was high and the waters were roaring savagely. She sat trembling on the veranda. What should she do? Where was she to go now? To go back inside would be to rob everything of meaning. She must destroy herself. "Come, evil spirits, devour me. Do not leave me to be discovered alive." As she sat hunched against the veranda, her mind in a turmoil, a very handsome man came up and announced that she was to go with him, and (she seemed to remember) took her in his arms. It would be Prince Niou, she said to herself.

And what had happened then? He carried her to a very strange place and disappeared. She remembered weeping bitterly at her failure to keep her resolve, and she could remember nothing more. Judging from what these people were saying, many days had passed. What a sodden heap she must have been when they found her! Why had she been forced against her wishes to live on?

She had eaten little through the long trance, and now she would not take even a drop of medicine.

"You do seem bent on destroying all my hopes," said the younger nun, the bishop's sister, not for a moment leaving her side. "Just when I was beginning to think the worst might be over. Your temperature has gone down—you were running a fever all those weeks—and you seemed a little more yourself."

Everyone in the house was delighted with her and quite unconditionally at her service. What happiness for them all that they had rescued her! The girl wanted to die; but the indications were that life had a stubborn hold on her. She began to take a little nourishment. Strangely, she continued to lose weight.

"Please let me be one of you," she said to the nun, who was ecstatic at the prospect of a full recovery. "Then I can go on living. But not otherwise."

"But you are so young and so pretty. How could you possibly want to become a nun?"

The bishop administered token orders, cutting a lock of hair and enjoining obedience to the five commandments.[193] Though she was not satisfied with these half measures, she was an unassertive girl and she could not bring herself to ask more.

---

193. Against killing, stealing, wantonness, deceit, and drunkenness.

"We shall go no further at the moment," said the bishop, leaving for his mountain cell. "Do take care of yourself. Get your strength back."

For his sister, these events were like a dream. She urged the girl to her feet and dressed her hair, surprisingly untangled after months of neglect, and fresh and lustrous once it had been combed out its full length. In this companionship of ladies "but one year short of a hundred,"[194] she was like an angel that had wandered down from the heavens and might choose at any moment to return.

"You do seem so cool and distant," said the nun. "Have you no idea what you mean to me? Who are you, where are you from, why were you there?"

"I don't remember," the girl answered softly. "Everything seems to have left me. It was all so strange. I just don't remember. I sat out near the veranda every evening, that I do half remember. I kept looking out, and wishing I could go away. A man came from a huge tree just in front of me, and I rather think he took me off. And that is all I remember. I don't even know my name." There were tears in her eyes. "Don't let anyone know I am still alive. Please. That would only make things worse."

Since it appeared that she found these attempts at conversation tiring, the nun did not press further. The whole sequence of events was as singular as the story of the old bamboo cutter and the moon princess,[195] and the nun was uneasy lest a moment of inattention give the girl her chance to slip away.

The bishop's mother was a lady of good rank. The younger nun was the widow of a high-ranking courtier. Her only daughter, who had been her whole life, had married another well-placed courtier and died shortly afterward; and so the woman had lost interest in the world, taken the nun's habit, and withdrawn to these hills. Yet feelings of loneliness and deprivation lingered on. She yearned for a companion to remind her of the one now gone. And she had come upon a hidden treasure, a girl if anything superior to her daughter. Yes, it was all very strange—unbelievably, joyously strange. The nun was aging but still handsome and elegant. The waters here were far gentler than at that other mountain village. The house was pleasingly furnished, the trees and shrubs had been set out to agreeable effect, and great care had obviously gone into the flower beds. As autumn wore on, the skies somehow brought a deepened awareness of the passing days. The young maidservants, making as if to join the rice harvesters at the gate, raised their voices in harvest songs, and the clacking of the scarecrows[196] brought memories of a girlhood in the remote East Country.

The house was set in against the eastern hills, some distance above the retreat of Kashiwagi's late mother-in-law, consort of the Suzaku emperor. The pines were thick and the winds were lonely. Life in the nunnery was quiet, with

---

194. In *The Tales of Ise*, sec. 63, the hero is pursued by a lady "but one year short of a hundred."

195. Kaguyahime, in the tenth-century *Tale of the Bamboo Cutter*, returns to the moon at the end of the story.

196. *Hita* are clappers of wood and bamboo manipulated from a distance by a string.

only religious observances to break the monotony. On moonlit nights the bishop's sister would sometimes take out a koto and a nun called Shōshō would join in with a lute.

"Do you play?" they would ask the girl. "You must be bored."

As she watched these elderly people beguiling the tedium with music, she thought of her own lot. Never from the outset had she been among those privileged to seek consolation in quiet, tasteful pleasures; and so she had grown to womanhood with not a single accomplishment to boast of. Her stars had not been kind to her. She took up a brush and, by way of writing practice, set down a poem:

> "Into a torrent of tears I flung myself,
>   and who put up the sluice that held me back?"

It had been cruel of them to save her. The future filled her with dread. On these moonlit nights the old women would recite courtly poems and talk of this and that ancient happening, and she would be left alone with her thoughts.

> "Who in the city, now bathed in the light of the moon,
>   will know that I yet drift on through the gloomy world?"

Many people had been in her last thoughts—or what she had meant to be her last thoughts—but they were nothing to her now. There was only her mother, who must have been shattered by the news. And Nurse, so desperate to find a decent life for her—how desolate she must be, poor thing! Where would she be now? She could not know, of course, that the girl was still alive. Then there was Ukon, who had shared all her secrets through the terrible days when no one else had understood.

It is not easy for young people to tell the world goodbye and withdraw to a mountain village, and the only women permanently in attendance were seven or eight aged nuns. Their daughters and granddaughters, married or in domestic service, would sometimes come visiting. The girl avoided these callers, for among them might be one or two who frequented the houses of the gentlemen she had known. It seemed absolutely essential that her existence remain a secret, and no doubt strange theories about her origins were going the rounds. The younger nun assigned two of her own maidservants, Jijū and Komoki, to wait upon the girl. They were a far cry from the "birds of the capital"[197] she had known in her other life. Had she found for herself the "place apart from the

---

197. In the ninth episode of *The Tales of Ise*, the exiled hero is reminded of home by the *miyakodori* (bird of the capital), the black-headed gull.

world" the poet speaks of?[198] The bishop's sister knew that such extreme reserve must have profound causes, and told no one of the Uji events.

Her son-in-law was now a guards captain. His younger brother, a court chaplain and a disciple of the bishop, was in seclusion at Yokawa. Members of the family often went to visit him. Once on his way up the mountain the captain stopped by Ono. Outrunners cleared the road, and the elegant young gentleman who now approached brought back to the girl, so vividly that it might have been he, the image of her clandestine visitor. Ono was little nearer the center of things than Uji, but the nunnery and its grounds showed that the occupants were ladies of taste. Wild carnations coyly dotted the hedge, and maiden flowers and bellflowers were coming into bloom; and among them stood numbers of young men in bright and varied travel dress. The captain, also in travel dress, was received at the south veranda. He stood for a time admiring the garden. Perhaps twenty-seven or twenty-eight, he seemed mature for his age. The nun, his mother-in-law, addressed him through a curtained doorway.

"The years go by and those days seem far away. It is good of you to remember that the darkness of our mountains awaits your radiant presence. And yet—" There were tears in her voice. "And yet I am surprised, I must admit, that you so favor us."

"I have not for a moment forgotten the old days; but I fear I have rather neglected you now that you are no longer among us. I envy my brother his mountain life and would like to visit him every day. But crowds of people are always wanting to come with me. Today I managed to shake them off."

"I am not at all sure that I believe you. You are saying what young people say. But of course you have not forgotten us, and that is evidence that you are not like the rest of them. I thank you for it, you may be sure, every day of the year."

She had a light lunch brought for the men and offered the captain lotus seeds and other delicacies. Since this was of course not the first time she had been his hostess, he saw no cause for reticence. The talk of old times might have gone on longer had a sudden shower not come up. For the nun, regret was added to sorrow, regret that so fine a young man had been allowed to become a stranger. Why had her daughter not left behind a child, a keepsake? Quite lost in the nostalgia these occasional visits induced, she sometimes said things she might better have kept to herself.

Looking out into the garden, alone once again with her thoughts, the girl was pathetic and yet beautiful in the white singlet, a plain, coarse garment, and drab, lusterless trousers in harmony with the subdued tones of the nunnery. What an unhappy contrast she must be with what she had once been! In fact, even these stiff, shapeless garments became her.

---

198. Anonymous, *Shūishū*, no. 506: "Would I might have a place apart from the world, there to hide what time has done to me."

"Here we have our dead lady back, you might almost think," said one of the women; "and here we have the captain too. It makes you want to weep, it really does. People will marry, one way and another, and it would be so nice if we could have him back for good. Wouldn't they make a handsome couple, though."

No, never, the girl replied silently. She had no wish to return to the past, and the attentions of a man, any man, would inevitably pull her toward it. She had been there, and she would have no more of it.

The nun having withdrawn, the captain sat looking apprehensively up at the sky. He recognized the voice of the nun Shōshō and called her to him.

"I am sure that all the ladies I knew are here, but you can probably imagine how hard it is for me to visit you. You must have concluded that I am completely undependable."

They talked of the past, on and on, for Shōshō had been in the dead lady's service.

"Just as I was coming in from the gallery," he said, "a gust of wind caught the blind, and I was treated to a glimpse of some really beautiful hair. What sort of damsel do you have hidden away in your nunnery?"

He had seen the retreating figure of the girl and found her interesting. How much more dramatic the effect would certainly be if he were to have a good look at her. He still grieved for a lady who was much the girl's inferior.

"Our lady was quite unable to forget her daughter, your own lady, and nothing seemed to console her. Then quite by accident she came on another girl, and she seems to have recovered somewhat from her grief. But it is not at all like the girl to have let you see her."

Now this was interesting, thought the captain. Who might she be? That single glimpse, a most tantalizing one, had assured him that she was well favored. He questioned Shōshō further, but her answers were evasive. . . .

Just as the moon came flooding over the hills the captain appeared. (There had been that note from him earlier in the day.) The girl fled aghast to the rear of the house.

"You are being a perfect fool," said Shōshō.[199] "It is the sort of night when a girl should treasure these little attentions. Do, I beg of you, at least hear what he has to say—or even a part of it. Are you so clean that his very words will soil you?"

But the girl was terrified. Though someone ventured to tell him that she was away, he probably knew the truth. Probably his messenger had reported that she was alone.

His recriminations were lengthy. "I don't care whether or not I hear her voice. I just want to have her beside me, prepared to decide for herself whether

---

199. Probably it is she, though no subject is given.

I am such an ugly threat. She is being quite heartless, and in these hills too, where it might be imagined that there would be time to cultivate the virtue of patient charity. It is more than a man should be asked to bear.

"In a mountain village, deep in the autumn night,
a lady who understands should understand.

"And I do think she should."

"There is no one here to make your explanations for you," said Shōshō to the girl. "You may if you are not careful seem rude and eccentric."

"The gloom of the world has been no part of my life,
and how shall you call me one who understands?"

The girl recited the poem more as if to herself than by way of reply, but Shōshō passed it on to him.

He was deeply touched. "Do ask her again to come out, for a moment, even."

"I seem to make no impression upon her at all," said Shōshō, who was beginning to find his persistence, and with it a certain querulousness, a little tiresome. She went back inside—and found that the girl had fled to the old nun's room, which she had not before so much as looked in upon.

Shōshō reported this astonishing development.

"With all this time on her hands," said the captain, "she should be more than usually alive to the pity of things, and all the indications are that she is a gentle and sensitive enough person. And that very fact, you know, makes her unfriendliness cut more cruelly. Do you suppose there is something in her past, something that has made her afraid of men? What might it be, will you tell me, please, that has turned her against the whole world? And how long do you expect to have her with you?"

Openly curious now, he pressed for details; but how was Shōshō to give them?

"A lady whom my lady should by rights have been looking after was lost for a number of years. And then, on a pilgrimage to Hatsuse, we found her again."

The girl lay face down, sleepless, beside the old nun, whom she had heard to be a very difficult person. The nun had dozed off from early evening, and now she was snoring thunderously. With her were two nuns as old as she, snoring with equal vigor. Terrified, the girl half wondered whether she would survive the night. Might not these monsters devour her? Though she had no great wish to live on, she was timid by nature, rather like the one we have all heard of who has set out across a log bridge and then changed her mind.[200] She had brought

---

200. A reference, apparently, to a story or proverb, not identified.

the girl Komoki with her. Of an impressionable age, however, Komoki had soon returned to a spot whence she could observe this rare and most attractive caller. Would she not please come back, would she not please come back? Ukifune was asking; but Komoki was little help in a crisis.

The captain presently gave up the struggle and departed.

"She is so hopelessly wrapped up in herself," said the women, "and the worst of it is that she is so pretty."

At what the girl judged would be about midnight the old nun awoke in a fit of coughing and sat up. In the lamplight her hair was white against her shawl. Startled to find the girl beside her, she shaded her eyes with her hand as the mink (or some such creature) is said to do[201] and peered over.

"Now this is strange," she said in a deep, menacing voice. "What sort of thing might you be?"

The moment had come, thought the girl. She was going to be devoured. When that malign being had led her off she had not resisted, for she had not had her senses about her. But what was she to do now? They had dragged her ignominiously back into the world, and black memories were a constant torment; and now came a new crisis, one which she seemed incapable of surmounting or even facing. Yet perhaps if she had had her way, if she had died, she would this moment be facing a crisis still more terrible. Sleepless, she thought back over her life, which seemed utterly bleak. She had not known her father and she had divided all those years between the capital and the remote provinces. And then she had come upon her sister. For a time she had been happy and secure; but that untoward incident had separated them. Some relief from her misfortunes had seemed in prospect when a gentleman declared himself ready to offer her a respectable position, and she had responded to his attentions with that hideous blunder. It had been wrong to permit even the smallest flutter of affection for Niou. The memory of her ultimate disgrace, brought on by his attentions, revolted her. What idiocy, to have been moved by his pledge and that Islet of Oranges and the pretty poem it had inspired![202] Her mind moved from incident to incident, and longing flowed over her for the other gentleman. He had not exactly burned with ardor, but he had seemed calm and dependable. From him above all she wanted to keep news of her whereabouts and circumstances. Would she be allowed another glimpse of him, even from a distance? But she sternly dismissed the thought. It was wrong. She must not harbor it for a moment.

After what had seemed an endless night, she heard a cock crowing. It was an immense relief—but how much greater a delight had it been her mother's voice awakening her! Komoki was still absent from her post. The girl lay in

---

201. The mink was believed to shade its eyes while scanning a stranger from afar.

202. A reference to the poem that Niou sent to Ukifune during the romantic excursion to the Islet of Oranges in the "A Boat upon the Waters" chapter.

bed, exhausted. The early snorers were also early risers, it seemed. They were noisily at work on gruel and other unappetizing dishes. Someone offered her a helping, but the donor was ugly and the food strange and unappetizing. She was not feeling well, she said, not venturing an open refusal. The old women did not sense that their hospitality was unwelcome.

Several monks of low rank came up to the nunnery. "The bishop will be calling on you today."

"What brings him so suddenly?"

"An evil spirit of some sort has been after the First Princess. The archbishop[203] has been doing what he can, but two messengers came yesterday to say that only His Reverence offers real hope." They delivered these tidings in proud voices. "Then late last night the lieutenant came, the son of the Minister of the Left, you know.[204] He had a message from Her Majesty herself. And so His Reverence will be coming down the mountain."

She must summon up her courage, thought the girl, and have the bishop administer final vows. Today there were no meddling women to gainsay them. "I fear I am very ill," she said, rousing herself, "and when he comes I hope I may ask him to let me take my vows. Would you tell him so, please?"

The old nun nodded vaguely.

The girl went back to her room. She did not like the thought of having anyone except the bishop's sister touch her hair, and she could not dress it without help. She loosened the cords that had bound it up for the night. Though of course she had no one but herself to blame for what was about to happen, she was sad that her mother would not see her again in lay dress. She had feared that her hair might be thinner because of her illness, but could detect no evidence that it was. Remarkably thick, indeed, it was a good six feet long, soft and smooth and beautifully even at the edges.

"I cannot think," she whispered to herself, "that she would have wished it thus."[205]

The bishop arrived in the evening. The south room had been readied for him. Suddenly full of shaven heads, it was an even less inviting room than usual. The bishop went to look in on his mother.

"And how have you been these last months? I am told that my good sister is off on a pilgrimage. And is the girl still with you?"

"Oh, yes. She didn't go along. She says, let me see, she's not feeling well. She'd like to take her vows, she says, and she'd like you to give them to her."

"I see." He went to the girl's room and addressed her through curtains. Shyly, she came forward.

---

203. Zasu, the chief abbot of Mount Hiei.

204. One of Yūgiri's sons and thus a first cousin of the princess.

205. Henjō, *Gosenshū*, no. 1241, upon taking holy orders: "I cannot think that she would have wished it thus, My aged mother, stroking my raven hair."

"I have felt that only a bond from a previous life could explain the curious way we met, and I have been praying my hardest for you. But I am afraid that as a correspondent I have not been very satisfactory. You will understand, I am sure, that we clerics are supposed to deny ourselves such pleasures unless we have very good reasons. And how have you been? It is not an easy life women lead when they turn their backs on the world."

"You will remember that I had no wish to live on, and my strange survival has only brought me grief. But of course I am grateful, in my poor way, for all you have done. Do, please, let me take my vows. I do not think I am capable of the sort of life other women lead. Even if I were to stay among them, I do not think I could follow their example."

"What can have brought you to such a conclusion, when you have your whole life ahead of you? No, it would be a grave sin. The decision may at the time seem a firm one, but women are irresolute creatures, and time goes by."

"I have never been happy, not since I was very young, and my mother often thought of putting me in a nunnery. And when I began to understand things a little better I could see that I was different from other people, and must seek my happiness in another world." She was weeping. "Perhaps it is because I am so near the end of it all—I feel as if everything were slipping away. Please, reverend sir, let me take my vows."

The bishop was puzzled. Why should so gentle a surface conceal such a strange, bitter resolve? But he remembered that malign spirit and knew that she would not be talking nonsense. It was remarkable that she was still alive. A terrible thing, a truly hideous thing, to be accosted by forces so evil.

"Your wish can only have gained for you the smiling approval of the powers above. It is not for me to deter you. Nothing could be simpler than administering vows. But I have come down on most pressing business, and must tonight be at the princess's side. The services begin tomorrow. In a week they will be over, and I shall see that your petition is granted."

But by then the younger nun would have come back, and she would surely object. It must be made to appear that the crisis was immediate.

"Perhaps I have not explained how unwell I am. I fear that vows will do me little good if I am beyond accepting them wholeheartedly. Please. I see my chance today, the only one I shall be blessed with."

Her weeping had touched his saintly heart. "It is very late. I used to have no trouble at all climbing up and down the mountain, but I am old, and matters are no longer so simple. I had thought to rest here awhile and then go on to the city. If you are in such a hurry, I shall see to your wishes immediately."

Delighted, the girl pushed scissors and a comb box toward him.

"Have the others come here, please." The two monks who had been with him that strange night at Uji were with him again tonight. "Cut the young lady's hair, if you will."

It was a most proper thing they were doing, they agreed. Given the perilous situation in which they had found her, they knew that she could have been meant for no ordinary life. But the bishop's favored disciple hesitated even as he raised the scissors. The hair pushed forward between the curtains was altogether too beautiful.

The nun Shōshō was off in another wing with her brother, a prefect who had come with the bishop. Saemon too was having a chat with a friend in the party; and such modest entertainment as they were capable of providing for these rare and most welcome visitors occupied most of the household.

Only Komoki was present. She scampered off to tell Shōshō what was in progress. A dismayed Shōshō rushed in just as the bishop was going through the form of bestowing his own robe and surplice upon the girl.

"You must now make obeisance, if you will, in the direction of your father and mother."

The girl was in tears, for she did not know in which direction that would be.

"And what, may I ask, are you doing? You are being utterly irresponsible. I cannot think what our lady will have to say when she gets back."

But the proceedings were at a point beyond which expressions of doubt could only disturb the girl. Shōshō said no more.

". . . as we wander the three worlds,"[206] intoned the bishop.

So, at length, came release. Yet the girl felt a twinge of sorrow: there had in fact been no bonds to break.

The bishop's assistant was having trouble with her hair. "Oh, well. The others will have time to trim it for you."

"You must admit no regrets for the step you have taken," said the bishop, himself cutting the hair at her forehead. He added other noble admonitions.

She was happy now. They had all advised deliberation, and she had had her way. She could claim this one sign of the Buddha's favor, her single reward for having lived on in this dark world.

The visitors left, all was quiet. "We had thought that for you at least," said her companions, to the moaning of the night wind, "this lonely life need not go on. We had looked forward to seeing you happy again. And this has happened. Have you thought of all the years that lie ahead of you? It is not easy for even an old woman to tell herself that life as most people know it has ended."

But the girl was serene. "Life as most people know it"—she need no longer think about that. Waves of peace flowed over her.

But the next morning she avoided their eyes, for she had acted selfishly and taken no account of their wishes. Her hair seemed to scatter wildly at the ends, and no one was prepared to dress it for her in charitable silence. She kept her curtains drawn.

---

206. Although the text from which the bishop is reciting has been lost, the reference would seem to be to the cycle of birth and rebirth.

She had never been an articulate girl, and she had no confidante with whom to discuss the rights and wrongs of what had happened. She seated herself at her inkstone and turned to the one pursuit in which she could lose herself when her thoughts were more than she could bear, her writing practice.

> "A world I once renounced, for they and I
> had come to nothing, I now renounce again.

"Finally, this time, I have done it."
The poem moved her to set down another:

> "I thought that I should see the world no more,
> and now, once more, 'no more' is my resolve."

The captain is disappointed to discover that the beautiful woman who has been hidden away among the elderly nuns has taken holy vows and is no longer within his reach. Meanwhile, the bishop visits the empress and informs her of the discovery of the mysterious woman at Uji. The empress realizes that the woman is the lover whom her brother Kaoru had lost and who is now presumed dead. Kosaishō, a female attendant to the empress, conveys this information to Kaoru, who is astounded.

"It sounds very much like someone I had been wondering about," Kaoru replied guardedly. "And is she still at Ono?"

"The bishop administered vows the day he came down from the mountain. She insisted on it, even though everyone wanted her to wait until she had regained a little of her strength."

The place was right, and not one of the circumstances was at variance with what he knew. Half hoping he would be spared the knowledge that it was indeed she, he cast about for a way to learn the truth. He would present an awkward figure if he were to lead the hunt himself. And if he were to treat Niou to the sight of his restlessness, his friend would no doubt seek ways to block the path the girl had chosen. Had Niou extracted a vow of silence from his mother? That would explain her curious reluctance to talk about a matter so extraordinary. And if Niou was already part of the conspiracy, then however strong the yearning, Kaoru must once again consign Ukifune to the realm of the dead. If indeed she still lived, then some chance turn of the wind might one day bring them together, to talk, perhaps, of the shores of the Yellow Spring.[207] He would not again think of making her his own.

Though the empress was evidently determined not to discuss these events, he found another occasion to seek her out.

"The girl I told you about, the one who I thought had died such a terrible death—I have heard that she is still alive. She has come on unhappy circumstances,

---

207. Yomi, Land of the Dead.

I am told. It all seems very unlikely—but then the way she disappeared was unlikely too. I find it hard to believe that she hated the world enough to think of such desperate measures. And so the rumors I have picked up may not be so unlikely after all." And he described them in more detail. He chose his words carefully when they touched upon Niou, and he did not speak at all of his own bitterness. "If he hears that I would like to find her he is sure to credit me with all the wrong motives. I do not propose to do anything even if I discover that she is still alive."

"I was rather frightened when I had the story from the bishop, and did not listen as carefully as I should have. But how could my son possibly have learned of it? I know all about his deplorable habits, and have no doubt that news of this sort would send him into a fever. The talk I pick up about his little escapades worries me terribly."

He knew that she would never, in what seemed to be the frankest of conversations, let slip something she had learned in confidence.

The mystery haunted him, day and night. In what mountain village would the girl be? How might he with dignity seek her out? He must have the facts directly from the bishop of Yokawa. He made solemn offerings on the eighth of every month, sometimes at the main hall on Mount Hiei, sacred to Lord Yakushi.[208] This time he would go on to Yokawa. He took the girl's brother with him. He did not mean to tell her family for the moment, not until he had more precise information. Perhaps he hoped that the boy's presence would bring an immediacy to an encounter that might otherwise seem unreal. If the girl in the bishop's story should indeed prove to be Ukifune, and if, further, she had already been the victim of improper advances, even in strange new dress, off among strange new women—the truth would not be pleasing.

Such are the thoughts that troubled him along the way.

In the next and final chapter, "The Floating Bridge of Dreams," Kaoru visits Yokawa and asks the bishop about the woman who took vows at Ono and comes to the conclusion that it must be Ukifune. Seeing Kaoru's reaction, the bishop regrets having given Ukifune the tonsure. The next day, Kaoru sends Ukifune's half-brother (Kogimi) to Ono with a message for Ukifune, who refuses to meet the visitor. The tale ends with Kaoru wondering if someone has been hiding Ukifune the way he had hidden her.

[Translated by Edward Seidensticker]

DAUGHTER OF TAKASUE

The author of the *Sarashina Diary* was the daughter (b. 1008) of Sugawara no Takasue, a provincial governor and a direct descendant of Sugawara no

---

208. Bhaisajyaguru, the buddha of medicine. The eighth of the month was one of his feast days.

Michizane, the noted literary figure and politician; she also was the niece of the author of the *Kagerō Diary*. In 1017, at the age of ten or so, the author went with her father to Kazusa Province (present-day Chiba Prefecture), where he had been appointed as governor. Then, at the age of thirteen, in 1020, she returned to the capital. The events of this journey are recorded in great detail at the beginning of the diary. In 1039, at the age of thirty-one, she went into court service as part of the entourage of Princess Yūshi, who was being raised in the Takakura Palace of her foster father, the regent Fujiwara no Yorimichi. A year later, the author's marriage to Tachibana no Toshimichi brought her back to her parents' home, but she continued to serve Yūshi intermittently, particularly while her husband, Toshimichi, was posted to Shimotsuke Province (present-day Tochigi Prefecture) in 1041/1042. Her marriage is only hinted at ambiguously in the diary itself, primarily with a sense of deep disappointment. It is apparent from the latter half of the diary, however, that her marriage and the subsequent birth of her son brought her both economic and spiritual security. She also continued to enjoy periodic visits to her colleagues at court, and her life provided ample opportunities for travel in the form of pilgrimages. But when her husband suddenly died in 1058, her situation took a turn for the worse, and in the latter part of the diary the author laments the loneliness of old age.

SARASHINA DIARY (*SARASHINA NIKKI*, CA. 1059)

The *Sarashina Diary* is known for its vivid, poetic description of the trip from Kazusa in the east to the capital, which occupies the first part of the narrative, and for its depiction of the author as a young girl absorbed in tales (monogatari). Indeed, the diary provides important evidence for the popularity of *The Tale of Genji* among readers one generation after its composition. In the *Sarashina Diary*, Daughter of Takasue reflects on more than fifty years of her life, making it, among the many kana diaries of the Heian period, the only work that covers such a long expanse, from girlhood to old age.

As a person brought up in the back of beyond, even farther than the end of the road to the East Country,[209] how uncouth I must have been, but however it was that I first came to know about them, once I knew that such things as tales existed in the world, all I could think of over and over was how much I wanted to read them. At leisure times during the day and evening, when I heard my elder sister and stepmother tell bits and pieces of this or that tale or talk about what the Shining Genji was like, my desire to read these tales for myself only increased—for how could they recite the tales to my satisfaction from memory alone? I became so impatient that I made an image of the Healing Buddha, in my own size, and performing purification rituals when no one else was around,

---

209. Kazusa, which occupied most of the Chiba Peninsula directly east of present-day Tokyo.

I would secretly enter the room. Touching my forehead to the floor, I would pray with abandon, "Please grant that I should go to the capital as soon as possible where there are so many tales, and please, let me get to read all of them." Then, the year I was thirteen, it did come about that we were to go up to the capital. On the third day of the Ninth Month, we made a preliminary start by moving to a place called Imatachi, Departing Now.[210]

At sunset, a heavy unsettling fog drifted in and covered the house where I had been so used to playing for years; it was turned inside out with goods all dismantled and scattered about in preparation for our departure. Looking back, I was so sad to leave behind the Buddha standing there where I used to go when no one else was looking and touch my forehead to the floor, and without others knowing, I burst into tears.

The place to which we decamped had no protective enclosures; it was just a temporary thatched hut without even shutters and the like. Bamboo blinds and curtains had been hung. To the south, one could gaze out far in the direction of the moor. To the east and west, the sea was nearby, so fascinating. Since it was wonderfully charming, when the evening mists rose over the scene, I did not fall even into a shallow slumber, so busy was I looking now here, now there. I even found it sad that we were going to have to leave this place. On the fifteenth day of that same month, as the rain poured out of a dark sky, we crossed the bor-der of the province and stopped at a place called Raft, and indeed the rain fell so hard it seemed as though our little hut might float away. I was so frightened I could not sleep a wink. In the midst of the moor, there was a place with a small hill on which there were only three trees standing. We stayed the day there dry-ing out the things that had been soaked in the rain and waiting for the others in our party who had got off to a later start.

We left early on the morning of the seventeenth. Long ago, a wealthy man named Mano lived in Shimousa Province. We crossed a deep river by boat where it is said there are the remains of the house where he had tens of thousands of bolts of cloth woven and bleached. There were four large pillars standing in the river's flow that apparently were the remains of his old gate pillars. Listening to the others recite poems, I composed to myself,

kuchi mo senu	Not rotted away,
kono kawabashira	if these pillars in the river
nokorazu wa	did not remain,
mukashi no ato o	how could we ever know
ikade shiramashi	the traces of long ago?

---

210. It was the custom in the Heian period to start journeys on astrologically auspicious days or from auspicious directions, which usually necessitated removal to a nearby temporary lodg-ing from which the actual trip could begin. The author is playing with the place-name Imata-chi, literally, "Departing Now."

That night we stayed at a place called Kuroto, Black Beach. On one side, there was a wide band of hills, and where the sand stretched whitely into the distance, groves of pine grew thickly; the moon was shining brightly; the sound of the wind was thrilling and unsettling. Moved by the scene, people composed poems:

madoromaji	I will not sleep a wink!
koyoi narade wa	If not for this evening, then when
itsuka mimu	could I ever see this?
Kuroto no hama	Kuroto's black beach beneath
aki no yo no tsuki	the moon of an autumn night.

We left there early the next morning and stopped at a ferry landing called Matsusato on the upper reaches of a river on the border of Shimousa and Musashi called Broad River; the whole night through, our goods were ferried across by boat. My nurse, whose husband had died, was about to give birth here at this border, so we were to leave her behind and go on up to the capital. Since I loved her so much, I wanted to visit her, so my elder brother carried me on horseback to her side. It could be said that our whole party was staying in temporary huts with only curtains hung up to try to keep the wind out, but this shelter for my nurse, since she had no husband accompanying her, was so ineptly constructed and rude. It had only one layer of reed screens that had been woven together; the moonlight poured in. She was covered with a scarlet robe and was lying there in some discomfort bathed in moonlight. This seemed not right for such a person; she was so white and fair; moved by the rarity of the moment, she stroked my hair and cried. Although I found it painful to abandon her, I could not help feeling pressed to return; my regrets were hard to bear. I was so sad when I recalled her face that not even feeling anything for the beauty of the moon, I lay down, in a gloomy frame of mind.

The next morning, the carts were lashed to boats and ferried across and then pulled up onto the other bank; those who had sent us off to this point all turned back. We who were going up to the capital halted until those returning were no longer in sight; those going, those staying behind, all were in tears. Even my young heart felt this very poignantly.

So now we were in Musashi Province.[211] There was nothing especially charming to be seen. There were no black beaches or white sand; it seemed very muddy, and although there was a moor on which I had heard the lavender-rooted gromwell[212] grew, there were only tall rushes and reeds growing so thickly and so high that one could not even see the tops of the bows of those mounted

---

211. This province covered most of the area now occupied by the city of Tokyo.

212. The gromwell (*murasaki*) is a wild perennial, whose roots yield a lavender color (*murasaki*) dye. The author refers to *Kokinshū*, no. 867: "Due to this single lavender root of the gromwell, all the wild grasses across Musashi Moor arouse a sigh as I gaze."

on horses. Parting our way through the midst of this, we went along and came
to a temple called Takeshiba. In the distance there were the remains of the
foundation of a commandary called Hahasou. When I asked "What kind of
place is this?" someone told this story:

"Long ago there was an estate called Takeshiba here. A man from this area
was sent to be a fire keeper for the fire huts of the palace. Once when he was
sweeping the imperial garden, he murmured to himself this complaint, 'Why,
oh why, have I met such a cruel fate? "On the seven, on the three, saké vats of
my home country, lie the straight handles of the gourd ladles. South blows the
wind, they drift to the north; north blows the wind, they drift to the south; west
blows the wind, they drift to the east; east blows the wind they drift to the west."[213]
None of which I see, stuck here just like this.' At that moment, the emperor's
daughter (a much treasured person) was standing by herself at the edge of the
bamboo blinds; leaning against a pillar, she gazed out and was much moved by
the serving man's solitary complaint. What kind of gourd ladles were they? How
did they drift one way and another? Since she became so curious about this, she
raised up the bamboo blind and summoned him, 'You over there, come here.'
Full of trepidation, when he came over beside the balustrade, she ordered him,
'What you just said, repeat it one more time for me.' And so he repeated the
words about the saké vats one more time. At this point, she ordered him, 'Take
me there and show me these things. I have a reason for asking you.' Although
he felt terribly afraid (but was this not something fated to happen?), he carried
her on his back and took her down to his home country. Now, thinking that
surely they would be followed, that night he set the princess down at the foot of
the Seta Bridge[214] and destroyed just one section of it. Leaping back over it, he
hoisted the princess on his back and seven days and seven nights later, they
arrived in the province of Musashi.

"The emperor and empress were distraught when they realized the princess
had disappeared. When they searched for her, someone said, 'There is a man
servant, a fire keeper from the province of Musashi, he flew away with a very
fragrant bundle around his neck.' When they inquired after this man servant,
he was gone. Surely he must have gone back to his home province, they thought.
When envoys from the court chased after him, finding the Seta Bridge broken,
they could not continue. Three months later, when they arrived in Musashi and
looked up this man servant, the princess summoned the imperial envoy into
her presence and made the following pronouncement: 'I, for it seems to have

---

213. This appears to be a folk song from his home region. It speaks of ladles for scooping saké
that are made of dried and split bottle gourds, with the narrow part of the gourd forming a
straight handle. They are light and float on the surface of the vats. Their moving to and fro
freely in response to the wind arouses a happy feeling.

214. The bridge across the narrow eastern neck of Lake Biwa, part of the main road to the
east country.

been meant to be, became very curious about this man's home, and when I said, "Take me there," he brought me here. I find it very pleasant here. If this man is punished for having committed a crime, then what about me? For me to have sought out this country must be a fate determined in a former existence. Quickly return to the court and report what has happened.' There was nothing he could say, so the envoy went back up to the capital and reported, 'It is such and so,' to the emperor. It was useless to say anything; even if this man had committed a crime, it was not as though now they could remove the princess and bring her back to the capital. So they put the Takeshiba man in charge of the province of Musashi for as long as he should live and exempted the province from public taxes and corvee duties, in effect making the princess the patron of the province. When the official proclamation came down, the man's house was renovated into a palace. Now this house where the princess lived, was turned into a temple after she passed away, and that is why it is called Takeshiba Temple. All the children born to the princess were given the surname Musashi, just like that. From that time forward, it is said that the imperial palace fires were attended by women."

There was nothing in particular to note as we passed through rushes and reeds, over moors and hills. Between the provinces of Musashi and Sagami, there is a river called Asuda (this is the river called Sumida in the *Ariwara Middle Captain Collection*,[215] where as he crossed it he composed the poem, "Come hither, I would ask you . . .").[216] When we crossed over it by boat, we were in Sagami Province.

The mountains of a place called Nishitomi all stood in a line just like scenes that are often depicted in screen paintings. On one side was the sea, and the lay of the beach as well as the waves rolling in was terribly beautiful. At a place called the Chinese Plains, the sand was amazingly white, and it took two or three days to pass by. Someone said, "In summer, Japanese pinks bloom all over, it looks like lengths of brocade in deep and pale colors. Since it is the end of autumn, we can't see them," yet still here and there were specks of color where they bloomed charmingly. "How about that, on the Chinese Plains, Japanese pinks are blooming all around"; people found this amusing.[217]

In the Ashigara Mountains, we passed through frighteningly dark forests for four or five days. The deeper we penetrated the foothills, we could not even see the complexion of the sky clearly, and the trees were indescribably thick; how

---

215. Reference to the personal poetry collection of Ariwara no Narihira (825–880).

216. The poem is also in *The Tales of Ise*, sec. 9, and the *Kokinshū* (no. 411). The poem's headnote records that it was written when Narihira was crossing the Sumida River and was told that the bird he saw was called the "Capital Bird." The poem reads: "Oh Capital Bird, if you bear the truth that goes with such a name, come hither, I would ask you, how fares the one I love?"

217. The play on the names containing Japanese and Chinese is amusing because the intertwining of Chinese and Japanese cultural elements was so much a part of Heian literary culture.

frightening it was. On a dark night with no moon, when anyone would lose their way in the darkness, out of nowhere appeared three female entertainers. One was about fifty, one about twenty, and the other about fourteen or fifteen. In front of our lodging, they set up a large umbrella and sat down. And when the men servants brought torches so that we could see, someone said, "This is the granddaughter of the famous Kohata of the old days." The woman's hair was very long with lovely sidelocks hanging down; her skin was white and clean. "She seems hardly suited for this sort of life, why, she would not be out of place as a maid servant for the nobility," people said, much impressed. The women's voices were incomparable as they sang wonderful songs that seemed to ring clear in the sky. Everyone was very moved and had the women move closer, so excited we were. When they overheard someone say, "There couldn't be entertainers as fine as these in the West Country," they sang in a splendid way, "When you compare us to those of Naniwa. . . ."[218] Their appearance was unsullied, and when they sang, their voices were incomparable. When they rose to go back into the mountains that were so frightening, everyone regretted their going and broke into tears. Young as I was, I regretted even the fact that we would also be leaving this temporary lodging.

At first light of dawn, we crossed the Ashigara Mountains. There is no way to describe how even more frightening it was in the middle of the mountains. Why, the clouds—we tread upon them under our feet. Right in the middle of the mountains in a small space under the trees, there were just three stalks of the *aoi* plant.[219] When someone said, "Here isolated from the world, it manages to grow," people found it very poignant. The river of that mountain flows in three courses.

Finally we crossed over those mountains and stopped at a mountain border station. From here on, we were in the province of Suruga. Beside the Yokohashi border station, there was a place called Rock Basin. In the middle of an amazingly large square rock, there was an opening from which flowed water that was extremely cold and clear.

Mount Fuji is in this province. It is the mountain we could see to the west of the province I grew up in. The appearance of that mountain is like nothing else in the world. Were I to try and describe this unusual appearance—its flanks are as though painted a deep indigo blue, and since eternal snow covers its summit, it is as though someone is wearing a white short robe over an indigo gown. From

---

218. The singers improvise a song about being compared with the entertainers of Naniwa, present-day Osaka, therefore the west country.

219. Stalks of the *aoi* plant are used as decorations for the Kamo Festival in Kyoto and therefore connote the splendor and liveliness of the capital at festival time. The name *aoi* is also understood as a pun for "meeting day" and evokes romantic affairs. To find three stalks of the plant in the isolated mountains strikes the party as incongruous and touching.

the slightly flat summit of the mountain, smoke rises. At dusk, one can even see flames shooting up.

They finally arrive in the capital on the second day of the Twelfth Month and take up residence in what is now the eastern ward of the city.

It was a large wild place, not inferior in wildness to the mountains we had passed through; there were huge frightening trees like those in the deep mountains; it was a place one could scarcely believe was in the capital. We were not settled yet and extremely busy with one thing or another, but it occurred to me, "If not now, then when?" so I pestered my mother,[220] "Please find me some tales to read, please!" She sent off a letter to a relative of ours known as Lady Emon no Myōbu who served at the Third Avenue Palace.[221] She was delighted with our news and sent us some tales "that her highness has deigned to pass down to me." These were particularly splendid scrolls packed in the lid of an inkstone box. I was beside myself with joy, day or night, the first thing I applied myself to was reading these tales. I wanted to read more and more. In this city, where we were not really settled yet, where might there be a person who could seek out more tales for me?

Now, as for my stepmother, she was a person who had left court service to go down to the provinces, but things had not worked out as she wished and she seemed to feel resentment about her situation, so she went elsewhere, taking along her child of about five years and some staff.[222] She said, "There will never come a time when I will forget the kindness of your heart." Pointing to a big plum tree close to the eaves, she said, "I will come and visit when this tree blossoms again," and leaving these words behind, she went away. In my heart, I kept missing her and feeling sad, stifling my sobs, I wept, and the new year came round again.[223] "Whenever will you bloom so that she will come for a visit? I

---

220. This is the first mention of the author's mother, who had not accompanied the father to the provinces but had maintained their residence in the capital. Her mother is the much younger sister, by a different mother, of Mother of Michitsuna, the author of the *Kagerō Diary.*

221. The Third Avenue Palace was the residence of Princess Shūshi (997–1050), daughter of the late ill-fated Empress Teishi, who had been Sei Shōnagon's patron.

222. From this passage, we understand why the author's stepmother was so familiar with the tales being circulated at court. The difficult situation of the stepmother is also explained between the lines. The author's father had taken the presumably younger woman down to the provinces with him and had had a child with her, but back in the capital the stepmother must have found it difficult to live in the shadow of the first wife. At any rate, the relationship between the author and her stepmother seems to have been atypically warm. Cruel stepmothers were stock characters in Heian fiction.

223. It is the year 1021, so the author is thirteen.

wonder if she really will." Such were my thoughts as I kept my eye on the tree and waited. Even when all the blossoms had opened, there was not a word from her. Suffering with longing, I broke off a blossoming branch and sent it to her,

tanomeshi o	Must I wait longer
nao ya matsubeki	for that which was promised, see—
shimogareshi	spring has not forgotten
ume o mo haru wa	even this plum tree
wasurezarikeri	that was withered by frost.

Since I had sent this poem, she wrote back and shared many touching thoughts,

nao tanome	Still wait, steadfast.
ume no tachi e wa	As for the plum's young branch tips,
chigiri okanu	with no pledge placed,
omoi no hoka no	I hear someone quite
hito mo tounari	unexpected will ask after you.[224]

That spring, when the world was in an uproar because of an epidemic, the nurse whom I had seen so poignantly in the moonlight at Matsusato Crossing died on the first day of the Third Month. I grieved for her helplessly; I even lost all interest in reading tales. All day long, I spent crying and when I glanced out, the evening sun was shining brilliantly on the cherry blossoms as they all fluttered down in confusion,

chiru hana mo	Scattering blossoms,
mata komu haru wa	when spring comes round again,
mimu ya semu	I may see them, but,
yagate wakareshi	oh, how I long for this one
hito zo kanashiki	from whom I am parted forever.

There was more news. The daughter of the major counselor[225] had died. Since I heard about how her husband, his lordship the middle captain,[226] grieved for her just at the same time as my own bereavement, I was deeply sad-

---

224. This poem alludes to a poem by Taira no Kanemori, *Shūishū*, no. 15: "The young branch tips of the plum tree in my garden must have come out in bloom; unexpectedly you seem to have deigned to visit." The stepmother may be referring to the author's birth mother or perhaps a future lover.

225. Fujiwara no Yukinari (972–1027), a famous calligrapher.

226. Yukinari's daughter had been married at the age of twelve to the youngest son of Fujiwara no Michinaga, Fujiwara no Nagaie. He was seventeen at the time of their marriage. She died only three years later, at the age of fifteen.

dened by the news. When we had come back to the capital, someone had given me some calligraphy in this young lady's own hand, saying, "Take this as a model for your own practice." She had written poems like "As night deepens, if I could not stay awake . . ."[227] and

Toribeyama	If the smoke rises from
tani ni keburi no	the valley of Toribeyama,
moe-tataba	I would have you
hakanaku mieshi	realize that it is me
ware to shiranamu.	who looked so fragile in life.[228]

Seeing this written in such a charming and skillful way, my tears flowed all the more.

My mother worried about the depression I had sunk into and thought to brighten my spirits by finding some more tales for me to read, and indeed as a matter of course, this did lighten my spirits. After I had read the part of *The Tale of Genji* about the lavender affinity,[229] I wanted even more to see what would happen next, but there was no one I could approach to obtain the rest of the tale, and everyone else in our household was as yet so new to the capital, they were unable to find it for me. Feeling so terribly impatient and eager to read more, I prayed in my heart, "Please grant that I may get to read *The Tale of Genji* from the first chapter the whole way through." Even when I went along with my parents into religious retreat at Uzumasa,[230] this was the only object of my prayers, and when we left the temple, I thought for certain I would get to see this tale, but it did not appear and I regretted this sorely. Then my parents had me go and meet an aunt who had come up from the countryside. "My, what a beautiful girl you have grown into," she said among other things and seemed to take a great liking to me. When I was about to return home, she said, "What shall I give you for a present? Certainly it should not be anything practical. I would like to give you something you really want." Then I received the fifty-odd chapters of *The Tale of Genji* in a large box,[231] as well as the tales *Ariwara Middle*

---

227. Mibu no Tadami, *Shūishū*, no. 104: "As night deepens, if I could not stay awake, the cuckoo's voice would be something I would only hear about from others."

228. Anonymous, *Shūishū*, no. 1324. Toribeyama is a place for cremation. The poem seems to foretell her own death.

229. Genji's mother was the Kiritsubo (Paulownia Court) consort. The paulownia tree has lavender flowers. Genji's stepmother, with whom he had a secret affair, was called the Fujitsubo (Wisteria Court) consort. The wisteria is also a lavender-color flower. Genji falls in love with young Murasaki because of her resemblance to Fujitsubo. The *murasaki* (gromwell) has roots that yield a lavender dye. The connection among these three characters is called the lavender affinity. The author is likely referring to the "Lavender" (Wakamurasaki) chapter of *The Tale of Genji*.

230. Uzumasa is in the western part of the city. The temple there is Kōryūji.

231. The comment is critical evidence that the full length of *The Tale of Genji* at this time

Captain,[232] Tōgimi, Serikawa, Shirara, Asōzu,[233] and others in a bag; carrying them home, the joy I felt was incredible.

With my heart pounding with excitement, I was able to read *The Tale of Genji* (this tale that had confused me and made me so impatient when I had read only a piece of it) right from chapter one. I did not have anything to do with the rest of the household; I just lay down inside my curtains, and the feeling I had as I unrolled scroll after scroll[234] was such that I would not have cared even if I had had a chance to become empress. I read all day long and as long as I could stay awake at night with the lamp pulled close to me. I found it quite amazing that passages I knew by heart would come floating unbidden into my head (since I did nothing but read, I suppose it was only natural). Then in a dream, I saw a pure-looking monk wearing a surplice of yellow cloth who said to me, "Quickly, memorize the fifth chapter of the Lotus Sutra." But I told no one, nor did I feel particularly inclined to memorize the Lotus Sutra. I was just infatuated with tales. I was rather ugly in those days, you know, but I was sure that when I grew up I would be extremely beautiful and my hair, too, would be splendidly long; I would just be like the Shining Genji's Yūgao or the Uji Captain's Ukifune—now it seems to me that my thoughts were frightfully frivolous.

Around the first of the Fifth Month, gazing at the scattered and ever so white petals of the nearby orange blossom tree, I composed this:

toki narazu	Gazing at this,
furu yuki ka to zo	I might think that snow had fallen
nagamemashi	out of season,
hanatachibana no	if it were not for the fragrance
kaorazariseba	of this orange blossom tree.

Since our place was as thick with trees as the dark woods on the flanks of the Ashigara Mountains, the crimson leaves of the Tenth Month were even more beautiful than those of the hills on all sides. When they were just like lengths of brocade spread over the forest, some visitors came who said, "There was a place on the way here that was simply beautiful with crimson leaves!" On the spot, it came to me,

izuko ni mo	It is not likely
otaraji mono o	inferior to anywhere else

---

was "fifty-odd" chapters. Textual scholars of *Genji* wish that the author had been more specific about the number.

232. *The Tales of Ise.*

233. None of these other tales survives.

234. It is known that women would often read tales aloud to one another, but this comment is evidence that they also read silently by themselves.

> *waga yado no*   this lodging of ours,
> *yo o akihatsuru*   yet you only speak of autumn scenery
> *keshiki bakari wa*   that wearies us of the world.[235]

I thought about tales all day long, and even at night as long as I could stay awake, this was all I had on my mind. Then, I had a dream in which a person said, "For the sake of Her Highness of the First Rank,[236] I constructed a small stream in the Hexagonal Hall."[237] When I asked, "Why is this so?" the response was, "Worship Amaterasu, Great Heaven Shining God."[238] Such was my dream, but I did not tell anyone and let it go without a thought; what a hopeless case I was.

Every spring I would gaze at the garden of Her Highness of the First Rank next door thinking "Ah they are about to bloom" and eagerly await them; "Ah, they have scattered," and regret their passing. It was as though those blossoms were in my own yard in the spring. Toward the end of the Third Month, to avoid the taboo of the earth god, we went to stay at someone else's house where the cherry trees were in full bloom, so lovely, not a one scattering even this late in the spring. Upon returning, the next day, I sent this to them,

> *akazarishi*   Not sated at all
> *yado no sakura o*   with the cherry blossoms of your house,
> *haru kurete*   spring drew to a close,
> *chirigata ni shimo*   you must have seen them
> *hitome mishi kana*   as they began to fall.

Always at about the time the cherry blossoms fell, since that was the season when my nurse had died, I could not help feeling sad; moreover, looking at the calligraphy of the major counselor's daughter who had died around the same time would also make me sad. Then, in the Fifth Month as night fell, when I was still up reading tales, I heard the soft mew of a cat coming from where I knew not. I was startled to see an incredibly charming cat. When I was looking around to see where the cat had come from, my elder sister said, "Hush, don't let

---

235. This poem involves puns on *yo wo aki* (weary of the world) and *aki hatsuru* (autumn ending). She playfully uses the Buddhist terminology "that wearies us of the world" to gently chide their guests for failing to praise their autumn scenery.

236. Princess Teishi (1013–1094), a granddaughter of Michinaga and not to be confused with the late Empress Teishi mentioned earlier.

237. Hexagonal Hall refers to the Chōhōji, a temple in central Kyoto that houses one of the "Seven Kannon of the Capital."

238. The tutelary god of the imperial family. The author's perception of the identity of Amaterasu seems to have been quite vague. It is not at all certain that she conceived of this being as a "goddess." The mention of Amaterasu in connection with a temple dedicated to Kannon may indicate the widespread belief at the time that Amaterasu was an avatar of Kannon.

anyone know. It is such a lovely cat, let's keep it for ourselves," and so we did. The cat got very used to us and would lie down right beside us. Since we wondered if someone might come looking for it, we hid it from others and did not let it go at all to the servant quarters. It stayed right with us all the time, and if something unclean was put before it to eat, it would turn its head away and refuse to eat it.

It stuck to the two of us; we were so happy and enchanted with it, but just around then, my sister fell ill. Since the house was in an uproar, I shut up the cat in the north wing[239] and did not summon it to our side, whereupon it raised a fuss, meowing noisily. Of course, this was understandable. Then my sister woke up from a painful slumber and said, "Where is the cat? Please bring it here." "Why?" I asked and she said, "In my dream, the cat came to my side and said, 'I am the daughter of the major counselor who has been reborn like this. Because of some small bond of fate from a former existence, I have somehow come to be loved by you two sisters. Just for a while, I could be with you here, but now you have shut me away with the servants, how awful it is!' and the appearance of the cat crying was just like a wellborn beautiful woman. I woke up with a start and hearing the cat meowing, I was smitten with pity." I was very moved by her story and brought the cat out of the north wing, treating it very kindly after that. When I was all by myself, the cat would come to me and I would stroke it saying, "So you are the beloved young daughter of the major counselor. How I would like to let him know." When I spoke like this, the cat would stare into my eyes mewing softly. There was no doubt about it, even from one glance one could tell this was not an ordinary cat. The way its face looked when it seemed to listen and understand was so touching.

I heard about someone who owned a copy of "The Song of Everlasting Sorrow"[240] that had been adapted into the form of a tale.[241] Although I was so curious to see it, the person was not someone I could approach directly. Seeking out a suitable intermediary, I sent over this poem on the seventh day of the Seventh Month,[242]

chirikemu	Curious this day
mukashi no kyō no	upon which long ago they
yukashisa ni	must have pledged their troth;
ama no kawa nami	like the waves rising on the
idetsuru kana	River of Heaven, this is sent out.

---

239. That is, the servant quarters.

240. Famous poem by the Tang poet Bo Juyi about the ill-fated love between Emperor Xuanzong and his concubine Yang Guifei.

241. Presumably, this is a vernacular Japanese translation of the poem with illustrations.

242. Tanabata, the festival of the stars when the Weaver Maid and Herdsman stars (Altair and Vega) are allowed to meet by crossing the bridge provided by the wings of magpies.

The reply,

tachi izuru	This is sent out to
ama no kawabe no	the one so curious
yukashisa ni	by Heaven's River;
tsune wa yuyushiki	one forgets this is a story
koto mo wasurenu	that was unhappy in the end.

On the night of the thirteenth of that same month, the moon shone brightly, lighting up every corner of the house. When everyone was asleep, my elder sister and I went out onto the veranda, and my sister stared intently at the sky, "How would you feel if I were to simply fly away and disappear right now?" Seeing the uncomfortable and fearful look on my face, she changed the subject and laughed merrily. Just then, at the house next door, a carriage for which the way had been cleared stopped, and someone called out, "Reed leaf, sweet reed leaf," but there was no answer. Tired of calling out, whoever it was played charmingly on a flute and moved on. I said,

fue no ne no	Since the voice
tada akikaze to	of the flute sounded just like
kikoyuru ni	the autumn wind,
nado ogi no ha no	why then did the reed leaf
soyo to kotaenu	not rustle in response?

With an air of "Well done," my sister responded,

ogi no ha no	That he did not keep
kotauru made mo	playing until the reed leaf responded,
fuki yorade	but passed by just
tada ni suginuru	like that, the voice of that flute,
fue no ne zo uki	it is really depressing.

In this way, right until dawn, we contemplated the brightness of the moon, and when dawn finally broke, we both went to bed.

That next year,[243] in the Fourth Month in the middle of the night, there was a fire and the cat on which we had lavished such care, thinking it to be the reincarnation of the major counselor's daughter, was burned to death. When I recalled how the cat would come when we called "Young Miss of the Major Counselor," looking as if it understood what we were saying (even father said, "This is truly marvelous; I should tell the major counselor about it"), I felt terribly bereft and thought what a shame it was to have lost her.

---

243. The year is 1023.

Since the spacious grounds of our house were like the scenery in the deep mountains, I had got used to seeing the flowers and crimson leaves of the passing seasons, which were as splendid as those of the mountains, on all sides. Now we had moved to an incomparably cramped place with hardly a garden at all and no trees; how depressing I found it. When the white and red plums of the house in front of this place were blooming in gay profusion, even when I was bathed in the fragrance brought by the wind, how much I missed the old home I was used to and yearned for it.

nioi kuru	Redolent with scent,
tonari no kaze o	the wind from the neighbor's yard
mi ni shimete	soaks into me,
arishi nokiba no	oh, how I yearn for the plum tree
ume zo koishiki	of the eaves I once knew well.

On the first day of the Fifth Month of that year,[244] my elder sister died in childbirth. Ever since I was a child, even the news that someone I did not really know had died would plunge me into deep sorrow; I grieved now with a sorrow that beggared all description. Mother and the others observed the wake with the departed one, so I took her young children, the keepsakes she had left behind, and put one on my left side and one on my right side. Through the cracks in the rough boards of the roof, the moonlight leaked in and shone on the face of one of the little ones. Finding this inauspicious, I covered his face with a sleeve and pulled the other one closer; how terrible were my thoughts!

An interval of about two years passes.

In this way, life went on and my mind was constantly occupied with nothing in particular. When on the rare occasion I went on a pilgrimage, even then I could not concentrate my prayers on becoming somebody in the world (nowadays people read sutras and devote themselves to religious practice even from the age of seventeen or eighteen, but I just could not put my mind to that sort of thing).[245] Somehow my thoughts were captivated by this scene—I would be a noble and elegant woman, beautiful in appearance and manner, whom some hero in a tale, someone like the Shining Genji, would hide away in the mountains like the Lady Ukifune and would visit, even if it were only once a year.[246] There I would gaze out at the blossoms, the crimson leaves, the moon, the snow;

---

244. The year is 1024, when the author is about seventeen years old.
245. The remark about "nowadays" indicates the retrospective nature of this entry.
246. Her imagined scene combines two characters in *The Tale of Genji* who are unconnected in the tale itself. Genji is the hero of the first forty-one chapters of the work; Ukifune makes her first physical appearance in chapter 49. It is Kaoru who hides Ukifune at Uji.

sunk in a melancholy languor, I would wait to read his occasional letters, which would of course be splendid—this was all I dreamed about, and I even felt this was the future I wanted for myself.

Then my father's life came to a turning point.[247] He had somehow hoped to see me settled in even a distinguished position, but time had just passed by without his intentions taking any direction, and now, finally, he was to take up a post far away in the distant East Country. "For years now, I have been expecting to receive a posting in the nearby provinces, and then with a mind free of worry, the first thing I could attend to would be taking care of you in fine style. I could take you with me on tours of duty, show you the seaside and mountain scenery, and, as a matter of course, see you settled into a higher social position than mine, in which all your needs would be met. This is what I wanted, but since it is our fate, both yours and mine, not to be blessed with good fortune, after all this waiting and hoping, now I am to take up a post far away. In your youth, even when I took you with me down to the East Country, I felt a little bad about it. I thought, 'What would happen if I have to abandon her to wander lost in this wild province? If it were just me alone facing the dangers of this alien country, I would be calm, but dragging her and the household with me, I cannot even say what I want to say, nor do what I want to do. How painful this is,' and my heart was torn to pieces with worry. Now this time, how much more am I concerned. I cannot take you off to the provinces as an adult when I cannot be certain about my own life (even though left behind in the capital, it is to be expected you will be living in reduced circumstances). Still that is preferable to imagining you adrift, wandering around as a country rustic in the East Country; that would be too terrible. Yet even in the capital, there is no relative or close friend on whom I can rely to take you in. Nonetheless, since I am not in a position to refuse this posting I have just barely been given, all I can do is leave you behind in the capital and resign myself to a long separation. Yet it is not as though even in the capital, I can leave you maintained in the style I should."[248] I felt so sad listening to my father lament like this day and night, I even lost my feeling for the blossoms and crimson leaves. Although I bemoaned this situation terribly, what could I do about it?

Father went down to his province on the thirteenth day of the Seventh Month. For five days before his departure, he had been unable to bear seeing me and so had not come into my room. On the day he was to leave, everyone was busy with the departure; how much worse I felt at the very moment when he raised the bamboo blind of my room and looked at me with tears pouring down his face. He left just like that. My eyes were blind with tears, and I had just lain

---

247. The year is 1032, when the author is twenty-five years old. Her father is sixty years old and has been expecting to get a provincial governorship in one of the provinces close to the capital, but instead he is appointed to Hitachi, the province next to his former post in Kazusa.

248. The father's rambling, repetitious speech shows the anxiousness of his mind.

down in my room when the household servants who were to remain behind had come back from seeing him off and delivered this letter written on folded note paper:

omou koto	If I were in a
kokoro ni kanau	position that fulfilled the
mi nariseba	wishes of my heart,
aki no wakare o	then would I savor deeply
fukaku shiramashi	the feeling of this autumn parting.[249]

This was all he had written, yet I could hardly read it through. Even at ordinary times, I can only think up verses with "broken backs,"[250] but somehow I felt I must say something, so in that state of mind I wrote almost unconsciously,

kakete koso	Never at all
omowazarishika	did I ever think that
kono yo nite	in this world,
shibashi mo kimi ni	even for a little while,
wakarubeshi to wa	I would be parted from you.

Now more than ever, no visitors came. I gazed constantly into space feeling lonely and bereft, imagining day and night how far he might have gone. Since I knew the path he was taking, as the distance grew between us, there was no limit to my yearning, loving thoughts. From dawn until dusk, I would spend my days staring at the rim of the mountains to the east. . . .

In this way as I drifted along in life, I wondered why I had not gone on pilgrimages. Of course, my mother was very old-fashioned. "A trip to Hatsuse Temple? How frightening the thought! What would I do if you were abducted on the slopes of the Nara hills? Ishiyama Temple? It would be terrifying to cross the Barrier Mountain. As for Kurama, the thought of taking you to that mountain is also frightening. Anyway, until your father gets back, it is out of the question." She seemed to think me troublesome as though I were some kind of outcast. Finally, she took me on a retreat to Kiyomizu Temple. But that time, too, as was my habit, I simply could not concentrate on my prayers. It was around the time of the equinox rites, and the temple was terribly noisy to the point of being frightening. When I finally fell into a fretful slumber, I dreamed that a monk, apparently a kind of steward, dressed in a blue woven robe and wearing a brocade

---

249. Parting in autumn, although sad, is celebrated in poetry. If her father had received the post he hoped for, he would have been able to appreciate the poetic feelings of parting in autumn. In his current situation, there is no such pleasure.

250. A fault in poetry composition in which the third line (thought of as the backbone of a poem) does not connect well with the fourth line.

headpiece and brocade shoes, came up to the railing where my curtain was and said in a chiding way, "Unaware of the sad future awaiting you, you just waste your time on idle concerns." Then he made as though to enter my curtains. Even having seen such a dream and having woke up with a start, I did not tell people, "I have seen such and so," and not even taking it particularly to heart, I went back home.

Then mother had a mirror cast one foot in circumference, and saying that it would be in place of taking me on a pilgrimage, she sent a monk on a pilgrimage to Hatsuse. She apparently told him, "Go perform devotions for three days. Please divine what future is in store for my daughter by having a dream." For that same period of time, she also had me maintain a regime of abstinence.

This monk returned and gave the following report: "Were I to come back without having at least seen one dream, it would be so disappointing, and what would I have to say for myself, so I made obeisances fervently and when I fell asleep, I saw a wonderfully noble and lovely looking woman emerge from behind curtains of state garbed in lustrous robes; she carried the offering mirror in her hand. 'Was there a letter of vows with this?' she asked. I respectfully replied, 'There was not. This mirror by itself is the offering.' 'How strange,' she said. 'This should be accompanied by a letter of vows.' Then she said, 'Look at what is reflected here in this mirror. When you look, it will be deeply sad!' and she wept and sobbed softly. When I looked in the mirror, there was the reflection of someone collapsed on the floor crying and lamenting. 'When you look at this reflection, it is very sad, is it not? Now, look at this,' and she showed me the reflection on the other side of the mirror.[251] Amid beautiful bamboo blinds and other hangings, various robes poured out from under curtains of state; plum and cherry blossoms were in bloom and from the tips of tree branches, warblers were singing. 'Looking at this makes one very happy, does it not?' she said. That is what I saw in the dream." Such was his report, but I did not really pay attention to what had been seen.

Even though I was of such a frivolous turn of mind, there was someone who was always telling me, "Pray to the Holy Deity Amaterasu." I had no idea of where Amaterasu might be or even whether this friend was speaking of a god or a Buddha.[252] Even so, gradually I began to be interested and asked about it. I was told, "It is a god; this god dwells in Ise. In the province of Kii, the one they call the 'Creator of Ki' is also the same holy god.[253] Moreover, it is also this god who is

---

251. A mirror would normally have only one polished side. This is a dream, however, so considerations of realism are not at issue.

252. Amaterasu, literally "Illuminating Heaven," is the Sun Goddess, titular deity of the imperial family. The author claims ignorance of whether Amaterasu is a god or Buddha. Certainly, she appears to have no consciousness of this deity as being gendered female.

253. This remark actually betrays a confusion between a pre-Nara-period official title, Creator of Ki, and the worship of the Sun Goddess in the province of Ki.

the guardian deity in the Sacred Mirror Room in the palace."[254] As far as going to the province of Ise to worship, that did not seem to be anything I could consider, and as for the Sacred Mirror Room of the palace, how could I go and worship there? Since it seemed that all there was to do was to pray to the light of the sky, I felt rather in the air.

Four years pass.

My father, who had been down in the East Country, finally came back up to the capital,[255] and since he settled down in a residence in the Western Hills, we all went to see him there. Wonderfully happy, on a bright moonlit night, we spent the whole night telling one another stories. I composed,

kakaru yo mo	That there could be
arikeru mono o	a night like this in a world like this,
kagiri tote	beyond the limit of joy—
kimi ni wakareshi	that autumn of parting from you,
aki wa ikani zo	it passed the limit too.

Father broke into tears and composed in return,

omou koto	Things not going
kanawazu nazo to	the way I had wished,
ito hikoshi	why live on? I thought;
inochi no hodo mo	now, to have lived as long as this
ima zo ureshiki	what happiness it is!

Ah this, compared with the sadness I felt when he came to tell me of his imminent departure, this joy of having him return safely after the long wait could not be exceeded by anything. Yet when father kept saying, "From what I have seen of people even in superior positions, when an old man whose abilities have declined mixes in society, he is regarded as foolish. So, as for myself, I have decided to close my gate and retreat from the world like this." The way he seemed to have given up all interest in the world made me quite unbearably forlorn. . . .[256]

In the Tenth Month, we moved into the capital. Mother became a nun; although she stayed in the same house with us, she lived apart in her own quarters.

---

254. This information is correct.

255. Takasue returned to the capital in 1036 at the age of sixty-four. The author is twenty-nine.

256. This seems to be a veiled reference to her own situation. Her father's leaving the world of political activity means that he will not be able to do anything positive about her prospects in the world, whether it be marriage or a career at court.

As for father, he just wanted to have me assume the position of mistress of the household, but when I saw that this would mean I would be hidden away and never mix with the world, I felt bereft of support. Around this time, a suggestion came from someone with whom we had a connection and who knew about me that I might serve at court,[257] "Surely it would be better than having her mope around the house with nothing to do." My old-fashioned parents found the idea of my becoming a serving woman most distasteful and so I stayed at home. However, several people said, "Nowadays, almost every young woman goes into service like that, and there have been cases of women who have done very well for themselves indeed. Why don't you give it a try?" So grudgingly father became willing to send me to court.

On the first occasion, I went into service for just one night.[258] I wore a not so deeply dyed ensemble of only eight layers with a jacket of lustrous silk. For me, who had only concentrated my mind on tales and aside from this had known nothing of the world and who, just living under the protection of my old-fashioned parents, had only visited with relatives and who was used only to gazing at the moon and the blossoms—as for my feelings at this moment of stepping out into court service—I could hardly believe it was me or that this was reality. In this state of mind, I returned home at dawn.

When I was a housebound woman, I used to occasionally feel that rather than being stuck forever at home, to go to serve at court would give me the opportunity to see interesting things and might even brighten my outlook, but now I felt uncertain. It seemed to me that indeed there would be things about this new life that might cause me sorrow. Nonetheless, what could I do about it?

In the Twelfth Month, I went again to serve. I was given my own sleeping quarters, and this time I performed duties during the day. Sometimes I would go up to my mistress's chambers and serve on night duty for a few nights. Having to lie down among strangers, I was unable to sleep a wink. I felt so embarrassed and on my guard not to make mistakes that I could not help weeping in secret from the strain. At the first light of dawn while it was still quite dark, I would go back to my own sleeping quarters and spend the whole day distractedly yearning for my family, thinking about my father who, now aged and in decline, depended especially on me. In fact we depended on each other. Then,

---

257. To serve at court means to take a position as lady-in-waiting in the entourages of any of the members of the imperial family.

258. She becomes a lady-in-waiting to Princess Yūshi (1038–1105), who is a child younger than two years old at the time. Princess Yūshi was the daughter of the reigning emperor GoSuzaku and the late Princess Genshi. Genshi was adopted by Fujiwara no Yorimichi after her mother, Empress Teishi, died. Thus Princess Yūshi was being raised in the Takakura Palace of her adoptive grandfather Yorimichi, who was the regent at the time. Service in that household had the potential of putting the author in touch with members of the inner circle of Heian aristocracy. It appears that she starts as a part-time lady-in-waiting for a trial period.

there were my orphaned nephews and niece[259] who had been with me since they were born and slept on my left and right side at night and got up with me in the morning; how poignantly I now recalled them. So I would end up spending my time lost in homesick reverie. My ears would prick up and sense that someone was peeking in at me; how terribly uneasy I was.

After a period of ten days of service, when I returned home, I found my father and mother waiting for me having kindled a fire in the brazier. At the moment of seeing me get down from the carriage, they broke into tears and said, "While you were here, we would see people from time to time, but since you have gone into service, days go by without the sound of human voices and we hardly see anyone; how forlorn and lonely we have been. If this goes on, what is going to become of us?"

Seeing them made me feel so sad. The next morning, they exclaimed, "Since you are home today, the family members and visitors are many; the house feels really lively." Face to face with them, I was moved; some indefinable joy brought me to the verge of tears.

Even for religious adepts, it is very difficult to learn about former lives through dreams, but somehow I felt that going on like this with no sense of direction was not very satisfying, so I had someone try to divine my former life in a dream. I was at the main hall of Kiyomizu Temple. A monk who was a kind of steward came out and reported, "You were actually once a monk in this very temple. As a monk artisan, you accumulated merit by making many Buddha statues. And so you were born into this life well above that lowly station. You built the thirty-foot Buddha[260] who resides in the east section of this hall. As a matter of fact, you died while you were applying the gold foil to this image." "My goodness! This means, does it, that I applied the gold foil to that Buddha over there?" "Since you died while you were doing it, it was a different person who applied the gold foil, and a different person who performed the offering ceremony when it was done." Having received the report of such a dream, afterward, had I made fervent pilgrimages to Kiyomizu Temple, on the strength of having worshiped the Buddha at that main hall in a former life, I would, as a matter of course, have done something good for my salvation. But there is really nothing I can say for myself; this affair ended with my being no more assiduous about making pilgrimages than before.

On the twenty-fifth of the Twelfth Month,[261] I was invited to attend the rite of Calling the Buddha's Names[262] at the princess's palace. I went expecting to

---

259. The children of her elder sister. It now has been fifteen years since her sister died.

260. The measurement mentioned is *ichijōrokushaku*, which is approximately thirty feet. From the size and description of its placement, the monk is likely referring to the central image of the Amida Buddha in the Kiyomizu Main Hall.

261. An intercalary Twelfth Month of 1039.

262. The "Calling the Buddha's Names" was an annual event at the imperial palace that involved reciting the names of all three thousand buddhas in order to expiate the sins of the past year. After the event at the imperial palace, the same event was repeated in the home palaces of

stay only that night. There were as many as forty attendants all in layers of white robes with jackets of lustrous silk. I hid myself behind the lady who was my guide at court and, after barely showing myself, returned home at dawn, Snow had begun to flutter down; in the amazingly severe freezing chill of the dawn light, the moon faintly reflected in my lustrous sleeves truly recalled the "face damp with tears" of long ago.[263] On the road back, I composed,

toshi wa kure	The year is ending,
yo wa akegata no	the night begins to dawn,
tsukikage no	both ephemeral
sode ni utsureru	as the rays of the moon
hodo zo hakanaki	reflected on these sleeves of mine.

Well, even if my debut had been like this, somehow I began to accustom myself to service at court. Although I was somewhat distracted by other things, it was not to the extent that people regarded me as eccentric, and as a matter of course, it seemed as though I had come to be regarded and treated as one of the company, but my parents did not understand, and before long, they ended up shutting me away at home.[264] Even so, it was not as though my way of life became suddenly bright and lively. Rather, although I was used to feeling very much at odds with life, now the situation I found myself in was utterly contrary to all my hopes.

ikuchi tabi	How many thousand times
mizu no ta zeri o	have I plucked the field parsley
tsumi shika wa	from the water thus,
omoishi koto no	without a dew drop falling
tsuyu mo kanawanu	in the direction of my hopes.[265]

With just this solitary complaint, I let matters go.

Meanwhile, I became distracted by this and that and completely forgot even about the world of the tales. I actually ended up feeling quite down to earth. Over the years and months, as I lay down and got up in meaningless activity, why had I not devoted myself to religious practices or pilgrimages? Ah, but, the things I had hoped for, the things I had wished for, could they ever really hap-

---

the imperial consorts. The ceremony that the author attends is presumably at the Takakura Palace.

263. An allusion to *Kokinshū*, no. 756: "Joining me in feeling at a time when I brood on things, the moon dwelling in these sleeves of mine also has a face damp with tears."

264. This is a veiled reference to her marriage to Tachibana no Toshimichi (1002–1058). From her following comments, it does not appear that it was a match to her taste at first.

265. "Plucking field parsley" was a proverbial expression for putting all one's heart into a project and having it come to nothing.

pen in this world? After all, was a man like the Shining Genji ever likely to exist in this world? No, this is a world in which being hidden away at Uji by Captain Kaoru could never happen.[266] Oh, how crazy I was and how foolish I came to feel. Such were the thoughts that sunk in, and had I then carried on with my feet on the ground, maybe things would have been all right, but it did not end up that way.

Some friends had informed the place at which I had first gone into court service that it did not appear staying cooped up at home like this was really my true wish, so there were endless requests for my attendance, and among them came a particular one, "Send the young lady to court,"[267] an order that could not be ignored, so I found myself drawn back into occasional service in the course of presenting my niece to court. However, it was not as though I could in the least entertain the vain and immodest hopes such as I had in the days gone by; after all, I was just being drawn along by my niece. On the occasions when I went to serve, the situation was like this. The women really familiar with court service are in a class by themselves and greet any occurrence with a knowing face, but as for me, although I could not be regarded as a novice, neither could I be treated as an old hand, so I was kept at a distance like an occasional guest. Although I was in this uncertain position, since I was not one who had to rely solely on that kind of work, I was not particularly envious of those who were so much better at it than me. In fact, I felt rather at ease, going to court just on suitable occasions, chatting with those women who happened to have time on their hands. On celebratory occasions, and interesting, pleasant occasions too, in my present situation I was able to mix with society in this way. Of course, since I had to maintain a reserve and take care not to push myself forward too much, I was privy only to the general goings-on at court. As I passed my time thus, there came a time when I accompanied the princess to the imperial palace.[268] One dawn when the moon was so bright, I thought to myself, "The god Amaterasu to whom I have been praying actually resides right here in the palace mirror room; I would actually like to take this occasion to worship here." So in the brightness of the moonlight of the Fourth Month, ever so secretly, I went to pay my respects with the guidance of an acquaintance, Lady Myōbu, who served as mistress of the inner chambers. In the very faint light of the lamp stand, she looked amazingly ancient and partook of a divine quality; as she sat there speaking of fine things as one might expect, she seemed scarcely like a human being, one might even think she was the god manifesting itself.

---

266. A reference to her youthful dream to be kept in a rural setting by someone as handsome as Genji.

267. A request to present the author's niece.

268. An occurrence in 1042.

The author recounts more service at the imperial palace, including a romantic conversa-
tion and correspondence with a courtier that fulfilled her fiction-inspired expectations.
The diary resumes after a gap of two or three years.

Now I had come to a sharp awareness of regretting only the absurd fancies
of long ago, and I also could not help recalling with vexation how I had ended
up not going along on my parents' pilgrimages and such. And now, too, I was
wealthy and full of energy, able to raise my "little sprout"[269] with the plentiful
care I wanted. My situation in the world exceeded that of the "Great Treasure
House" mountain, and so it spurred my concern and desires for the world to
come. Just past the twentieth of the Eleventh Month,[270] I went on a pilgrimage
to Ishiyama Temple.

Snow was falling; the scenery along the way was beautiful. When I saw the
Osaka Border Barrier, I suddenly recalled that the time we crossed this border long ago[271] it also was winter and, at that time, too, how wildly the wind
blew.

Ōsaka no	The voice of the
seki no seki kaze	border wind blowing now
fuku koe wa	through the barrier,
mukashi kikishi ni	from the one I heard long ago
kawarazarikeri	is no different at all.

When I saw how splendid the Barrier Temple had been built up, I recalled
how, that time before, one could only see the roughly hewn face of the Buddha.
How touching it was to realize how many months and years had passed.

The area around the beach of Uchiide and so forth looked no different than
before. We arrived at the goal of our pilgrimage just as it was getting dark. Getting down at the purification pavilion, we went up to the Sacred Hall. No one
spoke. I found the sound of the mountain wind to be frightening. I dozed off
while I was praying, and in a dream a person told me, "Some musk deer incense has been bestowed upon us by the Central Hall. Quickly announce this
over there." I woke up with a start and when I realized that it had been a
dream, I felt it must be auspicious, so I spent the whole night in religious
devotions.

---

269. A reference to a son she had with Toshimichi. Later in the diary, she mentions children
in the plural, and it is known that she had another son and one daughter with Toshimichi, but
the diary gives no precise information about the births. From other sources, it is also known that
Toshimichi was governor of Shimotsuke Province starting in 1041 and would have returned to
the capital around the time of this entry.

270. The year is 1045, when the author is thirty-eight years old.

271. The Osaka Barrier is in the mountains between the capital and Lake Biwa. The author
passed the barrier when she was thirteen years old on her way to the capital from the east.

The next day, too, snow fell heavily. Speaking with the friend I had got to know at court and who had accompanied me on the pilgrimage, I tried to soothe the feelings of uneasiness. We were in retreat for three days and then went back.

That following year, there was a great buzz about the procession for the Great Purification preceding the Great Festival of Thanksgiving that was to be held on the twenty-fifth day of the Tenth Months.[272] I had started fasting in preparation for a pilgrimage to Hatsuse Temple, and because I was to leave the capital on that very day, people whom one might expect to take an interest in my affairs said things like, "This is something one only gets to see once in a reign, even people from the countryside and all over the place are coming in to see it. After all, there are so many days in a month. For you to go off and desert the capital on that very day, why, it's crazy; it will certainly be a tale people will pass around." Although my brother fumed about it, the father of my children said, "No matter what, do what you think best."[273] I was quite moved by his willingness to send me off in accordance with what I had said. It seems that those who were to accompany me wanted very much to view the procession. Although it was sad for them, I thought to myself, "After all, what does sightseeing amount to? The zeal to want to make a pilgrimage on this kind of occasion will surely be recognized as such. I shall certainly see a sacred sign from the Buddha." I strengthened my will and left at first light of that day. Just as we were passing along the grand avenue of Nijō (I had had my attendants wear pilgrim's white garments and those in front carry holy lanterns), there were a lot of people going to and fro, some on horseback, some in ox carriages, some on foot, on their way to take up places in the viewing stands. Surprised and disconcerted at seeing us, people in the crowd murmured, "What on earth is this?" and even some laughed derisively and jeered.

When we passed in front of the house of the guard commander, Yoshiyori,[274] it seemed that he was just about to move to his viewing stand. The gates were pushed open wide and people were standing around. Someone said, "That seems to be somebody going on a pilgrimage. And to think of all the other days they could have chosen." Amid those laughing at this, there was one—I wonder what was in his heart—who said, "What is so important about delighting one's eyes for a moment? With such fervent zeal, someone like that is sure to receive the

---

272. The Great Festival of Thanksgiving is the grander version of the annual Festival of First Fruits. The Great Festival was held on years when a new emperor was officially enthroned. Emperor GoReizei (1025–1068) had assumed the throne the previous year. It was the custom to hold the official enthronement rites the year after the succession. The Great Purification preceding the festival had the new emperor perform a ritual ablution on the banks of the Kamo River. The pomp and pageantry made it a popular event for sightseeing.

273. This is the first direct mention of the author's husband in the diary, and it casts a surprisingly positive light on their relationship given her initially negative reaction to the marriage.

274. Eldest son of Fujiwara no Takaie (979–1044), brother of the late Empress Teishi.

Buddha's grace. Maybe we are the ones without sense. Giving up the sight-seeing and making up our minds to do something like that; that is what we ought to be doing." So, there was one person who could speak with some sense of seriousness.

Not to be exposed to the eyes of others on the road, we had left while it was still dark; now, in order to wait for those who had left later to catch up and hoping that the alarmingly deep fog would lift a little, we stopped at the main gate of Hōshō Temple. There we could really see the crowds of people coming in from the countryside to sightsee; they flowed on and on like a river. Everywhere, it was hard to make way. Even some rather strange-looking urchins who seemed hardly old enough to understand things looked askance at our carriage forcing its way against the stream of traffic. There was no end to it. Seeing all these people, I even began to wonder why on earth I had set out on this trip, but concentrating my thoughts single-mindedly on the Buddha, I finally arrived at Uji. There too, there was a crowd of people wanting to cross over to this side. The boat helmsmen were in no hurry to make the crossings; they stood around, sleeves rolled up, leaning on their oars, looking quite arrogant as though they were not even aware of all the people waiting to cross. Looking around, singing songs, they appeared very smug. We were unable to cross for an interminable amount of time. When I looked carefully around me, I recalled the daughters of the Uji prince in Murasaki's tale.[275] I always had been curious about what kind of place it was where she had had them live. So this must be it, and indeed it is a lovely place. Thinking these thoughts, finally I was ferried across. Also, when I went in to look at the Uji villa belonging to his lordship,[276] the first thing that sprang to mind was, "Would not the Lady Ukifune have lived in a place just like this?"[277]

Since we had left before light, my people were very tired, so we stopped at a place called Yahirouchi. While we were having something to eat, my attendants talked among themselves, "Say, isn't this the famous Mount Kurikoma?[278] It is getting on toward dusk. We had better get everyone ready to go." I listened to this with apprehension.

---

275. These are the daughters of the Eighth Prince in *The Tale of Genji*, who moved to Uji after his residence in the capital burned down. The courtship of these sisters, the untimely death of the elder sister, and finally the installation of their half sister Ukifune at Uji by Kaoru make up the content of the so-called Uji chapters of *The Tale of Genji*. This remark also is evidence that the author of *The Tale of Genji* was being referred to by the nickname Murasaki by this succeeding generation of readers.

276. This is the villa of Fujiwara no Yorimichi, Princess Yūshi's adoptive grandfather and therefore in a sense the author's employer. This is likely why she was able to tour the villa. Seven years after this date, Yorimichi rebuilt the villa magnificently and eventually had it consecrated as a temple, the Byōdō-in, which survives.

277. Another reference to the Uji chapters of *The Tale of the Genji*.

278. Mount Kurikoma was notorious for bandits.

We made it over that mountain; just as we arrived in the area of Nieno pond, the sun was just setting over the rim of the mountain. "Now let us stop for the night," said my attendants, and they spread out to seek lodging. "It is not a very suitable place, but there is only this rather poor and shabby little house," they said. "What else can we do?" I replied, and so we ended up lodging there. There were only two rather seedy-looking men servants in charge, who said, "Everybody else has gone up to the capital." That night, too, I barely got any sleep. The men servants kept walking around in and out of the house. I heard the maid servants in the rear of the house ask, "Why on earth are you roaming around like that?" "What do you mean? Here we are putting up people we don't know at all. Suppose they were to make off with the cauldron, what would we do? We can't sleep for worrying, so we are wandering around keeping an eye on things." They spoke thinking we were asleep. Listening to this was both strange and amusing.

Early the next morning, we left there and went to pray at Todai Temple. The Isonokami Shrine truly looked as old as its name makes one imagine;[279] it is all wild and overgrown.

That night we stayed at a place called Yamabe. Although I was tired, I tried to read the sutras a little. I dozed off, and in a dream I saw myself visiting an amazingly beautiful and noble lady. The wind was blowing hard. She looked at me and smiled, "What brings you here?" she asked. "How could I not pay my respects?" I replied. "It is to be expected that you will live at the imperial palace. It would be good for you to discuss this with Lady Myōbu"[280] is what I thought, she said. I felt very happy and putting much store by this dream, my faith strengthened more and more. We went along the Hatsuse River and that night arrived at the holy temple. After performing ablutions, we went up to the main hall. We stayed in retreat for three days. We were to start the return journey at dawn; night came and I dozed off. From the direction of the main hall came a voice, "You there, here is a sacred cedar branch bestowed by the Inari Shrine,"[281] and as the person appeared to reach out and throw me something, I woke up with a start and realized it was a dream.

At dawn, while it was still dark, we departed. We found it difficult to get lodgings that night but finally asked to stay at a house on this side of the Nara slope. My attendants talked among themselves, "This seems to be a suspicious place. Don't fall asleep at all. Something unexpected may happen. Whatever you do, do not look afraid or alarmed. Your Ladyship, please just lie here quietly." Just hearing this, I was miserable and afraid. I felt as though it took a

---

279. Isonokami Shrine was in the village of Furu, a place-name homophonous with the words "to age" and the "passing of time." Hence it became an *uta-makura*, a poetic toponym for growing old.

280. Lady Myōbu is the mistress of the inner chambers of the imperial palace.

281. The famous Inari Shrine at Fushimi, south of the capital.

thousand years for dawn to break. Finally, just as it began to get light, one of my attendants said, "This is the home of thieves. The woman who is our host acted suspiciously, you know."

On a day when the wind was blowing hard, we crossed the Uji River and rowed very close by the fish weirs.

oto ni nomi	Having only heard
kikiwatari koshi	of the sound of the waves
Uji kawa no	lapping against the
ajiro no nami mo	fish weirs of Uji River,
kyō zo kazouru	today, I can even count them.[282]

Since I have been writing consecutively in no particular order of events that were two, three or four years apart, it makes me look like a devout practitioner who was continually going on pilgrimages, but it was not like that; years and months separated these events.

The next section picks up the author's life around the year 1057, more than a decade after the pilgrimages just described.

In my life, one way or another, I had expended my heart on worry. As for my court service, how might it have turned out if only I had been able to devote myself to it single-mindedly? But since I went to serve only sporadically, it seems one could not expect it to have amounted to anything. I had gradually passed my prime and couldn't help feeling that it was unseemly for me to carry on as though I were still young. My body had become weak through illness, so I could no longer go on pilgrimages as I wanted. I had even stopped going out on rare occasions. While I hardly felt that I should live much longer, nonetheless, everyday, lying down, getting up, I was plagued with the thought, "How much I wish to live long enough in this world to see the young ones properly settled."[283] Meanwhile, I worried anxiously to hear news of a fortunate appointment for the one I relied on.[284] Autumn arrived, and it seemed that what we were waiting for had come, but the appointment was not what we expected.[285] It was a pity to be so disappointed. It did seem as though his post was a little closer than the eastern circuit my father had seen going to and fro on a number of occasions. Anyway, what could we do about it? We

---

282. The fish weirs at Uji were a favorite subject for poetry.

283. The three children that the author had with Toshimichi.

284. Toshimichi.

285. Toshimichi received a post as the governor of the province of Shinano (present-day Nagano Prefecture).

hurried with preparations for his imminent departure. He was to make his formal start a little after the tenth day of the Fifth Month from the residence to which his daughter had just moved.[286] His departure was a lively affair with lots of people bustling around.

Our son accompanied him when he left for the provinces on the twenty-seventh day.[287] Our son, with a sword at his side, wore purple trousers of a twill weave, with a hunting cloak of the bush clover color combination over a red robe that had been fulled to a glossy sheen. He walked behind his father, who wore dark blue trousers and a hunting coat. At the central gallery, they mounted their horses. After the lively procession had departed, I felt somehow at loose ends with nothing to do. Since I had heard that their destination was not so terribly far,[288] I did not feel quite as bereft as I had on previous occasions. Those who had gone along to see the party off came back the next day and said, "They departed in great splendor." And when they said, "This morning at dawn, a really large soul fire appeared and came toward the capital,"[289] I thought surely it must be from one of his attendants. Did an inkling of this being a bad omen come to me?

Now all I could think about was how to raise the young children into adults. My husband came back to the capital in the Fourth Month;[290] summer and autumn passed.

On the twenty-fifth day of the Ninth Month, my husband fell ill; on the fifth day of the Tenth Month, he died.[291] I felt as though it was a bad dream; I could not imagine something like this happening. The image that had been seen in the mirror offered to Hatsuse Temple[292] of a figure collapsed on the ground weeping; this was me now. The image of the joyous figure had never happened. Now, there was no hope of its ever happening. On the twenty-third day, the night when the evanescent clouds of smoke were to be kindled, the one whom I had watched go off with his father in such a magnificent costume now wore mourning white over a black robe and accompanied the funeral carriage crying and sobbing as he walked away. Seeing him off, remembering the other time—I had never felt like this before. I grieved as though lost in a dream; I wondered if my departed one could see me.

---

286. This is apparently an older daughter from an earlier marriage.

287. Their eldest son is about seventeen years old.

288. Shinano was a little more than half the distance to the east country.

289. "Soul fire" is the translation of *hitodama*, a bluish ball of light that was thought to depart from a person who was soon to die.

290. It seems that her husband was given permission to leave his post. His health may have been weakened by the severe winters of the mountainous Shinano region.

291. The text itself does not state explicitly that "he died" but merely speaks of feeling as though one were having a bad dream.

292. A reference to the mirror her mother had had cast and sent as an offering to Hatsuse Temple in order to try to divine her future as a young woman.

Long ago, rather than being infatuated with all those useless tales and poems, if I had only devoted myself to religious practice day and night, I wonder, would I have been spared seeing this nightmarish fate? The time that I went to Hatsuse Temple when someone in a dream threw something to me saying, "This is a sacred branch bestowed by the Inari Shrine," if I had just gone right then and there on a pilgrimage to Inari, maybe this would not have happened. The dreams that I had had over the years in which I had been told, "Worship the god Amaterasu" had been divined as meaning that I should become a nurse to an imperial child, serving in the palace and receiving the protection of the imperial consort.[293] But nothing like that had ever come to be. Only the sad image in the mirror had been fulfilled. Pitifully, I grieved. Since I had ended up as one without one thing going as I had wished, I drifted along without doing anything to accumulate merit.

Yet somehow it seemed that although life was sad, it would go on. I worried that perhaps even my hopes for the afterlife might not be granted. There was only one thing I could put my faith in. It was a dream I had had on the thirteenth day of the Tenth Month in the third year of Tenki.[294] Amida Buddha appeared in the front garden of the house where I lived. He was not clearly visible but appeared through what seemed like a curtain of mist. When I strained to look through gaps in the mist, I could see a lotus dais about three to four feet above the ground; the holy Buddha was about six feet in height. He glowed with a golden light, and as for his hands, one was spread open, and with the other he was making a mudra.[295] Other people could not see him; only I could see him. Unaccountably, I experienced a great sense of fear and was unable to move closer to the bamboo blinds to see. The Buddha deigned to speak, "If this is how it is, I will go back this time, but later I will return to welcome you." Only my ears could hear his voice, the others could not. Such was the dream I saw when I woke up with a start. It was the fourteenth. Only this dream is my hope for the afterlife.

My nephews, whom I had seen morning and evening when we lived in the same place, had gone off to live in different places after this sad event had occurred, so I rarely saw anyone. On a very dark night, the sixth youngest nephew[296] came for a visit; feeling this was unusual,

tsuki mo idede	Not even the moon
yami ni kuretaru	has come out in the dark shrouding
obasute ni	Abandoned Aunt, to which,

---

293. Here readers are finally given the precise content of the hopes she had entertained for practical success in the world.

294. The year 1055 was three years before the death of her husband. This is the only time in the diary that the author gives such a complete date.

295. A sacred hand gesture.

296. This reference has puzzled commentators because the author never before mentions having as many as six nephews.

| *nani tote koyoi* | with what on your mind this night, |
| *tazune kitsuramu* | might you have come visiting?[297] |

was what came spontaneously to my lips.

And to a friend with whom I had corresponded warmly before, but from whom I had not heard since I had come to this pass,

ima wa yo ni	Is it that you think
araji mono to ya	I am one no longer living
omouramu	in this world of ours?
aware naku naku	Sadly I cry and cry,
nao koso wa fure	yet I do indeed live on.

At the time of the Tenth Month, crying as I gazed out at the exceeding brightness of the full moon,

hima mo naki	Even to a heart
namida ni kumoru	clouded by tears that fall
kokoro ni mo	with no respite,
akashi to miyuru	the light pouring from the moon
tsuki no kage kana	can appear so radiant.

The years and months change and pass by, but when I recall that dreamlike time, my mind wanders, and it is as though my eyes grow dark so that I cannot recall clearly the events of that time.

Everyone has moved to live elsewhere; only I am left at the old house. One time when I stayed up all night in gloomy contemplation feeling so bereft and sad, I sent this to someone I had not heard from for a long time.

shigeri yuku	The mugwort grows more
yomogi ga tsuyu ni	and more rank, the dew on it
sobachitsutsu	soaks through and through;
hito ni towarenu	not visited by anyone,
ne o nomi zo naku	my voice is only raised in sobs.

---

297. Abandoned Aunt, or Obatsuteyama, literally, "the mountain where old aunts are abandoned," is an uta-makura, a poetic toponym with complex associations. Obatsuteyama is in the Sarashina District of Nagano and is famous both for its connection with the folk belief about an ancient custom of abandoning old women and for being a beautiful place to view the moon. The touchstone for the place-name's association with the moon is *Kokinshū*, no. 879: "My heart finds it hard to be comforted. Ah Sarashina! On Mount Abandoned Aunt, I see the bright moon shining." The place-name has a further personal association for the author because Sarashina and Obasuteyama are in the province of Shinano, the last posting for her husband. The traditional title for this diary, *Sarashina nikki*, is derived from this poem.

She was a nun and so replied,

yo no tsune no	Ah, yours is mugwort
yado no yomogi no	growing at an ordinary
omoiyare	dwelling in the world,
somuki hatetaru	imagine the clumps of weeds
niwa no kusa mura	in my garden of renunciation.

[Introduction by Itō Moriyuki and translation by Sonja Arntzen]

HEIAN LITERATI

In the Heian period, the ability to compose Chinese poetry and prose was a requirement for male officials. An earlier ideal (of which Sugawara no Michizane was perhaps the last major example) existed in which a person with literary ability was valued and rewarded in the world of bureaucracy and the court. This ideal was based on the belief that the ability to excel in belles lettres was linked to the ability to excel in government. But beginning in the tenth century with the dominance of the Fujiwara regency, this ideal existed only in name, and those officials who excelled in Chinese learning and belles lettres were not given an opportunity to rise in the bureaucracy or to be publicly rewarded for their talents. These men of letters, referred to here as literati (*bunjin*), tended to look at the sociopolitical hierarchy from the outside, with a critical eye. Among the literati leaders were Ōe no Asatsuna (886–957), Minamoto no Shitagō (911–983), Yoshishige no Yasutane (d. 1002), and Fujiwara no Akihira (989–1066), who appear in *Literary Essence of Our Country* (*Honchō monzui*).

LITERARY ESSENCE OF OUR COUNTRY
(*HONCHŌ MONZUI*, MID-ELEVENTH CENTURY)

The *Literary Essence of Our Country* is an anthology of Chinese prose and poetry by Japanese writers. It was edited by Fujiwara no Akihira (989–1066), a noted literatus and the author of *An Account of the New Monkey Music* (*Shinsarugakuki*) and *Akihira Letters* (*Meigō ōrai*). Following the model of the noted Chinese literary anthology the *Wen xuan* (J. *Monzen*), the *Honchō monzui* is a collection of texts written in Chinese over a two-hundred-year span, from 810 to 1037, divided into various genres and categories.

YOSHISHIGE NO YASUTANE

Yoshishige no Yasutane was born into the Kamo family, which specialized in yin-yang, but he pursued Confucian studies and became a low-ranking official.

Yasutane also was a key figure in forming the Kangaku-e, a group devoted to the study of Buddhism. When he came into contact with Genshin, the author of *Ōjōyōshū*, he was exposed to Jōdo (Pure Land) Buddhism and finally took holy vows in 986. (Yasutane's Buddhist name is Jakushin.) Yasutane is representative of mid-Heian literati who, becoming disillusioned with the low position of the literati in the aristocratic sociopolitical hierarchy, turned to the alternative of reclusion and Pure Land Buddhism.

RECORD OF A POND PAVILION (CHITEIKI, 982)

"Record of a Pond Pavilion," written in couplet-based, parallel-prose kanbun and one of the most famous texts in the *Honchō monzui*, anticipates Kamo no Chōmei's *An Account of a Ten-Foot-Square Hut (Hōjōki)* by two centuries.

. . . So, after five decades in the world, I've at last managed to acquire a little house, like a snail at peace in his shell, like a louse happy in the seam of a garment. The quail nests in the small branches and does not yearn for the great forest of Teng; the frog lives in his crooked well and knows nothing of the vastness of the sweeping seas. Though as master of the house I hold office at the foot of the pillar, in my heart it's as though I dwelt among the mountains.[298] Position and title I leave up to fate, for the workings of Heaven govern all things alike. Heaven and earth will decide if I live a long life or a short one—like Confucius, I've been praying for a long time now.[299] I do not envy the man who soars like a phoenix on the wind, nor the man who hides like a leopard in the mists. I have no wish to bend my knee and crook my back in efforts to win favor with great lords and high officials, but neither do I wish to shun the words and faces of others and bury myself in some remote mountain or dark valley. During such time as I am at court, I apply myself to the business of the sovereign; once home, my thoughts turn always to the service of the Buddha. When I go abroad I don my grass-green official robe, and though my post is a minor one, I enjoy a certain measure of honor. At home I wear white hemp undergarments, warmer than spring, purer than the snow. After washing my hands and rinsing my mouth, I ascend the western hall, call on the Buddha Amida, and recite the Lotus Sutra. When my supper is done, I enter the eastern library, open my books, and find myself in the company of worthy men of the past, those such as Emperor Wen of the Han, a ruler of another era, who loved frugal ways and gave rest to his people;

---

298. At this time, Yasutane held the post of *naiki*, or secretary in the Nakatsukasa-shō, a bureau of the government that handled imperial edicts, petitions, and other documents. "Clerk at the foot of the pillar" was a Chinese term for such a secretary.

299. When Confucius fell ill, one of his disciples asked to be allowed to pray for him, but Confucius replied, "I've been praying for a long time now" (*Analects*, 7:34).

Bo Juyi of the Tang, a teacher of another time, who excelled in poetry and served the Buddhist Law; or the Seven Sages of the Chin, friends of another age, who lived at court but longed for the life of retirement.[300] So I meet with a worthy ruler, I meet with a worthy teacher, and I meet with worthy friends, three meetings in one day, three delights to last a lifetime. As for the people and affairs of the contemporary world, they hold no attraction for me. If in becoming a teacher one thinks only of wealth and honor and is not concerned with the importance of literature, it would be better if we had no teachers. If in being a friend one thinks only of power and profit and cares nothing about frank exchange of opinions, it would be better if we had no friends. So I close my gate, shut my door, and hum poems and songs by myself. When I feel the desire for something more, I and my boys climb into the little boat, thump the gunwale and rattle the oars. If I have some free time left over, I call the groom and we go out to the vegetable garden to pour on water and spread manure. I love my house—other things I know nothing about.

Since the Ōwa era [961–964], people of the time have taken a fancy to building luxurious mansions and high-roofed halls, even going so far as to have the tops of the pillars carved in the shape of mountains and duckweed designs incised on the supports of the roof beam.[301] But though the expenditure runs into many millions in cash, they manage to live there barely two or three years. People in old times used to say, "The builder doesn't get to live in what he builds"— how right they were. Now that I am well along in years, I've finally managed to construct a little house, but when I consider it in light of my actual needs, even *it* seems somewhat too extravagant and grand. Above, I fear the anger of Heaven; below, I am ashamed in the eyes of men. I'm like a traveler who's found an inn along the road, an old silkworm who's made himself a solitary cocoon. How long will I be able to live here?

Ah, when the wise man builds a house, he causes no expense to the people, no trouble to the spirits. He uses benevolence and righteousness for his ridgepole and beam, ritual and law for his pillar and base stone, truth and virtue for a gate and door, mercy and love for a wall and hedge. Devotion to frugality is his family business, the piling up of goodness his family fortune. When one has such a house to live in, no fire can consume it, no wind topple it, no misfortune appear to threaten it, no disaster come its way. No god or spirit can peer within it, no thief or bandit can invade. The family who lives there will naturally grow rich, the master will enjoy a long life, and office and rank will be with it forever,

---

300. Emperor Wen reigned from 179 to 157 B.C.E.; Bo Juyi (772–846), whose poems were greatly admired in Japan, wrote prose pieces that provided the model for this work by Yasutane; the Seven Sages of the Bamboo Grove were a group of Chinese poet-philosophers of the third century who gathered to drink, play the lute, and discuss philosophy.

301. The latter part of the sentence is a conventional Chinese expression indicating architectural extravagance and should not necessarily be taken literally.

to be handed down to sons and grandsons. How can one fail, then, to exercise caution?

Composed and written in the hand of the master of the house, Yasutane, in the Tenth Month, the first month of winter, of the fifth year of Tengen (982).

[Translated by Burton Watson]

LATE HEIAN AND EARLY KAMAKURA MONOGATARI

The stories in the late Heian and early Kamakura periods are marked by their parodic and allusive nature, which makes them different from other short-story forms such as the sections (*dan*) found in poem tales like *The Tales of Ise* or the anecdotes. The contemporary aristocratic readers and writers of these monogatari shared their knowledge of earlier monogatari and their conventions, which become the source of variation, parody, and allusion. Significantly, *The Tale of Genji* was repeatedly mimicked and parodied, creating seemingly endless variations on this masterpiece. A noted characteristic of late Heian and early Kamakura monogatari is that at a time when the aristocracy was rapidly losing economic power and social status, the beleaguered aristocracy looked back to the Heian-court monogatari (and to a world that had become more ideal than reality) with detachment and irony as well as as a form of escape and fantasy.

THE STORIES OF THE RIVERSIDE MIDDLE COUNSELOR
(*TSUTSUMI CHŪNAGON MONOGATARI,*
CA. TENTH−FOURTEENTH CENTURIES)

The Stories of the Riverside Middle Counselor consists of ten short stories, which are not in a fixed order. The exact date of the stories is unknown but is thought to range from as early as the tenth century to as late as the fourteenth century. Only one of the short stories, "The Middle Counselor Who Could Not Cross Ōsaka," can be reliably dated. According to one record, it was presented by Koshikibu, a lady-in-waiting (*nyōbō*), at a monogatari contest sponsored by Princess Baishi in 1055.

The late Heian and early Kamakura monogatari assume a certain detachment toward the content of the Heian monogatari, making them the object of laughter and irony. If *aware* (pathos) was the pervading tone of the Heian-court monogatari, that of *The Stories of the Riverside Middle Counselor* and other late Heian monogatari mix in subtle and ironic humor. Significantly, "The Lady Who Preferred Insects" (Mushi mezuru himegimi) begins with the phrase "the lady who was fond of butterflies," which embodies the opposite of the protagonist. Fondness for butterflies represented the typical good taste of Heian aristocratic ladies, an attitude that here is inverted to reveal the underside of such a world. In fact, almost all the protagonist's views are either an implicit critique of or a form of resistance to aristocratic aesthetic and social standards, with the protagonist seeking her own individuality and identity in contradiction to these norms.

The Lady Who Preferred Insects (Mushi mezuru himegimi)

Next door to the lady who was fond of butterflies lived another lady, daughter of the Lord Inspector. She had been reared with uncommon love and attention. She said: "It is silly of people to make so much of flowers and butterflies. They would do far better to inquire seriously into the nature of things." Indiscriminately she gathered ugly specimens. "We will observe how they grow and change," she said, putting her specimens in cages in which she could observe them. "See how serious and intent the caterpillars seem to be." Her hair tucked out of the way behind her ears all the day long, she would hold them affectionately in her hand and gaze intently at them.

Her women being afraid of them, she gathered urchins of the lower orders who were afraid of nothing. She had them take out her insects and tell her their names, and when they had none she would invent names for them. It was her view that people should live the natural way. Against all common sense, she declined to pluck her eyebrows, and said that blackening the teeth was troublesome and unsanitary. Smiling an uncompromisingly white smile, she doted on her insects morning and night. Because her women were constantly fleeing, her room was in great confusion. Life was not easy for them. She was forever berating them and glowering at them through her thick black brows.

"Why can't she be like other girls?" her parents would say. "But she must have her reasons. It is all very strange. When you speak seriously to her the answers are sensible enough. So it is not that she is merely stupid." They were quite at a loss.

"This is all very well. But think what people are saying. They like a girl to be pretty. It does not do to have them say that you are devoted to repulsive caterpillars."

"I don't care in the least. Things make sense only when you observe and watch them develop. People are silly. A caterpillar becomes a butterfly." And she showed them how it was happening. "The silk that we wear is made by worms before they have wings. When they take wing it's all over." They had no answer.

Yet she was a lady. She did not address her parents openly. Devils and women were not to be looked upon. She would raise the blinds of the sitting room slightly and set out a post curtain, and thus discreetly receive them.

Her young women heard it all. "She may love her caterpillars, but they drive us to distraction. How pleasant it must be to work for the lady who likes butterflies."

A woman called Hyōei offered a poem:

> Am I to leave before she sees the light?
> A caterpillar is not that forever.

Laughing, a woman called Kodayū answered:

> Happy they with flowers and butterflies.
> For us it is the stench of caterpillars.

"How sad. Her eyebrows are genuine caterpillars. And her teeth are naked." Said a woman called Sakon:

> "So many furry creatures all about—
> we will survive the winter without coats.

and so, we may hope, will she."

An irritable old woman overheard. "And what are you children babbling about? I don't think it so fine that the lady next door likes butterflies. Indeed it seems stupid. Who could call a row of caterpillars a row of butterflies? The point is that they shed their skins and become butterflies. Watching it happen is a serious matter. When you take up a butterfly you get that nasty powder all over your hand. And you might get an attack of ague too. Isn't that reason enough to avoid butterflies?"

But this view of the matter only added to the shrillness of the criticism.

The boys meanwhile were kept busy. Knowing that there would be rewards, they brought in all manner of horrid creatures.

"The fur of the caterpillar is so interesting. Why don't the poets and the storytellers have more to say about it?"

The boys brought her mantises and they brought her snails, and sang loud songs about them, and the lady sang the loudest. "Why do the horns of the snail do battle?"

Thinking the names of her boys rather dull, she renamed them after specimens in her collection: Cricket, Toad, Mayfly, Grasshopper, Centipede.

Word of all this spread abroad, and there were extravagant rumors. One young man, son of a high courtier, dashing and gallant and handsome as well, said that he had something to frighten her with. He took a cutting from a fine sash and shaped it into a most life-like snake, even contriving that it would move. He put it in a pouch with a scale pattern and a drawstring and attached a poem to it.

> Crawling, crawling, it will stay beside you,
> telling of a heart forever steadfast.

As if it were nothing, a serving woman brought it to the lady. "There is this pouch. So heavy you can hardly open it."

The lady did open it, and the snake raised its head. Though all her women were hysterical, the lady was calm.

"Praise Amida Buddha, and let it be my guardian through this life. There is nothing to raise such a stir about." Her voice quavered and she looked away. "It is wrong to admire something only while it is beautiful." She brought it to her side, but she did after all seem uneasy about it. She jumped up and she sat down again, like a butterfly over a flower. Her voice was like a cicada's. Beside themselves with mirth, her women left the room. They reported these happenings to her father the Inspector.

"This is inexcusable. You have left her alone with the creature?"

Sword in hand, he rushed to her side. The snake was very realistic. He took it up and examined it.

"He is certainly very clever. He has played this trick on you because you are a scholar and connoisseur of insects and such. You must get off an answer immediately."

And he departed.

"What an unpleasant fellow," said the women, learning of the contrivance. "But indeed you must answer."

The answer was on stiff, inelegant paper. Not yet up to the flowing feminine script, she wrote in the angular masculine one.

> "Perhaps we are fated to meet in paradise.
> Uninviting is this form beside me.

Until then."

A most unusual letter, thought the man, who was a cavalry officer. "I must see her."

He consulted with a friend, a certain captain of the guards. Disguising themselves as women of the lower orders, they visited the Inspector's house at an hour when he would be away. They looked in through a crack in the partition to the north of the lady's room.

A boy stood in the undistinguished plantings. "This tree is crawling with bugs. I never saw anything like it. Come have a look." He raised her blind. "The best swarm of caterpillars you could hope to find."

"How splendid," she answered in a strong, clear voice. "Bring them here."

"There are too many. See. Right here. Come on over."

She emerged with a firm, masculine stride. Pushing the blind before her she gazed wide-eyed at the caterpillar branch. She had a robe pulled over her head. The flow of the hair was good, but, perhaps because it was untended, it had a bushy untidiness. The black eyebrows were rich and cool, though the whiteness of the teeth was disconcerting.

"She would be pretty if she took care of herself. What a shame."

Clearly she neglected herself. Yet she was not at all ugly, and gave an impression of fresh elegance, and a cleanness as of a summer sky. The pity of it all. She was wearing a figured robe of pale yellow, a cloak decorated with grasshoppers, and white trousers.

She leaned forward to examine the caterpillars. "How very nice. But we can't leave them out in the sunlight. Come, men. Herd them inside. Don't let a single one get away."

The boy shook the branch and they fell to the ground.

"Put them on this."

She offered a white fan on which someone had been practicing Chinese characters. He did as ordered.

The two young men looked on in amazement. The master of the house was a learned man, and he had quite a daughter. More, perhaps, than he could manage.

A boy espied the pair. "A couple of handsome young men [are] hiding behind that shutter. An odd-looking couple they are too."

"How awful," said Tayū. "There she is, chasing after those bugs of hers, completely exposed to the world. I must warn her."

Outside the blind as before, the lady was in a great stir getting caterpillars from leaves.

"Come inside." The woman was afraid to go near. "Someone might see you, way out there."

"What difference does it make?" said the lady, sure that this was merely a device to distract her.

"You think I'm lying? I'm told there are two fine young men behind that shutter. See, out there in back."

"Go have a look, Cricket."

"It's true," said the boy, running back.

Putting some caterpillars in her sleeve, the lady hurried inside.

She was neither too tall nor too short. Rich hair fell to the hem of her robe. Because the edges were untrimmed, it did not fall in perfect tresses. Yet it was good after its fashion, and rather charming.

Even someone less favored, thought the cavalry officer, could easily pass muster. She may not seem very approachable, but she is pretty and elegant, and there is a certain distinction even in her eccentricities. If only she did not have that peculiar hobby. It would be a pity to run off and not even let her know he had seen her. Using the juice from a grassy stem for ink, he set down a poem on a fold of paper:

> Having seen the fur of the caterpillar,
> I wish that I could take it for my own.

He tapped with his fan and ordered a boy to deliver it. The boy gave it to Tayū, saying that it was from the gentleman over there, for the lady.

"Frightful." Tayū was loud in her complaints. "I know who it's from. That cavalry man. Because of those stupid bugs you let him see you."

"When you look into the nature of things, there is nothing in the world to be ashamed of. This life of ours is a dream. Who can tell what is good in it and what is bad?"

What was a person to say? The women were in despair.

The young men waited, thinking there would surely be an answer. Presently, to their disappointment, all the boys were called inside.

There seems to have been at least one woman who saw the need for an answer. It would not do to have them wait in vain.

> I am not like others. Only having heard
> the name of the caterpillar do I wish to answer.

To this the cavalry officer replied:

> Like the fur of the caterpillar, possibly,
> there is no other who matters so much as a hair.

Laughing, he departed.

We will learn more of the lady in the next chapter.

[Translated by Edward Seidensticker]

THE MIRROR OF THE PRESENT (*IMAKAGAMI*, CA. 1170)

By the latter part of the twelfth century, *The Tale of Genji* had become the object of serious scholarship and commentary, particularly for those interested in Japanese poetry. But it stood in an uncertain position as a monogatari or work of fiction, which had long held a low position in the hierarchy of genres. "The Progress of Fiction" is the final chapter of the historical tale *The Mirror of the Present* and is cast in the form common to all works of the "mirror" series: an aged person, encouraged by an audience of inquisitive pilgrims, gives a rambling, firsthand account of times long past. The narrator of *The Mirror of the Present* is a toothless and doddering woman more than 150 years old, who as a young girl had served as a lady-in-waiting to Murasaki Shikibu. While gathering fern shoots near her home, she encounters a band of pilgrims returning from the temple at Hatsuse, who, upon learning her age and identity, begin to ask her questions. Toward the end of the day, one of the pilgrims laments the severity of Murasaki Shikibu's punishment for having written her "insinuating and suggestive" monogatari, and the work closes with the old woman's attempt to defend the writings of her former mistress. The ensuing conversation is an excellent epitome of the arguments for and against fiction that were rehearsed in a multitude of treatises on *The Tale of Genji* throughout the medieval period.

A strict interpretation of Buddhist moral precepts led to the conclusion that fictions of any sort were a form of "falsehood" (*mōgo*) and that writing of highly literary or poetic quality was a breach of the commandment against "specious, ornamented language" (*kigo*). As a tale of "amorous intrigues," *The Tale of Genji* was further censured for corrupting morals and exciting the passions. The cumulative force of these several strictures can be gauged by the widespread credence given the legend mentioned by the first pilgrim, that Murasaki Shikibu had been cast into hell for having written *Genji* and that her readers stood in danger of like retribution.

Defenders of *The Tale of Genji* argued not against the basic validity of these charges but for a more subtle interpretation of the precepts on which they were based. One line of reasoning held that *Genji*, though not "true" in the literal sense, was a moral fable and therefore a form of "expedient truth" (*hōben*), such as the Buddha had used in preaching to those incapable of grasping more sublime expressions of the Buddhist way. The immoral acts depicted in the novel could thus be seen as serving the same purpose as those related by the Buddha in his parables: to illustrate graphically the true nature and consequences of wrongdoing in order to inculcate in the reader an abhorrence of evil. A strong buttress to this argument was the popular belief in bodhisattvas who appeared in human form in order to "lead men to enlightenment." The narrator of *The Mirror of the Present* is one of many to suggest that Murasaki Shikibu was not an ordinary person but an incarnation of the bodhisattva Avalokiteśvara (J. Kannon).

Another line of argument used in "The Progress of Fiction" was based on the doctrine of the "Middle Way" expounded by the Indian sage Nagarjuna (ca. 150–250). In its original form this was a complex metaphysical postulate that held, among other things, that all sensory perceptions are illusory, hence all distinctions between true and false, right and wrong, good and evil, and so on, are meaningless. Seeming differences are only seeming; all partake ultimately of a single Absolute. In Japan, however, the doctrine was often interpreted in ways more utilitarian than metaphysical. Objections to literature could thus be confuted by citing, as the old woman does, the passage from the Nirvana Sutra that says "even coarse and insinuating language partakes of Absolute Truth," or the prayer by the Chinese poet Bo Juyi (772–846) that the "wild words and decorative phrases" (*kyōgen kigo*) of his poetry might "lead the way to enlightenment."

The Progress of Fiction

Yet another of the pilgrims said, "How true it is I do not know, but so often we hear that Murasaki Shikibu, for crafting so insinuating and suggestive a tissue of lies in her *Tale of Genji*, was in the afterlife doomed to be consumed in smoke, like seaweed in the salt fires. This so upsets me that, vain though it may be to hope for her deliverance, I should like to pray for the repose of her soul."

"Yes," the old woman replied, "that is indeed what everyone says. And yet, in Japan as in China, the writings of the wise have always brought comfort to men's hearts, and have illumined the way for dimmer minds; and this hardly deserves the name of falsehood [*mōgo.*] To describe what never did happen, protesting behind a face of innocence that it is actually true; to lead others to think well of evil—to utter any sort of lie [*soragoto*] is sinful indeed. But is *The Tale of Genji* really such an empty fabrication? Meretricious or specious you might call it; but these hardly seem the most monstrous of sins. To take the life of any living creature, or to steal even the least of a man's treasures—these are horrible sins for which the offender may be plunged to the very depths of hell. But I find it hard to imagine that such should be the lot of Murasaki Shikibu, though to be sure I have no knowledge of what retribution she might now be suffering. To stir men's hearts can, after all, be productive of virtue. And though to excite the passions may perhaps prevent one's release from the cycle of rebirth, this is hardly so serious a transgression as to send one to hell. It is difficult enough to comprehend the affairs of our own time; but in China the poet Bo Juyi composed a work in seventy volumes which greatly stirred men's hearts, with its elegant phrases and ingenious conceits—and this man, we are told, is the incarnation of Manjusri.[302] Indeed, the Buddha himself, when he preached in parables, invented stories of events that never occurred; and these certainly are not to be regarded falsehoods. For a mere woman to have written such a marvelous book as this, well, it does not seem to me she could have been any ordinary person. More than likely, she was Gadgadśvara or Avalokiteśvara or some other supernatural being, come to us in the form of a woman to preach the Doctrine and lead men to enlightenment."

A child in the company then said: "I can see how some women who have led others to enlightenment might indeed have been Avalokiteśvara incarnate—such as Queen Vimaladatta, who led the King before the Buddha and persuaded him to reform his wicked ways;[303] or Queen Shrimala, whose praise of the Buddha, inspired by her parents' epistles, will transmit the Doctrine to generations yet unborn.[304] But *The Tale of Genji* is such an assemblage of amorous intrigues, all set forth as the very truth, that it corrupts people's minds and excites their passion. How are we to regard this as the sacred and holy Doctrine?"

"Yes," the old woman said, "there is some truth in what you say. Yet when you consider what an extraordinary and marvelous work the *Genji* is; that she has written not just a scroll or two, but a book of sixty chapters;[305] that nowhere

---

302. *Bo Juyi's Collected Works.* Mañjuśrī (J. Monju) is the bodhisattva of wisdom.

303. Vimaladatta's (J. Jōtoku) conversion of her husband, with the help of an impressive magic display by her two sons, is the subject of the twenty-seventh chapter of the Lotus Sutra.

304. Alex Wayman and Hideko Wayman, trans., *The Lion's Roar of Queen Shrimala* (New York: Columbia University Press, 1974).

305. *The Tale of Genji* actually contains only fifty-four chapters. Medieval commentators, however, often ascribed sixty chapters, suggesting that this number had been selected by the author to correspond to the sixty chapters of the principal scriptures of the Tendai school of Buddhism.

is it flawed by frivolity; that in the past as in the present it has brought pleasure even to emperors and empresses, who have made magnificent copies of it, and have prized it above all their treasures—when you consider all these things, I say, what in fact strikes one as odd is that anyone could consider its author sinful. By showing the deeply sinful, it inspires one to chant the holy name of the Buddha, and thus can serve as a first step toward the enlightenment of those for whose deliverance we pray; by revealing to us the workings of a feeling heart, it wins over to the path of righteousness those mired in the miseries of this world; in demonstrating the evanescence of this world, it is by no means without effect as an exhortation to the Way of the Buddha. When you further consider that it depicts one who, though grieved at having to leave behind his loved ones, yet keeps the precepts of the Lay Disciple,[306] and a woman who guards her chastity until death in obedience to her father's dying injunctions,[307] it is plain to see that the tale was intended as an object lesson. When readers see how Genji, who enjoyed the boundless favor of the emperor, and was blessed with the best of all possible karmas, yet dies as though all this had been but a dream or an illusion, they cannot but realize how ephemeral are the things of this world. And then there is the emperor who relinquishes his throne to his younger brother and retires to a hermitage in the western hills[308]—here is another example of one that calls to mind that emperor of old in the Doctrine— one indeed that calls to mind that emperor of old in the Devadatta Chapter of the Lotus Sutra.[309] Vasubandhu has written at the beginning of his treatise[310] that naught but the wisdom to distinguish right from wrong can rescue the heart lost in darkness; for so deep are the depths of delusion that the ignorant only drift on as though upon a bottomless sea. And so the Buddha in his benevolence has given us this means to discern the true nature of things and turn us in the way of enlightenment, this seed of the propagation of his Doctrine—that even coarse and insinuating language can lead the way to the Truth of the Absolute. To be sure, *The Tale of Genji* is not the untainted holy word of the Doctrine. Yet under the pure morning light of the Doctrine, surely anyone possessed of such great compassion as to pray for the deliverance of Murasaki Shikibu—whether because he found comfort in her book or was deeply touched by it—surely such a person must form a very deep bond of good karma."

---

306. Hachinomiya, the Eighth Prince.

307. Ōigimi, the Eighth Prince's daughter.

308. The Suzaku emperor.

309. The twelfth chapter of the Lotus Sutra, in which the Buddha relates how he himself forsook his throne to seek enlightenment.

310. Probably referring to Vasubandhu's *Trsimika vijnapti-karika* (J. *Yuishiki sanjū ronju*, Daizōkyō 1586).

As she spoke, the pilgrims, in their eagerness to hear more, lost all thought of their destination. Yet loath though they were to part from her, the sun had begun to set, and they went their separate ways.

"Perhaps one day we shall all meet again," she said, "for I hope in some future life to become a buddha and preach the Doctrine as I have done here today under the Tree of Enlightenment."

These words convinced the pilgrims she could be no ordinary mortal. But when they later sought her at the place where she had said she lived, she was not to be found. Filled with regret that they had not sent one of their number to follow her, they proceeded on their way.

[Introduction and translation by Thomas J. Harper]

COLLECTION OF TALES OF TIMES NOW PAST
(KONJAKU MONOGATARI SHŪ, CA. 1120)

The *Collection of Tales of Times Now Past*, a monolithic collection of 1039 setsuwa, or anecdotes, was compiled in the late Heian period, in the early twelfth century. Of the thirty-one volumes, three (8, 18, 21) are missing. The collection is divided into three parts: the first five volumes are on India (Tenjiku); the next five volumes, on China (Shintan); and the remaining twenty-one volumes, on Japan (Honchō).

It is not clear whether the compiler was a Buddhist monk or an aristocrat, a single author or a group of writers. Traditionally, the compiler has been thought to be Minamoto no Takakuni (1004–1077), but the inclusion of stories dated after Takakuni died makes this improbable.

The anthology is the first world history of Buddhism to be written in Japanese; two-thirds of the anecdotes are Buddhist stories and the rest, secular stories. Volumes 1 through 4 describe the history of Buddhism in India, from the birth of Shakyamuni to the spread of Buddhism after Shakyamuni's death. Volumes 6 through 9 (with 8 missing) describe the transmission of Buddhism from India to China and relate various stories of miracles and karmic causality. Volumes 11 through 20 (with 18 missing) outline the history of Buddhism in Japan, beginning with the transmission of Buddhism from China.

The remaining volumes (5, 10, 21–32) depict secular life in India, China, and Japan. Volumes 5 and 10, which open the India and China sections, respectively, begin with stories about the emperor and the imperial court, followed by stories of ministers and then of warriors. Volume 21, the first of the secular-Japan section, is missing, but volume 22 provides biographies of powerful Fujiwara ministers; volume 23 depicts stories of military leaders; and volume 24 offers stories of doctors, diviners, and artists. The secular parts, in other words, are constructed with the imperial court and the emperor as the source of authority and the main sociopolitical axis. The secular volumes also reach beyond court society to include the samurai (vol. 25), who, though subservient to the nobility, rebel and commit violent acts. Volume 29, which focuses on those who commit evil acts (*akugyō*), takes this external perspective even further. Volumes 26 through 31 center on the themes of karmic retribution and reward, demons and spirits, humor, and love, depicting a diverse social world that contrasts with the aristocratic world of Heian monogatari and literary diaries.

The setsuwa in the *Konjaku monogatari shū* have two large purposes: religious (in leading the audience to a deeper understanding of Buddhism) and secular (for entertainment and practical purposes). In its religious aims, the *Konjaku monogatari shū* tries to appeal to commoners and the masses by presenting Buddhism in a simplified form. The rewards for faith are immediate, and the punishment for sin is direct and immediate. Stories about the Lotus Sutra, for example, make no or little attempt to explain the content of the sutra; instead, they focus on the efficacy and merit acquired by reciting the sutra or having faith in it. Indeed, the worldly efficacy—the belief in the power of Buddhism to protect human beings from disasters—is usually stressed. The Buddhist stories were probably compiled by Buddhist preachers as a means of instruction for illiterate audiences. These are not sermons but stories that could be used in sermons. The moral at the end usually applies to only part of the story, reflecting the multiple functions of these narratives. (Indeed, the same story often appears elsewhere in another setsuwa collection for a completely different purpose.)

The focus of the Buddhist stories generally is on the strange and the miraculous rather than on doctrinal matters. The same interest in the strange and mysterious marks the secular chapters, particularly volume 16 (karmic retribution/reward), volume 27 (demons and spirits), volume 28 (humor), volume 29 (evil and criminals), volume 30 (love stories), and volume 31 (stories of the strange). The setting of the setsuwa ranges from the ninth to the twelfth century, encompassing the same historical period in which the monogatari flourished but with a much broader social and environmental range.

The *Collection of Tales of Times Now Past* is written in a mixed Chinese–Japanese style (*wakan konkō bun*), which reflects a strong movement toward vernacular Japanese. The stories are presented not as words directly spoken by the narrator or editor but as transmissions of stories that have been heard and recorded.

Tales from India

Volume 5 contains stories about the birth of Shakyamuni, the historical Buddha, as well as many stories that took place before Shakyamuni achieved enlightenment. The story of Ikkaku sennin (One-Horned Immortal) had considerable impact on Japan and also appears in the *Taiheiki* (vol. 37) and in numerous setsuwa collections. The story became a nō play under the same name and in the mid-eighteenth century provided inspiration for the famous kabuki play *Narukami*.

HOW THE ONE-HORNED IMMORTAL CARRIED A WOMAN FROM
THE MOUNTAINS TO THE PALACE (5:4)

This story is derived from an early-fifth-century Chinese translation from Sanskrit known as *Dazhidu lun* (J. *Daichido-ron*).

The time is now long past when a certain immortal lived in the mountains of India.[311] He was called the One-Horned Immortal. A single horn protruded from his forehead. People called him the One-Horned Immortal because of the horn, you see. He had passed years and years in the depths of the mountains, devoting himself to various ascetic practices. He would hop on clouds and soar through the sky, and he moved giant mountains, and he caused the birds and beasts to do his bidding.

Then one day a great rain gushed from the sky and all the mountain paths were utterly ruined. Now as it happened, for reasons somewhat difficult to fathom—yes indeed, you really have to wonder what he was thinking!—the One-Horned Immortal was sauntering about on foot that day, not flying, and the slope was so steep that his feet slipped out from under him, and he fell. To think of an old immortal tumbling down a mountain like this! It made him furious. Then something occurred to him. It's because of all this rain! When rain falls, the paths get all messy—that's how it is in this world. How disgusting it feels having these drenched robes against my skin. And of course those dragon kings are responsible—they're the ones who make the rain fall! It was the work of an instant for the One-Horned Immortal to round up the various dragon kings and shut them up in his flask. Now that they were trapped in the flask, the various dragon kings started wailing and sobbed an infinity of tears.

Now since the One-Horned Immortal had taken all these giant dragon kings and stuffed them into such a small container, it had gotten intolerably cramped inside. It was quite impossible to move, and the pain was dreadful. But alas, the holy man had such marvelous powers that they couldn't do a thing against him. So that's how it was. Twelve years passed without so much as a tiny sprinkling of rain. And as a consequence all the land was parched, and everyone in all five of India's regions went about wailing and moaning.[312] The kings of the Sixteen Great Kingdoms[313] performed various rituals of supplication begging for rain,

---

311. According to the Chinese *Fayuan zhulin*, a certain mountain immortal was going to the bathroom in a bucket when he caught sight of two deer copulating and instantly became highly aroused. Afterward, the female deer came along and lapped up some of the mixture of urine and sperm, presumably mistaking it for water. She became pregnant. She gave birth to a human baby rather than a deer, a human with one horn: the One-Horned Immortal of this tale.

312. The five regions are the north, the south, the east, the west, and the center.

313. The sixteen kingdoms were located in the northwest of what is now India, centered on the Ganges River.

but none of these had any effect at all. None of the kings had any idea why things were like this.

And then a certain soothsayer spoke. Travel from here in the direction of the Cow and the Tiger and you will come to a forbiddingly large mountain.[314] There is an immortal who lives on this mountain. He has taken the various dragon kings that make the rain fall and bottled them up—that's why no rain falls anywhere in the land. Your majesties can order the venerable saints to pray all you like, their powers will never be able to compete with those of the other saint. That was what he said.

When the people of the various lands heard this, they let their minds circle the problem, considered it from all angles, wondering what they ought to do, but they were utterly unable to discover a solution. Then a certain minister spoke up. I don't care how venerable a saint this man is, there's no way he could be immune to physical allure or deaf to the charms of a lovely voice. That old mountain immortal people used to talk about way back when, Udraka-Ramaputra—would anyone even think of calling him a fraud?[315] I'd wager he was even greater than this current fellow. And yet Udraka-Ramaputra sank himself in the pleasures of the flesh, and no sooner had he done so than he lost his marvelous powers. So here's what I think we ought to do. We'll command all the elegant beauties with lovely voices to assemble here, and then we'll send them off to that mountain, and whenever they come to a particularly high peak or an especially deep valley—to places, I mean to say, where it seems a mountain immortal would make his abode or where a saint would live—when they find such a place they'll perform a heartrending, scintillating rendition of some song. Hearing that, even this exalted saint of ours is bound to melt. As soon as the minister had finished speaking, it was decided. See that it is done right away, said the king. And so they selected the most elegant and beautiful women with the loveliest voices, five hundred in all, and decked them out in the most exquisite clothing, covered them in sandalwood oil, sprinkled them with aloe, loaded them all into five hundred exquisitely decorated carriages, and sent them on their way.

The sight of all these women getting down out of their carriages way up there in the mountains and then gathering together in a crowd was so splendid there is simply no way to describe it. They wandered off this way and that way in groups of ten or twenty and went to stand in front of caves and under trees and between the peaks of mountains and in all sorts of places, and in these

---

314. The direction of the cow and the tiger is the northeast. This direction was the so-called demon's gate, from which supernatural forces mounted their attacks. Neither the direction of the cow and the tiger nor the soothsayer is mentioned in the source text.

315. Udraka-Ramaputra was so famous that he was sought out by Shakyamuni himself, but he lost his powers when he went to court and touched the hand of the king's favorite wife.

places they sang their heartrending songs. The mountains echoed and the valleys reverberated, and it was so wonderful you almost expected heavenly beings
and dragon gods to come look and listen.

While all this was going on, a saint dressed in rustic robes stood by a cave so
deep you could barely see into it. He was haggard and emaciated, totally without flesh. Nothing but skin and bones, that's all there was to him, so that looking at him you wondered where his soul could possibly be hiding. A single horn
protruded from his forehead. His appearance was infinitely frightening. He
hobbled out like a shadow hunched over his stick, a flask in his hand and a
misshapen grin on his face.

Here's what the immortal said. Who are you, you who come here and sing
such amazing songs? I've been living here on this same mountain for a thousand years, but never in my life have I heard anything like this. Are you beings
descended from heaven? Or demons from below?

A woman replied. We are neither beings from heaven nor demons from
below, but five hundred *kekara*-women—that's what we're called—who spend all
our time traveling across India in a big group like this.[316] We'd heard that these
mountains are magnificent beyond compare, that all sorts of flowers bloom here,
that the streams are thrilling to behold, and that in the midst of all this there lives
a most venerable saint. So we thought to ourselves, why don't we go sing our songs
for this sainted man? Living up there in the depths of those mountains, he's unlikely ever to have heard anything similar. If we do this, we'll be able to forge a
connection with him that may prove helpful in the future.[317] So you see, that's
why we've come.

Then the woman sang a song, and the holy man listened, and since her form
was truly unlike anything he had ever seen, either in the distant past or in more
recent times, and since she sang with such heartrending grace it would be futile
to try and describe it, he felt as if his eyes were swimming in light, and his heart
was profoundly moved, and his spirit didn't know which way to turn.

The holy man spoke. Listen, will you please do what I say? The woman decided that he seemed to have softened, and made up her mind to ruin him with
her cunning. Oh, yes, whatever you say! How could I possibly refuse? she said.
Well then, said the holy man, I think perhaps I'll just touch you a little here and
there, if that's all right with you. And with that he started galumphing awkwardly
toward her, his motions terribly stiff and utterly inappropriate, so that the woman
found herself struggling not to make this terrifying creature lose his temper,
even as she shuddered at the horn on his head. But since this was precisely what
the king of the land had told them to do when he sent them off, she finally
fought down her fear and managed to do the things the holy man told her to.

---

316. "Kekara" seems to be a corruption of Gandhara, which was a region of modern
Pakistan.

317. Their meeting with the immortal might encourage them to become Buddhist nuns.

And when that moment came, the various dragon kings were filled with joy, and they smashed their way out of the flask and ascended to the heavens. And no sooner had they done so than a layer of cloud swelled to fill the entire vast expanse of the sky, and bolts of lightning rained down amid crashes of thunder, and a tremendous deluge began. There was nowhere for the woman to hide herself, but then she had no means of getting back home either, and so despite her fear she remained with the holy man for a few days. During this time, his heart became deeply steeped in thoughts of the woman. Then on the fifth day the rain let up a little and the sky cleared, and the woman informed the holy man that she was leaving. Things can't go on like this, she said. I'm going to leave. The holy man was very sad that they would have to part. Well, he said, with a pained look on his face, if you must go you must go. The woman replied, I've never been out like this before and walking around on these rocks has caused my feet to swell up terribly. What's more, I don't know the way back. If that's the case, said the holy man, allow me to serve as your guide on the paths that cross the mountains. He started walking on ahead, and the woman gazed at him and saw how white his hair was, like a cap of snow on his head. His face was wrinkled like the surface of the sea, and a single horn protruded from his forehead. His back was so crooked he was folded in two, and he wore the most rustic of clothing. As she watched him hobble along, swaying from side to side as he leaned on his holy man's stick, she found him both ridiculous and, at the same time, terrifying.

They continued walking. And then they arrived at a path that led from one side of a certain valley to another, tracing the edge of a cliff so steep it was entirely beyond description. It was as if someone had set up an enormous folding screen. A giant waterfall plunged from the precipitous heights of the rock face, and way down at the bottom there was a pool of water. The white waves of water seemed to stream up from the bottom, falling backward, and when you tried to peer across to the other side your gaze got lost in a thick tide of fog and mist. There was really no way the woman would be able to get across this, not unless she grew wings or flew across on a dragon's back. And so when they arrived at this point, the woman called to the holy man. I'm not going to be able to make it. I get dizzy just looking—I can't even think. How on earth am I supposed to walk out there? Whereas you—you come here all the time, you're used to it. Please, oh please, you must carry me across! Since the holy man was so infatuated with her, he found it hard to say no to anything she suggested. Yes, that's all quite true, he replied. Let me carry you across.

The holy man's legs were so frail it looked like they would snap if you pinched them, and the fear that he might drop her left her even more terrified than she had been when she imagined crossing on her own, but still she let herself be carried. And though they made it across, the woman told him to keep carrying her a little farther, just a bit farther. In fact she ended up getting carried all the way to the palace.

People on the streets and everyone else who caught a glimpse of them started spreading the word that the One-Horned Immortal who lived in the mountains was heading for the palace with a kekara-woman on his back, and so people of all stations, high and low, both women and men, came from every corner of the vast land of India to see the sight. There the man was, a single horn protruding from his forehead, his hair so white it looked like a cap of snow on his head, his legs as skinny as pins. He held his walking stick under the woman's bottom, using it to wiggle her up again whenever she started to slip. Not one of the people who saw the sight refrained from laughing and jeering at the One-Horned Immortal.

When they had arrived at the palace, the king treated the One-Horned Immortal with great respect and even awe, since—though the old man looked like an ass—the king had heard he was a venerable saint. Feel free to return to your mountain right away, commanded the king, and though the holy man had felt as if he were walking on clouds all the way to the palace, he went back tottering and stumbling.

People say there really was a holy man as ridiculous as that.

[Translated by Michael Emmerich]

Tales from China

HOW WANG ZHAOJUN, CONSORT OF THE HAN EMPEROR YUAN, WENT TO THE LAND OF HU (10:5)

The source for this story is the early-twelfth-century poetic treatise *Toshiyori zuinō*, although it seems likely that other texts were consulted as well.

The time is now long past—it was in Han-dynasty China, during the reign of Emperor Yuan[318]—when His Majesty looked over the daughters of his ministers and the rest of the nobles and selected those with beautiful features and lovely figures and commanded that they be brought to the palace so he could get to know them intimately, and gave each of them a place to stay at court, so that the number of women quickly reached four or five hundred and ultimately climbed so extremely high that it was no longer always possible for him to get to know them as intimately as he should.

That's how things were when men from the land of Hu appeared in the capital.[319] They were barbarians—people rather like the Ebisu.[320] So everyone

---

318. The Han dynasty lasted from 202 B.C.E. to 220 C.E. Emperor Yuan, the tenth to rule the Han, lived from 75 to 33 B.C.E. and reigned from 49 B.C.E. to his death.

319. The land of Hu was found to the northwest of Han.

320. The Ebisu were inhabitants of what is now eastern Japan who refused to submit to the power of the center. It likely was a general term for rebellious people who live far from the capital.

from the emperor down to the ministers and the ordinary officials started debating the issue, trying to decide how these men should be dealt with, although without coming up with any acceptable plans. Except, that is to say, for one wise minister who was able to come up with a plan, which he explained to the emperor. It really doesn't bode at all well for our land that these men have come here from Hu, he said. It seems to me that we ought to find some way to send them back to the place from which they have come. You might accomplish this by choosing one of the less attractive women among the uselessly large population you've got at the palace now to present to these ruffians. I figure if you do that, they're bound to go back, and in the best of spirits. I doubt there could be a better plan than this. That's what the minister said.

The emperor thought it a very good idea when he heard it. He decided he had better go himself to take a look at these women and make up his mind which of them to send away. Except there were such huge crowds of them that just considering the task made his head ache. And then the emperor happened upon an idea of his own: He would summon crowds of painters and let them see the women and have them paint the women's portraits, and then he would compare these portraits and pick one of the less attractive of the women to present to the men from Hu! This was his idea. So he summoned the painters and showed them the women and gave them his orders. You must paint these women as they are, he said, and then give the pictures to me. The painters began painting, and the women—saddened and distressed at the notion that they might end up the plaything of barbarians and have to go off to some distant and unknown land—began competing with one another, each trying to load her own painter more heavily with gold and silver than anyone else or to give him more of all sorts of other treasures, and the painters got so swept up in the gift giving that they painted even the uglier women in such a way as to give them an air of great beauty, and they gave these paintings to the emperor. Now among all these women there was one named Wang Zhaojun.[321] Since her features were more beautiful than those of the other women, she figured there was really no need for her to give her painter anything at all, she would just let her beauty work its magic. So her painter didn't portray her as she really was but made her look dreadfully vulgar, and he gave this ugly painting to the emperor, who then promptly made up his mind. This woman, he announced, this woman here is the one to send!

Still, something about all this struck the emperor as strange. He commanded the woman to appear before him, and when he saw her . . . this Wang Zhaojun . . . why, she seemed to shoot out rays of light, that's how lovely she was. She was like a jewel, and the rest of the women were like dirt! The emperor was stunned and went about feeling terribly distressed because it was this woman he was going to have to present to the barbarians, and then after a few

---

321. The dates of Wang Zhaojun's birth and death are uncertain, but it is said that she was presented to Emperor Yuan at the age of seventeen. Later ages created legends about her beauty.

days the barbarians got wind of the fact that they were to be given—of all the emperor's women—Wang Zhaojun! So they came to the palace and asked the emperor to hand her over, and since he couldn't very well go through the whole process again and pick someone else, in the end he presented Wang Zhaojun to the men from Hu, who sat her on a horse and led her off.

Wang Zhaojun could weep and sigh, but that wouldn't help anything now. The emperor, too, was filled with pity and longing for Wang Zhaojun, but each time the extremity of his suffering drove him to go and look around the place she had lived, he found nothing but the willows of spring swaying in the wind, nightingales singing their sad songs, fallen leaves of autumn carpeting the garden, and the blossoms of the flower of forgetting clustered in tight profusion at the edge of the veranda, and all of these things moved him so profoundly he couldn't even have begun to describe the way he felt, and his pity and longing for Wang Zhaojun only increased.

The men from Hu were thrilled to have been given Wang Zhaojun, and as they led her away they played all sorts of songs on their lutes. And even though Wang Zhaojun continued to weep and sigh, listening to the music did make her feel a little bit better. The men arrived back in the land from which they had come, and they made Wang Zhaojun an empress and lavished infinite care and attention on her. Yet even so, you have to wonder whether Wang Zhaojun ever really enjoyed herself there.

People say that at the time all this happened, everyone heaped curses on Wang Zhaojun. They said it had all happened because she set too much store by her beauty and refused to give her painter any treasures.

[Translated by Michael Emmerich]

Buddhist Tales from Japan

HOW A MONK OF THE DŌJŌJI IN THE PROVINCE OF KII COPIED THE LOTUS SUTRA AND BROUGHT SALVATION TO SERPENTS (14:3)

Volume 14 describes miracles associated with the Lotus Sutra. At the end of this story, the aged monk copies the Lotus Sutra and dreams of the dead man and woman who have been freed of their serpent bodies and reborn in heaven. The tale claims to prove the efficacy and power of the Lotus Sutra, to reveal the compassion of the aged monk, and to demonstrate the "strength of the evil in the female heart." In typical Mahayana fashion, the story stresses the need for intermediaries (such as the Lotus Sutra) and the fact that even the most evil can be saved by Buddhism. But the actual interest of the story extends far beyond this didactic ending.

At a time now past, there were two monks on pilgrimage to Kumano. One was well along in years; the other was young and extraordinarily good-looking.

When they came to Muro District, the two of them rented lodgings and settled down for the night. The owner of the house was a widow and young, with two or three maids her only companions. When this woman saw the handsome young monk who had taken lodgings with her, her lustful desires were deeply aroused. She tended assiduously to his comfort. Night fell, and the monks went to bed. At midnight she secretly crept to where the young monk was sleeping, covered him with her dress, and lay down beside him. She nudged him awake; he opened his eyes in fright and confusion. "I never give lodging to travelers," said the woman, "but I let you stay here tonight because from the time I first saw you, this afternoon, I have longed to make you my spouse. I thought that by taking you in for the night I would achieve my aim, and now I have come to you. My husband is dead and I am a widow. Take pity on me!" Hearing her, the monk got up, terrified. He replied, "I have a longstanding vow; in accordance with it, in recent days I have purified myself in mind and body and set out on the distant journey to present myself before the deity of Kumano.[322] Should I carelessly break my vow here, the consequences would be dreadful for both of us. Abandon all such thoughts at once." He refused with all the strength at his command. The woman was greatly vexed, and all night long she kept embracing him and teasing and fondling him. The monk tried this argument and that argument to soothe her. "It is not that I refuse, my lady. But just now I'm on a pilgrimage to Kumano. I'll spend a few days there offering lamps and paper strips. Then, when I've turned homeward, I will do as you ask," he promised. The woman believed him and went back to her own bed. At daybreak the monks left the house and set out for Kumano.

The woman reckoned up the day of his promised return. She could think of nothing but her love for the monk and made all sorts of preparations in anticipation. But turning homeward, he stayed away for fear of her; he took a road she did not expect him to take and thus slipped past. She waited until she was weary, but he did not come; and she went to the side of the road and questioned passing travelers. Among them was a monk who had set out from Kumano. "There was a young monk and an old one, dressed in robes of such-and-such a color"—and she described them. "Have they started homeward?" "It is three days now since those two went home," said the monk. Hearing this, she struck her hands together. "He's taken another road and fled!" she thought. In great rage she returned to her house and shut herself into her bedroom. She stayed

---

322. Deity of Kumano, literally, "avatar of Kumano." The deity in question is a Shinto deity, and "avatar" (*gongen*) refers to the idea, widespread in the medieval period, that the Shinto kami are manifestations of buddhas. Pilgrimages to Kumano, in the Kii Peninsula (now Wakayama Prefecture), have been popular among all classes of society since the early tenth century. To have sexual relations with the woman would be not only a violation of the monk's Buddhist vows but a defilement, and thus highly offensive, in the eyes of the Shinto deity. The paper strips (*mitegura*, long strips of paper attached to either side of a pole) and lamps, in the following passage, are characteristic offerings at Shinto shrines.

there a little while without making a sound; and then she died. Her maidser-vants, who witnessed this, were weeping and wailing, when a poisonous snake forty feet long suddenly issued from her bedroom. It went out of the house and toward the road; then it slithered rapidly down the road by which pilgrims re-turn from Kumano. People saw it and were filled with terror.

The two monks had had a head start, but someone came up to them unasked and said, "Behind you a strange thing is happening. A serpent has appeared that is forty feet long. It crosses mountains and fields and is coming rapidly closer." At this the two monks thought, "Undoubtedly, because the promise to her was bro-ken, the mistress of that house let evil passions arise within her heart and be-came a poisonous snake and pursues us." Taking to their heels, they ran as fast as they could to a temple called Dōjōji and went in through the gate. "Why have you run here?" asked the monks of the temple. The two told them the story in detail and begged to be saved. The monks of the temple took counsel together; then they lowered a bell, concealed the young monk inside it, and shut the gate. The old monk hid himself in company with the monks of the temple.

After a little while, the serpent came to the temple. The gates were shut—no matter, she crossed over them and entered the compound. She went all around the halls once, twice; and when she came to the door of the bell-hall where the monk was sheltering, she rapped on it a hundred times with her tail. In the end, she smashed the leaves of the door and entered. She encircled the bell and beat upon the dragon head at its top with her tail; this lasted five or six hours. For all their fear, the monks were so amazed that they opened the doors on all four sides and gathered to watch. Tears of blood flowed from her eyes; raising her head, she licked her lips and slithered rapidly away whence she had come. Be-fore the eyes of the monks, the great bell of the temple blazed and was burned in the poisonous hot breath of the serpent. It was too hot to come near. But they threw water on it to cool it, and when they lifted it away to look at the monk, they saw that fire had consumed him utterly. Not even his skeleton remained. All that there was, was a little ash. Upon seeing this, the old monk returned home amid his tears.

Later, an aged monk, who was a senior monk of the temple, had a dream in which a serpent even larger than the one before came straight to him and ad-dressed him face to face: "Do you know who I am? I am the monk who was hidden inside the bell. The evil woman became a poisonous snake; in the end, I was made her captive and became her husband. I have been reborn in this vile, filthy body and suffer measureless torment. I now hope to free myself of this pain, but my own powers are insufficient—even though I honored the Lotus Sutra while I was alive. I thought that if only you, holy sir, would bestow on us the vastness of your mercy, I might escape this pain. I beseech you, on our account let limitless compassion arise within your heart; in purity copy the chapter of the Lotus Sutra called 'The Limitless Life of the Tathagata.' Dedi-cate its merit to us two serpents and free us thereby from our torments. Except by the power of the Lotus Sutra, how are we to escape them?" Thus he spoke, and departed. The monk awoke from his dream.

When the monk pondered this afterward, his piety was at once aroused. He himself copied out the chapter; and discarding his robe and bowl,[323] he invited a great many monks to celebrate a full day's Dharma assembly and dedicated its merit that the two serpents might be freed of their torments. Later, he dreamed that a monk and a woman, their happy faces wreathed in smiles, came to the Dōjōji and saluted him reverently. "Because you have cultivated the roots of enlightenment, we two were instantly rid of our snakes' bodies and set on the path of felicitous rebirth. The woman was reborn in the Trayastrimsa heaven, and the monk has ascended to the Tusita heaven." Having spoken, they departed separately, ascending into the sky. The monk awoke from his dream.

The aged monk rejoiced deeply, and he revered all the more the miraculous power of the Lotus Sutra. In truth, the Sutra's wonder-working powers are uncanny. That the serpents cast off their serpents' bodies and were reborn afresh in the heavens is due solely to the Lotus Sutra. Everyone who witnessed this affair or heard of it was moved to belief in the Lotus Sutra and copied and chanted it. Rare, too, was the heart of the aged monk. To have done such a compassionate deed, he must in a previous life have been their wise and good friend. Now think, that evil woman's passion for the young monk must also have come from a bond formed in a previous life.

You see, therefore, the strength of the evil in the female heart. It is for this reason that the Buddha strictly forbids approaching women. Know this, and avoid them. So the tale's been told, and so it's been handed down.

[Translated by Marian Ury]

HOW KAYA NO YOSHIFUJI, OF BITCHŪ PROVINCE, BECAME THE HUSBAND OF A FOX AND WAS SAVED BY KANNON (16:17)

Volume 16 focuses on miracles of Kannon, the bodhisattva of mercy. In this story, a layman with a cane, who is a transformation of the Kannon bodhisattva, appears and brings out a "strange, black, monkeylike creature" that turns out to be Yoshifuji, who has been seduced by a fox. The story reveals the power of Kannon and takes up the theme of attachment, which is blinding and deceiving. Here, as elsewhere, Buddhism evinces profound skepticism about external appearances and warns us not to be deluded.

At a time now past, in the village of Ashimori in Kaya District of Bitchū Province, there lived a man named Kaya no Yoshifuji. His household had gotten

---

323. In other words, at the cost of his last earthly possessions.

rich through the trade in coins.[324] He had a weakness for women and was prey to lustful thoughts.

Now, in autumn of the eighth year of Kanpei [896], while his wife was away in the capital and he, left by himself in his household, was a temporary widower, he went out for a stroll just at nightfall and suddenly caught sight of a beautiful young woman. She was someone he had never seen before. His lustful feelings were aroused, but the woman looked as though she would flee if he tried to touch her. He went up to her and took her by the hand. "Who are you?" he asked. She was brilliantly dressed, but she said, "I'm no one." How charming she looked as she said that! "Come to my house," said Yoshifuji. "That would be unseemly," she said, and tried to draw away. "Where do you live, then?" said Yoshifuji; "I'll go with you." "Just over there," she said, walking on. Yoshifuji walked with her, holding her hand.

Close by, there was a handsome house; inside, too, it was sumptuously furnished. "Odd," thought Yoshifuji, "I never knew there was anything like this here." Within, there was a great clamor, as men and women, persons of every degree, together cried, "Her Ladyship's come!" "This must be the daughter of the house," Yoshifuji thought, delightedly, and that night he slept with her.

The next morning a man who was evidently the master of the house appeared. "Congratulations," he said to Yoshifuji, "this bond was predestined! Now you must stay with us." Yoshifuji was treated very hospitably. He became utterly attached to the woman; they vowed eternal love, and waking and sleeping he spent all his time with her. He never wondered how his house and children might be faring.

In his own home, when he had not reappeared after nightfall, people thought, "Maybe he's crawling around somewhere in secret, in his usual way." But when it was quite dark and he still had not reappeared, there were some who took it amiss. "What a madman he is! Have the servants look for him." The night was more than half gone, but though they searched the neighborhood, he was not to be found. Could he have gone on a journey? But his clothing was still there; he had disappeared wearing only a light jacket. Day broke and the uproar continued. They looked everywhere that he might have gone but found absolutely nothing. "If he were a young man with unsettled ideas, he might have gone off suddenly to become a monk. But at his age? It's a very strange prank—if it is one." Meanwhile, where Yoshifuji was living, the years passed. His wife was pregnant, and after nine months she gave birth, without complications, to a son, so that he became even more deeply attached to her. It seemed to him indeed that time was passing swiftly; everything in his life was just as he desired it.

---

324. Coins imported from China.

In his own home, after he disappeared, he was sought for, but without success. His older brother, the Senior Officer Toyonaka, his younger brothers, the Supervisor Toyokage and Toyotsune, who was priest of the Kibitsuhiko shrine, and Yoshifuji's only son, Tadasada, were all affluent men. In their mutual grief, they decided to try at least to discover his corpse. Good resolves arose in them, and they felled a kae tree to make an image of the eleven-headed Kannon. The statue they made was the same height as Yoshifuji. They petitioned it. "At least let us see his corpse," they pleaded. Moreover, from the day on which he disappeared, they began invocations of the Buddha and sutra readings for the welfare of his soul in the next world.

A layman who walked with a staff came suddenly to the house where Yoshifuji was now living. At the sight of him, the whole household, from the master on down, fell into utter terror and fled. The layman jabbed Yoshifuji in the back with his staff, forcing him out through a narrow passageway. At twilight on the thirteenth day after Yoshifuji's disappearance, his people were mourning him. "What a strange way he disappeared! And it was just about this time of night, wasn't it?" they were saying to each other, when from underneath the storehouse in front of them a strange, black, monkeylike creature crawled out on all fours. "What's this, what's this!" They crowded in to look at it. "It's me," said the thing—and the voice was Yoshifuji's. His son, Tadasada, thought it uncanny, but since it was so obviously his father's voice, he dropped to the ground and pulled him up. "What happened to you?" he said. Yoshifuji said, "It was while I was a widower and by myself. All the time I kept thinking how much I wanted to have a woman.[325] And then, unexpectedly, I became the son-in-law of a high-ranking gentleman. During the years I've lived in his household I've gotten a son. He's a beautiful child. I held him in my arms day and night and wouldn't let go of him ever. I'm going to make him my heir. You, Tadasada, I'll make my second son. That's to show my regard for his mother's high rank." Tadasada heard this and said, "Where is your young son, sir?" "Over there," said Yoshifuji, and pointed to the storehouse.

Tadasada and all the rest of the company were dumbfounded. They saw that Yoshifuji had the appearance of a man emaciated by severe illness; and they saw that he had on the clothes that he was wearing when he disappeared. They had a servant look under the floor of the storehouse. A lot of foxes were there, and they scattered and fled. That was the place where Yoshifuji had lain. When they saw this they understood it all: Yoshifuji had been tricked by a fox and had become her husband and was no longer in his right mind. They immediately

---

325. Thus—by having sexual longings—making himself an easy victim for foxes, as the Japanese readers would have recognized. The original readers would have been expected to spot more subtle clues: when the young woman, asked her name, says "I'm no one"; when the worried relatives, wondering whether he is not off on a secret love affair, suggest jocosely (and all too accurately) that he may be "crawling" about somewhere.

summoned an eminent monk to pray for him and called in a yin–yang master to exorcise the evil influences; and they had Yoshifuji bathed repeatedly. But whatever they tried, he still bore no resemblance to his former self. Afterward, little by little, he returned to his senses; how ashamed he must have been, and how queer he must have felt. Yoshifuji had been under the storehouse for thirteen days, but to him it had seemed thirteen years. Moreover, the beams under the storehouse were only four or five inches above the ground; to Yoshifuji they had seemed high and broad. He had thought himself in a great house that one went in and out of freely. It was all because of the magic power of the spirit-foxes. As for the layman who entered and struck about with his cane, he was a transformation of the Kannon that had been made and dedicated to Yoshifuji's welfare.

This shows why everyone should invoke and meditate on Kannon. Yoshifuji lived more than ten years without illness and died in his sixty-first year.

This story was told to the Imperial Adviser Miyoshi no Kiyotsura[326] when he was governor of Bitchū. So the tale's been told, and so it's been handed down.

[Translated by Marian Ury]

Secular Tales from Japan

HOW A THIEF CLIMBED TO THE UPPER STORY OF RASHŌMON GATE AND SAW A CORPSE (29:18)

Volume 29 is about evil acts, particularly robbery and murder. The two stories here, "How a Thief Climbed to the Upper Story of Rashōmon Gate and Saw a Corpse" and "How a Man Who Was Accompanying His Wife to Tanba Province Got Trussed Up at Oeyama," were used by the modern author Akutagawa Ryūnosuke (author of *Rashōmon*) and then by the modern film director Kurosawa Akira in *Rashōmon*. Like many of the secular setsuwa, the story is about how to survive in this chaotic world. In the second story, instead of reprimanding the rapist, the setsuwa reprimands the husband for his stupidity. One must be alert for danger; anything can happen in this world.

At a time now past, there was a man who had come to the capital from the direction of Settsu Province[327] in order to steal. The sun was still high, so he concealed himself beneath Rashōmon Gate.[328] Shujaku Avenue, to the north,

---

326. Miyoshi no Kiyotsura (or Kiyoyuki, 847–918) was, among other things, a scholar of Chinese. Among his numerous works is a collection of anecdotes of the supernatural. This is one of the few places in which the compiler of the *Konjaku* may be explicitly acknowledging his immediate source.

327. That is, from the south. (Settsu is part of modern Hyōgo Prefecture.)

328. The Rashōmon Gate was at the southern end of the capital. In historical sources, it is described as splendidly ornamented, but it fell into disrepair at an early time, and its

was thronged, and he stood there waiting for the street to become quiet; but then as he waited he heard a great many people approaching from the other direction, and to avoid being seen by them he climbed silently to the upper story. There he saw the faint light of a torch.

This was strange, the thief thought, and he peered through the lattices. A young woman was lying dead. A torch had been lit at her pillow, and beside it sat a white-haired crone who was plucking and tearing the hair from the corpse's head.

The thief saw but could not comprehend. What could these be? he wondered. He was afraid, but he thought, "They may only be ghosts. I'll try scaring them off." He quietly opened the door and drew his sword. "You there, you there," he cried, and rushed in upon them.

The crone cowered in confusion and rubbed her hands together. "Who are you, old woman, and what are you doing here?" the thief asked.

"I lost my mistress, sir," she said, "and as there was no one to bury her, I brought her here. See what nice long hair she has. I'm plucking it out to make a wig. Spare me!"

The thief stripped the corpse and the old woman of the clothes they wore and stole the hair. He ran to the ground and made his getaway.

There used to be a lot of corpses in the upper story of that gate. It's a fact that when people died and for some reason or other couldn't be buried they were brought there.

The thief told someone what had happened, and whoever heard his story passed it on. So the tale's been told, and so it's been handed down.

[Translated by Marian Ury]

HOW A MAN WHO WAS ACCOMPANYING HIS WIFE TO TANBA PROVINCE GOT TRUSSED UP AT ŌEYAMA (29:23)

At a time now past, a man who lived in the capital had a wife who came from Tanba Province. He accompanied her on a journey to Tanba. The husband had his wife ride their horse while he himself walked along behind, keeping guard, with a quiver with ten arrows on his back and a bow in his hand. Not far from Ōeyama there fell in with them a brawny-looking young man with a sword at his waist.

They walked along together, each inquiring politely where the other was going and chatting about this and that. The new man, the one with the sword, said, "This is a famous sword that I'm wearing, an heirloom from Mutsu Province.

---

upper story—it had two stories—was thought to be the abode of supernatural beings and worse.

Look at it," and he unsheathed it. In truth it was a magnificent blade, and when the husband saw it he wanted it above all things. The new man saw the expression on his face and said, "Do you want this sword? I'll trade it for that bow you're carrying." The man with the bow knew his bow to be of no great value, while the sword was exceptionally fine. What with his desire for the sword and his greed for a profitable bargain, he made the exchange without a second thought.

Well then, as they were walking on the new man said, "I look ridiculous carrying a bow and nothing else. While we're in the mountains lend me a couple of arrows. After all, sir, we're traveling together, so it's all the same where you're concerned."

To the first man this seemed reasonable enough. He was in high good humor at having exchanged his worthless bow for a valuable sword, and so he took out two arrows and handed them over as he'd been asked. The new man walked behind, the bow and two arrows ready in his grasp. The first man walked ahead, with the sword at his waist and the useless quiver on his back.

After a time the travelers went into a grove to have their afternoon meal. The new man said, "It's not nice to eat where people can see. Let's go on a little," and so they went deep into the trees. Then, just as the husband had put his arms around his wife to lift her from the horse, the other man suddenly fitted an arrow to his bow, aimed at him, and pulled it taut. "I'll shoot if you move," he said.

The first man hadn't expected anything at all like this and stood looking at him dumbfounded. The other threatened him. "Go on into the mountains, go on!" Afraid for his life, he went with his wife perhaps half a mile farther into the mountains. "Throw away your sword and knife," the other commanded, and he threw them away. The other man approached, picked them up and knocked him down, and tied him fast to a tree with the bridle rope.

Then this man went up to the woman and looked at her closely. She was twenty or a little older and of humble station but adorably pretty. Her beauty aroused his desire, and forgetting any other purpose, he made her take off her clothes. The woman had no way of resisting, and so she stripped as he told her to. Then he too undressed and embraced her and lay with her. The woman was helpless and had to obey. All the while her husband watched in his trusses. What must he have thought!

Afterward, the man arose, dressed himself as before, strapped the quiver on his back and the sword to his waist and, bow in hand, hoisted himself onto the horse. To the woman he said, "I'm sorry, but I must go away. I have no choice. As a favor to you I'll spare your husband's life. I'm taking the horse so I can make a quick escape." And he galloped away, no one knows where.

After that, the wife went up to her husband and freed his bonds. He looked stupefied. "You wretch!" she exclaimed. "You good-for-nothing coward! From this day forward I'll never trust you again." Her husband said not a word, and together they went to Tanba.

The rapist had a sense of shame, for after all he did not rob the woman of her clothes. But the husband was a worthless fool: in the mountains to hand his bow and arrows to someone he'd never before laid eyes on was surely the height of stupidity.

No one knows what became of the other man. So the tale goes, and so it's been handed down.

[Translated by Marian Ury]

Chapter 3

THE KAMAKURA PERIOD

The Kamakura period began in 1183 with the establishment of the *bakufu*, or military government, in Kamakura, near present-day Tokyo, by Minamoto Yoritomo, the leader of the Minamoto (Genji) clan, which defeated the Heike (Taira) in 1185. The Genpei war between the Genji and the Heike is vividly recounted in the epic narrative *The Tales of the Heike*, part of which is translated here. After the end of the Genpei war, a struggle broke out between Yoritomo and his younger brother Yoshitsune, a prominent Minamoto military leader, who was killed in 1189 by Fujiwara no Yasuhira, a general of the Fujiwara clan in Ōshū (northeast Honshū). Yoritomo, in turn, destroyed the Fujiwara forces, thus ending all major domestic armed conflict. The legends surrounding Yoshitsune can be found in *The Story of Yoshitsune (Gikeiki)*.

After Yoritomo's death, control of the bakufu passed from the Minamoto to the Hōjō family, led by Hōjō Masako (1157–1225), the wife of Yoritomo and the mother of Minamoto Sanetomo (1192–1219), the third shogun and a noted waka poet. A key political turning point in the Kamakura period was the Jōkyū rebellion in 1221, when, in an attempt to regain direct imperial power from the military, the retired emperor GoToba (r. 1183–1198, 1180–1239) attacked the Hōjō but was soundly defeated and exiled to the small and remote island of Oki. The Jōkyū rebellion revealed the weakness of the nobility and the emperor and the growing strength of the samurai class, whose power had risen in the late Heian period. GoToba's exile to Oki is nostalgically recounted in *The Clear Mirror*

(*Masukagami*, 1338–1376), a vernacular historical chronicle, in a section translated in this book.

The Kamakura period ended in 1333 with the defeat of Hōjō Takatoki (1303–1333) and the Hōjō clan by Emperor GoDaigo (r. 1318–1339, 1288–1339), who gained power briefly, for two years, during the Kenmu restoration (1333–1336), before being defeated by another military clan, the Ashikaga. GoDaigo retreated to Yoshino, south of the capital, and established the Southern Court and the beginning of the rival court system known as the Northern and Southern Courts period (1336–1392). The political career of Emperor GoDaigo and his failed attempt at imperial restoration is one of the focal points of the *Taiheiki (Chronicle of Great Peace*, 1340s–1371), a major military chronicle whose highlights are included here.

The Kamakura period marks the beginning of the so-called medieval period, a four-hundred-year span from the fall of the Heike (Taira) clan in 1185 to the battle of Sekigahara in 1600, when Tokugawa Ieyasu (1542–1616) triumphed over his rivals and unified the country under his control. Sometimes the beginning of the medieval period is pushed back as far as the beginning of the Heian period (794–1185), and sometimes the end of the medieval period is pushed forward as far as the end of the Tokugawa (Edo) period (1600–1867). Generally, however, the Kamakura period (1183–1333), the Northern and Southern Courts (Nanbokuchō) period (1336–1392), and the Muromachi period (1392–1573), when warrior society came to the fore, are considered to be the three main historical divisions of the medieval period.

The Muromachi period extended from the rule by the Ashikaga clan, based in Kyoto (in the Muromachi quarter), through the end of the Northern and Southern Courts era to the defeat of the fifteenth shogun Ashikaga Yoshiaki by Oda Nobunaga in 1573. The latter half of the Muromachi period is referred to as the Warring States (Sengoku) period, from the beginning of the Ōnin war (1467–1477) to 1573, when Oda Nobunaga destroyed the Ashikaga bakufu and unified the country. The Azuchi-Momoyama period (1573–1598) refers to the short period of time when two powerful generals, first Oda Nobunaga and then Toyotomi Hideyoshi, gained national power before eventually succumbing to Tokugawa Ieyasu at the battle of Sekigahara in 1600. The most striking cultural and literary changes occurred between the early medieval period, from the fall of the Heike clan in 1185 to the fall of the Kamakura bakufu in 1333, and the late medieval period, from the Kenmu restoration onward, with a particularly significant break after the Ōnin war that forced the aristocratic culture, centered in the capital for many centuries, to disperse to the provinces.

THE SAMURAI AND LITERATURE

One of the principal aspects of medieval society was the emergence of a warrior government and culture. As a result of the Hōgen (1156) and Heiji (1159) rebellions, the Heike (Taira), a military clan, displaced the Fujiwara clan which had dominated the throne and the court for most of the Heian period. If the ascendance of the Heike is considered the beginning of the warrior rule then the medieval period begins with the first year of Hōgen (1156). But the Heike elite emulated the Fujiwara regents before them, continuing the court bureaucratic system based in Kyoto, and they soon were defeated by the Genji (Minamoto), who established a military government in Kamakura, between 1183 and 1185. Minamoto Yoritomo's establishment of a bakufu in Kamakura resulted in two political centers—a court government in Kyoto and a military government in the east—thereby laying the foundation for a system of dual cultures.

During the medieval period, the bakufu in the east gradually increased its control to the point that the court government in Kyoto lost its political power. Seeing their fortunes waning, the aristocrats in Kyoto occasionally tried to restore the imperial authority of the court-centered government. But the Jōkyū rebellion in 1221 ended in failure, and the Kenmu restoration lasted for only two years. The extended struggle during the Northern and Southern Courts period, when the imperial court was split, eventually ended these attempts and dispersed the nobility, with the political power permanently shifting to the military. The result in the Muromachi period was the full emergence of a samurai-based society and culture.

As the social and economic status of the samurai rose, their cultural activities multiplied as well. During the early medieval period, the samurai were drawn to aristocratic culture and the culture of the capital, which they tried to imitate. Although there were very few samurai waka poets during the Heian period, their number steadily increased during the medieval period. The most prominent was Minamoto Sanetomo (1192–1219), the third Kamakura bakufu shogun (1203–1219), who took an interest in *Man'yōshū*-style poetry. In the late medieval period, scholars and poets of samurai origin such as Imagawa Ryōshun (1326–1414), Tō no Tsuneyori (1401–1484), and Hosokawa Yūsai (1534–1610) became prominent, and a number of renga masters had samurai origins.

The first major works of "warrior" literature during the medieval period are the military chronicles (*gunki-mono*), which were organized chronologically and focused on the lives and families of samurai. Relatively few samurai actually helped produce these chronicles, however. More often, they were the work of fallen or lesser aristocrats (often recluses) or Buddhist priests, who gave military narratives like *The Tales of the Heike* a heavily Buddhistic and aristocratic coloring. Likewise, in the latter half of the medieval period, the founder of *kōwakamai* (ballad drama), Momonoi Kōwakamaru (1393–1470), the scion of a warrior family, gave kōwakamai a samurai flavor. The other playwrights of nō drama and kōwakamai were not samurai, although samurai did form an important part of the audience.

THE SPREAD OF BUDDHISM AND
THE WAY OF THE GODS

The Genpei war and subsequent military struggles left their survivors with a deep sense of the impermanence of the world. For followers of Buddhism, the situation was so apocalyptic that it signaled for them the latter age of the Buddhist law (*mappō*). Buddhism promised worldly benefits (protection, rewards in this life) as well as future salvation, a sense of sustenance amid turmoil and uncertainty. Buddhism had entered Japan from China as early as the sixth century and, especially Tendai and Shingon Buddhism, had become a central institution in Heian aristocratic society, but not until the late Heian period did it begin to penetrate commoner society at large.

Innovative priests who had become disillusioned with the older, established Buddhist institutions in the capitals of Nara and Kyoto created new Buddhist schools that appealed to commoners, who often were unable to read the Buddhist scriptures. Hōnen (1133–1212) founded the Jōdo (Pure Land) sect, which had a profound influence on medieval culture, and his disciple Shinran (1173–1262) created the Shinshū (New Pure Land) sect. A generation later, Ippen (1239–1289) founded the Jishū (Time) sect. These Pure Land sects, which stressed the recitation of the name of the Amida Buddha, promised an easily attainable way to salvation, relying on the power of grace and the benevolence of the Amida Buddha. The hymns and personal writings of these Pure Land leaders, particularly those by Hōnen, are included here both because of their high literary quality and as a necessary context for understanding medieval literary texts like *The Tales of the Heike*, which are based on Kamakura Pure Land beliefs. Zen Buddhism, which was imported from China in the medieval period and welcomed by the samurai in Kamakura, stressed meditation, non-dualism, and a frugal, minimalist lifestyle.

As the Buddhist sects (including Tendai, which continued to exert considerable institutional influence) rose in prominence, so too did belief in the native gods (*kami*), which laid the foundation for the institutional rise of Shinto (Way of the Gods) and its various local and national deities. Samurai leaders such as Minamoto Yoritomo, the founder of the Kamakura bakufu, worshiped and relied on both kami and buddhas. Kami were believed to bring worldly benefits and protections for the state, the community, and the clan, and they became the focus of worship at major shrines like the Ise Shrine. One result was the emerging doctrine of Japan as a "country of the gods" (*shinkoku*), evident in later Northern and Southern Courts-period texts such as Kitabatake Chikafusa's *Chronicle of the Gods* (*Jinnō shōtōki*, 1343). The rise of popular Buddhism and of cults of native gods led to a belief in *honji suijaku* (original ground—manifest traces), according to which Shinto gods are local manifestations (*suijaku*) of original buddhas (*honji*). This syncretist view had precedents in earlier periods but became prominent in the medieval period and is a frequent motif of the setsuwa of the Kamakura period and of the otogi-zōshi of the Muromachi period.

THE ARISTOCRACY AND LITERATURE

Even while their political and economic status declined, the aristocracy retained their prestige as the custodians of high culture and canonical literature, and the long tradition of aristocratic court literature continued to flourish in the early medieval period. Indeed, the first thirty or forty years of the Kamakura period, until the Jōkyū rebellion in 1221 when the power of the nobility was abruptly terminated, represents one of the peaks of aristocratic literature. Some of the greatest waka anthologies—beginning with the *Shinkokinshū* (*New Collection of Ancient and Modern Poems*, ca. 1205), the eighth imperial waka collection and often considered the finest of the twenty-one imperial waka anthologies—were compiled at this time. The best poetic treatises, such as Fujiwara Shunzei's *Poetic Styles from the Past* (*Korai fūteishō*, 1197) and Fujiwara Teika's *Essentials of Poetic Composition* (*Eiga taigai*, ca. 1222), were written during the early decades of the Kamakura period, an age of increased cultural production by the aristocracy. In fact, more *monogatari* (tales) were written during the early medieval period than in the Heian period, although many such works were imitative, drawing heavily on *The Tale of Genji*, which had become a model for literary and poetic composition. It was not until the Muromachi period that the monogatari received new stimulus from commoner culture, taking the form of what are now called *otogi-zōshi* (Muromachi tales).

Aristocratic literature in the medieval period was characterized by strong nostalgia for the Heian-court past and an emphasis on preserving court traditions. Indeed, literary production was the only means for many aristocrats to make a living on the basis of their heritage. The twenty-first and last imperial waka anthology, the *Shinshokukokinshū*, edited in 1439, symbolically marked the end of aristocratic literature. Not only did the aristocrats compose waka and monogatari in the medieval period, but they also turned their attention to preserving their cultural inheritance by collating, annotating, and commenting on earlier texts. Their scholarship extended from ancient texts such as the *Kojiki*, *Nihon shoki*, and *Man'yōshū* to major Heian texts like the *Kokinshū*, *The Tales of Ise*, and *The Tale of Genji*, which became the three most heavily annotated texts. The work by these aristocrats (beginning with Fujiwara Teika, who produced what became the most authoritative versions of *The Tale of Genji*) in constructing and transmitting the literary canon was eventually shared by other social groups, the priests and the samurai, who also had a strong nostalgia for the Heian classics. Two great literary figures of the late Muromachi period were Shōtetsu (1381–1459), a prolific and innovative poet who is regarded as one of the last distinguished exponents of classical waka, and the renga (linked verse) master Sōgi (1421–1502), of commoner birth, who wrote influential treatises on renga and numerous commentaries on the Heian classics. Such commentaries were motivated by the fact that Japanese poetry, specifically waka and renga, the two most important literary forms, required a knowledge of the diction and allusive associations of the Heian classics.

THE PRIESTHOOD AND LITERATURE

The contribution of the Buddhist priesthood to literature was enormous, especially in light of the dominant role that Buddhism played throughout the period. The first major contribution was the *hōgo*, teachings of the Buddhist law in kana prose. Although Buddhist writings such as the *Record of Miraculous Events in Japan (Nihon ryōiki)* and *The Essentials of Salvation (Ōjōyōshū)* appeared in the mid-Heian period, they were written in Chinese. In the Kamakura period, however, the priest-intellectuals of the new Buddhist sects wrote in kana, thereby producing vernacular Buddhist literature. Buddhist leaders like Shinran and Ippen also wrote *wasan* (Buddhist hymns), which made their teachings easily accessible and available for wide dissemination. Equally important was Zen Buddhism, introduced to Japan by Dōgen (1200–1253) and others. One product of Zen culture was the literature of the Five Mountains (*Gozan bungaku*), writings in Chinese by Zen priests from the late thirteenth to the sixteenth century, with which Ikkyū (1394–1481), whose poetry is included here, was associated. Zen Buddhism also had a profound impact on nō drama, as is evident in works such as *Stupa Komachi (Sotoba Komachi)*.

Equally important were the collections of setsuwa edited by Buddhist priests and used for preaching to commoners. Setsuwa were collected from as early as the Nara period, beginning with the *Nihon ryōiki*, and appeared in the late Heian period in the massive *Collection of Tales of Times Now Past (Konjaku monogatari shū)*, but it was in the Kamakura period that most of the setsuwa collections were edited and produced. At that time a new type of setsuwa emerged: the *engi-mono* (tales of origins), which describe the origins and miraculous benefits of the god or buddha worshiped by a specific temple or shrine complex. Engi-mono were produced by the priests or shrine officials at the religious site, using historical documents and popular legend to record, embellish, or reinvent the history of the temple or shrine and to advertise the powers of the enshrined deity. Almost all of them were preserved as illustrated scrolls (*emakimono*). A good example is "The Avatars of Kumano" in the *Shintōshū*, about the origin of the gods of the Kumano Shrine. Similar kinds of illustrated scrolls formed the basis for the later Muromachi otogi-zōshi. A *sekkyō* (sermon-ballad) tradition emerged in which priests narrated or chanted Buddhist teachings or engi-mono with a musical accompaniment. In the late medieval period this tradition was consolidated as *sekkyō-bushi* (ballads sung to the beat of the *sasara*), performed by commoner storytellers. This genre became the basis of *sekkyō jōruri* (ballads sung to shamisen accompaniment), a medium for narrating double suicides and revenge tales that eventually evolved into *jōruri* (puppet theater) in the Tokugawa period. Buddhist priest-storytellers (*monogatari sō*) also became specialists in narrating military chronicles like the *Taiheiki* (*Chronicle of Great Peace*).

Buddhist priests were also prominent composers of waka and renga. In fact, there is probably no genre in the medieval period that was not related to the Buddhist clergy. One consequence is that Buddhist thought permeates medieval literature: warrior tales, historical chronicles, setsuwa, essays (*zuihitsu*), nō drama, otogi-zōshi, and sekkyō-bushi. Even the treatises on waka, renga, and nō drama are permeated by Buddhist perspectives. In sum, all forms of cultural production in the medieval period were inseparable from Buddhist concepts and worldviews. This is why the notion that literature amounts to nothing more than *kyōgen kigo* (wild words and decorative phrases) came to the fore. On the one hand, in the Buddhist context, literature and its production were thought to be illusory and even an impediment to salvation, encouraging worldly attachments. On the other hand, it could, as argued in the selections from the *Collection of Sand and Pebbles* (*Shasekishū*, 1279–1283), be rationalized by Buddhist writers as an expedient means (*hōben*) of teaching the Buddhist law and leading readers (or listeners) to insight and, ultimately, enlightenment.

SAIGYŌ

Satō Norikiyo, now known as Saigyō (1118–1190), was the son of a wealthy family of hereditary warrior aristocrats. At the age of fifteen, he entered the service of the powerful Tokudaiji family, and later he served the retired emperor Toba as one of the Northern Guard (Hokumen no bushi), a select group of military bodyguards. Members of the Northern Guard also served as cultural companions to the retired emperor, exhibiting skill in poetry, music, *kemari*,[1] and other aristocratic pastimes. For reasons still being debated, in 1140, at the age of twenty-three, Saigyō suddenly abandoned his post and his family to become a Buddhist monk. For the next fifty years, Saigyō alternately lived in seclusion, traveled about the country, spent time in the capital, and carried out various Buddhist activities. Throughout his tonsured life, Saigyō continued to compose poetry, increasing his fame. The pinnacle of Saigyō's poetic influence came fifteen years after his death, when ninety-four of his poems (more than those of any other poet) were included in the imperially sponsored *Shinkokinshū* (*New Collection of Ancient and Modern Poems*, ca. 1205).

Although reliable historical documents concerning Saigyō's life are scarce, the autobiographical nature of many of his poems has fed the imagination of

---

1. Kemari is the aristocratic game of hacky-sack, or sepia. Saigyō is known to have been a master kemari player.

readers for centuries, giving rise to a vast body of semilegendary material. "The Woman of Pleasure at Eguchi," from the *Tales of Renunciation (Senjūshō)*, is a good example of how Saigyō's poems became the object of legends. It now is nearly impossible to separate the legend Saigyō from the actual poet and his poems. Saigyō spent many years in and around the capital and nearly thirty years in relative seclusion near Mount Kōya, the headquarters of the Shingon Buddhist establishment. He is best known as a travel poet, making the long and arduous trip to Michinoku (northeastern Honshū) twice—once shortly after becoming a monk and again when he was around sixty-nine years of age. He also traveled to Shikoku, Kumano, and Ise, where he spent the duration of the Genpei (Heike/Genji) war (1180–1186). After the fighting ended, Saigyō returned to the capital and then to Kawachi (near present-day Osaka), where he lived out his remaining years, dying on the sixteenth day of the Second Month in 1190.

Although Saigyō composed poetry covering the entire range of traditional waka topics, his most famous poems are on travel, reclusion, cherry blossoms, and the moon. Travel was an established category in both waka composition and the imperially sponsored anthologies. Later interpreters and scholars have perceived a special sense of immediateness in Saigyō's travel poetry. Many waka poets never saw the poetic sites they described in their poems, relying instead on established associations of poetic place-names. Even though Saigyō is known for his travels, he also composed many poems on famous places without visiting them.

Similarly, it is not entirely clear just how secluded from the world Saigyō was. He likely lived alone in the capital or far away in Kōya or Ise, but he probably was never in total seclusion. Rather, he lived near and associated with others who had abandoned the world. Furthermore, Saigyō nourished ties with the poetic establishment; he maintained relationships with high-ranking aristocrats and imperial personages from the time of his service as a samurai; and he actively participated in poetic and Buddhistic activities in and around the capital as well as at Kōya and Ise.

SELECTED POEMS

Saigyō is noted for his poetry on cherry blossoms, being especially fond of the blossoms in the mountainous region of Yoshino, not far from Mount Kōya. Saigyō's cherry blossom poems often express a sense of attachment to the blossoms and have been interpreted as self-remonstrative in the Buddhist sense. Saigyō's moon poems also carry Buddhist overtones, for in both Buddhist sutras and waka, the moon is the symbol of enlightenment. Many of Saigyō's moon poems also, however, retain the traditional association of love or longing.

Saigyō's poetry is marked by unadorned self-expression, seeming simplicity of diction, self-reflection, and the interweaving of nature imagery with Buddhist motifs and ideals. These traits have made his poems among the most popular and influential in the poetic canon.

SANKASHŪ, MISCELLANEOUS, NO. 723

At the time that I decided to abandon the world, some people at Higashiyama composed on the topic "expressing one's feelings on mist."

sora ni naru	The empty sky
kokoro wa haru no	of my heart
kasumi ni te	enshrouded in spring mist
yo ni araji to mo	rises to thoughts of
omoi tatsu kana	leaving the world behind.[2]

SHINKOKINSHŪ, LOVE, NO. 1267; SANKASHŪ, MISCELLANEOUS, NO. 727

When I was staying somewhere far away, I sent the following to someone in the capital around the time of the moon.

tsuki nomi ya	Only the moon
uwa no sora naru	in the sky above
katami ni te	a vacant reminder,
omoi mo ideba	should you think of me,
kokoro kayowamu	perhaps it will link your heart to mine.[3]

SHINKOKINSHŪ, MISCELLANEOUS, NO. 1535

sutsu to naraba	If I've forsaken
ukiyo o itou	the world of sorrows
shirushi aramu	there must be proof I despise it—

---

2. This poem was composed seven months before Saigyō took vows. The opening phrase (*sora ni naru kokoro*) literally means "my heart that is the sky" or "my heart that is empty," which suggests that the poet's heart is becoming the sky, spreading infinitely until it becomes clear and empty. The verb *tatsu* means both for a person "to resolve" (on leaving the world) and for the spring mist "to rise." The combined image suggests that Saigyō wishes to rise above the world, where he can freely gaze on the clear and empty sky of his own heart.

3. "The time of the moon" is autumn. Although Saigyō was a monk, it was not unusual for Buddhist priests to compose love poetry, based on experience or imagination. This poem is thought to have been sent to someone in the capital, most likely Saigyō's wife. *Uwa no sora* (sky above) can also mean "vacant," "restless," or "distracted." The poem implies that the poet is always thinking of the former loved one, although that loved one has likely forgotten the poet.

<table>
<tr><td>ware ni wa kumore</td><td>shroud yourself for me,</td></tr>
<tr><td>aki no yo no tsuki</td><td>autumn night moon.[4]</td></tr>
</table>

SHINKOKINSHŪ, MISCELLANEOUS, NO. 1611; *SANKASHŪ*, MISCELLANEOUS, NO. 728

When I abandoned the world and was on my way to Ise, I composed this at Suzuka-yama (Bell Deer Mountain).

<table>
<tr><td>Suzuka-yama</td><td>Suzuka Mountain,</td></tr>
<tr><td>ukiyo o yoso ni</td><td>I've tossed aside the world of sorrows</td></tr>
<tr><td>furisutete</td><td>as a stranger to myself,</td></tr>
<tr><td>ika ni nariyuku</td><td>so what note will I now sound,</td></tr>
<tr><td>waga mi naruran</td><td>what will become of me?[5]</td></tr>
</table>

SANKASHŪ, SPRING, NO. 66

<table>
<tr><td>Yoshino yama</td><td>Since the day</td></tr>
<tr><td>kozue no hana o</td><td>I saw the treetop blossoms</td></tr>
<tr><td>mishi hi yori</td><td>in Yoshino's mountains</td></tr>
<tr><td>kokoro wa mi ni mo</td><td>my heart has not stayed</td></tr>
<tr><td>sowazu nari ni ki</td><td>with my body at all.[6]</td></tr>
</table>

SHINKOKINSHŪ, MISCELLANEOUS, NO. 617

<table>
<tr><td>Yoshino yama</td><td>Mount Yoshino,</td></tr>
<tr><td>yagate ideji to</td><td>I'd like to stay</td></tr>
</table>

---

4. Like the moon of the previous poem, this moon is associated with worldly thoughts. As one who has forsaken the world, Saigyō must have some proof that he is free of worldly emotions. This proof is in Saigyō's not thinking of the world, or of love, when he looks at the moon. This is not possible, Saigyō implies, if the moon is clear and beautiful.

5. Poems about Suzuka (Bell Deer) Mountain use words related to bells. *Furisutete* means "to toss away" but also implies ringing a bell (*furu*). *Naru* and *nari* imply the sound of a bell being rung, as well as "becoming." This poem calls on a long history of poetry by imperial princesses chosen to become the high priestess of the Ise shrines. Suzuka Mountain was on the route to the Ise shrines as well as being a checkpoint along the Eastern Sea Road (Tōkaidō), and a popular place to compose a poem expressing feelings concerning the journey ahead. The poet seems concerned about his future now that he has broken all ties with the world. Recent commentators, however, have pointed out that often bells were rung when praying for the fulfillment of a wish.

6. The spirit was thought to wander away from the body when deeply disturbed or fraught with jealousy. Here Saigyō's spirit has left his body in ecstatic excitement at seeing the cherry blossoms of Mount Yoshino, famous for its mountain cherries. The poem suggests that Saigyō is disappointed that he cannot control his thoughts and desires, but Yoshino is also known as a sacred space and a site of religious training, where spiritual feats are not uncommon.

omou mi o	and never leave,
hana chirinaba to	though some are surely waiting, thinking
hito ya matsuran	"once the blossoms have fallen . . ."[7]

SANKASHŪ, SPRING, NO. 76

hana ni somu	Why should my heart
kokoro no ikade	remain stained
nokorikemu	by blossoms,
sutehateteki to	when I thought
omou waga mi ni	I had tossed all that away?[8]

SANKASHŪ, SPRING, NO. 87

When I thought I'd like some peace and quiet, people came to see the cherry blossoms.

hanami ni to	Wanting to see the blossoms
muretsutsu hito no	people come in droves
kuru nomi zo	to visit—this alone
atara sakura no	regrettably
toga ni wa arikeru	is the cherry tree's fault.[9]

SANKASHŪ, SPRING, NO. 139

On the topic "cherry blossoms scattering in a dream," composed with others at the residence of the former Kamo Priestess.

harukaze no	When I dream
hana o chirasu to	of spring wind

---

7. The poet has gone to Mount Yoshino to see the cherry blossoms. However, since Mount Yoshino is traditionally a place of religious retreat as well, perhaps he really wants to escape the world altogether. But someone waits, thinking that he will simply return to the capital once the blossoms fall. He is caught between his desire to escape the world and his thoughts for the people waiting for him at home.

8. This poem, perhaps composed shortly after Saigyō took Buddhist vows, expresses his consternation at his remaining attachments. The phrase "stained by blossoms" (*hana ni somu*), which has also been interpreted as referring to a romantic or worldly attachment, implies a deep attachment to the cherry blossoms. This internal conflict is a hallmark of Saigyō's style.

9. This is one of Saigyō's most famous poems, primarily because it forms the basis of *Saigyō zakura (Saigyō and the Cherry Tree)*, one of the most beloved nō plays. In the play, the spirit of the cherry tree appears to rebuke Saigyō for blaming the blossoms for his discomfort. But Saigyō is stating that the *only* fault to be found in a cherry tree is that it is so beautiful that crowds of people come to see it and destroy the serenity of a monk in retreat.

miru yume wa	scattering cherry blossoms
samete mo mune no	my heart stirs
sawagu narikeri	even after waking.[10]

SHINKOKINSHŪ, MISCELLANEOUS, NO. 1471

yo no naka o	When I think of
omoeba nabete	this world
chiru hana no	all is scattering blossoms,
waga mi o satemo	so where else
izuchi kamo semu	might I choose to be?[11]

SHINKOKINSHŪ, MISCELLANEOUS, NO. 1846;
SANKASHŪ, SPRING, NO. 77

negawaku wa	My wish is
hana no shita nite	to die in spring
haru shinan	under the cherry blossoms
sono kisaragi no	on that day in the Second Month
mochizuki no koro	when the moon is full.[12]

SANKASHŪ, SPRING, NO. 78

hotoke ni wa	Offer up
sakura no hana o	cherry blossoms
tatematsure	to the deceased,
waga nochi no yo o	if anyone wishes to mourn me
hito toburawaba	after I'm gone.[13]

---

10. The Kamo Priestess was an imperial princess chosen to serve as the high priestess of the Kamo Shrine in the capital. The poem alludes to a late spring poem by Ki no Tsurayuki, *Kokinshū*, no. 117: "That night when I lodged and slept in the spring foothills, the blossoms scattered even in my dreams." Saigyō's poem describes the state of the poet after waking from that dream. The verb "to stir" (*sawagu*) is a word associated in the poetic tradition with "wind," but it also implies a racing heart.

11. Saigyō draws a direct parallel between the scattering blossoms and himself (*waga mi*). If we take *waga mi* to mean the poet's body specifically, the poem can be read as foreseeing death. Most commentators see a more general expression of uncertainty: if the whole world is as impermanent as scattering blossoms, then he cannot escape that uncertainty.

12. "That day in the Second Month" refers to the fifteenth day of the Second Month in the lunar calendar, the day that Shakyamuni, the historical Buddha, is said to have died. Saigyō here combines his three central devotions—cherry blossoms, the moon, and the Buddha—in one poem. Saigyō actually died on the sixteenth day of the Second Month. At least four other monks of the medieval period are said to have successfully entered nirvana on the same day as the Buddha, and it was not unusual for many to try.

13. Although cherry blossoms are not usually chosen as offerings to the dead, Saigyō here insists on his favorite flower. Saigyō's request has been seen as further evidence of his lingering

SHINKOKINSHŪ, AUTUMN 1, NO. 362; SANKASHŪ,
AUTUMN, NO. 470

Composed along the way to somewhere in autumn.

kokoro naki	Even one
mi ni mo aware wa	with no heart could not help
shirarekeri	but know pathos:
shigi tatsu sawa no	a snipe takes flight in a marsh
aki no yūgure	this autumn evening.[14]

SHINKOKINSHŪ, WINTER, NO. 625

Tsu no kuni no	Was spring at Naniwa
Naniwa no haru wa	in Tsu Province
yume nare ya	a dream?
ashi no kareha ni	Wind blows
kaze wataru nari	over the withered reeds' leaves.[15]

SHINKOKINSHŪ, MISCELLANEOUS, NO. 1676

furuhata no	From a tree
soba no tatsu ki ni	standing on a cliff
iru hato no	by an old field

---

attachment to the world, but the cherry blossoms can also be associated with the death of Siddhartha (the historical Buddha) beneath the sala blossoms.

14. This poem is one of the "three evening poems" (sanseki no uta) of the Shinkokinshū. The other two poems are by Jakuren and Teika. Autumn evenings (aki no yūgure) are associated with loneliness in classical poetry. The sound of the wings of the snipe(s) fading into the approaching darkness deepens the sense of loneliness in the autumn dusk. According to the headnote, Saigyō composed this poem while traveling, which also connotes loneliness. The phrase kokoro naki mi (body/self without heart/spirit) has basically two interpretations: one who has taken Buddhist vows and has presumably transcended joy and sadness, or one who has no aesthetic or poetic sensibility and does not understand the pathos (aware) of things. Either way, this scene would move even such a person. More specifically, the speaker has been caused to know (shirarekeri) the pathos of things through this scene.

15. This poem is an allusive variation on Nōin's famous poem on Naniwa, or Osaka Bay, in the Goshūishū, vol. 1, Spring 1, no. 43: "To someone with a heart I'd like to show this scene of spring at Naniwa in the province of Tsu." Saigyō rarely alluded directly to earlier poems, but he was fond of Nōin's poetry. Here the allusion establishes a seasonal contrast between spring at Naniwa and the barrenness of winter. The implied sound of the wind through the reeds, which always are associated with Naniwa, adds to the sense of loneliness. Fujiwara no Shunzei described this poem as an example of yūgen (mystery and depth) style.

tomo yobu koe no	the voice of a dove calling a friend
sugoki yūgure	in the eerie twilight.[16]

SANKASHŪ, AUTUMN, NO. 414

With a certain purpose in mind, I went to Ichinomiya in Aki. Along the way, at a place called Takatomi Bay, I was stopped for a while by the wind. Upon seeing moonlight filtering through a rush-thatched hut, I composed the following:

nami no oto o	My heart troubled
kokoro ni kakete	by the sound of the waves,
akasu kana	I spend the night,
toma moru tsuki no	my only friend the moon's light
kage o tomo ni te	winnowing through this hut.[17]

SHINKOKINSHŪ, AUTUMN 1, NO. 472

kirigirisu	Cricket,
yosamu ni aki no	as the autumn night cold
naru mama ni	wears on,
yowaru ka koe no	are you weakening?
tōzakariyuku	Your voice grows more distant.[18]

SHINKOKINSHŪ, WINTER, NO. 627

sabishisa ni	I wish there were another here
taetaru hito no	who could bear
mata mo are na	this loneliness;

---

16. *Soba* is a slope, bluff, or precipice, suggesting that this field is in the hills or mountains. The combination of images—the sound of the dove, the abandoned fields, evening, and so forth—suggests autumn. The dove crying to a friend is an implicit metaphor for the poet, implying both loneliness and love. The use of the word *sugoki*, suggesting fright, cold, and isolation, is highly unusual in waka but common in prose.

17. Aki is part of present-day Hiroshima Prefecture. Ichinomiya is the Itsukushima Shrine on Miyajima Island. The subject of moonlight filtering through the roof or eaves of a thatched hut was a favorite of Saigyō's. A night in a hut on a beach almost always implies wind, waves, and the moon. Saigyō was known for making friends out of inanimate objects like the moon and pine trees.

18. The voice of an insect, especially a gradually weakening voice, is commonly used to suggest the loneliness of autumn and the gradual loss of life. Saigyō, however, is engaging the cricket directly in a conversational mode. The cricket may be a cricket, a friend of the poet, or the poet himself.

iori narabemu	we'd build our huts side by side
fuyu no yamazato	in this wintry mountain village.[19]

SHINKOKINSHŪ, SUMMER, NO. 262

michinobe ni	In the shade
shimizu nagaruru	of a roadside willow
yanagi kage	near a clear flowing stream
shibashi tote koso	I stopped,
tachidomaritsure	for just a while, I thought.[20]

KIKIGAKISHŪ, NO. 165

When I was living in Saga, I and others wrote poems in a light vein.

unaiko ga	The sound of children
susami ni narasu	playfully blowing
mugibue no	straw whistles
koe ni odoroku	wakes me from my
natsu no hirubushi	summer afternoon nap.[21]

SHINKOKINSHŪ, TRAVEL, NO. 987

Composed when going to the eastern provinces.

toshi takete	Did I ever imagine
mata koyubeshi to	I would make this pass again
omoiki ya	in my old age?

---

19. The poet wishes for a friend who, like himself, can bear the loneliness. Saigyō does not wish to escape the loneliness but, rather, to share it with another. Implicitly the thatched hut of a recluse is a place for reflection, meditation, and composition.

20. Much of the effect of this poem derives from the repetition of the *i* sound in *michinobe ni shimizu* and in *shibashi* and from the series of *a* sounds in *nagaruru yanagi kage*. The *koso . . . tsure* construction leaves out the logical conclusion, "but I lingered much longer than planned." Later interpreters read this as a travel poem, with willow trees becoming part of the legend (as in the nō play *Yugyō yanagi* and Matsuo Bashō's *Oku no hosomichi*). Both the shade of the willow and the flowing stream are cool images appropriate to summer.

21. This is the first of a series of thirteen poems written by Saigyō late in life. It is thought that they were composed shortly after his second trip to Michinoku, around 1188. They are unusually playful and colloquial in tone and are thus called *tawabure uta* (playful poems). Some commentators believe, however, that these play poems contain deeper Buddhist connotations and that this poem in particular describes a moment of awakening analogous to enlightenment.

| *inochi narikeri* | Such is life! |
| *Sayanonaka yama* | Sayanonaka Mountain.[22] |

SHINKOKINSHŪ, MISCELLANEOUS, NO. 1613

On Mount Fuji, composed when carrying out religious practices in the eastern provinces.

kaze ni nabiku	Trailing in the wind,
Fuji no keburi no	Fuji's smoke
sora ni kiete	fades into the sky
yukue mo shiranu	destination unknown,
waga omoi kana	just like my own thoughts![23]

SHINKOKINSHŪ, MISCELLANEOUS, NO. 1536

fuke ni keru	As I ponder
waga yo no kage o	my waning shadow
omou ma ni	of life far gone,
haruka ni tsuki no	in the distance
katabuki ni keri	the moon sets.[24]

---

22. Sayanonaka Mountain, in present-day Shizuoka Prefecture, was a difficult pass along the Eastern Sea Road. This poem was composed on Saigyō's second trip to Michinoku and refers to his amazement at being able to cross Sayanonaka some forty years after his first trip. The key to the poem lies in the fourth line, translated here as "Such is life!" *Inochi* refers to the poet's life or lifespan, but it can also mean "fate" or "destiny." Long life is remarkable when one assumes that life is fleeting and insubstantial.

23. *Nabiku* (trailing), *keburi* (smoke), *yukue mo shiranu* (destination unknown), and *omoi* (thoughts/longing) are all words traditionally used in love poems. The *hi* of *omo(h)i* also suggests fire (*hi*). Mount Fuji was long a symbol of smoldering passion. Hence, this poem is placed in the love section of *Saigyō shōninshū*, but it is placed in the miscellany category of the *Shinkokinshū*, and most commentators go out of their way to deemphasize the love imagery. According to Saigyō's friend Jien, Saigyō himself considered this perhaps his best poem (*jisanka*), and it has received critical and popular acclaim. The nexus of meaning is thought to be in the word *omohi*. In a traditional love poem, these "thoughts" would imply a lover or longing. The first half of the poem, while suggesting love imagery, can also be interpreted as funerary, with the image of smoke fading away suggesting the smoke of a funeral pyre. The death imagery suggests that it is not only his thoughts but also himself that is trailing toward extinction, or nirvana. "Destination unknown" is a pivot phrase that modifies both the smoke and the poet's thoughts.

24. *Fuke ni keru* is generally used to mean night or autumn "growing deep." It can also mean "growing old." Saigyō puns on the word *yo*, which can mean "one's life" as well as "night." *Kage* can mean "shadow" or "one's physical form" (or face). If we take *yo* to be one's lifetime, then *kage* would be the accumulation of one's life experiences. If we take *ma* to be a moment, this becomes a sudden awakening to the reality of old age. If we take *ma* to be a period of time, we can imagine

SHINKOKINSHŪ, BUDDHIST POEMS, NO. 1978

On looking at one's heart.

yami harete	Darkness dispels,
kokoro no sora ni	and the moon shining clear
sumu tsuki wa	in my heart's sky
nishi no yamabe ya	now seems to near
chikaku naruramu	the western hills.[25]

[Introduction and translations by Jack Stoneman]

FUJIWARA NO TEIKA

Fujiwara no Teika (1162–1241), or Sadaie, was the son of Shunzei and heir to the Mikohidari house of poetry. Teika was recognized at a fairly early age as one of the most controversially innovative poets of his generation, and he was one of the four primary compilers of the *Shinkokinshū*. From the age of eighteen to the age of seventy-four, he kept a diary entitled the *Meigetsuki*. Between 1185 and 1199, he began to explore a new poetic style, which was criticized as *"daruma"* poems, or "incomprehensible" poems. Despite his audacious experiments with syntax and disdain for convention, Teika could also be remarkably conservative, especially in his later years, and notoriously called for a return to early classical models of composition. His dictum "new meanings, old words" is an emblem of the difficult demands he made for originality within the constraints of precedent. Few poets were able to follow Teika's demands without resorting to tedious conventionalism. This fact, combined with his overwhelming influence as the patriarch of the dominant schools of court poetry for several centuries, is often blamed for the stultification of courtly waka after the thirteenth century. Forty-six of Teika's poems were included in the *Shinkokinshū*.

ESSENTIALS OF POETIC COMPOSITION
(*EIGA NO TAIGAI*, CA. 1222)

Essentials of Poetic Composition explains Teika's approach to waka composition in his later years and reflects a fundamental technique of medieval aristocratic literature:

---

the poet pondering his long life throughout the night, only to notice that in the meantime the moon has begun to set.

25. The topic of this poem is *kanjin* (looking at one's heart)—that is, meditation on the heart and self-realization. Often in Buddhist discourse, the heart is compared to a mirror that, when clear and unspotted, is able to reflect the full bright moon, a symbol of the Buddha and the Buddhist law. The darkness is that of attachment and sin. The "western hills" symbolize the Western Paradise of Amida Buddha. This poem was chosen as the final entry in the *Shinkokinshū*, occupying a privileged position.

allusive variation. *Essentials of Poetic Composition* divides poetic technique into three key notions: meaning (*kokoro*), diction (*kotoba*), and style (*fūtei*). The meaning (*kokoro*) of a poem should be neither "old" (*inishie*) nor "modern" (*ima*); instead, it should be "new" (*atarashi*). Teika usually uses the word *kokoro* in close relation to the "topic" (*dai*). Thus a more elaborate translation of the opening line would be: "For the meaning of the poem as it relates to the essence of the given topic, one should, above all, be innovative." Diction (*kotoba*), by contrast, should be "old." What *kokoro* and *kotoba* have in common here is that neither can be "modern."

Teika also contrasts "modern poets"—from the latter half of the twelfth century—with "ancient poets" and strictly forbids drawing on either the diction or the meaning introduced by "modern poets"—that is, those writing in the past seventy or eighty years. For him, diction must be circumscribed and publicly recognized. "Old diction" is not a matter of age but of the canon. "Old words" refers to the poetic diction exemplified in the *Three Collections* (*Sandaishū*): the *Kokinshū*, *Gosenshū*, and *Shūishū*, the first three imperial collections of waka. The only exceptions are the poems of the *Man'yōshū*, primarily those by Hitomaro, Akahito, and Yakamochi, which are included in the *Thirty-six Poets' Collection* (*Sanjūrokuninshū*), compiled by Fujiwara no Kintō in the mid-Heian period. With regard to "style" (*fūtei*), however, Teika notes that one should learn from poets both "old and new." In summary, the meaning of the poem should be new; its diction should derive from the superior poems in the *Three Collections*: and the superior poems of both old and new poets should provide a model for poetic style.

Teika also is concerned about plagiarism and the lack of originality. His rules for allusive variation (*honkadori*) on a base poem are an extension of those he prescribed for *kotoba* and represent a solution to the difficulties imposed by the necessity of using only "old" diction. At the end of the preface, which is written in kanbun, Teika notes that "one should always keep in mind the scene [*keiki*] of old poetry and let it sink deep into the heart." *Keiki* refers to not just the poetic scenes and images that appear in the poetic world but also its poetic associations. Significantly, Chinese poetry, which played a significant role in the development of Heian waka, became a major source for these associations. In the original text, certain lines appear to be notes—as they are in smaller print than that of the main text—and have been placed in parentheses in the translation.

As for the meaning [*kokoro*] of poetry, newness must come first. (One must seek a conception or an approach that has yet to be used.) When it comes to diction [*kotoba*], one must use old words. (One must not use anything not found in the *Three Collections*. The poems of ancient poets collected in the *Shinkokinshū* can be used in the same way.) The style [*fūtei*] of poetry can be learned from the superior poems of superior poets of the past. (One should not be concerned about the period but just learn from appropriate poems.)

Regarding the conception and diction of recent poets, even if it is a new phrase, one should be careful and leave it alone. (In regard to the poetry of those poets, one should never use the words from poems composed in the last seventy or eighty years.)

Poets frequently use and compose with the words of the poetry of the ancients. That already is a trend. But when using old poems and composing new poems, taking three out of the five measures [ku][26] is too much, and these poems will lack freshness. It is permissible to take three or four syllables more than two measures [ku]. However, it is too much if the content is the same and one uses words from old poems. (For example, using a foundation poem on flowers to compose on flowers or using a foundation poem on the moon to compose on the moon.) One should take a foundation poem on the seasons and compose on love or miscellaneous topics, or take a foundation poem on love and miscellaneous topics and compose on the four seasons. If done in this way, there probably will be no problems with borrowing from old poetry. . . .

One should always keep in mind the scene [keiki] of old poetry and let it sink deep into the heart. One should learn in particular from the Kokinshū, The Tales of Ise, Gosenshū, Shūishū, and from superior poets in the Thirty-six Poets' Collection. (Those who should come to mind from the Thirty-six Poets' Collection are Hitomaro, Ki no Tsurayuki, Tadamine, Ise, Ono no Komachi, and so on.)

Even if one is not a master of Japanese poetry, in order to understand the seasonal scenes, the ups and downs of the human world, and the essence of things, one should always be sure to absorb the first twenty volumes of Bo Juyi's Collected Works.[27] (These deeply resonate with Japanese poetry.)

Poetry has no master. One simply makes the old poems one's teacher. If one dyes one's heart in the old style and learns from the words of one's predecessors, who would not be able to learn to compose poetry? No one.

SHINKOKINSHŪ
(NEW COLLECTION OF ANCIENT
AND MODERN POEMS, CA. 1205)

The Shinkokinwakashū, better known as the Shinkokinshū, is an anthology of nearly two thousand Japanese poems (waka), all in the same standard prosodic form, thirty-one syllables in five measures. It was compiled and edited during the first two decades of the thirteenth century and was the eighth in what became a series of twenty-one anthologies of classical poetry created in response to an imperial edict, beginning with the Kokinshū (ca. 905) and ending with the Shinshokukokinshū (1439). Its title—literally, New Collection of Ancient and Modern Poems or New Kokinshū—implies that the Shinkokinshū was conceived and edited in calculated emulation of the first such imperially commissioned collection. The attempt to produce an anthology that would match, if not sur-

---

26. There are five (5/7/5/7/7) measures (ku) in a thirty-one-syllable waka.
27. Seventy-one volumes in all, of which the first twenty consist of Chinese poetry.

pass, the achievements of the *Kokinshū* was widely deemed successful in the judgment of later generations. Its chronological scope is broader, not only because it postdates the *Kokinshū* by three centuries, but also because it includes poetry by authors of earlier periods deliberately excluded from the *Kokinshū*, and the range of styles encompassed is arguably richer. The question of which of these collections is superior, makes for better reading, or serves as a more reliable model for aspiring poets has been the subject of debate for several centuries and has not yet been resolved.

Following the precedent of the *Kokinshū*, the *Shinkokinshū* has two prefaces, one in Sino-Japanese kanbun and one in kana. The poems are arranged by topics into twenty volumes. The topics or poetic themes of these books generally follow the conventions established by the *Kokinshū* but, in their details, are much closer to the precedent of the *Senzaishū* (1187), the seventh imperially commissioned anthology. In chronological order from one through twenty, the topics consist of two books on spring; one on summer; two on autumn; one on winter; one each on felicitations, mourning, parting, and travel; five on love; three of miscellany; and one each on poems on Shinto and Buddhist topics. Quantitatively, the emphasis is on seasonal poems and poems of love, the favored genres for public, formal poetic composition. But the *Shinkokinshū* allows for considerably more coverage, compared with the *Kokinshū*, of "miscellaneous" topics, which tend to consist of personal reflections on the contingencies of life. The typology of the *Shinkokinshū*'s twenty books was sufficient to encompass the entire range of topics considered suitable, as of the late twelfth century, for the composition of court poetry and thus gives a rough overview of how the world of poetic experience was partitioned at the time. Given the immense authority accorded to the *Kokinshū* in the construction of this world, even the less conspicuous departures from its precedent are significant. That is, the *Kokinshū* contains virtually no poetry on specifically Buddhist topics, and its few more or less explicitly Shinto-inspired poems are mainly in the two books of miscellany. Anagrammatic (*mono no na*) poems, which make up the entire tenth book of the *Kokinshū*, have disappeared. All the poems in variant prosody (*zōtai*) have been omitted as well.

In each of the twenty books, but most noticeably in the books of seasonal and love poems and those on miscellaneous topics, the compilers took great care to arrange their materials into clusters of poems on the same conventional topics, such as "Beginning of Autumn" (*risshū*, the first seventeen poems in the first book of autumn), with common images or motifs (in this instance, "Autumn Winds"). These clusters were often linked by word associations (*engo*) to adjacent clusters. The effect of this was a sense of progression, with intermittent digressions, through the phases of seasonal change or movement toward the inevitable disappointments of a courtly love affair. The subtleties of such patterns were complicated and sometimes undermined by efforts to alternate sequences of recent poems—the "modern" of the anthology's title—with those by "ancient" poets, and by deleting individual poems during the ultimately unfinished process of revising the anthology over many years.

Especially significant for appreciating the changes in the topography of decorum that the editors of the *Shinkokinshū* sought is the resulting exclusion of *haikai* (dissonant poems), which were included among poems of variant prosody (*zōtai*) in the *Kokinshū*.[28] The question raised by the exclusion of haikai from the *Shinkokinshū* is one of many about the designs of this collection's editors and, by extension, about the meaning of its title. Was the "renewal" of courtly poetic traditions suggested by its title meant to be a return to the origins, a restoration of the hallowed traditions of early court poetry, or an affirmation of new directions in poetic practice? Numerous and diverse answers have been proposed, but it is up to the reader to decide.

The poems translated here were selected from works by poets of the late twelfth century most prominently represented in the anthology, those who defined its distinctive aesthetic. As far as possible, the translations are literal in the sense that each word of the English answers to some word or wording of the Japanese. The poems are parsimonious in form and extravagant in sense, and if the English is ambiguous or occasionally obscure, it is (ideally) because the text is so to more or less the same degree. The poems achieve their depths and breadth through the exploitation of a received array of figures and an accepted vocabulary of connotations, as well as through techniques of punning (*kakekotoba*) and allusions to earlier classical poems (*honka-dori*) and subtexts (*honsetsu*), all of which made it possible for a single phrase or word to resonate well beyond its denotative sense. The commentary attempts to explicate some of what the poets presumably expected their readers to take for granted or recognize anew, supplies the *honka* (base poem) or *honsetsu* (subtext) in translation, and provides occasional citations from early commentaries or from the judgments of the poetry matches in which many of the poems originally were presented.

Spring 1

1

On the motif "Spring Begins."

Miyoshino wa	Fair Yoshino, mountains
yama mo kasumite	now wrapped in mist:
shirayuki no	to the village where snow

---

28. Haikai poems as represented in the *Kokinshū* are not, in fact, prosodically different from conventional waka but, rather, violate the aesthetic ideals of court poetry, lexically or thematically, through their use of archaic or "inelegant" diction, tendentious humor, or extravagant conceits—and thus they served by contraries to define the bounds of decorum. The exclusion of haikai is notable because even though Fujiwara no Shunzei, the sole editor of the *Senzaishū*, had demoted "poems in variant prosody" (*zōtai*), the topic of a separate book (no. 19) in the *Kokinshū*, to the subtitle of his third book of miscellany (*zōka*), he followed the precedent of the *Kokinshū* to the extent of including twenty-two haikai poems in his collection.

furinishi sato ni   was falling
haru wa kinikeri   spring has come.[29]

The Regent Prime Minister[30]

3

When the poet presented a hundred-verse set of poems, a poem on "Spring."

yamafukami   By a gate of pine
haru to mo shiranu   in mountains too deep
matsu no to ni   to know spring has come,
taedae kakaru   one by one they fall,
yuki no tamamizu   jewel drops of melting snow.[31]

Princess Shokushi[32]

---

29. A poem on the topic *risshun* ("Spring Begins," the first day of spring by the solar calendar) became conventional for the opening of an imperial waka anthology. Yoshino, a mountainous area in Yamato and near the capital, was noted in poetry for deep snow as well as for cherry blossoms and autumn foliage. It was also the site of a seventh-century "detached" imperial palace, which qualified it for recognition as a former capital, acknowledged in the conventional phrase *furinishi sato* (literally, "old village"), with a pun on *furinishi* meaning "[snow] was falling." The imperial association, underscored by the laudative prefix *mi-* in *miyoshino*, may well have been one reason this poem was chosen for first place in the anthology, which was compiled under the attentive gaze of the retired emperor GoToba. The base text (*honka*) is the first poem from the third imperial anthology, *Shūishū*: "'Spring begins today'—is it only saying so that makes the snowy mountains of fair Yoshino look draped in mist, this morning?" (Mibu no Tadamine). Yoshitsune's poem affirms that indeed mist, an auspicious sign of spring, has replaced snow even in the cold mountains of Yoshino and that therefore spring has arrived in due time. It was the prerogative of the imperial household to issue the calendar, and the implicit moral responsibility of the emperor to ensure that the seasons followed it. Signs that they did so were taken as a cause for celebration.

30. Fujiwara no Yoshitsune (1169–1206). Born into an illustrious and powerful branch of the Fujiwara clan, Yoshitsune became regent-prime minister at the early age of thirty-six and then died under mysterious circumstances two years later. An enthusiastic and gifted poet, he used his position at court to patronize Teika and other major poets of the age and to sponsor numerous events, including the monumental Poetry Match in Six Hundred Rounds, a source of many poems for the *Shinkokinshū*. Seventy-four of his poems were included in the anthology.

31. Spring comes late to deep mountains: the first sign of its arrival here is the melting of winter snow rather than the appearance of mist. "Gate of pine" is a metonymy for a recluse's dwelling too remote from the capital to rely on an official calendar to announce the coming of spring, while the evergreen pines by their nature do not "know" and hence cannot inform the speaker of the change of seasons.

32. Princess Shokushi (d. 1201), the third daughter of Emperor GoShirakawa, studied poetry as a disciple of Shunzei, whose major treatise on waka, *Korai fūteishō*, was dedicated to her. She was admired as one of the most accomplished exponents of the *Shinkokinshū* style, and forty-nine of her poems were included in the anthology, more than for any other female poet.

4

For a fifty-verse set of poems composed for presentation to the
retired emperor.

kakikurashi	Cloud-darkened,
nao furusato no	this ancient village:
yuki no uchi ni	in falling snow
ato koso miene	not a trace of spring,
haru wa kinikeri	yet surely it has come.[33]

Kunaikyō[34]

23

On the topic "Lingering Cold," for a hundred-verse poetry
match at the poet's residence.

sora wa nao	Under skies still
kasumi mo yarazu	awaiting mist,
kaze saete	the wind chills
yukige ni kumoru	a spring night's moon
haru no yo no tsuki	hiding in snow-fraught clouds.[35]

The Regent Prime Minister

24

At the Bureau of Poetry, on the motif "Spring Mountain Moon."

yama fukami	In mountains deep
nao kage samushi	a spring moon's light

---

33. Snow is still falling from a sky darkened with clouds, and if spring personified has indeed
made its way to this village, the tracks it should have left are covered in fresh snowfall and darkness. No visible evidence supports the poet's confidence in the arrival of the season. None is
needed: winter must yield to convention and let the calendar prevail.

34. Kunaikyō (ca. 1185–1204?). Her earliest recorded poems are those presented in a poetry
match sponsored by the retired emperor GoToba in 1200, when she was fourteen or fifteen, and
during the next five years she enjoyed a reputation as a leading adept of intricately wrought and
complexly allusive poems in the *Shinkokinshū* style. Legend had it that her death at the age of
nineteen or twenty was caused by intense concentration on poetic composition. Fifteen of her
poems were included in the anthology.

35. The poetry match of the headnote, completed in 1194, has come to be known as the Poetry
Match in Six Hundred Rounds. It was sponsored by the author of this poem, the regent–prime
minister Fujiwara no Yoshitsune, and was a major source of poems for this collection. Instead of
the longed-for mist of early spring, it is snow-laden clouds that obscure the light of the moon.

haru no tsuki　　　　still cold—
sora kakikumori　　　the sky thickens with clouds
yuki wa furitsutsu　　as snow falls and falls.[36]

Echizen

25

On the topic "Spring Vista at a Waterside Village," when Japanese poems were matched with poems in Chinese.

Mishima-e ya　　　　　By the Bay of Mishima
shimo mo mada hinu　　even as frost lingers
ashi no ha ni　　　　　spring winds
tsunogumu hodo no　　call forth new shoots
harukaze zo fuku　　　from withered reeds.[37]

Michiteru

26

On the topic "Spring Vista at a Waterside Village," when Japanese poems were matched with poems in Chinese.

yūzukuyo　　　　　　　Evening of a new moon—
shio michikuru rashi　　the tide must be rising
Naniwa-e no　　　　　in the Bay of Naniwa:
ashi no wakaba ni　　　over the young shoots of reeds
koyuru shiranami　　　crests of white waves.[38]

Hidetō

36

When some courtiers were making verses in Chinese and matching poems to them, a poem on "Water."

miwataseba　　　　　　Gazing out over
yamamoto kasumu　　　mist-shrouded foothills

---

36. The poet has opted to address the nominal topic of this poem, "Spring Mountain Moon," with imagery—moonlight chilled by snow clouds—drawing the poem into alignment with the formal topic of the previous poem, "Lingering Cold."

37. The topic of this poem breaks away from the previous two. The link is maintained by contrasts: a shift from mountain depths to seaside village, snow replaced by frost, and chill winds by those proper to the season.

38. The budding reed-shoots of the previous poem are now leaved in green as frost becomes froth. The contrast of green against white underscores the progression from lingering cold to early spring proper.

Minasegawa	beyond the river Minase,
yūbe wa aki to	who could have thought
nani omoiken	evenings are autumn?[39]

The Retired Emperor GoToba

37

For a poetry match at the residence of the regent prime
minister, on the motif "Spring Dawn."

kasumi tatsu	Mist rises over
Sue no Matsuyama	Far Pine Mountain—
honobono to	faintly aglow,
nami ni hanaruru	a sky of drifting clouds
yokogumo no sora	parts from the waves.[40]

Fujiwara no Ietaka[41]

38

For a fifty-verse set of poems composed at the request
of the cloistered Prince Shukaku.

| haru no yo no | A spring night's |
| yume no ukihashi | floating bridge of dreams |

---

39. This spring poem alludes to and challenges the famous assertion in Sei Shōnagon's *Pillow Book* that evening is the most poignant moment of an autumn day and thus best appreciated in that season. Compare nos. 361 and 363. The broader context is a timeless debate over which season, spring or autumn, is aesthetically more interesting.

40. "Far Pine Mountain" (Sue no Matsuyama) is an *utamakura*, a place-name with well-defined poetic connotations. This one is traditionally identified with Michinoku, in northeastern Honshu. It first appeared in an anonymous folk song in the *Kokinshū* that may be paraphrased as "Should I ever set you aside and let my heart stray, then might the waves surge over Far Pine Mountain," implying that the former is as improbable as the latter and, in turn, that Far Pine Mountain rises near the shore well above sea level on the coast in Michinoku. As so many later poets did, Karyū imagined conditions under which the impossible takes place as waves of mist rise over the mountain at dawn. This poem shares with the previous few poems the season word "mist" but begins a new sequence of three poems on the topic *akebono* (spring dawn).

41. Ietaka (or Karyū, 1158–1237) became a disciple of Shunzei at about the age of twenty and soon was recognized for his technical expertise in what was to become known as the *Shinkokinshū* style. Several of his most admired poems are paired with Teika's in the anthology, underscoring the impression that he was acknowledged by Teika as a rival and predecessor. He was one of the four chief compilers of the anthology, in which forty-three of his poems were included.

todaeshite	breaks:
mine ni wakaruru	sky of cloud drift
yokogumo no sora	parting from a mountain peak.[42]

Fujiwara no Teika[43]

44

When the poet presented a hundred-verse set of poems.

ume no hana	On sleeves scented
nioi o utsusu	by blossoms of plum
sode no ue ni	moonlight spilling
noki-moru tsuki no	through the eaves
kage zo arasou	claims its place.

Fujiwara no Teika

45

When the poet presented a hundred-verse set of poems.

ume ga ka ni	When I ask of the past
mukashi o toeba	in the scent of the plum,
haru no tsuki	the spring moon

---

42. Numerous interpretations have been proposed for this poem, one of Teika's best known, especially for the phrase "floating bridge of dreams," an allusion to the last chapter of *The Tale of Genji*. One suggestion is of fleeting, perhaps unrequited, love, imaged in the sky at dawn by a cloud drifting away from a mountain peak. In this context, however, in which the topic of the poem is "Spring Dawn," the "floating bridge" is usually taken as a broader image of human life and its evanescence. In the late-thirteenth-century poetic treatise *Chikuenshō*, Fujiwara no Tameaki (a grandson and poetic heir of Teika) acknowledges the fame of this poem while also offering it as exemplary of one of the traditional "eight poetic faults" (*ranshibyō*, or "disordered thoughts"). Perhaps in response, Tameyo (a great-grandson and heir in another poetic lineage) is reported as having asserted that this poem is so superior that its meaning could not help but be uncertain, in the same way that music is able to move the heart, even though it carries no meaning (*kotowari*) as such.

43. The son of Fujiwara no Shunzei and heir to the Mikohidari house of poetry, Teika (1162–1241) was recognized at a fairly early age as one of the most controversially innovative poets of his generation and was one of the four primary compilers of the *Shinkokinshū*. Despite his audacious experiments with syntax and disdain for convention, he could also be remarkably conservative, especially in his later years, and notoriously called for a return to early classical models of composition. His dictum "new meanings, old words" is an emblem of the difficult demands he made for originality within the constraints of precedent. Forty-six of his poems were included in the anthology.

> *kotaenu kage zo*   keeps still
> *sode ni utsureru*   glistening on my sleeves.[44]

Fujiwara no Ietaka

47

For the Poetry Match in Fifteen Hundred Rounds.

> *ume no hana*   Never do I tire of their
> *akanu iro kamo*   color or their scent:
> *mukashi ni te*   plum blossoms
> *onaji katami no*   the spring night's moon
> *haru no yo no tsuki*   recalling the past.[45]

Master of the Household of the
Dowager Empress, Shunzei

58

For the hundred-verse poetry match at the regent prime
minister's residence.

> *ima wa tote*   The wild geese in the field,
> *tanomu no kari mo*   knowing it's time to leave,
> *uchiwabinu*   cry plaintively:

---

44. Both nos. 44 and 45 are striking examples of the innovative early poems that shocked their more conservative contemporaries and earned them recognition as young poets whose departures from precedent delineated what came to be known as the *Shinkokinshū* style. What is disturbing is that the spare but fluent syntax so successfully enfolds an obtrusive conceit—the prosopopoeia of moonlight competing with the scent of plum blossoms—within an impeccably decorous scene of high classicism, the speaker assuming the attitude, pensive regret, of Ariwara no Narihira in the fourth episode of *The Tales of Ise*. In that story, Narihira returns to an abandoned house one year after visiting to call on a woman who had been abducted to the imperial palace. It is a night in the first month of the year by the lunar calendar, early spring. The plum trees are in blossom. The moon is in the sky. Narihira looks around in vain for some trace of his long-absent lover and of the past, lies down weeping under the ruined eaves as the moon sets, and offers a poem: "Is there no moon? Is the spring not the spring of the past? I alone am as I was." It is only the confluence of imagery and mood (*omokage*) that may recall *The Tales of Ise* for the reader. The compilers of the *Shinkokinshū* apparently decided to propose the allusion by placing this poem at the beginning of a sequence of four (nos. 44–47), none of which cites Narihira's poem but each of which can be taken as evoking it. The creation of the sequence effectively imposes on each of the four poems a reference to *The Tales of Ise* that none of the authors may have meant but that readers of the anthology must keep in mind.

45. Part of a longer sequence of poems on the topic "Flowering Plums," the first three belong to a cluster of four poems (no. 46 is omitted here) drawing on images of plum blossoms and the spring moon to evoke, indirectly, the famous love poem by Ariwara no Narihira—"Is there no moon? Is the spring not the spring of the past? I alone am as I was"—and to suggest the motif of longing for the past.

oborozukiyo no mist-shrouded moon
akebono no sora lingering in the dawn sky.[46]

Priest Jakuren

Spring 2

133

For a picture of Mount Yoshino on a sliding screen panel at
Saishōshitennō-in.

Miyoshino no Flowers must be falling
takane no sakura on Yoshino's peaks:
chirinikeri this spring dawn's
arashimo shiroki gusting winds
haru no akebono blossom in white.[47]

The Retired Emperor GoToba

134

For the Poetry Match in Fifteen Hundred Rounds.

sakurairo no Of winds of spring in my garden
niwa no harukaze of the color of cherry blossoms
ato mo nashi not a trace, nor visitor
towaba zo hito no to take these petals
yuki to dani min for fallen snow.[48]

Fujiwara no Teika

---

46. This verse was composed on the topic "Spring Dawn," but the editors have taken advantage of the season words *oborozukiyo* (mist-shrouded moon) and *kari* (wild geese) to place the poem here as a link between a sequence of poems on the former and latter topics in turn. Regretting that the moon lingering at dawn must depart from the sky, the speaker takes the cries of the geese readying to depart for the north as empathetic with his own feelings, perhaps also taking the departing moon as emblematic of the geese's plight.

47. Lines 1 and 2 in the translation offer a rational inference—that the cherry blossoms at the peaks of Yoshino must be falling—to explain something seemingly irrational: the startling image of white wind blowing down to the foot of the mountain. Yoshino was famous for both its relatively steep mountains and its cherry blossoms.

48. The awkward translation attempts to suggest the complex syntax of the poem, which yokes a series of words into overlapping images to suggest—by allusion to the "yesterday" and "today" of the base poem—a concrete succession of moments in time. The first image is a pale pink garden, "the color of cherry blossoms," and then a pink spring wind blowing through the garden. No trace of the wind remains except for a carpet of pale pink petals, and the speaker wishes only for the tracks of a visitor, someone imaginative enough to share with the poet the illusion (via *mitate*) of the fallen flowers as a late spring snowfall. The base poem, an ironic reply

Summer

179

Composed as a poem on "Beginning of Summer."

orifushi mo	As seasons change
utsureba kaetsu	they too change
yo no naka no	their flowered robes:
hito no kokoro no	the fickle hearts of
hanazome no koromo	men of this world.[49]

Daughter of Shunzei[50]

Autumn 1

361

Topic unknown.

sabishisa wa	Loneliness has no
sono iro to shi mo	color of its own:
nakarikeri	pine trees
maki tatsu yama no	on a darkening mountain
aki no yūgure	evening of autumn.[51]

Priest Jakuren

to a poem chiding Ariwara no Narihira for visiting with even less frequency than the cherry blossoms, is by Narihira, *Kokinshū*, no. 63: "Had I not come today, and tomorrow they fell like snowflakes, though they did not melt, could I yet see them as blossoms? (Hardly.)" Teika's poem changes the tone of key images of the base poem from ironic to elegiac while reversing Narihira's irony to chide him for lacking the sensibility to mistake fallen flowers for snow. The link to the preceding poem, also on the topic of falling cherry blossoms, is the conceit of colored wind.

49. The fifth and last poem in a sequence on the topic "Changing Robes," which had become the conventional opening topic for the book of summer in imperially commissioned anthologies. The honka, or base poem, is a well-known poem by Ono no Komachi, *Kokinshū*, no. 797: "All too visibly its color fades: the flower of the heart of one passing through this world of love."

50. A granddaughter of Shunzei, Daughter of Shunzei (ca. 1171–ca. 1252) was apparently adopted by him as a daughter, hence the designation by which she is best known. She is the author of some of the most exquisitely contrived and technically innovative poems in the *Shinkokinshū* style. One of her poems was placed at the beginning of the second book of love of the *Shinkokinshū* at the express command of the retired emperor GoToba. Twenty-nine of her poems appear in the anthology.

51. This belongs to a series of ten poems on the topic "Autumn Evening" and is the first of three in particular that later became known as the famous *sanseki* (three evening poems) by Jakuren, Saigyō, and Teika, respectively. As of the twelfth century and after, this topic was considered especially challenging because the compound appeal of the season and of evening or dusk made it difficult to do justice to the topic, and it was especially difficult to do so inventively.

363

For a hundred-verse set of poems composed at the suggestion of
Priest Saigyō.

miwataseba	Looking out across
hana mo momiji mo	the shore
nakarikeri	no flowers, no autumn leaves:
ura no tomaya no	a thatched hut's
aki no yūgure	evening of autumn.[52]

Fujiwara no Teika

380

When the poet presented a hundred-verse set of poems, a poem
on "The Moon."

nagame-wabinu	Gazing till weary of these skies
aki yori hoka no	I long for a dwelling
yado mogana	away from autumn:
no ni mo yama ni mo	must the moon light
tsuki ya sumuran	every field and mountain?[53]

Princess Shokushi

Jakuren's poem has been the subject of much interpretive debate. As do many poems of this era, it consists of an abstract assertion followed by a concrete observation with a *soku* (distanced link) relation between the first three and last two measures, a logical or rhetorical gap the reader is forced to explore. Evergreen trees seem impervious to the coming of autumn, but as dusk consumes the light, they fade into a monochrome perfectly consonant with the mood of an autumn evening.

52. The logic of this most famous of Teika's poems has affinities with Jakuren's preceding poem. In rejecting the familiar emblems of seasonal beauty—spring flowers and autumn foliage—in favor of a monochrome scene containing only a humble cottage by the shore, the poem has been taken to anticipate the minimalist aesthetics of *sabi* and *wabi*, associated later with the way of tea and the poetics of Shinkei and Bashō, among many others. Teika himself did not seem to consider this a particularly memorable poem and included it in neither *Teika hachi-daishō* nor *Hyakuban jika-awase*, which include those poems he seemed most interested in preserving.

53. The base poem (honka) for this composition is Sosei, *Kokinshū*, no. 947: "Where might I find distaste for this world? In pastures and hills alike my heart yearns to stray." Sosei's poem, partly by its placement in the *Kokinshū*, Miscellaneous, book 2, clearly implies the familiar ethical dilemma of a Buddhist ascetic seeking to leave the world. That nuance is attenuated by the placement of Princess Shokushi's poem here in the first book of autumn. The speaker's "weariness" is due to the aesthetic conflict between the moon and the season of autumn in which it "dwells" (and shines most clearly, by the pun on *sumu*) or between beauty and sadness.

419

When the poet had a fifty-verse set of poems on "The Moon"
composed for delivery at his residence.

tsuki dani mo	Heedless that the moon
nagusamegataki	brings sadness enough
aki no yo no	to this autumn night,
kokoro mo shiranu	the wind
matsu no kaze kana	sighs in the pines.[54]

The Regent Prime Minister

420

When the regent prime minister had a fifty-verse set of poems
on "The Moon" composed for delivery at his residence.

samushiro ya	On a mat of rush
matsu yo no aki no	as autumn winds deepen
kaze fukete	her night of waiting,
tsuki o katashiku	the Maiden of Uji Bridge
Uji no Hashihime	spreads a robe of moonlight.[55]

Fujiwara no Teika

Winter

671

When the poet presented a hundred-verse set of poems.

koma tomete	No shelter to rest my horse
uchiharau	or brush my sleeves,

---

54. The logic of this verse places it in a category of conceit much favored by *Shinkokinshū*
poets: as though X were not enough, here is the moon, or the wind, or the crying birds or insects, to bring something more.

55. This is an example of Teika's ability to combine the techniques of ellipsis, verbal association, and allusion with strongly inventive figural language. The *honka* (base poem) is an anonymous love poem in the *Kokinshū*, no. 689: "Spreading her robe on a mat of rush, will she await
me again tonight—the Maiden of Uji Bridge?" *Aki no kaze* (autumn's wind) retains—from the
honka—the conventional metaphorical sense of fading or sated passion, inevitably called forth
by the phrase *matsu yo* (night of waiting). Allusive variation was usually expected to begin from
a displacement across topical categories, as here from love to autumn. This poem was regarded
as an example of Teika's so-called new-fangled, unfounded Daruma (Zen) style, which provoked such anxiety among conservative critics.

kage mo nashi	not a shadow
Sano no watari no	at Sano Crossing
yuki no yūgure	in snow-falling dusk.[56]

Fujiwara no Teika

Mourning

788

In the autumn of the year his mother died, on a day of wind-storms, the poet went to the place where he had once lived with his mother.

tamayura no	Not fleeting drops
tsuyu mo namida mo	of dew nor tears will pause:
todomarazu	winds of autumn
nakihito kouru	sweep the dwelling
yado no akikaze	loved by one now gone.

Fujiwara no Teika

Travel

939

For a fifty-verse set of poems composed for presentation [to the retired emperor].

akeba mata	Yet another mountain peak
koyubeki yama no	to be crossed after dawn?

---

56. The poem, one of Teika's most admired, becomes fully intelligible only when the reader recalls the base poem in the *Man'yōshū*, vol. 3, no. 265: "How dismal this endless rain at Sano Crossing in Miwa no Saki, no trace of a house that might offer shelter." Apart from the poetic place-name, Sano Crossing, none of the language of the base poem is introduced into Teika's poem, and the season is changed (from autumn to winter and rain into snow). The primary connotation of the place-name, judging from a contemporary poetic lexicon, was "desolation," signified by the absence of dwellings (the base poem is evidently the source of this association). Teika's poem evokes the connotation with the phrase *kage mo nashi* (not a shadow), which in the context implies the absence of any building to cast a shadow (any shelter) but literally refers also to the setting: snowfall at dusk, a scene from which all shadow is, perforce, absent. The single most telling effect, however, is achieved by the absence in Teika's poem of any emotional or evaluative word, as found in the base poem. It was a rule of late classical poetics that such words were to be avoided: a well-wrought poem could evoke a feeling or mood without naming it. Teika usually follows this rule, and in this instance it enables him to alter the tone of his own poem to distinct advantage: what was merely privative (steady rainfall and no shelter=desolation) in the base poem is inverted to become an occasion for exalted contemplation (absence of shelter forces the speaker's attention toward the austere beauty of the setting).

mine nareya	White clouds touched
sorayuku tsuki no	by the distant reach
sue no shirakumo	of the setting moon.

Fujiwara no Ietaka

Love 1

1034

For a hundred-verse set of poems, on the topic "Love Endured."

tama no o yo	If this jewel thread of life
taenaba taene	is to break, let it break:
nagaraeba	living on
shinoburu koto no	would be to endure
yowari mo zo suru	love's torment alone.[57]

Princess Shokushi

1035

For a hundred-verse set of poems, on the topic "Love Endured."

wasurete wa	Another evening's sighs:
uchinagekaruru	have I forgotten
yūbe kana	this hidden longing
ware nomi shirite	is mine alone to suffer
suguru tsukibi o	as days become months?[58]

Princess Shokushi

Love 2

1136

Among the poems for the Minase-koi Poetry Match on fifteen topics, on the motif "Spring Love."

omokage no	My loved one's image
kasumeru tsuki zo	shimmers in the misted moon

---

57. *Tama no o* (literally, "a thread of beads or jewels") was a familiar periphrasis for "(human) life." Words linked to "thread . . . break" (*tae*) and "living on" (*nagarae*, or "extend, endure") help invigorate the cliché.

58. This poem is based closely on Ki no Tsurayuki, *Kokinshū*, no. 606: "Keeping this longing hidden within is what hurts—with only me to hear my sighs."

yadorikeru   of a spring now past
haru ya mukashi no   dwelling in tears
sode no namida ni   on my sleeves.[59]

Daughter of Shunzei

Love 3

1206

Composed as a poem of love.

kaeru sa no   Does he now gaze
mono to ya hito no   as one returning might
nagamuran   on the moon at dawn
matsu yo-nagara no   of this night
ariake no tsuki   I waited in vain?[60]

Fujiwara no Teika

Miscellaneous Topics 3

1764 (1762)

At the Bureau of Poetry, on the motif "Regretting."

oshimu to mo   I do not regret these
namida ni tsuki mo   heartfelt tears
kokoro kara   nor the earnest moon
narenuru sode ni   shining on my sleeves
aki o uramite   resenting autumn.[61]

---

59. This poem is based on the same base poem (Narihira's "Is there no moon?") to which nos. 44, 45, and 47 loosely allude. There is a difference in the treatment in this poem, which belongs to the same category (love) as the honka, but the allusion still is based on just the single phrase *haru ya mukashi* (of a spring now past).

60. The poet feigns the persona of a woman who waited past dawn for a faithless lover. Her sole consolation, the moon lingering after dawn, is marred by the thought that he may be enjoying the same moon's light on his way home from another lover's home.

61. This complicated net of puns and syllepses weaves at least three more or less distinguishable statements—two of them approximated in the translations—into one of the most tantalizing poems of the collection. For centuries, commentators have offered widely discrepant interpretations. The paratactic style exemplified here is close to that of the brief collection of admonitory poems, "Notes from the Future" (Miraiki), purportedly composed by Fujiwara no Teika to demonstrate what might happen if the more radical tendencies of the late-twelfth-century avant-garde were pursued to their limits.

The same poem might be translated as

oshimu to mo	I do not grudge autumn
namida ni tsuki mo	nor my sleeves drenched
kokoro kara	in heartfelt tears,
narenuru sode ni	too familiar moonlight
aki o uramite	resenting both.

Daughter of Shunzei

[Introduction and translations by Lewis Cook]

RECLUSE LITERATURE (*SŌAN BUNGAKU*)

During the late Heian and early Kamakura periods, many aristocrats took holy vows and retreated from the secular world, not to the busy Buddhist monasteries in Nara and the capital (such as Mount Hiei, the headquarters of the Tendai sect), but to retreats outside the cities, which they believed to be a purer form of renunciation. The physical separation from the secular world freed the "recluses" from heavy obligations to their families or superiors and allowed for devotion to their own interests, which often included literary and cultural pursuits. Many of these recluse monks were intellectuals and artists who produced what is now referred to as "recluse literature" (*sōan bungaku*). Recluse literature, which contains some of the finest writing in this period, is characterized by a deep interest in nature and in self-reflection. Prominent figures are Saigyō in the late Heian period; Kamo no Chōmei, author of *An Account of a Ten-Foot-Square Hut* (*Hōjōki*) in the early Kamakura period; and Kenkō, who wrote *Essays in Idleness* (*Tsurezuregusa*) in the fourteenth century. Prominent recluse figures in the late medieval period include Sōgi (1421–1502), a renga master and literary scholar; and Yamazaki Sōkan (1465–1533), one of the founders of haikai (comic or popular linked verse).

KAMO NO CHŌMEI

Kamo no Chōmei (1155?–1216) was born into a family of hereditary Shinto priests who had served many generations at the Shimogamo (Kamo) Shrine, a prestigious shrine just north of the capital. Chōmei was the second son of Kamo no Nagatsugu, the head administrator of the shrine. As a child, Chōmei lived in comfortable circumstances and studied classical poetry (waka) and music, but his father died young while Chōmei was still in his teens, leaving him without the means for social advancement. Chōmei, however, continued to devote himself to the study of poetry and music, two fields in which he excelled.

In 1200, Chōmei began composing with the prominent poets of the day and was invited in 1201 by the retired emperor GoToba to take a prestigious position in the Imperial Poetry Office, where the imperial waka anthologies were edited and compiled. In the spring of 1204, at around the age of fifty, Chōmei suddenly took holy vows. It is generally believed that the cause for his sudden retirement was his disillusionment in not having received a high position at the Tadasu Shrine, part of the Shimogamo Shrine complex, a position for which he had long hoped but which was blocked by the shrine's existing head administrator.

AN ACCOUNT OF A TEN-FOOT-SQUARE HUT (*HŌJŌKI*, 1212)

Chōmei wrote *An Account of a Ten-Foot-Square Hut* at the end of the Third Month of 1212 while in retirement at Hino, in the hills southeast of Kyoto. It is written in a mixed Japanese–Chinese style that draws heavily on Chinese and Buddhist words and sources. Probably the most noticeable rhetorical feature of this style is the heavy use of parallel phrases and of metaphors. The work is noted for its vivid descriptions of a series of disasters in the capital during a time of turmoil (the war between the Taira and Minamoto at the end of the twelfth century) and for its description of the law of impermanence of all things, one of the central tenets of Buddhism, which had a profound impact on Japan at this time. As a recluse who retreats from society and turns toward the pursuit of the Pure Land, a western paradise envisioned by the Pure Land Buddhist sect, the author is representative of a larger movement among the cultural elite at this time. In the end, however, Chōmei finds himself in the paradoxical position of advocating detachment and rebirth in the Pure Land while at the same time becoming attached to the beauties of nature and the four seasons and the aesthetic life of his ten-foot-square hut at Hino.

The current of the flowing river does not cease, and yet the water is not the same water as before. The foam that floats on stagnant pools, now vanishing, now forming, never stays the same for long. So, too, it is with the people and dwellings of the world. In the capital, lovely as if paved with jewels, houses of the high and low, their ridges aligned and roof tiles contending, never disappear however many ages pass, and yet if we examine whether this is true, we will rarely find a house remaining as it used to be. Perhaps it burned down last year and has been rebuilt. Perhaps a large house has crumbled and become a small one. The people living inside the houses are no different. The place may be the same capital and the people numerous, but only one or two in twenty or thirty is someone I knew in the past. One will die in the morning and another will be born in the evening: such is the way of the world, and in this we are like the foam on the water. I know neither whence the newborn come nor whither go the dead. For whose sake do we trouble our minds over these temporary dwellings, and why do they delight our eyes? This, too, I do not understand. In competing for impermanence, dweller and dwelling are no different from the morning glory and the dew. Perhaps the dew will fall and the blossom linger.

But even though it lingers, it will wither in the morning sun. Perhaps the blossom will wilt and the dew remain. But even though it remains, it will not wait for evening.

In the more than forty springs and autumns that have passed since I began to understand the nature of the world, I have seen many unexpected things. I think it was on the twenty-eighth of the Fourth Month of Angen 3 [1177]. Around eight o'clock on a windy, noisy night, a fire broke out in the southeastern part of the capital and spread to the northwest. Finally it reached Suzaku Gate, the Great Hall of State, the university, and the Popular Affairs Ministry, and in the space of a night they all turned to dust and ash. The source of the fire is said to have been the intersection of Higuchi and Tominokōji, in makeshift housing occupied by *bugaku* dancers. Carried here and there in the violent wind, the fire spread outward like a fan unfolding. Distant houses choked on smoke; nearby, wind drove the flames against the ground. In the sky, ashes blown up by the wind reflected the light of the fire, while wind-scattered flames spread through the overarching red in leaps of one and two blocks. Those who were caught in the fire must have been frantic. Some choked on the smoke and collapsed; some were overtaken by the flames and died instantly. Some barely escaped with their lives but could not carry out their possessions. The Seven Rarities and ten thousand treasures all were reduced to ashes.[62] How great the losses must have been. At that time, the houses of sixteen high nobles burned, not to mention countless lesser homes. Altogether, it is said that fire engulfed one-third of the capital. Thousands of men and women died, and more horses, oxen, and the like than one can tell. All human endeavors are foolish, but among them, spending one's fortune and troubling one's mind to build a house in such a dangerous capital is particularly vain.

Then, in the Fourth Month of Jishō 4 [1180], a great whirlwind arose near the intersection of Nakanomikado and Kyōgoku and raged as far as the Rokujō District. Because it blew savagely for three or four blocks, not a single house within them, large or small, escaped destruction. Some were flattened; some were reduced to nothing more than posts and beams. Blowing gates away, the wind carried them four or five blocks and set them down; blowing fences away, it joined neighboring properties into one. Naturally, all the possessions inside these houses were lifted into the sky, while cypress bark, boards, and other roofing materials mingled in the wind like winter leaves. The whirlwind blew up dust as thick as smoke so that nothing could be seen, and in its dreadful roar no voices could be heard. One felt that even the winds of retribution in hell could be no worse than this. Not only were houses damaged or lost, but countless men were injured or crippled in rebuilding them. As it moved toward the south-southwest, the wind was a cause of grief to many people. Whirlwinds often

---

62. "Seven Rarities and ten thousand treasures" here means "things of value." The Seven Rarities of Buddhist texts are gold, silver, lapis lazuli, crystal, coral, agate, and clamshell.

blow, but are they ever like this? It was something extraordinary. One feared that it might be a portent.

Then, in the Sixth Month of the same year, the capital was abruptly moved.[63] The relocation was completely unexpected. According to what I have heard, Kyoto was established as the capital more than four hundred years ago, during the reign of the Saga emperor.[64] The relocation of the capital is not something that can be undertaken easily, for no special reason, and so it is only natural that the people were uneasy with this move and lamented together about it. Objections having no effect, however, the emperor, the ministers, and all the other high nobles moved. Of those who served at court, who would stay behind in the old capital? Those who vested their hopes in government appointments or in rank, or depended on the favor of their masters, wasted not a day in moving, while those who had missed their chance, who had been left behind by the world, and who had nothing to look forward to, stayed sorrowfully where they were. Dwellings, their eaves contending, went to ruin with the passing days. Houses were disassembled and floated down the Yodo River as the land turned into fields before one's eyes. Men's hearts changed; now they valued only horses and saddles. No one used oxen and carriages any more. People coveted property in the southwest and scorned manors in the northeast. At that time I had occasion to go to the new capital, in the province of Tsu. I saw that there was insufficient room to lay out a grid of streets and avenues, the area being small. To the north, the city pressed against the mountains and, to the south, dropped off toward the sea. The roar of waves never slackened; a violent wind blew in off the saltwater. The palace stood in the mountains. Did that hall of logs look like this?[65] It was novel and, in its way, elegant. Where did they erect the houses they had torn down day by day and brought downstream, constricting the river's flow? Open land was still plentiful, houses few. Even though the old capital had become a wasteland, the new capital was yet unfinished. Everyone felt like the drifting clouds. Those who had lived here before complained about losing their land. Those who had newly moved here bemoaned the pains of construction. In the streets, I saw that those who should have used carriages rode on horses, and most of those who should have dressed in court robes and headgear wore simple robes instead. The ways of the capital had changed abruptly; now they were no different from the ways of rustic samurai. I heard that these developments were portents of disorder in the land, and it turned out to be so: day by day the world grew more unsettled and the people more uneasy, and their fears proved to be

---

63. Kiyomori, the leader of the Taira clan, had the capital moved from Kyoto to Fukuhara (now Kobe) in 1180.

64. It was Emperor Kanmu (r. 781–806) who actually relocated the capital from Nagaoka to Heian-kyō (Kyoto), in 794. Perhaps Chōmei saw the failed attempt to return the capital to the former capital, Nara—in 810, during the reign of Emperor Saga (r. 809–823)—as serving to establish the capital at Kyoto once and for all.

65. Empress Saimei (r. 655–661) built a temporary palace of logs in Kyushu in 661.

well founded, so that in the winter of the same year the court returned to this capital.[66] But what became of all the houses that had been torn down? Not all of them were rebuilt as they had stood before.

I have heard that in venerable reigns of ancient times, emperors governed the nation with compassion: roofing his palace with thatch, Yao[67] of China refrained from even trimming the eaves; seeing how thin the smoke that rose from the people's hearths, Nintoku[68] of Japan forgave even the lowest taxes. They did so because they took pity on the people and tried to help them. By measuring it against the past, we can know the state of the present.

Then, was it in the Yōwa era [1181–1182]?—long ago, and so I do not remember well, the world suffered a two-year famine, and dreadful things occurred. Droughts in spring and summer, typhoons and floods in fall—adversities followed one after another, and none of the five grains ripened. In vain the soil was turned in the spring and crops planted in the summer, but lost was the excitement of autumn harvests and of the winter laying-in. Consequently, people in the provinces abandoned their lands and wandered to other regions, or forgot their houses and went to live in the mountains. Various royal prayers were initiated and extraordinary Esoteric Buddhist rites were performed, to no effect whatever. It was the habit of the capital to depend on the countryside for everything, but nothing was making its way to the capital now. How long could the residents maintain their equanimity? As their endurance wore down, they tried to dispose of their valuables as if throwing them away, but no one showed any interest. The few who did engage in barter despised gold and cherished millet. Beggars lined the streets, their pleas and lamentations filling one's ears. In this way, the first year struggled to a close. Surely the new year would bring improvement, one thought, but on top of the famine came an epidemic, and conditions only got worse. The metaphor of fish in a shrinking pool fit the situation well, as people running out of food grew more desperate by the day.[69] In the end, well-dressed men wearing lacquered sedge hats, their skirts wrapped around their legs, went intently begging house to house. One would see them walking, exhausted and confused, then collapse, their faces to the ground. The corpses of people who had starved to death lay along the earthen walls and in the streets; their numbers were beyond reckoning. A stench filled the world, as no one knew how to dispose of so many corpses, and often one could not bear to look

---

66. The people's fears were realized when Minamoto no Yoritomo raised an army in the Eighth Month of 1180.

67. Yao was one of the legendary sage kings of antiquity in the Confucian tradition on which emperors were meant to model their rule.

68. According to the *Kojiki* (712) and *Nihon shoki* (720), Emperor Nintoku was the legendary sixteenth emperor of Japan who also had a reputation for sage rulership for his remittance of taxes every third year.

69. Chōmei probably borrowed the metaphor from *The Essentials of Salvation* (*Ojōyōshū*, 985), by Genshin (942–1017).

at the decomposing faces and bodies. There was not even room for horses and carriages to pass on the Kamo riverbed. As lowly peasants and woodcutters exhausted their strength, firewood, too, came to be in short supply, and so people with no other resources tore apart their own houses and carried off the lumber to sell at market. I heard that the value of what one man could carry was not enough to sustain him for a single day. Strangely, mixed in among the firewood were sticks bearing traces here and there of red lacquer, or of gold and silver leaf, because people with nowhere else to turn had stolen Buddhist images from old temples and ripped out temple furnishings, which they broke into pieces. I saw such cruel sights because I was born into this impure, evil age.[70] There were many pathetic sights as well. Of those who had wives or husbands from whom they could not part, the ones whose love was stronger always died first. The reason is that putting themselves second and pitying the others, they gave their mates what little food they found. So it was that when parents and children lived together, the parents invariably died first. I also saw a small child who, not knowing that his mother was dead, lay beside her, sucking at her breast.

The eminent priest Ryūgyō of Ninna Temple,[71] grieving over these countless deaths, wrote the first letter of the Sanskrit alphabet on the foreheads of all the dead he saw, thereby linking them to the Buddha. Wanting to know how many had died, he counted the bodies he found during the Fourth and Fifth Months.[72] Within the capital, between Ichijō on the north and Kujō on the south, between Kyōgoku on the east and Suzaku on the west, more than 42,300 corpses lay in the streets. Of course, many others died before and after this period, and if we include those on the Kamo riverbed, in Shirakawa, in the western half of the capital, and in the countryside beyond, their numbers would be limitless. How vast the numbers must have been, then, in all the provinces along the Seven Highways. I have heard that something of the sort occurred in the Chōjō era [1134], during the reign of Emperor Sutoku, but I do not know how things were then. What I saw before my own eyes was extraordinary.

Then—was it at about the same time?—a dreadful earthquake shook the land.[73] The effects were remarkable. Mountains crumbled and dammed the

---

70. The last of the three Buddhist periods: the first is the age of the true law, during which enlightenment was possible and correct practice could be performed; the second is the age of the simulated law, during which correct practice could be performed and the Buddha's teaching existed; and the last is the age of the degenerated law or latter age of the Buddhist law (mappō), during which only the Buddha's teaching remained. In Japan, it was believed that mappō began in 1051.

71. Ninna Temple is a large Buddhist institution in northwestern Kyoto that was commissioned by Emperor Kōkō (830–887, r. 884–887) and built by Emperor Uda (867–931, r. 887–897) in 888. The temple maintained particularly close ties to the imperial family in the twelfth and thirteenth centuries.

72. The subject might be Ryūgyō; the text is ambiguous.

73. The earthquake hit on the ninth day of the Seventh Month, 1185.

rivers; the sea tilted and inundated the land. The earth split open and water gushed forth; boulders broke off and tumbled into valleys. Boats rowing near the shore were carried off on the waves; horses on the road knew not where to place their hooves. Around the capital, not a single shrine or temple survived intact. Some fell apart; others toppled over. Dust and ash rose like billows of smoke. The sound of the earth's movement and of houses collapsing was no different from thunder. People who were inside their houses might be crushed in a moment. Those who ran outside found the earth splitting asunder. Lacking wings, one could not fly into the sky. If one were a dragon, one would ride the clouds. I knew then that earthquakes were the most terrible of all the many terrifying things. The dreadful shaking stopped after a time, but the aftershocks continued. Not a day passed without twenty or thirty quakes strong enough to startle one under ordinary circumstances. As ten and twenty days elapsed, gradually the intervals grew longer—four or five a day, then two or three, one every other day, one in two or three days—but the aftershocks went on for perhaps three months. Of the four great elements, water, fire, and wind constantly bring disaster, but for its part, earth normally brings no calamity. In ancient times—was it during the Saikō era [855]?—there was a great earthquake and many terrible things occurred, such as the head falling from the Buddha at Tōdai Temple,[74] but, they say, even that was not as bad as this. Everyone spoke of futility, and the delusion in their hearts seemed to diminish a little at the time; but after days and months piled up and years went by, no one gave voice to such thoughts any longer.

All in all, life in this world is difficult; the fragility and transience of our bodies and dwellings are indeed as I have said. We cannot reckon the many ways in which we trouble our hearts according to where we live and in obedience to our status. He who is of trifling rank but lives near the gates of power cannot rejoice with abandon, however deep his happiness may be, and when his sorrow is keen, he does not wail aloud. Anxious about his every move, trembling with fear no matter what he does, he is like a sparrow near a hawk's nest. One who is poor yet lives beside a wealthy house will grovel in and out, morning and evening, ashamed of his wretched figure. When he sees the envy that his wife, children, and servants feel for the neighbors, when he hears the rich family's disdain for him, his mind will be unsettled and never find peace. He who lives in a crowded place cannot escape damage from a fire nearby. He who lives outside the city contends with many difficulties as he goes back and forth and often suffers at the hands of robbers. The powerful man is consumed by greed; he who stands alone is mocked. Wealth brings many fears; poverty brings cruel hardship. Look to another for help and you will belong to him. Take someone

---

74. Tōdai Temple is one of the seven great Nara temples and served as the head of the national temple system instituted in Nara times. It is famous for its large statue of Vairocana Buddha, known popularly as the Great Buddha.

under your wing, and your heart will be shackled by affection. Bend to the ways of the world and you will suffer. Bend not and you will look demented. Where can one live, and how can one behave to shelter this body briefly and to ease the heart for a moment?

I inherited my paternal grandmother's house and occupied it for some time. Then I lost my backing,[75] came down in the world, and even though the house was full of fond memories, I finally could live there no longer,[76] and so I, past the age of thirty, resolved to build a hut. It was only one-tenth the size of my previous residence. Unable to construct a proper estate, I erected a house only for myself.[77] I managed to build an earthen wall but lacked the means to raise a gate. Using bamboo posts, I sheltered my carriage. The place was not without its dangers whenever snow fell or the wind blew. Because the house was located near the riverbed, the threat of water damage was deep and the fear of robbers never ebbed. Altogether, I troubled my mind and endured life in this difficult world for more than thirty years. The disappointments I suffered during that time awakened me to my unfortunate lot.[78] Accordingly, when I greeted my fiftieth spring, I left my house and turned away from the world. I had no wife or children, and so there were no relatives whom it would have been difficult to leave behind. As I had neither office nor stipend, what was there for me to cling to? Vainly, I spent five springs and autumns living in seclusion among the clouds on Mount Ōhara.[79]

Reaching the age of sixty, when I seemed about to fade away like the dew, I constructed a new shelter for the remaining leaves of my life. I was like a traveler who builds a lodging for one night only or like an aged silkworm spinning its cocoon. The result was less than a hundredth the size of the residence of my middle age. In the course of things, years have piled up and my residences have steadily shrunk. This one is like no ordinary house. In area it is only ten feet square; in height, less than seven feet. Because I do not choose a particular place to live, I do not acquire land on which to build. I lay a foundation, put up a simple, makeshift roof, and secure each joint with a latch. This is so that I can easily move the building if anything dissatisfies me. How much bother can it be to reconstruct it? It fills only two carts, and there is no expense beyond payment for the porters.

---

75. Chōmei is probably referring to the death of his father, in 1172 or 1173.

76. Suō Naishi, *Kin'yōshū*, no. 581: "I cannot live here any longer, and I leave: like the grass of remembrance growing thickly at the eaves, this dwelling is lush with fond memories."

77. A proper estate would have included guest quarters, storehouses, and other outbuildings.

78. Chōmei's family were hereditary priests of the Tadasu Shrine, part of the Shimogamo complex of Shinto shrines, just north of the capital. His greatest disappointment seems to have been his failure to succeed to this position.

79. Chōmei implies that these five years were vain because even though he had taken Buddhist vows, he had not made any progress toward enlightenment. Ōhara lies to the north of the capital.

Now, having hidden my tracks and gone into seclusion in the depths of Mount Hino,[80] I extended the eaves more than three feet to the east, making a convenient place to break and burn brushwood. On the south I made a bamboo veranda, on the west of which I built a water-shelf for offerings to the Buddha, and to the north, behind a screen, I installed a painting of Amida Buddha,[81] next to it hung Fugen,[82] and before it placed the Lotus Sutra. Along the east side I spread soft ferns, making a bed for the night. In the southwest, I constructed hanging shelves of bamboo and placed there three black leather trunks. In them I keep selected writings on Japanese poetry and music, and the *Essentials of Salvation*. A koto and a biwa stand to one side. They are what are called a folding koto and a joined lute.[83] Such is the state of my temporary hut. As for the location: to the south is a raised bamboo pipe. Piling up stones, I let water collect there. Because the woods are near, kindling is easy to gather. The name of the place is Toyama. Vines cover all tracks.[84] Although the ravines are overgrown, the view is open to the west. The conditions are not unfavorable for contemplating the Pure Land of the West. In spring I see waves of wisteria. They glow in the west like lavender clouds. In summer I hear the cuckoo. Whenever I converse with him, he promises to guide me across the mountain path of death.[85] In autumn the voices of twilight cicadas fill my ears. They sound as though they are mourning this ephemeral, locust-shell world. In winter I look with deep emotion upon the snow. Accumulating and melting, it can be compared to the effects of bad karma. When I tire of reciting the Buddha's name or lose interest in reading the sutras aloud, I rest as I please, I dawdle as I like. There is no one to stop me, no one before whom to feel ashamed. Although I have taken no vow of silence, I live alone and so surely can avoid committing transgressions of speech.[86]

---

80. Southeast of the capital, in what is now Fushimi Ward, Kyoto.

81. It was believed that Amida Buddha presided over the Pure Land paradise to the west, where anyone who sought refuge in him by reciting his name would be reborn. Amida was thought to ride on lavender clouds when he came from his Pure Land to receive the dying.

82. The bodhisattva Fugen (Skt. Samantabhadra) is often shown seated on an elephant with six tusks, symbolizing the slow, steady progress with which one moves toward enlightenment.

83. The koto could be folded up, and the biwa (lute) disassembled, making them portable.

84. Although Chōmei uses "Toyama" as a proper noun here, the word also denotes "outer mountains," or slopes near town, as opposed to "deep mountains" (*miyama*). The association of *toyama* with vines (*masaki no kazura*) derives from Anonymous, *Kokinshū*, no. 1077: "Deep in the mountains hail must be falling. Vines on the outer mountains have turned red."

85. Chōmei alludes to an exchange between the Horikawa lady and the monk Saigyō (1118–1190). From the lady, *Sankashū*, no. 750; *Gyokuyōshū*, no. 2809: "Let us speak together now, in this world, and make a vow—oh cuckoo—be my guide on the mountain path of death." Saigyō's reply, *Sankashū*, no. 751: "The weeping cuckoo will sing to keep his vow with you if you set out upon the mountain path of death."

86. Underlying this and the next two sentences is the Buddhist tradition of ascetic practice aimed at achieving correct action in speech, body, and mind. Chōmei suggests that because of his way of life, he cannot help but act correctly.

Although I do not go out of my way to observe the rules that an ascetic must obey, what could lead me to break them, there being no distractions here? In the morning, I might gaze at the ships sailing to and from Okanoya, comparing myself to the whitecaps behind them, and compose verses in the elegant style of the novice-priest Manzei;[87] in the evening, when the wind rustles the leaves of the *katsura* trees, I might turn my thoughts to the Xunyang River and play my biwa in the way of Gen Totoku.[88] If my enthusiasm continues unabated, I might accompany the sound of the pines with "Autumn Winds" or play "Flowing Spring" to the sound of the water.[89] Although I have no skill in these arts, I do not seek to please the ears of others. Playing to myself, singing to myself, I simply nourish my own mind.

At the foot of the mountain is another brushwood hut, the home of the care-taker of this mountain. A small child lives there. Now and then he comes to visit. When I have nothing else to do, I take a walk with him as my companion. He is ten years old; I am sixty. Despite the great difference in our ages, our plea-sure is the same. Sometimes we pluck edible reed-flowers, pick pearberries, break off yam bulbils, or gather parsley. Sometimes we go to the paddies at the foot of the mountain, collect fallen ears of rice, and tie them into sheaves. If the weather is fair, we climb to the peak and gaze at the distant sky above my former home, or look at Mount Kohata, the villages of Fushimi, Toba, and Hatsukashi. Because a fine view has no master,[90] nothing interferes with our pleasure. When walking is no problem and we feel like going somewhere far, we follow the ridges from here, crossing Mount Sumi, passing Kasatori, and visit the temple at Iwama or worship at the Ishiyama temple. Then again, we might make our way across Awazu Plain and go to see the site where Semimaru lived, or cross the Tanakami River and visit the grave of Sarumaru Dayū.[91] On our return, de-pending on the season, we break off branches of blossoming cherry, seek out autumn foliage, pick ferns, or gather fruit. Some we offer to the Buddha, and some we bring home to remind us of our outing. When the night is quiet, I look

---

87. Okanoya was on the east bank of the Uji River, in what is now the city of Uji. Manzei (or Mansei), a poet who took Buddhist vows in 721, is best remembered for the waka to which Chō-mei alludes: *Shūishū*, no. 1327: "To what shall I compare the world? Whitecaps behind a ship that rows out at dawn."

88. The Xunyang River is in Jiangxi Province, China, where the poet Bo Juyi (772–846) wrote his famous *Biwa Song*. Gen Totoku (Minamoto no Tsunenobu, 1016–1097), poet and musician and founder of the Katsura school of biwa playing, lived in the village of Katsura, southwest of the capital.

89. "Autumn Winds" is a well-known piece of court music. "Flowing Spring" is a biwa com-position reserved for specially initiated musicians.

90. Bo Juyi, *Wakan rōeishū*, no. 492: "A fine view has no particular master. Mountains be-long to those who love mountains."

91. Semimaru, said to have been a blind lutenist, and Sarumaru Dayū were early Heian poets to whom many legends have attached. "Tanakami" refers to the upper reaches of the Uji River.

at the moon at the window and think fondly of my old friends;[92] I hear the cries of the monkey and wet my sleeve with tears.[93] Fireflies in the grass might be taken for fishing flares at distant Maki Island; the rain at dawn sounds like a gale blowing the leaves of the trees. When I hear the pheasant's song I wonder whether it might not be the voice of my father or mother;[94] when the deer from the ridge draws tamely near I know how far I have withdrawn from the world.[95] Sometimes I dig up embers to keep me company when, as old men do, I waken in the night. This is not a fearful mountain, and so I listen closely to the owl's call.[96] Thus from season to season the charms of mountain scenery are never exhausted. Of course one who thinks and understands more deeply than I would not be limited to these.

When I came to live in this place, I thought that I would stay for only a short time, but already five years have passed. Gradually my temporary hut has come to feel like home as dead leaves lie deep on the eaves and moss grows on the foundation. When news of the capital happens to reach me, I learn that many of high rank have passed away since I secluded myself on this mountain. There is no way to know how many of lower rank have died. How many houses have been lost in the frequent fires? Only a temporary hut is peaceful and free of worry. It may be small, but it has a bed on which to lie at night and a place in which to sit by day. Nothing is lacking to shelter one person. The hermit crab prefers a small shell. This is because he knows himself. The osprey lives on rugged shores. The reason is that he fears people. I am like them. Knowing myself and knowing the world, I have no ambitions, I do not strive. I simply seek tranquillity and enjoy the absence of care. It is common practice in the world that people do not always build dwellings for themselves. Some might build for their wives and children, their relations and followers, some for their intimates and friends. Some might build for their masters or teachers, even for valuables, oxen, and horses. I now have built a hut for myself. I do not build for others. The reason is that given the state of the world now and my own circumstances, there is neither anyone I should live with and look after, nor any dependable servant. Even if I had built a large place, whom would I shelter, whom would I have live in it?

When it comes to friends, people respect the wealthy and prefer the suave. They do not always love the warmhearted or the upright. Surely it is best simply

---

92. Bo Juyi, *Wakan rōeishū*, no. 242: "On the fifteenth night, the glow of a new moon. Two thousand miles away, the heart of my friend."

93. It was a convention of Chinese poetry that monkey cries are sad.

94. The priest Gyōki (Gyōgi), *Gyokuyōshū*, no. 2627: "When I hear the voice of the pheasant singing I think—is it my father? is it my mother?"

95. Saigyō, *Sankashū*, no. 1207; *Gyokuyōshū*, no. 2240: "Deep in the mountains the deer draws tamely near and I know how far I have withdrawn from the world."

96. Saigyō, *Sankashū*, no. 1203: "Deep in the mountains there are no friendly birdsongs— the fearful call of the owl."

to make friends with strings and woodwinds, blossoms and the moon. When it comes to servants, they value a large bonus and generous favors. They do not seek to be nurtured and loved, to work quietly and at ease. It is best simply to make my body my servant. How? If there is something to be done, I use my own body. This can be a nuisance, but it is easier than employing and looking after someone else. If I have to go out, I walk. This can be painful, but it is not as bad as troubling my mind over the horse, the saddle, the ox, the carriage. Now I divide my single body and use it in two ways. My hands are my servants, my legs my conveyance, and they do just as I wish. Because my mind understands my body's distress, I rest my body when it feels distressed, use it when it feels strong. [And] though I use it, I do not overwork it. When my body does not want to work, my mind is not annoyed. Needless to say, walking regularly and working regularly must promote good health. How can I idle the time away doing nothing? To trouble others is bad karma. Why should I borrow the strength of another? It is the same for clothing and food. Using what comes to hand, I cover my skin with clothing woven from the bark of wisteria vines and with a hempen quilt, and sustain my life with asters of the field and fruits of the trees on the peak. Because I do not mingle with others, I am not embarrassed by my appearance. Because food is scarce, my crude rewards taste good. My description of these pleasures is not directed at the wealthy. I am comparing my own past only with my present.

The Three Worlds exist only in the one mind.[97] If the mind is not at peace, elephants, horses, and the Seven Rarities will be worthless; palaces and pavilions will have no appeal. My present dwelling is a lonely, one-room hut, but I love it. When I happen to venture into the capital, I feel ashamed of my beggarly appearance, but when I come back and stay here, I pity those others who rush about in the worldly dust. Should anyone doubt what I am saying, I would ask them to look at the fishes and birds. A fish never tires of water. One who is not a fish cannot know a fish's mind.[98] Birds prefer the forest. One who is not a bird cannot know a bird's mind. The savor of life in seclusion is the same. Who can understand it without living it?

Well, now, the moon of my life span is sinking in the sky; the time remaining to me nears the mountaintops. Soon I shall set out for the darkness of the

---

97. Chōmei here echoes a basic tenet of Mahayana Buddhism, that the phenomena around us, lacking any independent, objective existence, exist only as concepts or distinctions constructed by our minds. His wording derives from a line in the Kegon (Skt. Avatamsaka) Sutra: "All things in the Three Worlds exist only in the one mind." "The Three Worlds" are the world of desire, the world of form, and the world of formlessness, a division of the universe according to the level of enlightenment reached by the beings who exist in each realm. Human beings exist in the world of desire.

98. *Zhuangzi*, "Autumn Floods": "Not being a fish, how can you know that the fish are happy?"

Three Paths.[99] About what should I complain at this late date? The essence of the Buddha's teachings is that we should cling to nothing. Loving my grass hut is wrong. Attachment to my quiet, solitary way of life, too, must interfere with my enlightenment. Why then do I go on spending precious time relating useless pleasures?

Pondering this truth on a tranquil morning, just before dawn, I ask my mind: one leaves the world and enters the forest to cultivate the mind and practice the Way of the Buddha. In your case, however, although your appearance is that of a monk, your mind is clouded with desire. You have presumed to model your dwelling after none other than that of Vimalakirti,[100] but your adherence to the discipline fails even to approach the efforts of Suddhipanthaka.[101] Is this because poverty, a karmic retribution, torments your mind,[102] or is it that a deluded mind has deranged you? At that time, my mind had no reply. I simply set my tongue to work halfheartedly reciting the name of the compassionate Amida Buddha two or three times, and that is all.

The monk Ren'in wrote this late in the Third Month of Kenryaku 2 [1212], at his hut on Toyama.[103]

[Translated by Anthony H. Chambers]

TALES OF AWAKENING
(HOSSHINSHŪ, CA. 1211)

Tales of Awakening, a collection of Buddhist *setsuwa*, or anecdotes, was edited by Kamo no Chōmei (1155?–1216), who also wrote the preface. It contains a little over a hundred stories set in Japan. According to the preface, the aim of the collection was to lead those like Chōmei, who were wandering in darkness, to salvation. As the title suggests, several of the stories are about awakening to the Buddhist truth (*hosshin*) and being reborn in the Pure Land. Some of the stories illustrate how and why the precepts of Buddhism are to be observed; others are about reclusion or the failure to be reborn in the Pure Land. Kamo no Chōmei's career as a writer peaked around 1212, when he wrote his noted essay

---

99. The Three Paths are Hells, the Animal Path, and the Path of Hungry Ghosts, into which human beings who had committed bad actions were thought to be reborn.

100. Vimalakirti (J. Yuima), the central figure of the sutra named for him, was a wealthy townsman who achieved enlightenment without becoming a monk and who welcomed the bodhisattva Mañjuśrī (J. Monjūshiri) and thousands of followers in a humble room that in Chinese and Japanese tradition was ten feet square. In the sutra, Vimalakirti demonstrates the doctrine of nonduality by remaining silent when asked to explain it.

101. Suddhipanthaka was the most foolish of the Buddha's disciples, although in the end he, too, achieved enlightenment.

102. The passage has also been interpreted to mean, "Is it perhaps that you torment yourself as a result of your poverty?"

103. Ren'in is the name Chōmei received when he took Buddhist vows.

An Account of a Ten-Foot-Square Hut and when he became even more deeply committed to Buddhism. In the following story about Rengejō, Chomei suggests, as he does in *An Account of a Ten-Foot-Square Hut*, that the key to salvation and rebirth in the Pure Land is just a single issue: one's prevailing spiritual state, particularly at the point of death. This position, in which the individual determines his or her fate, predates the type of Pure Land Buddhism advocated by Hōnen (1133–1212) and others that relies on the other and on the *nenbutsu*, intoning the Amida Buddha's name as an expression of faith in his power to save.

Rengejō's Suicide by Drowning

Not long ago there lived a rather well known holy man named Rengejō. He was on friendly terms with the priest Tōren, who over the years had now and then had occasion to be helpful to him in one way or another.[104] This holy man, however, was now beginning to get on in years, and he spoke to Tōren, saying, "I now grow weaker with each passing year and have little doubt that my death is drawing near. As my most earnest wish is to pass away with a clear mind fully focused on rebirth in the Pure Land, I have resolved that I shall end my life by drowning myself while my mind is in a state of composure."[105]

Tōren was astonished to hear this and remonstrated with him, saying, "You mustn't do that! Your aim should be to devote yourself, if for even one more day, to accruing spiritual merit by reciting the nenbutsu, the name of the Amida Buddha. What you propose is the sort of thing the ignorant do!" But seeing that Rengejō was absolutely unbending in his determination, Tōren said, "Well, if you are this resolute, I suppose there is no stopping you. It may be that this was predestined by karma." And he worked together with Rengejō, helping him make various arrangements in preparation for death.

---

104. No dates are available for the priest Tōren, but he is known to have been an esteemed waka poet, active in the capital in poetic circles during the 1160s and 1170s. Nothing is known about Rengejō, but the thirteenth-century historical chronicle *Skimmings One Hundred Times Tempered* (*Hyakurenshō*) mentions a similarly named Rengejō (with one character written differently) as the prime mover in a group of eleven clerics who drowned themselves in the Katsura River in September 1176, on the day of the equinoctial full moon.

105. The notion of the state of mind at the exact moment of death being a crucial factor in determining one's rebirth dates back to early Buddhism. Moreover, the Lotus Sutra, enormously influential in Japan, relates numerous laudatory tales of Buddhists who expressed their zeal by gestures such as setting themselves alight to make "human offering lamps" of their own bodies. Under the influence of the Lotus Sutra and such texts as Genshin's *Essentials of Salvation* (*Ōjōyōshū*), the practice of deliberately taking one's own life while one's mental faculties were still clear gained considerable currency as a means of both ensuring a favorable rebirth and demonstrating one's spiritual commitment. By the late eleventh century, this kind of religious suicide, especially by drowning, had developed into a fad of sorts and at the same time had become the subject of some controversy.

When the time came, they went to a stretch of the Katsura River where the water was deep, and Rengejō began reciting the nenbutsu in a loud voice and, after a time, submerged himself and sank to the bottom of the river. By this time, word about Rengejō's intentions had gotten around, and so many people were gathered there that it looked like market day. Their expressions of boundless admiration and sorrow for him went on for some time. Tōren was deeply grief-stricken. "And we'd known each other for so many years!" he lamented and returned home, fighting back the tears.

Some days after this, Tōren fell ill with a sickness that appeared to be the result of possession by some sort of malignant spirit. Those around him were just beginning to sense that this was no ordinary illness, that something strange was going on, when the spirit manifested and identified itself, saying, "I am he who was once Rengejō." Tōren said, "I cannot believe that this is true. We were friends for many years, and to the very end I did nothing whatsoever to arouse your resentment. What's more, the level of your spiritual dedication was extraordinary, and your end was most exemplary. So why would you come here in this totally unexpected form?"

The spirit replied, "That's just it! Although you had tried so hard to stop me, I did not fully understand my own heart, and so I went and threw my life away. I wasn't particularly doing it for anybody else's sake, so I never imagined that when it came down to it I might have a change of heart; but through whatever trick of Tenma, at the very moment when I was about to enter the water I was suddenly assailed by misgivings.[106] But with all those people there, how could I just feel free to change my mind? 'Ah, if only you would try to stop me *now!*' I thought, attempting to catch your eye; but as your face gave no indication of noticing, it seemed as though you were urging me, 'Now, hurry up and get on with it!' so I felt compelled to submerge myself—and in my bitterness at that, my mind held no thought whatsoever of Pure Land rebirth. Now I find myself in a rebirth that I had not bargained for at all. This was my own foolish error, so I have no business blaming anyone else for it; but because my final thought was of unwillingness to go, I have ended up coming back here like this."

Now this affair may indeed be a matter of karmic seeds sown in a previous existence. Yet it still ought to serve as a warning to the people of this degenerate age. The hearts of others are difficult to fathom and are not always motivated by attitudes that are pure and honest. Caught up in competitiveness and ambition or driven by pride and jealousy, some foolishly believe that immolating themselves as human-offering lamps or drowning themselves in the sea will secure them rebirth in the Pure Land, and so they rashly take it into their heads to commit this sort of act. This is, in fact, identical to "the ascetic practices of the

---

106. The demon Tenma (Skt. Devaputramara) is an evil trickster who here personifies the various temptations, obstacles, doubts, and distractions that can seduce the Buddhist practitioner away from the true path.

heretics" and should be labeled as a major perverse view.[107] For this reason, such a person's suffering on entering into the flames or water is by no means insignificant. If his resolution is not exceedingly deep, how will he be able to endure it? And due to that agony, his heart will not be serene. Not only begging for the Buddha's aid but also maintaining a mind of unwavering conviction[108] will be extremely difficult.

It seems that even among the silly prattlings of ignorant people, they say things like "I could never bring myself to become a human-offering lamp, but I could easily submerge myself in water." No doubt this is because from an on-looker's standpoint, it appears as though there is practically nothing to it; but in fact they have no idea what the experience is really like. One holy man relates, "I was drowning in the water and had already begun to die when somebody rescued me, and I just barely survived. On that occasion, so intense was the torment of the water's assault as it came in through my nose and mouth that it seemed to me that the agonies of hell itself could not possibly be this excruciating. The fact that people can nevertheless believe that water is a soft and gentle thing is because they are not yet acquainted with water as a killer."

Someone once observed, "All the various actions that we perform lie in the hearts of each of us. It is we alone who perform these actions, and we alone can know them. They are difficult for an outside observer to judge. In regard to past karmic causes, future karmic effects, and the Buddha's protection, if we just concentrate on composing our own state of mind, it will become obvious how to judge them. But let us at least clarify one thing.[109] In order to practice the way of the Buddha, if a person secludes himself in mountain forests or dwells alone in open fields yet still cherishes an attitude of fearing for his body and clinging to survival, it is by no means certain that he will be able to depend on the Buddha's protection. He should adopt the attitude that it is necessary to withdraw from the world, hiding himself behind fences and walls; and by protecting his own body and saving his own self from sickness, he should aspire to make gradual progress in his spiritual practice. If you regard your body as

---

107. "The ascetic practices of the heretics" (gedō no kugyō) refers to radically ascetic religious practices, such as the near-total abstinence from food and bathing and sleeping on spike mattresses. The practice of such austerities was widespread among spiritual seekers in India in the time of the Buddha, who vigorously repudiated them, preaching instead a "middle way" between the two extremes of self-mortification and self-indulgence. "Perverse views" (J. jaken) may refer specifically to denial of the reality of karmic cause and effect or, more generally, to various heterodox misapprehensions of reality, which are viewed as impediments to spiritual liberation.

108. By this period, the term shōnen (literally, "right mindfulness") had come to encompass a range of meanings, including "a mind of unwavering faith in the Amida Buddha."

109. The author seems to suggest that one's actions, their causes and effects, and the question of whether or not the Buddha would extend his protection all boil down to a single issue: one's present spiritual condition.

entirely consecrated to the Buddha—so that even if a tiger or wolf tries to harm you, you will not be overly fearful and so that even if you run out of food and are starving to death, you will not become disheartened—then without fail the Buddha will extend to you his protection, and the host of bodhisattvas, too, will come to protect you.[110] Dharma-obstructing demons and venomous beasts will find no opening for attack. Robbers will have a change of heart and go away, and through the power of the Buddha your diseases will be healed. But if you do not realize this and allow your heart to remain as shallow as ever, yet still count on the protection of the Buddha, then you will do so at your own peril."

And this, it seems to me, is indeed the truth of the matter.

[Translated by Herschel Miller]

ANECDOTES (SETSUWA)

Collections of *setsuwa* (anecdotes) existed from as early as the *fudoki* (provincial gazetteers) in the Nara period and the *Nihon ryōiki* (ca. 822), but the great period of setsuwa is the late Heian period, beginning with the *Collection of Tales of Times Now Past* (*Konjaku monogatari shū*, ca. 1120), through the Kamakura period (1185–1333), when several setsuwa collections were compiled. The most famous of the Kamakura-period setsuwa collections, at least today, is *A Collection of Tales from Uji* (*Uji shūi monogatari*, early thirteenth century). These collections, which were edited by aristocrats or priests of aristocratic origin, mark the emergence of a new, robust form of literature, reflecting new values and social groups, which ranged from commoners, warriors, and priests to aristocrats. They embraced a wide variety of topics, from poetry to violence to sex.

Yanagita Kunio (1875–1962), one of the founders of modern Japanese folklore studies, once defined setsuwa both as a narration that is spoken and heard and as written literature, as collections of recorded stories. All setsuwa now are in written form, though they reveal traces of their original oral transmission.

In contrast to monogatari, which admit to their fictionality, setsuwa present the narration as history, as a record of past events, even when these events tend to be about the strange, miraculous, or unusual, causing surprise. In the medieval and Tokugawa periods, setsuwa collections were considered to be a kind of historical record or vernacular Buddhist writing (*hōgo*), and it was not until the modern period that they were considered a type of literature (*bungaku*) comparable to the monogatari.

The setsuwa also differ from monogatari and military chronicles by their brevity. They tend to be action oriented (plot centered) and compact, often

---

110. This refers to the host of bodhisattvas who attend the Amida Buddha in the Pure Land and who are said to accompany the Amida when he comes, at the believer's moment of death, to escort and welcome the believer to the Pure Land.

focusing on a single event, much like a short story. The collections or antholo-gies of setsuwa, however, can be very large, such as the *Collection of Tales of Times Now Past* and *A Collection of Tales from Uji*, and have their own complex thematic structure. Like the poems in a poetry collection, setsuwa can be read both independently and as part of a larger sequence or section.

The setsuwa genre is also marked by didactic endings. The editor of each setsuwa collection gives each setsuwa a particular function. Thus the same set-suwa may appear in one collection as a Buddhist setsuwa, in another collection as a secular setsuwa, and in yet another collection as part of a poetry handbook. About half the extant setsuwa collections are Buddhist, beginning with the *Nihon ryōiki*, reflecting the large role they played in preaching and teaching the Buddhist law. Although we sometimes know the editors, such as Priest Mujū (1226–1312), the editor of *Shasekishū* (*Collection of Sand and Pebbles*, 1279–1283), the setsuwa themselves, which were constantly recycled and reworked, are anon-ymous. In contrast to those in the early fudoki and the *Nihon ryōiki*, which are written in Chinese, the collections from the late Heian through the Kamakura period, the heyday of the setsuwa, are written in vernacular Japanese.

In the late medieval period, the setsuwa were replaced by *otogi-zōshi* (Muro-machi tales), which are a longer narrative form that incorporates more elements of the monogatari. Both during and after their peak, setsuwa provided a constant and deep source of material for other genres, such as the literary diary (*nikki*), monogatari, warrior tale, historical chronicle, nō drama, *kōwakamai* (ballad drama), *kyōgen*, otogi-zōshi, and *sekkyō-bushi*. A closely related genre is the war-rior tale or chronicle, which often integrates setsuwa into a longer chronological narrative.

A COLLECTION OF TALES FROM UJI
(*UJI SHŪI MONOGATARI*, EARLY THIRTEENTH CENTURY)

A Collection of Tales from Uji is the most popular and widely read of the medieval set-suwa collections. The quality of the writing was considered to be unsurpassed among setsuwa collections, and it was widely printed and read in the Tokugawa period. Al-though the author and date of composition are uncertain, it is generally considered to be an early-thirteenth-century work. A late-Heian-period aristocrat, the senior counselor (*dainagon*) Minamoto no Takakuni, who lived in the twelfth century at the Byōdō-in at Uji, south of the capital, is thought to have written a work entitled *Tales of the Senior Counselor* (*Uji dainagon monogatari*), which was very popular but was lost. The at-tempt to reconstruct the lost text in the early thirteenth century resulted in *Uji shūi monogatari*. The *Uji* in this title refers to the Byōdō-in, and *shūi* (collection of remains) probably refers to collecting the remains of the *Uji dainagon monogatari*.

Uji shūi monogatari contains 197 stories, of which 80 also appear in the Heian-period *Collection of Tales of Times Now Past* (*Konjaku monogatari shū*), and a number appear in other setsuwa collections. The fact that so many of these stories appear elsewhere is an indication of how popular they were at the time. Fifty of the stories are not duplicated elsewhere, however, including humorous tales with sexual content and folktales, such as "How Someone Had a Wen Removed by Demons."

The stories in *Uji shūi monogatari* are not arranged according to subject matter, as they are in *Konjaku monogatari shū*, nor does the collection seem to have any particular order or plan, except to include the most interesting stories. They are of many kinds: serious and humorous, Japanese and foreign (India and China), Buddhist (about one-third to one-half of the stories), and secular, with many of the most noted being secular. Unlike the Buddhist anecdotes in *Konjaku monogatari shū*, these Buddhist-related stories do not appear to be intended for immediate religious use. Instead, the interest is in looking at individuals and human society with an ironic eye and a love of good storytelling. Whereas in the late Heian and early Kamakura periods, setsuwa were collected as part of the attempt to preserve artifacts of court culture that was rapidly disappearing, in *Uji shūi monogatari* the point of view is not at all fixed, instead exploring different classes and social groups from different angles.

The stories in *Uji shūi monogatari* are not records of oral performances but are written narratives that assume the characteristics of such a performance. Accordingly, they open with set phrases like "Now, long ago" (*Ima wa mukashi*) and end with "so it has been told" (*to ka, to zo, to nan*). Both "Wen Removed by Demons" and "How a Sparrow Repaid Its Debt of Gratitude" finish with a didactic message, but these were probably added as part of the convention of storytelling.

"How Someone Had a Wen Removed by Demons" (1:3) is a variation on a folktale (*mukashi-banashi*) that reappears in myriad forms across the centuries. Although most of the *oni* (demons) that appear in *Uji shūi monogatari* are fearful in appearance, here they dance, drink, and enjoy themselves, so much that the old man joins them, an image that no doubt appealed to commoner audiences.

"How a Sparrow Repaid Its Debt of Gratitude" (3:16) is another variation on a folktale. The sparrows (like other creatures) provide rewards and punishments in accordance with actions of the humans. Like "Wen Removed by Demons," this setsuwa draws on a familiar folktale pattern, of neighbors who stand in contrast to one another in moral character, in which the rewards and punishments directly reflect their contrasting moral character.

"How Yoshihide, a Painter of Buddhist Pictures, Took Pleasure in Seeing His House on Fire" (1:38), which also appears in the *Jikkinshō* (1:6), provided the basis for the famous short story "Hell Screen" (Jigokuhen), by Akutagawa Ryūnosuke (1892–1927). Although Yoshihide's house is burning, he makes no effort to put out the fire and thus is able to create a great painting of the Fudōmyō Buddha in the midst of flames. In Akutagawa's story, the author takes the story of absolute dedication to one's artistic path one step further: the painter watches his daughter burn to death. "About the Priest with the Long Nose" (2:7), which also is included here, was adapted by Akutagawa as well, into a noted short story entitled "Nose" (Hana).

How Someone Had a Wen Removed by Demons (1:3)

Again, there was once an old man who had a big wen on his right cheek, the size of an orange. On account of this he avoided mixing with people and made his living gathering firewood. When in the mountains one day, he was caught in such a violent storm that he was unable to get home and had no choice but to stay where he was, out there in the wilds. Having no other woodcutter with him, he was scared out of his wits, so he got inside a nearby hollow tree and squatted down, though he made no attempt to sleep. Suddenly he heard in the distance a noisy crowd of people approaching. It put new life into him to find some signs of humanity when he was all alone in the wilds, and he looked out— only to find a swarm of some hundred creatures of all sorts and descriptions, red ones dressed in blue, black ones wearing red loincloths, some with only one eye and some with no mouth—the whole lot hideous beyond words. In a noisy, jostling throng, carrying torches that blazed as brightly as the sun, they seated themselves in a circle before the hollow tree where he was sheltering. He was almost beside himself with terror.

One demon who appeared to be the leader sat at the head, and in two rows on his right and left were countless other demons, every single one of them indescribably horrible to look at. They were offering each other wine and enjoying themselves just like ordinary people. The wine jar went round many times, and the chief demon seemed particularly drunk. A young demon at the end of a row got up and walked slowly out in front of the chief, holding up a tray and evidently chattering away in a low voice—though what it all was that he was saying, the old man could not make out. The chief demon looked just like any ordinary person as he sat with a cup in his left hand and his face wreathed in smiles. The young demon performed a dance and sat down, then, beginning from the ends of the rows, the other demons danced in turn, some of them well, some badly. Watching in amazement, the old man heard the chief say, "Tonight's entertainment has been even better than usual. But what I should like to see is some dance that's really special." At these words—perhaps some spirit took possession of him, or some god or Buddha put the thought into his mind— the old man suddenly felt an urge to rush out and do a dance. At first he thought better of it, but then the rhythm that the demons were chanting sounded so attractive that he said to himself, "I don't care what happens, I'll rush out and dance. If I die, I die." And with his hat down over his nose and his woodchopper's axe stuck in his belt, he left his hollow tree and danced out in front of the chief. The demons leapt to their feet with loud shouts of surprise. The old man danced with all his might, jumping in the air and bending low, twisting this way and that, and marking the time with loud yells, until he had danced right round the clearing. The chief and the whole company of demons watched in delighted astonishment.

"We've been having these parties for many years now," the chief said, "but we've never had anything like this before. Old man, from now on you must always attend our parties." "You don't need to tell me, sir," replied the old man, "I shall be there. This time I was unprepared and forgot the last steps. But if it pleases you so much, sir, I'll do it again in less of a hurry." "Well said," declared the chief. "You must come again, without fail." "The old man may promise this now," said a demon three places away from the chief, "but I am afraid he may not come. Shouldn't we get some pledge from him?" "Yes, we certainly should," the chief agreed, and they all began to discuss what they should take. "What about taking the wen off his face?" said the chief. "A wen is a lucky thing, so I doubt if he'd want to lose that." At this, the old man begged, "Take an eye or my nose, but please allow me to keep this wen, sir. It would be very hard on me to be robbed for no reason at all of something I've had for so many years." "If he's that unwilling to part with it, take it from him," said the chief, whereupon a demon went up to the old man and with a "Here goes!" twisted the wen and pulled. The old man felt no pain at all. "Now then, see to it that you attend our next party," he was told. By this time it was nearly dawn, and as the cocks were crowing, the demons went away. When he felt his face, the old man could find no trace of the wen he had had for so long. It had disappeared completely, as if it had been just wiped away. All thought of going to cut wood went out of his mind, and he returned to his home. When his aged wife questioned him about what had happened, he told her the story of the demons. "Who would have thought such a thing possible?" she exclaimed.

Now the old man who lived next door to them had a large wen on his left cheek, and when he found that his neighbor no longer had one, he asked him how he had got rid of it. "Where did you find a doctor to take it away? I wish you would tell me, then I could have mine taken away too." "It wasn't taken away by a doctor," replied the old man, and he explained what had happened and how the demons had removed it. "I'll get rid of mine in the same way," said the other, and he persuaded his neighbor to tell him all the details of what had happened.

The second old man, following his instructions, got into the hollow tree and waited; then, just as he had been told, the demons appeared and sat round in a circle, enjoying themselves drinking. "Where is he? Is the old man here?" called the chief, and the second old man tottered out, trembling with fright. "Here he is," shouted the demons, and the chief ordered him to be quick and dance. Compared with the first old man's dance, this was a very poor and clumsy effort, and the chief demon said, "This time his dance was bad, very bad indeed. Give him back that wen we took from him as a pledge." A demon came out from the end of a row and shouting, "The chief's giving you back the wen we took as a pledge," threw the wen at the old man's other cheek, so that he now had one on each side of his face.

Never be envious of others, they say.

About the Priest with the Long Nose (2:7)

Once there lived at Ikenoo[111] a court priest named Zenchin.[112] He was a very saintly man, being thoroughly versed in the esoteric teachings of Buddhism and having practiced its rites for many years, and thus he was in great demand to say all manner of prayers. As a result he was very prosperous, and there was never a sign of dilapidation in the temple buildings or in the priests' living quarters. The offerings to the Buddha and the votive lamp were never neglected. The periodic banquets to the priests and the temple sermons—all were held regularly. And so the priests' quarters in the temple were always fully occupied. Never a day passed without the bath being heated and a noisy crowd of priests bathing. In the neighborhood, too, a number of small houses were built and a flourishing village grew up.

Now Zenchin had a long nose, five or six inches long, in fact, so that it seemed to hang down beyond his chin. It was purply-red in color, swollen and pimply like the peel of an orange. It itched terribly, and he used to boil water in a kettle and put his nose into it, protecting his face from the fire by means of a tray in which he had cut a hole just large enough to allow the nose to pass through. He would give it a good boiling, and when he took it out it was a deep purple hue. Then he would lie down on his side, and putting something underneath the nose, he would get someone to tread on it, whereupon something like smoke oozed out from the hole in each of the pimples. As the treading grew heavier, white maggots emerged from each of the holes and were pulled out with a pair of hair-tweezers—a white maggot about half an inch long from each hole. You could even see the open holes they had come from. Then the nose was put back into the same water and boiled up again, which made it shrink until it was the size of an ordinary person's nose. But within two or three days it would swell up again to its former size.

This same process went on over and over again, so that there were a great many days when it was swollen. At mealtimes, therefore, Zenchin would get one of his acolytes to sit opposite him and hold a strip of wood about a foot long and an inch wide under his nose to keep it up, staying like that until the meal was over. When Zenchin got anyone else to hold his nose up, they were not gentle in the way they did it and he got so annoyed that he lost his appetite. Accordingly this one priest was given the job of holding his nose up at every meal. One day, however, he was feeling unwell, and when Zenchin sat down to his breakfast gruel there was no one to support his nose. While he was wondering what to do, a lad who was one of his servants volunteered to hold the nose up for him. "I'm sure I shall do just as well as that priest," he said. He was overheard

---

111. In Uji, on the outskirts of and to the southeast of Kyoto.

112. The priest was a *naigu(bu)*, one of the "Ten Chosen Buddhist Priests." His identity is obscure, although one theory is that he was a great-grandson of Murasaki Shikibu's husband.

by one of the acolytes, who reported his offer to Zenchin, and the boy, a good-looking lad in his middle teens, was summoned to come and sit in front of his master, where he took up the nose-supporter and, holding himself very formally and correctly, kept the nose at just the right height, not too high and not too low, so that Zenchin could drink his gruel. As he drank, Zenchin remarked how skillful the lad was, even better than the priest. But just then the boy turned aside to sneeze, and as he sneezed, his hand shook, the stick supporting the nose wobbled, and the nose slipped off and fell plop into the gruel, which splashed up all over their faces. Zenchin was furious, and as he wiped his head and face with paper, he ordered the boy out, bellowing, "You confounded idiot! A stupid lout, that's what you are. Just you go and hold up some bigwig's nose, instead of mine, then I'll bet you wouldn't do this. You stupid great fool! Get out, get out!" "Certainly, I'll go and hold his nose up," called the lad, as a parting shot, "—if there is anybody else with a nose like yours. You don't know what you're talking about, sir." The acolytes all went where they could not be seen and had a good laugh.

How Yoshihide, a Painter of Buddhist Pictures, Took Pleasure in Seeing His House on Fire (3:6)

Again, long ago there was a painter of Buddhist pictures named Yoshihide. His neighbor's house caught fire, and when the flames threatened to engulf Yoshihide's house too, he saved himself by running out into the street. Inside the house he had some pictures of Buddhist divinities that he had been commissioned to paint. Also inside were his wife and children, all caught there without even having time to dress. But Yoshihide did not give them a thought, he simply stood on the other side of the street congratulating himself on his own escape. As he watched, he could see that the fire now had a grip on his own house, and he continued to watch from the other side of the street until the house was a mass of billowing smoke and flame. Several people came up to him to express their sympathy at this awful disaster, but he was completely unperturbed, and when asked why, all he did was to go on standing there on the other side of the street watching his house burn, nodding his head and every now and then breaking into a laugh. "What a stroke of luck!" he said. "This is something I've never been able to paint properly for all these years." The people who had come to express their condolences asked him how he could just stand there like that. "What a shocking way to behave! Has some demon got into you?" they asked. Yoshihide, however, only stood laughing scornfully, and replied, "Of course not. For years now I've not been able to paint a good halo of fire in my pictures of the god Fudō.[113] Now that

---

113. Fudō Myōō (Skt. Acala) was one of the Five Great Guardian Kings and a figure of particular importance to esoteric Buddhism.

I've seen this, I've learned what a fire really looks like. That's a real stroke of luck. If you want to make a living at this branch of art, you can have any number of houses you like—provided you're good at painting Buddhas and gods. It's only because you have no talent for art that you set such store by material things."

It was perhaps from this time on that he began to paint pictures of his "Curling Fudō," which even nowadays people praise so highly.

How a Sparrow Repaid Its Debt of Gratitude (3:16)

Long ago, one fine day in spring, a woman of about sixty was sitting cleansing herself of lice when she saw a boy pick up a stone and throw it at one of the sparrows that were hopping around in the garden. The stone broke the bird's leg, and as it floundered about, wildly flapping its wings, a crow came swooping down on it. "Oh, the poor thing," cried the woman, "the crow will get it," and snatching it up, she revived it with her breath and gave it something to eat. At night, she placed it for safety in a little bucket. Next morning, when she gave it some rice and also a medicinal powder made from ground copper, her children and grandchildren ridiculed her. "Just look," they jeered, "Granny's taken to keeping sparrows in her old age."

For several months she tended it, till in time it was hopping about again, and though it was only a sparrow, it was deeply grateful to her for nursing it back to health. Whenever she left the house on the slightest errand, the woman would ask someone to look after the sparrow and feed it. The family ridiculed her and wanted to know whatever she was keeping a sparrow for, but she would reply, "Never you mind! I just feel sorry for it." She kept it till it could fly again, then, confident that there was no longer any risk of its being caught by a crow, she went outside and held it up on her hand to see if it would fly away. Off it went with a flap of its wings. Everyone laughed at the woman because she missed her sparrow so much. "For so long now I've been used to shutting it up at night and feeding it in the morning," she said, "and oh dear, now it's flown away! I wonder if it will ever come back."

About three weeks later, she suddenly heard a sparrow chirruping away near her house, and wondering if all this chirruping meant that her sparrow had come back, she went out to see, and found that it had. "Well I never!" she exclaimed. "What a wonderful thing for it to remember me and come back!" The sparrow took one look at the woman's face, then it seemed to drop some tiny object out of its mouth and flew away. "Whatever can it be, this thing the sparrow has dropped?" she exclaimed, and going up to it, she found it was a single calabash-seed. "It must have had some reason for bringing this," she said, and she picked it up and kept it. Her children laughed at her and said, "There's a fine thing to do, getting something from a sparrow and treating it as if you'd got a fortune!" "All the same," she told them, "I'm going to plant it and see what happens," which she did. When autumn came, the seed had produced an enormous crop of calabashes, much larger and more plentiful than usual. Delighted, the woman gave some to her neighbors, and however many she picked, the supply was inexhaustible. The children who had laughed at her were now eating the fruit from morning to night, while everyone in the village received a share. In the end, the woman picked out seven or eight especially big ones to make into gourds, and hung them up in the house.

After several months, she inspected them and found that they were ready. As she took them down to cut openings in them, she thought they seemed rather heavy, which was mysterious. But when she cut one open, she found it full to the brim. Wondering whatever could be inside it, she began emptying it out— and found it full of white rice! In utter amazement, she poured all the rice into a large vessel, only to discover that the gourd immediately refilled itself. "Obviously some miracle has taken place—it must be the sparrow's doing," she exclaimed, bewildered but very happy. She put that gourd away out of sight before she examined the rest of them, but they all proved to be crammed full of rice, just like the first one. Whenever she took rice from the gourds, there was always far more than she could possibly use, so that she became extremely rich. The people in the neighboring villages were astonished to see how prosperous she had become, and were filled with envy at her incredible good fortune.

Now the children of the woman who lived next door said to their mother, "You and that woman next door are the same sort of people, but just look where she's got to! Why haven't you ever managed to do any good for us?" Their criticism stung the woman into going to see her neighbor. "Well, well, however did you manage this business?" she asked. "I've heard some talk about it being something to do with a sparrow, but I'm not really sure, so would you tell how it all came about, please?" "Well, it all began when a sparrow dropped a calabash-seed and I planted it," said the other woman, rather vaguely. But when her neighbor pressed her to explain the whole story in detail, she felt she ought not to be petty and keep it to herself, so she explained how there had been a sparrow with a broken leg that she had nursed back to health, and how it must have been so grateful that it had brought her a calabash-seed, which she had planted; and that was how she had come to be wealthy. "Will you give me one of the seeds?" she was asked, but this she refused to do. "I'll give you some of the rice that was in the gourds," she said, "but I can't give you a seed. I can't possibly let those go." The neighbor now began to keep a sharp lookout in case she too might find a sparrow with a broken leg to tend. But there were no such sparrows to be found. Every morning as she looked out, there would be sparrows hopping around pecking at any grains of rice that happened to be lying about outside the back door—and one day she picked up some stones and threw them in the hope of hitting one. Since she had several throws and there was such a flock of birds, she naturally managed to hit one, and as it lay on the ground, unable to fly away, she went up to it in great excitement and hit it again, to make sure that its leg was broken. Then she picked it up and took it indoors, where she fed it and treated it with medicine. "Why, if a single sparrow brought my neighbor all that wealth," she thought to herself, "I should be much richer still if I had several of them. I should get a lot more credit from my children than she did from hers." So she scattered some rice in the doorway and sat watching, then when a group of sparrows gathered to peck at it, she threw several stones at them, injuring three. "That will do," she thought, and putting the three sparrows with broken legs into a bucket, she fed them a medicinal powder made from ground copper. Some months later, feeling very pleased with herself now that they had all recovered, she took them outdoors and they all flew away. In her own estimation she had acted with great kindness. But the sparrows bitterly resented having had their legs broken and being kept in captivity for months.

Ten days went by, and to the woman's great joy the sparrows returned. As she was staring at them to see if they had anything in their mouths, they each dropped a calabash-seed and flew off. "It's worked," she thought exultantly, and picking up the seeds, she planted them in three places. In no time, much faster than ordinary ones, they had grown into huge plants, though none of them had borne much fruit—not more than seven or eight calabashes. She beamed with pleasure as she looked at them. "You complained that I had never managed to do any good for you," she said to her children, "but now I'll do better than that woman next door," and the family very much hoped that she would. Since there were only a few calabashes, she did not eat any herself or let anyone else eat any, in the hope of getting more rice from them. Her children grumbled, "The woman next door ate some of hers and gave some to her neighbors. And we've got three seeds, which is more than she had, so there ought to be something for ourselves and the neighbors to eat." Feeling that perhaps they were right, the woman gave some away to the neighbors, while she cooked a number of the fruit for herself and her family to eat. The calabashes tasted terribly bitter, however; they were just like the *kihada* fruit that people use as a medicine, and made everyone feel quite nauseated. Every single person who had eaten any, including the woman herself and her children, was sick. The neighbors were furious and came round in a very ugly mood, demanding to know what it was she had given them. "It's shocking," they said. "Even people who only got a whiff of the things felt as if they were on their last legs with sickness and nausea." The woman and her children, meanwhile, were sprawled out half-unconscious and vomiting all over the place, so that there was little point in the neighbors' complaining, and they went away. In two or three days, everyone had recovered, and the woman came to the conclusion that the peculiar things which had happened must have been the outcome of being overhasty and eating the calabashes which should have given rice. She therefore hung the rest of the fruit up to store. After some months, when she felt they would be ready, she went into the storeroom armed with buckets to hold the rice. Her toothless mouth grinning from ear to ear with happiness, she held the buckets up to the gourds and went to pour out the contents of the fruit—but what emerged was a stream of things like horseflies, bees, centipedes, lizards, and snakes, which attacked and stung her, not only on her face but all over her body. Yet she felt no pain, and thought that it was rice pouring over her, for she shouted, "Wait a moment, my sparrows. Let me get it a little at a time." Out of the seven or eight gourds came a vast horde of venomous creatures which stung the children and their mother— the latter so badly that she died. The sparrows had resented having their legs broken and had persuaded swarms of insects and reptiles to enter the gourds; whereas the sparrow next door had been grateful because when it had broken its leg it had been saved from a crow and nursed back to health.

So you see, you should never be jealous of other people.

[Translated by Douglas E. Mills]

TALES OF RENUNCIATION
(*SENJŪSHŌ*, EARLY THIRTEENTH CENTURY)

Tales of Renunciation is a collection of 121 Buddhist setsuwa divided into nine volumes. Although the date of 1183 is given in its colophon, it probably was composed about a century later. The collection has been popularly attributed to Saigyō (1189– 1190), a noted late Heian monk and waka poet, probably because Saigyō figures prominently in the collection. He appears as the first-person narrator in one of the tales, and poems from *Sankashū*, Saigyō's poetry collection, are incorporated into several tales, whereas several other tales appear to be based on headnotes from *Sankashū*. But it is clear that Saigyō was not the author or compiler.

The collection is unified by the theme of renunciation. The tales in *Senjūshō* usually begin with an anecdote, followed by an exposition or a commentary on the main theme of the anecdote. The first tale, which is included here, is representative of the tales' format. The commentary, which is almost as long as the anecdote itself, argues that attachment to worldly possessions and reputation leads to sin and must be overcome, which Zōga does in an extreme fashion. Significantly, the eccentric Zōga is inspired by Amaterasu, the Sun Goddess, whose presence reflects the Shinto–Buddhistic syncretism typical of the medieval period. The second example, Saigyō's encounter with a prostitute at Eguchi, is the most famous of the Saigyō episodes and became the source for the nō play *Eguchi*.

The Venerable Zōga (1:1)

Long ago there lived a man known as the Venerable Zōga who had been deeply religious from an early age.[114] For a thousand nights he kept vigil in the Main

---

114. Zōga (917–1003) was the son of Tachibana no Tsunehira, the "consultant" (*saishō*) mentioned later. After becoming a Tendai monk, he lived for a while on Mount Hiei and then set-

Hall on Mount Tendai,[115] praying that he might attain perfect sincerity of heart, but he still found this difficult to accomplish. Once, when he had gone alone to the Great Shrine of Ise and was praying, he received, as if in a dream, this revelation: "If you would give rise to a heart that follows the Way, you must not regard your body as a body."

Zōga was astonished and thought, "This means, 'Rid yourself of all desire for fame and fortune.' Well then, I shall do just that." So he took off his priestly robes and gave them all away to beggars. He did not keep even his unlined underrobe but left the shrine completely naked.

Those who saw him were amazed. They crowded around to look at him, exclaiming, "He's going mad. What a sad and dreadful sight!" But Zōga was not at all disturbed. He set out on his travels, begging as he went, and on the fourth day of the month again climbed the mountain to the chambers of Master Jie, where he had once lived.[116] It is said that some of his fellow monks watched him, thinking, "The son of the consultant has gone mad," while others viewed him with pity.

When no one was watching, the Master, who was Zōga's teacher, invited him in and admonished him, "You have learned that a person should disregard fame and fortune. Still, you shouldn't go to such extremes. Just behave properly, without desiring fame and fortune."

But Zōga replied, "This is the way that a person who has long ago completely abandoned desire for fame and fortune should behave." Then he cried out, "Oh, oh, I'm so happy," and ran off.

The Master, too, went out the gate and wept as he watched Zōga disappear in the distance.

Zōga wandered until at last he reached Tōnomine in Yamato. There he lived in the ruins of the hermitage in which Zen Master Chirō had dwelt.

Ambition for fame and fortune is fearful indeed. Grave troubles also result from the three poisons of greed, anger, and ignorance. We believe that our bodies really exist, and so we create many other fictions to support them. Men born into military families wage war; fitting arrows to the bowstring in quick succession and wielding their long swords, they lose their lives in quest of the glory and gain that come from overpowering others. Women paint on fine, willow-leaf brows and perfume their robes with orchid and musk, calculating that their appearance will dispel the last traces of the autumn breezes of their lovers' fickleness, and they, too, do this for no other reason than glory and fortune.

---

tled on Tōnomine, a mountain on the southern edge of the Nara basin. Known as an eccentric, he is the subject of many setsuwa found in collections such as the *Konjaku monogatari shū* and *Hosshinshū*.

115. That is, the Enryaku-ji temple on Mount Hiei, the headquarters of the Tendai sect.

116. Jie Daishi (Master Jie) was the posthumous name of Ryōgen (912–985). He is noted for his treatise *Sōmoku hosshin shugyō jōbutsu ki*, which teaches that nonsentient things, such as plants, possess buddhahood. He appears in many setsuwa.

Furthermore, there are those who don the drab, dark robes of a priest and, fingering their rosary beads, preach to people as a way of supporting themselves. Or else they aspire to the highest rank and office in the hope that they will sit with nobles at religious assemblies and be honored by three thousand disciples. They, too, are not free from the desire for fame and profit.

But in addition to those who are not aware of this truth, there also are people who have seen the Yuishiki and Shikan texts[117] and have the capacity to understand the ultimate truths of the scriptures. Despite this, they do not reject fame and fortune and so remain drifting in the ocean of birth and death. Everyone who tries to discard his reputation finds it difficult to change a habit of many lifetimes. It is truly wonderful that the Venerable Zōga was finally able to discard all longing for fame and fortune. How could he have ever reached that resolve without the aid of the Great Shrine of Ise? How impressive and awesome it is that a man in the eternal night of worldly desires was cleansed by the waves of the Isuzu River[118] and that the clustered clouds of greed, anger, and ignorance vanished in the light of Amaterasu, the Sun Goddess. This incident should never be forgotten.

[Translated by Jean Moore]

The Woman of Pleasure at Eguchi (9:8)

Once around the twentieth of the Ninth Month, as I passed by a place called Eguchi, the sight of houses squeezed together on the north and south banks of the river and the hearts of the pleasure women set on the comings and goings of travelers made me think, "How pitiful and hopeless!" As I was thus gazing at the scene, an unseasonably wintry shower suddenly darkened the skies, so I approached the dwelling of one of these unseemly folk and asked for shelter until the skies cleared, but because the woman of pleasure of the house showed no sign of letting me in, I casually recited the following:

yo no naka o	It may be difficult
itou made koso	for you to despise
katakarame	this fleeting world,
kari no yadori o	but you begrudge me
oshimu kimi kana	even momentary lodging!

---

117. Yuishiki, "Consciousness Only" or "Mere Ideation," is the teaching of the Hossō sect, which attributes the existence of the outer world to inner ideation. Shikan, "Concentration and Insight," is a teaching propounded by Zhiyi (538–597), founder of the Tiantai (Tendai) sect, according to which meditation allows insight and the realization of truth.

118. A clear stream that flows through the Ise Shrine. Visitors rinse their hands and mouth in its waters as a ritual of purification.

The woman of pleasure of the house then replied despairingly:

ie o izuru	Because I heard
hito to shi kikeba	that you had taken vows
kari no yado	my only thought was:
kokoro tomu na to	do not set your heart
omou bakari zo	on this momentary lodging![119]

She then quickly let me in.

Although I had intended to seek shelter only during the rain, this poem was so wonderful that I stayed through the night. This woman of pleasure must have been more than forty at the time. Her appearance and manner were quite elegant and graceful. As we talked throughout the night about this and that, the woman of pleasure said: "I became a pleasure girl when I was quite young, and although I've carried on for many years this way, I still find it piteous. I've heard that women are particularly sinful, and the fact that on top of that I have carried on in this way makes me think that it must have been the result of karma from a previous existence, and that leaves me very depressed. But in the last two or three years my feelings have greatly deepened, and furthermore, since I've grown old, I don't engage in such practices at all any more. Even though the same bell sounds each night from the temple in the fields, tonight I am filled with sorrow, and for some reason I am blinded by tears. When I wonder how long I might linger in this impermanent world of sorrows, how fleeting it all seems! At dawn my heart is clear, and I am deeply moved by the voices of birds bidding their fond farewells. Likewise in the evening I think to myself, 'What will become of me when this night passes?' And with the break of dawn I think, 'Once this night has passed I'll take on a nun's appearance and make my resolve,' but for years now I've grown accustomed to this world and its ways, and I feel like a bird in snowy mountains. What sorrow it is to have so helplessly fretted all this time!"

So saying, she wept uncontrollably. When I heard this, I was deeply moved and found it so rare and wonderful that I was unable to wring the tears from my own darkly dyed sleeves.[120] When the night had turned to dawn, though with great regret, we promised to meet again and parted.

Now, on the road back, I thought several times of how noble she was and shed more tears. Even now my heart is moved, and even at the sight of grasses or trees,

---

119. Eguchi, a heavily frequented port on the Yodo River near Osaka, was famous for its brothels, and the composer of the reply is one of the women of pleasure (*yūjo*). Later legends say that the pleasure woman Tae was actually the bodhisattva Fugen in disguise, which explains the Buddhist qualities of her reply. Saigyō rebukes Tae for not letting him in, but she rebukes Saigyō for letting his mind dwell on something so trivial as a little shelter from the rain.

120. "Darkly dyed sleeves" refers to the dark robes of a monk.

I feel as though surrounded by darkness.[121] Is this perhaps what is meant by "the amusement of wild words and decorative phrases is the cause for praise of the Dharma"?[122] If I had not recited my poem, "but you begrudge me even momentary lodging," this woman of pleasure probably would not have given me shelter. And so how else should I have met this wonderful person? How glad I was, for thanks to this lady my heart was inspired in a small way for a moment, and why shouldn't this, in some small way, cause the seed of unsurpassed enlightenment to sprout?

Now, in the promised month, just as I was thinking I should visit her, a certain holy man came from the capital, and so I was completely distracted. Disappointed at my failed intentions, I related the situation to someone I could trust and then wrote a letter to send with which I included the following:

karisome no	"Don't leave any
yo ni wa omoi o	thoughts behind
nokosu na to	in this fleeting world!"
kikishi koto no ha	These words I heard
wasurare mo sezu	have not been forgotten.

After sending this, the following reply came with her letter:

wasurezu to	"Not forgotten,"
mazu kiku kara ni	as soon as I heard this
sode nurete	my sleeves were wet.
waga mi mo itou	I too despise
yume no yo no naka	this world of dreams.

At the end she had also written, "I have changed my appearance,[123] and yet my heart remains unchanged," to which she added:

kami oroshi	I've cut my hair
koromo no iro wa	and the color of my robes
somenuredo	has changed.[124]
nao tsurenaki wa	What remains the same, though,
kokoro narikeri	is my heart.

---

121. By this, he means that his tears prevent him from seeing. The darkness does not have negative connotations.

122. "Wild words and decorative phrases" (*kyōgen kigo*) was a phrase coined by the eighth-century Chinese poet Bo Juyi.

123. She means that she has become a nun, cutting her hair and wearing dark robes.

124. The implication is that the robes have been dyed a darker hue than before. To highlight the contrast between the changed color of the robes and the unchanged heart, the verb *somu* (to dye) has been translated here as "change."

When I read this, for some reason the tears flowed so freely that my sleeves could not absorb them all. Such a remarkable woman of pleasure she was! Such women of pleasure usually hope to become familiar with someone who would love them, but she distanced herself from such desires and devoted herself with all her heart to the next world—how could this not be rare and wonderful? Surely this was not the result of just a little good karma here and there. Although her many observations of the precepts had accumulated over many lives and had been blessed by the waters of Eguchi, even her poetry was remarkable. "In the evening I think, *when the night has passed* . . . and at dawn I weep, thinking, *when the day comes* . . ." So she told me, and yet I wonder whether those sentiments continue? No, for she has become a nun![125] I wanted to visit her after she had taken vows, but when I heard that she no longer lived in Eguchi after becoming a nun, my hopes in the end were in vain. Quite often I can't help but wonder what that woman of pleasure's final moments must have been like.

[Translated by Jack Stoneman]

WARRIOR TALES (*GUNKI-MONO*)

Warrior tales or chronicles (*gunki* or *gunki-mono*) are one of the main genres of medieval literature. In *Notes on Foolish Views* (*Gukanshō*), written in the early Kamakura period, Jien (1155–1225) distinguishes between historical chronicles like *The Great Mirror* (*Ōkagami*) and those that describe the world of warriors and battle.

The first period of warrior tales is the mid-Heian, beginning with the *Record of Masakado* (*Shōmonki*, ca. 940) and the *Record of the Deep North* (*Mutsuwaki*, ca. 1062), both written in kanbun by Buddhist monks or middle-rank intellectuals. *Shōmonki* describes the uprising by Taira no Masakado (d. 940) and reveals the attempt to save his spirit from hell.

The second period began with texts like *The Tales of Heiji* (*Heiji monogatari*, 1221?), *The Tales of Hōgen* (*Hōgen monogatari*, 1221?), and *The Tales of the Heike* (*Heike monogatari*, mid-thirteenth century), marking the transition from the early period to medieval warrior society. Both *Hōgen monogatari* and *Heiji monogatari*, which describe military conflicts leading up to the Genpei war, resemble *Shōmonki* and *Mutsuwaki* as narratives about warriors who caused major disturbances. But in contrast to *Shōmonki* and *Mutsuwaki*, which are "records" (*ki*) written in kanbun (Chinese prose) with a documentary focus, *Hōgen monogatari* and *Heiji monogatari* have the quality of Heian monogatari in trying to

---

125. The narrator is paraphrasing the words of the *yūjo* from the conversation they had earlier, in which she said: ". . . in the evening I think to myself, 'What will become of me when this night passes?' And with the break of dawn I think, 'Once this night has passed I'll take on a nun's appearance and make my resolve.'"

re-create the interior life of the participants. The perspective of *Shōmonki* and *Mutsuwaki* was of those at the center looking out at the rebels in the provinces, whereas the military narratives in the second period (such as *The Tales of the Heike*) were written or recited from the perspective of those who had sometimes experienced the war at first hand or who sympathized with the fate of the defeated warriors. These texts were written in the so-called mixed Japanese–Chinese style, which combines Japanese prose and Chinese compounds and phrases, including allusions to Chinese classics and history.

The *Rise and Fall of the Genji and the Heike* (*Genpei seisuiki* or *Genpei jōsuiki*) describes *Hōgen monogatari* and *Heiji monogatari* as "diaries [*nikki*] of the Hōgen and Heiji periods," revealing that in the Kamakura period they were still considered to be reliable records of events, despite their monogatari character. Like other military narratives, *Hōgen monogatari* and *Heiji monogatari* include setsuwa, following a tradition that goes back to the late Heian *Collection of Tales of Times Now Past* (*Konjaku monogatari shū*), which devotes one volume to warrior stories. Most of the military narratives have three parts, describing the causes of the military conflict, the conflict itself, and the aftermath, a structure apparent in *The Tales of Hōgen* and *The Tales of Heiji*.

The second period climaxed with the *Record of the Jōkyū Disturbance* (*Jōkyūki*), which describes the failed attempt in 1221 (Jōkyū 3) by the retired emperor GoToba (r. 1183–1198) to seize power from the Kamakura bakufu, and the *Taiheiki* (*Chronicle of Great Peace*, 1340s–1371), which describes the collapse of the Kamakura bakufu in 1333 and the subsequent rule by the Ashikaga clan.

The military narratives in the second period were heavily influenced by the Heian monogatari but differed in that they reveal the impact of various forms of recitation or oral performance practices (*katari*). These practices had an important ritual function: to celebrate (*shūgen*) the preservation or restoration of order and to pacify the souls (*chinkon*) of those warriors who had died terrible deaths on the battlefield. In the former capacity, the warrior tales affirmed those who had established or preserved order and peace, and in the latter capacity, they tried to console the spirits of the defeated, hoping to calm their angry and sometimes vengeful spirits, and to offer them salvation, thereby incorporating them into the new social order.

During the third period, in the late medieval period, were written such works as *The Record of the Meitoku Disturbance* (*Meitokuki*), on the Meitoku disturbance (1390–1394); *The Record of the Ōnin War* (*Ōnin-ki*), about the Ōnin war (1467–1477); and *The Tale of Mikawa* (*Mikawa monogatari*, 1622). The third period also produced texts that, though about war, focused on the fate of a single warrior or small group. *The Story of Yoshitsune* (*Gikeiki*, early fifteenth century?) describes Yoshitsune's flight to the Tōhoku region and Yoshitsune himself, his family, and his retainers. *The Tales of the Soga Brothers* (*Soga monogatari*, mid-fourteenth century), which was recited by *goze* (blind female singer-musicians), likewise is centered on the life of the Soga brothers as they avenge their father's death. In contrast to *The Story of Yoshitsune*, which reflects the interests of Kyoto urban audiences, *The Tales of the Soga Brothers* reflects the interests of those who lived in the east.

Many of these warrior chronicles have no identifiable authors and actually were written by several people. For example, *The Tales of the Heike* draws on numerous setsuwa and has many variants. The *Taiheiki* also is the product of many writers, who did not know how the events would end, resulting in an open and unfinished work. The author(s) of these military tales did not, however, write the narratives from beginning to end; instead, they edited and re-wrote the transmitted texts, much as the editors of the setsuwa collections did, to suit their own ends.

Another notable characteristic of warrior chronicles like *The Tales of the Heike* and the *Taiheiki* is that they often allude to Chinese history and Chinese texts, comparing the disorder and dangers of the present with those in the past and drawing lessons from this comparison or pointing to similarities. In this regard, they belong to a larger tradition of historical narrative.

The military narratives were transmitted in two ways: as read text (*yomi-mono*), which could be used for sermons and other functions, and as orally recited material (*katari-mono*) performed by *biwa hōshi* (blind lute minstrels) or storytelling monks (*monogatari sō*) attached to armies. *Hōgen monogatari*, *Heiji monogatari*, and *Heike monogatari* were recited by biwa hōshi, and the *Taiheiki* and the *Meitokuki* were recited by monogatari sō.

These warrior tales, which belonged to performative traditions, later were heavily used and absorbed by other genres such as nō, kōwakamai, otogi-zōshi (Muromachi tales), jōruri, kabuki, Tokugawa fiction, and modern novels.

Chronology of Major Incidents in Warrior Tales

Jōhei–Tengyō disturbance (935–941)	*Shōmonki*
Hōgen disturbance (1156)	*Hōgen monogatari*
Heiji disturbance (1159)	*Heiji monogatari*
Struggle between Heike and Genji lineages (1180), with Heike destroyed at Dan-no-ura (1185)	*Heike monogatari*
Jōkyū disturbance (1221)	*Jōkyūki*
Kenmu restoration (1334), with Ashikaga Takauji as Seii taishogun (barbarian-subduing generalissimo) (1338)	*Taiheiki*

THE TALES OF THE HEIKE
(*HEIKE MONOGATARI*, MID-THIRTEENTH CENTURY)

The Tales of the Heike is about the Genpei war (1180–1185), fought between the Heike (Taira) lineage, led by Taira no Kiyomori, and the Genji (Minamoto) lineage, whose head became Minamoto no Yoritomo. The Taira's initial, rapid ascent to power was followed by a series of defeats, including their abandonment of the capital in 1183 (taking with them Antoku, the child emperor). By 1183 Yoritomo had gained control of the Kantō, or eastern, region; Kiso no Yoshinaka, another Minamoto leader, had brought Kyoto under his power; and the Taira had fallen back to the Inland Sea. In an interlude of fighting among the Minamoto, Yoritomo and his half brother (Minamoto) Yoshitsune defeated Yoshinaka in 1184. In a decisive battle at Ichi-no-tani in 1184, near the present-day city of Kobe, Yoshitsune, leading the Minamoto forces, decisively turned back the Taira, driving them into the Inland Sea. Finally, in 1185, the last of the Taira forces were crushed at Dan-no-ura, in a sea battle at the western end of the Inland Sea. In the same year, Rokudai, the last potential heir of the Taira clan, was captured and eventually executed.

This war between the Taira and the Minamoto marked the beginning of the medieval period and also became the basis for *The Tales of the Heike*, which focuses on the lives of various warriors from both military houses, particularly those of the defeated. The narrative also includes numerous non-samurai stories drawn from anecdotes (setsuwa), many of which deal with women and priests, that were frequently transformed by the composers of the *Heike* into Buddhist narratives, much like the anecdotes in Buddhist setsuwa collections. Therefore, even though *The Tales of the Heike* is a military epic, it has strong Buddhist overtones, which are especially evident in the opening passage on impermanence, in many of the stories of Buddhistic disillusionment and awakening (such as those about Giō or Koremori), and in the final "Initiates' Book" (Kanjō no maki) leading to the salvation of Kenreimon'in, the daughter of Kiyomori, who has a vision of the fall of her clan.

The first variants of *The Tales of the Heike* were probably recorded by writers and priests associated with Buddhist temples who may have incorporated Buddhist readings and other folk material into an earlier chronological, historically oriented narrative. These texts, in turn, were recited from memory, accompanied by a lute (*biwa*) played by blind minstrels (referred to as *biwa hōshi*), who entertained a broad commoner audience and had an impact on subsequent variants of *The Tales of the Heike*, which combined both literary texts and orally transmitted material. The many variants of *The Tales of the Heike* differ significantly in content and style, but the most famous today is the Kakuichi text, part of which is translated here. This variant was recorded in 1371 by a man named Kakuichi, a biwa hōshi who created a twelve-book narrative shaped around the decline of the Heike (Taira) clan. At some point "The Initiates' Book," which unifies the long work and gives it closure as a Buddhist text, was added, as well as sections that were inspired by Heian monogatari and centered on women and the private life of the court.

Thanks largely to Kakuichi, the oral biwa performance of *The Tales of the Heike* eventually won upper-class acceptance and became a major performing art, reaching its height in the mid-fifteenth century. After the Ōnin war (1467–1477), the biwa performance declined in popularity and was replaced by other performance arts, such as nō and kyōgen (comic drama), but *The Tales of the Heike* continued to serve as a rich source for countless dramas and prose narratives. Indeed, most of the sixteen warrior pieces (*shuramono*) in today's nō drama repertoire are from *The Tales of the Heike*. *Heike* heroes began appearing in the ballad dramas (*kōwakamai*) in the sixteenth century, and in the Tokugawa period, stories from *The Tales of the Heike* became the foundation for a number of important kabuki and jōruri (puppet) plays, thus making it one of the most influential works of premodern Japanese culture.

The first half of the *Heike*, books one through six, relates the history of Kiyomori, the head of the Taira (Heike) clan, who comes into conflict with the retired emperor GoShirakawa and then with various members of the Minamoto (Genji) clan. The second half, books seven through twelve, is about three important Minamoto (Genji) leaders: Yoritomo, the head of the Genji in the east; Yoshinaka, who becomes a Genji leader farther to the west; and Yoshitsune, Yoritomo's brother. However, the real focus of the narrative is not on the Genji victors—in fact, Yoritomo, the ultimate victor, plays almost a peripheral role—but on a series of defeated Taira figures: Shigemori, Shigehira, Koremori, Munemori, and Kenreimon'in—all descendants of Kiyomori—who, bearing the sins of the forefather, suffer different fates on their way to death. In short, in the first half, *The Tales of the Heike* centers on the Taira, on Kiyomori, the clan leader, and, in the second half, on the various defeated Taira, almost all of whom die or are executed. (Also important in the second half is the fall of the former Genji leader, Kiso Yoshinaka, who is defeated by Yoritomo.) It is not until "The Initiates' Book" that the tragedy of the Taira becomes an opportunity for reconciliation, between Kenreimon'in, Kiyomori's daughter, and the retired emperor GoShirakawa, who had been victimized by Kiyomori.

Key Figures

Imperial Family

ANTOKU (r. 1180–1185): emperor and son of Emperor Takakura and Kenreimon'in; is held by the Taira clan and drowns at Dan-no-ura.

GOSHIRAKAWA (1127–1192, r. 1155–1158): retired emperor, head of the imperial clan, and son of Retired Emperor Toba.

KENREIMON'IN (1155–1213): daughter of Kiyomori and Tokiko (Nun of the Second Rank), consort of Emperor Takakura, mother of Emperor Antoku, and full sister of Munemori, Tomomori, and Shigehira; is taken prisoner at Dan-no-ura and dies a nun.

MOCHIHITO, PRINCE (1151–1180): second son of Retired Emperor Go-Shirakawa and leader of an anti-Taira revolt in 1180; also called Prince Takakura.

NUN OF THE SECOND RANK: principal wife of Kiyomori and mother of Munemori, Shigehira, and Kenreimon'in; dies at Dan-no-ura.

TAKAKURA: emperor and son of Retired Emperor GoShirakawa.

TOBA: retired emperor and father of Retired Emperor GoShirakawa.

Taira (Heike)

ATSUMORI: nephew of Kiyomori; dies at Ichi-no-tani.

KIYOMORI: son of Tadamori and, after his father's death, Taira clan head; dominates the court even after taking vows.

KOREMORI: eldest son of Shigemori; commits suicide after taking vows.

MUNEMORI: son of Kiyomori and Nun of the Second Rank and, after Shigemori's death, Taira clan head.

ROKUDAI: son of Koremori, grandson of Shigemori, and presumptive Taira clan head after the Genpei war.

SHIGEHIRA: son of Kiyomori and Nun of the Second Rank; a Taira leader largely responsible for the burning of Nara; captured at Ichi-no-tani and later executed.

SHIGEMORI: eldest son of Kiyomori and, until his early death, a restraining influence on Kiyomori.

TADAMORI: father of Kiyomori and a former Taira clan head.

TADANORI: younger brother of Kiyomori.

Genealogy of key figures in *The Tales of the Heike*.

Minamoto (Genji)

YORITOMO: leader of the Minamoto in the east and founder of the Kamakura shogunate after the Genpei war.

YOSHINAKA: cousin of Yoritomo and leader of the Minamoto in the north; captures Kyoto and later is killed by Yoritomo's forces; also called Lord Kiso.

YOSHITSUNE: younger half brother of Yoritomo and one of Yoritomo's chief commanders; defeats the Heike at Dan-no-ura.

Priests

MONGAKU: monk; incites Yoritomo to rebel against the Taira.

SHUNKAN: bishop and Shishi-no-tani conspirator.

Book One

THE BELLS OF GION MONASTERY (1:1)

The bells of the Gion monastery in India echo with the warning that all things are impermanent.[126] The blossoms of the sala trees teach us through their hues that what flourishes must fade.[127] The proud do not prevail for long, but vanish like a spring night's dream. The mighty too in time succumb: all are dust before the wind.

Long ago in a different land, Zhao Gao of the Qin dynasty in China, Wang Mang of the Han, Zhu Yi of the Liang, and An Lushan of the Tang all refused to be governed by former sovereigns. Pursuing every pleasure, deaf to admonitions, unaware of the chaos overtaking the realm, ignorant of the sufferings of the common people, before long they all alike met their downfall.

More recently in our own country there have been men like Masakado, Sumitomo, Gishin, and Nobuyori, each of them proud and fierce to the extreme. The tales told of the most recent of such men, Taira no Kiyomori, the lay priest of Rokuhara and at one time the prime minister, are beyond the power of words to describe or the mind to imagine.

Kiyomori was the oldest son and heir of Taira no Tadamori, the minister of punishments, and the grandson of Masamori, the governor of Sanuki. Masamori was a ninth-generation descendant of Prince Kazurahara, a first-rank prince and the minister of ceremonies, the fifth son of Emperor Kanmu.

---

126. According to Buddhist legend, the Gion monastery, which was built by a rich merchant in a famous garden in India, was the first monastery in the Buddhist order. It is also said that the temple complex included a building known as the Impermanence Hall, which contained four silver and four crystal bells.

127. The Buddha is said to have died under sala trees, at which time the trees' blossoms, ordinarily yellow, turned white to express their grief.

KIYOMORI'S FLOWERING FORTUNES (1:5)

Not only did Kiyomori himself climb to the pinnacle of success, but all the members of his family enjoyed great good fortune as well. Kiyomori's eldest son, Shigemori, became a palace minister and a major captain of the left; his second son, Munemori, became a junior counselor and a major captain of the right; his third son, Tomomori, rose to the level of middle captain of the third court rank; and his grandson, Shigemori's heir Koremori, rose to that of lesser captain of the fourth court rank. In all, sixteen members of the family became high-ranking officials; more than thirty were courtiers; and a total of more than sixty held posts as provincial governors, guards officers, or officials in the central bureaucracy. It seemed as though there were no other family in the world but this one. . . .

In addition, Kiyomori had eight daughters, all of whom fared well in life. . . . One of them was made the consort of Emperor Takakura and bore him a son who became crown prince and then emperor, at which time she received the title of Kenreimon'in. Daughter of the lay priest and the prime minister, mother of the ruler of the realm, nothing further need be said about her good fortune. . . .

GIŌ (1:6)

As prime minister, Kiyomori now held the entire realm within the four seas in the palm of his hand. Thus ignoring the carpings of the age and turning a deaf ear to censure, he indulged in one caprice after another. An example was the case of Giō and Ginyo, sisters renowned in the capital at that time for their skillful performance as *shirabyōshi* dancers. They were the daughters of a *shirabyōshi* dancer named Toji. Giō, the older sister, had succeeded in winning extraordinary favor with Kiyomori. Thus the younger sister, Ginyo, also enjoyed wide repute among the people of that time. Kiyomori built a fine house for their mother, Toji, providing her with a monthly stipend of a hundred piculs of rice and a hundred strings of coins, so that the entire family prospered and lived a life of ease.

The first *shirabyōshi* dancers in our country were two women, named Shima-no-senzai and Waka-no-mai, who introduced this type of dancing during the time of the retired emperor Toba. Such dancers originally wore white jackets of the kind called *suikan* and tall black hats and carried silver-hilted daggers, pretending to be male dancers. Later they dropped the black hat and dagger and simply retained the *suikan* jacket, at which time they became known as *shirabyōshi*, or "white tempo," dancers.

As Giō became renowned among the *shirabyōshi* of the capital for the extraordinary favor she enjoyed, some people envied her and others spoke spitefully of her. Those who envied her would say, "What splendid good fortune this Lady Giō enjoys! Any woman entertainer would be delighted to be in her place. Her good fortune doubtless derives from the Gi element that makes up the first part of her name. We should have a try at that too!" Giichi, Gini, Gifuku, and Gitoku were some of the names that resulted.

The scorners took a different view. "How could fortune come from a name alone?" they asked. "It is due solely to good karma acquired in a previous existence!" and for the most part they declined to change their names.

After some three years had passed, another highly skilled *shirabyōshi* dancer appeared in the capital, a native of the province of Kaga named Hotoke, or "Buddha." She was said to be only sixteen. Everyone in the capital, high and low alike, exclaimed over her, declaring that among all the *shirabyōshi* dancers of the past, none could rival her.

Lady Hotoke thought to herself, "I have won fame throughout the realm, but I have yet to realize my true ambition, to be summoned by this prime minister of the Taira clan who is now at the height of power. Since it is the practice among entertainers, why should I hold back? I will go and present myself!" Accordingly she went and presented herself at Kiyomori's Nishihachijō mansion.

When Kiyomori was informed that the Lady Hotoke who enjoyed such renown in the capital at that time had come to call, he retorted, "What does this mean? Entertainers of that type should wait for a summons—they simply do not take it upon themselves to appear! I don't care whether she's a god or a buddha—I already have Giō in my service! Send her away!"

Refused admission in this summary manner, Hotoke was preparing to take her leave when Giō spoke to the prime minister. "It is quite customary for entertainers to present themselves in this way. Moreover, the girl still is young and just has happened to hit on this idea; it would be a shame to dismiss her so coldly. I, for one, would be greatly distressed. Because we are devotees of the same art, I cannot help feeling sympathy for her. Even if you do not let her dance or listen to her singing, at least admit her into your presence before you send her away. That would be the kind thing to do. Bend your principles a bit and call her in."

"If you insist," replied Kiyomori, "I will see her," and he sent word to have her admitted.

Having been rudely dismissed, Lady Hotoke was about to get into her carriage and leave, but at the summons she returned and presented herself.

"I had no intention of admitting you," Kiyomori announced when they met. "But for some reason Giō was so adamant that, as you see, I agreed to the meeting. And since you are here, I suppose I should find out what sort of voice you have. Try singing an *imayō* for me."

"As you wish," replied Lady Hotoke, and she obliged with the following song in the *imayō* style:

> Since I met you,
> I'm like the little pine destined for a thousand years!
> On turtle-shape isles of your pond,
> how many the cranes that flock there![128]

She repeated the song, singing it over three times while all the persons present listened and looked on in wonder at her skill.

Kiyomori was obviously much impressed. "You are very good at *imayō*," he said, "and I have no doubt that your dancing is of the same order. Let's have a look. Call in the musicians!"

When the musicians appeared, Hotoke performed a dance to their accompaniment. Everything about her was captivating, from her hairdo and costume to her appearance as a whole, and her voice was pleasing and artfully employed, so her dancing could not fail to make an impression. In fact, it far exceeded Kiyomori's expectations, and he was so moved by her performance that he immediately fell in love with her.

"This is somewhat troubling," said Hotoke. "Originally I was not to be admitted but was sent away at once. But through the kind offices of Lady Giō, I was allowed to present myself. Having done so, I would be most reluctant to do anything that would counter Lady Giō's intentions. I beg to be excused as soon as possible so that I may be on my way."

"There is no reason for that!" replied Kiyomori. "But if you feel uneasy in Giō's presence, I will see that she leaves."

"But how would that look?" objected Hotoke. "I was uneasy enough to find that the two of us had been summoned here together. If now, after all her kindness, she were dismissed and I were to remain behind, think how dreadful I would feel! If by chance you happen to remember me, perhaps you might summon me again at some future time. But for today I beg to take my leave."

Kiyomori, however, would not hear of this. "Nonsense!" he said. "You will do no such thing. Have Giō leave at once!"

Three times he sent an attendant with these instructions.

Giō had long been aware that something like this might happen, but she was not expecting it "this very day."[129] But faced with repeated orders to leave the house at once, she resigned herself to doing so and set about sweeping and tidying her room and clearing it of anything unsightly.

Even those who have only sought shelter under the same tree for a night or have merely dipped water from the same stream will feel sorrow on parting.

---

128. Pines, turtles, and cranes are symbols of longevity.

129. This is an allusion to Ariwara no Narihira's death poem, which appears in both the *Kokinshū* (no. 861) and the final section of *The Tales of Ise*: "I had heard there is a path that all must follow but didn't think yesterday that I'd be going today."

How sorrowful, then, Giō's departure must have been from the place where she had lived these three years. Her tears, futile though they were, fell quickly. Since there was nothing she could do, however, she prepared to depart. But perhaps wanting to leave behind some reminder of herself, she inscribed the following poem on the sliding panel of the room, weeping as she did so:

> Those that put out new shoots, those that wither are the same
> grasses of the field—come autumn, is there one that will not fade?

Getting into her carriage, she returned to her home and there, sinking down within the panels of the room, began weeping.

"What has happened? What is wrong?" her mother and sister asked, but she did not reply. It was only when they questioned the maid who had accompanied her that they learned the truth.

Before long, the monthly stipend of a hundred piculs of rice and a hundred strings of coins ended, and for the first time Hotoke's friends and relations learned the meaning of happiness and prosperity. Among high and low, word spread throughout the capital. "They say that Giō has been dismissed from the prime minister's service," people said. "We must go call on her and keep her company!" Some sent letters, others dispatched their servants to make inquiries. But faced with such a situation, Giō could not bring herself to receive visitors. The letters she refused to accept; the messengers she sent off without a meeting. Such gestures served only to deepen her mood of melancholy, and she passed all her time weeping. In this way the year came to an end.

The following spring Kiyomori sent a servant to Giō's house with this message: "How have you been since we parted? Lady Hotoke appears to be so hopelessly bored that I wish you would come and perform one of your *imayō* songs or your dances to cheer her up."

Giō declined to give any answer.

Kiyomori tried again. "Why no answer from you, Giō? Won't you come for a visit? Tell me if you won't come! I have ways of dealing with the matter!"

When Giō's mother, Toji, learned about this, she was very upset and, having no idea what to do, could only plead tearfully with her daughter. "Giō, at least send an answer," she begged. "Anything is better than being threatened!"

But Giō replied, "If I had any intention of going, I would have answered long ago. It is because I have no such intention that I'm at a loss as to how to reply. He says that if I do not respond, he has ways of dealing with the matter. Does this mean I will be banished from the capital? Or that I will be put to death? Even if I were expelled from the capital, I would have no great regrets. And if he wants to deprive me of my life, what of that? He once sent me away a despised person—I have no heart to face him again." She thus refused to send an answer.

But the mother continued begging. "As long as you continue to live in this realm, you cannot hope to defy the prime minister's wishes! The ties that bind man and woman are decreed from a past existence—they do not originate in this life alone. Those who vow to be faithful for a thousand or ten thousand years often end by parting, whereas those who think of this as merely an affair of the moment find themselves spending their whole lives together. In this world of ours there's no predicting how things will turn out between a man and a woman.

"For three whole years you enjoyed favor with the prime minister. That was a stroke of fortune hardly to be matched. Now if you refuse to answer his summons, it is scarcely likely you will be put to death. Probably you will merely be banished from the capital. And even if you are banished, you and your sister are young and can manage to live even in the wildest and most out-of-the-way spot. But what about your mother? I am a feeble old woman—suppose I am banished too? Just the thought of living in some strange place in the countryside fills me with despair. Let me live out the rest of my days here in the capital. Think of it as being filial in this world and the next."

Much as it pained her, Giō did not feel that she could disobey these pleas from her mother, and so weeping all the while, she set out for the prime minister's mansion. But her heart was filled with foreboding. It would be too difficult to make the trip alone, Giō felt, and therefore she took her younger sister, Ginyo, with her, as well as two other *shirabyōshi* dancers, the four of them going in one carriage to Nishi-hachijō.

Upon her arrival, Giō was not shown to the seat she had previously been accustomed to occupy, but instead to a far inferior place where makeshift arrangements had been made. "How can this be?" she exclaimed. "Although I was guilty of no fault, I was driven out of the house. And now I find that even the seat I had occupied has been demoted! This is too heartless! What am I to do?" In an effort to hide her confusion, she covered her face with her sleeve, but the trickle of tears gave her away.

Moved to pity by the sight, Lady Hotoke appealed to Kiyomori. "What is the meaning of this?" she asked. "If this were someone who had never been summoned before, it might be different. But surely she should be seated here with us. If not, I beg your permission to go where she is."

"That will not be necessary!" replied Kiyomori, and Hotoke was thus helpless to move.

Later, Kiyomori, apparently quite unaware of Giō's feelings, asked how she had been faring since they met last. "Lady Hotoke seems so terribly bored," he remarked. "You must sing us an *imayō*."

Having come this far, Giō did not feel that she could disregard the prime minister's wishes. And so holding back her tears, she sang the following song in the *imayō* style:

Buddha was once a common mortal,
and we too one day will become buddhas.
All alike endowed with the Buddha nature,
how sad this gulf that divides us!

Weeping all the while, she sang the song two more times. All the members of the Taira clan who were present, from the ministers of state, lords, and high-ranking courtiers down to the lowly samurai, were moved to tears. Kiyomori himself listened with keen interest. "A song admirably suited to the occasion," he commented. "I wish we could watch you dance, but unfortunately today there are other things to be attended to. In the future you must not wait to be summoned but come any time you like and perform your *imayō* songs and dances for Hotoke's amusement."

Giō made no answer but, suppressing her tears, withdrew.

Reluctant to disobey her mother's command, Giō had made the trip to the prime minister's mansion, painful as it was, and exposed herself a second time to callous treatment. Saddened by the experience and mindful that as long as she remained in this world similar sorrows likely awaited her, she turned her thoughts to suicide.

"If you do away with yourself," said her sister, Ginyo, "I will do likewise!"

Ordered by Kiyomori to return to his residence, Giō (*left*) appears and performs for Kiyomori and Lady Hotoke (*right*). (A 1656 Meireki woodblock edition, by permission of Shogakukan)

Learning of their intentions, their mother, alarmed, had no choice but to plead with Giō in tears. "You have every reason to be resentful," she said. "I forced you to go and thereby inflicted this pain, though I could hardly have known what would happen. But now, if you do away with yourself, your sister will follow your example, and if I lose both my daughters, then old and feeble as I am, I would do better to commit suicide myself rather than live alone. But by inducing a parent to carry out such an act before the destined time for death has come, you will be committing one of the Five Deadly Sins.[130] We are mere sojourners in this life and must suffer one humiliation after another, but these are nothing compared with the long night of suffering that may await us hereafter. Whatever this life may entail, think how frightful it would be if you should condemn yourself to rebirth in one of the evil paths of existence!"

Faced with these fervent entreaties, Giō, wiping back her tears, replied, "You are right. I would be guilty of one of the Five Deadly Sins. I will abandon any thought of self-destruction. But as long as I remain in the capital, I am likely to encounter further grief. My thought now is simply to leave the capital."

Thus at the age of twenty-two, Giō became a nun and, erecting a simple thatched retreat in a mountain village in the recesses of the Saga region,[131] she devoted herself to reciting the Buddha's name.

"I vowed that if you committed suicide, I would do likewise," said her sister, Ginyo. "If your plan now is to withdraw from the world, who would hesitate to follow your example?" Accordingly, at the age of nineteen she put on nun's attire and joined Giō in her retreat, devoting all her thoughts to the life to come.

Moved by the sight of them, their mother, Toji, observed, "In a world where my daughters, young as they are, have taken the tonsure, how could I, old woman that I am, cling to these gray hairs of mine?" Thus at the age of forty-five she shaved her head and, along with her two daughters, gave herself wholly to the recitation of Amida Buddha's name, mindful only of the life hereafter.

And so spring and the heat of summer passed, and as the autumn winds began to blow, the time came for the two star lovers to meet, the Herd Boy poling his boat across the River of Heaven, and people gazed up into the sky and wrote down their requests to them on leaves of the paper mulberry.[132]

As the nuns watched the evening sun sinking below the hills to the west, they thought to themselves that there, where the sun went down, was the Western

---

130. The Five Deadly Sins are killing one's father, killing one's mother, killing a Buddhist saint (*arhat*), injuring the body of a buddha, and harming the Buddhist ecclesiastical community.

131. Saga is an area to the immediate west of the capital.

132. The lovers, two stars known as the Herd Boy and the Weaving Maiden, are permitted to meet on only one night a year, when the Herd Boy crosses the River of Heaven, or the Milky Way, in his boat. Another version of the legend has him crossing over a bridge formed by sympathetic magpies. The occasion, known as Tanabata, takes place on the seventh night of the seventh lunar month, at which time celebrants write their wishes on leaves and dedicate them to the lovers.

Paradise of Amida. "One day we, too, will be reborn there and will no longer know these cares and sorrows," they said. Giving themselves up to melancholy thoughts of this kind, their tears never ceased flowing.

When the twilight hour had passed, they closed their door of plaited bamboo, lit the dim lamp, and all three, mother and daughters, began their invocation of the Buddha's name.

But just then they heard someone tap-tapping at the bamboo door. The nuns started up in alarm. "Has some meddling demon come to interrupt our devotions, ineffectual as they are?" they wondered. "Even in the daytime, no one calls on us in our thatched hut here in the remote hills. Who would come so late at night? Whoever it is can easily batter down the door without waiting for it to be opened, so we may as well open it. And if it should be some heartless creature come to take our lives, we must be firm in our faith in Amida's vow to save us and unceasingly call his holy name. He is certain to heed our call and come with his sacred host to greet us. And then surely he will guide us to his Western Paradise. Come, let us take heart and not delay pronouncing his name!"

When they had thus reassured one another and mustered the courage to open the bamboo door, they discovered that it was no demon at all but Lady Hotoke who stood before them.

"What do I see?" said Giō. "Lady Hotoke! Am I dreaming or awake?"

"If I tell you what has happened, I may seem merely to be making excuses," said Lady Hotoke, straining to hold back her tears. "But it would be too unkind to remain silent, and so I will start from the beginning. As you know, I was not originally summoned to the prime minister's house but went of my own accord, and if it had not been for your kind intervention, I would never have been admitted. We women are frail beings and cannot always do as we wish. I was far from happy when the prime minister detained me at his mansion, and then when you were summoned again and sang your *imayō* song, I felt more than ever the impossibility of my position. I could take no delight in it because I knew that sooner or later my turn would come to fall from favor. I felt it even more when I saw the poem you wrote on the sliding panel with its warning that 'come autumn, all alike must fade!'

"After that, I lost track of your whereabouts. But when I heard that you and your mother and sister all had entered religious life, I was overcome with envy. Again and again I asked the prime minister to release me from service, but he would not hear of it.

"What joy and delight we have in this world is no more than a dream within a dream, I told myself—what could such happiness mean to me? It is a rare thing to be born a human being and rarer still to discover the teachings of the Buddha. If because of my actions now I were to be reborn in hell or to spend endless aeons transmigrating through the other realms of existence, when would I ever find salvation? My youth could not be counted on, that I knew, for neither young nor old can tell when death may overtake them. One may breathe one instant and then not live to breathe the next: life is as fleeting as the shimmering heat of summer or a flash of lightning. To revel in a moment's happiness and not be heedful of the life to come would be a pitiful course of action indeed! So this morning I stole away from the prime minister's mansion and have come here."

With these words she threw off the cloak that she had around her. She had assumed a nun's tonsure and habit.

"I have come dressed in this fashion," she told them, "because I wish to ask pardon for my past offenses. If you say you can forgive me, I would like to join you in your devotions, and perhaps we may be reborn on a single lotus leaf in the Western Paradise. But if you cannot bring yourself to forgive me, I will make my way elsewhere. Wherever I may settle, on a bed of moss or by the roots of a pine tree, I will devote what life is left to me to reciting the Buddha's name, hoping, as I have done for so long, for rebirth in his paradise."

Near tears, Giō replied, "I never dreamed you felt this way. In a world of sadness, we all are, no doubt, fated to endure such trials. And yet I could not help envying you, and it seemed that such feelings of envy would prevent me from ever achieving the salvation I yearned for. I was in a mean and merely half-resolved frame of mind, one suitable for neither this life nor the life to come.

"But now that I see you dressed in this manner, these past failings of mine fall away like so much dust, and at last I am certain of gaining salvation. Hereafter, all my joy will be to strive for that long-cherished goal. The whole world was puzzled when my mother and sister and I became nuns, deeming it an unprecedented step, and we too wondered in a way, and yet we had good reasons for doing what we did. But what we did was nothing compared with what you have done! Barely turned seventeen, with neither hatred nor despair to spur you on, you have chosen to cast aside the world of defilement and turn all your thoughts toward the Pure Land. How fortunate we are to meet such a fine guide and teacher! Come, we will work toward our goal together!"

So the four women, sharing the same hut, morning and evening offered flowers and incense to the Buddha, all their thoughts on their devotions. And sooner or later, it is said, each of the four nuns attained what she had so long sought, rebirth in the Western Paradise.

Thus, on the curtain that lists the departed in the Eternal Lecture Hall founded by the retired emperor GoShirakawa are found, inscribed in one place, the names of the four: "The honored dead, Giō, Ginyo, Hotoke, Toji."

Theirs was a moving story.

The stability in the capital gradually breaks down. Disagreements erupt within the imperial family as well as among temple-shrine complexes. In addition, tensions between Kiyomori, head of the now ascendant Taira clan, and the imperial court, led by the retired emperor GoShirakawa, peak in the Shishi-no-tani incident, in which Narichika, a

Fujiwara courtier favored by GoShirakawa, becomes the principal conspirator in a plot to eliminate Kiyomori. He is joined by Shunkan, Yasuyori, and Saikō, a member of GoShirakawa's staff. A conflict breaks out between the court and Mount Hiei, a key Buddhist center, over a delayed court decision in which the warrior monks of Mount Hiei are routed. In 1177 a great conflagration consumes much of Kyoto and its cultural treasures.

Book Five

SHIGEHIRA (Taira): son of Kiyomori; leads punitive expedition against Nara.
YORITOMO (Minamoto): future leader of the Minamoto (Genji).
YOSHITOMO (Minamoto): father of Yoritomo.

Kiyomori moves the capital to Fukuhara, an isolated area west of the capital (near present-day Kobe), causing considerable hardship. The Taira, led by Koremori and Tadanori, gather troops and march against Yoritomo in the east. However, the Taira army, which has been put on edge by stories of the easterners' martial prowess, scatters in fear when a flock of birds suddenly takes flight at Fuji River. Kiyomori moves the capital back to its earlier location, which again causes havoc.

THE BURNING OF NARA (5:14)

In the capital, people were saying, "When Prince Takakura went to Onjō-ji, the monks of Kōfuku-ji in Nara not only expressed sympathy with his cause but even went to Onjō-ji to greet him. In doing so they showed themselves to be enemies of the state. Both Kōfuku-ji and Onjō-ji will surely be attacked!"

When rumors of this kind reached the monks of Kōfuku-ji, they rose up like angry hornets. Regent Fujiwara no Motomichi assured them that "if you have any sentiments you wish to convey to the throne, I will act as your intermediary on whatever number of occasions may be required." But such assurances had no effect whatsoever.

Motomichi dispatched Tadanori, the superintendent of the Kangaku-in, to act as his emissary, but the monks met him with wild clamor, shouting, "Drag the wretch from his carriage! Cut off his topknot!" Tadanori fled back to the capital, his face white with terror. Motomichi then sent Assistant Gate Guards Commander Chikamasa, but the monks greeted him in similar fashion, yelling, "Cut off his topknot!" He dropped everything and fled back to the capital. On that occasion, two lackeys from the Kangaku-in had their topknots cut off.

In addition, the Nara monks made a big ball, of the kind used in New Year's games, dubbed it "Prime Minister Kiyomori's head," and yelled, "Hit it! Stomp on it!" Easy talk is the midwife of disaster, and incautious action is the highway to ruin, people say.[133] This prime minister, Kiyomori, as the maternal grandfather of

---

133. This is a reference to *Chengui*, a Tang-period ethical text.

the reigning emperor, was someone to be spoken of with the utmost respect. It seemed as though only the Devil of the Sixth Heaven[134] could have inspired the Nara monks to use such language in referring to him.

When news of these events reached Prime Minister Kiyomori, he began making plans to deal with the situation. In order to bring an immediate halt to the unruly doings in Nara, he appointed Senoo Kaneyasu as the chief of police of Yamato Province, where Nara is situated, and sent him with a force of five hundred horsemen under his command. "Even if your opponents resort to violence, you must not retaliate in kind!" he warned the men when they set off. "Do not wear armor or helmets, and do not carry bows and arrows!"

But the Nara monks were not, of course, aware of Kiyomori's private instructions, and, seizing some sixty of Kaneyasu's men who had become separated from the main force, they cut off their heads and hung them in a row around the border of Sarusawa Pond.

Enraged at this, Kiyomori commanded, "Very well, then, attack Nara!"

He dispatched a force of more than forty thousand horsemen to carry out the attack, with Shigehira as commander in chief and Michimori as second in command. Meanwhile more than seven thousand monks, both old and young, had put on helmets and dug trenches across the road at two places, one at the slope called Narazaka and the other at Hannya-ji temple, and fortified them with barricades of shields and thorned branches. There they awaited the attackers.

The Heike, their forty thousand men split into two parties, swept down on the two fortified points at Narazaka and Hannya-ji, shouting their battle cries. All the monks were on foot and armed with swords. The government forces, being mounted, could thus charge back and forth among them, chasing some this way, driving others that, showering arrows down on them until countless numbers had been felled. The ceremonial exchange of arrows signaling the start of hostilities took place at six in the morning, and the battle continued throughout the day. By evening, both the fortified points at Narazaka and Hannya-ji had been captured. . . .

The fighting continued into the night. Darkness having fallen, the Heike commander in chief, Shigehira, who was standing in front of the gate of Hannya-ji temple, called for torches to be lit. A certain Tomokata, a minor overseer of the Fukui estate in Harima, broke his shield in two and, using it as a torch, set fire to one of the commoners' houses in the area. It was the twenty-eighth night of the Twelfth Month and a strong wind was blowing. Although only one fire had been set, it was blown by the wind this way and that until it had spread to many of the temples in the vicinity.

---

134. According to Buddhist cosmology, the Devil of the Sixth Heaven is the lord of the highest of the six realms of desire and, together with his followers, hinders people from adhering to Buddhism.

Monk soldiers and the Heike clash near Hannya-ji temple in Nara (*right*). The temples, which have been set on fire by the Heike, burn while the monk soldiers flee (*left*). (A 1656 Meireki woodblock edition, by permission of Shogakukan

By this time, those monks who were ashamed to be thought cowardly and who cared what kind of name they left behind them had died in the fighting at Narazaka or Hannya-ji. Those who could still use their legs fled in the direction of Mount Yoshino and Totsukawa. The older monks who were unable to walk any great distance, along with the special students in training at the temples, the aco-lytes, and the women and children all fled as fast as they could to Kōfuku-ji or Tōdai-ji, some thousand or more persons climbing up to the second story of the latter temple's Hall of the Great Buddha. To prevent any of their pursuers from reaching them, they then threw down the ladders by which they had ascended. When the flames from the fire came roaring down on them, their shrieks and cries could hardly have been surpassed by even those of the sinners being tor-tured in the Hell of Scorching Heat, the Great Hell of Scorching Heat, or the Hell of Never-Ceasing Torment.

Kōfuku-ji was founded at the behest of Lord Tankai, Fujiwara no Fuhito,[135] and thereafter served generation after generation as the temple of the Fujiwara clan. Its Eastern Gold Hall contained an image of Shakyamuni Buddha brought to Japan when Buddhist teachings were first introduced. The Western Gold Hall contained an image of the bodhisattva Kannon that, on its own accord,

---

135. By becoming the father of an empress, Fujiwara no Fuhito (659–720) was one of the first of his clan to rise to great power in the aristocracy.

had risen out of the earth. These, along with the corridors strung like emerald gems surrounding them on four sides, the two-story hall with its vermilion and cinnabar trimmings, the two pagodas with their nine-ring finials shining in the sky, all went up in smoke in the space of an instant.

In Tōdai-ji was enshrined the one-hundred-and-sixty-foot gilt-bronze image of the Buddha Vairochana—burnished by the hand and person of Emperor Shōmu[136] himself—the representation of the Buddha who abides eternally, never passing away, as he manifests his living body in the Land of Actual Reward and the Land of Eternally Tranquil Light. The protuberance on the top of his head towering on high, half-hidden in the clouds; the tuft of white hair between his eyebrows, an object of veneration:[137] this hallowed figure was as perfect as the full moon. Now amid the flames, the head fell to the ground, and the body melted and fused into one mountainlike mass. The eighty-four thousand auspicious marks of the Buddha were suddenly obscured like an autumn moon by the clouds of the Five Cardinal Sins; the garlands of jewels adorning the forty-two stages of bodhisattva practice were blown away like stars in the night sky by the winds of the Ten Evil Actions.[138] Smoke rose to blanket the sky, flames filled every corner of the empty air. Those who witnessed with their own eyes what was happening turned their gaze aside; those far off who heard reports of the disaster felt their spirits quail. All the doctrines and sacred writings of the Hossō and Sanron schools of Buddhism were lost, with not one scroll remaining.[139] Never before in India or China, it seemed, to say nothing of our land of Japan, had the Buddhist law suffered such terrible destruction.

King Udayana fashioned an image of fine gold, and Vishvakarman carved one out of red sandalwood, but these Buddha figures were merely life-size.[140] How could they compare with the Buddha of Tōdai-ji, unique and without equal anywhere in the entire continent of Jambudvipa in which we humans live? Yet this Buddha, who no one thought would ever suffer injury or decay whatever ages might pass, had now become mingled with and defiled by worldly dust, leaving behind only a legacy of unending sorrow. Brahma, Indra, the Four Heavenly Kings, the dragons, spirits, and others of the eight kinds of guardian beings, the wardens of the underworld, all those who lend divine protection to Buddhism must have looked on with alarm and consternation. The god Daimyō-jin of the nearby Kasuga Shrine, who guards and protects the Hossō sect—what

---

136. Emperor Shōmu (701–756, r. 724–749) was famous for his acts of Buddhist piety.

137. The protuberance and the tuft of hair are two of the thirty-two distinguishing marks of the body of the Buddha.

138. The Ten Evil Actions are killing, stealing, commiting adultery, lying, using duplicitous language, slandering, equivocating, coveting, becoming angry, and holding false views.

139. The Kōfuku-ji temple and the Tōdai-ji temple were centers for Hossō school and Sanron school studies, respectively.

140. According to Buddhist mythology, King Udayana was the creator of the first Buddhist statue. Vishvakarman is the patron god of artisans.

could he have thought? Little wonder, then, that the dew that fell on Kasuga meadow now had a different color, and the storm winds over Mount Mikasa sounded with a vengeful roar.

When the number of persons who perished in the flames was tallied up, it was found that more than seventeen hundred had died in the second story of the Hall of the Great Buddha, more than eight hundred at Kōfuku-ji, more than five hundred at this hall, more than three hundred at that hall—a total, in fact, of more than three thousand, five hundred persons. Of the thousand or more monks who died in the fighting, some had their heads cut off and exposed by the gate of Hannya-ji, while the heads of others were carried back to the capital.

On the twenty-ninth day of the month that the commander in chief, Taira no Shigehira, having destroyed the Southern Capital of Nara, returned to the Northern Capital of Heian, only Prime Minister Kiyomori, his anger now appeased, delighted in the outcome. But the empress, Retired Emperor GoShirakawa, Retired Emperor Takakura, Regent Motomichi, and the others below them in station all deplored what had happened, declaring, "It was one thing to punish the evil monks, but what need was there to destroy the temples?"

The heads of the monks killed in battle were originally intended to be paraded through the main streets of the capital and then hung on the tree in front of the prison, but those in charge were so shocked at the destruction of Tōdaiji and Kōfuku-ji that these orders were never issued. Instead, the heads were simply discarded here and there in the moats and drainage ditches.

In a document written in his own hand, Emperor Shōmu had declared, "When these temples prosper, the entire realm shall prosper. When these temples fall to ruin, the realm, too, shall fall into ruin." It thus appeared that without doubt these events must presage the downfall and ruin of the nation.

Thus this terrible year [1180] came to an end, and the fifth year of the Jishō era began.

Book Six

GoShirakawa: retired emperor and head of the imperial clan.
Kiyomori (Taira): lay priest, prime minister, and retired Taira clan head.
Munemori (Taira): son of Kiyomori and Taira clan head.
Nun of the Second Rank (Taira): wife of Kiyomori.
Yoritomo (Minamoto): leader of the anti-Taira forces in the east.
Yoshinaka (Minamoto): cousin of Yoritomo and leader of the anti-Taira forces in the north; also called Lord Kiso.

The New Year's ceremonies are shortened and do not have their normal luster owing to the burning of Nara. The gloom is deepened by the death of Retired Emperor Takakura.

Yoshinaka of Kiso, working to overthrow the Taira, begins to gather allies in the north. The Taira's rule continues to weaken, and rebellions break out in Kyushu, Shikoku, and elsewhere.

THE DEATH OF KIYOMORI (6:7)

After this, all the warriors of the island of Shikoku went over to the side of Kōno no Michinobu. Reports also came that Tanzō, the superintendent of the Kumano Shrine, had shifted his sympathies to the Genji side, despite the many kindnesses shown him by the Heike. All the provinces in the north and the east were thus rebelling against the Taira, and in the regions to the west and southwest of the capital the situation was the same. Report after report of uprisings in the outlying areas came to startle the ears of the Heike, and word repeatedly reached them of additional impending acts of rebellion. It seemed as though the "barbarian tribes to the east and west"[141] had suddenly risen up against them. The members of the Taira clan were not alone in thinking that the end of the world was close at hand. No truly thoughtful person could fail to dread the ominous turn of events.

On the twenty-third day of the Second Month, a council of the senior Taira nobles was convened. At that time Lord Munemori, a former general of the right, spoke as follows: "We earlier tried to put down the rebels in the east, but the results were not all that we might have desired. This time I would like to be appointed commander in chief to move against them."

"What a splendid idea!" the other nobles exclaimed in obsequious assent. A directive was accordingly handed down from the retired emperor appointing Lord Munemori commander in chief of an expedition against the traitorous elements in the eastern and northern provinces. All the high ministers and courtiers who held military posts or were experienced in the use of arms were ordered to follow him.

When word had already gotten abroad that Lord Munemori would set out on his mission to put down the Genji forces in the eastern provinces on the twenty-seventh day of the same month, his departure was canceled because of reports that Kiyomori, the lay priest and prime minister, was not in his customary good health.

On the following day, the twenty-eighth, it became known that Kiyomori was seriously ill, and people throughout the capital and at Rokuhara whispered to one another, "This is just what we were afraid of!"

From the first day that Kiyomori took sick, he was unable to swallow anything, not even water. His body was as hot as though there were a fire burning inside it: those who attended him could scarcely come within twenty-five or

---

141. A phrase used in China to refer to provinces in all four directions.

thirty feet of him so great was the heat. All he could do was cry out, "I'm burning! I'm burning!" His affliction seemed quite unlike any ordinary illness.

Water from the Well of the Thousand-Arm Kannon on Mount Hiei was brought to the capital and poured into a stone bathtub, and Kiyomori's body was lowered into it in hopes of cooling him. But the water began to bubble and boil furiously and, in a moment, had all gone up in steam. In another attempt to bring him some relief, wooden pipes were rigged in order to pour streams of water down on his body, but the water sizzled and sputtered as though it were landing on fiery rocks or metal, and virtually none of it reached his body. The little that did so burst into flames and burned, filling the room with black smoke and sending flames whirling upward.

Long ago, the eminent Buddhist priest Hōzō was said to have been invited by Enma, the king of hell, to visit the infernal regions. At that time he asked if he might see the place where his deceased mother had been reborn. Admiring his filial concern, Enma directed the hell wardens to conduct him to the Hell of Scorching Heat, where Hōzō's mother was undergoing punishment. When Hōzō entered the iron gates of the hell, he saw flames leaping up like shooting stars, ascending hundreds of yojanas into the air. The sight must have been much like what those attending Kiyomori in his sickness now witnessed.

Kiyomori's wife, the Nun of the Second Rank, had a most fearful dream. It seemed that a carriage enveloped in raging flames had entered the gate of the mansion. Stationed at the front and rear of the carriage were creatures, some with the head of a horse, others with the head of an ox. To the front of the carriage was fastened an iron plaque inscribed with the single word *mu*, "never."

In her dream the Nun of the Second Rank asked, "Where has this carriage come from?"

"From the tribunal of King Enma," was the reply. "It has come to fetch His Lordship, the lay priest and prime minister of the Taira clan."

"And what does the plaque mean?" she asked.

"It means that because of the crime of burning the one-hundred-and-sixty-foot gilt-bronze image of the Buddha Vairochana[142] in the realm of human beings, King Enma's tribunal has decreed that the perpetrator shall fall into the depths of the Hell of Never-Ceasing Torment. The 'Never' of Never-Ceasing is written on it; the 'Ceasing' remains to be written."

The Nun of the Second Rank woke from her dream in alarm, her body bathed in perspiration, and when she told others of her dream, their hair stood on end just hearing about it. She made offerings of gold, silver, and the seven precious objects to all the temples and shrines reputed to have power in such matters, even adding such items as horses, saddles, armor, helmets, bows, arrows, long swords, and short swords. But no matter how much she added as accompaniment to her supplications, they were wholly without effect. Kiyomori's sons and daughters

---

142. This refers to the Great Buddha of the Tōdai-ji Temple.

gathered by his pillow and bedside, inquiring in anguish if there were something that could be done, but all their cries were in vain.

On the second day of the second intercalary month, the Nun of the Second
Rank, braving the formidable heat, approached her husband's pillow and spoke
through her tears. "With each day that passes, it seems to me, there is less hope
for your recovery. If you have anything you wish to say before you depart this
world, it would be good to speak now while your mind is still clear."

In earlier days the prime minister had always been brusque and forceful
in manner, but now, tormented by pain, he had barely breath enough to utter
these words. "Ever since the Hōgen and Heiji uprisings, I have on numerous
occasions put down those who showed themselves enemies of the throne, and I
have received rewards and acclaim far surpassing what I deserve. I have had the
honor to become the grandfather of a reigning emperor and to hold the office of
prime minister, and the bounties showered on me extend to my sons and grandsons. There is nothing more whatsoever that I could wish for in this life. Only
one regret remains to me—that I have yet to behold the severed head of that
exile to the province of Izu, Minamoto no Yoritomo! When I have ceased to be,
erect no temples or pagodas in my honor, conduct no memorial rites for me!
But dispatch forces at once to strike at Yoritomo, cut off his head, and hang
it before my grave—that is all the ceremony that I ask!" Such were the deeply
sinful words that he spoke!

On the fourth day of the same month, the illness continuing to torment
him, Kiyomori's attendants thought to provide some slight relief by pouring
water over a board and laying him on it, but this appeared to do no good whatsoever. Moaning in desperation, he fell to the floor and there suffered his final
agonies. The sound of horses and carriages rushing about seemed to echo to the
heavens and to make the very earth tremble. Even if the sovereign of the realm
himself, the lord of ten thousand chariots, had passed away, there could not
have been a greater commotion.

Kiyomori had turned sixty-four this year. He thus was not particularly advanced in age. But the life span decreed him by his actions in previous exis-
tences had abruptly come to an end. Hence the large-scale ceremonies and secret ceremonies performed on his behalf by the Buddhist priests failed to have
any effect; the gods and the Three Treasures of Buddhism[143] ceased to shed
their light on him; and the benevolent deities withdrew their guardianship.

And if even divine help was beyond his reach, how little could mere human
beings do! Although tens of thousands of loyal troops stationed themselves inside his mansion and in the grounds around it, all eager to sacrifice themselves
and to die in his place, they could not, even for an instant, hold at bay the

---

143. The Three Treasures of Buddhism are the Buddha, the Buddhist law, and the community of Buddhist priests.

deadly devil of impermanence, whose form is invisible to the eye and whose power is invincible. Kiyomori went all alone to the Shide Mountains of death, from which there is no return; alone he faced the sky on his journey over the River of Three Crossings to the land of the Yellow Springs. And when he arrived there, only the evil deeds he had committed in past days, transformed now into hell wardens, were there to greet him. All in all, it was a pitiful business.

Since further action could not be postponed, on the seventh day of the same month Kiyomori's remains were cremated at Otagi in the capital.[144] The Buddhist priest Enjitsu placed the ashes in a bag hung around his neck and journeyed with them down to the province of Settsu, where he deposited them in a grave on Sutra Island.

Kiyomori's name had been known throughout the land of Japan, and his might had set men trembling. But in the end his body was no more than a puff of smoke ascending in the sky above the capital, and his remains, after tarrying a little while, in time mingled with the sands of the shore where they were buried, dwindling at last into empty dust.

The Taira are able to beat back a Minamoto advance but cannot press the attack into the Minamoto strongholds in the east. Several obvious signs—the death of the leader of a Taira campaign, the deaths of priests praying for Taira victory and prosperity—foreshadow defeat for the Taira. Nevertheless, Munemori, the leader of the Taira clan and commander in chief of their armies, spends his time solidifying his position in the court bureaucracy.

Book Seven

The Taira summon warriors from all the provinces, but those who gather are mainly from the west. This army goes north to attack Yoshinaka and his troops. Yoshinaka traps and crushes the Taira army at both Kurikara Valley and Shinohara. Sanemori, an elderly Taira vassal, had pledged to die fighting during the battle at Shinohara.

TADANORI LEAVES THE CAPITAL (7:16)

Taira no Tadanori, the governor of Satsuma, returned once more to the capital, although where he had been in the meantime is uncertain. Accompanied by five mounted warriors and a page, a party of seven horsemen in all, he rode along Gojō Avenue to the residence of Fujiwara no Shunzei.[145] The gate of Shunzei's mansion was closed and showed little sign of opening.

When Tadanori announced his name, there was a bustle inside the gate, and voices called out, "Those men who fled from the city have come back!" Tadanori

---

144. Otagi is a famous crematorium and cemetery in the eastern part of Kyoto.
145. Fujiwara no Shunzei (1114–1204) was a famous poet, scholar, and judge of waka contests.

dismounted from his horse and spoke in a loud voice. "There is no cause for alarm. I have come back merely because I have something I would like to say to His Lordship. You need not open the gate—if you could just have him come here a moment. . . ."

"I was expecting this," said Shunzei. "I'm sure he won't make any trouble—let him in."

The gate was opened and Shunzei confronted his caller, whose whole bearing conveyed an air of melancholy.

"You have been good enough to give me instruction for some years," said Tadanori, "and I hope I have not been entirely unworthy of your kindness. But the disturbances in the capital in the last two or three years and the uprisings in the provinces have deeply affected all the members of my clan. Although I have not intended in any way to neglect my poetry studies, I fear I have not been as attentive to you as I should have been.

"The emperor has already left the capital, and the fortunes of my family appear to have run out. I heard some time ago that you were going to compile an anthology of poetry at the request of the retired emperor. I had hoped that, if you would be so kind as to give your assent, I might have perhaps one poem included in it in fulfillment of my lifelong hopes. But then these disorders descended on the world and the matter of the anthology had to be put aside, a fact that grieves me deeply.

"Should the state of the world become somewhat more settled, perhaps work on the anthology can be begun. I have here a scroll of poems. If in your kindness you could find even one of them to be worthy of inclusion, I will continue to rejoice long after I have gone to my grave and will forever be your guardian in the world beyond."

Reaching through the opening in his armor, Tadanori took out a scroll of poems and presented it to Lord Shunzei. From among the poems he had composed in recent years, he had selected some hundred or so that he thought were of superior quality and had brought them with him now that he was about to take final leave of the capital.

As Shunzei opened the scroll and looked at it, he said, "Since you see fit to leave me with this precious memento of your work, you may rest assured that I will not treat it lightly. Please have no doubts on that score. And that you should present it to me now, as a token of your deep concern for the art of poetry, makes the gesture more moving than ever—so much so that I can scarcely hold back the tears!"

Overjoyed at this response, Tadanori replied, "Perhaps I will find rest beneath the waves of the western ocean; perhaps my bones will be left to bleach on the mountain plain. Whatever may come, I can now take leave of this uncertain world without the least regret. And so I say good-bye!"

With these words he mounted his horse, knotted the cords of his helmet, and rode off toward the west. Shunzei stood gazing after until the figure had receded far into the distance. And then it seemed that he could hear Tadanori reciting in a voice loud enough to be heard from afar:

> Long is the journey before me—my thoughts race
> with the evening clouds over Wild Goose Mountain.

Deeply grieved at the parting, Shunzei wiped back the tears as he turned to reenter his house.

Later, after peace had been restored and Shunzei had begun compiling the anthology known as the *Senzaishū* [*The Collection of a Thousand Years*],[146] he recalled with deep emotion his farewell meeting with Tadanori and the words that the latter had spoken on that occasion. Among the poems that Tadanori had left behind were several that might have been included in the anthology. But since the anthology was being compiled by imperial command, Shunzei did not feel that he could refer to Tadanori by name. Instead, he selected one poem entitled "Blossoms in the Old Capital" and included it with the notation "author unknown." The poem read:

> In ruins now, the old capital of Shiga by the waves,
> yet the wild cherries of Nagara still bloom as before.

Because Tadanori was among those branded as enemies of the sovereign, perhaps less might have been said about him. And yet there is great pathos in his story.

Book Eight

Retired Emperor GoShirakawa chooses his fourth son to be the new crown prince and installs him as emperor, a rival to the Taira's sovereign, Antoku. No longer able to muster an army, the Taira are forced to take to the sea. Yoritomo is appointed shogun by Emperor GoShirakawa and subsequently requests an order to subjugate Yoshinaka, whose men have been plundering the capital. After Yoshinaka commits other excesses, Yoritomo is given permission to move against him and sends an army westward under the command of his brother Yoshitsune.

Book Nine

KANEHIRA (Imai): retainer of Yoshinaka and son of his wet nurse.
KUMAGAE NAOZANE (Minamoto): warrior.
MUNEMORI (Taira): son of Kiyomori and Taira clan head.
NORITSUNE (Taira): nephew of Kiyomori.
SHIGEHIRA (Taira): son of Kiyomori; accused of the crime of burning Nara.

---

146. *Senzaishū* (1187) is the seventh imperial waka collection, edited by Shunzei.

TADANORI (Taira): brother of Kiyomori, warrior, and avid poet.

YOSHINAKA (Minamoto): commander who defeats the Taira but is later attacked by Yoritomo; also called Lord Kiso.

YOSHITSUNE (Minamoto): half brother of Yoritomo; sent to the capital to destroy Yoshinaka.

Yoshitsune's punitive army arrives just as Yoshinaka's forces are at their weakest. Yoshinaka tries to set up defensive positions at Seta and Uji, outside the capital, but Yoshitsune is able to enter the capital and rescue Emperor GoShirakawa. Yoshinaka, who had earlier entered the capital with fifty thousand warriors, is forced to flee on horseback with six other riders.

THE DEATH OF LORD KISO (9:4)

Lord Kiso had brought with him from Shinano two women attendants, Tomoe and Yamabuki. Yamabuki had remained in the capital because of illness. Of these two, Tomoe, fair complexioned and with long hair, was of exceptional beauty. As a fighter she was a match for a thousand ordinary men, skilled in arms, able to bend the stoutest bow, on horseback or on foot, ever ready with her sword to confront any devil or god that came her way. She could manage the most unruly horse and gallop down the steepest slopes. Lord Kiso sent her into battle clad in finely meshed armor and equipped with a sword of unusual size and a powerful bow, depending on her to perform as one of his leading commanders. Again and again she emerged unrivaled in feats of valor. And this time too, even though so many of Lord Kiso's other riders had fled from his side or been struck down, Tomoe was among the six who remained with him.

Certain reports claimed that Yoshinaka was heading toward Tanba by way of Long Slope; others, that he had crossed over Ryūge Pass and was proceeding to the northern provinces. In fact he was fleeing west toward Seta, anxious to discover where Imai Kanehira and his men were. Meanwhile, Imai had been defending his position at Seta with the eight hundred or more men under him. But when his forces had been reduced by fighting to a mere fifty riders, he furled his banners and started back toward the capital, thinking that his superior in command, Yoshinaka, must be wondering about him. In Ōtsu, at a place on the Lake Biwa shore called Uchide, he met up with Lord Kiso as the latter was headed west.

While still some distance apart, Lord Kiso and Imai recognized each other and spurred their horses forward in anticipation of the meeting. Seizing Imai's hand, Lord Kiso exclaimed, "I had intended to die in the fighting in the riverbed at Rokujō, but I wanted so much to find out what had become of you. That's why I dodged my way through all those enemy troops and slipped off so I could come here!"

"Your words do me great honor," replied Imai. "I, too, had fully expected to die in the encounter at Seta, but I hastened here in hopes of finding out how you were faring."

"The bonds that link us have not come to an end yet!" said Lord Kiso. "My own forces have been broken up and scattered by the enemy, but they have most likely taken shelter in the hills and woods hereabouts and are still in the vicinity. Unfurl those banners you are carrying and raise them high!"

When Imai hoisted the banners, more than three hundred friendly horsemen, spotting them, gathered around, some having escaped from the capital, others from the troops that had fled from Seta.

Yoshinaka was overjoyed. "With a force this size, there's no reason we can't fight one last battle!" he said. "Whose men are those I see massed there in the distance?"

"I believe they're under the command of Lord Ichijō Tadayori of Kai."

"How many men would you say there are?"

"Some six thousand or more, I would judge."

"They will make an excellent opponent. If we are to die in any case, let's confront a worthy foe and meet death in the midst of a great army!" With these words, he spurred his horse forward.

That day Yoshinaka was wearing a red brocade battle robe and a suit of finely laced armor. He had a horned helmet on his head and carried a sword of forbidding size. On his back was a quiver containing the arrows left from the day's fighting, fledged with eagle tail-feathers, their tips projecting above his head, and in his hand he grasped a bow bound with rattan. He rode his famed horse Oniashige or Demon Roan, a powerful beast of brawny build, and was seated in a gold-rimmed saddle.

Raising himself up in his stirrups, he called out his name in a loud voice. "From times past you've heard of him: Kiso no Kanja. Now take a look at him! Minamoto no Yoshinaka, director of the Imperial Stables of the Left, governor of Iyo, the Rising Sun Commander! And you, I hear, are Ichijō of Kai. We are well matched. Come attack me and show that man in Kamakura—Yoritomo— what you can do!" Shouting these words, he galloped forward.

Ichijō of Kai addressed his troops. "The one who just spoke is the commander. Don't let him get away, men! After him, you young fellows! Attack!" Vastly superior in number, Ichijō's troops surrounded Yoshinaka, each man eager to be the first to get at him.

Encircled by more than six thousand enemy horsemen, Yoshinaka's three hundred galloped forward and backward, left and right, employing the spider-leg formation and the cross-formation in their efforts to escape from the circle. When they finally succeeded in breaking through to the rear, only fifty of them were left.

Free at last, they then found their path blocked by more than two thousand horsemen under the command of Toi no Jirō Sanehira. Battling their way through them, they confronted four or five hundred of the enemy here, two or three hundred there, a hundred and fifty in another place, a hundred in still another, dashing this way and that until only five riders, Yoshinaka and four of his followers, remained. Tomoe, still uninjured, was among the five.

Lord Kiso turned to her. "Hurry, hurry now! You're a woman—go away, anywhere you like!" he said. "I intend to die in the fighting. And if it looks as though I'm about to be captured, I'll take my own life. But I wouldn't want it said that Lord Kiso fought his last battle in the company of a woman!"

But Tomoe did not move. When Lord Kiso continued to press her, she thought to herself, "Ah! If only I had a worthy opponent so I could show him one last time what I can do in battle!"

While she was hesitating, they encountered thirty horsemen under the command of Onda no Moroshige, a warrior of the province of Musashi who was renowned for his strength. Tomoe charged into the midst of Onda's men, drew her horse up beside his, and, abruptly dragging him from his seat, pressed his head against the pommel of her saddle. After holding him motionless for a moment, she wrenched off his head and threw it away. Then she threw off her helmet and armor and fled somewhere in the direction of the eastern provinces.

Of the other remaining horsemen, Tezuka Tarō was killed in the combat and Tezuka no Bettō fled. Only two men, Lord Kiso and Imai, remained.

"Up until now I never gave a thought to my armor, but today it seems strangely heavy!" said Lord Kiso.

"You can't be tired yet, my lord," said Imai, "and your horse is in good shape. A few pounds of choice armor could not weigh on you that heavily. It's just that your spirits are flagging because we have so few men left. You still have me, though, and you should think of me as a thousand men. I still have seven or eight arrows, and I'll use them to keep the enemy at bay. Those trees you see there in the distance are the pine groves of Awazu. Go over among those trees and make an end of things!"

As they spurred their horses onward, they spied a new group of some fifty mounted warriors heading toward them. "Hurry over to that grove of pines! I'll hold off these men!" he repeated.

"I ought to have died in the fighting in the capital," said Lord Kiso, "but I've come this far because I wanted to die with you. Rather than dying one here and the other there, it's better that we die together!"

When Lord Kiso insisted on galloping at his side, Imai leaped to the ground, seized the bit of Lord Kiso's horse, and declared, "No matter how fine a name a warrior may make for himself at most times, if he should slip up at the last, it could mean an everlasting blot on his honor. You are tired and we have no more men to fight with us. Suppose we become separated in combat and you are surrounded and cut down by a mere retainer, a person of no worth at all! How terrible if people were to say, 'Lord Kiso, famous throughout the whole of Japan—done in by so-and-so's retainer!' You must hurry to that grove of pines!"

"If it must be—" said Lord Kiso, and he turned his horse in the direction of the Awazu pines.

Imai, alone, charged into the midst of the fifty enemy horsemen. Rising up in his stirrups, he shouted in a loud voice, "Up to now you've heard reports of me—now take a look with your own eyes! Imai no Shirō Kanehira, foster brother of Lord Kiso, thirty-three years of age. Even the lord of Kamakura has heard of me. Come cut me down and show him my head!"

Then, fitting his eight remaining arrows to his bow in rapid succession, he sent them flying. With no thought for his own safety, he proceeded to shoot down eight of the enemy riders. Then, drawing his sword, he charged now this way, now that, felling all who came within reach of his weapon, so that no one dared to face him. He took many trophies in the process. His attackers encircled him with cries of "Shoot him! Shoot him!" But although the arrows fell like rain, they could not pierce his stout armor or find any opening to get through, and so he remained uninjured.

Meanwhile, Lord Kiso galloped off alone toward the Awazu pine grove. It was the twenty-first day of the first lunar month, and evening was approaching. The winter rice paddies were covered with a thin layer of ice, and Lord Kiso, unaware of how deep the water was, allowed his horse to stumble into one of them. In no time the horse had sunk into the mud until its head could not be seen. He dug in with his stirrups again and again, laid on lash after lash with his whip, but could not get the animal to move.

Wondering what had become of Imai, he turned to look behind him, when one of the enemy riders who had been pursuing him, Ishida Tamehisa of Miura, drew his bow far back and shot an arrow that pierced the area of Lord Kiso's face unprotected by his helmet. Mortally wounded, he slumped forward, the bowl of his helmet resting on the horse's head, whereupon two of Ishida's retainers fell on him and cut off his head. Ishida impaled the head on the tip of his sword and, raising it high in the air, shouted, "Lord Kiso, famed these days throughout all of Japan, has been killed by Ishida no Jirō Tamehisa of Miura!"

Although Imai had continued to battle the enemy, when he heard this, he asked, "Who is left now to go on fighting for? You lords of the eastern provinces, I'll show you how the bravest man in all Japan takes his life!" Then he thrust the tip of his sword into his mouth and flung himself down from his horse in such a way that the sword passed through his body, and so he died. Thus there was no real battle at Awazu.

As the Genji fight among themselves, the Taira return to the old capital at Fukuhara and establish a stronghold at Ichi-no-tani near the shore (of what is now the city of Kobe), protected to the north by steep mountains and to the south by the Inland Sea.

Yoshitsune prepares to attack, but the Taira's position at Ichi-no-tani seems impervious to a direct assault.

THE DEATH OF ATSUMORI (9:16)

The Heike had lost the battle. "Those Taira lords will be heading for the shore in hopes of making their getaway by boat!" thought Kumagae Naozane to himself. "Fine! I'll go look for one of their generals to grapple with!" and he turned his horse in the direction of the beach.

As he did so, he spotted a lone warrior riding into the sea, making for the boats in the offing. He was wearing a battle robe of finely woven silk embroidered in a crane design, armor of light green lacing, and a horned helmet. He carried a sword with gilt fittings and a quiver whose arrows were fledged with black and white eagle feathers and held a rattan-wound bow in his hand. He was seated in a gold-rimmed saddle, astride a gray horse with white markings.

The lone warrior's horse had swum out about two hundred feet from the shore when Kumagae, waving with his fan, called out, "Ho there, General! I see you. Don't shame yourself by showing your back to an enemy. Come back!"

The rider, acknowledging the call, turned toward the beach. As he was about to ride up out of the waves, Kumagae drew alongside and grappled with him, dragging him from his horse. Pinning him down so as to cut off his head, Kumagae pushed aside his helmet. The face he saw was that of a young man of sixteen or seventeen, lightly powdered and with blackened teeth.

Gazing at the boy's handsome face, Kumagae realized that he was just the age of his own son Kojirō, and he could not bring himself to use his sword. "Who are you? Tell me your name and I'll let you go!" he said.

"Who are you?" asked the young man.

"No one of great importance—Kumagae Naozane of the province of Musashi."

"Then there's no need for me to tell you my name," the young man replied. "I'm worthy enough to be your opponent. When you take my head, ask someone who I am—they will know all right!"

"Spoken like a true general!" thought Kumagae. "But simply killing this one man can't change defeat into victory or victory into defeat. When my son Kojirō has even a slight injury, how much I worry about him! Just think how this boy's father will grieve when he hears that he's been killed! If only I could spare him."

But as he glanced quickly behind him, he saw some fifty Genji horsemen under Toi and Kajiwara coming toward him. Fighting back the tears, he said, "I'd like to let you go, but our forces are everywhere in sight—you could never get away. Rather than fall into someone else's hands, it's better that I kill you. I'll see that prayers are said for your salvation in the life to come."

"Just take my head and be quick about it!" the boy said.

Kumagae was so overcome with pity that he did not know where to strike. His eyes seemed to dim, his wits to desert him, and for a moment he hardly knew where he was. But then he realized that, for all his tears, no choice was left him, and he struck off the boy's head.

"We men who bear arms—how wretched is our lot!" he said. "If I had not been born of a warrior family, would I ever have faced a task like this? What a terrible thing I have done!" Again and again, he repeated the words as he raised his sleeve to brush the tears from his face.

After some time, aware that he must get on with the business, he removed the boy's armor and battle robe and wrapped the head in them. As he was doing so, he noticed a brocade bag with a flute in it that had been fastened to the boy's waist. "Ah, how pitiful!" he said. "Those people I heard at dawn this morning playing music in the enemy stronghold—he must have been one of them! Among all the ten thousand troops from the eastern provinces fighting on our side, is there anyone who carries a flute with him into battle? These highborn people—how gentle and refined they are!"

Later, when Kumagae's battle trophies were presented to Yoshitsune for inspection, there were none among the company who did not weep at the sight.

It was subsequently learned that the young man slain by Kumagae was Atsumori, the seventeen-year-old son of the master of the Palace Repair Office, Taira no Tsunemori. From that time onward, Kumagae's desire to become a Buddhist monk grew even stronger. The flute in question had been presented by Retired Emperor Toba to Atsumori's grandfather, Tadamori, who was a skilled player. From him it had been passed down to the son, Tsunemori, and in turn had been given to Atsumori because of his marked aptitude for the instrument. It was known by the name Saeda, Little Branch.

It is moving to think that for all their exaggerated phrases and flowery embellishments, even music and the arts can in the end lead a man to praise the Buddha's way.

After a resounding defeat, the Taira forces scatter in their attempt to flee by sea.

Book Eleven

ANTOKU: emperor and son of Emperor Takakura and Kenreimon'in.

GOSHIRAKAWA: retired emperor and head of the imperial clan.

KAGETOKI (Kajiwara): deputy commander of Minamoto forces and rival of Yoshitsune.

KENREIMON'IN (Taira): daughter of Kiyomori and Nun of the Second Rank.

MUNEMORI (Taira): son of Kiyomori, Taira clan head, and leader of the Taira forces at Yashima.

NUN OF THE SECOND RANK (Taira): widow of Kiyomori and grandmother of Emperor Antoku.

YOSHITSUNE (Minamoto): younger half brother of Yoritomo and leader of the Genji forces at Yashima and Dan-no-ura.

After landing with a small force on the island of Shikoku, Yoshitsune leads his Genji troops to the rear of the Taira camp at Yashima, where the Taira have set up their head-quarters. With a small force, he manages to bluff the Taira, led by Munemori, into re-treating to their boats. The tide finally turns against the Taira at the sea battle at Dan-no-ura, on the western tip of the Inland Sea.

THE DROWNING OF THE FORMER EMPEROR (11:9)

By this time the Genji warriors had succeeded in boarding the Heike boats, shooting dead the sailors and helmsmen with their arrows or cutting them down with their swords. The bodies lay heaped in the bottom of the boats, and there was no longer anyone to keep the boats on course.

Taira no Tomomori boarded a small craft and made his way to the vessel in which the former emperor was riding. "This is what the world has come to!" he exclaimed. "Have all these unsightly things thrown into the sea!" Then he began racing from prow to stern, sweeping, mopping, dusting, and attempting with his own hands to put the boat into proper order.

"How goes the battle, Lord Tomomori?" asked the emperor's ladies-in-waiting, pressing him with questions.

"You'll have a chance to see some splendid gentlemen from the eastern region!" he replied with a cackling laugh.

"How can you joke at a time like this!" they protested, their voices joined in a chorus of shrieks and wails.

Observing the situation and evidently having been prepared for some time for such an eventuality, the Nun of the Second Rank, the emperor's grand-mother, slipped a two-layer nun's robe over her head and tied her glossed silk trousers high at the waist. She placed the sacred jewel, one of the three imperial regalia, under her arm, thrust the sacred sword in her sash, and took the child emperor in her arms. "I may be a mere woman, but I have no intention of fall-ing into the hands of the enemy! I will accompany my lord. All those of you who are resolved to fulfill your duty by doing likewise, quickly follow me!" So saying, she strode to the side of the boat.

The emperor had barely turned eight but had the bearing of someone much older than that. The beauty of his face and form seemed to radiate all around him. His shimmering black hair fell down the length of his back.

Startled and confused, he asked, "Grandma, where are you going to take me?"

Gazing at his innocent face and struggling to hold back her tears, the nun replied, "Don't you understand? In your previous life you were careful to observe the ten good rules of conduct, and for that reason you were reborn in this life as a ruler of ten thousand chariots. But now evil entanglements have you in their power, and your days of good fortune have come to an end.

"First," she told him tearfully, "you must face east and bid farewell to the goddess of the Grand Shrine at Ise. Then you must turn west and trust in Amida Buddha to come with his hosts to greet you and lead you to his Pure Land. Come now, turn your face to the west and recite the invocation of the Buddha's name. This far-off land of ours is no bigger than a millet seed, a realm of sorrow and adversity. Let us leave it now and go together to a place of rejoicing, the paradise of the Pure Land!"

Dressed in a dove gray robe, his hair now done in boyish loops on either side of his head, the child, his face bathed in tears, pressed his small hands together, knelt down, and bowed first toward the east, taking his leave of the deity of the Ise Shrine. Then he turned toward the west and began chanting the *nenbutsu*, the invocation of Amida's name. The nun then took him in her arms. Comforting him, she said, "There's another capital down there beneath the waves!" So they plunged to the bottom of the thousand-fathom sea.

How pitiful that the spring winds of impermanence should so abruptly scatter the beauty of the blossoms; how heartless that the rough waves of reincarnation should engulf this tender body! Long Life is the name they give to the imperial palace, signaling that one should reside there for years unending; its gates are dubbed Ageless, a term that speaks of a reign forever young. Yet before he had reached the age of ten, this ruler ended as refuse on the ocean floor.

Ten past virtues rewarded with a throne, yet how fleeting was that prize! He who once was a dragon among the clouds now had become a fish in the depths of the sea. Dwelling once on terraces lofty as those of the god Brahma, in palaces like the Joyful Sight Citadel of the god Indra, surrounded by great lords and ministers of state, a throng of kin and clansmen in his following, now in an instant he ended his life beneath this boat, under these billows—sad, sad indeed!

Yoshitsune returns to the capital with the imperial regalia and the Heike prisoners. The praise and awards showered on him arouse the suspicions of Yoritomo, and the situation is exacerbated when Kajiwara Kagetoki slanders Yoshitsune. Meanwhile, Munemori and his son, as well as Shigehira and other leading members of the Taira family, are executed.

The Initiates' Book

GOSHIRAKAWA: retired emperor, head of the imperial clan, and paternal grandfather of Emperor Antoku.

KENREIMON'IN (Taira): daughter of Kiyomori, consort of Emperor Takakura, and mother of the deceased emperor Antoku; taken prisoner at Dan-no-ura.

THE MOVE TO ŌHARA

. . . The place where Kenreimon'in was living was not far from the capital, and the bustling road leading past it was full of prying eyes. She could not help feeling that fragile as her existence might be, mere dew before the wind, she might better live it out in some more remote mountain setting where distressing news of worldly affairs was less likely to reach her. She had been unable to find a suitable location, however, when a certain lady who had called on her mentioned that the Buddhist retreat known as Jakkō-in in the mountains of Ōhara was a very quiet spot.

A mountain village may be lonely, she thought to herself, recalling an old poem on the subject, but it is a better place to dwell than among the world's troubles and sorrows. Having thus determined to move, she found that her sister, the wife of Lord Takafusa, could probably arrange for a palanquin and other necessities. Accordingly, in the first year of the Bunji era, as the Ninth Month was drawing to a close, she set off for the Jakkō-in in Ōhara.

As Kenreimon'in passed along the road, observing the hues of the autumn leaves on the trees all around her, she soon found the day coming to a close, perhaps all the sooner because she was entering the shade of the mountains. The tolling of the evening bell from a temple in the fields sounded its somber note, and dew from the grasses along the way made her sleeves, already damp with tears, wetter than ever. A stormy wind began to blow, tumbling the leaves from the trees; the sky clouded over; and autumn showers began to fall. She could just catch the faint sad belling of a deer, and the half-audible lamentations of the insects. Everything contrived to fill her with a sense of desolation difficult to describe in words. Even in those earlier days, when her life had been a precarious journey from one cove or one island to another, she reflected sadly, she had never had such a feeling of hopelessness.

The retreat was in a lonely spot of moss-covered crags, the sort of place, she felt, where she could live out her days. As she looked about her, she noted that the bush clover in the dew-filled garden had been stripped of its leaves by frost, that the chrysanthemums by the hedge, past their prime, were faded and dry— all reflecting, it seemed, her own condition. Making her way to where the statue of the Buddha was enshrined, she said a prayer: "May the spirit of the late emperor attain perfect enlightenment; may he quickly gain the wisdom of the buddhas!" But even as she did so, the image of her dead son seemed to appear before her, and she wondered in what future existence she might be able to forget him.

Next to the Jakkō-in she had a small building erected, ten feet square in size, with one room to sleep in and the other to house the image of the Buddha. Morning and evening, day and night, she performed her devotions in front of the image, ceaselessly intoning the Buddha's name over the long hours. In this way, always diligent, she passed the months and days.

On the fifteenth day of the Tenth Month, as evening was approaching, Kenreimon'in heard the sound of footsteps on the dried oak leaves that littered the garden. "Who could be coming to call at a place so far removed from the world as this?" she said, addressing her woman companion. "Go see who it is. If it is someone I should not see, I must hurry to take cover!" But when the woman went to look, she found that it was only a stag that had happened to pass by.

"Who was it?" asked Kenreimon'in, to which her companion, Lady Dainagon no Suke, struggling to hold back her tears, replied with this poem:

> Who would tread a path to this rocky lair?
> It was a deer whose passing rustled the leaves of the oak.

Struck by the pathos of the situation, Kenreimon'in carefully inscribed the poem on the small sliding panel by her window.

During her drab and uneventful life, bitter as it was, she found many things that provided food for thought. The trees ranged before the eaves of her retreat suggested to her the seven rows of jewel-laden trees that are said to grow in the Western Paradise, and the water pooled in a crevice in the rocks brought to mind the wonderful water of eight blessings to be found there. Spring blossoms, so easily scattered with the breeze, taught her a lesson in impermanence; the autumn moon, so quickly hidden by its companion clouds, spoke of the transience of life. Those court ladies in the Zhaoyang Hall in China who admired the blossoms at dawn soon saw their petals blown away by the wind; those in the Changqiu Palace who gazed at the evening moon had its brightness stolen from them by clouds. Once in the past, this lady too had lived in similar splendor, reclining on brocade bedclothes in chambers of gold and jade, and now in a hut of mere brushwood and woven vines—even strangers must weep for her.

The retired emperor GoShirakawa visits Kenreimon'in.

THE DEATH OF THE IMPERIAL LADY

While they were speaking, the bell of the Jakkō-in sounded, signaling the close of the day, and the sun sank beyond the western hills. The retired emperor, reluctant though he was to leave, wiped away his tears and prepared to begin the journey back.

All her memories of the past brought back to her once more, Kenreimon'in could scarcely stem the flood of tears with her sleeve. She stood watching as the imperial entourage set out for the capital, watching until it was far in the distance. Then she turned to the image of the Buddha and, speaking through her tears, uttered this prayer: "May the spirit of the late emperor and the souls of all my clanspeople who perished attain complete and perfect enlightenment; may they quickly gain the wisdom of the Buddhas!"

In the past she had faced eastward with this petition: "Great Deity of the Grand Shrine of Ise and Great Bodhisattva Hachiman, may the Son of Heaven be blessed with most wonderful longevity, may he live a thousand autumns, ten thousand years!" But now she changed direction and, facing west with palms pressed together, in sorrow spoke these words: "May the souls of all those who have perished find their way to Amida's Pure Land!"

On the sliding panel of her sleeping room she had inscribed the following poems:

> When did my heart learn such ways?
> Of late I think so longingly of palace companions I once knew!

> The past, too, has vanished like a dream—
> my days by this brushwood door cannot be long in number!

The following poem is reported to have been inscribed on a pillar of Kenreimon'in's retreat by Minister of the Left Sanesada, one of the officials who accompanied the retired emperor on his visit:

> You who in past times were likened to the moon—
> dwelling now deep in these faraway mountains, a light
>   no longer shining—.

Once, when Kenreimon'in was bathed in tears, overwhelmed by memories of the past and thoughts of the future, she heard the cry of a mountain cuckoo and wrote this poem:

> Come then, cuckoo, let us compare tears—
> I, too, do nothing but cry out in a world of pain.

The Taira warriors who survived the Dan-no-ura hostilities and were taken prisoner were paraded through the main streets of the capital and then either beheaded or sent into exile far from their wives and children. With the exception of Taira no Yorimori, not one escaped execution or was permitted to remain in the capital.

With regard to the forty or more Taira wives, no special punitive measures were taken—they were left to join their relatives or to seek aid from persons they had known in the past. But even those fortunate enough to find themselves seated within sumptuous hangings were not spared the winds of uncertainty, and those who ended in humble brushwood dwellings could not live free of dust and turmoil. Husbands and wives who had slept pillow to pillow now found them-

Amida Buddha and bodhisattvas arrive on a lavender cloud to meet the dying retired empress. (A 1656 Meireki woodblock edition, by permission of Shogakukan)

selves at the far ends of the sky. Parents and children who had nourished each other no longer even knew each other's whereabouts. Although their loving thoughts never for a moment ceased, lament as they might, they had somehow to endure these things.

And all of this came about because the lay priest and prime minister Taira no Kiyomori, holding the entire realm within the four seas in the palm of his hand, showed no respect for the ruler above or the slightest concern for the masses of common people below. He dealt out sentences of death or exile in any fashion that suited him, took no heed of how the world or those in it might view his actions—and this is what happened! There can be no room for doubt—it was the evil deeds of the father, the patriarch, that caused the heirs and offspring to suffer this retribution!

After some time had gone by, Kenreimon'in fell ill. Grasping the five-color cord attached to the hand of Amida Buddha, the central figure in the sacred triad, she repeatedly invoked his name: "Hail to the Thus Come One Amida, lord of teachings of the Western Paradise—may you guide me there without fail!" The nuns Dainagon-no-suke and Awa-no-naishi attended her on her left and right, their voices raised in unrestrained weeping, for they sensed in their grief that her end was now at hand. As the sound of the dying woman's recitations grew fainter and fainter, a purple cloud appeared from the west, the room became filled with a strange fragrance, and the strains of music could be heard in the sky. Human life has its limits, and that of the imperial lady ended in the middle days of the Second Month in the second year of the Kenkyū era [1191].

Her two female attendants, who from the time she became imperial consort had never once been parted from her, were beside themselves with grief at her passing, helpless though they were to avert it. The support on which they had depended from times past had now been snatched from them, and they were left destitute, yet even in that pitiable state they managed to hold memorial services each year on the anniversary of her death. And in due time they, too, we are told, imitating the example of the dragon king's daughter in her attainment of enlightenment and following in the footsteps of Queen Vaidehi, fulfilled their long-cherished hopes for rebirth in the Pure Land.

[Translated by Burton Watson]

TRAVEL DIARIES

From the late twelfth century through the end of the sixteenth century, legislative and judicial power gradually came to rest in the hands of the warrior class, even though the courtier class continued to exert political influence well into the Muromachi period (1392–1573). This dual-polity system, with the bakufu headquarters in Kamakura and the court capital in Kyoto, required constant travel between Kamakura and Kyoto. A system of highways, checkpoints, and inns developed to facilitate, monitor, and house the increase in traffic. There also was a renewed interest in pilgrimages to major shrines and temples. Following the lead of the itinerant poet Saigyō (1118–1190) and the ascetic Ippen (1239–1289), travel itself came to be regarded as a form of religious practice (yugyō). The growing interest in travel extended to medieval poets (peripatetic waka and renga poets) and diarists who followed the tracks of legendary poets and wrote travel diaries.

From the early thirteenth into the fourteenth century, the production of travel literature (kikōbun) developed to an unprecedented degree. From the Jōkyū rebellion of 1221 until the early fourteenth century, a large number of Japanese literary works refer to journeys both actual and imagined. Travel appears as a literary topic in every major genre of the time, from military chronicles to anecdotes, diaries, classical poetry, linked verse, and nō drama. Among these literary travelers were a growing number of female writers. Two literary examples that exemplify this new trend are The Diary of the Sixteenth Night Moon (Izayoi nikki, 1283), a travel diary describing Nun Abutsu's (1225–1283) trip to Kamakura, and The Confessions of Lady Nijō (Towazugatari, 1306?), which describes the author's travels after being banished from the imperial palace.

In the poetic maps charted by medieval poets and writers, the capital forms the central axis from which all other locations were measured. Authors who recorded their journeys viewed themselves within a history of travel poetry, which included The Tales of Ise, The Tale of Genji, and the poetry of Saigyō, which served as inspiration for their journeys. In other words, medieval travelers perceived their journeys through the double lens of their own experience and that of their predecessors whose journeys they retraced through visits to poetic sites. This tradition continued in the Muromachi period with texts like Sōgi's Journey to Shirakawa (Shirakawa kikō, 1468).

LADY NIJŌ

Lady Nijō (1258–1329?) was the daughter of a mid-Kamakura-period aristocrat, the senior counselor (*dainagon*) Koga Masatada, who raised her as a child and to whom she was very close. Her mother, who died when Nijō was only two, was the daughter of the senior counselor Shijō Takachika. Both the Koga and the Shijō families were noted poets. Nijō (literally, Second Avenue) was the name she was given as a lady-in-waiting (*nyōbō*) at court. After her mother's death, Nijō was raised in the imperial palace, at the imperial residence of the retired emperor GoFukakusa (r. 1246–1259, 1243–1304), who referred to her as "my child" (*agako*).

In 1271, at the age of fourteen, Nijō became intimate with GoFukakusa, whom her mother had earlier served and apparently initiated into the ways of love. (The memoirs imply that the mother's death wish was that Nijō be given to GoFukakusa, making Nijō a kind of surrogate for the lost lover-mother.) A year later, in 1272, Nijō's father passed away. According to her memoirs, Nijō became romantically or sexually involved with various men while remaining GoFukakusa's lover and bore children to at least three of the men, including GoFukakusa. Although Nijō's position among GoFukakusa's women remained secondary to that of his principal consort (Empress Higashi-Nijō), she apparently was given privileges, such as riding in GoFukakusa's carriage, that were allowed only to women of the highest status.

According to her memoirs, Nijō had a secret affair with Yuki no Akebono (Snow Dawn), or Akebono, who is thought to be Saionji Sanekane (1249–1322), a powerful politician who was close to GoFukakusa and a noted man of letters, with fifty-seven poems in the imperial waka anthology the *Gyokuyōshū* (1312). In 1275, at the age of eighteen, Nijō began another secret affair with a priest nicknamed Ariake no Tsuki (Dawn Moon), or Ariake. Ariake is assumed to be Shōjo (1247–1282), a prince and a Shingon priest at Ninna Temple. In 1283, after altercations with Higashi-Nijō and with GoFukakusa's dwindling interest in her, Nijō was forced out of the imperial court, and around 1288 she took holy vows. She then traveled to the eastern provinces, the first of many journeys, some of which were directly inspired by the priest Saigyō. GoFukakusa died in 1304, and the last recorded date in Nijō's memoirs is 1306, the third anniversary of the retired emperor's death.

THE CONFESSIONS OF LADY NIJŌ (*TOWAZUGATARI*, 1306?)

The Confessions of Lady Nijō was discovered in 1938, but because the content would have been considered scandalous by the wartime government, it was ignored until 1950, when it was first printed. It was not until the 1960s that *Confessions* was considered a significant part of the history of Japanese literature, particularly as a major contribution by a woman writer. *Confessions* appears to have remained an unread or a secret text throughout the medieval period, and only *The Clear Mirror* (*Masukagami*, 1338–1376), a historical tale describing the history of imperial succession in the Kamakura period, alludes to it.

Towazugatari (literally, "narrated without being asked") consists of five books, which describe the life of the author from the age of fourteen to forty-nine. The text takes the form of a memoir of a woman of an advanced age looking back on the last thirty-five years of her life. The first three volumes (until the age of twenty-eight) focus on her love life at the imperial court: her relationships with five different men, beginning with the retired emperor GoFukakusa, Akebono, and Ariake, and her bearing children to each of them. The last two volumes, or the second half, describe her life after she becomes a nun and depict her travels throughout the country, with the text often taking the form of a travel diary. In these last two volumes, Nijō periodically traces the footsteps of Saigyō, the late Heian poet-priest traveler, traveling between Kyoto and Kamakura as well as going to Zenkō-ji temple, Nara, Kōchi, Itsukushima, Shikoku, and other places. She prays for the spirits of her dead children, for the deceased Ariake, for her father, and, most of all, for the spirit of GoFukakusa, who dies in volume 5. Shortly before his death, Nijō's father tells Nijō that even if things do not go well with GoFukakusa, she must never serve two masters and that if the relationship sours, she should take holy vows and dedicate herself to her own salvation as well as that of her parents—a last testament that has a profound effect on her later life.

At the beginning of *Towazugatari*, the reigning emperor is Kameyama (r. 1259–1274), and the retired emperor is GoFukakusa (r. 1246–1259). GoFukakusa (b. 1243), fifteen years older than Nijō, was the son of Emperor GoSaga (r. 1242–1246) and became emperor in 1246, at the age of four. But in 1259, he was forced by the retired emperor GoSaga to cede the throne to his younger brother Kameyama, which set off a bitter rivalry between two imperial lines. *Towazugatari* begins in 1271, twelve years after GoFukakusa was forced to abdicate the throne.

At the beginning of the diary, Nijō's father and the retired emperor GoFukakusa arrange to give Nijō, fourteen at the time, to GoFukakusa. Her father considers this an honor, but apparently his daughter is not informed of the details and is shocked when the relationship is consummated. After Nijō has been reintroduced at court, Empress Higashi-Nijō, GoFukakusa's principal consort, becomes jealous and makes life difficult for Nijō. While serving GoFukakusa, Nijō has a secret relationship with Akebono, a politician in the service of GoFukakusa. Later, seemingly with GoFukakusa's implicit approval, she also begins a relationship with Ariake, a priest who is assumed to be GoFukakusa's half brother.

Book 1 (1271)

As the mist rose among the spring bamboo heralding the dawn of the new year, the ladies of GoFukakusa's court,[147] who had so eagerly awaited this morning,

---

147. In 1271 GoFukakusa was a twenty-nine-year-old retired emperor, and Lady Nijō, fourteen years old, was one of his ladies-in-waiting. According to the lunar calendar, the first day of the new year came in late January or February, marking the beginning of spring.

made their appearances in gorgeous costumes, each trying to surpass the others in beauty. I too took my place among them. I recall wearing a layered gown shaded from light pink to dark red, with outer gowns of deep purple and light green and a red formal jacket. My undergown was a two-layered small-sleeved brocade patterned with plum blossoms and vines, and embroidered with bamboo fences and plum trees.

My father, a senior counselor, served today's medicinal saké.[148] After the formal ceremonies everyone was invited in, the ladies were summoned from the tray room, and a drinking party began. Earlier Father had proposed the customary three rounds of saké with three cups each time, which meant that the participants in the formal ceremonies had already had nine cups. Now he proposed the same again, but His Majesty revised the suggestion: "This time we'll make it three rounds of nine cups each." As a result, everyone was quite drunk when GoFukakusa passed his saké cup to my father and said, "Let 'the wild goose of the fields' come to me this spring."[149] Accepting this proposal with great deference, my father drank the cups of saké offered to him and retired. What did it all mean? I had seen them speaking confidentially, but I had no way of knowing what was afoot.

After the services had ended, I returned to my room and found a letter:[150] "Snowbound yesterday, today spring opens new paths to the future. I shall write you often." With the letter was a cloth-wrapped package containing an eight-layered gown shaded from deep red to white, a deep maroon undergown, a light green outer gown, a formal jacket, pleated trousers, and two small-sleeved gowns of two and three layers. This unexpected gift upset me, and I was preparing to return it when I noticed a piece of thin paper on one of the sleeves. It contained this poem:

> Unlike the wings of love birds, our sleeves may never touch,
> yet wear this plumage that you may feel my love.

It seemed cruel to reject a gift prepared and sent with such feeling, yet I returned it with this note:

> Were I to wear these gowns in your absence, I fear
> the sleeves would rot away from muffling my sobs.
> If only your love does not vanish.

---

148. On the first three mornings of the new year, various kinds of spiced saké, specially prepared by the Bureau of Medicine and tasted by young maidens, were formally served to the emperor and certain officials. This ceremony, known as the medicinal offering (onkusuri), was performed to ward off illness in the coming year.

149. The retired emperor suggests that Lady Nijō become his concubine by alluding to The Tales of Ise, sec. 10, in which a mother asks the protagonist to marry her daughter. In the poems they exchange, a wild goose is used as a metaphor for the girl.

150. This seems to be from Akebono, whose relationship to Lady Nijō at this point is unclear. Lady Nijō's reaction to his gift suggests that their future affair is still in its early stages.

Late that night, while I was out on duty,[151] someone came and knocked on the back door to my room. The young serving girl who rashly opened the door told me later that a messenger had thrust something inside and immediately vanished. It was the same package with another poem:

> Our hearts were pledged. If yours remains unchanged,
> spread out these gowns and sleep on them alone.

I did not feel I could return the present a second time.

On the third of the month, when the cloistered emperor GoSaga came to visit GoFukakusa, I wore those gowns. My father noticed them and said, "The colors and sheen are especially fine. Did you receive them from His Majesty?"

My heart throbbed, but somehow I replied calmly, "They are from Her Highness, Lady Kitayama."

On the evening of the fifteenth, a messenger arrived from my father's house in Kawasaki saying he was to escort me home.[152] I was annoyed by this urgent summons, but saw no way to decline it. When I arrived at my home I could tell that something was about to happen—though I did not know what—for the furnishings were much more elaborate than usual. Folding screens, bordered mats, portable curtains, and even hanging curtains had been arranged with special care. "Is all this just for New Year's?" I wondered as I retired for the night.

At dawn there was much talk about what should be served and how the courtiers' horses and the nobles' oxen should be cared for, and even my grandmother, a nun, came and joined in the bustle. I finally asked what all the fuss was about. My father smiled at me: "His Majesty has announced that he will come here this evening because of a directional taboo, and since it's the first of the year, we'd like everything to be exactly right.[153] I summoned you expressly to serve him."

"But it's not the eve of a seasonal change. What directional taboo brings him out here?"

"What a naïve child you are," he replied amid the general laughter. How was I to understand?

They were setting up folding screens and small portable curtains in my bedroom. "Such preparations! Is my room going to be used too?" But my questions were met with smiles instead of answers. No one would tell me a thing.

That evening a three-layered white gown and deep maroon pleated trousers

---

151. Court ladies took turns sleeping outside the room of their master or mistress at night.

152. Kawasaki was an area on the northeastern edge of the capital, just west of the Kamo River.

153. To satisfy complex taboos pertaining to the avoidance of unlucky directions, people were often forced to spend a night away from their permanent residences. This was especially common on the eve of spring, a date determined by a solar calendar rather than the official lunar one.

were laid out for me to wear, and elaborate care was taken in scenting the house and placing the incense burners where they would be unnoticed. After the lamps had been lit, my stepmother brought me a gay small-sleeved gown and told me to put it on. Later my father came in, hung several gowns about the room for their decorative effect, and said to me, "Don't fall asleep before His Majesty arrives. Serve him well. A lady-in-waiting should never be stubborn, but should do exactly as she's told." Without the least idea what these instructions were all about and feeling bewildered by all the commotion, I leaned against the brazier and fell asleep.

What happened after that I am not sure. His Majesty GoFukakusa arrived without my knowing it, and there must have been great excitement when my father welcomed him and refreshments were served, but I was innocently sleeping. When GoFukakusa overheard the flustered cries of "Wake her up!" he said, "It's all right, let her sleep," so no one disturbed me.

I don't know how long I had slept leaning against the brazier just inside the sliding door, my outer gown thrown up over my head, but I suddenly awakened to find the lights dim, the curtains lowered, and inside the sliding door, right beside me, a man who had made himself comfortable and fallen fast asleep.

"What is this?" I cried. No sooner did I get up to leave, than His Majesty wakened. Without rising he began to tell me how he had loved me ever since I was a child, how he had been waiting until now when I was fourteen, and so many other things that I have not words enough to record them all. But I was not listening; I could only weep until even his sleeves were dampened with my tears as he tried to comfort me. He did not attempt to force me, but he said, "You have been indifferent to me for so long that I thought on this occasion perhaps . . . How can you continue to be so cold, especially now that everyone knows about this?"

So that's how it was. This was not even a secret dream, everyone knew about it, and no doubt as soon as I woke my troubles would begin. My worries were sad proof that I had not completely lost my senses at least, but I was wretched. If this was what was in store for me, why hadn't I been told beforehand? Why didn't he give me a chance to discuss it with my father? How could I face anyone now? I moaned and wept so much that he must have thought me very childish, but I could not help myself, for his very presence caused me pain.

The night passed without my offering him even a single word of response. When at dawn we heard someone say, "His Majesty will be returning today, won't he?" GoFukakusa muttered, "Now to go back pretending something happened!" and prepared to leave. "Your unexpected coldness has made me feel that the pledge I made long ago—when you still wore your hair parted in the middle—was all in vain.[154] You might at least behave in a way that other people

---

154. A girl wore shoulder-length hair parted in the middle until her coming-of-age ceremony, when a section of it was tied up on top of her head.

won't find too strange. What will people think if you seclude yourself?" He tried both scolding and comforting me, but I refused to answer. "Oh, what's the use!" he said at last; then he got up, put on his robe, and ordered his carriage. When I heard Father inquiring about His Majesty's breakfast, I felt as though I could never face him again. I thought longingly of yesterday.

After GoFukakusa had gone, I lay utterly still with my outer gown pulled up over my head, pretending to sleep, until the arrival of a letter from him threw me into even greater misery. To add to my wretchedness my stepmother and grandmother came in full of questions. "What's the matter?" they asked. "Why don't you get up?"

"I don't feel well after last night," I blurted out, only to realize with dismay that they thought it was because I had shared my pillow with a man for the first time.

In great excitement someone entered with the letter I had no intention of reading. The royal messenger was waiting uneasily for a reply, and my attendants were wringing their hands not knowing what to do, until finally someone suggested, "Go tell her father." This, I knew, would be the most unbearable ordeal of all.

"Aren't you feeling well?" Father asked when he arrived. When they brought up the matter of the letter he said, "What childishness is this? Surely you intend to answer it?" I heard him opening the letter. It was a poem written on thin purple paper:

> Friends for many years, yet now your perfume haunts
> my last night's sleeves that never lay on yours.

When my attendants read this they gossiped among themselves about how different I was from most young people these days. Still tense and uneasy I refused to get up. After much fretting they agreed that it would not be appropriate to have someone else reply for me, whereupon they gave the messenger a gift and entrusted him with this message: "She's such a child that she's still in bed and hasn't even looked at His Majesty's letter yet."

Around noon a letter came from an unexpected source. I read these lines:

> I might well die of grief if now
> the smoke trails off entirely in that direction.[155]

To this the writer added, "Thus far I have survived this meaningless life, but now what is there?" This was written on thin, light blue paper, which had as a background design the old poem:

---

155. This poem from Akebono alludes to *The Tales of Ise*, sec. 12: "After many earnest declarations of devotion to a certain man, a lady fell in love with someone else. The first man composed this poem: 'Captured by the gale, the smoke from the salt-fires of the fisherfolk at Suma has drifted off in an unforeseen direction.'"

If I could cease to be, no longer would these clouds
cling to the secret mountains of my heart.[156]

I tore off a piece of the paper where the words "secret mountains" appeared,
and wrote: Can you not understand?

My thoughts scattered and confused,
my heart has not gone drifting off, a wisp of evening smoke.

After I sent this I began to wonder what I had done.

My refusal that day to take any kind of medicine gave rise to idle gossip
about my "strange illness." Shortly after dusk fell, I was informed that His Majesty had arrived. Before I had time to wonder what might happen at this meeting, he pushed open the door and entered my room with an air of intimacy.
"I understand you're ill. What's the trouble?" he inquired. Feeling not the least
inclination to reply, I lay motionless where I was. He lay down beside me and
began to talk of what was uppermost in his heart, but I was so dazed that I could
only worry about what would happen next. I was tempted to acquiesce quoting
the line, "If this were a world without lies,"[157] except for my fear that the person
who had claimed he might die of grief would consider my behavior vulgar when
he learned that the evening smoke had so quickly trailed off in a certain direction. Tonight, when GoFukakusa could not elicit a single word of reply from me,
he treated me so mercilessly that my thin gowns were badly ripped. By the time
that I had nothing more to lose, I despised my own existence. I faced the dawn
with dread.

My undersash untied against my will,
At what point will my name be soiled?

What surprised me, as I continued to brood, was that I still had wits enough to
think of my reputation.

GoFukakusa was expressing his fidelity with numerous vows. "Though from
life to life our shapes will change," he said, "there will be no change in the
bond between us; though the nights we meet might be far apart, our hearts will
never acknowledge separation." As I listened, the short night, barely affording
time to dream, gave way to dawn and the tolling of bells. It was past daybreak.
"It will be embarrassing if I stay," GoFukakusa said, getting up to leave. "Even
if you are not sorry we must part, at least see me off."

Unable to refuse his insistent urgings, I slipped a thin, unlined gown over
the clothes I had on, which were damp from a night of weeping, and stepped

---

156. Fujiwara no Masatsune, *Shinkokinshū*, Love 2, no. 1094.

157. An allusion to *Kokinshū*, no. 712: "If this were a world without lies, how happy your
words would make me."

outside. The moon of the seventeenth night was sinking in the west, and a narrow bank of clouds stretched along the eastern horizon. GoFukakusa wore a
green robe, scarlet-lined, over a pale gown. He had on heavily figured trousers.
I felt more attracted to him than I ever had before, and I wondered uneasily
where these new feelings had come from.

The imperial carriage was ordered by Lord Takaaki, a senior counselor, who
was dressed in a light blue robe. The only courtier in attendance was Lord
Tamekata, an assistant chief investigator. While several guards and servants
were bringing the carriage up, some birds sang out noisily as though to warn me
of the new day, and the tolling bell of Kannon Temple seemed meant for me
alone. Touched by two kinds of sadness, I remembered the line, "Tears wet my
sleeves both left and right."[158]

GoFukakusa still did not leave. "It will be lonely," he said. "See me home."
Knowing who he was, I could hardly claim to be "unaware of the shape of the
mountain peak,"[159] so I stood there in confusion as the brightening dawn
spread through the sky. "Why do you look so pained?" he asked as he helped
me into his carriage and ordered it driven away. Leaving this way, without a
word to anybody, seemed like an episode from an old tale. What was to become of me?

> Dawn's bell did not awaken me for I never went to sleep.
> Yet the painful dream I had streaks the morning sky with grief.

I suppose our ride might be considered amusing, for all the way to the palace
GoFukakusa pledged his affection to me as if he were a storied lover making off
with his mistress, but for me the road we traveled seemed so dreary I could do
nothing but weep.

After the carriage had been drawn through the middle gate to the Corner
Mansion,[160] GoFukakusa alighted and turned to Takaaki: "I brought her along
because she was too unreasonable and childish to leave behind. I think it would
be better if no one learned of this for a while." Then, leaving orders that I was to
be taken care of, he retired to his living quarters.

It hardly seemed the same palace where I had lived for so many years as a
child. Frightened and ill at ease now, I regretted having come and wondered
blankly what I might expect. I was sobbing when I heard the comforting sound

---

158. An allusion to the "Suma" chapter of *The Tale of Genji*, from a poem Genji composed
in exile at Suma when he shed tears of bitterness and affection as he thought about the emperor
who had banished him.

159. An allusion to the "Evening Faces" (Yūgao) chapter of *The Tale of Genji*, from the poem
of foreboding that Yūgao composed when Genji, without revealing his identity, took her to a
deserted mansion where she later died: "Unaware of the shape of the mountain peak, the moon
courses through the sky. Will its light be blotted out?"

160. This was one of the buildings on the grounds of GoFukakusa's Tomi Street Palace.

of my father's voice expressing concern over me. When Takaaki explained Go-Fukakusa's instructions, Father replied, "This kind of special treatment won't do. Things should go on as usual. To be secretive now will only lead to trouble when word gets out." Then I heard him leave. After his visit I brooded uneasily about the future. GoFukakusa interrupted my painful musings and poured out so many words of affection that I was gradually comforted. The thought that my fate was inescapable began to resign me to it.

I remained at the palace for about ten days, during which time His Majesty never failed to visit me at night; yet I was still foolish enough to think about the author of that poem, which had questioned the direction the smoke was taking. My father, meanwhile, kept insisting on the impropriety of my situation, and finally had me return home. I could not bear to see anyone, so I pretended to be ill and kept to my own quarters.

GoFukakusa wrote an affectionate letter saying, "I have grown so accustomed to you that I'm depressed now you are gone. Come back immediately."

> I doubt you yearn for me this much.
> If only I could show you the many teardrops on my sleeves.

Although I usually thought his letters disagreeable, I found myself eagerly reading this one. My answer was perhaps too artificial:

> Perhaps they were not for me, those drops upon your sleeves,
> yet word of them makes my tears flow.

Several days later I returned to the palace—this time openly, in the usual fashion—yet I grew uncomfortable when people immediately began to talk. "The Senior Counselor certainly treasures her," they would say. "He's sent her with all the ceremony due an official consort."

The gossip spread, and before long Empress Higashi-Nijō began to be unpleasant. As the days dragged by I became wretched. I cannot claim that His Majesty really neglected me, but I was depressed when days passed between his visits, and although I didn't feel I could complain—as his other ladies did—about who kept him company at night, every time it fell to my lot to conduct another woman to him I understood anew the painful ways of this world. Yet I was haunted by a line of poetry that kept coming to mind: "Will I live to cherish memories of these days?"[161] The days passed, each dawn turned to dusk, and autumn arrived. . . .

Was it because of the rains of the Fifth Month, which left nothing untouched, that my father's spirits were damper than the wettest autumn day? Or was he so

---

161. Fujiwara no Kiyosuke, *Shinkokinshū*, no. 1843: "Will I live to cherish memories of these days too? What once was sad now seems dear."

thin and worn because he had given up his custom of never spending a night alone and had even stopped going to drinking parties? On the night of the fourteenth, as he was coming home in his carriage from Buddhist services at Ōtani, the outriders accompanying him noticed that he looked sallow and they knew something was seriously wrong. The doctor they summoned made a diagnosis of jaundice caused by too much worry and began administering moxa treatments. I began to worry about him when I saw that his health was gradually deteriorating. Then in the Sixth Month, when I was already at my wits' end, I discovered that my own condition was not normal. But how could I mention it at such a time?

Father did not order any prayers for his recovery. "Since my condition seems hopeless anyhow, I don't want to waste a single day in joining His Majesty," he explained. For a few weeks he remained at his house at the corner of Rokkaku and Kushige streets before returning on the fourteenth of the Seventh Month to his Kawasaki home. He left his younger children behind so that he could quietly prepare for the end. I alone accompanied him, proud of having such responsibility. Father noticed that I was not my usual self, but at first he supposed I was not eating because of my worry for him. He tried to console me until he recognized my real condition and suddenly began to hope that his life might be prolonged for a while. For the first time he had religious services performed: a seven-day service to the God of Mount Tai at the central hall of the Enryaku Temple, seven performances of outdoor *dengaku* dances at the seven shrines of Hie, and an all-day recitation of the Great Wisdom Sutra at the Iwashimizu Hachiman Shrine. He also had a stone monument constructed at the riverbed. All these acts of piety were inspired not by any love of his own life, but by concern for my future. I had become, alas, an impediment to his salvation.

Though still seriously ill, my father was out of immediate danger by the twentieth, at which time I returned to the palace. When GoFukakusa learned of my condition, he was especially kind, and yet I was well aware that nothing, not even the so-called "eternal ivy," lasts forever, and I was afraid lest my fate be like that of the mistress of the wardrobe, who had died in childbirth last month. As the Seventh Month drew to a close my father was showing no improvement, and I was uncertain as to what my own fate would be. On the night of the twenty-seventh, when fewer people were in attendance than usual, GoFukakusa asked me to come to his room. I accompanied him there, and he took the opportunity of our privacy to talk quietly of things past and present. "The uncertainty of life is cruel," he began. "Your father's case seems hopeless, and if worse comes to worst, you will be left with no one to depend on. Who besides me will take pity on you?" He wept as he talked of this. How sad that even consolation brings pain.

It was a moonless night. We were talking alone in the darkened room lit only by a dim lantern when suddenly we heard a voice calling my name. It was very late, and I was puzzled until I learned that it was a messenger from Kawasaki. He announced, "The end is imminent."

I left at once, without any preparations, and feared all the way that I would find Father already dead. Though I knew we were hurrying, the carriage seemed to crawl. When we finally arrived I learned to my great relief that he was still alive.

My father spoke to me, sobbing weakly. "The dew, not yet quite gone, awaits the wind. This life is painful, but knowing your condition I cannot face death without regrets."

Bells were tolling a late hour when GoFukakusa's arrival was announced. This was so completely unexpected that even my father, desperately ill though he was, became excited. I hurried out when I heard his carriage being drawn up, and saw that he had come in secret, accompanied by a single courtier and two junior guards. The late moon had just appeared over the rim of the mountains when I saw His Majesty standing in the brilliant moonlight dressed in a light violet robe with a woven flower design. What a splendid honor it was to receive such a sudden visit from the retired emperor.

Father sent this word: "Lacking even the strength to slip on a robe, I am unable to receive you, but the fact that you have honored me with this visit will be one of my fondest memories of this life."

At this GoFukakusa unceremoniously slid open the doors and entered the room. Father attempted to sit up but could not. "Stay as you are," GoFukakusa said as he laid a cushion beside Father's pillow and sat down. Before long, tears were streaming down GoFukakusa's cheeks. "You have served me intimately since I was a child. News that the end is near grieved me so much I wanted to see you once more."

"The joy your visit has brought me is more than I deserve, yet I am so concerned for this child I don't know what to do. Her mother left her behind when she was only two, and knowing that I was all she had, I raised her carefully. Nothing grieves me more than the thought of leaving her in this condition." Father wept as he spoke.

"I am not sure how much I can do, but at least I am willing to help. Don't let these worries block your path to paradise." His Majesty spoke kindly. "You should rest," he said and got up to leave.

It was now past daybreak and the retired emperor, anxious to leave before he was observed in his informal attire, was on the point of departing when a messenger came out to his carriage with a *biwa* that had belonged to my grandfather, Prime Minister Michimitsu, and a sword that once belonged to Emperor GoToba and had been presented to my grandfather about the time of GoToba's exile.[162] A note on light blue paper was attached to the thong of the sword:

> Master and man, our ties span three worlds they say;
> departing, I commit the future to your hands.

---

162. Emperor GoToba was banished in 1221 to Oki Island in the Japan Sea for his part in the Jōkyū rebellion.

GoFukakusa was deeply moved by this. Several times over he assured me that I had no reason to worry. Shortly afterward a letter arrived written in His Majesty's own hand:

> The next time we shall meet beyond this world of sorrow,
> under the brightening sky of that long-awaited dawn.[163]

His Majesty's concern was our only pleasure in this sad and painful time.

GoFukakusa sent me a maternity sash earlier than was customary so my father could witness the ceremony.[164] It was formally presented to me by his emissary, the senior counselor Takaaki, on the second day of the Eighth Month. Takaaki wore a court robe, having been instructed by GoFukakusa not to wear mourning on this occasion, and was accompanied by outriders and attendants. My father, who was immensely pleased by this, ordered saké to be prepared. I wondered sadly if this would be the last such occasion. Father made Takaaki a present of Shiogama, the highly prized ox he had received from the prince who headed the Ninna Temple.

Because Father had felt better on this day, I had a glimmer of hope that he might improve. When it grew late I lay down beside him to rest and promptly fell asleep. He awakened me abruptly: "It's useless. I am able to forget the grief of setting out, perhaps even today or tomorrow, on an unknown path, but my thoughts keep dwelling on the one thing that grieves me. Just to watch you innocently sleeping there makes me wretched. Ever since your mother died when you were only two, I alone have worried about you. Although I have many other children, I feel that I have lavished on you alone the 'love due three thousand.' When I see you smile, I find 'a hundred charms'; when you are sad, I too grieve.[165] I have watched the passing of fifteen springs and autumns with you, but now I must depart. If you would serve His Majesty and not incur his displeasure, always be respectful; never be negligent. The ways of this world are often unexpected. If you should incur the ill will of your Lord and of the world and find you are unable to manage, you are immediately to enter holy orders where you can work toward your own salvation, repay your debts to your parents, and pray that we might all be together in paradise. But if, finding yourself forsaken and alone, you decide to serve another master or try to make your way by entering any other household whatsoever, consider yourself disowned even though I am already dead. For the truth is that relationships between men and women are not to be

---

163. The dawn of salvation, a time in the immensely distant future when Miroku Buddha is to descend to earth to teach salvation.

164. This congratulatory ceremony expressed the father's recognition of the unborn child.

165. These phrases are from the Chinese poet Bo Juyi's poem "The Song of Everlasting Sorrow," which describes the love of the emperor for his concubine Yang Guifei.

tampered with, inasmuch as they are not limited to this world alone. It would be shameful indeed if you remained in society only to blacken the name of our great family. It is only after retiring from society that you can do as you will without causing suffering." Father spoke at such length that I took these as his final instructions to me.

The bells were tolling daybreak when Nakamitsu[166] came in with the steamed plantain leaves that were regularly spread under the patient's mat.

"Allow me to change the plantain," he said to my father.

"It doesn't matter now. The end is near," my father said. "Anything will do. First see to it that Nijō eats. I want to watch her. Hurry!" I did not see how I could eat, but my father insisted. I wondered sadly what would happen later when he was no longer around to watch me. Nakamitsu returned bringing a yam dish called *imomaki* in an unglazed pottery bowl. Everyone knows that *imomaki* is said to be an unhealthy food for a pregnant woman, and when the dish was set before me it looked so unappetizing that I merely pretended to eat it.

At daybreak we decided to send for a priest. In the previous month the chief priest of the Yasaka Temple had come to shave Father's head and administer his vows. He had also given Father the religious name Renshō. Therefore, that priest seemed the logical one to summon for the last rites, but for some reason my grandmother, the Koga nun, insisted instead on calling Shōkōbō, the chief priest of the Kawara Temple. Even though he had been informed that Father was rapidly failing, he did not hurry.

The end appeared imminent. My father called to Nakamitsu, "Sit me up." Nakamitsu, the eldest son of Nakatsuna, had been raised from childhood by my father and had always served at Father's side. He lifted Father up and sat down behind him. The only other person present, a lady-in-waiting, sat before Father while I sat at his side. "Hold my wrist," Father said. When I had taken it he asked, "Where is the surplice the priest gave me?" After I draped the surplice over the informal silk robe he wore without trousers, he instructed Nakamitsu to join him in prayer. Together they prayed for about an hour, and then as the sun began to shine into the room Father dozed off, leaning over to the left. Intending to rouse him and help him continue his meditation, I shook his knee. He awoke with a start, raised his head, and looked directly into my eyes. "I wonder what will happen," he started to say, but he died before he could finish the sentence. It was eight o'clock in the morning on the third day of the Eighth Month of 1272. My father was fifty years old.

Had Father died saying his prayers, his future would have been assured; but as it was I had uselessly awakened him only to see him die with other words upon his lips. The thought of this plagued me. So black was my own mood that when I looked up at the heavens I thought the sun and moon must have fallen

---

166. The eldest son and heir of Nakatsuna, Masatada's faithful steward.

from the sky, and as I lay on the ground sobbing, my tears seemed to be a river flowing out of me.

When I was two years old I lost my mother, but at that time I was too young to realize what had happened. However, my father and I had spent fifteen years together—ever since the forty-first day of my life, when I was first placed upon his knee. In the morning, looking in my mirror, I was happy to realize whose image I reflected; and in the evening, changing my gowns, I thought of my indebtedness to him. The debt I owed him for my life and my position was greater than the towering peak of Mount Sumeru, and the gratitude I felt toward him for taking my mother's place in raising me was deeper than the waters of the four great seas. How could I ever show my gratitude or repay him who gave me so much? Things he said at various times kept coming back to my mind. I could not forget them. Nothing I could ever do would erase the grief of this parting. . . .

[Introduction by Christina Laffin and translation by Karen W. Brazell]

KENKŌ

Kenkō (ca. 1283–ca. 1352) is thought to have been born in the Kōan era (1278–1288), in the late Kamakura period (1185–1333), and died in the Northern and Southern Courts period (1336–1392). Kenkō came from the Urabe, a noted Shinto family, but he did not enter the Shinto profession. Instead, during his teens, he served Emperor GoNijō (r. 1301–1308) as a sixth-rank *kurōdo* (chamberlain), in turn as an archivist or a secretary in charge of sundry affairs. In 1313, at around the age of thirty, Kenkō took the tonsure. He traveled a number of times to the east, to the Kantō area, and in 1319 his poetry was included in the *Zoku senzai-shū*, a semi-imperial anthology. Kenkō became a poet of the Nijō school and was referred to as one of the "four kings of waka," of whom the most notable was Ton'a (1289–1372). But in his treatise *Comments on Recent Poetic Styles* (*Kinrai fūteishō*, 1387), the noted scholar-poet Nijō Yoshimoto (1320–1388) disparagingly refers to Kenkō as below the other "four kings" in quality. In addition to *Essays in Idleness* (*Tsurezuregusa*), he left behind a collection of his own poetry, *Collection of Priest Kenkō* (*Kenkō hōshi shū*, ca. 1343). In the latter part of his life, Kenkō was closely affiliated with the Ashikaga house, which was in power, and interacted with waka poets, intellectuals, warriors, and nobility. In other words, Kenkō both lived in seclusion and continued to mingle with the most powerful figures of the time, including cultural luminaries like Nijō Yoshimoto, one of the founders of classical renga.

ESSAYS IN IDLENESS
(TSUREZUREGUSA, 1329–1333)

Essays in Idleness now consists of a preface and 243 sections (*dan*). The shortest section is only one sentence long, and the longest one—"Are We to Look at Cherry Blossoms Only in Full Bloom?"—is about four pages. (These sections were created in the Tokugawa period, to make the text easier to read.) On the eve of the Northern and Southern Courts period, Kenkō, an intellectual who was neither completely secular nor completely a priest, casts a sharp eye on a chaotic, *Taiheiki* type of world. In 1331, when Kenkō probably wrote the bulk of *Tsurezuregusa*, Emperor GoDaigo's second plan to overthrow the bakufu was discovered, and the Kasagi and Akasaka castles fell. The period of the *Taiheiki* was a time when friend and foe, outsider and insider, establishment and nonestablishment, war and peace, were constantly changing and replacing each other.

Of the more than two hundred sections, about half directly reveal Kenkō's views of life and the world, which were based on a strong sense of impermanence and impending death. Good examples of this type are "Determined to Take the Great Step" (sec. 59) and "Gathering Like Ants" (sec. 74), both of which are included here. Another third of the sections, which have the character of anecdotes, describe people from all walks of life who have caught Kenkō's attention. These sections also provide information about court or warrior rules and precedents.

It is not clear when *Tsurezuregusa* was composed. Today the dominant view is that Kenkō wrote most of the text in two or three years during the Gentoku era (1329–1331), when he was in his late forties. Scholars, however, point to significant differences in vocabulary, style, and content between the first and second parts, and many believe that *Tsurezuregusa* was written over a longer period of time. They believe that the first part, what might be called the original *Tsurezuregusa*, from section 1 through about section 30, was probably written as early as the Bunpō era (1317–1319), when Kenkō was young, immediately after he had left court life. This part reveals a strong yearning for Heian aristocratic culture, uses Heian aesthetic terms such as *aware* (moving) and *wokashi* (charming), and expresses great admiration for *The Tale of Genji* as well as *The Pillow Book*. In section 19, "Changing of the Seasons," for example, Kenkō describes the beauties of the four seasons as they are embodied in Heian literature and poetry.

The second part of *Tsurezuregusa*, the main body, sections 31 through 240, was probably written later, in 1330/1331. This second part makes more use of Sino-Japanese (*kanbun kundoku*) expressions, shows the influence of Daoism, advocates renunciation and reclusion, and confronts life and death. In contrast to the first part of *Tsurezuregusa*—in which Kenkō draws on his rich knowledge of Chinese classics, Japanese poetry, and Heian classical texts and discusses classical topics such as love and friendship—in the second part Kenkō gradually breaks away from classical aesthetics and includes more medieval anecdotes, focusing on eccentric, highly individualized characters.

The inherent contradictions of *Tsurezuregusa* reflect the changes in Kenkō's per-spective between his youth and his middle years, as well as the larger tensions of the period, particularly between the court culture and the culture in the east (with its distinctive setsuwa and folk songs). Because Kenkō traveled frequently between Kyoto and Kamakura, he was exposed to both the imperial court culture of Kyoto and the new warrior culture. Despite his interest in the new eastern culture, Kenkō's general preference was for the refined culture of the capital, as evident in the famous section 137: "Are We to Look at Cherry Blossoms Only in Full Bloom?"

Today *Tsurezuregusa* is generally referred to as a *zuihitsu* (miscellany) and is regarded as part of a literary lineage starting with *The Pillow Book* and extending through *An Account of a Ten-Foot-Square Hut (Hōjōki)*. Indeed, *Tsurezuregusa* bears certain similarities to *The Pillow Book* in that it reveals the author's opinions and musings on a wide range of subjects, expressed in very short and independent passages. In contrast to *Hōjōki*, which is a unified essay on the theme of reclusion and salvation, however, *Tsurezuregusa* has no central theme or order. *Tsurezuregusa* can also be read as one of the last setsuwa collec-tions, resembling such Buddhist collections as Mujū Ichien's *Collection of Sand and Pebbles (Shasekishū, 1279–1283)* and *Collection of Sundry Conversations (Zōtanshū, 1305)*, which is considered to be one of the later medieval setsuwa collections.

Tsurezuregusa consists of roughly three different worlds: the secular world in which most people live, the world of the Buddhist priesthood, and the world of the recluse (*tonseisha*). Although Kenkō apparently took vows, he did not belong to any particular sect or school, nor was he a lay person who lived in regular society. In-stead, he moved freely among these three worlds, particularly enjoying that of the recluse. The term *tsurezure*, which means "idleness," was usually used negatively. But in section 75, "A Person Who Complains of Having Nothing to Do," Kenkō praises this condition as an ideal, since it allows solitude, avoids entanglements, and brings peace to the heart—ideals of the recluse. In contrast to the *hijiri* (holy man), as exemplified by someone like Priest Zōga and other Buddhist heroes, tonseisha, though wanting to separate themselves from the preoccupations of the secular world, cannot tolerate the kinds of hardships endured by these holy men, nor do they have their deep faith. Furthermore, tonseisha like Kenkō regarded reclusion as a means of devoting themselves to learning and the arts. Unlike Kamo no Chōmei in *Hōjōki*, Kenkō has little interest in being reborn in the Pure Land; rather, he is interested in this life, in the present. His intense awareness of impermanence turns his attention not to the next world but to this world, in an effort to make memorable every minute in this life.

Preface

What a strange, demented feeling it gives me when I realize I have spent whole days before this inkstone, with nothing better to do, jotting down at random whatever nonsensical thoughts have entered my head.

If the Dews of Adashino Never Faded (7)

If man were never to fade away like the dews of Adashino,[167] never to vanish like the smoke over Toribeyama,[168] but lingered on forever in the world, how things would lose their power to move us![169] The most precious thing in life is its uncertainty. Consider living creatures—none lives so long as man. The mayfly waits not for the evening, the summer cicada knows neither spring nor autumn. What a wonderfully unhurried feeling it is to live even a single year in perfect serenity! If that is not enough for you, you might live a thousand years and still feel it was but a single night's dream. We cannot live forever in this world; why should we wait for ugliness to overtake us? The longer man lives, the more shame he endures. To die, at the latest, before one reaches forty, is the least unattractive. Once a man passes that age, he desires (with no sense of shame over his appearance) to mingle in the company of others. In his sunset years he dotes on his grandchildren, and prays for long life so that he may see them prosper. His preoccupation with worldly desires grows ever deeper, and gradually he loses all sensitivity to the beauty of things, a lamentable state of affairs.

Leading the Heart Astray (8)

Nothing leads a man astray so easily as sexual desire. What a foolish thing a man's heart is! Though we realize, for example, that fragrances are short-lived and the scent burnt into clothes lingers but briefly, how our hearts always leap when we catch a whiff of an exquisite perfume! The holy man of Kume[170] lost his magic powers after noticing the whiteness of the legs of a girl who was washing clothes; this was quite understandable, considering that the glowing plumpness of her arms, legs, and flesh owed nothing to artifice.

Beautiful Hair, of All Things (9)

Beautiful hair, of all things in a woman, is most likely to catch a man's eye. Her character and temperament may be guessed from the first words she utters, even if she is hidden behind a screen. When a woman somehow—perhaps unintentionally—has captured a man's heart she is generally unable to sleep

---

167. Adashino was a crematorium in the northwest of the capital. The word *adashi* (impermanent), contained in the place-name, accounted for the frequent use of Adashino in poetry as a symbol of impermanence. The dew also is often used with that meaning.

168. Toribeyama was also another major crematorium in the capital.

169. *Mono no aware* (literally, "the pathos of things") is here translated as the "power [of things] to move us."

170. The holy man of Kume, a legendary figure dating back to the tenth century, had the ability to fly through the air.

peacefully. She will not hesitate to subject herself to hardships, and will even endure cheerfully what she would normally find intolerable, all because love means so much to her.

The love of men and women is truly a deep-seated passion with distant roots. The senses give rise to many desires, but it should be possible to shun them all. Only one, infatuation, is impossible to control; old or young, wise or foolish, in this respect all seem identical. That is why they say that even a great elephant can be fastened securely with a rope plaited from the strands of a woman's hair, and that a flute made from a sandal a woman has worn will infallibly summon the autumn deer. We must guard against this delusion of the senses, which is to be dreaded and avoided.

A Proper Dwelling (10)

A house, I know, is but a temporary abode, but how delightful it is to find one that has harmonious proportions and a pleasant atmosphere. One feels somehow that even moonlight, when it shines into the quiet domicile of a person of taste, is more affecting than elsewhere. A house, though it may not be in the current fashion or elaborately decorated, will appeal to us by its unassuming beauty—a grove of trees with an indefinably ancient look; a garden where plants, growing of their own accord, have a special charm; a verandah and an openwork wooden fence of interesting construction; and a few personal effects left carelessly lying about, giving the place an air of having been lived in. A house which multitudes of workmen have polished with every care, where strange and rare Chinese and Japanese furnishings are displayed, and even the grasses and trees of the garden have been trained unnaturally, is ugly to look at and most depressing. How could anyone live for long in such a place? The most casual glance will suggest how likely such a house is to turn in a moment to smoke.

A man's character, as a rule, may be known from the place where he lives. The Gotokudaiji minister[171] stretched a rope across his roof to keep the kites from roosting. Saigyō,[172] seeing the rope, asked, "Why should it bother him if kites perch there? That shows you the kind of man this prince is." I have heard that Saigyō never visited him again. I remembered this story not long ago when I noticed a rope stretched over the roof of the Kosaka palace,[173] where Prince Ayanokōji[174] lives. Someone told me that, as a matter of fact, it distressed the prince to see how crows clustering on the roof would swoop down to seize frogs in the pond. The story impressed me, and made me wonder if Sanesada may not also have had some such reason.

---

171. Fujiwara no Sanesada (1139–1191), a poet.

172. Saigyō (1118–1190), a noted waka poet.

173. Another name for the Tendai temple Myōhō-in.

174. The prince was a son of Emperor Kameyama (1249–1305) and was also known by his Buddhist name, Shōe.

Changing of the Seasons (19)

The changing of the seasons is deeply moving in its every manifestation. People seem to agree that autumn is the best season to appreciate the beauty of things. That may well be true, but the sights of spring are even more exhilarating. The cries of the birds gradually take on a peculiarly spring-like quality, and in the gentle sunlight the bushes begin to sprout along the fences. Then, as spring deepens, mists spread over the landscape and the cherry blossoms seem ready to open, only for steady rains and winds to cause them to scatter precipitously. The heart is subject to incessant pangs of emotion as the young leaves are growing out.

Orange blossoms are famous for evoking memories,[175] but the fragrance of plum blossoms above all makes us return to the past and remember nostalgically long-ago events. Nor can we overlook the clean loveliness of the *yamabuki*[176] or the uncertain beauty of wisteria, and so many other compelling sights.

Someone once remarked, "In summer, when the Feast of Anointing the Buddha[177] and the Kamo Festival come around, and the young leaves on the treetops grow thick and cool, our sensitivity to the touching beauty of the world and our longing for absent friends grow stronger." Indeed, this is so. When, in the Fifth Month, the irises bloom and the rice seedlings are transplanted, can anyone remain untroubled by the drumming of the water rails? Then, in the Sixth Month, you can see the whiteness of moonflowers glowing over wretched hovels, and the smoldering of mosquito incense is affecting too. The purification rites of the Sixth Month[178] are also engrossing.

The celebration of Tanabata is charming.[179] Then, as the nights gradually become cold and the wild geese cry, the under leaves of the *hagi*[180] turn yellow, and men harvest and dry the first crop of rice. So many moving sights come together, in autumn especially. And how unforgettable is the morning after an equinoctial storm!—As I go on I realize that these sights have long since been enumerated in *The Tale of Genji* and *The Pillow Book*, but I make no pretense of trying to avoid saying the same things again. If I fail to say what lies on my mind it gives me a

---

175. According to the Japanese poetic tradition, the scent of orange blossoms (*tachibana*) was believed to bring back old memories.

176. Sometimes translated as "kerria roses," a yellow flower.

177. On the eighth day of the Fourth Month, the birthday of Shakyamuni, his statues were anointed with perfumed water. The Kamo Festival was held in the middle of the Fourth Month. Both were summer events because, in the lunar calendar, summer began with the Fourth Month.

178. On the last day of the Sixth Month, the last day of summer, palace officials sent little floats down the Kamo River, intended to symbolize sins accumulated during the year.

179. Tanabata, a feast celebrated on the seventh night of the Seventh Month, commemorated the annual meeting of two stars.

180. Bush clover. The lavender or white flower is traditionally associated with the autumn rains. The turning of the colors of its underleaves is often mentioned in poetry as a sign of approaching winter.

feeling of flatulence; I shall therefore give my brush free rein. Mine is a foolish diversion, but these pages are meant to be torn up, and no one is likely to see them.

To return to the subject. Winter decay is hardly less beautiful than autumn. Crimson leaves lie scattered on the grass beside the ponds, and how delightful it is on a morning when the frost is very white to see the vapor rise from a garden stream. At the end of the year it is indescribably moving to see everyone hurrying about on errands. There is something forlorn about the waning winter moon, shining cold and clear in the sky, unwatched because it is said to be depressing. The Invocation of the Buddha Names and the departure of the messengers with the imperial offerings[181] are moving and inspiring. How impressive it is that so many palace ceremonials are performed besides all the preparations for the New Year! It is striking that the Worship of the Four Directions follows directly on the Expulsion of the Demons.[182]

On the last night of the year, when it is extremely dark, people light pine torches and go rushing about, pounding on the gates of strangers until well after midnight. I wonder what it signifies. After they have done with their exaggerated shouting and running so furiously that their feet hardly touch the ground, the noise at last fades away with the coming of the dawn, leaving a lonely feeling of regret over the departing old year. The custom of paying homage to the dead,[183] in the belief that they return that night, has lately disappeared from the capital, but I was deeply moved to discover that it was still performed in the East. As the day thus breaks on the New Year the sky seems no different from what it was the day before, but one feels somehow changed and renewed. The main thoroughfares, decorated their full length with pine boughs, seem cheerful and festive, and this too is profoundly affecting.

World as Unstable as the Asuka River (25)

The world is as unstable as the pools and shallows of the Asuka River.[184] Times change and things disappear: joy and sorrow come and go;[185] a place that once

---

181. For three days, beginning on the nineteenth day of the Twelfth Month, rites were performed at the Seiryōden to purify the sins of the six senses. The names of the Buddhas of the Three Worlds were invoked. Messengers were sent from the provinces in the middle of the Twelfth Month with offerings of the harvest for the imperial tombs.

182. The Expulsion of the Demons (Tsuina) took place on the last day of the year. The next morning, the emperor worshiped the Four Directions and the imperial tombs and prayed for a safe and prosperous year.

183. The last night of the year was one of six times during the year when the dead were believed to return. The Bon Festival preserves that belief today.

184. The Asuka River, a stream near Nara, figures prominently in Japanese poetry. Reference is made here to an anonymous poem in the Kokinshū, "In this world what is constant? In the Asuka River yesterday's pools are today's shallows."

185. These phrases are borrowed from the Japanese preface to the Kokinshū.

thrived turns into an uninhabited moor; a house may remain unaltered, but its occupants will have changed. The peach and the plum trees in the garden say nothing[186]—with whom is one to reminisce about the past? I feel this sense of impermanence even more sharply when I see the remains of a house which long ago, before I knew it, must have been imposing.

Whenever I pass by the ruins of the Kyōgoku Palace,[187] the Hōjō-ji temple,[188] and similar buildings, it moves me to think that the aspiration of the builders still lingers on, though the edifices themselves have changed completely. When Fujiwara Michinaga erected so magnificent a temple, bestowing many estates for its support, he supposed that his descendants would always assist the emperor and serve as pillars of the state; could he have imagined that the temple would fall into such ruin, no matter what times lay ahead? The Great Gate and the Golden Hall were still standing until recent years, but the Gate burned during the Shōwa era,[189] and the Golden Hall soon afterward fell over. It still lies there, and no attempt has been made to restore it. Only the Muryōju Hall[190] remains as a memento of the temple's former glory. Nine images of Amida Buddha,[191] each sixteen feet tall,[192] stand in a row, most awesomely. It is extremely moving to see, still plainly visible, the plaque inscribed by the Major Counselor Kōzei[193] and the door inscription by Kaneyuki. I understand that the Hokke Hall[194] and perhaps other buildings are still standing. I wonder how much longer they too will last?

Some buildings that lack even such remains may survive merely as foundation stones, but no one knows for certain to what they once belonged. It is true in all things that it is a futile business attempting to plan for a future one will never know.

When I Sit Down in Quiet Meditation (29)

When I sit down in quiet meditation, the one emotion hardest to fight against is a longing in all things for the past. After the others have gone to bed, I pass the time on a long autumn's night by putting in order whatever belongings are at hand. As I tear up scraps of old correspondence I should prefer not to leave

---

186. From a kanshi by Sugawara no Fumitoki (899–981), *Wakan rōeishū*, no. 548.

187. The palace of the powerful Fujiwara no Michinaga (966–1027).

188. Michinaga lived in this temple after retiring from public office in 1018.

189. The era lasted from 1312 to 1317. The date of the burning of the gate is not known.

190. The formal name of the Amida Hall within the Hōjō-ji, which burned down in 1331, indicating that Kenkō wrote this section before then.

191. Each statue represented one level of paradise.

192. Sixteen feet (*jōroku*) was the legendary height of the Buddha.

193. Fujiwara no Yukinari (972–1027), known by his artistic name of Kōzei, was a celebrated calligrapher.

194. A building used by Tendai priests for contemplation on the Lotus Sutra.

behind, I sometimes find among them samples of the calligraphy of a friend who has died, or pictures he drew for his own amusement, and I feel exactly as I did at the time. Even with letters written by friends who are still alive I try, when it has been long since we met, to remember the circumstances, the year. What a moving experience that is! It is sad to think that a man's familiar possessions, indifferent to his death, should remain unaltered long after he is gone.

To Be Governed by a Desire for Fame and Profit (38)

What a foolish thing it is to be governed by a desire for fame and profit and to fret away one's whole life without a moment of peace. Great wealth is no guarantee of security. Wealth, in fact, tends to attract calamities and disaster. Even if, after you die, you leave enough gold to prop up the North Star,[195] it will only prove a nuisance to your heirs. The pleasures that delight the foolish man are likewise meaningless to the man of discrimination who considers a big carriage, sleek horses, gold, and jeweled ornaments all equally undesirable and senseless. You had best throw away your gold in the mountains and drop your jewels into a ravine. It is an exceedingly stupid man who will torment himself for the sake of worldly gain.

To leave behind a reputation that will not perish through long ages to come is certainly to be desired, but can one say that men of high rank and position are necessarily superior? There are foolish and incompetent men who, having been born into an illustrious family and, being favored by the times, rise to exalted position and indulge themselves in the extremes of luxury. There are also many learned and good men who by their own choice remain in humble positions and end their days without ever having encountered good fortune. A feverish craving for high rank and position is second in foolishness only to seeking wealth.

One would like to leave behind a glorious reputation for surpassing wisdom and character, but careful reflection will show that what we mean by love of a glorious reputation is delight in the approbation of others. Neither those who praise nor those who abuse last for long, and the people who have heard their reports are likely to depart the world as quickly. Before whom then should we feel ashamed? By whom should we wish to be appreciated? Fame, moreover, inspires backbiting. It does no good whatsoever to have one's name survive. A craving after fame is next most foolish.

If I were to address myself to those who nevertheless seek desperately to attain knowledge and wisdom, I would say that knowledge leads to deceit, and artistic talent is the product of much suffering. True knowledge is not what one

---

195. The phrase is borrowed from a Chinese poem by Bo Juyi containing the lines "Even if, by the time you die, you have amassed gold enough to support the North Star, it is not as good as having a cask of wine while you are alive."

hears from others or acquires through study. What, then, are we to call knowl-edge? Proper and improper come to one and the same thing—can we call any-thing "good"?[196] The truly enlightened man has no learning, no virtue, no ac-complishments, no fame.[197] Who knows of him, who will report his glory? It is not that he conceals his virtue or pretends to be stupid; it is because from the outset he is above distinctions between wise and foolish, between profit and loss.

If, in your delusion, you seek fame and profit, the results will be as I have described. All is unreality. Nothing is worth discussing, worth desiring.

A House Should Be Built for Summer (55)

A house should be built with the summer in mind. In winter it is possible to live anywhere, but a badly made house is unbearable when it gets hot.

There is nothing cool-looking about deep water; a shallow, flowing stream is far cooler. When you are reading fine print you will find that a room with sliding doors is lighter than one with hinged shutters. A room with a high ceiling is cold in winter and dark by lamplight. People agree that a house which has plenty of spare room is attractive to look at and may be put to many different uses.

Determined to Take the Great Step (59)

A man who has determined to take the Great Step should leave unresolved all plans for disposing of urgent or worrisome business.

Some men think, "I'll wait a bit longer, until I take care of this matter," or "I might as well dispose of that business first," or "People will surely laugh at me if I leave such and such as it stands. I'll arrange things now so that there won't be any future criticism," or "I've managed to survive all these years. I'll wait till that matter is cleared up. It won't take long. I mustn't be hasty." But if you think in such terms the day for taking the Great Step will never come, for you will keep discovering more and more unavoidable problems, and there will never be a time when you run out of unfinished business.

My observation of people leads me to conclude, generally speaking, that even people with some degree of intelligence are likely to go through life sup-posing they have ample time before them. But would a man fleeing because a fire has broken out in his neighborhood say to the fire, "Wait a moment, please!"? To save his life, a man will run away, indifferent to shame, abandon-ing his possessions. Is a man's life any more likely to wait for him? Death attacks

---

196. The expression is from Zhuangzi, a Daoist philosopher, whose works were widely read by Zen monks of Kenkō's time.

197. This sentence, too, is from Zhuangzi.

faster than fire or water, and is harder to escape. When its hour comes, can you refuse to give up your aged parents, your little children, your duty to your master, your affections for others, because they are hard to abandon?

Gathering Like Ants (74)

They flock together like ants, hurry east and west, run north and south. Some are mighty, some humble. Some are aged, some young. They have places to go, houses to return to. At night they sleep, in the morning get up. But what does all this activity mean? There is no ending to their greed for long life, their grasping for profit. What expectations have they that they take such good care of themselves? All that awaits them in the end is old age and death, whose coming is swift and does not falter for one instant. What joy can there be while waiting for this end? The man who is deluded by fame and profit does not fear the approach of old age and death because he is so intoxicated by worldly cravings that he never stops to consider how near he is to his destination. The foolish man, for his part, grieves because he desires everlasting life and is ignorant of the law of universal change.

Are We to Look at Cherry Blossoms Only in Full Bloom? (137)

Are we to look at cherry blossoms only in full bloom, the moon only when it is cloudless? To long for the moon while looking on the rain, to lower the blinds and be unaware of the passing of the spring—these are even more deeply moving. Branches about to blossom or gardens strewn with faded flowers are worthier of our admiration. Are poems written on such themes as "Going to view the cherry blossoms only to find they had scattered" or "On being prevented from visiting the blossoms" inferior to those on "Seeing the blossoms"? People commonly regret that the cherry blossoms scatter or that the moon sinks in the sky, and this is natural; but only an exceptionally insensitive man would say, "This branch and that branch have lost their blossoms. There is nothing worth seeing now."

In all things, it is the beginnings and ends that are interesting. Does the love between men and women refer only to the moments when they are in each other's arms? The man who grieves over a love affair broken off before it was fulfilled, who bewails empty vows, who spends long autumn nights alone, who lets his thoughts wander to distant skies, who yearns for the past in a dilapidated house—such a man truly knows what love means.

The moon that appears close to dawn after we have long waited for it moves us more profoundly than the full moon shining cloudless over a thousand leagues. And how incomparably lovely is the moon, almost greenish in its light, when seen through the tops of the cedars deep in the mountains, or when it hides for a moment behind clustering clouds during a sudden shower! The sparkle on hickory or white-oak leaves seemingly wet with moonlight strikes one to the heart. One suddenly misses the capital, longing for a friend who could share the moment.

And are we to look at the moon and the cherry blossoms with our eyes alone? How much more evocative and pleasing it is to think about the spring without stirring from the house, to dream of the moonlit night though we remain in our room!

The man of breeding never appears to abandon himself completely to his pleasures; even his manner of enjoyment is detached. It is the rustic boors who take all their pleasures grossly. They squirm their way through the crowd to get under the trees; they stare at the blossoms with eyes for nothing else; they drink saké and compose linked verse; and finally they heartlessly break off great branches and cart them away. When they see a spring they dip their hands and feet to cool them; if it is the snow, they jump down to leave their footprints. No matter what the sight, they are never content merely with looking at it.

Such people have a very peculiar manner of watching the Kamo Festival. "The procession's awfully late," they say. "There's no point waiting in the stands for it to come." They go off then to a shack behind the stands where they drink and eat, play go or backgammon, leaving somebody in the stands to warn them. When he cries, "It's passing now!" each of them dashes out in wild consternation, struggling to be first back into the stands. They all but fall from their perches as they push out the blinds and press against one another for a better look, staring at the scene, determined not to miss a thing. They comment on everything that goes by, with cries of "Look at this! Look at that!" When the procession has passed, they scramble down, saying, "We'll be back for the next one." All they are interested in is what they can see.

People from the capital, the better sort, doze during the processions, hardly looking at all. Young underlings are constantly moving about, performing their masters' errands, and persons in attendance, seated behind, never stretch forward in an unseemly manner. No one is intent on seeing the procession at all costs.

It is charming on the day of the festival to see garlands of hollyhock leaves carelessly strewn over everything. The morning of the festival, before dawn breaks, you wonder who the owners are of the carriages silently drawn up in place, and guess, "That one is his—or his," and have your guesses confirmed when sometimes you recognize a coachman or servant. I never weary of watching the different carriages going back and forth, some delightfully unpretentious, others magnificent. By the time it is growing dark you wonder where the rows of carriages and the dense crowds of spectators have disappeared to. Before you know it, hardly a soul is left, and the congestion of returning carriages is over. Then they start removing the blinds and matting from the stands, and the place, even as you watch, begins to look desolate. You realize with a pang of grief that life is like this. If you have seen the avenues of the city, you have seen the festival.

I suddenly realized, from the large number of people I could recognize in the crowds passing to and fro before the stands, that there were not so many people in the world, after all. Even if I were not to die until all of them had gone, I should not have long to wait. If you pierce a tiny aperture in a large vessel filled with water, even though only a small amount drips out, the constant leakage will empty the vessel. In this capital, with all its many people, surely a day never passes without someone dying. And are there merely one or two deaths a day? On some days, certainly, many more than one or two are seen to their graves at Toribeno, Funaoka, and other mountainsides, but never a day passes without a single funeral. That is why coffin makers never have any to spare. It does not matter how young or how strong you may be, the hour of death comes sooner than you expect. It is an extraordinary miracle that you should have escaped to this day; do you suppose you have even the briefest respite in which to relax?

When you make a *mamagodate*[198] with backgammon counters, at first you cannot tell which of the stones arranged before you will be taken away. Your count then falls on a certain stone and you remove it. The others seem to have escaped, but as you renew the count you will thin out the pieces one by one, until none is left. Death is like that. The soldier who goes to war, knowing how close he is to death, forgets his family and even forgets himself; the man who has turned his back on the world and lives in a thatched hut, quietly taking pleasure in the streams and rocks of his garden, may suppose that death in battle has nothing to do with him, but this is a shallow misconception. Does he imagine that, if he hides in the still recesses of the mountains, the enemy called change will fail to attack? When you confront death, no matter where it may be, it is the same as charging into battle.

[Translated by Donald Keene]

---

198. A kind of mathematical puzzle. Fifteen white and fifteen black stones are so arranged that eliminating the tenth stone, counting in one direction, will result after fourteen rounds in only one white stone remaining. If the count is then resumed in the opposite direction, all the black stones will be eliminated, leaving the one white stone. The Japanese name *mamagodate* (stepchild disposition) derives from the story of a man with fifteen children by one wife and fifteen by another; his estate was disposed of by means of the game, one stepchild in the end inheriting all.

Chapter 4

THE MUROMACHI PERIOD

The late medieval period extends from the beginning of the Kenmu restoration (1333–1336) to the battle of Sekigahara in 1600, roughly 270 years that can be further subdivided into the Northern and Southern Courts (Nanboku-chō) period (1336–1392), the Muromachi period (1392–1573), and the Azuchi–Momoyama period (1573–1598).

In 1333 the Kamakura shogunate was overthrown by warrior forces that rallied to the royalist cause of Emperor GoDaigo (r. 1318–1339). GoDaigo saw the overthrow of the Kamakura shogunate as a mandate to revive what he believed to be the direct imperial rule that had existed before the rise of the Fujiwara regents in the mid-Heian period, the powerful retired emperors in the late Heian period, and the *bakufu* (military government) in the Kamakura period. The "imperial restoration," known as the Kenmu restoration, lasted for only three years, until 1336, when a struggle broke out between Nitta Yoshisada (1301–1338) and Ashikaga Takauji (1305–1358), the leaders of two branches of the Minamoto, both of whom had initially rallied to GoDaigo's cause. In 1336 Takauji defeated Yoshisada and captured Kyoto. GoDaigo fled to Yoshino, in the mountains to the south. Takauji then had a member of another branch of the imperial family named as emperor in Kyoto, making two emperors, one in the north (Kyoto) and one in the south (Yoshino), a situation that was not resolved until 1392 when the two lines were rejoined. Meanwhile, Takauji established a new shogunate, known later as the Ashikaga or Muromachi shogunate (1336–1573), with its offices in the Muromachi quarters of Kyoto.

The sixty years of the Northern and Southern Courts was probably the bloodiest period in Japanese history. The depth of its chaos and internal conflict are vividly depicted in the *Taiheiki* (1340s–1371), a military history that bears the seemingly ironic title *Chronicle of Great Peace*. Nonetheless, despite the constant bloodshed and upheaval, a new culture emerged. A new form of poetry, *renga* (classical linked verse), led by Nijō Yoshimoto (1320–1388), became popular; historical chronicles written in the vernacular appeared; Zen priests wrote their finest kanshi (Chinese) poetry; kyōgen (comic drama) were performed; and nō theater was first established as a high art form by Kan'ami (1333–1384).

Noteworthy among the historical chronicles of the Nanboku-chō period are *The Clear Mirror* (*Masukagami*, 1338–1376), which recounts the history of the Kamakura period, especially the Jōkyū rebellion (1221), which resulted in Emperor GoToba's exile, and Kitabatake Chikafusa's *Chronicle of Gods and Sovereigns* (*Jinnō shōtōki*, 1339, 1343), which, under the influence of Ise Shinto, argues for the legitimacy of the imperial succession from the perspective of the Southern Court. But the outstanding military chronicle is the *Taiheiki*, a history of the throne and the different samurai houses involved in the turmoil of the Northern and Southern Courts period. The *Taiheiki* was recited widely, and beginning in the Muromachi period, it had a great impact on popular culture.

Until the thirteenth century, *renga* (linked verse) had been monopolized by court aristocrats, but from the end of the Kamakura period (1185–1333), it suddenly spread to samurai, temple-shrines, and commoners across the country. In response to this new market, texts like the *Tsukuba Collection* (*Tsukubashū*, 1356), an anthology of renga edited by Nijō Yoshimoto, one of the leading intellectuals and poets of the day, were compiled.

The Muromachi period—named after the Ashikaga clan that established the *bakufu*, or military government, in Muromachi, a section of Kyoto—lasted for about 180 years, from 1392, when the two imperial courts were unified, to 1573, when Oda Nobunaga (1534–1582) drove out the fifteenth and last Ashikaga shogun, Ashikaga Yoshiaki (1537–1597). The latter half of the Muromachi period is sometimes referred to as the Sengoku (Warring States) period (1467–1573), beginning with the Ōnin war (1467–1477) and ending with the unification of the country under Oda Nobunaga in 1573. The Azuchi–Momoyama period, when Oda Nobunaga and his successor Toyotomi Hideyoshi (1537–1598) held control of the country, began with the fall of the Muromachi shogunate in 1573 and ended with the battle of Sekigahara, which unified the country in 1600 under Tokugawa Ieyasu and ushered in the Tokugawa, or Edo, period.

During the Northern and Southern Courts period, classical court culture gradually disappeared, replaced by the rise of linked verse (pioneered by Nijō Yoshimoto and others), the flourishing of Chinese poetry by Zen monks, and the emergence of nō drama, kyōgen, and such dance (*mai*) forms as *kowakamai* (ballad drama). These dramatic forms prospered in the Muromachi-period and were patronized by and became the favorite pastimes of powerful domain lords and shoguns. Otogi-zōshi (the narrative successor to monogatari and setsuwa) and *kouta* (little songs) were popular as well. Theories of art and drama became highly developed during the Muromachi period, with Zeami's (1363?–1443?) and Zenchiku's (1405?–1470?) treatises on nō drama, Shōtetsu's (1381–1459) treatise on waka, and Sōgi's (1421–1502) and Shinkei's (1406–1475) writings on renga. The short Azuchi–Momoyama period represents a transition to the Tokugawa or early modern period, in which *sekkyō-bushi* (sermon ballads) were popular and jōruri (puppet theater) and kabuki first appeared. In the late medieval period, haikai (popular linked verse) and renga (classical linked verse) found large audiences, and by the seventeenth century, haikai had become the most widely practiced literary genre in Japan. In 1549 the Jesuit order (Societas Jesu, J. Yasokai), which was founded in 1540, sent missionaries to Japan, and they brought with them Western culture and produced a romanized version of *Aesop's Fables*.

THE PATRONAGE OF THE ASHIKAGA

The Muromachi bakufu came of age with the third shogun, Ashikaga Yoshimitsu (r. 1368–1394), who unified the Northern and Southern imperial courts. Yoshimitsu was also a great patron of the arts and is especially remembered for the retreat that he built at Kitayama, north of the capital, and for the construction of the Kinkaku-ji (Golden Pavilion). The cultural efflorescence under Ashikaga Yoshimitsu and his son Ashikaga Yoshimochi, the fourth shogun (r. 1394–1423), is referred to as Kitayama culture. In the Muromachi period, both nō and kyōgen matured into major genres, particularly under the leadership of Zeami, whose patron was Yoshimitsu. Another notable period of cultural activity was the so-called Higashiyama period, in the latter half of the fifteenth century, primarily during the rule of Ashikaga Yoshimasa (1436–1490, r. 1449–1473), the eighth shogun. In 1483 he built a retreat at Higashiyama (the Ginkaku-ji, or Silver Pavilion), where he led an elegant life and supported nō drama, tea ceremony, flower arrangement, renga, and landscape gardening. Higashiyama culture, as it is called, is noted for its fusion of warrior, aristocratic, and Zen elements, particularly the notions of *wabi* and *sabi*, which found beauty and depth in minimalist, seemingly impoverished, material.

The origins of nō drama were the *sarugaku* (literally, "monkey/comic art") schools associated with shrines and temples (such as the Kasuga Shrine) in Ōmi and Yamato Provinces. The actors belonged to groups attached to private estate owners (*ryōshu*) and large temples and shrines in the Kinai region (Yamato, Yamashiro, Kawachi, Izumi, and Settsu Provinces). A number of nō plays are based on *engi-mono*, stories about the origins of local gods. During the Northern and Southern Courts period, when nō and kyōgen matured, Kan'ami (1333–1384) and Zeami were being patronized by the Ashikaga shogunal family, which stood at the apex of power. At that point, nō and kyōgen broke away from their earlier dependence on temples and shrines and from their function as religious performances supporting the private estate system. Of particular interest here is that in their mature phase, nō and kyōgen, which had developed in the provinces as commoner entertainment, now were the province of the Muromachi military government, situated in the capital, which was actively absorbing the court culture. At this time, nō reflected Heian court culture and aesthetics and developed the aesthetics of *yūgen* (mystery and depth), which included evocations of the classical past. Characteristic of this phase of nō was the woman play (*katsura mono*), including plays about characters from *The Tales of Ise* and *The Tale of Genji*. Despite first taking shape in the provinces and outside the central spheres of power, nō now was helping enforce the authority of the center, of the Muromachi bakufu, and of the revival of imperial court culture.

ZEN AND SAMURAI CULTURE

From the latter half of the thirteenth century and peaking in the fourteenth century, Song and Yuan Zen culture was imported into the world of the shrines and temples in both Kamakura and Kyoto. Zen Buddhism influenced such art forms as dry stone gardens (*karesansui*), monochromatic ink-painting, Chinese poetry (kanshi), and tea ceremony. Using the Chinese cultural forms that the Zen institutions had imported, the temples and shrines created a new culture distinct from that established by the Heian court aristocrats.

Likewise, samurai culture used Zen culture to transform itself. Until the thirteenth century—despite the outstanding samurai waka poets like Minamoto Sanetomo (1192–1219); the third Kamakura shogun (r. 1203–1219), who produced the *Poetry Collection of the Minister from Kamakura* (*Kinkaishū*), in a neo-*Man'yōshū* style; and the bakufu rituals imitating those of the Kyoto nobility—they all remained within the framework of aristocratic culture. Then, beginning in the latter half of the thirteenth century, when the bakufu had as much authority as the imperial court, the samurai slowly began to produce their own culture, particularly through the medium of Zen. The bakufu invited Zen intellectual leaders to Kamakura, and under its patronage the Zen priests imported texts and utensils from Song and Yuan China. After the Northern and Southern Courts period, this Zen-inspired samurai culture developed rapidly, creating a distinctive culture that was more than merely an imitation of Zen culture.

THE RISE OF PROVINCIAL CULTURE

One of the main characteristics of the late medieval period is that the various genres that had originated in Heian court culture—the imperial anthologies of Japanese poetry (*chokusenshū*), the vernacular court tales (*monogatari*), and women's court diaries (*nikki*)—and that had continued to flourish in the Kamakura period, almost completely died out. The editing and collecting of *setsuwa* (anecdotes), which were popular in the late Heian and Kamakura periods, also ended with the compilation of the *Records of Three Countries* (*Sangoku denki*), in the first half of the fifteenth century.

Perhaps one of the most salient characteristics of the Muromachi culture was its focus on commoner life and values in the provinces. In the late Heian period, setsuwa collections such as the *Tales of Times Now Past* (*Konjaku monogatari shū*, ca. 1120) provided a window onto life in the provinces, but the values remained largely those of the capital and the aristocracy. But in the late medieval period, the perspectives of the provinces and of the commoners formed a counterbalance to those of the capital and aristocrats.

At the beginning of the medieval period, the establishment of the bakufu, the seat of the military government, in the east in Kamakura, far from the capital, had a great impact on medieval culture. Although cultural activity continued to be centered in Kyoto, a new community of intellectuals gathered in Kamakura, making it a separate cultural center. The spread of culture outside the capital increased dramatically during the Warring States period (1467–1573). The Ōnin war (1467–1477), which arose over an inheritance issue involving the Ashikaga shogun and which pitted daimyō (military lords) from the west against those in the east, took place mainly in Kyoto and destroyed the city, leading aristocrats and cultural figures to flee to the provinces.

The rise of a new culture was closely related to the development of roads and travel, the reasons for which are various. Many people wanted to escape the ravages of war, and the aristocracy, particularly after being driven out of the capital during the Ōnin war, sought the patronage of wealthy provincial lords. Buddhist and Shinto followers frequently went on pilgrimages to shrines and temples, the most famous of which was the pilgrimage to Ise Shrine. Various religious groups—such as monks from Mount Kōya (*Kōya hijiri*), monks soliciting donations for temple building (*kanjin hijiri*), and nuns (*bikuni*)—also traveled, as did *biwa hōshi* (lute-playing minstrels), *etoki* (picture storytellers), nō actors, kyōgen players, and puppeteers (*tekugutsu*). Renga masters, who often were half layperson and half priest, also traveled to compose with different groups throughout the country, to give lessons on the Japanese classics, and to inspire their own poetry.

The culture of the capital was thus carried to the provinces while the culture of the provinces was brought to the capital, giving new life to both. This interaction of oral and written, aristocratic and commoner, led, particularly in the late medieval period, to the juxtaposition of the elegant, refined sensibility (*ushin*) and the common or popular (*mushin*), the serious and the comic, the elite and the popular—what in the Tokugawa period was called *ga* (high) and *zoku* (low). This dialectic is evident in the relationship of nō to kyōgen, and of renga (classical linked verse) to haikai (popular linked verse). Sometimes a commoner genre (such as *sarugaku*, a form of mime) evolved into an elite genre like nō, shedding its comic, vulgar, or commoner roots. Sometimes, however, a genre continued to cultivate its own popular base (as with kyōgen and haikai).

NŌ DRAMA

Nō drama consists of dance, song, and dialogue and is traditionally performed by an all-male cast. Sometime in the late Kamakura period (1192–1333), *sarugaku* (literally, "monkey/comic art"), a performance art that includes comic mime and skits, evolved into nō drama. Sarugaku troupes served at temples, and it is believed that their roles in religious rituals have been preserved in the oldest and most ritualistic piece in the current nō repertoire, *Okina* (literally, *Old Man*), in which the dances of deities celebrate and purify a world at peace.

By the mid-fourteenth century, nō had gained wide popularity and was performed not only by sarugaku but also by *dengaku* troupes. Dengaku had originally been a type of musical accompaniment to the planting of rice, but its troupes came to specialize in acrobatics and dance as well. In the late fourteenth century, a period of intense competition (among troupes and between sarugaku and dengaku), the Kanze troupe, a sarugaku troupe from Yamato Province (now Nara Prefecture), led first by Kan'ami (1333–1384) and later by his son Zeami (1363?–1443?), shaped the genre into what is seen on today's stage.

Kan'ami attracted audiences with his rare talent as a performer and a playwright. Among his innovations was the introduction of the *kusemai*, a popular genre combining song and dance, in which the dancing performer rhythmically chants a long narrative. By incorporating the rhythms of kusemai singing into his troupe's performances, Kan'ami transformed the hitherto rather monotonous nō chanting into a more dramatic form, one that became very popular and was soon emulated by other sarugaku and dengaku troupes.

In 1374, Kan'ami's growing popularity finally inspired the seventeen-year-old Yoshimitsu (1358–1408, r. 1368–1394), the third Ashikaga shogun, to attend a performance by Kan'ami's troupe in Imagumano (in eastern Kyoto). From that time on, the young shogun became a fervent patron of Kan'ami's troupe. Yoshimitsu also was charmed by a beautiful boy actor, the twelve-year-old Zeami. Zeami soon began serving the shogun as his favorite page, mixing with court nobles and attending linked-poetry (renga) parties and other cultural events. After Kan'ami's death, however, Yoshimitsu's patronage shifted from Zeami, now a mature nō performer and the head of his own troupe, to Inuō (also known as Dōami, d. 1413), a performer in a sarugaku troupe from Ōmi Province (now Shiga Prefecture). Inuō had gained a reputation for his "heavenly maiden dance" (*tennyo-no-mai*), an elegant dance that was said to epitomize *yūgen*, a term signifying profound and refined beauty and the dominant aesthetic among upper social circles.

In order to maintain the shogun's favor, Zeami had to keep producing new plays and reforming his troupe's performing style in accordance with shifting aesthetic trends. Zeami's plays, of which he wrote nearly forty (or more than fifty, if his revisions of existing plays are included), are marked by exquisite phrasing and frequent allusions to Japanese classical texts. In addition, Zeami incorporated Inuō's elegant dance into his own plays, even though his troupe had originally specialized in wild demon plays and realistic mimicry. In an effort to adjust his troupe's performances to the principle of yūgen, Zeami created plays with elegant dances and refined versification, which poetically represented aristocratic characters often drawn from Heian monogatari. In his twenty or so theoretical treatises on nō, he also emphasized the importance of using yūgen in every aspect of nō.

Another of Zeami's innovations was the *mugen-nō* (dream play or phantasmal play), which typically consists of two acts. In the first, a traveler (often a traveling monk) meets a ghost, a plant spirit, or a deity, who, in the guise of a local commoner, recalls a famous episode that took place at that location, and in the second act, the ghost, spirit, or deity reappears in its original form in the monk's dream. The ghost usually recalls a crucial incident in its former life, an incident that is now causing attachment and obstructing its path to buddhahood. By reenacting that incident, the ghost seeks to gain enlightenment through the monk's prayers. The focus of these plays thus is less on the interaction between the characters than on the protagonist's emotional state.

Ashikaga Yoshinori (Yoshimitsu's son), who became the sixth Ashikaga shogun in 1429, favored Zeami's nephew On'ami, eventually placing him at the head of the Kanze troupe. With the loss of the shogun's patronage, Zeami's second son took the tonsure and left the theater. His elder son Motomasa, the author of *Sumida River* (*Sumidagawa*) and Zeami's last hope, died in 1432, in his early thirties. In 1435 Zeami was exiled to Sado, a remote island in northeastern Japan. The year of his death is not certain, nor is it known whether he died on Sado or was pardoned and permitted to return to Kyoto.

After his death, Zeami's plays were recognized as central to the repertoire and were followed especially faithfully by Zeami's son-in-law Zenchiku (1405?–1470?), the author of *Shrine in the Fields* (*Nonomiya*). In the late Muromachi period, following the Ōnin war (1467–1477), audiences began to exhibit a taste for different types of nō, spurring the creation of more spectacular plays, such as those depicting dramatic events occurring in the present (for example, *Ataka*) and often featuring realistic battle scenes.

Nō became especially popular among the warrior class. When Tokugawa Ieyasu founded his shogunate in Edo in 1603, he bestowed his official patronage on four sarugaku troupes: Kanze, Hōshō, Konparu, and Kongō, all from Yamato (later the Kita troupe was added). As a result, only those performers affiliated with these four (or five) troupes were officially allowed to perform nō. It also became customary among provincial lords (daimyō), following the shogun's lead, to employ performers of official nō troupes, who performed on ceremonial occasions. One of the direct outcomes of this ceremonialization of nō was a lengthening of performance times, as a result of which the plays came to be performed with much more rigorous precision. The intention was not to bring nō into line with changing trends but to preserve and refine the established plays and performance styles.

Although around 2,000 nō plays still exist, the current repertoire consists of only about 240 plays, most of which were written between the fourteenth and sixteenth centuries. And even today, many of the most frequently performed plays are those written by Zeami.

THEATRICAL ELEMENTS

The *shite*, or protagonist, is often a supernatural being such as a ghost, plant spirit, deity, or demon. Most nō plays center on the shite's words and deeds— that is, his or her telling of a story, usually about the shite's own past, in the form of a monologue and dance. The characters subordinate to the shite are called *shite-tsure* (companions to the shite) or simply *tsure*. In two-act plays, the shite in the first act is called the *mae-shite* (or *mae-jite* [shite before]), and in the second act, the *nochi-shite* (or *nochi-jite* [shite after]). The nochi-shite usually appears in a different costume, signifying the revelation of his or her true identity, and sometimes even as a different character altogether.

The *waki* is the character opposite—although not necessarily antagonistic to—the shite. When the shite is a supernatural being, the waki is usually a traveling monk who listens to the shite's retelling of the past. But when the shite is a living warrior, the waki is most often a warrior of the opposing camp. Unlike the shite, the waki is always a living person. The characters subordinate to the waki, often their retainers or traveling companions, are called *waki-tsure* (or *waki-zure*). The *ai* or *ai-kyōgen* is a minor character in a nō play, such as a local villager, who might provide the waki, and thus the audience, with a relatively colloquial, prose recapitulation of what the shite has already recounted in poetry. In some plays, especially those written in the late Muromachi period, comical characters appear *during* the acts as, for example, in *Ataka*. These characters are also called *ai*.

The chorus consists of six to ten members who sit motionless throughout the play on the right side of the stage and do not have a specific role in the play.

Sometimes they chant the words of one or another of the characters, and at other times they describe the scene. The main nō stage is a square about nineteen by nineteen feet. During a performance, the actors usually enter and exit the stage along the bridgeway (*hashigakari*) to the left. Nō never uses painted scenery or backdrops. The setting is depicted only verbally, and many plays have no stage props at all. Others have only a symbolic prop used for the most significant element of a play's setting. When placed on the bare stage, this prop attracts the audience's attention and becomes the play's focal point. The characters sometimes hold swords, rosaries, or willow boughs that signify that the holder is crazed (as with the mother in *Sumida River*). All performers carry fans, which are sometimes used as substitutes for other props, such as a writing brush, a saké flask, or a knife.

Most actors wear masks, although the waki and waki-tsure, who always portray living male characters, never do. A performer without a mask must never show any facial expression or use makeup; he is expected to use his own face as if it were a mask. Except for some masks that are made for specific characters (such as the shite's mask in *Kagekiyo*), most masks represent generic types. For example, *waka-onna* masks, which show a young female face, are used for both the female saltmaker in *Pining Wind* (*Matsukaze*) and Lady Rokujō in *Shrine in the Fields*.

Demon masks, with their ferocious faces and large, protruding eyes, express fierce supernatural power, while masks of human characters (including ghosts), whose feelings and emotions are often the focus of a play, usually display a static and rather neutral expression instead of a specific emotion. These masks are paradoxically said to be both "nonexpressive" and "limitlessly expressive," since the expression appears to change according to the angle of a performer's face. The actor's unchanging "face" also encourages audience members to project onto his mask the emotional content that they detect from the chanting. Interestingly, the nō masks are slightly smaller than the human faces they cover, revealing the tip of the performer's lower jaw and thus disrupting the audience's full immersion in dramatic illusion.

Nō costumes are famous for their splendor and exquisite beauty. Most are made of stiff, heavy materials that are folded around the performer's body like origami. A lighter kimono, made from a translucent fabric and with long, wide sleeves, is sometimes worn over these costumes. Thus, just as masks conceal the actor's facial individuality, so the costumes conceal his physical individuality. The beauty and expressiveness of his performance thus are not in the particular features of his own face and body but in the grace and expressiveness of his movements.

Movements on the nō stage are strictly choreographed and are generally very slow and highly stylized. Weeping, for example, is expressed merely by slowly lifting one hand toward the eyes and then lowering it again. This strict economy of movement infuses each gesture with meaning. One step forward can express

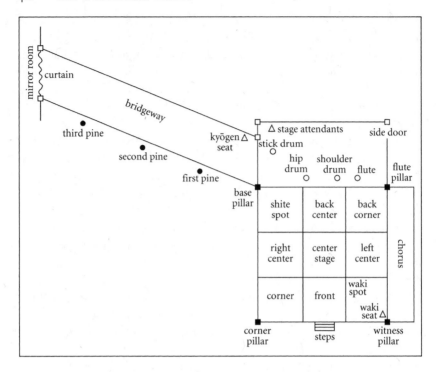

Diagram of a nō stage.

joy, resolution, or any other feeling that seems to fit the context. The fundamental basis for the dances and gestures of nō is the standing posture (*kamae*) and a stylized manner of walking called *hakobi*. Shite actors play characters of both sexes, with gender expressed by subtle variations of the angles of the performer's limbs and, above all, by the way he stands and walks. Differences in age, social status, and mental state are indicated similarly. Because so much emphasis is placed on a simple movement like walking, nō has often been characterized as "the art of walking."

Dance in nō is performed to musical accompaniment, by either the musicians alone or the musicians and chorus together. In many plays, dances set to the chanting of the chorus appear in the *kuse* section and at the end of the play. The dance in the kuse section consists mostly of abstract movements. Because they do not have any fixed meanings, dances can be interpreted according to the general context or to that of the lines that accompany them, in much the same way that a single nō mask can project a broad range of emotions. By contrast, the dance at the end of the play usually includes many specifically representational movements that mimetically render the words of the text. Dances set to instrumental music generally are abstract as well and usually are similar in both movement and music. The same series of movements can appear in a rapid, exuberant "deity dance" (*kami-mai*), an elegant and gentle dance (*chū-no-mai*), or a tranquil and meditative dance (*jo-no-mai*), depending on the tempo and mood of otherwise very similar music. As with the masks, these dances, too, are generic. The same chū-no-mai, for example, is performed by a noble youth in *Atsumori* and by the female saltmaker in *Pining Wind*.

The chanting styles of nō are divided into speech (*kotoba*) and song (*fushi*), with the speech actually more intoned than spoken. Song can be further subdivided into "congruent song" (*hyōshi ai*), which is chanted in a steady rhythm, keeping precise time with the drums, and "noncongruent song" (*hyōshi awazu*), which incorporates prolonged grace notes into important phrases and is not chanted in measured time. There also are two modes of singing: a "dynamic mode" (*tsuyogin* or *gōgin*) and a "melodic mode" (*yowagin* or *wagin*). The dynamic mode is generally used for the roles of warriors and demons, and the melodic mode is reserved for female and elderly roles. In many plays, however, the same character may use both modes. For example, in *Kiyotsune*, even though the shite chants mainly in the dynamic mode, he frequently switches to the melodic mode (in segments indicated, for example, as *ge-no-ei*, *kakeai*, *jō-no-ei*, or *uta*) in order to convey two different aspects of the same character: warrior and loving husband.

Except for the preceding modes, which were introduced only after the Tokugawa period, the distinctions in chanting styles, as well as the rhythmic patterns and the degree of regularity of the syllabic meter, are necessary for distinguishing subsections (*shōdan*) of plays. In the following translations, the names of subsections are indicated in parentheses preceding the text. Each subsection has its own pattern of musical structure and/or content, which remains consistent from play to play. For example, the subsection called the *nanori* is a self-introduction by a character and is chanted mostly in the speech style, while a kuse is a congruent song with narrative elements that starts in a lower register and then moves to a higher one.

Instrumental music accompanies the dances and some of the chanting, as well as the entrance and exit of the characters. The music is provided by one flute and three different types of drums, each played by a single musician. With this dominance of percussion instruments, the music of nō consists more of silence than of sound. In fact, silence (*ma* ["interval" or "gap"]) is traditionally regarded as the principal element of nō music. The sounds of the instruments, as well as the intermittent cries of the drummers, are introduced in order to interrupt the flow of time in nō plays and to make the silence between sounds all the more noticeable.

Among the several ways in which nō plays are categorized, the one most widely used today is the "five categories," which generally are differentiated according to the type of shite. The first category is the "deity play" (*waki-nō* or *kami-nō*), in which a deity explains the origin of a shrine, or a related legend, and celebrates the peaceful reign of an emperor. The second is the "warrior play" (*shura-nō*), in which the ghost of a warrior, now tormented in the hellish realm of constant battle known as the *shura* realm, reenacts a battle scene from his previous life. The third is the "woman play" (*kazura-mono*), whose protagonists are mostly elegant female figures, including the ghosts of women or female plant spirits. The "fourth-category plays" (*yobanme-mono*), also referred to as "miscellaneous plays" (*zō mono*), include all plays that do not fit into any of the other four categories, including plays about mad people, living warriors, or the spirits of the dead who linger in this world because of their excessive attachments. The fifth category is "demon plays" (*oni-nō*), also called "ending plays" (*kiri-nō*), in which the protagonists usually are demons.

This categorization scheme originated in the late seventeenth century. From that time until the present, a formal program for a nō-play performance usually includes one play from each of the five categories, performed in the preceding order, with a kyōgen play between each nō play. Today, however, performances in this full formal configuration are staged only on special occasions, such as New Year's Day.

Many nō plays draw on and allude to classical texts like *The Tales of Ise*, *The Tale of Genji*, or folk legends of such famous figures as Ono no Komachi. Since classical texts were largely disseminated through medieval commentaries, many plays also reflect contemporary interpretations of their source material. In addition, playwrights often introduced their own new twists to familiar narratives. Indeed, the mugen-nō structure gave playwrights the perfect format for such reinterpretations, as famous episodes could be subjectively reconstrued through the personal recollections of a ghost.

Nō plays are also interlarded with citations from famous poems and classic tales. *Atsumori*, for example, offers an analogy between its eponymous hero, who is a character from *The Tales of the Heike*, and the protagonist of *The Tale of Genji*; similarly, the crazed mother in *Sumida River* compares herself with the nobleman protagonist of *The Tales of Ise*. Such heavy dependence on classical allusions is especially noticeable in Zeami's and Zenchiku's plays and suggests an audience with a high level of literary erudition. In fact, the most popular literary activity at the time in high society—also practiced, to some extent, even among commoners—was the composition of linked verses (renga), which required the participants to allude constantly to a wide range of earlier literary works. It was in such a cultural milieu that nō developed.

The following plays are presented in chronological order, so as to give some sense of the historical development of the genre.

[All nō introductions by Akiko Takeuchi]

Subsections
According to Styles

Primary Speech Styles

katari	story narration
yomimono	recitation
mondō	question and answer
nanori	self-introduction
tsuki-zerifu	arrival speech

Noncongruent Song Styles

ei	chanted poem
ge-no-ei	waka recited in the lower register
jō-no-ei	waka recited in the upper register
issei	song in regular 7/5 meter mostly in the upper register, typically chanted right after the entrance of a character
kakeai	segment chanted alternately by two characters
kudoki	song sung mostly in the lower register, expressing lament or sorrow
kuri	short segment sung mostly in the high register, incorporating the highest pitch (also called *kuri*) and prolonged grace notes
kudoki-guri	*kuri* just before *kudoki*
nanori-guri	*kuri* that delivers a character's self-introduction
sashi	song that starts in the upper register, narrating a scene in a relatively plain rhythm and melody
waka	recitation of a waka just after a dance

Congruent Song Styles

uta	song in regular 7/5 meter
age-uta	song sung in the upper and middle registers
sage-uta	song sung in the middle and low registers
dan-uta	song starting in the fashion of *age-uta* but developing into a different pattern
chū-noriji	song sung in vigorous *chū-nori* rhythm, in which each syllable matches a half beat; typically used in the ending scene of a warrior play
kiri	simple song sung in the middle register with almost no grace notes, at the end of a play
kuse	song with narrative elements, which starts in the low register and then moves to a higher one

noriji	song sung in ōnori rhythm, characterized by an especially steady, rhythmical beat, with each syllable lasting a whole beat
rongi	segment chanted alternately by characters (or a character and a chorus)
shidai	short song in regular meter, starting in the upper register and ending in the lower one

Subsections that do not fit the preceding categories are listed as "unnamed."

LADY AOI (AOI NO UE)
Anonymous, revised by Zeami

Lady Aoi is the oldest of the numerous nō plays that draw on *The Tale of Genji*. In the nō treatise *Conversations on Sarugaku* (*Sarugakudangi*), Zeami recalls watching the play performed by Inuō (d. 1413), a senior sarugaku performer from Ōmi Province. The text included here is probably Zeami's revision of a play that was originally written for Inuō's troupe.[1] Since the play still preserves what are regarded as basic characteristics of nō theater from Ōmi Province—such as a female demon as the protagonist and a struggle between a monk and a vengeful spirit—Zeami's contribution was probably rather minor and may have been largely limited to refinements in phrasing.

The play is based on a famous episode in *The Tale of Genji*, in the "Heartvine" (Aoi) chapter, in which the young Genji has an affair with Lady Rokujō, a widow of the late crown prince known for her sophistication and beauty. Before long, his visits to her become less frequent, and she feels deeply wounded, particularly since their relationship has come to be widely known. Nevertheless, on the day before the Kamo Festival, she decides to view the procession, hoping to secretly glimpse Genji. In order to conceal her identity, she appears in an inconspicuous carriage, which is roughly pushed to the back of the crowd by Aoi's drunken male attendants (who do in fact recognize Rokujō) to give their own mistress a front-row view. Genji passes Rokujō without noticing her half-wrecked carriage, instead acknowledging Lady Aoi, his principal wife, who is pregnant with his first child. Soon thereafter, Aoi is possessed by an evil spirit, which later kills her shortly after she has given birth to Genji's son. The evil spirit turns out to be the jealous and vengeful spirit of Lady Rokujō, which, without her conscious knowledge, had wandered from her body and attacked her rival.

In the first act of the play, Teruhi, a shaman who summons "possessing spirits" (*mononoke*) with the twanging of a bow, identifies the possessing spirit as that of Lady Rokujō. In the second act, the holy man of Yokawa, a renowned mountain ascetic,

---

1. Zeami lists the play's title in his treatise *Five Sounds* (*Go-on*), but without mentioning its author. Because Zeami refers in this treatise to the author whenever he mentions a play that is not his own, the extant version of *Lady Aoi* is most likely his revision.

dispels the possessing spirit. A careful comparison with *Genji* reveals how freely the play has adapted its original material. There is scarcely any direct citation from the original text except in one section (the *kudoki*), which refers to some well-known chapter titles. Aoi's pregnancy, one reason for her vulnerability and for Rokujō's jealousy, is not mentioned at all in the play. The shaman does not appear in the original, in which the spirit of Lady Rokujō speaks with Aoi's voice directly to Genji and various monks. Neither does the mountain ascetic play a significant role in the original. In *Genji*, the spirit, far from being conquered by a monk, finally succeeds in killing Aoi, and even after Rokujō's own death, her spirit continues to torment and kill Genji's other wives.

Several tales contemporaneous with this play depict exorcisms of vengeful spirits in a surprisingly similar manner, suggesting that the play followed an existing pattern of exorcism tales and borrowed the names of characters from *Genji*. On the one hand, because the text of *Genji* was largely inaccessible to the general population, the play is written in such a way as to entertain even those who might not be familiar with the original. On the other hand, the text of the play repeatedly refers to a carriage and to the humiliation associated with it (without recounting the incident itself), which allows those familiar with the original *Genji* episode to appreciate these cryptic allusions to Lady Rokujō's carriage.

In early performances of the play, a carriage was used as a stage prop, with a weeping young lady-in-waiting clinging to its shaft. Later, both the carriage and the lady-in-waiting were omitted, giving rise to certain discrepancies between the text and the action on stage. For example, although Lady Rokujō appears alone on stage, the shaman refers to a weeping lady-in-waiting. Moreover, in the *mondō* section, the shaman sympathizes with Rokujō and joins her in tormenting Aoi. Originally, it was presumably the lady-in-waiting, not the shaman, who chanted this section and acted as Rokujō's accomplice. The reason for eliminating the lady-in-waiting and the carriage is not entirely clear, but it may have been to avoid the difficult task of getting both of them off the stage without disrupting the performance.

In the first act, the performer who plays Lady Rokujō wears a *deigan* mask, whose golden eyes indicate her repressed jealousy. In the second act, he wears a *hannya*, a mask of a woman with two horns and a wide mouth, signifying that her spirit has now been transfigured into a demon. On stage, Aoi herself is represented only by a folded kimono. This stage prop is said to have inspired William Butler Yeats, who used a similarly folded cloth to symbolize the well in his nō-inspired play *At the Hawk's Well*. The following translation is based on the current text of the Kanze school.

Characters in Order of Appearance

TERUHI, a shaman (*ko-omote* mask)	*tsure*
A COURTIER in the service of Emperor Suzaku	*waki-tsure*
VENGEFUL SPIRIT OF LADY ROKUJŌ in the form of a noblewoman (*deigan* mask)	*mae-shite*

A MESSENGER of the minister of the left   *ai*
THE HOLY MAN of Yokawa   *waki*
LADY ROKUJŌ as an evil spirit (*hannya* mask)   *nochi-shite*

Place: Mansion of the minister of the left in the capital

Act 1

Stage attendant places toward the front of the stage an embroidered kosode *kimono, which represents Lady Aoi on her sickbed. Teruhi, wearing a* ko-omote *mask, wig, gold-patterned underkimono, brocade outer kimono, and white wide-sleeved robe, and the Courtier, wearing a cavity cap, heavy silk kimono, lined hunting robe, and white wide divided skirt, appear, cross the bridgeway, and enter the stage. Teruhi sits at the waki spot, and the Courtier stands at the shite spot.*

COURTIER: (*nanori*) I am a courtier in the service of Emperor Suzaku.[2] The demon that has possessed Lady Aoi, daughter of the minister of the left, is intransigent. His Lordship has invited the most revered and eminent priests to perform secret and solemn rites of exorcism as well as cures. They have tried everything but to no avail. I have been ordered to call in Teruhi, a shaman, who is known far and wide for her skill in birch-bow divination. She will ascertain by the bow whether the evil spirit is that of a living or a dead person. I shall ask her.

Teruhi faces the kosode *kimono and, to azusa music, chants an incantation for calling forth an evil spirit.*

TERUHI:
    (*unnamed*) May Heaven be cleansed,
    May Earth be cleansed,
    May all be cleansed within and without,
    The Six Roots, may they all be cleansed.[3]
    (*jō-no-ei*) Swiftly, on a dapple gray horse,
    Comes a haunting spirit
    Tugging at the reins.

To issei entrance music, the spirit of Lady Rokujō, wearing a mask with gold-painted eyes, long wig, serpent-scale-patterned underkimono, embroidered outer kimono in the koshimaki *style, and brocade outer kimono in the* tsubo-ori *style, appears, advances along the bridgeway, and stops by the first pine.*

---

2. In *The Tale of Genji*, Suzaku is Genji's elder brother.
3. The six organs of perception are eye, ear, nose, tongue, body, and mind.

ROKUJŌ:

> (*issei*) Riding the Three Vehicles of the Law,
> Others may escape the Burning House.[4]
> Mine is but a cart
> In ruins like Yūgao's house;[5]
> I know not how to flee my passions.[6]
> (*Enters the stage and stands in the shite spot.*)
> (*shidai*) Like an ox-drawn cart, this weary world,
> Like an ox-drawn cart, this weary world
> Rolls endlessly on the wheels of retribution.
> (*sashi*) Like the wheels of a cart forever turning
> Are birth and death for all living things;
> Through the Six Worlds[7] and the Four Births[8]
> You must journey;
> Strive as you will, there is no escape.
> What folly to be blind
> To the frailty of this life,
> Like the banana stalk without a core,
> Like a bubble on the water![9]
> Yesterday's flowers are today but a dream.[10]
> How sad my fate!
> Upon my sorrow others heap their spite.
> Now, drawn by the birch bow's sound,

---

4. A reference to a famous parable in the Lotus Sutra: a fire once broke out in the home of a wealthy man. His children, absorbed in their play, did not understand the danger and would not listen when he warned them to get out of the house. He then told them that waiting for them outside the gate were a cart drawn by sheep, another drawn by deer, and a third drawn by oxen. Beguiled by this trick, the children rushed out of the burning house. This parable allegorizes Buddha's various "expedient" doctrines for saving mankind.

5. Genji's affections had earlier shifted to Yūgao (Evening Faces), whom Rokujō's wandering spirit had killed, before carrying out a similar attack on Aoi. Yūgao was staying in a shabby house, with yūgao flowers clinging to the eaves, in a squalid alley.

6. Jijū Chūnagon, *Shirakawadono shichihyakushu*, no. 688: "I know not how to escape my lovelorn thoughts. It is like a broken-down cart, this sad heart of mine!"

7. The six worlds (or realms)—those of heavenly creatures, human beings, fighting demons, animals, hungry ghosts, and hell beings—through which a soul, unless enlightened, must transmigrate eternally according to the merits or demerits of its deeds done in successive lives.

8. Viviparous birth (for example, humans), oviparous birth (for example, birds), birth from moisture (for example, worms, mosquitoes), and apparitional birth—that is, sudden birth—by spontaneous generation, without any apparent cause. These are the ancient Indian classifications for all sentient beings.

9. An allusion to a passage in the Vimalakirti Sutra (J. Yuima-kyō): "How should a bodhisattva regard sentient beings? Like . . . a cloud in the sky, like a bubble on the water . . . ; like the [frail] core of a plantain tree . . . —thus does a bodhisattva regard sentient beings."

10. An echo from Bo Juyi's line: "The glory of yesterday declines today."

The ghost has come
To find a moment of respite.
(*sage-uta*) Ah, how shameful that even now
I should shun the eyes of others
As on that festive day.[11]
(*age-uta*) Though all night long I gaze upon the moon,
Though all night long I gaze upon the moon,
I, a phantom form, remain unseen by it.
Hence, by the birch bow's upper end,
I shall stand to tell of my sorrow,
I shall stand to tell of my sorrow. (*As if listening, steps forward.*)
(*unnamed*) From where does the sound of the birch bow come,
From where does the sound of the birch bow come?

TERUHI:

(*ge-no-ei*) Though by the mansion gate I stand,

ROKUJŌ:

As I have no form, people pass me by. (*Steps back and weeps.*)

TERUHI:

(*unnamed*) How strange! I see a gentle-born lady,
Though I know not who she is,
Riding in a decrepit cart,
And one who seems a waiting-maid,
Clutching the shaft of the ox-less cart
And weeping, bathed in tears.
Oh! pitiful sight! (*Speaks to the Courtier.*)
(*mondō*) Is this the evil spirit?

COURTIER:

Now I can guess who it is. Tell me your name.
(*Not seeing Rokujō's spirit, turns to Teruhi.*)

ROKUJŌ:

(*kudoki-guri*) In this world
Where all passes like lightning,
There should be none for me to hate
Nor any fate for me to mourn;
Why did I leave the way of truth? (*Speaks to Teruhi.*)
(*kudoki*) Attracted by the birch bow's sound,
Here I now appear. Do you still not know me?
I am the spirit of Lady Rokujō.
In days of old when I moved in society,
On spring mornings I was invited
To the flower feasts at the palace,

---

11. Refers to the day of the incident involving Rokujō's cart.

And on autumn nights
I viewed the moon in the royal garden.
Happily thus I spent my days
Among bright hues and scents.
Fallen in life, today I am no more
Than a morning glory that withers with the rising of the sun.[12]
My heart knows no respite from pain;
Bitter thoughts grow like fern shoots
Bursting forth in the field.
I have appeared here to take my revenge.

CHORUS:

(*sage-uta*) Do you not know that in this life
Charity is not for others?
(*age-uta*) Be harsh to another,
Be harsh to another,
And it will recoil upon you.[13]
Why do you cry?
(*Rokujō gets up and, gazing at the* kosode *kimono and stooping down, weeps. She stares at it again.*)
My curse is everlasting,
My curse is everlasting.

ROKUJŌ:

(*mondō*) Oh, how I hate you!
I will punish you.

TERUHI:

What shame!
For Lady Rokujō, gentle born,
To seek revenge[14]
And act as one lowborn:
Are you not ashamed?
Stop and say no more.

ROKUJŌ:

Say what you will, I must strike her now.
(*Walks to the* kosode *and defiantly strikes it with the fan.*)
So saying, I walk toward the bedside of Lady Aoi and strike her.
(*Returns to her seat.*)

---

12. Kii, *Horikawa hyakushū*, no. 767: "I must get up at dawn to see the morning glory in flower, whose beauty will be gone before the sun begins to shine."

13. Refers to a poem by Owari, *Shinkokinshū*, Love 5, no. 1401: "Remembering my harshness to others, I will not grieve my lot; this is a retribution that has come while I am still alive."

14. This refers to "beating the new wife," a Muromachi-period custom in which, when a man remarried, his divorced wife or her relatives would vent their anger by forcing their way into her former husband's home and beating his new wife.

TERUHI:

> Now that things have come to such a pass,
> There is nothing more to do.
> So saying, I walk toward Lady Aoi's feet
> And torment her.

ROKUJŌ:

> Present vengeance is the retribution
> For past wrongs you did to me.

TERUHI:

> The flame of consuming anger

ROKUJŌ:

> Scorches only my own self.[15]

TERUHI:

> Do you not feel the fury of my anger?

ROKUJŌ:

> You shall feel the fullness of its fury. (*Fixes her gaze on the* kosode.)

CHORUS:

> (*dan-uta*) This loathsome heart!
> This loathsome heart!
> My unfathomable hatred
> Causes Lady Aoi to wail in bitter agony.
> But as long as she lives in this world,
> Her bond with the Shining Genji will never end—
> The Shining Genji, more beautiful than a firefly
> That flits across the marshland.

ROKUJŌ:

> I shall be to him

CHORUS:

> A stranger, as I was once,
> And I shall pass away
> Like a dewdrop on a mugwort leaf.
> When I think of this,
> How bitter I feel!
> Our love is already an old tale,
> Never to be revived even in a dream.
> Yet all the while my longing grows
> Until I am ashamed to see my love-torn self.
> Standing by her pillow,
> I shall place Lady Aoi
> In my wrecked cart

---

15. From a verse in the *Dai-Shōgon-ron:* "Man's self is like dried-up wood, his anger a flaming fire; before the fire destroys another, it first consumes its own self."

> (*Rokujō pulls the outer kimono over her and,*
>> *stooping, withdraws to the stage-attendant position.*)
> And secretly carry her off,
> And secretly carry her off.

Act 2

A Messenger of the minister of the left, wearing a striped kimono, sleeveless robe, and trailing divided skirt, is seated at the kyōgen seat.

COURTIER: (*mondō*) Is anyone here?

MESSENGER: I am at your service. (*Comes forward in front of the Courtier.*)

COURTIER: Lady Aoi, who is possessed by an evil spirit, is grievously ill. Go! Fetch the holy man of Yokawa.

MESSENGER (*returns to the shite spot*): (*unnamed*) I understood that Lady Aoi, though possessed by an evil spirit, was very much better. Now I am told that she is more ill than ever. Therefore I am ordered to go to Yokawa and bring the holy man back with me. I must make haste. (*Goes to the first pine and, turning toward the curtain, calls out.*) I have arrived. If you please, I wish to be announced.

The Holy Man, wearing a small round cap, brocade stole, heavy silk kimono, wide-sleeved robe, and wide white divided skirt and carrying a short sword and a rosary of diamond-shaped beads, appears and advances along the bridgeway, stopping at the third pine.

HOLY MAN:

> (*mondō*) Before the window of the Nine Ideations,[16]
> On the seat of the Ten Vehicles[17]
> I am filled with the waters of *yoga*,[18]
> Reflecting the Moon of Truth in the Three Mysteries.[19]
> Who is it that seeks admission?

---

16. The nine categories of consciousness in Buddhist psychology: the five sense perceptions (sight, hearing, smell, taste, and touch), the conscious mind, the two different aspects of the subconscious mind, and the undefiled consciousness.

17. The ten "vehicles" of spiritual disciplines that, according to Buddhist doctrine, carry one to nirvana.

18. *Yoga*, a Sanskrit word meaning "union," refers to perfect union of oneself with the Buddha, and thus with ultimate truth, attained by properly regulating one's mind and body.

19. The Three Mysteries are body, speech, and mind. To attain the state of yoga, one forms the mystic hand gestures known as *mudras* (yogas of the body), recites *mantras* (yogas of speech), and mentally visualizes the Buddha (the yoga of mind).

MESSENGER: I am a messenger from the minister. Lady Aoi, who is possessed by an evil spirit, is grievously ill, and I am commanded to ask you to come at once and perform an exorcism.

HOLY MAN: Of late I have been engaged in performing special rites and cannot leave, but since it is a request from the minister, I will go immediately. You may return at once.

MESSENGER: I will lead the way.

I have returned, my lord, accompanied by the holy man.

The Holy Man enters the stage and stands in the shite spot, where the Courtier turns to him.

COURTIER: I am much obliged to you for coming.

HOLY MAN: I received your message. Where is the lady who is ill?

COURTIER: She is there in the gallery. (*Turns to the* kosode.)

HOLY MAN: I shall perform the exorcism at once.

COURTIER: Pray do so.

To notto *music, the Holy Man moves in front of the musicians, tucks up his sleeves, and advances toward the* kosode.

HOLY MAN:

> (*unnamed*) He now performs the healing rites,
> Wearing his cloak of hemp,
> In which, in the footsteps of En-no-Gyōja,[20]
> He scaled the peaks[21]
> Symbolic of the sacred spheres
> Of Taizō and Kongō,[22]
> Brushing away the dew that sparkles like the Seven Jewels,[23]
> And with a robe of meek endurance[24]

---

20. The Nara-period originator of mountain asceticism (*shugendō*).

21. Referring to a range of mountains called Ōmine, extending more than thirty miles in Yamato and Kii Provinces. It contains several high peaks above five thousand feet, and the head temple of mountain asceticism is located there. Those who have undergone mortification and asceticism in these mountains and have been initiated into the mysteries of the sect are regarded as master ascetics, and their prayers and invocations are said to possess superhuman powers. The holy man in the present play is such an accomplished master.

22. Taizō-kai (Womb World, All-Embracing Realm) is a view of the sentient world, including all states of existence, from buddhas to devils, as embraced in the infinite love of the Great Sun Buddha (Mahavairocana), of whom all sentient beings are manifestations. The pictorial representation of this view is one of the most important mandala of Esoteric Buddhism. The other is the Kongō-kai (Diamond World), representing the powers and works of the Great Sun Buddha's supreme wisdom, which is likened to a diamond, since it is immutable and can destroy the attachments of mortals.

23. The Buddhist paradise is said to be adorned with seven jewels (treasures).

24. Endurance of all insults and injuries from others. The Lotus Sutra says, "The garment of the Buddha is the spirit of meekness and forbearance."

To shield him from defilements,
Fingering his reddish wooden beads,
And rubbing them together, he intones a prayer: *Namaku, samanda,*
basarada.

The spirit of Lady Rokujō, having exchanged the golden-painted-eyes mask for
a hannya *mask and covered her head with her brocade outer kimono, stands*
behind the Holy Man with a hammer-shaped staff in her hand and fixes her
gaze on him.
    (*Quasi dance:* inori)
    The Holy Man turns toward Rokujō and tries to vanquish her by his incan-
tation, but she wraps her brocade outer kimono around her waist and takes a
defiant attitude. Then she kneels, supporting herself with her hammer-shaped
staff.

ROKUJŌ:
    (*kakeai*) Return at once, good monk, return at once.
    Otherwise you will be burdened with regret.
HOLY MAN:
    However evil the evil spirit,
    The mystic power of a holy man will never fail.
    With these words I once again finger my sacred rosary.
CHORUS:
    (*chū-noriji*) Gōzanze Myōō, Wisdom Kings of the East,
ROKUJŌ:
    Gundari-yasha Myōō of the South,
CHORUS:
    Daiitoku Myōō of the West,
ROKUJŌ:
    Kongō-yasha Myōō
CHORUS:
    Of the North,
ROKUJŌ:
    The most Wise Fudō Myōō of the Center—[25]

---

25. Myōō (*vidyaraja* [wisdom kings]) are manifestations of the Great Sun Buddha. They
assume features of terrible anger in order to quell the rebellious spirits of men and demons.
The five mentioned here are especially venerated in Esoteric Buddhism. Gōzanze (Trailokya)
Myōō sits in the east, has three faces and eight arms expressing great anger, and destroys the three
vices of covetousness, anger, and folly. Gundari-yasha (Kundali-yaksa) Myōō sits in the south,
has one face and eight arms, and destroys all angry spirits and devils. Daiitoku (Yamantaka)
Myōō sits in the west; has six faces, six arms, and six feet; rides a great white ox; and carries
various weapons in his hands to destroy all poisonous serpents and evil dragons. Kongō-yasha
(Vajra-yaksa) Myōō sits in the north, enveloped in flames, has three faces and six arms, carries various weapons in his hands, and destroys all fierce *yaksa* (demons). Finally, the Great

In act 2, the prayers of the Holy Man of Yokawa prevent Lady Rokujō's spirit, wearing a *hannya* mask, from harming Aoi (represented by a folded kimono). (From *Meiji-Period Nō Illustrations* by Tsukioka Kōgyo, in the Hōsei University Kōzan Bunko Collection)

CHORUS:

> *Namaku samanda basarada senda makaroshana sowatayauntara takamman!*[26]
> Whoever hears my teaching
> Shall gain profound wisdom;
> Whoever knows my mind
> Shall gain the purity of buddhahood.[27]

Rokujō, subdued, drops her staff and covers her ears.

Holy One—that is, Fudō Myōō (Acalanatha, the Immovable One)—sits in the center, expressing great anger; he is in reality a form that Dainichi Nyorai (Mahavairocana Tathagata) takes in order to conquer all evil spirits. His right hand clasps a sword, which symbolizes the infinite wisdom of the Great Sun Buddha, and his left hand holds a lasso, which symbolizes the Buddha's supreme compassion. He stands on a rock, amid flames.

26. A romanized transcription of a *dharani*, a passage of Sanskrit that, in Chinese and Japanese Buddhist sutras, is left untranslated because it would lose the mystical power of its sounds. This dharani is a formula for subduing evil spirits and is used in exorcism by a devotee of Fudō Myōō. A very rough translation might read: "Homage to all indestructible ones. Wrathful destroyer of evil, may you crush the evil demons within our hearts!"

27. The latter half of Fudō Myōō's vow, which was often cited by mountain ascetics in their prayers.

Rokujō:

> (*unnamed*) How fearful is the chanting of the sutra!
> My end at last has come.
> Never again will this evil spirit come.

Chorus:

> (*kiri*) Hearing the voice of incantation,
> Hearing the voice of incantation,
> The demon's heart grows gentle. (*Rokujō rises, as if rid of her curse.*)
> Forbearance and mercy incarnate,
> The Bodhisattva comes to meet her.
> She enters nirvana,
> Released from the cycle of death and rebirth—Buddha be praised!
> Released from the cycle of death and rebirth—Buddha be praised!

Rokujō goes to the shite spot, joins her hands in prayer, and stamps twice.

[Adapted from a translation by Gakujutsu shinkōkai]

STUPA KOMACHI (*SOTOBA KOMACHI*)
Attributed to Kan'ami and revised by Zeami

The image of Ono no Komachi as a flawlessly beautiful poet has prevailed for more than a thousand years. The *Kana* Preface to the *Kokinshū* (ca. 905) praises her as a successor to Sotoori-hime, a legendary princess of peerless beauty who was regarded as the goddess of poetry. But aside from Komachi's excellent poems, which are the source of the diverse legends about her, nothing certain is known about her life. From those poems in which she laments her lost beauty and youth, the legend arose that late in her life she became exceedingly ugly and haggard. The poems describing her unrequited passion gave rise to her image as an amorous woman (in the medieval period, she was sometimes even depicted as a courtesan), while in other pieces she scolds and rejects her suitors, suggesting the opposite image, that of a coldhearted beauty. The image of Komachi as a *belle dame sans merci* took shape in the legend of Fukakusa no Shōshō's visits of a hundred nights, in which Komachi is said to have once promised to reciprocate this courtier's love on the condition that he appear outside her home for a hundred nights in succession. As the legend goes, however, he died on the ninety-ninth night, the eve of the fulfillment of his quest.

Subsequently, in the medieval period, the Buddhist exemplum *The Flowering and Decline of Tamatsukuri Komachi* (*Tamatsukuri Komachi sōsuisho*) came to be regarded as the definitive historical document of the poet's life. Written around the year 1000, most likely by a Buddhist preacher, this story relates a monk's encounter with an ugly old beggar, who, it turns out, was born into a wealthy family. She explains to the monk how she once boasted of her beauty and cruelly rejected her suitors but then lost her youth and family fortune, ending up as a beggar. Scholars disagree as to whether this story originated independently of the legend of Ono no Komachi. In any case, *Tamatsukuri* contributed to the enduring image of Komachi as a decrepit, hundred-year-old beggar.

These legends are evident in *Stupa Komachi*, which draws heavily on *Tamatsukuri* and the tale of Shōshō's hundred nightly visits. The play opens with an encounter between two traveling monks and the wandering beggar Komachi. (Unlike in *Tamatsukuri*, in the play Komachi roundly refutes the monks' shallow preaching.) The play also borrows or paraphrases many passages from *Tamatsukuri* contrasting the tattered clothes and miserable life of the aging Komachi with her past glory and beauty. In the latter part of the play, Komachi is suddenly possessed by the spirit of the dead Shōshō (Lesser Captain), who makes her reenact in front of the monks his hundred nights of visits to her, as if to bring home to her how cruel her treatment of him was.

The play was originally written by Kan'ami and then revised by his son Zeami. Since the original by Kan'ami is now lost, the extent of Zeami's contribution is not certain, except for his brief comment in *Conversations on Sarugaku* (*Sarugaku dangi*) that the original was much longer and included a scene in which a messenger of Tamatsushima—a god of poetry—appears in the form of a bird.

Such ambiguity in authorship is a problem common to early nō plays, almost none of which remained untouched by Zeami. It is not that Zeami was unusually fond of revising others' plays; rather, adapting old plays was a common practice among nō playwrights, including Kan'ami. The concept of authorship was not as strict at that time as it is now, and it was necessary to continually revise plays for new troupes and for audiences' changing tastes. It was only after Zeami had established the basic aesthetic principles and structure of nō plays that the practice of revising the plays subsided.

Although Zeami revised all the extant plays by Kan'ami, they still retain characteristics of Kan'ami's style, such as the vivid and witty conversation and the realistic representation of dramatic story lines, which often include confrontations between characters. These characteristics, which can clearly be seen in *Stupa Komachi*, are in fact the remnants of sarugaku from Yamato Province. Later, Zeami attenuated these features through his reformation of nō, bringing it more in line with the principle of yūgen.

The play's antiquity is indicated also by Shōshō's possession of Komachi. In *Teachings on Style and the Flower* (*Fūshikaden*), Zeami classifies "derangement" (*monogurui*) into two types, one due to possession by a spirit or god and the other to an emotional crisis, usually precipitated by the loss of a lover or child. For female protagonists, Zeami recommends the latter type of derangement but rejects the former. He in fact wrote numerous nō plays that feature a distraught female protagonist seeking her lost child or lover, which became the standard for later generations of playwrights. Before Zeami, however, presumably many plays dealt with female characters whose derangement was caused by possession, but most were gradually omitted from the repertoire and eventually disappeared altogether. *Stupa Komachi* is a rare exception. With such diverse scenes, presented one after the other—the fiery and witty debate between the monks and Komachi, her bemoaning her lost beauty and current misery, her possession by Shōshō's spirit, and her reenactment of his one hundred nightly visits—the play remains one of the most popular in today's repertoire, even though only a few performers, of mature years and superior skill, are permitted to play this highly prized and prestigious role.

Characters in Order of Appearance

MONK	*waki*
COMPANION, also a monk	*waki-tsure*
ONO NO KOMACHI, a poet, now a very old woman (*uba* mask)	*shite*

To shidai *music, enter slowly Monk with Companion. They stand side by side at the front of the stage and then face each other.*

MONK AND COMPANION:
(*shidai*) Mountains are but shallow hideaways;
mountains are but shallow hideaways; what hermitage
is deeper than the heart?

Monk faces forward.

MONK: (*nanori*) I am a monk come from the monasteries of Mount Kōya. I thought I'd pay a visit to the capital, and am on my way there now.
(*sashi*) The Buddha that once was has now passed on;
the Buddha that shall be is not yet come into the world.[28]

Monk and Companion face each other again.

MONK AND COMPANION:
Born into such a dreamlike in-between,
what can we take for real?
By chance we have obtained this human body,
so difficult to obtain,
and have encountered the teachings of the Buddha,

---

28. Buddhas are said to be born into the world periodically, but very infrequently, in order to benefit human beings by teaching them the path to enlightenment. Thus "the buddha that once was" refers to the buddha of the current period—that is, the historical buddha Shakyamuni, who, being dead, "has now passed on"—while "the buddha that shall be" refers to the coming Buddha Maitreya (J. Miroku), who, according to Shakyamuni Buddha's prophecy, will not be born in the world for many aeons to come.

so difficult to encounter.
That this is the seed of enlightenment we know,
as tokened by these robes as black as ink
in which we drape ourselves.[29]
(age-uta) Knowing our self-nature before birth,
Knowing our self-nature before birth,
we have no parents who can claim our love.
We have no parents; and we have
no children to constrain their hearts
with worry for our sakes. (Monk mimes walking.)
This self that goes a thousand leagues
and does not count it far,
bedding down in meadows,
dwelling in the mountains:
this is our true home,
this is our true home.

MONK: (tsuki-zerifu) Having hastened along, already we have come, it seems, to the pine forest of Abeno, in the province of Settsu. Let us rest here for a bit.[30]

COMPANION: Yes, by all means.

Monk and Companion sit in the waki spot.

Stage assistant brings out a stool from backstage and places it center stage. It represents a decaying stupa. To narai no shidai *music, Ono no Komachi enters, moving very slowly with the aid of a walking stick and pausing to rest as she moves down the bridgeway. Stopping at the shite spot, she stands facing the rear.*

KOMACHI:

(shidai) Were there but a stream to woo this floating water plant,
were there but a stream to woo this floating water plant . . .
But there is none—only a lonely, aching heart.[31] (Faces forward.)

---

29. Human birth is regarded as a very rare and precious opportunity to hear and practice Buddhism, attain enlightenment, and thus save oneself from the otherwise endless round of rebirth and suffering known as *samsara.* Thus the human body is the "seed" of enlightenment, to be nurtured, not squandered. The monks are saying that they have responded to this poignant realization by renouncing the world and taking monastic vows, as signaled by their clerical garb.

30. The *tsuki-zerifu* (arrival speech) is taken from the version of *Sotoha Komachi* found in *Yōkyokushū,* SNKBZ 59:116–127.

31. This is a partial paraphrase of a famous poem in the *Kokinshū* (no. 938), attributed to Ono no Komachi and, if its prose prelude is to be believed, written in response to the eminent early Heian poet Funya no Yasuhide (fl. ca. 860), who had playfully invited her to go away with him to the provinces. It reads: "Steeped in misery, a forlorn, floating plant, I would break off from my root; if there were but a coaxing current I believe I'd drift away."

(*sashi*) Ah, but oh so long ago
I was the proudest of them all,
my raven tresses sensually rippling
like weeping-willow streamers
wafted lightly on spring breezes.
And the trilling of this warbler
was more exquisite even than
the dew-drenched *itohagi* blossoms,
their petals only just begun to fall.
But now, despised even by lowly common wenches,
my shame exposed for one and all to see,
as joyless days and months heap up upon me,
I have become a hundred-year-old hag.
(*sage-uta*) In the capital I hide myself from people's gaze;
"Can that be she?" they murmur, faint
light of the gloaming in which,
(*age-uta*) with the moon for company, I venture forth,
with the moon for company, I venture forth.
The men who guard the palace—
that grand abode among the clouds, built from myriad stones
upon the heights—
will surely pay no heed to such a wretch as I;
why then, there is no need for slinking, hidden
in the shadows of the trees
of the Tomb of Love[32]
at Toba, and the Autumn Hill,
and moonlit Katsura riverboat—(*Facing stage right, peers into the distance
    from under her wide sedge hat.*)
rowing it away, who can that be?
rowing it away, who can that be? (*Plants her walking stick before her,
    right hand atop the stick, left hand atop the right, and gazes into the
    distance.*)
(*tsuki-zerifu*) I am in such pain— (*Looks over at the stool.*) I think I'll just
sit down and rest upon this moldering piece of wood.

*Removes her sedge hat and, holding it in her hand, slowly makes her way to the
stool and sits down on it. Monk and Companion stand up.*

---

32. The Toba Tomb of Love (Toba no Koi-zuka) memorializes Lady Kesa (J. Kesa Gozen), a
twelfth-century Heian noblewoman who sacrificed her own life to save those of her mother and
husband.

Komachi, holding a walking stick and a wide sedge hat, sits on a stupa and rebuts a sermon by two monks. (From *Meiji-Period Nō Illustrations* by Tsukioka Kōgyo, in the Hōsei University Kōzan Bunko Collection)

MONK: (*mondō*) Why, already the sun has set. We must hasten on our way. But look! that beggar there: surely that is a stupa she is sitting on.[33] Let us teach her the error of her ways and have her move away from it.

COMPANION: Yes, by all means.

Companion passes behind Komachi and moves toward the corner pillar so that the three characters form a triangle, with Komachi at its apex and Monk and Companion forming its base.

MONK: (*mondō*) How now, you beggar, there! That place where you are sitting—do you not know that you are profaning a stupa, the form of Buddha's body? Get up from there; go rest some other place!

KOMACHI (*to Monk*): Profane—the form of Buddha's body, you say! But I see no writing here, no carven image; it looks like just a moldering piece of wood to me.

---

33. The stupa on which Komachi is sitting would not be a full-size tower but, rather, a replica: either a small, sculpted wooden stupa or else a tall, slim wooden board meant to stand upright as a grave marker and typically carved into a stupa-like shape at the top. Either would typically have sacred Sanskrit characters carved or painted onto its surface. The stupa appears to have slid down into a leaning or fallen position.

MONK:

>   (*kakeai*) Though but a moldering piece of wood
>   in mountains deep,
>   when the tree has blossomed
>   there's no hiding what it is.

>   And all the more so when the wood's carved in the form of Buddha's body—how can you say there was no indication?

Komachi remains seated during the ensuing exchange as she responds to Monk and Companion, speaking slowly throughout, with pretended ignorance.

KOMACHI:

>   I am myself a lowly, buried tree,
>   yet still the blossom of my heart remains;
>   why, then, should this not be my offering?[34]
>   But tell me: why is this to be viewed as Buddha's body?

COMPANION:

>   You see, a stupa is how Vajrasattva,
>   provisionally manifesting in the world,
>   embodied the Buddha's sacred vow
>   in symbolic form: as a *samaya* body.[35]

KOMACHI:

>   This form it is embodied in: what is it?

MONK:

>   Earth, water, fire, wind, and space.

KOMACHI:

>   Those Five Great Elements' five rings
>   make up the body of a person—so between us
>   why should there be any separation?[36]

---

34. An allusion to a famous waka by Ono no Komachi, *Kokinshū*, no. 797: "What fades away, its color unseen, is the flower of the heart of those of this world." Komachi's "flower(s) of the heart" can mean "the heart of a person of refined aesthetic sensibilities," "a fickle heart," or the hidden blossom of an enlightened mind, all of which resonate here. "Flower," as suggested in the following line, can also denote the offering flowers presented to the Buddha at altars and thus prefigures the final image of "offering up a flower to the Buddha."

35. According to Esoteric Shingon, the enlightened bodhisattva Vajrasattva (J. Kongōsatta) compiled the teachings of Mahavairocana (J. Dainichi), the cosmic buddha who vowed to save all sentient beings from samsaric suffering. Vajrasattva then temporarily hid Mahavairocana's teachings for safekeeping in an iron stupa in southern India. The stupa is thus regarded as a *samaya-gyō* (unification body), a concrete manifestation of Mahavairocana's compassionate vow.

36. Each tier of a five-tier stupa represents one of the "five great elements"—earth, water, fire, wind, and space—that, in Buddhist cosmology, constitute the material world, including the human body.

COMPANION:

>It may not be dissimilar in form,
>but in mind and merit it is clearly different.[37]

KOMACHI:

>And what, pray, is a stupa's merit?

MONK:

>One glimpse of a stupa frees you forever
>from rebirth in the three lower realms.[38]

KOMACHI:

>The essence of enlightened mind
>that flashes in one instant:
>now how is that inferior?[39]

COMPANION:

>But if you claim enlightened mind,
>why have you not renounced this world of suffering?[40]

KOMACHI (*unaffectedly and clearly*):

>You think it is the outward form
>that renounces the world?
>It is the mind that renounces.

MONK:

>Yours is a body with no mind;
>no doubt that's why
>you do not know the body of the Buddha.

KOMACHI: Indeed, it is because I know this as the Buddha's body that I come near to a stupa.

COMPANION:

>In that case why did you sit down on it
>without so much as bowing?

Komachi looks at the stupa.

KOMACHI (*with growing force*):

>In any case this stupa is reclining;
>can it object that I too should relax?

---

37. "Mind" (J. *kokoro*) here can also mean "meaning" or "content." "Merit" refers to actions, both physical and mental, that are conducive to the attainment of enlightenment. Venerating a representation of the Buddha or an enlightened human being is considered meritorious, and disrespecting such representations or persons is unmeritorious.

38. The three lower realms are the hungry-ghost realm, the animal realm, and the hell realm, in which sentient beings' suffering is most intense.

39. "Arousing the essence of enlightened mind for a single instant is superior [in merit] to erecting a hundred thousand stupas" (cited in the *Manbō jinshin saichō busshin hōyō* [*Essentials of Buddha-Mind of Myriad Phenomena, Profound and Exalted*]).

40. That is, renounced the world and became a nun.

MONK:

> That is a far from proper connection
> to the Buddha.

KOMACHI:

> Even a backward connection can lead to enlightenment.[41]

COMPANION:

> Even Daiba's evil

KOMACHI:

> is Kannon's compassion.[42]

MONK:

> Even Handoku's stupidity

KOMACHI:

> is Monju's wisdom.[43]

COMPANION:

> Even what we call evil

KOMACHI:

> is good.

MONK:

> Even what we call the passions

KOMACHI:

> is enlightenment.[44]

---

41. In *gyakuen* (backward karmic connection), perverse actions such as rejecting the Buddhist teachings and reviling Buddhist teachers become the occasion for glimpsing the enlightened mind, coming to understand and practice the Buddhist teachings, and (eventually) attaining enlightenment.

42. Daiba (Skt. Devadatta), a cousin and disciple of Shakyamuni Buddha, attempted to assassinate the Buddha and was reborn in hell as a result. Nevertheless, in the Devadatta chapter of the Lotus Sutra, the Buddha prophesies even Devadatta's eventual attainment of buddhahood and describes how in lives past Devadatta helped Shakyamuni Buddha's spiritual development toward buddhahood. Thus it is possible to view Devadatta as a manifestation of the bodhisattva Kannon (Skt. Avalokiteshvara), the embodiment of compassion.

43. Handoku (Shurihandoku; Skt. Cudapanthaka) was the Buddha's most dim-witted disciple, who was nevertheless able to attain enlightenment by following the Buddha's instructions. Monju (Monjushiri; Skt. Manjushri) is a bodhisattva regarded as the embodiment of transcendent knowing.

44. Enlightenment (J. *bodai*; Skt. *bodhi*) in Mahayana Buddhism refers to a supremely lucid and naturally compassionate state of mind eternally free of the suffering of "the passions" (desire, aggression, ignorance, and so on). From a relative viewpoint, the emotional "defilements" of the passions may appear to obstruct enlightenment, but the more sophisticated perspective of absolute truth reveals that actually they are, in essence, expressions of enlightened mind itself, as Chinese Zen master Huineng (J. Enō, 638–713) proclaims in fascicle 26 of the *Rokuso hōbōdan-gyō* (*Luyi-zu-da-shi fa bao tan jing* [*The Dharma-Treasure Platform Sutra of the Sixth Patriarch*, ca. 820]): "If you practice [transcendent knowing] for a single instant, your dharma-body will be the same as [that of] the Buddha. Good friends, the very passions are themselves bodhi."

COMPANION:

Enlightenment, at its root,

KOMACHI:

is not a tree.

MONK:

And the clear mirror—

KOMACHI:

—mind's mirror-on-a-stand—there's no such thing. (*Decisively turns to face forward.*)

CHORUS:

(*uta*) Indeed, when in the first place not one thing exists,

there is no separation between

buddhas and sentient beings.[45] (*Companion moves back next to Monk and sits down.*)

(*age-uta*) To this, the Buddha's

solemnly sworn vow of compassion,[46]

this expedient devised

for saving ignorant, deluded beings,

even a backward connection

can lead to enlightenment. (*She turns earnestly toward Monk.*)

—Thus she explains,

at which the monk cries,

Truly, an enlightened mendicant! (*As though unable to help himself, Monk falls back two or three steps, sinks to his knees, and deferentially lowers his forehead to the earth.*)

and lowering his forehead to the earth,

three times he makes obeisance,

whereupon:

KOMACHI:

I now feel stronger, so I shall make bold

to compose a frivolous verse:

(*ge-no-ei*) (*easily, in a low voice*) If we were in the heaven of Supreme Bliss:

---

45. The foregoing discussion of the nature of bodhi reenacts an episode found in both the *Keitoku dentōroku* (*Jingde chuan deng lu* [*The Jingde Record of the Transmission of the Lamp,* 1004]) and the Dharma-Treasure Platform Sutra of the Sixth Patriarch. A monk at the Zen temple where Huineng lived, who was thought to be the most advanced of the Fifth Patriarch's disciples, wrote the poem: "The body is the bodhi tree; the mind like a clear mirror-on-a-stand. Time and time again, diligently wipe it; do not let there be upon it any dust." In response, Huineng, a lowly disciple who was young and illiterate, dictated the following poem: "Bodhi, at its root, is not a tree; nor yet is mind a mirror-on-a-stand. Since from the start no single thing exists, from what surface could one wipe off any dust?" This led to the Fifth Patriarch's selecting Huineng as his dharma heir.

46. "This" refers to the stupa.

it would no doubt be a sin;
but here outside,
whatever can you be objecting to?[47]

Abruptly rising, she turns her back to Monk as though in annoyance and moves away several steps toward the base pillar.

CHORUS:

(*uta*) Presumptuous priest, who would
"teach me the error of my ways"!
Presumptuous priest, who would
"teach me the error of my ways"!

MONK: (*unnamed*) (*to Komachi's back*) But what manner of person are you? Please tell us your name!

Komachi turns to face Monk.

KOMACHI: Embarrassing though it is, I shall tell you my name. (*Moves slowly to center stage and sits facing forward.*)

(*nanori-guri*) (*haughtily, yet sadly*) I am what has become of
Ono no Komachi,
daughter of Ono no Yoshizane,
governor of Dewa Province.

MONK AND COMPANION:

(*sashi*) My heart goes out to her.
Komachi—ah, truly, long ago
she was a lady of surpassing beauty:
her visage like a flower, radiant,
her eyebrows two slim blue crescents,
her face invariably powdered white,
she had so many fine silk robes,
they overflowed her mansion.

KOMACHI:

Thus I remained absorbed in my appearance,

CHORUS:

and men far away ached for me,
while men close by were plunged in utter gloom;

KOMACHI:

and I, in robes whose turquoise breakers foamed
upon a cobalt coast,

---

47. "Supreme Bliss" (J. Gokuraku), also known as the Western Pure Land, is the buddha-field of the Amida Buddha. The waka turns on a pun involving *soto wa* (outside) and *sotowa* (*sotoba* [stupa]).

CHORUS:

> like sunset-painted clouds ringed round with cobalt peaks,

KOMACHI:

> resplendent

CHORUS:

> as a floating lotus blossom
> lapped by daybreak waves,[48]

KOMACHI (*slowly*):

> Composing Japanese poems
> and writing Chinese verse, . . .

CHORUS:

> When she raised a cup of heady wine,
> the stars and moon would tarry on her sleeves.
> That peerless grace and beauty—
> when was it so utterly transformed?
> (*age-uta*) Her head's crowned with a frosted, drooping thatch,
> and at her temples those once-lovely, flowing locks
> cling limply to her skin in random streaks;
> her gently curving brows, twin butterflies,
> have lost their hue that was like distant hills.
> (*sage-uta*) A year short of a hundred—ninety-nine—
> oh, that the grief of these white, straggly locks
> should have come to her one day![49]—
> wan daylight moon: (*Komachi hides her face with her hat.*)
> how mortifying her appearance now! (*She rises and moves toward the shite spot.*)
> (*rongi*) The pouch that you have hung around your neck—
> what do you have in it?

KOMACHI:

> Although I know not whether life may end today,
> to save me from hunger tomorrow I've brought along
> some dried millet-and-beans inside this bag.

CHORUS:

> And in the bag you carry on your back?

---

48. The preceding exchange between Komachi and the chorus appears only in the texts of the so-called Shimo-gakari schools (Konparu, Kongō, and Kita schools) of nō.

49. Komachi's age is given as one hundred. However, this passage makes a pun on the fact that if the character *momo* (one hundred) were "one short"—that is, lacking its top brushstroke, which resembles the one-stroke character *hito* (one)—it would then not only be one short of a hundred but also now form the character *shiro* (white [hair]). This conceit underscores the retribution in which Komachi suffered through one year of increasingly onerous life for each of the ninety-nine nights to which she once subjected her suitor Fukakusa no Shōshō.

KOMACHI:

A garment soiled with dirt and grease.

CHORUS:

And in the basket in the crook of your arm?

KOMACHI:

Kuwai roots, both black and white.[50]

CHORUS:

With tattered cloak of straw

KOMACHI:

and tattered hat of sedge, (*Looks at the hat in her hand.*)

CHORUS:

you cannot so much as hide your face, (*She looks down, betraying some emotion.*)

KOMACHI:

much less keep out the frost, snow, rain, dew,

CHORUS:

tears—even her tears

she has not cuffs and sleeves enough to staunch! (*Examines first one sleeve and then the other.*)

And now she wanders by the roadside, (*With both hands, Komachi thrusts out her hat, turned upside down, and moves purposefully toward the corner pillar.*)

begging from passersby.

When she cannot beg what she needs, (*Komachi peers searchingly into her hat.*)

an evil mood, (*With a deranged air, takes two or three steps.*)

a crazy wildness, takes her mind,

and her voice grows weirdly altered. (*Abruptly throws down her walking stick.*)

KOMACHI (*again thrusting out her hat with both hands, and advancing toward Monk*):

(*mondō*) I pray you, sir, vouchsafe me something.

I beg of you, reverend monk, I beg of you. (*Presses toward Monk, to around center stage.*)

MONK: What is it you want?

KOMACHI: Let us go calling on Komachi—oh yes, please!

MONK: But you yourself are Komachi! Why do you speak such nonsense?

KOMACHI (*facing forward*): Ah, but that Komachi, what exquisite charms were hers! (*Looking this way and that.*) Love letters from here, missives from there, (*Backing away slightly.*)

---

50. *Kuwai* roots, an edible rootstalk grown in rice paddies, were regarded as coarse fare, the kind of food an indigent might eat.

written by love-beclouded hearts,

poured down upon her

like the summer rains

darkening the heavens.

Yet she would not answer even once,

not even in words empty as the sky. (*Turns her face downward, evidently
holding back strong emotion.*)

Now she is one hundred years of age—

her karmic retribution.

Ah, how I long for her!

Ah, how I long for her!

MONK: "I long for her," you say? What manner of being is it, then, possesses
you?

KOMACHI (*turning toward Monk*):

Of all the many men who staked their hearts on Komachi, (*Faces decisively forward.*)

the deepest love was that of Shii no Shōshō,

of Fukakusa's deep grasses;

CHORUS:

(*uta*) for Shii no Shōshō

the tally of love's grievances

rolls round again; (*Advances slightly, then stops, caught in the throes of
attachment.*)

to her carriage-shaft bench

I must go courting![51] (*She looks off to the west, toward the bridgeway.*)

(*age-uta*) What time of day is it?—twilight.

With the moon as my companion,

I shall set out on the road to her.

Though there be barrier guards to block the way,[52]

I will not let that stop me; off I go. (*Goes to the stage-assistant position and
turns her back to the audience.*)

(*Costume change*)

While monogi-ashirai *music is played, the actor playing Komachi lengthens
his sleeves by lowering the shoulders of his outer robe; or he may exchange it for*

---

51. A carriage-shaft bench was a stool used for getting into and out of an ox-drawn carriage
and also a stand on which to rest the shafts of the carriage. According to the tale on which this
play is based, a man (Shōshō) is smitten by the charms of a woman (Komachi), but she rebuffs
him, declaring that only after he has come and slept on her shaft bench for a hundred consecutive nights will she agree to see him. The man keeps a tally of the nights, each dawn recording
his visit by leaving a new mark on the shaft bench.

52. Barrier guards (*sekimori*) were soldiers placed at strategic checkpoints along major
thoroughfares to stop and inspect travelers.

a chōken *(man's overrobe)*. *He then dons an* eboshi *(black-lacquered court hat), takes up a fan, and proceeds to the shite spot.*

KOMACHI *(looking down at her trouser hems and stamping once)*:
(*uta*) Hitching up the legs of my white trousers,[53]

(*Quasi dance:* iroe)
To musical accompaniment, she moves very slowly to the corner pillar, then circles left to back center and stops, facing forward. Although her movements have no meaning in themselves, the romantic ardor of the Shōshō as he makes his way to Komachi is perceptible. She continues dancing and miming as the text resumes.

KOMACHI:
Hitching up the legs of my white trousers,
folding down my tall court hat, (*Raises fan and points with it to her head.*)
and draping my robe's sleeve over my head,[54] (*Flips left sleeve over her head and half-hides her face with fan.*)
I make my way to her in stealth, avoiding the world's gaze,
going in bright moonlight or in darkness, (*Lowers her hands and faces forward, gazing up into the sky.*)
on rainy nights and windy nights,
when chilly autumn leaves come drizzling down,
and when the snow lies deep.
(*unnamed*) As from the eaves the jewel drops melt and patter
quick-quick-quick-quick (*Looks upward and around.*)
CHORUS:
(*uta*) go and then return, (*Komachi moves away two or three steps.*)
return, then go again: (*Bends the fingers of her left hand, counting.*)
one night, two nights, three nights, four,
seven nights, eight nights, nine nights—
to attend the harvest feast, the Light of Plenty,
I did not appear at court,
and yet neither did she appear to me—
at cockcrow, timely as the rooster with each dawn,
I inscribed the nightly count
upon the edge of her shaft bench.
I'd sworn to go to her a hundred nights; (*Stamps several times.*)
so came the ninety-ninth night. (*Extends her left hand and looks at her still unbent little finger.*)

---

53. The image of hitching up his clean white trousers (*hakama*) to keep them free of mud is of a young, elegant, manly figure.

54. The Shōshō throws his sleeve (which is extremely long and broad) over his head in order to hide his face. He folds his tall court hat over to one side to indicate the informal, private nature of his excursion.

Oh, agony! The world grows dark before my eyes. . . . (*Falls back to center stage, pressing her fan to her breast as though in pain.*)

A pain within my breast, he cried in sorrow, and,
not tarrying that one last night, so died (*Drops to one knee, then sits.*)
the Shōshō, of Fukakusa's deep grasses, he
whose bitter indignation (*Sits bolt upright, then rises.*)
takes possession of Komachi, (*Earnestly facing Monk, stamps her foot.*)
visiting on her this state of frenzy.

Komachi's attitude now shifts, and she becomes completely tranquil.

(*kiri*) And thus we see that aspiration for the life to come
is the true way. (*Slowly extends fan, as though beckoning from afar.*)
Piling up sand to make a stupa tower,[55]
burnishing the Buddha's golden skin
with loving care,
offering up a flower, (*Slowly closes fan, joins her hands as if in prayer.*)
let us enter the path of awakening,
let us enter the path of awakening.

[Translated by Herschel Miller]

PINING WIND (*MATSUKAZE*)
Attributed to Zeami

The play's title, *Matsukaze*, is taken from the name of its protagonist, the ghost of a female saltmaker. *Matsukaze* means "wind (*kaze*) in the pines (*matsu*)" as well as "the wind (*kaze*) that awaits (*matsu*)." Poetic puns on this homonym recur throughout the play. The protagonist is the ghost of a rural girl, lingering on the desolate seashore of Suma—like a lonely wind blowing through the coastal pines—awaiting the return of her lover, who long ago set off for the capital and never returned.

The play's authorship has long been the subject of scholarly debate, but it is now generally accepted that it was probably written by Zeami, although he seems to have borrowed several chanting sections from earlier compositions.[56] The precise relationship between the play and its original source also remains obscure. The image of two saltmakers drawing seawater under the moon was probably taken from *Drawing of*

---

55. The image of piling up sand, grain by grain, is one of untiringly and sincerely continuing to practice meritorious actions.

56. In *Conversations on Sarugaku* (*Sarugakudangi*), the play is referred to as Zeami's own. However, in one of Zeami's treatises, *Books on Playwriting* (*Sakunō-sho*), he explains that the *rongi* section of the play was borrowed from an older version of *Tōei*. Nonetheless, the *sashi-sageuta-ageuta* sequence is thought to derive from an independent song composed by his father Kan'ami: in *The Five Sounds* (*Go-on*), Zeami cites a phrase from this sequence as an example of his father's compositions.

Seawater (*Shiokumi*), a play now lost. *Pining Wind*'s central plot—an affair between Ariwara Yukihira (818–893), a noble exiled from the capital, and two sisters from Suma Bay, his place of exile—cannot be found anywhere else and was probably Zeami's own invention. Yukihira, a grandson of Emperor Heizei, was exiled to Suma for some unknown reason. One account of his life in exile, in an anthology of Buddhist anecdotes (setsuwa) entitled *Senjūshō*, recounts an episode in which Yukihira exchanged words with a local fisherperson (*ama*).[57] Although this account offers no hint of any love affair, certain romantic connotations are associated with fisherwomen in literature and legends, some of which depict a girl by the sea marrying a noble aristocrat and bearing his child.

The "Suma" chapter of *The Tale of Genji* links the image of Yukihira in Suma—a nobleman lamenting his exile to a desolate seashore—to the romantic portrayal of fisherwomen. Like Yukihira, Genji, in self-imposed exile, spends a period of time in Suma, after which he moves on to Akashi, a nearby coastal province. While there, he becomes involved with the Akashi lady, who likens her own status to that of rural girls working by the seashore. This lady, however, bears Genji his only daughter, a child who later becomes the mother of a crown prince, cementing Genji's political power and worldly glory. *Pining Wind* borrows from *Genji* this relationship between a noble exile and a local girl at the seacoast and re-creates it as a story about Yukihira, who stays in Suma for three years, has an affair with two local girls, and leaves behind his robe and court cap as keepsakes before making the journey back to the capital, just as Genji left his robe with Lady Akashi before his own return to the capital. The play is replete with citations from *Genji*, especially in its description of the Suma seashore.

According to one medieval linked-verse (renga) manual, the "Suma" chapter, which recounts Genji's sojourn at Suma, bears a close literary association (*yoriai*) with "The Wind in the Pines" chapter, in which the Akashi lady and her daughter finally move to the capital. According to another contemporaneous renga manual, wind in the pines is associated also with autumn rain, since both are representative autumn poetic topoi. At the same time, wind and rain allude to the goddess of Mount Wu in China, famously portrayed in a Chinese poem entitled "Ode to Gaotang." The goddess, who appears to Emperor Huai in a dream and sleeps with him, promises to manifest herself as "clouds in the morning and rain in the evening" on Mount Wu, which subsequently remains obscured by a mysterious haze. This tale, which suggests erotic beauty in hazy clouds and misty rain engulfing distant mountains, became a popular example of the concept of *yūgen* (mystery and depth). Through the association with the goddess of Mount Wu, the two sisters' names, Pining Wind and Autumn Rain, suggest that they, too, might be amorous incarnations of natural phenomena along the Suma coast.[58]

---

57. *Ama*, translated here as "fisherperson," includes, besides saltmakers, divers who gather seaweed and shellfish.

58. This was the way the play was appreciated by Zeami's son-in-law Zenchiku (1405?–1470?) and Ikkyū Sōjun (1394–1481), a monk famous for his poems written in Chinese.

Another pair of natural images is implicitly erotic as well; the moon and the pails. The moon was sometimes a metaphor for a beautiful young man, and some popular medieval songs compare a young girl to a flower basket; one even uses the combination of the moon and a basket as a metaphor for coitus.[59] Here there may be erotic implications in the scene in which the two sisters rejoice on seeing the moon reflected in their water-filled pails.

Pining Wind is the oldest example of extant nō plays that depict love not merely negatively, as a sinful attachment, but also positively, as an illogical yet irresistible human passion.[60] In earlier plays, those obsessed with the fervent passion of love in their former lives end up tormented in hell. In *Pining Wind*, the sisters' longing for Yukihira is repeatedly referred to as a sinful attachment. At the end of the play, however, both surrender to their passion and to the illusion that a pine tree standing on the seashore *is* Yukihira, who has come back to them at last. Instead of representing torturous retribution in hell, the play displays the deranged dance of a girl (Pining Wind) enraptured by an illusory reunion with her lover. *Pining Wind* thus marks Zeami's significant departure from the purely negative treatment of earthly desires, a remnant of nō's original religious function, toward a more poetic representation of human emotions.[61]

Characters in Order of Appearance

A Monk	*waki*
A Villager	*ai*
Pining Wind (*waka-onna* mask)	*shite*
Autumn Rain (*ko-omote* mask)	*tsure*

Stage attendant places a small pine tree, set in a stand, at front of stage; a poem-slip hangs from its branches. To shidai *music, the Monk enters and stands in the shite spot.*

Monk:

> (*shidai*) Suma! and on down the shore to Akashi
> Suma! and on down the shore to Akashi
> I will go roaming with the moon.

---

59. Nakamura Itaru, "*Matsukaze* no henbō: Muromachi makki shodenpon wo chūshin ni," *Kokubungaku: Gengo to bungei*, no. 78 (1974).

60. Yamanaka Reiko, "Nyotainō ni okeru 'Zeami-fū' no kakuritsu: *Matsukaze* no hatashita yakuwari," *Nō: Kenkyū to hyōron*, no. 14 (1986).

61. The opening *shidai*, *nanori*, and *tsukizerifu* are from a manuscript in the hand of Konparu Zenpō (1454–1532). The *mondō* that follows is the *Ai shimai tsuke* version published by Itō Masayoshi (*Yōkyokushū* 3, SNKS, 239–240). The rest of the play is based on NKBT.

(*nanori*) You have before you a monk who is looking at every province. Since I have not yet seen the lands of the west,[62] I have decided this autumn to make my way there and watch the moon over Suma and Akashi.

(*tsuki-zerifu*) Having come so swiftly, I have already reached Suma shore, as I believe it is called, in the province of Settsu. On the beach, I see a single pine with a sign placed before it and a poem-slip hanging in its branches. There must be a story about this tree. I will ask someone what it is.

(*mondō*) Is any resident of Suma shore nearby?

Villager, who has slipped in to sit at the kyōgen *seat, now rises and comes to the first pine.*

VILLAGER: What do you need, reverend sir, from a resident of Suma shore?

MONK: I see this pine has a tablet planted before it, and a poem-slip hanging in its branches. There must be a story about it. Would you kindly tell it to me?

VILLAGER: Why, certainly. Long ago there were two young women—two saltmakers[63]—named Pining Wind and Autumn Rain. This pine stands in their memory. People who wished to honor them put this tablet here and hung in the pine's branches the poem-slip you see. Such people also give them comfort and guidance as they pass. Of course, reverend sir, you yourself have no connection with them,[64] but it would be good of you to do so, too, as you pass by.

MONK: Thank you for your account. Then I will go to the pine and comfort the spirits of those two young women.

VILLAGER: If there is anything else you need, reverend sir, please let me know.

MONK: I promise to do so.

VILLAGER: Very well.

Exit Villager. Monk comes to center and stands facing the pine.

MONK: (*unnamed*) So, this pine is the relic of two saltmakers who lived long ago: Pining Wind, one was called, and the other Autumn Rain.

> A sad, sad story!
> There they lie buried deep in the earth,
> yet their names still linger, and in sign,
> ever constant in hue, a single pine

---

62. *Saigoku*, a vague term for the region west of Kyoto and along the Inland Sea.

63. Saltmakers cut seaweed offshore or raked it up from the beach and then repeatedly poured brine over it. Next, they burned this salt-saturated seaweed, mixed the ashes with water, let the ashes settle, and skimmed off the salt solution. Only then did they boil down this elaborately prepared brine.

64. If the monk were a relative of the two sisters, he would have a natural duty to comfort their spirits. Since he is not, he could choose to pass on without doing so.

leaves a green autumn.[65]
Ah, very moving!

And now that I have comforted them by chanting the sutra and by calling for them upon our Lord Amida, the sun—as it will on these short autumn days—has all too quickly set. That village below the hills is still a good way off. I will go instead to this salt-house and see the night through here.

Stage attendant places the brine wagon near the corner pillar: a small, light evocation of a wagon, with a pail on it and a long brocade "rope" to pull it by.

To shin-no-issei music,[66] Autumn Rain enters and stops at the first pine. She is followed by Pining Wind, who stops at the third pine. Autumn Rain carries a second pail. Both are dressed in white robes over red trouser-skirts. They stand facing each other.

PINING WIND AND AUTUMN RAIN:
(*issei*) A brine wagon wheels meagerly
our dreary world round and round:[67]
O sorry life!

They face the audience.

RAIN:
Waves here at our feet: on Suma shore

They face each other.

BOTH:
the very moon moistens a trailing sleeve.[68]

To ashirai music, both come on stage. Autumn Rain stands at the center, Pining Wind in the shite spot.

(*shidai*) We of Suma, long familiar with fall,
we of Suma, long familiar with fall—
come, under the moon, let us draw brine!

---

65. The pine that stands "in sign" of the sisters' memory "leaves a green autumn" because it alone remains green amid the red autumn foliage.

66. *Shin-no-issei* music, which is normally reserved for the entrance of the shite in a god play and which probably dates from about 1700, underscores the exceptional beauty and purity of the two sisters, who are dressed mainly in white.

67. *Kuruma* means both "wheel" and "wagon." These two lines evoke not only the drearily repetitious cycle of their daily labor but also their sufferings on the wheel of birth and death.

68. The sisters' sleeves are wet with the brine they gather, but even the moon moistens their sleeves because, seeing it, they recall the past and weep.

Face audience.

WIND:

> (*sashi*) Fall winds were blowing, to call forth sighs,[69]
> and although the sea lay some way off,
> Yukihira, the Middle Counselor,

Face each other.

BOTH:

> sang of the breeze from Suma shore
> blowing through the pass; and every night,
> waves sound so near the saltmakers' home,
> apart and lonely. On the way to the village,
> besides the moon, there is no company.

WIND:

> The sorry world's labors claim us,
> and wholly wretched the seafolk's craft

BOTH:

> that makes no way through life, a dream
> where, bubbles of froth, we barely live,
> our wagon affording us no safe haven:
> we of the sea, whose grieving hearts
> never leave these sleeves dry!

Face audience.

CHORUS:

> (*sage-uta*) So thoroughly
> this world of ours
> appears unlivable,
> one only envies
> the brilliant moon[70]
> rising now, come, draw the rising tide, (*Pining Wind steps forward, as
> though toward the sea.*)

---

69. This is the beginning of the *sashi-sageuta-ageuta* passage probably set to music by Kan'ami. The following passage draws on the "Suma" chapter of *The Tale of Genji*. At Suma, Genji lived in a house some way back from the sea. Finding the noise of the waves still very loud, he recalled a poem by Yukihira, who had preceded him at Suma and who (as *The Tale of Genji* suggests) had lived at the same spot. Since Yukihira had spoken in verse of the breeze from Suma shore blowing through the pass (over the hills along the beach), Genji realized that this breeze must stir up the waves. This *sashi* intimates that the two sisters (there was probably only one saltmaker in Kan'ami's piece) live roughly where Genji, and Yukihira before him, lived.

70. A slight modification of a poem by Fujiwara no Takamitsu, *Shūishū*, Miscellaneous 1, no. 435.

rising now, come, draw the rising tide! (*Notices her reflection in a tide pool.*)

(*age-uta*) Image of shame, my reflection,
image of shame, my reflection
shrinks away, withdrawing
tides leave behind stranded pools, (*Gazes at the water again.*)
and I, how long will I linger on?
Dew agleam on meadow grasses
soon must vanish in the sun,
yet on this stony shore
where saltmakers rake seaweed in,
trailing fronds they leave behind,
these sleeves can only wilt away,
these sleeves can only wilt away. (*Retreats to the shite spot.*)

WIND:

(*sashi*) How lovely, though so familiar,
Suma as twilight falls!
Fishermen's calls echo faintly;

They face each other.

BOTH:

out at sea, their frail craft loom
dim, the face of the moon:
wild geese in silhouette,
flocks of plovers, cutting gales,
salt sea winds—yes, each one
at Suma speaks of autumn alone.[71]
Ah, the nights' long, heart-chilling hours!

Face the audience.

WIND:

(*kakeai*) But come, let us draw brine!
At the sea's edge flood and ebb
clothe one in salt robes:

RAIN:

tie the sleeves across your shoulders

WIND:

to draw brine[72]—or so we wish,

---

71. All these sights and sounds of Suma recall what Genji sees in the "Suma" chapter.

72. The long, dangling sleeves had to be tied back in order to allow freedom of movement for work.

RAIN:

> yet no, try as we may,

WIND:

> a woman's wagon

CHORUS:

> > (*age-uta*) rolled in, falls back, weak and weary, (*Autumn Rain goes to the back center. Pining Wind advances slightly, gazes after the cranes.*)
> > rolled in, falls back, weak and weary.[73]
> > Cranes start from the reeds with cries
> > while all four storm winds add their roar.[74]
> > The dark, the cold: how can they be endured? (*Pining Wind looks at the moon, then glances into the buckets on the brine wagon.*)
> > As night wears on, the moon shines so bright!
> > Now we draw the moon's reflections!
> > Salt-fire smoke—O do take care![75]
> > This is the way we of the sea
> > live through the gloom of fall. (*Kneels by the brine wagon.*)
> > (*sage-uta*) Pine Islands! where Ojima's seafolk,[76]
> > beneath the moon, (*With her fan, mimes drawing brine, then gazes at the moon's reflection in her pail.*)
> > draw reflections, ah, with keen delight
> > draw reflections, ah, with keen delight! (*To the shite spot.*)
> > (*rongi*) Far away they haul their brine[77]
> > in Michinoku: though the name
> > is "near," Chika, where workers tend
> > the Shiogama salt-kilns.[78]

WIND:

> And where the poor folk carried salt-wood:
> Akogi beach, that was, and the tide withdrawing

---

73. The two lines beginning with "a woman's wagon" also contain the fleeting image of a great "male wave" approaching the shore, only to recede, and this wave might conceivably point to Yukihira.

74. Storm winds from the four directions.

75. "Take care lest the smoke of the salt fires drift across the moon and hide it."

76. "Pine Islands" is Matsushima, a celebrated scenic spot on the northeast coast of Honshu, near the Shiogama mentioned later. The name Ojima is associated with Matsushima in poetry.

77. *Tōei*, the play from which Zeami transplanted this *rongi* passage, is set at Ashiya. In their aesthetic exaltation, Pining Wind and Autumn Rain play with fragments of poems that eulogize places associated with saltmaking.

78. Michinoku is northern Honshu, where Matsushima and Shiogama are to be found. *Shiogama* means "salt kiln," and the name Chika, near Shiogama, resembles *chika[shi]*, which means "near." Zeami developed the poetic value of Shiogama in his play *Tōru* and, to a lesser extent, in *Akoya no matsu* (no longer performed).

CHORUS:

> on down the same Ise coast lies Futami shore,
> and its Paired Rocks: O I would pair
> a past life in the world with one renewed![79]

WIND:

> When pines stand misty in spring sun,
> the sea-lanes seem to stretch away
> past the tide-flats of Narumi,
> Bay of the Sounding Sea.[80]

CHORUS:

> Ah, Narumi, that was,
> but here at Naruo,[81]
> beneath the shadowing pines,
> no moon ever shines to touch
> the village huts roofed with rushes
> at Ashinoya,[82]

WIND:

> drawing brine from Nada seas
> sorely burdens me with care
> though none will tell, and I am come,
> no boxwood comb in my hair,[83]

CHORUS:

> while in comb the rolling billows (*Autumn Rain places her pail on the
>   brine wagon. Pining Wind gazes at it.*)
> for us to draw brine, and look:
> the moon is in my pail!

WIND:

> In mine, too, there is a moon!

---

79. Akogi Beach is near the Grand Shrine of Ise, on Ise Bay. Just off Futami-ga-ura (Futami, or "Twice-See" Shore), also near the Ise Shrine, two tall rocks rise from the water. They are called the Husband-and-Wife Rocks, and a sacred straw rope encircles them. The "poor folk" carrying "salt wood" (wood to fuel the saltmakers' fires) on Akogi Beach recall several classical poems.

80. Narumi-gata is a spot on the coast near present-day Nagoya. Its name (if the characters used to write it are taken literally) means something like "Bay of the Sounding Sea."

81. Naruo, the name of which sounds like Narumi, is along the coast east of Suma.

82. Ashinoya (or Ashiya), literally "rush houses," is a well-known locality on the coast east of Suma, now between Kobe and Osaka.

83. The line "at Ashinoya" begins a five-line passage that is a variant of a poem in *The Tales of Ise*, episode 87. Nada is the name of the shore near Ashinoya. The passage puns elaborately on *tsuge* (boxwood) and *tsugeji* (will not tell [of my plight]) and on *sashi* ("insert" a comb in one's hair) and *sashi-kuru* ([waves] come surging in). In the original poem, the girl explains to her lover that she has been so busy gathering brine, she has not been able even to dress her hair with a comb before coming to meet him.

CHORUS:

> How lovely! A moon here, too!

Pining Wind looks into the other pail, then up to the sky, then again at the two pails. Having received the wagon-rope from Autumn Rain, she pulls the wagon up to the drums, then looks back at it one more time.

WIND:

> The moon is one,

CHORUS:

> reflections two, three the brimming tide,
> for tonight we load our wagon with the moon.[84]
> O no, I do not find them dreary,
> the tide-roads of the sea!

Stage attendant removes the wagon. Pining Wind sits on a stool in front of the drums, while Autumn Rain sits directly on stage, slightly behind her and to her left. They are in the salt-house.

MONK: (*unnamed*) The people of the salt-house have returned. I will ask them to give me shelter for the night.

> (*mondō*) I beg your pardon, there in the salt-house! Excuse me, please!

RAIN (*rises*): What is it?

MONK: I am a traveler, and now the sun has set. May I have shelter for the night?

RAIN: Please wait a moment. I will ask the owner. (*Turns to Pining Wind, kneels on one knee.*) I beg your pardon, but a traveler is here. He says he wants shelter for the night.

WIND: We could easily give him shelter, but our house simply is not fit to be seen. No, we cannot let him stay.

RAIN (*rises, turns to Monk*): I gave your request to the owner. She says that our house is not fit to be seen and that we cannot offer you lodging for the night.

MONK: I understand, of course, but please realize that I do not mind what condition your house is in. I am a monk, after all. Do pass on again my urgent request for shelter here tonight.

RAIN (*turns to Pining Wind, kneeling on one knee*): The traveler is a monk, and he insists on asking again for a night's shelter.

WIND: What? The traveler is a monk, you say? Why yes, the moonlight shows me one who has renounced the world. Well, it will do, this saltmakers' home, with its posts of pine and fence of bamboo.[85] The night is cold, I know. Tell him he may stay and warm himself at our rush fire.

---

84. To "one [moon]" and "two [reflections]," the original adds the puns *mitsu* ("three" or "brimming") and *yo* ("four" or "night"). "For" is meant to be homophonous with "four."

85. Genji's house at Suma is described in this way in the "Suma" chapter.

Pining Wind pulls a small wagon carrying two pails of seawater. (From *Meiji-Period Nō Illustrations* by Tsukioka Kōgyo, in the Hōsei University Kōzan Bunko Collection)

RAIN (*rises, turns to Monk*): Do please come in.
MONK: Thank you for your kindness.

> *Autumn Rain sits as before. Monk rises, advances a few steps, sits again. He too is now in the salt-house.*

WIND: From the start I wanted to have you stay, but this house is simply not fit to be seen. That is why I refused.
MONK: It is very good of you to have me. Since I am a monk and have always been one, my travels have no particular goal. On what grounds, then, should I prefer one lodging to another? Besides, here on Suma shore, any sensitive person ought actually to prefer a somewhat melancholy life:

> Should one perchance
> ask after me,
> say that on Suma shore,
> salt, sea-tangle drops
> are falling as I grieve.[86]

Yes, that was Yukihira's poem. By the way, I noticed that pine tree on the shore. When I asked a man about it, he told me that it stands in memory of

---

86. According to the *Kokinshū* (ca. 905), Yukihira, in exile at Suma, sent this poem back to someone in the capital. The "salt, sea-tangle drops" are both the brine that drips from the seaweed gathered by saltmakers along the beach and the poet's own tears.

two saltmakers named Pining Wind and Autumn Rain. (*Pining Wind and Autumn Rain weep.*) I have no connection of my own with them, of course, but I prayed for them before going on. Why, how strange! When I mentioned Yukihira, both of you seemed overcome with sorrow. What is the meaning of your grief?

WIND AND RAIN: Oh, it is true! When love is within, love's colors will show without![87] The way you quoted his poem, "Should one by chance inquire for me," brought on such pangs of longing! So tears of attachment to the human world once more moistened our sleeves. (*They weep.*)

MONK: Tears of attachment to the human world? You talk as though you were not of the living. And Yukihira's poem seems to afflict you with feelings of painful longing; I do not understand. Please, both of you, tell me your names!

WIND AND RAIN:

> (*kudoki-guri*) I am ashamed!
> As the tale rises to my lips,
> I whom none ask after, ever,
> rejoin a world gone long ago,
> where, brine drenched, I learn no lesson
> but suffer on in bitterness of heart.[88]
> (*kudoki*) Yet having spoken,
> perhaps we need dissemble no more.
> Some while ago, as twilight fell,
> you kindly comforted those who lie
> under that pine, beneath the moss:
> two young women,
> Pining Wind and Autumn Rain.
> We before you are their phantoms.
> Yes, Yukihira, those three years,
> lightened his leisure with pleasant boating
> and watched the moon here on Suma shore.
> While seafolk maidens each night drew brine,
> he chose and courted us, two sisters.
> Pleased with names that fit the season,
> he called us Pining Wind and Autumn Rain.
> We Suma seafolk, familiars of the moon,

WIND:

> found our saltburners' clothing suddenly changed

---

87. A well-known saying, ultimately derived from the Chinese classic *Mencius.*

88. The brine that drenches her in her daily work also represents the memories from which she can never be free. This kudoki-guri passage uses language from the "Suma" chapter of *The Tale of Genji.*

BOTH:

> to silken summer robes censed with sweet fragrance.

WIND:

> So those three years slipped quickly by.
> Then Yukihira went up to the capital

RAIN:

> and, not long after, came the news

BOTH:

> that he, so young, had passed away.[89]

WIND:

> O how I love him!
> But perhaps once, in another life (*Weeps.*)
> he again will come,

CHORUS:

> (*uta*) pining. Wind and Autumn Rain
> wet these sleeves, helpless, alas,
> against a love so far beyond us.
> We of Suma are deep in sin:[90] (*They appeal to Monk with palms pressed together.*)
> O in your kindness, give us comfort!
> (*age-uta*) Upon passion's tangled grasses,
> dew and longing mingle wildly, (*Below, Autumn Rain goes to sit in left center while Monk moves to the waki spot.*)
> dew and longing mingle wildly,
> till the heart, spellbound, yields to madness.
> The Day of the Serpent brings purification,[91]
> yet sacred streamers to ask the god's help
> wave on, useless, wave-borne froth,
> we melt into grief and lasting sorrow. (*Below, stage attendant gives Pining Wind a man's hat and robe. Carrying them, she dances and mimes in consonance with the text.*)
> (*kuse*) Ah, as those old days return to mind,
> I miss him so!
> Yukihira, the Middle Counselor,
> three years dwelt on Suma shore,
> then went away up to the capital,

---

89. Zeami invented this death. Yukihira actually died at the age of seventy-five.

90. This "sin" is neither social (love across class lines) nor moral. It is the sin of "wrongful clinging" (*mōshu*): the error of desiring intensely what one cannot possibly have. Such clinging leads only to misery.

91. A purification rite was regularly performed on the Day of the Serpent early in the third lunar month. Evil influences were transferred onto dolls that were then floated down rivers or out to sea. The same rite appears in the "Suma" chapter.

but left as keepsakes of our love
his tall court hat, his hunting cloak.
Each time I see them, ever more
passion grasses spring,
the pale dewdrops on each blade
so swiftly gone—might I so soon
forget this agony!

    His parting gifts,
    O they are enemies:
    were they gone from me,
    a moment of forgetfulness
    might even now be mine[92]
so someone sang. O it is true!
My love for him only deepens. (*Lowers her hat and cloak, which she had
    clasped to her, and weeps. Below, she continues miming.*)

WIND:

    Night after night,
    I remove on lying down
    this, my hunting cloak,[93]

CHORUS:

    and on and on I only pray
    that he and I might share our life—
    but fruitlessly.
    His keepsakes bring me no joy!
    She throws them down but cannot leave them;
    picks them up, and his own face
    looms before her. Do as she may,
    From the pillow,
        from the foot of the bed,
        love comes pursuing.[94]
        Down she sinks in helpless tears,
    lost in misery.

(*The donning of the robe*)
    *In the shite spot, Pining Wind collapses into a sitting position and weeps.
To ashirai music, the stage attendant clothes her in the robe and places the hat
on her head. She weeps once more.*

---

92. Anonymous, *Kokinshū*, Love 4, no. 746.
93. The first half of a poem by Ki no Tomonori, *Kokinshū*, Love 2, no. 593. The speaker of
the poem says that each night before retiring, as he removes his hunting cloak and hangs it on
its stand, he cannot help thinking of his love. The key words in the poem are *kakete* (hang [the
cloak on its stand]) and "constantly," here rendered as "on and on."
94. Anonymous, *Kokinshū*, Haikai Poems, no. 1023.

WIND:

> (*ge-no-ei*) River of Three Crossings:[95]
> the grim ford of ceaseless weeping
> yet conceals a gulf of churning love!
> (*kakeai*) O what happiness! Yukihira is standing there, calling my name,
>> Pining Wind!
> I am going to him!

She rises and starts toward the pine. Autumn Rain comes up behind her and catches her right sleeve.

RAIN: How awful! This state you are in is exactly what drowns you in the sin of clinging! You have not yet forgotten the mad passion you felt when we still belonged to the world. That is a pine tree. Yukihira is not there.

WIND:

> You are too cruel, to talk that way! That pine *is* Yukihira!
> Though for a time we may say goodbye,
> should I hear you pine, I will return:
> so said his poem, did it not?[96]

RAIN:

> Why, you are right! I had forgotten!
> A while, perhaps, we may say goodbye,
> but should you miss me, I will come:
> those were the words

WIND:

> I had not forgotten, pining
> wind is rising now:
> he promised he will come—

RAIN:

> news to start an autumn rain,
> leaving sleeves a moment moistened;

WIND:

> yes, pining still, he will return:

RAIN:

> we rightly trusted

WIND:

> his dear poem:

---

95. The river that the soul must cross to reach the afterworld. It has three fords (deep, medium, and shallow), depending on the sins that burden the soul.

96. Pining Wind quotes Yukihira's poem inaccurately, and so does Autumn Rain a few lines later. It is a climactic moment when a little later still, their mounting excitement recalls it to them perfectly.

BOTH:

> (*waka*) Now I say goodbye,

(*Dance*: chū-no-mai)

In tears, Pining Wind runs on to bridgeway, while Autumn Rain, also weeping, goes to sit in left center. Pining Wind then returns to the stage, pauses in the shite spot, and performs a chū-no-mai *dance.*

WIND:

> bound for Inaba's
> far green mountains;
> yet, my love, pine
> and I will come again.[97]
> (*noriji*) Yonder, Inaba's far mountain pines;

CHORUS:

> here, my longing, my beloved lord
> here on Suma shore pines:[98] Yukihira
> back with me once more, while I,
> beside the tree, rise now, draw near:
> so dear, the wind-bent pine—
> I love him still!

(*Dance*: ha-no-mai)

Pining Wind ceases weeping, then lifts her head and dances a ha-no-mai *around the pine. As the text continues, she continues to dance and mime.*

CHORUS:

> In the pine a wind blows wild.
> The Suma breakers rage nightlong
> While wrongful clinging brings you this, our dream.
> In your kindness, give us comfort!
> Now, farewell:
> (*uta*) receding waves fall silent
> along Suma shore
> a breeze sweeps down from off the hills.
> On the pass, the cocks are crowing.
> The dream is gone, without a shadow
> night opens into dawn.
> It was autumn rain you heard,
> but this morning see:

---

97. This poem, from the *Kokinshū*, is generally taken as a farewell addressed by Yukihira to a friend or friends in the capital, when he set out for Inaba Province in 855 as the new governor.

98. This "pines" is meant to include the meaning "is a pine."

    pining wind alone lingers on,
    pining wind alone lingers on.

Facing the side from the shite spot, stamps the final beat.

[Translated by Royall Tyler]

ATSUMORI
Attributed to Zeami

The protagonists of warrior plays are the ghosts of those who have fallen in battle. In earlier versions, they usually seem to have been portrayed as denizens of a hellish realm of never-ending battle in the afterlife.[99] However, in *The Three Paths (Sandō)*, Zeami recommends selecting protagonists of warrior plays from *The Tales of the Heike* and depicting them in an elegant manner. In this way, Zeami transformed warrior plays to suit the tastes of his cultural patrons in the capital, such as court nobles and high-ranking samurai, who favored elegant beauty over the rough mimicry of demonic battles between long-dead warriors.

The Tales of the Heike was enormously popular at the beginning of the medieval period. Earlier versions of this narrative are closer to historical documents in their descriptions of actual battles between the Heike (Taira) and the Genji (Minamoto) clans, whereas later versions highlight the aristocratic refinement of the Heike and the tragedy of the deaths of the clan's noblemen and -women. In addition, Zeami often changed details of the original plot in order to accentuate the elegance of the protagonists.

Atsumori is Zeami's adaptation of a famous episode from the *Heike*. Near the end of the battle at Ichi-no-tani on Suma Bay, Naozane, a follower of the rival Genji clan, catches sight of an apparently high-ranking warrior of the Heike alone on the seashore. Wrestling his enemy to the ground and removing his helmet, Naozane realizes that the soldier—Atsumori—is a boy of only about fifteen, nearly the same age as his own son. Although his first impulse is to spare the boy's life, he sees other Genji followers fast approaching and knows that they will surely kill the boy. Thinking it better for the boy that he be the one to strike the final blow, Naozane is compelled to cut off the boy's head. When he tears off a piece of Atsumori's garment to wrap the head, he notices a flute, a symbol of courtly elegance, hidden under the boy's armor. Some time afterward, revolted by the calling that has led him to commit such a brutal act, Naozane takes the tonsure. Later descriptions of this episode emphasize young Atsumori's nobility, his almost feminine beauty, and his musical talent, as well as Naozane's regret for having killed such an exquisite youth.

---

99. In *Teaching on Style and the Flower (Fūshikaden)*, Zeami notes that warrior plays "tend to be demonic" and "are not interesting."

The nō play *Atsumori* revisits the encounter at Suma Bay between Naozane, who is now a monk named Renshō, and the ghost of Atsumori, disguised as a reaper. In the first act, the ghost of Atsumori shows his love for music by playing the flute. A question about the sound of his flute opens the conversation between the monk and the ghost, which soon leads to a song reciting the names of famous flutes in Japanese literature. Recurrent references to the flute function as allusions to the one that Atsumori kept close to his person during his life, even on the field of battle.

The play also alludes frequently to the "Suma" chapter of *The Tale of Genji*. Its background scene, the shore at Suma, is thus portrayed as a highly poetic landscape with strong associations with aristocratic culture rather than a bloody battlefield. These associations even suggest an analogy between Atsumori and the protagonist of the Heian-period tale of the Shining Genji, as both characters fled the capital for this remote seashore under adverse circumstances. The climax of the second act, unlike that of typical warrior plays, describes not the warriors' torment in hell but Atsumori's recollection of a banquet he enjoyed with his family the night before his death. Atsumori's ghost reenacts the singing, flute playing, and dancing during the banquet.

Atsumori is a dream play (mugen-nō) in two acts, a structure that Zeami invented, although he did not follow it strictly here. For example, in a standard mugen-nō, the monk would simply be a passerby with no personal connection with the ghost, whereas in *Atsumori*, the monk is Naozane, the murderer of Atsumori. Such an exceptional personal relationship between the ghost and the monk is based on the fact that the original episode in the *Heike* is a tragedy for both Atsumori and Naozane, who is forced by circumstances to kill the young boy. Consequently, just as Atsumori needs to be saved from the torment of hell, Naozane is desperate to be delivered from his own anguish. This double salvation is attained at the end of the play, when Atsumori forgives Naozane and expresses his strong hope that, through Naozane's prayers, Atsumori will attain buddhahood.

Characters in Order of Appearance

THE MONK RENSHŌ, formerly the Minamoto warrior Kumagai no Jirō Naozane	*waki*
A YOUTH, the ghost of Atsumori appearing as a grass cutter	*mae-shite*
TWO OR THREE COMPANIONS to the Youth	*tsure*
A VILLAGER	*ai*
THE GHOST OF THE TAIRA WARRIOR ATSUMORI (*Atsumori*, *jūroku*, or *chūjō* mask)	*nochi-shite*

Place: Ichi-no-tani, in Settsu Province

Act 1

To shidai *music, Renshō enters, carrying a rosary. He stands in the shite spot, facing the rear of the stage.*

RENSHŌ:

> (*shidai*) The world is all a dream, and he who wakes
> the world is all a dream, and he who wakes,
> casting it from him, may yet know the real. (*Turns to audience.*)

> (*nanori*) You have before you one who in his time was Kumagai no Jirō Naozane, a warrior from Musashi Province. Now I have renounced the world, and Renshō is my name. It was I, you understand, who struck Atsumori down; and the great sorrow of this deed moved me to become the monk you see. Now I am setting out for Ichi-no-tani, to comfort Atsumori and guide his spirit toward enlightenment.

> (*age-uta*) The wandering moon,
> issuing from among the Ninefold Clouds,[100]
> issuing from among the Ninefold Clouds, (*Mimes walking.*)
> swings southward by Yodo and Yamazaki,
> past Koya Pond and the Ikuta River,
> and Suma shore, loud with pounding waves,
> to Ichi-no-tani, where I have arrived,
> to Ichi-no-tani, where I have arrived.

> (*tsuki-zerifu*) Having come so swiftly, I have reached Ichinotani in the province of Settsu. Ah, the past returns to mind as though it were before me now. But what is this? I hear a flute from that upper field. I will wait for the player to come by and question him about what happened here.

Sits below the witness pillar. To shidai *music, the Youth and Companions enter. Each carries a split bamboo pole with a bunch of mown grass secured in the cleft. They face each other at the front.*

YOUTH AND COMPANIONS:

> (*shidai*) The sweet music of the mower's flute,
> the sweet music of the mower's flute
> floats, windborne, far across the fields.

YOUTH:

> (*sashi*) Those who gather grass on yonder hill
> now start for home, for twilight is at hand.

---

100. The moon suggests the monk Renshō himself. The "Ninefold Clouds" refer to the capital. "Ninefold," an epithet for the imperial palace, and hence for the capital, refers to the nine gates of ancient Chinese palaces.

YOUTH AND COMPANIONS:

> They too head back to Suma, by the sea,
> and their way, like mine, is hardly long.
> Back and forth I ply, from hill to shore,
> heart heavy with the cares of thankless toil.
> (*sage-uta*) Yes, should one perchance ask after me,
> my reply would speak of lonely grief.[101]
> (*age-uta*) On Suma shore
> the salty drops fall fast, though were I known,
> the salty drops fall fast, though were I known,
> I myself might hope to have a friend.[102]
> Yet, having sunk so low, I am forlorn,
> and those whom I once loved are strangers now.

While chanting these lines, Youth goes to stand in the shite spot, Companions in front of the chorus.

> But I resign myself to what life brings,
> and accept what griefs are mine to bear,
> and accept what griefs are mine to bear.

Renshō rises.

RENSHŌ: (*mondō*) Excuse me, mowers, but I have a question for you.

YOUTH: For us, reverend sir? What is it, then?

RENSHŌ: Was it one of you I just heard playing the flute?

YOUTH: Yes, it was one of us.

RENSHŌ: How touching! For people such as you, that is a remarkably elegant thing to do! Oh yes, it is very touching.

YOUTH: It is a remarkably elegant thing, you say, for people like us to do? The proverb puts the matter well: "Envy none above you, despise none below." Besides,

> the woodman's songs and the mower's flute

YOUTH AND COMPANIONS:

> are called "sylvan lays" and "pastoral airs".[103]
> they nourish, too, many a poet's work,
> and ring out very bravely through the world.
> You need not wonder, then, to hear me play.

---

101. These lines allude to the poem by Ariwara no Yukihira in the *Kokinshū* (Miscellaneous 2, no. 962) that figures so prominently in *Pining Wind*. Yukihira was exiled to Suma.

102. Yukihira's poem alludes to a friend in the capital, and the youth is probably longing for a similar friend, in the capital now lost to him, who would know his true quality. In fact, his only possible friend, Renshō, is already present.

103. From a line of Chinese verse by the Japanese poet Ki no Tadana, *Wakan rōeishū*, no. 559.

RENSHŌ:

    (*kakeai*) I do not doubt that what you say is right.

    Then, "sylvan lays" or "pastoral airs"

YOUTH:

    mean the mower's flute,

RENSHŌ:

    the woodman's songs:

YOUTH:

    music to ease all the sad trials of life,

RENSHŌ:

    singing,

YOUTH:

    dancing.

RENSHŌ:

    fluting—

YOUTH:

    all these pleasures

Youth begins to move and gesture in consonance with the text.

CHORUS:

    (*age-uta*) are pastimes not unworthy of those
    who care to seek out beauty: for bamboo,
    who care to seek out beauty: for bamboo,
    washed up by the sea, yields Little Branch,
    Cicada Wing, and other famous flutes;
    while this one, that the mower blows,
    could be Greenleaf, as you will agree.[104]
    Perhaps upon the beach at Sumiyoshi,
    one might expect instead a Koma flute;[105]
    but this is Suma. Imagine, if you will,
    a flute of wood left from saltmakers' fires
    a flute of wood left from saltmakers' fires.

Exeunt Companions. Youth, in the shite spot, turns to Renshō.

RENSHŌ: (*kakeai*) How strange! While the other mowers have gone home, you have stayed on, alone. Why is this?

---

104. It was felt that bamboo washed up by the sea yielded particularly fine flutes. Atsumori's own was, in fact, the one named Little Branch (Saeda). The divine music of Greenleaf was legendary.

105. Because Sumiyoshi was where ships from Koma (Korea) once used to set anchor. The *Koma-bue* (Koma flute) is used in the ancient court music known as *gakaku*.

In act 2, Atsumori's ghost, appearing in his original form, refrains from attacking Kumagai and drops to one knee. (From *Meiji-Period Nō Illustrations* by Tsukioka Kōgyo, in the Hōsei University Kōzan Bunko Collection)

YOUTH: You ask why have I stayed behind? A voice called me here, chanting the Name. O be kind and grant me the Ten Invocations![106]

RENSHŌ: Very gladly. I will give you Ten Invocations, as you ask. But then tell me who you are.

YOUTH: In truth, I am someone with a tie to Atsumori.

RENSHŌ:

> One with a tie to Atsumori?
>
> Ah, the name recalls such memories! (*Presses his palms together in prayer over his rosary.*)
>
> "Namu Amida Butsu," I chant in prayer:

Youth goes down on one knee and presses his palms together.

YOUTH AND RENSHŌ:

> "If I at last become a Buddha,
> then all sentient beings who call my Name

---

106. The Name is that of Amida, the Buddha of Infinite Light, whose invocation is *Namu Amida Butsu* (Hail Amida Buddha). The Ten Invocations (ten callings of the Name for the benefit of another) were often requested of holy persons even by the living. Renshō's teacher, Hōnen, was an outstanding Amida devotee. In *Pining Wind*, too, the monk invokes Amida for the spirits of the dead.

in all the worlds, in the ten directions,
will find welcome in Me, for I abandon none."[107]

CHORUS:

(*uta*) Then, O monk, do not abandon me!
One calling of the Name should be enough,
but you have comforted me by night and day—
a most precious gift! As to my name,
no silence I might keep could quite conceal
the one you pray for always, dawn and dusk; (*Youth rises.*)
that name is my own. And, having spoken,
he fades away and is lost to view,
he fades away and is lost to view.

Exit Youth.

Interlude

Villager passes by and, in response to Renshō's request for information, describes how Atsumori was defeated by Kumagai on this very coast. He expresses deep sympathy for the former and a fierce hatred for the latter. Renshō reveals his identity. Greatly surprised, the Villager apologizes for his previous indignation, advises Renshō to pray for the peace of Atsumori's spirit, and exits.

Act 2

RENSHŌ:

(*age-uta*) Then it is well: to guide and comfort him,
then it is well: to guide and comfort him,
I shall do holy rites, and through the night
call aloud the Name for Atsumori,
praying that he reach enlightenment,
praying that he reach enlightenment.

To issei *music, Atsumori enters, in the costume of a warrior. He stops in the* shite *spot.*

ATSUMORI:

(*jō-no-ei*) Across to Awaji the plovers fly,
while the Suma barrier guard sleeps on;
yet one, I see, keeps night-long vigil here.

---

107. The canonical vow made by Amida before he became a Buddha, to save all beings by his grace. These lines, in Chinese, are from the sutra known in Japan as Kammuryōju-kyō.

O keeper of the pass, tell me your name.[108]
    (*kakeai*) Behold, Renshō: I am Atsumori.
RENSHŌ:

    Strange! As I chant aloud the Name,
    beating out the rhythm on this gong,
    and wakeful as ever in broad day,
    I see Atsumori come before me.
    The sight can only be a dream.

ATSUMORI:

    Why need you take it for a dream?
    For I have come so far to be with you
    in order to clear karma that is real.

RENSHŌ:

    I do not understand you: for the Name
    has power to clear away all trace of sin.
    Call once upon the name of Amida
    and your countless sins will be no more:
    so the sutra promises. As for me,
    I have always called the Name for you.
    How could sinful karma afflict you still?

ATSUMORI:

    Deep as the sea it runs. O lift me up,

RENSHŌ:

    that I too may come to buddhahood!

ATSUMORI:

    Let each assure the other's life to come,

RENSHŌ:

    for we, once enemies,

ATSUMORI:

    are now become,

RENSHŌ:

    in very truth,

ATSUMORI:

    fast friends in the Law.

Below, Atsumori moves and gestures in consonance with the text.

---

108. The barrier on the pass through the hills behind Suma was well known in poetry, as was its nameless guard. In the language of poetry, an older man seen at night at Suma can only be this guard, so that Atsumori's playful challenge, "O keeper of the pass, tell me your name," seems intended to remind the more rustic Renshō of his place. His words, based on a twelfth-century poem, are as elegant as the music of his flute.

CHORUS:

> (*uta*) Now I understand!
>> "Leave the company of an evil friend,
>> cleave to the foe you judge a good man":
> and that good man is you! O I am grateful!
> How can I thank you as you deserve?
> Then I will make confession of my tale,
> and pass the night recounting it to you,
> and pass the night recounting it to you. (*Atsumori sits on a stool at the center, facing the audience.*)
> (*kuri*) The flowers of spring rise up and deck the trees
> to urge all upward to illumination;
> the autumn moon plumbs the waters' depths
> to show grace from on high saving all beings.

ATSUMORI:

> (*sashi*) Rows of Taira mansions lined the streets:
> we were the leafy branches on the trees.

CHORUS:

> Like the rose of Sharon, we flowered one day;
> but as the Teaching that enjoins the Good
> is seldom found,[109] birth in the human realm
> quickly ends, like a spark from a flint.
> This we never knew, nor understood
> that vigor is followed by decline.

ATSUMORI:

> Lords of the land we were, but caused much grief;

CHORUS:

> blinded by wealth, we never knew our pride. (*Atsumori rises now and dances through the* kuse *passage below.*)
> (*kuse*) Yes, the house of Taira ruled the world
> twenty years and more: a generation
> that passed by as swiftly as a dream.
> Then came the Juei years, and one sad fall,
> when storms stripped the trees of all their leaves
> and scattered them to the four directions,
> we took to our fragile, leaflike ships,
> and tossed in restless sleep upon the waves.
> Our very dreams foretold no return.
> We were like caged birds that miss the clouds,

---

109. It is only rarely, and by great good fortune, that a sentient being is able to hear the Buddha's teaching; and it is only as a human being that one can reach enlightenment.

or homing geese that have lost their way.
We never lingered long under one sky,
but traveled on for days, and months, and years,
till at last spring came round again,
and we camped here, at Ichinotani.
So we stayed on, hard by Suma shore,

ATSUMORI:

while winds swept down upon us off the hills.

CHORUS:

The fields were bitterly cold. At the sea's edge
our ships huddled close, while day and night
the plovers cried, and our own poor sleeves
wilted in the spray that drenched the beach.
Together in the seafolk's huts we slept,
till we ourselves joined these villagers,
bent to their life like the wind-bent pines.
The evening smoke rose from our cooking fires
while we sat about on heaps of sticks
piled upon the beach, and thought and thought
of how we were at Suma, in the wilds,
and we ourselves belonged to Suma now,
even as we wept for all our clan.

Atsumori stands in front of the drums.

ATSUMORI:

(*kakeai*) Then came the sixth night of the Second Month.
My father, Tsunemori, summoned us
to play and dance, and sing *imayō*.[110]

RENSHŌ:

Why, that was the music I remember!
A flute was playing so sweetly in their camp!
We, the attackers, heard it well enough.

ATSUMORI:

It was Atsumori's flute, you see:
the one I took with me to my death

RENSHŌ:

and that you wished to play this final time,

ATSUMORI:

while from every throat

RENSHŌ:

rose songs and poems

---

110. The popular songs (much appreciated at court) of the late twelfth century.

CHORUS:

> (*issei*) sung in chorus to a lively beat.

(*Dance:* chū-no-mai)
> *Atsumori performs a lively* chū-no-mai, *ending in the shite spot. Below, he continues dancing and miming in consonance with the text.*

ATSUMORI:

> (*unnamed*) Then, in time, His Majesty's ship sailed,

CHORUS:

> (*noriji*) with the whole clan behind him in their own.
> Anxious to be aboard, I sought the shore,
> but all the warships and the imperial barge
> stood already far, far out to sea.

ATSUMORI:

> (*unnamed*) I was stranded. Reining in my horse,
> I halted, at a loss for what to do.

CHORUS:

> (*chū-noriji*) There came then, galloping behind me,
> Kumagai no Jirō Naozane,
> shouting, "You will not escape my arm!"
> At this Atsumori wheeled his mount
> and swiftly, all undaunted, drew his sword.
> We first exchanged a few rapid blows,
> then, still on horseback, closed to grapple, fell,
> and wrestled on, upon the wave-washed strand.
> But you had bested me, and I was slain.
> Now karma brings us face to face again.
> "You are my foe!" Atsumori shouts, (*Brandishes sword.*)
> lifting his sword to strike; but Kumagai (*He drops to one knee.*)
> with kindness has repaid old enmity, (*Rises, retreats.*)
> calling the Name to give the spirit peace.
> They at last shall be reborn together
> upon one lotus throne in paradise.
> Renshō, you were no enemy of mine. (*He drops his sword and, in the shite spot, turns to Renshō with palms pressed together.*)
> Pray for me, O pray for my release!
> Pray for me, O pray for my release!

Facing right center from the shite spot, stamps the final beat.

[Translated by Royall Tyler]

SHRINE IN THE FIELDS (*NONOMIYA*)
Attributed to Konparu Zenchiku

Zeami's elegant style was most faithfully followed by Konparu Zenchiku (1405?–1470?), head of the Konparu-za sarugaku troupe in Yamato Province, as is obvious in both Zenchiku's plays and his aesthetic treatises. Having lost his father while still young, Zenchiku turned to Zeami as his mentor and married Zeami's daughter. While Zeami was in exile on Sado Island, Zenchiku supported him financially and looked after his wife, who remained in Yamato.

Although there is no documented evidence of the authorship of *Shrine in the Fields*, a third-category or "woman" play, it is generally attributed to Zenchiku, as it contains many characteristics common to his works. The setting of the play, a lonely field on an autumn night, reflects Zenchiku's predilection for desolate settings. Zenchiku's plays also frequently use the word *iro* (color), often signifying metaphysical instead of visible colors, as in *kokoro no iro* (the shades of my heart), which is a convention he probably borrowed from the famous poet Fujiwara no Teika (1162–1241), whom he greatly admired. Here, however, this convention is also an allusion to a remark made in *The Tale of Genji*, about the "unchanging color" of the sacred *sakaki* branch.

The overall composition and details of the play also resemble *The Well Cradle* (*Izutsu*), one of Zeami's most popular works, such as the arrangement of subsections (*shōdan*), the way in which a traveling monk encounters a female ghost, and the use of relatively large stage props (in *Izutsu*, a well; in *Nonomiya*, the gate and fences of a shrine). Although Zeami often incorporated whole or revised portions of earlier plays, he rarely created a new play by duplicating the structure of an earlier one of his own. Instead, each of his plays seems to be a new composition or contain a new theatrical device. Conversely, Zenchiku often copied the structure of Zeami's popular plays, as if teaching himself how to write by patterning his own works after Zeami's.

Nonomiya is based on an episode in "The Sacred Tree" (Sakaki) chapter of *The Tale of Genji*, a sequel to the episode that inspired the nō play *Lady Aoi*. In *Genji*, the daughter of Lady Rokujō and the late crown prince is appointed as the Ise Shrine's priestess. Lady Rokujō (or the "Consort," as she is referred to in the play), who has by now realized that her own wandering, resentful spirit killed Aoi and that Genji is well aware of this, makes the highly unorthodox decision to accompany her daughter to distant Ise. Before setting off on their long journey, mother and daughter seek purification at Nonomiya, a shrine in a desolate field north of Kyoto. One autumn night while they are there, Genji pays Lady Rokujō a last visit to bid her farewell. In *Nonomiya*, a traveling monk visits Nonomiya and there encounters the ghost of Lady Rokujō, who has been returning to this place on this very night in autumn every year since her death.

Although they share the same protagonist, *Lady Aoi* and *Nonomiya* differ in other respects. *Lady Aoi* presents Lady Rokujō as an obsessive female demon, whereas *Nonomiya* depicts her as a proud and noble lady who quietly recalls her past love. In *Lady Aoi*, Genji is rarely cited directly, whereas in *Nonomiya* the night of Genji's visit is described in detail, with several quotations from the original. *Lady Aoi* also does not refer directly to the earlier episode of the "clash of the carriages," in which Lady Rokujō conceives an ultimately deadly animosity toward Aoi, but alludes to it only vaguely, through its frequent references to a carriage. The audience thus can enjoy the play even if they are not familiar with the original story. By contrast, in the second act of *Nonomiya* the ghost of Lady Rokujō reenacts this incident but does not explain how it relates to her relationship with Genji. Clearly, *Nonomiya* assumes its audience is sufficiently familiar with *Genji* to understand the significance of this scene, for otherwise they would be completely lost in the second act of the play. This change in expectations regarding nō audiences' literary knowledge may have reflected the rapid rise in nō performances' social status.

Although it follows the original narrative more closely than *Lady Aoi* does, *Nonomiya* introduces a new twist in its presentation of the relationship between Lady Rokujō and Genji from the viewpoint of her ghost. In the original, Genji finally decides to sever his ties with Rokujō when he realizes that her living spirit has murdered his wife. But he continues to visit her at Nonomiya, and when she is about to set out for Ise, he sends her a letter asking that she remain in the capital. These gestures can be viewed less as sincere demonstrations of affection than as formal expressions of the prevailing etiquette. As is clear in the original text, Genji's intention in comforting Lady Rokujō is to avoid acquiring a reputation for heartlessness. In *Nonomiya*, however, the ghost of Lady Rokujō never mentions her attack on Aoi but recalls Genji's visit as a token of his genuine affection for her. She even regrets not having heeded his request to stay in the capital. It is as if that night—and her whole relationship with Genji—has become idealized in her memory over the many centuries since her death.

Toward the end of the play, the ghost of Lady Rokujō performs a dance (*jo-no-mai*) that serves no clear purpose in the plot. Indeed, such purely ornamental dance was introduced only after Zeami, who had always provided in his plays social situations in which female characters might plausibly dance. Since the social code of that time did not permit ordinary women to dance, the female characters who dance in his plays are deities, professional dancers, or deranged women. But through such plays, in which ordinary women, or sometimes even women of high rank, dance in derangement or after being reborn as deities, both playwrights and audiences gradually grew accustomed to seeing female characters dance in nō. By Zenchiku's time, dancing by female characters had become little more than a theatrical convention of nō.

Another characteristic of Zenchiku's style can be found in *Nonomiya*'s ending, which suggests that the ghost of Lady Rokujō may not attain buddhahood after all. At the end of many of his other plays, ghosts do not relinquish their earthly desires and thus fail to attain buddhahood. This type of ending may have resulted from the decreasing emphasis on one of nō's original religious purposes: *chinkon*, the pacification of the unsettled spirits of the dead.

Characters in Order of Appearance

A Monk	*waki*
A Lady (*waka-onna* mask)	*mae-shite*
A Villager	*ai*
The ghost of the Consort, Lady Rokujō (*waka-onna* mask)	*nochi-shite*

Act 1

Stage attendant places a model of a torii *(shrine gate) with a brushwood fence to either side of it at front center stage. To* nanori-bue *music, the Monk enters, stands at the shite spot, and faces the audience.*

MONK: (*nanori*) I am a monk who is visiting all the provinces. Of late I have been in the capital and have seen each of the capital's famed places and ancient sites. Now that autumn is drawing to its close, I think I shall go and see Sagano[111] while at its charming best.[112] When I asked someone about these woods, he said this old site is that of Nonomiya[113] or some such place, and so I shall have a look in passing.

Moves to the center, stands in front of the torii.

MONK:

    (*unnamed*) Having come to these woods,
    I see that the rough-hewn log torii[114]
    And the low brushwood fence
    Have not changed from long ago, (*Kneels, puts hands together as in prayer.*)
    But how can this be?
    Never mind, for I am glad
    Of this chance to come and worship.
    (*uta*) Ise's sacred fence forms no barrier,[115]

---

111. Sagano, or Saga, is a rural area west of the capital, well known as a place of retreat and reclusion. Because of its desolate reputation, Sagano is commonly associated with autumn in Japanese poetry.

112. A strict grammatical rendering would be "because I am drawn to Sagano."

113. *Nonomiya* literally means "shrine in the fields."

114. "Rough-hewn log" means a log not completely stripped of its bark and is a phrase borrowed from the Nonomiya episode in "The Sacred Tree" (Sakaki) chapter of *The Tale of Genji*. A *torii* is a shrine gate consisting of two upright pillars crossed at the top by one or more horizontal beams (in this case, logs).

115. In other words, the deities worshiped at the Ise shrines do not distinguish between Shinto and Buddhist worship.

Straight is the Way of the Law's teaching,
And straight is the way I came to see this holy shrine.[116]
How clear is the twilight, and clear my heart!
How clear is the twilight, and clear my heart! (*Stands, moves to the waki spot, and sits.*)

To shidai *music, Lady enters, holding a branch of leaves in her left hand, and stands at the shite spot.*

LADY:[117]

> (*shidai*) Nonomiya, so used to flowers,
> O Nonomiya, so used to flowers,
> What will become of you when autumn has passed?[118] (*Faces audience.*)
> (*sashi*) Then will the lonesome autumn end
> And at last my sleeves wither with dew.[119]
> In the dusk I am broken.
> The shades of my heart,
> Like all flowers, fade,
> Destined, alas, to decline! (*Still facing audience.*)
> (*sage-uta*) No one knows, but this day each year
> I return to these traces of the past.
> (*age-uta*) As autumn deepens and bitter winds blow
> In these woods of Nonomiya,
> As autumn deepens and bitter winds blow
> In these woods of my soul,
> The deeply dyed shades of my heart
> Vanish, then returning,
> I think of long ago, but
> What of this grass robe of longing I wear,
> These lingering thoughts of the past
> I bring to this transient world, (*Moves slightly to right center.*)

---

116. The "Law's teaching" refers to Buddhist teachings. The phrase "straight is the way" forms a pivot word modifying both the Law and the actual road the monk has taken to Nonomiya. This also implies that the straight way of the Buddhist law leads also to the Shinto shrines of Ise. Both this passage and the "sacred fence" passage highlight the syncretic nature of Buddhist and Shinto worship in the medieval period.

117. The *shite* is referred to as "Lady" for the first half of the play and "Consort" for the second half.

118. Nonomiya can be interpreted here as both the shrine in the fields and Lady Rokujō, and the flowers can be seen as Shining Genji. A double meaning is afforded by the pun on *aki*, which means "autumn" or "to grow weary." Rokujō questions what will become of her when Genji's affections have waned.

119. Dew implies tears.

to which I return again with bitter rue,
return again and again with bitter rue![120]

Monk remains sitting while Lady stands.

MONK: (*mondō*) In the shade of this grove as I ponder the past, my heart clear,
a glamorous[121] lady suddenly appears. What person might this be?

LADY: Who am I, you ask? I should ask you the same. This is the Shrine in
the Fields, where long ago the appointed Ise priestess would temporarily reside. Though later this practice came to an end, still on the seventh day of
the long month,[122] on this day, each year, as I think of long ago, (*Faces
audience.*)

Unknown to others
I come to clean this shrine
And serve the gods here, (Faces Monk.)
Where a wandering stranger has now come
And caused offense,123 so
Quickly, quickly, take your leave!

MONK: (*kakeai*) No, no, I mean no offense, but I am indeed a wanderer with no
certain future in this uncertain world which I've renounced. Well now, each
year on this day you come to these ruins and ponder the past. What is the
reason for this?

LADY: Shining Genji visited here on the seventh day of the long month, this
very day, and pushed through the sacred fence a small branch of *sakaki*[124]
he had brought, whereas the Consort[125] quickly replied with this poem
that day:

No cedar marks this sacred fence,
So why have you mistakenly broken a branch of sakaki?

MONK:

Quite an elegant leaf of verse,
And the branch of sakaki you hold now,
Its color is unchanged from long ago!

LADY:

Color unchanged from long ago—a clever thought,
But only the sakaki remains unchanged
In the immutable shadowed

---

120. It is Lady Rokujō's regrets and attachments that cause her to wander as a spirit back into
the world of the living rather than proceeding to rebirth or salvation.

121. *Namamekeru*, which also implies "alluring."

122. *Nagazuki*, the ninth month of the lunar calendar, roughly equivalent to October.

123. She is implying that a Buddhist presence at the shrine is offensive to the Shinto gods.

124. The *sakaki*, an evergreen tree of the camellia family, is used in Shinto ritual, often as an
offering placed before a shrine. Here Genji is using it as a token of the "unchanging color" of his
feelings for her.

125. Miyasudokoro, Rokujō's title, given to the principal wife of a crown prince.

In act 1, Lady Rokujō's ghost retells the story of the past to the traveling monk in front of the shrine gate. (From *Meiji-Period Nō Illustrations* by Tsukioka Kōgyo, in the Hōsei University Kōzan Bunko Collection)

MONK:

    Path of this grove as fall comes to its close

LADY:

    And the autumn leaves turn and scatter,

    Turn and scatter;

MONK:

    And the reeded plain too,

CHORUS:

    (*age-uta*) Withers, Nonomiya grown wild with weeds,

    Nonomiya has grown wild with weeds. (*She moves in front of the torii, bends one knee, and lays down a leaf.*)

    Here, to these ruins

    Where my heart is drawn in longing, (*Stands.*)

    That seventh day of the long month

    Has come round again.

    Somehow so makeshift, (*Looks at fence.*)

    This little brushwood fence,

    This transient dwelling. (*Looks through the torii.*)

    Now, too, in the faint light

    Of the fire from the watchman's hut (*Sees the fire to the right.*)

    You can see the inmost glow

    Of my heart's longing revealed. (*Moves to the shite spot.*)

    Ah, the lonely shrine, (*She gazes forward.*)

How lonely is this shrine! (*Moves to center and sits.*)
(*kuri*) Now, this Consort was the wife
Of the Kiritsubo emperor's younger brother,
Known as the Former Crown Prince,
Who for a time prospered as a colorful, fragrant flower,
Their love never shallow; but

LADY (*still sitting*):

(*sashi*) "Those who meet must surely part,"[126]
As the old saying goes, and so

CHORUS:

Should I wonder now at this world of dreams?
No, I should have known; but
So soon, he left me behind.

LADY:

I could not weep forever, my tears like shimmering dew,

CHORUS:

Then Shining Genji,
Stealthily he forced his way
To see her, but

LADY (*still sitting*):

What became of his heart

CHORUS:

As the bond between us broke?
(*kuse*) But how moving, indeed,
Making his way o'er the moors
To distant Nonomiya
Because he could not disfavor her altogether.
The autumn flowers all faded,
The insects' voices too have died away,
Even the sound of the wind blowing in the pines,
Along his lonely path, autumn sorrows know no end.
Thus he came to this place,
And how touching the
Inmost feelings of his heart
As he poured out his love in
Words like so many dewdrops.

LADY:

Then at the Katsura lustration[127]

---

126. *Esha jōri*, a popular Buddhist phrase indicating the impermanence of all things, also found in *The Tales of the Heike*.

127. A ceremonial purification in the Katsura River southwest of Kyoto before the Ise priestess's departure for Ise. The white strands mentioned later are usually attached to *sakaki* branches and are Shinto ritual objects. They carry away impurities as they are set adrift in the river.

CHORUS:

> The sacred white strands
> Afloat upon the waves, and
> Myself, like floating grass, with
> No one to rely upon, my heart
> Drawn by the water's current:[128]
> Who will think to ask when I've gone to Ise
> If Suzuka River's waves[129] wet my sleeves or not?[130]
> Leaving these words,
> Mother and child together,
> Though it was unprecedented,[131]
> Followed the road to the Take capital,[132]
> Her heart heavy with regret. (*Still sitting.*)
> (*rongi*) I see, just hearing your words,
> You are no ordinary person,
> With no ordinary air about you.
> Please tell me your name.

LADY:

> Even though I tell you my name,
> How ashamed this worthless one,
> But surely in time it will be known
> To others outside this grove, and so
> If you must know,
> That name belongs to one who is no more.
> Oh, mourn for me!

CHORUS:

> "One who is no more," I hear—how strange.
> Well then, that one who passed so vainly from this world,

LADY:

> Only her name so long remaining—

CHORUS:

> The Consort

---

128. The previous three lines allude to a poem by Ono no Komachi, *Kokinshū*, no. 938: "Steeped in misery as I am, a forlorn, floating plant, I would break off from my root; if there were but a coaxing current, I believe I'd drift away."

129. Suzuka River, in present-day Mie Prefecture, is a major stopping point along the journey to Ise and a popular poetic topos. "Waves" is preceded here by a pillow word (*makurakotoba*) that makes the literal meaning "waves of the eighty rapids" (*yasose no nami*).

130. A slight modification of the poem Lady Rokujō sends to Genji as she departs for Ise in *The Tale of Genji*.

131. It was not customary for the mother of the Ise priestess to accompany her daughter to Ise.

132. A name for the priestess's residence at Ise, which was located in the Take District of Ise, in present-day Taki County.

LADY (*to Monk*):

    Is me!

CHORUS:

    She says, the autumn wind at dusk, (*Stands.*)

    And the evening moon's pale light (*Looks to the right.*)

    Winnowing through the grove, (*Moves forward.*)

    In the darkness near the twin pillars (*Gazes at the torii.*)

    Of the rough-hewn log torii standing, (*Moves back slightly.*)

    She vanishes! Leaving no trace, (*Lowers face and quietly exits.*)

    She vanishes!

Interlude

Villager passes by and, in response to the Monk's request for information, relates the brief relationship between the Shining Genji and Lady Rokujō and the story of Genji's visit to her at Nonomiya. When the Monk tells him about the mysterious lady he has just met, the Villager opines that she must be the ghost of Lady Rokujō, advises the Monk to pray for the repose of her spirit, and exits.

Act 2

MONK (*still sitting*):

    (*age-uta*) My sleeve spread,

    In the shadow of this grove these robes of moss,

    In the shadow of this grove these robes of moss

    Match the color of this grass mat,[133]

    And, my thoughts reaching out through the night,

    I mourn her memory,

    I mourn her memory.

To issei *music, the Consort enters as if riding in a carriage. She moves to the shite spot and faces the audience.*

CONSORT:

    (*ge-no-ei*) To Nonomiya turns the carriage decked with

    All the flowers of fall, as I too return to long ago.

MONK (*to Consort*):

    (*kakeai*) How strange! In the pale moonlight

    The faint sound of a carriage approaching;

---

133. Monks were said to wear moss-color robes. The grass mat implies the monk is sleeping outdoors.

An unexpected sight I see: a wickerwork carriage
With its blind lowered. Now there can be no doubt;
Are you then the Consort?
And even so, what kind of carriage might this be?

CONSORT (*to Monk*):

"What kind of carriage?" you ask,
And so I recall the past—
The Kamo Festival and the carriage brawl.[134]
Not knowing whose carriage belonged to whom,

MONK:

All lined up in narrow rows;

CONSORT:

Among the onlookers' carriages was that of
The highly favored Lady Aoi.[135]

MONK:

Saying "Make way for the lady's carriage!"
They push people aside, raising a racket,

CONSORT:

But there is no place to put
Even my small carriage,
I answered, and so we held our ground, (*Looks around to the right.*)

MONK:

When front and back of my carriage

CONSORT:

They rushed, (*Moves forward.*)

CHORUS:

(*uta*) Seizing the wheel shafts and shoving (*With sleeve upturned, mimes with fan.*)
My carriage behind her attendants' carriage, (*Moves to the back as if pushed.*)
So that I was powerless to see anything
But my own powerless position. (*Suppresses tears.*)
Alas, as I consider it, (*Circles stage.*)
In all things one can never escape
Retribution for the sins of former lives.
Still turning round and round
In this ox-drawn carriage of sorrow,

---

134. The aforementioned struggle between Rokujō and Genji's principal wife Aoi for a prime spot along the route of the Kamo Festival parade. Both women wished to see Genji in the parade, but Rokujō was forced to watch from behind the other carriages.

135. Genji's principal wife, who later became the victim of Rokujō's malevolent wandering spirit.

Returning again and again,
How long must this go on?[136]
Oh, dispel the darkness of my delusion! (*Faces Monk, joining her palms in supplication.*)
Dispel the darkness of my delusion!

CONSORT (*faces audience*):
(*ei*) I recall the past,
My flowered sleeves (*Moves to the shite spot.*)

CHORUS:
I toss to the moon,
And the past returns.

(*Dance:* jo-no-mai)
Consort performs a very tranquil jo-no-mai *dance and continues to dance and mime as the text resumes.*

CONSORT (*in the shite spot, raises fan*):
(*waka*) Might the moon above Nonomiya too
Remember the past?

CHORUS:
The lonely light of the moon
Shimmers in the dew beneath the trees,
Shimmers in the dew beneath the trees

CONSORT:
(*nori-ji*) Where once I too like the dew
Stayed so long ago, and, oh (*Points forward, moves forward, and looks to left and right.*)

CHORUS:
The look of that garden,

CONSORT:
Like no other,

CHORUS:
Seems so fleeting, (*Nears the fence.*)

CONSORT:
And so makeshift the brushwood fence

CHORUS:
From which he wipes the dewdrops, (*Brushes away dew with fan.*)
He and I, like this world of dreams, (*Follows after Genji's visage through the torii.*)
Only aging remnants. (*Points with fan and moves to corner, then looks down.*)

---

136. The turning refers to the wheels of the carriage as well as the "wheel" of endless rebirth. Rokujō keeps returning to this world because of her strong attachments and bitterness.

Who is it I await?

As the pine cricket cries shrill,

And the wind blusters and blows (*Fanning with both hands, moves forward.*)

Through the night at Nonomiya, (*Gazes through the torii.*)

How I long for long ago! (*Suppressing tears, moves back.*)

(*Dance:* ha-no-mai)

Consort performs a brief ha-no-mai *dance.*

CHORUS:

(*nori-ji*) In and out of the torii gate (*Points to the torii with fan.*)

Graced by the divine wind of Ise (*Moves forward.*)

She goes, perhaps feeling rejected by the gods (*Holds torii pillar with left hand.*)

For treading the path of death and rebirth; (*Puts right foot through torii.*)

She mounts again her carriage, (*Stamps foot.*)

And will she leave the Burning Mansion's gate?[137] (*Faces audience.*)

The Burning Mansion's gate?

Faces right center, turns out sleeve, then stamps.

[Translated by Jack Stoneman]

COMIC THEATER (*KYŌGEN*)

Of the traditional performance arts, *gagaku* from the ancient period, nō and kyōgen from the medieval period, and jōruri (puppet theater) and kabuki from the Tokugawa period, kyōgen remains the easiest for modern audiences and nonspecialists to understand. The simple stage, the limited number of character actors, the straightforward acting, the humor, and a language close to modern Japanese make it an easily accessible performance art. Of all the traditional performative arts, kyōgen, a Chinese compound meaning "crazy words," is the only one devoted to comedy.

Both nō and kyōgen originated from the earlier dramatic forms known as sarugaku and dengaku, which included mime and improvisational comedy. Nō dropped the comic dimension and turned into a serious form incorporating song and dance. Kyōgen, by contrast, maintained its comic roots and emphasis on mime. Kyōgen as we now know it began in the Northern and Southern Courts period (1336–1392) and achieved maturity in the Muromachi period. About 80 percent of the more than one hundred kyōgen plays mentioned in the

---

137. A reference to the parable of the burning mansion in the Lotus Sutra. The burning mansion is a symbol for this world of delusion and desire.

Tenshō kyōgen bon (1578), the only Muromachi text that describes kyōgen in detail, are close in content to those performed today.

In the Northern and Southern Courts period, the nobility and the large shrine-temple institutions, both of which relied on the private estate (*shōen*) system for their economic base, finally collapsed and were replaced by a new samurai class represented by the Ashikaga bakufu. In the process, a number of new cultural forms such as kyōgen emerged, not from aristocratic or court society in the capital, as most of the earlier cultural forms had, but from the villages and the life of urban commoners.

By Zeami's (1363?–1443?) day, nō plays alternated with kyōgen on the same stage. Kyōgen actors performed the *ai-kyōgen* (supplementary dialogue or meta-commentary) in the nō, and Sanbasō (one of the three old men) in the *Okina (Old Man)* nō play was performed by a kyōgen actor. Kyōgen actors were attached to nō troupes and also formed professional houses or families. The Ōkura school arose in the late Muromachi period, and in the Tokugawa period, when no and kyōgen were officially patronized by the Tokugawa bakufu, two more schools, the Izumi and the Sagi, based on the *iemoto* (house) system, became prominent. In the Tokugawa period, kyōgen became a form of classical theater, with the plays written down and acted according to each school's performance traditions. Ōkura Toraakira's *Ōkura Toraakirabon* (1642) was the first collection of scripts. With the Meiji Restoration, the Sagi school disappeared, but the Ōkura and Izumi schools have continued to this day.

Kyōgen has a close, contrastive relationship to nō. If nō is a serious drama based on song and dance, performed to the accompaniment of a chorus and musicians, kyōgen focuses on dialogue and comedy, only occasionally using a chorus and musicians. In contrast to the main nō actor, who wears a mask, the actors in kyōgen plays do not wear masks, except when portraying supernatural beings and some women. Kyōgen plays are short, about twenty to forty minutes, as opposed to the much longer nō performances. Unlike nō, which elevated itself to a high art by developing the aesthetics of yūgen, incorporating poetic language, and borrowing from and alluding to such classical texts such as *The Tales of Ise* and *The Tale of Genji*, kyōgen was based on contemporary life and used colloquial speech. Kyōgen plays generally portray an everyday world, unlike the dreams and other-worldly realms that characterize much of the nō. Similarly, the characters in kyōgen are anonymous, unlike the famous or legendary figures who often appear in the nō. Furthermore, kyōgen had no dominant and easily identifiable dramatists like nō's Kanami, Zeami, and Motomasa. Instead, the plays are identified primarily by the kyōgen actors' school. In short, unknown actor-playwrights created unnamed characters, thereby providing the basis for a dramatic form expressing popular sentiments.

The historical relationship between kyōgen and nō drama parallels that of linked verse, which started as a popular pastime and then, in the late medieval period, split into two genres: renga (classical linked verse), which was based on

classical waka poetry and poetics and alluded extensively to Heian classical literature, and haikai (popular linked verse), which emphasized humor, parodied
the classics, used the vernacular, and reflected contemporary life.

Today the Ōkura school has about 200 plays, and the Izumi school has about
250. A record of kyōgen plays in 1792 lists seven broad categories of kyōgen,
variations of which are used today by the two major schools: (1) celebratory
(waki) plays, (2) big landlord (daimyō) plays, (3) minor landlord (shōmyō) plays,
(4) husband/woman (muko/onna) plays, (5) demon/mountain priest (oni/yama-
bushi) plays, (6) priest/blind man (shukke zatō) plays, and (7) miscellaneous
(atsume) plays. Waki kyōgen (which resemble waki/god plays in nō) are celebratory kyōgen, represented by, for example, the plays of gods of good fortune (fu-
kujin mono), in which a god of good fortune typically appears before worshipers
and gives them his blessings. Daimyō plays, like Buaku, have a daimyō (big
landlord) for their chief protagonist In shōmyō kyōgen, by contrast, a shōmyō
(small landlord) is the lord and the servant (Tarō Kaja) is the main character.
These are also referred to as Tarō Kaja (servant) plays. Delicious Poison (Busu),
translated here, is the archetypal Tarō Kaja play.

The daimyō or shōmyō in these lord-servant plays are not powerful provincial lords but samurai who own land (myōden) in a village. Depending on the
size of the land and the number of servants, the lord could be referred to as a
daimyō (large owner) or a shōmyō (small owner). These low-level samurai were
not necessarily on the side of authority, and in the farmers' uprisings (ikki), they
often sided with the commoners. In kyōgen, the daimyō and shōmyō are often
depicted as parvenu daimyō, a new class that was often seen at that time as reaching beyond their actual power. In the Tarō Kaja, or shōmyō, plays, the servant
provides a critical perspective on the master, pulling him down to reality.

Kyōgen appeared in the Northern and Southern Courts period, during the
time of gekokujō (the overcoming of the high by the low), in which people of a
lower status often rose beyond those of higher status. In the fourteenth and fifteenth centuries, the kyōgen audience, predominantly of low social status (though
later made up of upper-rank samurai), no doubt identified with the "lower" figures
like the servant (Tarō Kaja), who reveals the weaknesses and the contradictions
of his social superiors. The Tarō Kaja plays often suggest that the bottom is the
reality and the top is a self-imposed illusion. Kyōgen also goes beyond class distinctions to make fun of human foibles or weaknesses in general and thus do not
represent actual daimyō or shōmyō so much as all those who think too highly of
themselves.

Kyōgen frequently debunks traditional authority figures, revealing incompetent samurai, weak gods and demons, impotent mountain ascetics, ignorant
priests, and pathetic husbands henpecked by strong wives. In the demon plays
like The Thunder God (Kaminari), a demon or god, thought to be awesome
and fearful, is revealed to be weak or very human. In the mountain priest (yamabushi) plays like Mushrooms (Kusabira), the yamabushi, who were thought to

possess superhuman and magical powers, are found humorously lacking in this regard. The humor of kyōgen also comes from parody, particularly of nō; for example, *Buaku* satirizes the conventions of the dream/ghost (*mugen-nō*) nō play.

DELICIOUS POISON (BUSU)

Delicious Poison is the most popular play in the kyōgen repertory and the canonical play of the genre. No character better represents kyōgen than Tarō Kaja, the leading character in this play. He is the archetypal clever servant, willing to exhaust every stratagem in order to outwit his master. Even though Tarō and his fellow servant Jirō destroy two of their master's treasured art objects in this play, the audience's sympathy clearly lies with the servants because of the master's deceitful treatment of the pair. Tarō shows that his trickery is far more clever and effective than anything his master can imagine.

Kyōgen's humor walks the fine path between the psychologically real and the physically and vocally ridiculous, and no action better demonstrates this than the two servants desperately exhorting each other and waving their fans as they fearfully approach the poison, hoping to blow its deadly fumes in the other direction. This activity is executed with the elegance and precision that characterize all kyōgen performances and that make it impossible to mistake for clowning or buffoonery. Unlike most kyōgen plays, *Busu* has an identifiable literary source, the *Collection of Sand and Pebbles* (*Shasekishū*, 1279–1283), a collection of setsuwa compiled by the priest Mujū Ichien (1225–1312). The play adds a second servant, enabling a complex interaction and contrast between the characters that does not exist in the original.[138]

Characters in Order of Appearance

MASTER, a wealthy man	*ado*/side role
TARŌ, his servant	*shite*/lead role
JIRŌ, his servant	*ado*/side role

The Master, Tarō, and Jirō enter down the bridgeway, or hashigakari. *The Master goes to the shite spot, and his two servants kneel down side by side about eight feet behind him.*

MASTER: I am a man who lives in this area. Today I must go over the mountains on business. Now I will call my two servants and order them to look after the house while I am away. (*Walking to the waki spot*) Hey, hey, the both of you, come here!

---

138. This translation is from the Ōkura school text of *Busu*. Jirō is cowardly throughout in the Izumi school text, whereas in the Ōkura school he occasionally attempts to be as brave as his friend Tarō.

TARŌ AND JIRŌ: Yeeeees. (*They rise and go to the shite spot, standing on either side of it, facing the Master, who is at the waki spot.*)

MASTER: Are you there?

TARŌ AND JIRŌ: We both are at your service.

MASTER: I didn't call you about anything special. I have to go over the mountains on a little business, and I want you to look after the house while I'm away.

TARŌ: Wait. I'll go with you, so have Jirō look after the house.

JIRŌ: No, no, I'll go with you, so have Tarō look after the house.

MASTER: No, today my business is such that I need neither of you to accompany me. Now both of you wait here.

TARŌ AND JIRŌ: Yes, sir.

MASTER (*speaks his next line while going to the stage assistant, picking up a large, lidded, cylindrical lacquer barrel, and carrying it to downstage center, where he places it*): This is poison, so take special care when you guard the house. (*He returns to the waki spot.*)

TARŌ: In that case both of us . . . right?

JIRŌ: Right . . .

TARŌ AND JIRŌ: Will go with you.

MASTER: And why is that?

TARŌ: After all, if that *person* will watch the house while you're gone, no one else . . . right?

JIRŌ: Right . . .

TARŌ AND JIRŌ: Is needed to guard the house.

MASTER: You both have terrible ears. I didn't say "person," I said "poison." This is Busu, a poison so deadly that if a breeze blows over it and even a whiff of it reaches your noses, you will die instantly. Be aware of this and guard it carefully.

TARŌ: In that case, we'll do as you command.

JIRŌ: I have one small question.

MASTER: And what is that?

JIRŌ: Well, if this Busu is so deadly that even a whiff is fatal, how is it that *you* are able to handle it?

TARŌ: You asked a very good question.

JIRŌ: I sure did.

MASTER: Your uncertainty is most reasonable. This poison is the Master's treasured possession, and as long as I touch it, it will do no harm. But if you two come anywhere near, it will kill you for sure. So be aware of this while you guard the house.

TARŌ: In that case . . .

TARŌ AND JIRŌ: We will do as you command.

MASTER: Well, I'm going now.

TARŌ AND JIRŌ: Are you going already?

MASTER: I'm counting on you to look after the house.

TARŌ: Don't worry about the house, we'll take good care of everything. Please take your time . . .

TARŌ AND JIRŌ: And enjoy yourself while you are away.

MASTER: I'm depending on you. I'm depending on you. (*The Master exits down the bridgeway, and the two servants turn to watch him leave.*)

TARŌ: My, he sure left in a hurry.

JIRŌ: You're right. He sure left in a hurry.

TARŌ: First of all, let's sit down.

JIRŌ: Right.

TARŌ AND JIRŌ: *Ei ei yattona. (Uttering this expression of physical effort, they sit alongside each other upstage, facing straight out at the barrel and the audience.)*

TARŌ: Actually, what I said to Master about wanting to go with him was a lie. Really, staying at home and guarding the house is a lot easier than working, isn't it?

JIRŌ: You're right. Nothing is easier than what we're doing right now.

TARŌ (*slapping the stage and then running down the bridgeway*): Quick, run away, run away!

JIRŌ (*following Tarō*): What happened, what happened?

TARŌ: Just now there was a cold breeze blowing from the direction of the Busu.

JIRŌ: That's pretty scary.

TARŌ: Let's move a little farther away from it.

JIRŌ: Good idea.

TARŌ: Around here would be good.

JIRŌ: Right.

TARŌ AND JIRŌ: *Ei ei yattona. (They sit side by side on a diagonal line in front of the flute position, facing the corner pillar.)*

JIRŌ: You know, I asked Master about it, but don't you think it's strange that poison so deadly a breeze passing over it can kill you, is harmless when the Master handles it? I wonder why that's so?

TARŌ: You're right. There's something strange about all this.

JIRŌ (*slapping the stage and then running down the bridgeway*): Quick, run away, run away!

TARŌ: What happened, what happened? (*Following Jirō onto the bridgeway.*)

JIRŌ: Just now a warm, damp breeze blew from the direction of the Busu.

TARŌ: This is getting worse and worse. You know what I think? Why don't we take a quick look and see what's inside that Busu?

JIRŌ: What do you mean? How do you expect to get a look at it when even a whiff of it means sudden death?

TARŌ: We'll fan the wind blowing toward us back the other way and that's when we take a peek.

JIRŌ: That's a fine idea!

TARŌ: OK, help me by fanning with all your might.

JIRŌ: Right.

TARŌ: Fan hard, fan hard!

JIRŌ: I'm fanning, I'm fanning!

> *Tarō takes the lead position, advancing toward the Busu while hiding his head behind his raised left arm and fanning under his left sleeve. Jirō follows, holding his fan in both hands and fanning with an up-and-down motion.*

TARŌ: Fan hard, fan hard!

JIRŌ: I'm fanning, I'm fanning!

TARŌ: All right. I'm ready to loosen the cord, so fan with all your might.

JIRŌ: Right, right!

TARŌ: Fan hard, fan hard!

JIRŌ: I'm fanning, I'm fanning!

TARŌ: Run away, run away! (*He runs back onto the bridgeway, Jirō following him.*)

JIRŌ: What happened, what happened?

TARŌ: I managed to untie the cord. Please, you go and take off the lid.

JIRŌ: No, taking off the cord was just the first step in taking off the lid. You go do it.

TARŌ: No, no. The two of us have to take turns doing the dangerous work. Please, this time you have to go and take off the lid.

JIRŌ: In that case, I'll go take it off, but please fan for me with all your might.

TARŌ: Right.

JIRŌ: Fan hard, fan hard!

TARŌ: I'm fanning, I'm fanning! (*This time Jirō takes the lead fanning position, with Tarō in the following position.*)

JIRŌ: Fan hard, fan hard!

TARŌ: I'm fanning, I'm fanning!

JIRŌ: All right, I'm ready to take the lid off, so fan with all your might!

TARŌ: Right.

JIRŌ: Fan hard, fan hard!

TARŌ: I'm fanning, I'm fanning!

JIRŌ: Quick, run away, run away!

TARŌ: What happened, what happened?

JIRŌ: I got the lid off.

TARŌ: That's a relief.

JIRŌ: Why do you say that?

TARŌ: If something alive were inside it would have jumped out. At least we know it's not something alive.

JIRŌ: It might be playing possum, you know.

TARŌ: It's scary, but I'm going to go look at what's inside.

JIRŌ: That's a good idea.

TARŌ: You help me fan the breeze the other way with all your might, OK?

JIRŌ: Right.

TARŌ: Fan hard, fan hard!

JIRŌ: I'm fanning, I'm fanning! (*Tarō takes the lead position with Jirō following.*)

TARŌ: Fan hard, fan hard!

JIRŌ: I'm fanning, I'm fanning!

TARŌ: I'm ready to look in now. Keep fanning with all your might.

JIRŌ: Right.

TARŌ: Fan hard, fan hard!

JIRŌ: I'm fanning, I'm fanning!

TARŌ: Quick, run away, run away!

JIRŌ: What happened, what happened?

TARŌ: You know what? It's brown and sticky, and looks delicious!

JIRŌ: What's that? It looks delicious?

TARŌ: That's right.

JIRŌ: In that case, I'll go take a look too. You help me fan with all your might.

TARŌ: Right.

JIRŌ: Fan hard, fan hard!

TARŌ: I'm fanning, I'm fanning! (*Jirō takes the lead position, with Tarō following.*)

JIRŌ: Fan hard, fan hard!

TARŌ: I'm fanning, I'm fanning!

JIRŌ: Fan hard, fan hard!

TARŌ: I'm fanning, I'm fanning!

JIRŌ: Quick, run away, run away!

TARŌ: What happened, what happened?

JIRŌ: Just like you said, it looks delicious.

TARŌ: You know what? Suddenly, I want to eat that Busu. I'll go eat it up.

JIRŌ: What's the matter with you? That's a poison so deadly a breeze passing over it will kill you. How do you think you can eat it?

TARŌ: Maybe I've been possessed by the Busu because I have a terrible craving for it. I'll go eat it up!

JIRŌ: Wait! As long as I'm by your side, I won't let you go. (*He seizes Tarō's sleeve.*)

TARŌ: Let go of me!

JIRŌ: I won't let go!

TARŌ: I'm telling you to let go!

JIRŌ: And I say I won't! (*Tarō shakes loose from Jirō's grip and sings as he approaches the barrel.*)

TARŌ:

> Casting off my darling's sleeves I bid farewell . . .
> And approach the deadly Busu poison.

JIRŌ: Oh, no, you've gone near the Busu! Now you're doomed!

Tarō kneels on one knee behind the bucket. He sticks the bamboo handle of his closed fan into the barrel, stirs, and then says the following as he mimes eating a sticky substance off the handle of his fan.

TARŌ: *Ahm ahm ahm ahm.*

JIRŌ: Oh no! You're eating the Busu. Now you are truly doomed!

TARŌ: Ooooh, I'm dying. (*Tarō strikes his forehead with his left hand and slumps forward.*)

JIRŌ (*runs to Tarō's side and supports him*): Tarō, what happened? Pull yourself together.

TARŌ (*in apparent pain*): Who is it, who is it?

JIRŌ: It's me, Jirō.

TARŌ (*gleefully*): Hey, Jirō.

JIRŌ: What happened?

TARŌ: It's so *delicious*, I'm dying.

JIRŌ: What's that? It's delicious?

TARŌ: Yes.

JIRŌ: So what is the poisonous Busu?

TARŌ: Here, take a look, it's *sugar!*

JIRŌ: Let me see it. It really *is* sugar!

TARŌ: So, let's dig in!

JIRŌ: Right you are.

TARŌ AND JIRŌ (*stirring with closed fans, then miming eating the sugar off the handles*): *Ahm ahm ahm ahm.*

TARŌ: Well, well, isn't it delicious?

JIRŌ: You're right. It is delicious.

TARŌ: And because it's so delicious, master tried to stop us from eating it, saying it was "Busu" . . .

JIRŌ: "Poison" . . .

TARŌ AND JIRŌ (*laugh*): Ha, ha, ha, ha, ha.

TARŌ: It sure was nasty of him. *Ahm ahm ahm ahm.*

JIRŌ: Let's keep eating and stuff ourselves. *Ahm ahm ahm ahm.*

TARŌ: It's so delicious I'm afraid my chin will drop off! *Ahm ahm ahm ahm.*

Tarō takes the barrel off to stage left, where he continues to eat alone. Jirō notices this and when Tarō isn't looking, he takes it to stage right and proceeds to eat alone.

JIRŌ: I can't stop eating it. *Ahm ahm ahm ahm.*

TARŌ (*notices the barrel is gone and confronts Jirō*): Hey! Aren't you going to let me have any?

JIRŌ: You were hogging it. I've got to eat some too!

TARŌ: No, I've got to eat it. Give it here! (*They tussle over the Busu.*)

JIRŌ: Give it here!

TARŌ: Give it here!

JIRŌ: Give it here!

TARŌ: All right, let's place it here, right between us and share it.

JIRŌ: That's fine with me.

TARŌ: Well, well, let's dig in!

JIRŌ: Yes, let's.

TARŌ AND JIRŌ: *Ahm ahm ahm ahm.*

TARŌ: All my life I've never tasted anything this good. *Ahm ahm ahm ahm.*

JIRŌ: It's so delicious I'm afraid my chin will drop off! *Ahm ahm ahm ahm.*

TARŌ: Eat up, eat up. *Ahm ahm ahm ahm.*

JIRŌ: Right you are, right you are. *Ahm ahm ahm ahm.*

> *Tarō notices the Busu is almost gone and leaves. He goes to the shite spot, where he stands facing forward.*

JIRŌ (*stirring with a clattering sound as he scrapes the inside of the barrel*): There's still some left, there's still some left. *Ahm ahm ahm ahm.* Hey, what's this? The Busu is all gone. (*He goes to the waki spot and turns to face Tarō.*)

TARŌ: What?! You've just done something fine.

JIRŌ: What do you mean "something fine?"

TARŌ: Well, Master didn't want you and me to eat the Busu. That's why he told us it was deadly poison. Now you've gone and eaten it all up, and I don't think he will be very pleased about it. When the Master comes home, I'm going to tell him right away.

JIRŌ: Hey, wait, wait! It was *you* who first looked at the Busu and first ate the Busu, and when the Master comes home, I'll tell him about it right away.

TARŌ: Now wait, wait! What I just said was a joke.

JIRŌ: You shouldn't be telling bad jokes like that. So, what should we do for an excuse?

TARŌ (*pointing to the right of the waki pillar*): Tear up that hanging scroll.

JIRŌ: What? If I rip it up, will it give us an excuse?

TARŌ: Oh, it will, it will!

JIRŌ: In that case, I'll tear it up. (*He goes to the right of the waki pillar, where, to the following vocalization, he mimes pulling down a scroll, ripping it up, and throwing the pieces away.*) *Zarrari, zarrari, bassari!* There, I've ripped it to shreds.

TARŌ: What?! You just did something fine again.

JIRŌ: What do you mean?

TARŌ: Now it's true that I was the first to see and the first to eat the Busu. But because the Master treasures that scroll more than any other, I don't think he'll be pleased when he sees it ripped up like that. When he returns, I'll tell him right away just who it was that ripped it up.

JIRŌ: Hey, what do you mean?! It was you who told me to rip it up, and when the Master returns, I'll tell him about it right away.

TARŌ: Now wait, wait! That was another joke.

JIRŌ: How many times do I have to tell you this is no time for bad jokes. Now what's our excuse?

TARŌ: Smash that huge Chinese vase. (*He points in the direction of the corner pillar.*)

JIRŌ: I'm not going to do anything you tell me anymore.

TARŌ: And why is that?

JIRŌ: You'll tell on me, right? (*Both laugh.*)

TARŌ: So, let's get together, and *both* smash it.

JIRŌ: That's a good idea.

TARŌ: Come over here.

JIRŌ: Right. (*They walk downstage, to the left of the corner pillar.*)

TARŌ AND JIRŌ (*they crouch down together and mime lifting a heavy object*): Ei ei yattona.

TARŌ: For this we need three lifts, and on the third we'll let it go.

JIRŌ: Right.

TARŌ AND JIRŌ: *Iiiiyaaaa. Eiii.*

TARŌ: That was one.

TARŌ AND JIRŌ: *Iiiiyaaaa. Eiii.*

JIRŌ: That was two.

TARŌ: This is the important one. Don't forget to drop it.

JIRŌ: I won't forget to drop it.

TARŌ AND JIRŌ: *Iiiiiyaaaaaa. Eiii!*

TARŌ: *Garari!* (Crash!)

JIRŌ: *Chin!* (Tinkle, tinkle!)

TARŌ: There's a lot more of it now!

JIRŌ: It's in smithereens!

> *Tarō and Jirō laugh together as they return to their respective places at the shite and waki spots.*

JIRŌ: Well, now what do we do for an excuse?

TARŌ: My, you are a weakling. When the Master comes home, burst into tears!

JIRŌ: What? Will crying be an excuse?

TARŌ: Oh, it will, it will. (*He looks toward the bridgeway.*) Oh, look, he'll be back soon. Come over here and sit down. (*The two sit side by side in front of the left side of the orchestra position, up-stage center, facing the audience.*)

MASTER (*at the first pine*): My business is finally over. (*Walking toward the main stage*) Even though I told Tarō AND Jirō to guard the house, I'm worried about them so I'll hurry home. (*Arriving at the main stage*) What do you know, I'm home already.

TARŌ: He's back. Start crying.

TARŌ AND JIRŌ: *Eheh, eheh, heh, heh, heh, heh.* (*This is the vocalization used for weeping.*)

MASTER: Hey, Tarō, Jirō, I'm home! (*The two servants continue to weep as the Master takes his place at the waki spot.*) Something's wrong. You should be happy to see your Master return. Why are you crying like that?

TARŌ: Jirō, please, you explain it to him.

JIRŌ: No Tarō, please, you do it. (*They continue to weep.*)

MASTER: Enough! You two are making me very angry. Either one of you tell me what is going on right away.

TARŌ: In that case, I guess I'll tell you. We had important work to do guarding the house, and we knew we shouldn't fall asleep, so I sumo-wrestled Jirō to keep awake. He was stronger and lifted me up higher than his head. I didn't want to be thrown, so I grabbed onto that scroll, and—look—that's what's become of it. (*The two servants weep.*)

MASTER (*looking at the remains of the scroll on the ground*): What's this? My precious scroll is torn to shreds!

JIRŌ: Then we had a rematch, and I fell with a crash onto the big Chinese vase, and there—it's in smithereens. (*The two servants weep.*)

MASTER (*moving to stage right and looking at the shards of the vase on the ground*): Oh my god! You smashed my precious vase to bits! (*Returning to the waki spot*) The two of you don't deserve to live!

TARŌ: We knew we had no right to live, and so we hoped to kill ourselves by eating the Busu. Right, Jirō?

JIRŌ: Riiiiiight!

MASTER: What's this? You even ate all the Busu. What useless wretches!

TARŌ AND JIRŌ (*singing*):
>We took one mouthful
>But we did not die.
>Two mouthfuls, and still we did not die.
>Three mouthfuls, four mouthfuls, five mouthfuls,
>Ten mouthfuls and more. (*They begin dancing.*)
>We ate up all the Busu
>And still we could not die.
>Destined to live, what lucky fellows!
>Aren't we sturdy guys?

Tarō and Jirō end the dance by striking the head of the standing Master with their open fans. They then run off stage, down the bridgeway.

MASTER: What do you mean, "sturdy guys"? You rascals! I'll get you, I'll get you.

TARŌ AND JIRŌ (*exiting down the bridgeway*): Please forgive us, forgive us!

MASTER (*chasing the servants and exiting down the bridgeway*): Where are you going? Someone stop them please! I'll get you, I'll get you!

[Introduction and translation by Laurence Kominz]

LINKED VERSE (RENGA)

SŌGI

Sōgi (1421–1502), a poet in the late Muromachi period, was born into a family of the warrior class, probably in Ōmi Province just east of Kyoto. At a young age Sōgi was placed in one of the premier Zen temples of the day, where he evidently contemplated life as a cleric. Only fairly late, in his thirties, did he decide instead to make a living as a *rengashi*, a master of linked verse. Sōgi's first teacher was the renga master Sōzei (d. 1455), also of warrior background, although of much higher rank, who was important for not only guidance in poetry but also social contacts, enabling Sōgi to ask courtiers such as Ichijō Kanera (Kaneyoshi, 1421–1520) for instruction. With his teacher's encouragement, Sōgi studied linked verse as well as waka and court classics like *The Tale of Genji* and *The Tales of Ise*. Like Ton'a and other commoner poets, he never attained a dominant position in court circles, but by the end of his life he had achieved a position of respect seldom afforded one of such modest social origins.

During the Ōnin war (1467–1477), Sōgi spent much of his time traveling in the east country (Azuma) and the Kantō area and befriending powerful warlords, many of whom became his chief patrons. Staying sometimes for extended periods with one clan, he lectured, led linking sessions, and served as a mentor to samurai eager to acquire elite culture. As a partial record of this first great tour of the eastern regions, he composed a short travel journal, *Journey to Shirakawa (Shirakawa kikō*, 1468). The Shirakawa Pass, the entry into the northern frontier since ancient times, was a place that many famous poets of the past had visited, and he was anxious to add his name to the list of those who had recorded their impressions of the place in verse.

It was during his time in the east country that Sōgi met Shinkei (1406–1475), another refugee from the capital and a noted poet whose linked verse, characterized by the qualities of *yūgen* (mystery and depth) and *hiesabi* (chilled loneliness), he regarded as the finest of that of his contemporaries. In his own work, Sōgi tried in many ways to combine the strengths of his two teachers: Sōzei's verbal ingenuity and Shinkei's profundity. Although Shinkei was rather critical of Sōzei's work, he recognized Sōgi's talent and did all he could to encourage him.

After peace returned to Kyoto in the late 1470s, Sōgi set up his own practice there, in the tradition of poets like Ton'a and Shōtetsu. Sōzei, Shinkei, and their peers of the previous generation had died, and Sōgi marked their passing with an anthology of their work entitled *Notes from the Bamboo Grove (Chikurinshō*, 1476). By this time, he was indisputably the premier renga master in the capital and had students even among the traditional aristocracy. His unprecedented success was symbolized by two events: his appointment as steward of the Kitano Shrine's renga office in 1488, and a commission to compile a second imperially sanctioned anthology of linked verse, the *New Tsukuba Collection (Shinsen Tsukubashū*, 1495).

Even during the years when he was most in demand as a master in Kyoto, Sōgi spent a great deal of time on the road, visiting patrons for whom he acted as a teacher of linked verse and the classics of court literature and waka. One of his journeys, through Kyushu in 1480 and 1481, is recorded in detail in *Record of a Journey to Tsukushi* (*Tsukushi no michi no ki*). In his early years, traveling to attend patrons had been a necessity; later it became part of the rhythm of Sōgi's life and a crucial element of his literary practice.

Sōgi was a prolific writer. He left four major collections of his own linked verse, numerous full sequences that he had directed as senior participant (including *Three Poets at Minase* [*Minase sangin hyakuin*, 1488]) and that soon became required reading for aspiring poets, a personal collection of waka, more than a dozen essays on linked verse, and various lectures on court classics. He also was instrumental in reforming the *Kokin denju* (secret teachings of the *Kokinshū*) under the instruction he received from another warrior literatus named Tō no Tsuneyori (1401–1484?) during his first extended trip to the east country. In later years, these esoteric teachings assumed a central role in elite poetic culture, among both courtiers and warrior poets.

Many of Sōgi's writings on linked verse are handbooks or compendia of notes intended for poets preparing to compose in a *za* (linked-verse session). As aesthetic theory, none of his work rises to the level of Shinkei's *Whisperings* (*Sasamegoto*, 1463). But in *East Country Dialogues* (*Azuma mondō*, 1467–1470), Sōgi addresses both practical questions concerning technique and the history of the genre and its aesthetic ideals; and in *An Old Man's Diversions* (*Oi no susami*, late 1470s), he offers sensitive readings of links by his teachers that reveal him as both a scholar and an astute critic. The number of disciples he attracted is an indication that he was a dedicated and respected teacher.

Sōgi left Kyoto in the summer of 1500 to visit friends in the east country, and he died at Hakone (in present-day Kanagawa Prefecture) in 1502. His last days are recorded in a short essay, "A Record of Sōgi's Passing" (*Sōgi shūen ki*, 1502), written by a disciple, Sōchō (1448–1532), a distinguished renga poet.

EAST COUNTRY DIALOGUES
(*AZUMA MONDŌ*, 1467–1470)

As a master of linked verse, Sōgi was first of all a teacher of many disciples, some of them training to become professionals, others content to be amateurs. Most of his essays were written for such students, usually for specific individuals. The most famous of Sōgi's treatises is best known by the title *East Country Dialogues* and was written in response to questions by members of the Nagao clan of Musashi Province (in present-day Tokyo and Saitama Prefecture). The mondō (question–answer) format was a well-established didactic genre, and we cannot be sure whether the questions in the text were recorded verbatim, but the answers serve the purpose of introducing the basics of renga. The title East *Country Dialogues*—probably not chosen by Sōgi but by a later scribe—suggests that the text was regarded as a successor to Nijō Yoshimoto's *Tsukuba Dialogue* (*Tsukuba mondō*, 1372), which was widely accepted as the first and foremost critical text in the renga tradition.

Most of Sōgi's critical writings are handbooks on technique, but *Azuma mondō* touches also on questions of history, philosophy, and aesthetics. The following are three sections from the text, two dealing with matters of training and the third with the proper pace of composition in the *za*, in the linked-verse session.

QUESTION: What writings should be read as part of the renga poet's training [*keiko*]?

ANSWER: This is a difficult question. My own opinion is that all the imperial anthologies of the various reigns, beginning with the *Man'yōshū*, as well as the personal collections of the several families of poetry, are suitable for training. Still, it depends on the individual. Since the world counts on me for expertise,[139] I have collected texts of the *Man'yōshū*, *The Eight Anthologies*,[140] *The Tale of Genji*, *The Tales of Ise*, *The Tales of Yamato*, *The Tale of Sagoromo*, *Utsuho* [*The Tale of the Hollow Tree*], *The Tale of the Bamboo Cutter*,[141] and the like, which I refer to in case questions arise—although, having said that, the unfortunate fact is that I can't claim that my efforts have been of much benefit to others or myself.

Perhaps those preoccupied with government duties, or busy with administrative service, cannot hope to engage in such broad training. I do believe, however, that all students should at the very least peruse *The Three Collections*,[142] *Senzaishū*, *Shinkokinshū*, and catalogs of poems about famous places.[143] Of course, even that may be too much for the elderly and for children. In such cases, they should just use the *Kokinshū*, *Shinkokinshū*, and books on famous places.

QUESTION: One hears of beginning, intermediate, and advanced stages of training. What do these stages entail?

ANSWER: I haven't ever seen anything written down about beginning, intermediate, and advanced stages of training.[144] But a young person will begin by

---

139. *Utsuwa* (vessel) is a term originally used in Confucian discourse to refer to an expert in one field, rather than a proper "gentleman," who by definition is above specializing. Here Sōgi uses the term self-effacingly to refer to his role as a master of linked verse expected to have specialized knowledge.

140. The first eight imperial waka anthologies, from the *Kokinshū* to the *Shinkokinshū*.

141. All these texts are from the "golden age" of courtly culture, ending around the middle of the thirteenth century, and most are represented in this anthology. This list shows a general bias among poets of the late medieval age against the work of more recent times. In fact, the rules of linked verse explicitly advised against alluding to texts later than the *Shokugosenshū* (1251).

142. The first three imperial waka anthologies: *Kokinshū*, *Gosenshū*, and *Shūishū*.

143. "Famous places" (*nadokoro*) mentioned in literary texts. Many medieval treatises and handbooks contained lists of such literary topoi.

144. In fact, references to such "stages" in training are fairly common in the writings of earlier renga masters, but Sōgi's treatment here is more comprehensive than earlier statements.

perusing the *Kokinshū* innocently,[145] committing to memory poems that will be useful later on, and play chain games[146] with friends, always chanting poems. I would call this the beginning stage.

In the intermediate stage, students ask people about the meanings of classical waka, and when the words thus learned come up in linking sessions, they will take care to use them in making links. By doing so, one will acquire the respect of others and be pleased with oneself, until one gradually develops the heart of a connoisseur.[147] This is what should be called the intermediate stage.

Once beyond that level, you need no longer think about borrowing words from particular waka but, instead, putting all your efforts into the work of attaining moments of intense feeling [*ushin*], seek beauty of form and grandeur of style.[148] In this way, you will stay effortlessly within the realm of waka, without drawing on the diction of specific poems. Once you have entered this deeply into the art, all the texts will be in your heart. You will no longer need to tire your eyes with reading. I would call this the advanced stage of training.

QUESTION: Which would you say is better—favoring a rapid pace in the *za* or a slow pace?

ANSWER: The Way of linked verse is to ponder deeply and, indeed, to brood over your links. Nevertheless there are times when, judging the needs of a whole sequence, you may produce a simple verse that surpasses a distinctive verse in total effect. In the distant past it appears that most people felt they must ponder carefully in the *za*. Lord Sōzei,[149] however, said that you should polish your talents through practice [*keiko*][150] and then compose quickly when in the *za*.

Surely, without practice, you will not produce an outstanding link in the *za*, no matter how you agonize over it. It is particularly unfortunate when someone, at a promising point in a sequence, as if to keep anyone else from coming up with a link, produces a verse with an earnest look on his face even before the scribe has had time to read the previous verse aloud. You

---

145. "With no special intentions or preconceptions." Young poets, in particular, were encouraged to do practice without preconceived notions. As the next phrases suggest, repetition, under a master's direction, was deemed the most important form of preparation.

146. A game in which one person would quote an ancient poem, with the next person being required to quote another poem beginning with the last syllable of the first poem.

147. *Suki*, a true devotee and not just a casual participant.

148. *Sugata utsukushiku taketakaki tei.* The vocabulary here is that of the courtly waka tradition, showing that for Sōgi, as for his teachers Sōzei and Shinkei, linked verse was a genre whose aesthetic goals were identical with those of waka.

149. A warrior-poet (d. 1455) who served as commissioner of the shogunal renga office. He was Sōgi's first teacher.

150. In the medieval period, constant practice was considered essential to success not only in linked verse but also in waka and other such practices. Only with the accumulation of experience in actual practice could a poet hope to become proficient in the Way.

should understand that when pursuing this Way, you must weigh your own attainments against the circumstances of the *za* and compose appropriately, without being either overly modest or too forward.

Anyone wishing to pursue this Way should first seek the aid of the gods and buddhas. Dedicate oneself to Sumiyoshi and Tamatsushima,[151] embrace the straight and forsake the crooked, abandon distinctions between self and other, and, whether as a teacher of others or as a disciple, pray only to become skillful in the end.

In the Way of Japanese poetry, embrace above all the mind of compassion, so that seeing the red blossoms of spring gives way to the yellow leaves of autumn; meditating on the principle that all that lives must die, the demons of the heart will be calmed; and the mind will return to the truth of Original Enlightenment and Thusness.[152] All phenomenal appearances are manifestations of absolute reality, and whichever Way you pursue, your heart must never depart from this thought.[153]

THREE POETS AT MINASE (*MINASE SANGIN HYAKUIN*, 1488)

In the spring of 1488, three renga masters—Sōgi (1421–1502) and his disciples Sōchō (1448–1532) and Shōhaku (1443–1527)—met at Minase, in Settsu Province (present-day Osaka) to compose a hundred-verse renga sequence. When completed, the sequence was presented to the nearby Minase Shrine as a votive offering in memory of Emperor GoToba (1180–1239), who had built a noted detached imperial villa in that area centuries earlier. As the emperor whose court had produced the *Shinkokinshū* and countless other poetic masterpieces, GoToba was one of the most honored literary sovereigns.

Although Sōgi was clearly the leader in the group, Sōchō and Shōhaku also were mature and experienced poets. Even though they were from radically different backgrounds—Sōgi from a military family, Shōhaku from an aristocratic lineage (the Nakanoin), and Sōchō from a provincial family of swordsmiths—the men shared an education in the classical canon and a dedication to linked verse as a courtly art form. The work they produced together soon became a model text for younger poets trying to improve their skills in linking. The sequence obeys all the complex and detailed rules of renga, thereby enforcing the idea of variety and constant change. All the major thematic categories of the courtly tradition—the four seasons, love, travel, Buddhism, Shinto, and lamentation—are represented, but none is allowed to dominate the sequence. The most prominent images of the imperial anthologies—cherry blossoms and the moon—are used as well but are spaced to keep them from overpowering the

---

151. The shrines whose deities were worshiped as patron gods by poets.

152. *Hongaku shinnyo*, the doctrine that human beings are already enlightened and that all worldly experience is a manifestation of absolute reality ("thusness").

153. In other words, appearances may differ, but in essence all things are identical.

whole. In this way, the three poets worked together to create a sequence that formed a seamless aesthetic whole. Many forms of linking technique (from the simple expansion of a scene to a complete recasting) and many different personae (travelers, old men, lovers, and the like) create a dialectical movement that is the essence of the genre.

Translated here are three sections of the hundred-verse sequence: the first six verses, five verses from the middle, and the four verses with which it concludes. The comments on the links begin with an old commentary that appeared very early in the text's history, written by an unidentified renga master.

1

yukinagara	Some snow still remains
yamamoto kasumu	as mist covers the foothills
yūbe kana	toward evening.[154]

Sōgi

2

yuku mizu tōku	Flowing water, far away—
ume niou sato	and a plum-scented village.[155]

Shōhaku

3

kawakaze ni	Wind off the river
hitomura yanagi	blows through a clump of willows—
haru miete	and spring appears.[156]

Sōchō

---

154. Old Commentary: "An allusion to the base poem [*honka*], 'Gazing out over mist-shrouded foothills beyond the river Minase, who could have thought evenings are autumn?' 'Mist covers the foothills toward evening' is interesting [*omoshiroshi*] enough on its own; and the image 'snow remains' is even more outstanding." The opening verse (hokku) alludes to the poem, quoted earlier as the honka, by the retired emperor GoToba, chief architect of the *Shinkokinshū*, to whom the sequence is dedicated. As required by the rules, the first verse refers to the season in which the sequence was composed—spring—and sets the tone with its lofty imagery. "Mist" (*kasumu*) is a spring word.

155. Old Commentary: "On the peaks above, snow remains, while down below, water from melting snow flows gently. The village would be at the foot of the mountain." To the scene established by the hokku, Shōhaku adds a river flowing from the foothills and, on its banks, a village with fragrant plum trees.

156. Old Commentary: "Plum blossoms are associated with riverbanks and inlets. By itself, the verse means that the green of the willows doesn't appear when the wind isn't blowing; thus spring 'appears' with the wind." In the context of the link, the wind carries the scent of plum.

4

| fune sasu oto mo | A boat being poled along, |
| shiruku akegata | sounding clear at the break of dawn.[157] |

Sōgi

5

tsuki ya nao	Still there, somewhere:
kiri wataru yo ni	the moon off behind the fog
nokoruran	traversing the night.[158]

Shōhaku

6

| shimo oku nohara | Out on frost-laden fields |
| aki wa kurekeri | autumn has come to its end.[159] |

Sōchō

37

kimi o okite	While I have you,
akazu mo tare o	why tire of you and think
omouran	of anyone else?[160]

Sōchō

---

157. Old Commentary: "In the faint light of dawn, with the sound of a boat being poled, a stand of willows appears. 'Appears' is thus crucial to the verse by itself and for the link. The connection between 'break of dawn' and 'spring appears' is interesting [omoshiroshi]." To the sight of the wind blowing in the willows, Sōgi adds the sound of a boat passing and also establishes a temporal context: daybreak. The first three verses presented spring scenes; this one contains no seasonal imagery and is thus categorized as miscellaneous.

158. Old Commentary: "Though night has ended, the fog is so dark the moon seems to linger in the night sky." What by itself is a night scene becomes a description of daybreak. Unless otherwise qualified, "moon" is always an autumn image.

159. Old Commentary: "The moon always 'remains' of course, but here the author has linked a lingering moon to late autumn. The moon remains in the night engulfed by mist as autumn comes to its end on frosty fields. 'Mist' and 'frost' complement each other."

160. Old Commentary: "I already have you to love, why should I long for anyone else?" The verse could be taken as a literal question, but in the context is more likely meant rhetorically.

38

sono omokage ni   No resemblance do I see
nitaru dani nashi   to that other countenance.[161]

                                                 Shōhaku

39

kusaki sae   Shrubs and grasses—
furuki miyako no   even these make me long bitterly
urami nite   for the old capital.[162]

                                                 Sōgi

40

mi no uki yado mo   Even here in my house of pain
nagori koso are   I still have some attachments.[163]

                                                 Sōchō

41

tarachine no   Before time passes,
tōkaranu ato ni   remember your parent fondly—
nagusameyo   and take comfort now.[164]

                                                 Shōhaku

---

161. Old Commentary: "How unlikely that there could be anyone better than you." Inevitably, the mind seeks a comparison. The conclusion here is that the one he or she loves is beyond compare.

162. Old Commentary: "The courtyard garden has grown old, no image of what I once saw there." The word "even" in the maeku is taken here to mean "too," not "let alone. . . ." The previous verse by itself is a love verse, but in the link "that visage" becomes the appearance of a ruined capital, overgrown with shrubs and grasses.

163. Old Commentary: "Still recalling the garden of my old dwelling, which I can't bring myself to abandon, I resent even those shrubs and grasses." A lament by someone who has not been able to sever attachments to the world.

164. Old Commentary: "Since you are within three years of your father's death, take comfort in what you still recall." This world is a place of pain, but there are some memories for which to be thankful.

97

yama wa kesa   Mountains at morning—
iku shimoyo ni ka   how many nights of frost
kasumuran   preceded the mist?[165]

Sōchō

98

keburi nodoka ni   Smoke rises quietly
miyuru kariio   around a makeshift hut.[166]

Shōhaku

99

iyashiki mo   Among the lowborn, too,
mi o osamuru wa   must be some who live
aritsubeshi   in prosperity.[167]

Sōgi

100

hito ni oshinabe   For people everywhere
michi zo tadashiki   the Way lies straight ahead.[168]

Sōchō

[Introductions and translations by Steven Carter]

---

165. Old Commentary: "Until just recently the groves were withered by frost, but this morn-ing, mist begins to appear." Winter has been long and hard, but now spring mist rises through the groves.

166. Old Commentary: "The smoke is seen as mist." In the winter, smoke rising from a hut only reminds one of the surrounding cold, but as spring begins, the smoke—really spring mist— makes a serene impression.

167. Old Commentary: "The poet recasts [*torinashi-zuke*] the meaning of 'quietly' as 'in pros-perity.'" Even among the peasants, the speaker says, some are prosperous enough to live in peace. Smoke rising from hearth fires is a conventional symbol of peace and prosperity in the nation.

168. Old Commentary: "If all is in order, then everyone, from the lowest to the highest, is able to live in peace." The Way lies clear before all, even the peasants, who live in peace as long as the state maintains order. The first verse alludes to a poem by the retired emperor GoToba, and the last verse evokes the imperial way as a force for stability. The verse is meant to be taken as a prayer for peace in a time of political uncertainty.

MUROMACHI TALES (*OTOGI-ZŌSHI*)

Muromachi tales (*otogi-zōshi*, sometimes translated as "companion books") constitute an extremely diverse genre of short to middle-length narratives dating from the early fourteenth to the early seventeenth century (Northern and Southern Courts, Muromachi, and early Tokugawa periods).[169] Alternatively referred to as *Muromachi monogatari* (Muromachi tales) and *chūsei shōsetsu* (medieval novels), otogi-zōshi differ from their Heian and neoclassical antecedents in their thematic variety, their abundant and often vibrant illustrations, their plot-centered narratives, and their broad popular appeal. Since the early twentieth century, bibliographers have identified more than four hundred separate otogi-zōshi, most of which survive in numerous manuscripts in multiple textual lines. *The Tale of Bunshō* (*Bunshō sōshi*), for example, is preserved in at least eighty-two manuscripts in ten textual lines, and *Little One-Inch* (*Issun bōshi*) survives in a mere three manuscripts in a single textual line.[170] Of largely unknown authorship, otogi-zōshi incorporate a seemingly endless range of characters, from buddhas, nobles, warriors, and commoners to monsters, fish, and sentient plants, all set in a variety of domestic, foreign, and imagined locales.

The Northern and Southern Courts period (1336–1392), when court traditions dramatically declined and those of commoners came to the fore, marks the great divide between the early medieval and the late medieval age. Even though Heian literary genres—imperial anthologies, diaries of court women, and neoclassical monogatari—survived and even flourished during the Kamakura period, they began to disappear around the fourteenth century.

The editing and collecting of setsuwa, one of the principal cultural phenomena of the late Heian and Kamakura periods, declined precipitously at this time as well. But the earlier literary forms were reborn as otogi-zōshi, many of which—particularly the commoner tales—embraced elements of both setsuwa, with their focus on commoner life, and Heian monogatari, with their emphases on waka (classical poetry) and the refinements of court culture. Indeed, the otogi-zōshi absorbed a wide range of earlier narrative forms, including stories about the origins of shrines and temples (engi-mono) and warrior tales (gunki-mono). Viewed historically, otogi-zōshi thus bridge the gap between the Heian aristocratic and Tokugawa popular literary forms, the latter represented by the *kana-zōshi* and *ukiyo-zōshi* (tales of the floating world) that emerged in the seventeenth century.

---

169. The term *otogi-zōshi* derives from the name of a boxed-set anthology of short medieval fiction (*Otogi bunko* [*The Companion Library*, ca. 1716–1729]) published by the Osaka bookseller Shibukawa Seiemon. In its strictest sense, it refers only to the twenty-three works in Shibukawa's collection. Since at least the early nineteenth century, however, the term has also been used to refer to the larger corpus of medieval tales from which the *Otogi bunko* texts were drawn.

170. Matsumoto's 1982 catalog of extant otogi-zōshi, 122–124.

As noted earlier, one of the main differences between early medieval culture and late medieval culture was the new audience, epitomized in the term *gekokujō* (overthrowing of the upper by the lower). This term applies most appropriately to the period from the Kenmu restoration (1333–1334), when Emperor GoDaigo tried to restore direct imperial rule, through the Warring States period (1467–1573). Gekokujō could be found on a number of levels: social, political, economic, and military. In the provinces, for example, the *shugo daimyō* (military governors) became daimyō (semiautonomous warlords ruling over one or more provinces), and it was people like them who may have sponsored the production of the many lavishly illustrated otogi-zōshi martial tales that survive today, including the numerous *Demon Shuten Dōji* and *Little Atsumori* picture scrolls. Like the protagonists often found in kyōgen, some of the characters in otogi-zōshi reflect this spirit of gekokujō, in which individuals of lower status rise above or otherwise get the better of their superiors.

In the Heian and Kamakura periods, the aristocrats and the clergy, many of whom were of aristocratic origin, produced the texts. But as a result of various wars, particularly during the Northern and Southern Courts period, the nobility lost its power, the capital was damaged, and many cultural treasures were lost. With the decline of the capital and its surrounding culture, new authors and audiences appeared, and otogi-zōshi were subsequently produced by what seems to have been a wide range of social groups: fallen nobility, Buddhist priests, renga masters, literate samurai, recluses, and well-to-do urban commoners. The new, largely commoner audiences for whom they wrote had diverse interests and ambitions. Some, having suddenly risen in social status or attained material wealth, were especially interested in culture—classical aristocratic culture—but lacked the means to acquire a classical education. Otogi-zōshi, particularly the tales of the nobility, likely functioned for them as popular digests of the classics, providing a means of enjoying formerly aristocratic mores without the necessity of requiring a formal education.

The otogi-zōshi encompass an astonishing range of subject matter. One type derives from Heian monogatari, particularly *The Tale of Genji*, and includes such evil stepmother tales as *Head Bowl* (*Hachikazuki*).[171] This category also covers tales about poetry and famous waka poets. Another prominent category is priest tales, which include tales of awakening (*hosshin*) and confession, such as *The Three Priests* (*Sannin hōshi*), and stories about relationships between an older Buddhist priest and a young boy acolyte (*chigo*), in which love is often presented as a means to help the priest achieve enlightenment. The most famous of these is *A Long Tale for an Autumn Night* (*Aki no yo no naga monogatari*), in which a priest from Mount Hiei and a chigo from Mii-dera temple are

---

171. Translated by Chigusa Steven in "*Hachikazuki*: A Muromachi Short Story," *Monumenta Nipponica* 32 (1977): 303–331.

caught in a tragic struggle between the two temples.[172] Another subgenre is the "breaking of vows" stories (*hakaidan*), in which a priest violates monastic rules, as in *Errand Nun* (*Oyō no ama*).[173]

Otogi-zōshi also encompass a number of tales about samurai, which can be considered offshoots of the earlier warrior tales (gunki-mono). Here the most popular figure by far is Yoshitsune. The otogi-zōshi warrior tales recount legends about struggles with monsters and villains such as *The Demon Shuten Dōji* (*Shuten Dōji*) as well as many tales of commoners, which often involve courtship and social climbing. The most notable of these are *The Tale of Bunshō* (*Bunshō sōshi*); *Lazy Tarō* (*Monogusa Tarō*), which is included here; and *Little One-Inch* (*Issun bōshi*). Otogi-zōshi also may be about nonhumans or animals (*irui mono*), like *Urashima tarō*, *The Clam's Tale* (*Hamaguri no sōshi*), and *The Tale of Mice* (*Nezumi no sōshi*).

A recurrent characteristic of otogi-zōshi is their didacticism, often in the form of heavy-handed lessons revealing how readers' spiritual and material ambitions might best be attained. Except for all-too-typical cases in which characters find themselves torn between duty to their families and aspirations to the Buddhist Way, as in *Chūjōhime* (*Chūjōhime no honji*), internal moral conflicts are rare. Characters are usually depicted as either inherently good or bad, in some cases alternating between the two. The apparently overriding purpose of many otogi-zōshi is to encourage the cultivation of specific virtues or devotional practices by depicting exemplary lives and promising grandiose rewards; but the purpose of others is to simply entertain. Some audiences may have believed that by merely reading or listening to these texts, they could achieve the things described in them. Thus *Lazy Tarō* concludes with the line "The god has vowed that those who daily read this story or tell it to others will be filled with riches and achieve their hearts' desires. How wonderfully blessed!" *The Story of Bunshō* was similarly read by young women at New Year's in the hope that they, too, would receive auspicious returns.

LAZY TARŌ (*MONOGUSA TARŌ*)

Like a number of the commoner tales in otogi-zoshi, such as *The Tale of Bunshō* (*Bunshō sōshi*) and *Little One-Inch* (*Issun bōshi*), *Lazy Tarō* is a story of upward social mobility and ends on a celebratory note. And like these other two otogi-zōshi, it also is a tale of courtship. In a manner typical of the gekokujō (overcoming the higher by the

172. Margaret H. Childs, *Rethinking Sorrow: Revelatory Tales of Late Medieval Japan* (Ann Arbor: Center for Japanese Studies, University of Michigan, 1991), 26–27.

173. Virginia Skord, trans., *Tales of Tears and Laughter: Short Fiction of Medieval Japan* (Honolulu: University of Hawai'i Press, 1991), 205–220.

lower) spirit of the late medieval period, there are a number of inversions: from out-sider to insider, from low to high, and from profane to sacred. The protagonist, who looks repulsive and is from the lowest order, turns out to be very good at poetry, a sign of high culture and a key to his successful courtship. Much of the humor and interest of the narrative derives from these various paradoxes.

Lazy Tarō represents a popular form of the "exile of the young noble" found in earlier narratives such as the Kojiki and The Tale of Genji. The important differ-ence here is that in contrast to the earlier exiles, in which the hero is already of high status, the protagonist begins in a low social position and ends with wealth and high social status. Significantly, Lazy Tarō attains success as a result of his own efforts, but his spectacular success is reinforced by the revelation that he is a god. Often the protagonist has a patron god, as Little One-Inch (Sumiyoshi) and Bunshō the Salt-maker (Kashima) do, but here they are united in the body of Tarō, who turns out to be a god of longevity. In this sense, Lazy Tarō may be seen as a variation on the honji-mono (tale of a god's origins), in which a male protagonist typically encounters great difficulties, is exiled from his parents and familiar surroundings, reveals his strength, and is recognized as a deity who provides benefit to the people. Lazy Tarō brings con-siderable humor to this plot paradigm, suggesting that it may even be a parody of that convention.

At the furthest reaches of the Tōsen route, in a place called Atarashi village, in Tsukama, one of the ten districts of Shinano Province, lived a peculiar man called Lazy Tarō Hijikasu,[174] so dubbed because no one in the province could equal him in sheer laziness. He may have been called lazy, but he had a won-derful idea for building a house. He would construct a clay enclosure with a gate in three of the four sides. Inside, to the north, south, east, and west, he would create ponds and islands planted with pines and cedars. Arched bridges, their pillars crowned in shining ornamentation, would link the islands to the garden. It was truly a marvelous plan! There would be a retainers' quarters twelve ken wide, connecting corridors nine ken[175] long, a water-viewing pavilion, galleries, and plum, paulownia, and bamboo courtyards abloom with myriad varieties of flowers. There would be a main chamber of twelve ken, roofed in cypress bark, with damask-covered ceilings, gold- and silver-studded beam ends and rafters, and splendid woven hanging blinds. Everything would be magnificent, right down to the stables and servants' quarters. If only he could build such a fine man-sion! But he utterly lacked the means, and so he was obliged to make do with a straw mat upheld by four bamboo poles—a most uncomfortable residence in either rain or shine. As if the lean-to wasn't wretched enough, Tarō had more

---

174. The name Hijikasu may be a combination of hiji (dirt) and kasu (dregs). Now a common personal name, Tarō was once associated with the first and best among many, hence in the pres-ent context, the filthiest or dirtiest.

175. The ken was a linear measure about six feet in length.

than his due share of chilblains, fleas, lice, and even elbow grime. He had no assets, so he couldn't set up shop; he tilled no land, so he had no food. For days on end he would lie there without rising once.

On one occasion, a kind soul said to him, "Here, take this, you must be hungry," and gave him five rice cakes left over from a wedding feast. Tarō received food so rarely that he immediately devoured four of them. As for the last, however, if he kept it and didn't eat it, he could rely on it later; if he ate it now and left nothing, his stomach might be full, but then he could not expect more later. Just looking at that rice cake provided a certain solace, so he decided to keep it until he received something else. Lazy Tarō would lie there playing with it, rolling it around on his chest, polishing it with oil blotted from his nose, wetting it with spit, and balancing it on his head. While he was thus amusing himself, the rice cake slipped from his grasp and rolled over to the side of the road. Tarō looked at it and pondered. He was too lazy to get up and retrieve it. Figuring that sooner or later someone was bound to come by, he waited for three days, waving around a bamboo stick to ward off the dogs and crows who came to nibble at it, but not one person came along.

Finally, on the third day, there came the awaited passerby, none other than the local Land Steward, Saemon no jō Nobuyori,[176] off on an autumn hunting expedition accompanied by a host of some fifty to sixty mounted retainers carrying white-eyed falcons. When Tarō spotted him, he craned his neck and called, "Hey you! Excuse me, but there's a rice cake over there. Would you mind fetching it for me?"

But Nobuyori paid no heed and continued on his way.

"How in the world can such a lazy man possibly manage an entire domain?" thought Tarō. "It isn't that much trouble to get down and pick up a rice cake. I thought I was the only lazy fellow around, but there must be many of us."

"What a heartless lord!" he grumbled aloud, quite provoked.

Had Nobuyori been a short-tempered man, he would have taken offense, and there is no telling what he might have done. But instead he reined in his horse and asked his retainer, "Is that fellow the notorious Lazy Tarō?"

"There couldn't possibly be two of them, sir. That must be him."

"You there, how do you make a living?" asked Nobuyori directly.

"When people give me something, I'll eat anything at all. When they don't, I go without for four, five, as many as ten days."

"What a sorry plight! You must do something to help yourself! There is a saying that those who rest under the shade of the same tree and who drink of the same water share a karmic connection from a former life. That of all places in the world you were born into my domain must mean there is a bond between us. Cultivate some land and live off that."

176. "Saemon no jō" refers to his formal court post, sixth rank or below, which was granted to men of his position.

"But I have no land."

"Then I'll give you some."

"I'm too lazy—I don't want to work."

"Then set up a shop."

"I have nothing to sell."

"Then I'll give you something."

"It's hard to do something you're not used to, and I've never done it before."

"What an odd fellow!" thought Nobuyori. "I must do something to help him out." Pulling out an inkstone, he wrote the following edict and had it distributed throughout his lands:

"Lazy Tarō is to be fed daily: three measures of rice twice a day and wine once a day. Those who fail to comply will be expelled from this domain." Everyone thought this a prime example of the saying, "The unreasonableness of a lord's decree," but for three years they fed Tarō as ordered.

At the end of spring of the third year, Arisue, Governor of Shinano and Major Counselor of Nijō, ordered the village of Atarashi to supply a laborer to work in the capital. All the villagers gathered together to decide which household should provide the laborer. It had been such a long time since this sort of demand had been imposed that they were at a loss about what to do.

Then someone suggested, "How about sending Lazy Tarō?"

Another objected, "That's ridiculous! He's so lazy he wouldn't even pick up a rice cake lying in the road—he waited for the Steward to pass by and asked him to get it!"

"Convincing someone like Tarō to do it just might be the answer. Come on, let's give it a try," said another. So four or five elders got together and went to Tarō's hovel.

"Hey there, Lord Lazy Bones! Please help us out! It's our turn to send a man for public labor."

"What's that?" asked Tarō.

"We have to find a laborer—sort of like a longshoreman."

"How long is that? It must be awfully big!"[177]

"No, no! It's nothing like that! A laborer is someone we send from among the villagers to go serve in the capital. You should go out of gratitude to us for having fed you for three years."

"That's not something you cooked up yourselves, is it? I'll bet the Steward put you up to this." Tarō was not at all inclined to go.

"Look at it this way: it's for your own good," said one of them. "I mean, a fellow becomes a man when he takes a wife, and a girl becomes a woman when she has a husband. So, rather than live all alone in this broken-down shack, why

---

177. Tarō presumes that the *naga* of *nagabu* (laborer) refers to a long object, which is suggested here in the English translation by the word "longshoreman" but, of course, does not appear in the original.

don't you start making plans to be a responsible adult? You know, they say that there are three times in a man's life when he comes into his own: when he first wears adult trousers,[178] when he holds a job, and when he takes a wife. And you grow up even more when you travel. Country folks have no sense of human warmth, but city folks do. In the capital, no one is despised, and fine-looking people will live with anyone as husband and wife. So why don't you take off to the capital, get together with a woman who suits your fancy, and make a man of yourself?" he urged, presenting a fine array of arguments.

"Fine with me! If that's the case, then please send me there as soon as possible!" said Lazy Tarō. He was ready to depart immediately. The delighted villagers got together some traveling money and sent him off. ·

Lazy Tarō went along the Tōsen road, and, as he passed through each successive way station, he showed not a trace of laziness. On the seventh day, he arrived in the capital. "I'm the laborer come from Shinano," he announced proudly.

Everyone stared at him and laughed. "Can such a grimy, filthy creature possibly exist in this world?" they snickered among themselves. But the Major Counselor took him on. "It matters not how he looks," he said. "As long as he's a hard worker, he'll be fine."

Kyoto far surpassed anything Tarō had ever seen in Shinano. The mountains to the east and west, the palaces, temples, and shrines—everything was endlessly fascinating. Tarō was not lazy in the least; indeed, never had there been a more diligent worker than he. They kept him seven months, although he was obliged to serve only three. Finally, in the eleventh month, he was released from duty and decided to return home.

Tarō went to his lodgings to contemplate his situation. He had been told to bring back a good wife; the prospect of returning home all alone was too bleak. Wondering how he might find a wife, he approached his landlord for advice.

"I'm going back to Shinano. If you can, would you please find a woman willing to be the wife of a man like me?"

The landlord laughed and thought to himself, "I'd like to see any woman who would marry the likes of you!" But aloud he replied, "It's easy enough to ask around and find a woman, but marriage is quite another matter. What you really want is a streetwalker."

"What's a streetwalker? What do you mean by that?"

"Someone without a husband, who meets you for money—that's a streetwalker."

"Well, then, please find one for me. I have some money for my trip, some twelve or thirteen *mon*. Please use it for her."

---

178. Genpuku, a coming-of-age ceremony performed when a youth was between twelve and fifteen years of age, at which time he puts on adult trousers, ties up his hair, and takes an adult name.

The landlord thought that he had never met a bigger fool. "If you want one, you'll have to go out and cruise around."

"Cruise around? What's that supposed to mean?"

"That's when you look at all the women who don't have men with them and who aren't riding in carriages, and then you pick out a nice-looking one who catches your fancy. It's all right—you're allowed to do it."

"If that's the case, then I'll give it a try."

Tarō set out to try his luck at Kiyomizu Temple on the eighteenth of the Eleventh Month,[179] just as his landlord had suggested. He was dressed in the same rags he had long worn even in Shinano: a rough hempen singlet, so ancient that the color and pattern were indistinguishable, a straw rope wrapped around his waist, a pair of old frayed scuffs on his feet, and a bamboo staff in his hand. It was late in the year, and the bitter winds were so fierce that Tarō's nose ran. He looked like a sooty stupa as he waited by the main gate, standing rigidly with his arms outstretched. The returning worshipers thought him a frightful sight. Whatever could he be waiting for? All took care to avoid him, and not a single person ventured near. Groups of women ranging in age from seventeen to twenty surged by, but not one spared him a glance. Thousands of people must have passed as he stood there vacillating from dawn to dusk, rejecting one woman after another.

Then a young lady emerged. She might have been seventeen or eighteen years old, a veritable blossom of spring. With her raven locks and lovely midnight blue eyebrows, she looked just like a mountain cherry in bloom. Her sidelocks curved as gracefully as the wings of an autumn cicada; she was blessed with the beauty of the myriad marks of the angels and was as radiant as a golden buddha.[180] Her charm extended from her arching eyebrows right down to the hem of her robes, which danced with every step she took. She wore a crimson skirt over her gaily-colored robe and light, unlined sandals on her feet. The scent of plum blossoms rose from her hair, which was longer than she was tall. She had come to worship at the temple, accompanied by a maidservant almost as pretty as she was. To Lazy Tarō, here indeed had come his bride. He waited eagerly, arms outstretched, ready to embrace and kiss her. The lady caught sight of him and leaned over to her maid.

"What's that?" she asked.

"It's a person," came the reply.

"How dreadful! How can I avoid him?" she thought in a panic, hastily taking another path.

---

179. A monthly festival day at Kiyomizu-dera, a popular trysting place that houses the Tsuma Kannon, a deity believed to provide wives for single men and, by extension, companions for any supplicants.

180. Literally, the thirty-two physical marks and eight minor marks of a buddha or heavenly being.

"Oh, no!" thought Tarō. "She's heading that way! I have to catch up with her!" He went up to her with open arms and poked his dirty head under her lovely sedge hat. Bringing his face up to hers, he cried, "Hey, lady!" and threw his arms around her. Taken by surprise, she was speechless with confusion. People in the bustling crowd cried out, "How terrible! Isn't it frightful?" but everyone was careful to give them a wide berth.

Tarō held on tightly. "Hey, lady! It's been a long time! I've seen you all over the place—at Ōhara, Seryū and Shizuhara, Kōdō, Kawasaki, and Nakayama, Chōrakuji, Kiyomizu, Rokuhara, and Rokkakudō, Hōrinji, Saga, Daigo, Uzumasa, Kobata, Kurusu, Yahata, Yodo, Kuramadera, Sumiyoshi, Gojō Tenjin, Kibune Myōjin, Hiyoshi Sannō, Kitano, Gion, Kasuga, Kamo[181]—what do you think? Huh? Huh?"

At this, the lady decided that he was just another country bumpkin whose landlord had told him to go out cruising around. She could outwit someone like that.

"Is that so?" she said coolly. "There are so many people looking on now; why don't you come visit me at my home?"

"Where do you live?" he asked.

The lady assumed that she could confuse him with some fancy phrases and make her escape while he was puzzling them out. "I live in a place called Underpine," she replied.

"Oh, I see. Under a pine torch is bright, so you must live at Brightstone Bay."[182]

She was taken aback. Well, he might understand that, but he certainly wouldn't be able to guess another. "It's in a village where the sun sets."

"Ah, a village where the sun sets. I can guess that one, too. It must be deep in Dark Mountain.[183] Whereabouts?"

"That indeed is my home. You must look for Lampwick Lane."

"Tallow Lane?[184] Whereabouts?"

"That indeed is my home. It is a shy village."

"Hidden Village?[185] Whereabouts?"

"That indeed is my home. It is a village of cloaks."

"Brocade Lane?[186] Whereabouts?"

---

181. A list of famous sites in and around the capital.

182. Underpine (Matsu no moto); Brightstone Bay (Akashi no ura). In this and the following riddles, the places that Tarō correctly identifies are genuine place-names, translated into English to preserve the point of the riddles.

183. A village where the sun sets would be dark, so it must lie in the depths of Dark Mountain (Kurama no oku).

184. Because lamps are lit with tallow, Lampwick Lane (Tomoshibi no kōji) indicates Tallow Lane (Abura no kōji).

185. A shy village (*hazukashi no sato*) would be hidden from sight, hence Hidden Village (Shinobu no sato).

186. Robes are made of fabric, so a village of cloaks (*uwagi no sato*) indicates Brocade Lane (Nishiki no kōji).

"That indeed is my home. It is in a land of solace."

"Love-Tryst Province?[187] Whereabouts?"

"At an unclouded village of cosmetics." . . .

As long as he was responding like this, there was no way for the lady to escape. Perhaps she could recite some poetry and flee while he was working it out. Taking her cue from his bamboo stick, she recited:

> Rather hard to join with the man I see
> carrying a staff of many-jointed bamboo.[188]

"Oh, dear!" thought Tarō. "The lady's saying that she doesn't want to sleep with me." And he replied:

> Each and every stalk is nightly linked together.
> Why, then, can there be no joining with this bamboo bough?[189]

"Oh, no!" thought the lady. "This man is saying that he wants to sleep with me! But his poetic sensitivity does make him much more refined than he looks." And she said:

> Loosen your net! The eyes are fixed too tightly.
> Release your hand, then we shall speak.[190]

Tarō understood that she was asking him to let her go and wondered what to do. So he responded:

> So what if the network of eyes is fixed on you?
> Let me kiss you, then my hand will loosen.

At this, the lady realized that poetic repartee was getting her nowhere. And so she recited:

> If you love me, then call on me.
> Mine is the house with the orange-blossom gate.[191]

---

187. Meeting a love brings solace, so a land of solace (*nagusamu kuni*) would be in Love-Tryst Province (Afumi no kuni, a pun on Ōmi Province).

188. The verse puns on *fushi* (lie down) and *fushi* (bamboo joint).

189. The verse incorporates the puns of the preceding poem, extending it with puns on *yo*: "world," "stalk," and "night."

190. The verse puns on *itome* (eyes [of a net]) and *hitome* (eyes of others).

191. The meaning of the last two lines is unclear. *Karatachibana* refers to Chinese orange blossoms, reddish or white in color, and *murasaki* is lavender. Here *murasaki* may refer to *murasaki-sō*, a flower with white blossoms similar to Chinese orange blossoms. Alternatively, the gate may simply be planted with both types of flowers.

As Tarō took note of her words, he gradually allowed his grip to relax. She shook herself free and dashed off, leaving her sedge hat, cloak, sandals, and servant behind. Tarō was devastated at the disappearance of his lady love. He grabbed his staff, called out, "Lady, where are you going?" and took off in pursuit.

The lady was familiar with the streets, and, sure that this was her last chance, made her getaway by crisscrossing back and forth, through this alley and around that corner, like a cherry petal scattering in the spring wind.

"Hey, where are you going, sweetie?" Tarō called out again. He headed down an alley so as to meet up with her at the next corner, but somehow lost track of her. Retracing his steps, he found nothing, and passersby all denied having seen her. Finally, he returned to his post at Kiyomizu. "Now," he told himself, "she was standing facing this way, then she turned that way, said such and such . . . oh, wherever did she go?"

His burning love seemed to be hopeless until he suddenly remembered that she had spoken of an orange-blossom gate. He would have to find out where that was. So he wrapped a piece of paper around his stick[192] and went into a soldiers' guard post.

"I'm up from the country and have forgotten an address. It's a place called Orange-Blossom Gate, or something like that. Where might that be?"

"Seems that there's a place by that name back of Seventh Avenue, at the residence of the Lord Governor of Buzen. Go down this lane and ask there," he was told.

And indeed it was the place. Tarō felt as if he had already found his lady, and he was filled with joy. Here people were absorbed in all sorts of amusements: polo, chess, sugoroku, music, and song. Tarō searched everywhere in vain for his beloved. Hoping that she might yet emerge, he concealed himself beneath a veranda and waited.

Here, the lady was known as Jijū no Tsubone.[193] Late that night, she returned to her quarters after serving at the Governor's court. She stood in the outer corridor and called to her maid, Nadeshiko.

"Hasn't the moon risen yet? I wonder what happened to that man from Kiyomizu? If it had been this dark when I ran into him, it would have been the end of me."

"How detestable he was!" replied Nadeshiko. "He couldn't possibly come here! But do be careful—speak of the devil, and he's sure to appear, you know!"

Lazy Tarō was listening from under the veranda. Here was his bride! In his joy that their bond had not been severed, he pranced out and leaped up beside her. "Hey, lady! I've been pretty worried about you, sweetie! Darned near broke my neck trying to find you!"

---

192. Tying paper to a stick may have been a medieval practice demonstrating humility to an unknown person when making inquiries.

193. It was common for a high-ranking woman to be referred to by the office of a male relative. *Jijū* (chamberlain) was of middle rank; *tsubone* was a term of respect for aristocratic women.

The lady was utterly aghast. She scrambled behind her screen to escape and remained there in a state of shock, her face as vacant as the sky above. Presently, she moaned to her maid, "How dreadfully tenacious he is! He's actually here! Of all the men in the world, that such a dirty, disgusting creature should fall in love with me! How awful!"

Just then a company of watchmen came by. "Have you seen a stranger around?" they asked. "The dogs are in an uproar!"

"Oh, no!" she thought, "What if they kill him? As a woman, my sins are already deep enough, what with the Five Hindrances and Three Duties."[194] She wept bitter tears. What harm could there be in putting him up for the night, then slipping him out at dawn? She told the maid to put out an old mat for him to sit on. So the maid went to Tarō and informed him that he could remain until dawn, when he must leave quietly, taking care that no one saw him. She spread out a mat trimmed with elaborately patterned edging, the likes of which Tarō had never seen, and bade him sit on it.

Lazy Tarō was quite exhausted from all the running around he had done that day. He hoped that they would bring him something—anything—soon. What might it be? If it were chestnuts, he would first roast, then eat them; if persimmons, pears, or rice cakes, he would gobble them down right away. If they gave him wine, he would drink almost twenty cups of it. As he was sitting there musing expectantly, the maid brought out a knife, salt, and a rough-edged basket filled with chestnuts, persimmons, and pears.

"Darn it," said Tarō to himself. "In spite of her fine looks, she's treating me like a horse or an ox, giving me this fruit all jumbled together in a basket without setting it out nicely on a lid or paper. It's too much! There must be something more to it. Let's see: she gave me the fruit all together, so that must mean that she wants to get together with me. And the chestnuts mean that she won't repeat the nutty things she said before,[195] the pears that she wishes to be paired only with me.[196] But what about the persimmons and salt? Well, I can use them together in a poem:

> Since this is the fruit of Naniwa Bay in Tsu,
> it has crossed no seas but is well pickled in salt.[197]

---

194. Women were thought to be burdened by the Five Hindrances (*goshō*), which prevented them from becoming a Brahma god-king, the god Sakra, King Mara, a sage-king turning the wheel, or a buddha-body. The Three Duties (*sanjū*) refer to the teaching that women are subordinate first to their fathers, then to their husbands, and finally to their sons. The Five Hindrances and the Three Duties often appear together in medieval literature to express the inferiority of women.

195. This involves a pun on *kuri* (chestnut) and *kurigoto* (repetition). I have altered the original wording to create a pun in English.

196. This is a pun on *nashi* (pear) and *nashi* (none) (she has no other men).

197. The verse puns on *umiwataru* (to ripen) and *umi wataru* (to cross the sea). Tsu is an old name for Settsu, in the vicinity of Osaka, and thus the persimmons would not have been transported by sea.

The lady overheard this and marveled at his exceptional sensitivity. Here indeed was an example of the proverbial "lotus blooming from the mire" and "gold wrapped in straw." "Here, take this," she said, passing him some ten sheets of paper. Tarō wondered at this, but concluded that, although she had written no message, she must want him to write a response. And so he composed:

> You give me mighty divine paper for my use.
> Could this mean that you think me a sacred shrine?[198]

"I can't hold out any longer!" she cried. "Bring him in!" She gathered together a pair of wide trousers, a robe, a court hat, and a sword for him to wear.

Delighted at this happy turn of events, Tarō Hijikasu wrapped his old hand-me-downs around his staff. She probably meant to lend him the new attire just for the night, and he would need his old rags again in the morning.

"Dogs, don't you dare eat these! Thieves, don't you dare steal these!" he thought, tossing the bundle under the veranda. Then, confronted with the problem of putting on the trousers and robe, he looped the ties around his neck and draped the pants over his shoulders, such that the maid was obliged to help him out of his predicament. As she was about to put the court hat on his head, she saw that his hair was such a tangle of dirt, fleas, and lice that it looked as if it had never known a comb. But somehow she managed to straighten it out, perched the hat on his head, and led him inside.

Tarō had been able to navigate the mountains and cliffs of Shinano, but never before had he encountered such a slippery smooth surface as these oiled floor boards, and he skidded and slipped to and fro as he walked. Nadeshiko led him behind the lady's screen and disappeared. Just as he was about to approach her, he lost his footing, tumbled head over heels, and landed squarely on top of her cherished koto, Tehikimaru, smashing it to smithereens. The lady was heartsick. Tears streaming down a face turned as red as the leaves of autumn, she said:

> Whatever can I do now
> to while away my idle hours?

Gazing up at her from his prone position, Tarō returned:

> The koto's smashed; my hopes are dashed—
> I'm so abashed![199]

With this, the lady realized that Tarō had the soul of a gentleman. So moved was she that they must have shared a karmic bond, for this could not be the shallow connection of a single lifetime. She pledged herself to him.

---

198. Tarō puns on *kami* (paper) and *kami* (god).

199. Tarō's response puns on *kotowari* ("reason, excuse" and "to break a koto").

Dawn broke all too soon, and as Tarō was making ready for a hasty departure, she said, "I was moved in spite of myself to invite you in. Surely this means that we share a bond from a former life. If you hold me dear to your heart, please remain here. I may be a court lady, but what difference does that make?" And so Tarō agreed to stay.

Together the lady and her maid worked day and night setting him to rights. They had him bathe every day for a week, and by the seventh day he sparkled like a jewel. Each successive day thereafter he shone more brilliantly and came to acquire a reputation as a handsome man and an accomplished poet of linked verse. As his lady was of high rank, she was able to instruct him in all matters of gentlemanly deportment. His dress was impeccable: from the hang of his trousers to the angle of his court hat and the coif of his hair, he easily outdid the highest of nobility. The Governor of Buzen heard about him and summoned him to an audience. Seeing Tarō so beautifully dressed, he remarked, "You are indeed a handsome man. What is your name?"

"Lazy Tarō."

This was so inappropriate that the Governor renamed him Uta no Saemon.[200]

Eventually, word reached the inner sanctum of the palace, and Tarō was summoned to report there at once. He tried to decline the honor, but to no avail. He rode in a carriage to the palace, and on his arrival he was ushered into the formal audience hall.

"I hear that you are a prodigy at linked verse. Compose a couple of links," ordered the Emperor. Just then, a warbler flew down, perched on a plum branch, and sang. Hearing this, Tarō recited:

> Is it because spring rain has spilled over the umbrella
> of plum blossoms that the warbler is bathed in tears?

"Do they call it a plum where you come from?" asked the Emperor. Without hesitation, Tarō replied:

> In Shinano the flower is called *baika*;
> in the capital what might they call the plum?

The Emperor was very impressed. "Who are your ancestors?" he asked.

"I have no ancestors."

The Emperor ordered him to inquire of the Deputy Governor of Shinano about his ancestry. The Deputy Governor in turn gave the commission to the local steward, and eventually the results were brought to the Emperor in a missive wrapped in rush matting. On examination, the Emperor learned that the Middle Captain of the Second Rank, the second son of the fifty-third emperor,

---

200. The meaning of the office title is unclear.

Ninmyō,[201] also known as Fukakusa, had been exiled to Shinano, where he lived for many years. He had no children, and his desperation led him to make a pilgrimage to Zenkō Temple, where he petitioned the Amida Buddha. As a result, he was blessed with a son. When the child was but three years old, his parents died, and thus he dropped to a lowly status and was tainted with the dirt of humble commoners.

On reading this, the Emperor saw that Tarō was not far removed from the imperial line itself. He dubbed him the Middle Captain of Shinano and granted him the domains of Kai and Shinano. Accompanied by his wife, the Middle Captain went to the village of Asahi in Shinano. Since Nobuyori, the Steward of Atarashi, had been so kind to him, he made him General Administrator of his domains and awarded land to each of the farmers who had fed him for three years. For the site of his own mansion, he selected Tsukama, and there set up his household. Everyone, regardless of social standing, obeyed him, and he governed his domains in peace and tranquillity under the protection of the gods and buddhas. He lived for 120 years, producing many descendants, and his household overflowed with the Seven Treasures and abundant wealth. He became a god of longevity and the Great Deity of Odaka, while his wife was a manifestation of the Asai Gongen.

This occurred during the reign of Emperor Montoku.[202] Tarō was a manifestation of a god who brought together those who had gathered karmic merit from a previous life. He vowed that when anyone, man or woman, came to worship him, he would fulfill the request. Usually, ordinary men are provoked to anger at talk of their origins, but, when the origins of a god are revealed, the torments of the Three Heats[203] are quelled, and he is immediately delighted. As revealed in this tale, even a lazy man may be pure and sincere at heart.

The god has vowed that those who daily read this story or tell it to others will be filled with riches and achieve their hearts' desires. How wonderfully blessed!

[Translated by Virginia Skord]

POPULAR LINKED VERSE (*HAIKAI*)

Haikai (literally, "popular or unorthodox poetry") usually take the form of interlinking verses, alternating between seventeen-syllable and fourteen-syllable verses. Haikai also appear earlier in the form of the thirty-one-syllable waka in

---

201. Ninmyō (833–850) is usually listed as the fifty-fourth emperor. He had many sons, some of whom succeeded to the throne, but nothing is known about the exile in question.

202. Reigned from 850 to 858.

203. The Three Heats (*sannetsu*) are torments that gods of the earth, owing to their association with dragons, must undergo. They are a hot wind and a sandstorm that burns them, an evil wind that strips them, and an attack by a phoenix.

the *Kokinshū* (ca. 905), in which the term applies to thirty-one-syllable waka that either are humorous or diverge from courtly standards in diction, content, or aesthetics. Here haikai were largely characterized by what they were not: elegant, refined, and aristocratic.

As linked verse, haikai developed alongside classical or orthodox linked verse (renga) but without its restrictions in diction and rules. The typical form was a fourteen-syllable (7/7) previous verse (*maeku*) followed by a seventeen-syllable (5/7/5) added verse (*tsukeku*), which combined with and twisted the first verse. The seventeen-syllable (5/7/5) opening verse (*hokku*), which required a seasonal word (*kigo*) and a cutting word (*kireji*), also became an independent form (and eventually the modern haiku). For most of history, haikai were scorned as beneath the notice of serious anthologizers, and so most haikai verses have been lost. But with the advent of the Warring States period (1467–1573), when "inferior overcame superior" in a massive political, economic, and cultural upheaval, haikai became popular. Like the kyōgen plays performed between the more rarified no dramas, haikai reveled in the daily, comedic, and vulgar, taking particular pleasure in skewering pretensions, religious ideals, and courtly romance. The increasingly rule-bound and sophisticated form of classical linked verse likewise contributed to the growth of haikai linked verse, which was simpler and addressed the interests and concerns of a wider cross section of society.

The oldest extant collection of haikai linked verse appears in book 19 of the first court-sponsored anthology of linked verse, the *Tsukuba Collection* (*Tsukubashū*, 1356–1357). Its compilers, the court literatus Nijō Yoshimoto (1320–1388) and his poetic adviser Gusai (also read as Kyūsei, 1282?–1376?), were intent on raising the reputation of verse to rival that of waka, and so they modeled the anthology, including its haikai linked-verse section, on the *Kokinshū*. Interest in haikai grew, and gradually the genre began to be perceived as a separate enterprise. It was at this point that the first extant anthology completely devoted to haikai, the *Hobbyhorse Collection of Mad Songs* (*Chikuba kyōginshū*, 1499), was compiled. The *Hobbyhorse Collection* is divided into sections of hokku and linked-verse couplets of maeku and tsukeku. In order to elevate classical linked verse, Sōgi (1421–1502), an influential fifteenth-century renga master, did not include haikai in his *New Tsukuba Collection* (*Shinsen tsukubashū*, 1495). The fact that *Chikuba kyōginshū* was compiled only four years after *Shinsen tsukubashū* suggests that it was a counterpoint to classical renga.

The most famous anthology of early haikai is the *Newly Selected Mongrel Tsukuba Collection* (*Shinsen inu tsukubashū*, ca. 1530), which came to be known as the *Mongrel Tsukuba Collection* (*Inu tsukubashū*). The editor of the *Mongrel Tsukuba Collection* is thought to have been Yamazaki Sōkan (1465–1533). The first extended haikai sequence is the "Moritake Thousand Verses" (*Moritake senku*), composed by Arakida Moritake (1473–1549), a colleague of Sōkan. Although the *Hobbyhorse Collection* was not circulated widely in the Tokugawa period, the *Mongrel Tsukuba Collection* and the "Moritake Thousand Verses" became well known, with the result that Sōkan and Moritake were regarded by later generations as the founders of haikai. As a genre, haikai reached its apex in the Tokugawa period, when it became the most popular poetic and literary form of that time.

HOBBYHORSE COLLECTION OF MAD SONGS
(*CHIKUBA KYŌGINSHŪ*, 1499)

The *Hobbyhorse Collection of Mad Songs*, whose compiler is not known, is the first extant anthology devoted to haikai. Roughly patterned on the imperial waka collections, it begins with sections on the seasons, followed by sections on love (*koi*) and miscellaneous topics. Selections of two-verse links are translated here. The witty and often ribald approach to the classical topics makes an interesting contrast with more formal waka and renga anthologies. Many of the selections in the *Hobbyhorse Collection* also appear in the *Mongrel Tsukuba Collection*. The preface to the anthology—which is rich in puns, presaging the later haikai prose (*haibun*)—is an important early manifesto regarding the value of haikai.

Preface

This is an age in which all have a taste for linked verse, in which poetry is pounded out like rice cakes near and far upon Mount Tsukuba; it is even in the mouths of the gods, and the buddhas do not turn their faces from it.[204] My verse is bent to breaking, a bad reed at Naniwa, and I just sit breaking wind beside the rush of the waves at Waka Bay.[205] But poetry in China does not deviate from the right path, and in Japan it is as seeds in the heart; so like one of those Chinese poet-sages living in lofty madness or feigned lunacy, I have assembled verses just as wild and intoxicated, and entitled the whole *Hobbyhorse Collection of Mad Songs*.[206]

I had no way to search throughout the eight Kantō provinces to the east, nor could I inquire in the nine of Kyushu to the west; I simply copied down what people told me or I happened to hear. They are shallow, like the water at the bottom of a well in which lives a frog of a lay priest; scentless and bland like a dried plum of a monk in a forest.[207] But even so, they may help guide those who look for pears but pick up chestnuts, or amuse those who cannot tell gems from

---

204. An allusion to a song of the east country, *Kokinshū*, no. 1095, which also mentions Mount Tsukuba: "There is shade near and far on the peak of Mount Tsukuba, but none better than the protecting shade of my lord's grace."

205. Both Naniwa (Osaka) and Waka Bay (Wakanoura) appear in poems quoted in the preface to the *Kokinshū*.

206. The preface refers here to lines from the "Weizheng" book of the Confucian *Analects* and to the preface to the *Kokinshū*.

207. "A frog in the well knows nothing of the sea," a proverb about parochial ignorance, appears in *Zhuangzi*. "A dried plum of a monk in a forest" combines a pun on *umeboshi* (dried plum) and *hōshi* (monk) with overtones of a legend in *Shishuo xinyu* in which Cao Cao (Emperor Wu) tells his thirsty men that he knows of a plum tree up ahead, at the mere mention of which his men's mouths start to water.

stones.[208] So I view them as noble, just as the barking of a village dog can lead to enlightenment, or as the belling of a stag can reveal the Truth. Perhaps he who takes up this collection will find it a morsel to whet a drinker's thirst.

Autumn

81–82

keikai sureba	When debts pile up,
aki zo nao uki	autumn is even sadder.

tsuyu shimo no	As frosty dew falls,
furu ni sode sae	he gives up even his robe
shichi ni shite	as a pledge for a loan.[209]

87–88

tsubururu mo ari	Some are ruined;
tsuburenu mo ari	some are not.

akikaze ni	From the branches
kozue no jukushi	in the autumn wind,
mata ochite	another ripe persimmon falls.[210]

91–92

osorenagara mo	Trying to insert it
irete koso mire	while filled with awe.

wa ga ashi ya	My foot
tarai no mizu no	in a water basin
tsuki no kage	reflecting the moon.[211]

---

208. "Those who look for pears but pick up chestnuts" refers to the *kurinomotoshū* (literally, "those beneath the chestnut tree"), meaning those who pursue haikai, in contrast to the *kakinomotoshū*, those who follow Kakinomoto (literally, "beneath the persimmon tree") Hitomaro— that is, classical renga poets. "Look for pears" (*nashi o motome*) is homophonic with "look for nothingness." "Pears" and "chestnuts" are associated words.

209. In classical poetry, autumn was closely associated with sadness. The link here parodies that aesthetic association by making the cause of sadness a very secular matter of accumulating debt.

210. "Ruined" (*tsuburu*) can suggest any number of disasters, such as going bankrupt or losing face. The added verse unexpectedly invokes ripe persimmons, an autumn delicacy, some of which have fallen and some of which have not.

211. "While filled with awe" (*osorenagara mo*) in the previous verse suggests a forbidden coupling between a low-ranking man, perhaps a servant, and a highborn woman. This scene is subverted by the added verse in which the man's diffidence comes from his reluctance to defile

Love

135–136

muma no ue ni te	Making love to a temple boy
chigo to chigireri	on top of a horse.

yamadera no	At a mountain temple
shōgi no ban o	they use a chess board
karimakura	for a pillow.[212]

145–146

kaki no anata o	Through a hole in the fence
nozokite zo miru	he steals a look.

ware hitori	Getting a grip on himself,
nigirite netaru	he lies alone
yomosugara	all night long.[213]

Miscellaneous

227–228

shukke no soba ni	Beside the monk
netaru nyōbō	lies a lady.

Henjō ni	Hidden from Henjō
kakusu Komachi ga	is Komachi's
utamakura	poem-pillow.[214]

---

with his dirty foot the water, an image of purity in Buddhism, and the reflection in the basin of the moon, a Buddhist symbol of enlightenment. A variant is in *Inu Tsukubashū*, nos. 140–141.

212. In the medieval male monastery, pederasty was common, and haikai depict the relationships between priests and temple boys (*chigo*) in varying degrees of explicitness. The acrobatic improbability of the first verse is explained in the second by the use of the *shōgi* (Japanese chess) board as a pillow, with a horse piece finding its way beneath them. The mountain temple suggests Enryaku-ji on Mount Hiei, center of the Tendai Buddhist sect.

213. The first verse recalls the way that many romances begin in *The Tale of Genji* and other classical tales, when a young noble peeps at a lady through a fence. But in the added verse here, the man is only frustrated by the titillating view of the lady's private parts, and so takes matters into his own hands. *Anata* (across the way) phonically implies *ana* (hole).

214. Two of the so-called Six Poetic Immortals of the *Kokinshū* era were Priest Henjō and Ono no Komachi. The added verse implies that despite their intimacy, Komachi remains concerned about her poetic rival's reading her "poem-pillow" (*utamakura*), a list or handbook of

371–372

nigiri hosomete   Gripping it, squeezing it,
gutto irekeri   plunging it in!

hachatsubo no   Into a small-mouthed
kuchi no hosoki ni   jar, a big bag
ōbukuro   of tea leaves.[215]

MONGREL TSUKUBA COLLECTION
(*INU TSUKUBASHŪ*, CA. 1530)

The *Newly Selected Mongrel Tsukuba Collection* (*Shinsen inu Tsukubashū*), better known as the *Mongrel Tsukuba Collection*, is the best-known haikai collection from the medieval period. The *inu* (mongrel) in the title implies something both similar to and radically different from the *Tsukuba Collection* (mid-fourteenth century), the classical renga anthology edited by Nijō Yoshimoto in the Northern and Southern Courts period. Attributed to Yamazaki Sōkan (1465–1533), the *Mongrel Tsukuba Collection* is thought to have been started around 1530, after which it was added to incrementally, by both Sōkan (in whose hand several different manuscripts survive) and later editors, with the result that no single text is authoritative. Although early manuscripts are entitled *Haikai renga* (*Haikai Linked Verse*) or *Haikai rengashō*, by the time versions of the work began to be printed in the Tokugawa period, it had come to be known by its current title. Little is known about Sōkan except that he served the Ashikaga shogun and later took holy vows and lived west of the capital, in Yamazaki.

The variant used here has 322 linked-verse couplets divided into six sections: the four seasons (spring, summer, autumn, winter), love, and miscellaneous. These are followed by a section of ninety-three hokku (opening verses), also ordered by the seasons. Even though the writers of the poems are listed as anonymous, many have been identified as the renga poets Sōgi, Kensai, and Sōchō, and the noted haikai poets Sōkan and Moritake.

---

poetic material, a term doubly appropriate in the context of sleeping together. The scene recalls an episode related in both *Gosenshū* and *Yamato monogatari* (NKBT 9:335–341) in which Komachi, on a pilgrimage, has a chance encounter with Henjō, whom she had known before he took the tonsure. She composes a waka asking to borrow a robe against the cold, and he responds with another saying that since he has only one, they will have to share it as they sleep. In that story, their relationship goes no further.

215. An implicitly lewd verse is wittingly transformed into something surprisingly innocent. A hidden joke lies in the fact that a woman's private parts were vulgarly known as the "tea jar" (*chatsubo*) and the man's parts as a "big bag" (*ōbukuro*). A variant appears in *Inu Tsukubashū* (Tōkyō daigaku toshokan ms.), no. 257.

Spring

1–2

kasumi no koromo	The robe of haze
suso wa nurekeri	is soaked at the hem

Saohime no	Spring has come,
haru tachinagara	and the goddess Saohime
shito o shite	pisses where she stands.[216]

Love

193–194

oyobanu koi o	A love beyond one's reach
suru zo okashiki	is certainly ridiculous!

ware yori mo	In bed behind
ōwakazoku no	a young man
ato ni nete	too tall for him![217]

Miscellaneous

kiritaku mo ari	To cut down
kiritaku mo nashi	or not to cut down[218]

nusubito o	Catching a thief
toraete mireba	and finding him
waga ko nari	to be your own child.

---

216. The maeku, identified as a spring verse by the seasonal word "haze" (*kasumi*), is a puzzle, asking the next verse to explain how the "robe of haze" (*kasumi no koromo*, an elegant waka expression) can be soaked at the hem. The poet, perhaps Sōkan himself, rises to the challenge by clothing Saohime, the eminently refined goddess of spring, in the robe of haze and then abruptly undercutting the elegant image with the earthy last line, introduced by a *kakekotoba* (pivot word) between "Spring has come" (*haru tachi*) and "stands" (*tachinagara*).

217. The first verse indicates impossible love due to differences in social station. The second verse twists that into impossible male–male sex because the difference in height is insurmountable. This also appears in *Chikuba kyōginshū*, nos. 139–140.

218. This fourteen-syllable maeku is followed by three alternative seventeen-syllable tsukeku, each of which gives a different interpretation to the same maeku. This set and the next are from a different variant than that of the SNKS.

sayakanaru   The bright moon
tsuki o kakuseru   hidden by branches
hana no eda   of a cherry tree.

kokoro yoki   An arrow that turns
matoya no sukoshi   out well but is a bit
nagaki o   too long.

. . .

ke no aru naki wa   Finding out if there is hair
sagurite zo shiru   or not by groping.

deshi motanu   A priest without
bōzu wa kami o   disciples shaves
jizori   his own head.[219]

Hokku

Summer

373

tsuki ni e o   If you stick
sashitaraba yoki   a handle in the moon,
uchiwa kana   it makes a good fan!

[Introductions and translations by H. Mack Horton]

---

219. The previous verse about groping for hair has lewd implications, which are humorously transformed into a priest trying to find out whether he has shaved his head completely.

ENGLISH-LANGUAGE BIBLIOGRAPHY

THE ANCIENT PERIOD

Kojiki

Fuminobu, Murakami. "Incest and Rebirth in *Kojiki.*" *Monumenta Nipponica* 43, no. 4 (1988): 455–463.

Kawai, Hayao. "The Hollow Center in the Mythology of *Kojiki.*" *Review of Japanese Culture and Society* 1, no. 1 (1986): 72–77.

Kōnoshi, Takamitsu. "The Land of Yomi: On the Mythical World of the *Kojiki.*" *Japanese Journal of Religious Studies* 11, no. 1 (1984): 57–76.

Philippi, Donald L. "Ancient Tales of Supernatural Marriage." *Journal of the Association of Teachers of Japanese* 5 (1960): 19–23.

Philippi, Donald L. "Four Song-Dramas from the *Kojiki.*" *Journal of the Association of Teachers of Japanese* 5 (1960): 81–88.

Philippi, Donald L., trans. *Kojiki.* Tokyo: University of Tokyo Press, 1968.

Nihon shoki

Aston, W. G, trans. *Nihongi: Chronicles of Japan from the Earliest Times to* A.D. 697. Tokyo: Turtle, 1972.

Mythohistory

Akima, Toshio. "The Myth of the Goddess of the Undersea World and the Tale of Empress Jingū's Subjugation of Korea." *Japanese Journal of Religious Studies* 20, nos. 2–3 (1993): 95–185.

Aoki, Michiko Y. *Ancient Myths and Early History of Japan: A Cultural Foundation.* New York: Exposition Press, 1974.

Ellwood, Robert S. "A Japanese Mythic Trickster Figure: Susa-no-o." In *Mythical Trickster Figures: Contours, Contexts, and Criticisms,* edited by William J. Hynes and William G. Doty, 141–158. Tuscaloosa: University of Alabama Press, 1993.

Grapard, Allan G. "Visions of Excess and Excesses of Vision: Women and Transgression in Japanese Myth." *Japanese Journal of Religious Studies* 18, no. 1 (1991): 3–22.

Kato, Genchi, and Hikoshiro Hoshino, trans. *Kogoshūi: Gleanings from Ancient Stories.* 3rd and enlarged ed. New York: Barnes & Noble Books, 1972.

Kurosawa, Kōzō. "Myths and Tale Literature." *Japanese Journal of Religious Studies* 9, nos. 2–3 (1982): 115–125.

Littleton, C. Scott. "Yamato-takeru: An 'Arthurian' Hero in Japanese Tradition." *Asian Folklore Studies* 54, no. 2 (1995): 259–274.

Matsumae, Takeshi. "The Heavenly Rock-Grotto Myth and the *Chinkon* Ceremony." *Asian Folklore Studies* 39, no. 2 (1980): 9–22.

Nakanishi, Susumu. "The Spatial Structure of Japanese Myth: The Contact Point Between Life and Death." In *Principles of Classical Japanese Literature,* edited by Earl Miner, 106–129. Princeton, N.J.: Princeton University Press, 1985.

Ancient Songs

Akima, Toshio. "The Songs of the Dead: Ritual Poetry, Drama, and Ancient Death Rituals of Japan." *Journal of Asian Studies* 41, no. 3 (1982): 485–509.

Brannen, Noah, and Wm. Elliott, trans. *Festive Wine: Ancient Japanese Poems from the Kinkafu.* New York: Walker/Weatherhill, 1969.

Philippi, Donald L., trans. *This Wine of Peace, This Wine of Laughter: A Complete Anthology of Japan's Earliest Songs.* New York: Grossman, 1968.

Provincial Gazetteers

Aoki, Michiko Yamaguchi. *Records of Wind and Earth: A Translation of Fudoki, with Introduction and Commentaries.* Monograph and Occasional Papers Series, no. 53. Ann Arbor, Mich.: Association for Asian Studies, 1997.

Prayers to the Gods

Philippi, Donald L. *Norito: A Translation of the Ancient Japanese Ritual Prayers.* Tokyo: Institute for Japanese Culture and Classics, Kokugakuin University, 1959.

Man'yōshū

Cranston, Edwin A. "Five Poetic Sequences from the *Man'yōshū.*" *Journal of the Association of Teachers of Japanese* 13 (1980): 5–40.

Cranston, Edwin A. "The River Valley as *Locus Amoenus* in Man'yō Poetry." In *Studies in Japanese Culture,* edited by Saburo Ota and Rikutaro Fukuda, 1:14–37. Tokyo: Japan P.E.N. Club, 1973.

Cranston, Edwin A. "Water Plant Imagery in *Man'yōshū.*" *Harvard Journal of Asiatic Studies* 31 (1971): 137–178.

Cranston, Edwin A., trans. *A Waka Anthology: The Gem-Glistening Cup.* Stanford, Calif.: Stanford University Press, 1993, 1998.

Doe, Paula. *A Warbler's Song in the Dusk: The Life and Work of Ōtomo Yakamochi (718–785).* Berkeley: University of California Press, 1982.

Ebersole, Gary L. *Ritual Poetry and the Politics of Death in Early Japan.* Princeton, N.J.: Princeton University Press, 1989.

Levy, Ian Hideo. *Hitomaro and the Birth of Japanese Lyricism.* Princeton, N.J.: Princeton University Press, 1984.

Levy, Ian Hideo, trans. *The Ten Thousand Leaves: A Translation of the Man'yōshū, Japan's Premier Anthology of Classical Poetry.* Vol. 1. Princeton, N.J.: Princeton University Press, 1981.

Miller, Roy Andrew. "A Korean Poet in Eighth-Century Japan." *Korea Journal* 25, no. 11 (1985): 4–21.

Miller, Roy Andrew. "The Lost Poetic Sequence of the Priest Manzei." *Monumenta Nipponica* 36, no. 2 (1981): 133–172.

Nippon gakujutsu shinkōkai, ed. *The Man'yōshū: One Thousand Poems.* New York: Columbia University Press, 1983.

Wright, Harold, trans. *Ten Thousand Leaves: Love Poems from the Man'yōshū.* Woodstock, N.Y.: Overlook Press, 1986.

Yasuda, Kenneth K., trans. *Land of the Reed Plains: Ancient Japanese Lyrics from the Man'yōshū.* Rutland, Vt: Turtle, 1960.

THE HEIAN PERIOD

LaMarre, Thomas. *Uncovering Heian Japan: An Archeology of Sensation and Inscription.* Durham, N.C.: Duke University Press, 2000.

Ramirez-Christensen, Esperanza, and Rebecca L. Copeland, eds. *The Father/Daughter Plot: Japanese Literary Women.* Honolulu: University of Hawai'i Press, 2001.

Stevenson, Barbara, and Cynthia Ho, eds. *Crossing the Bridge: Comparative Essays on Medieval European and Heian Japanese Women Writers.* New York: Palgrave, 2000.

Yoda, Tomiko. *Gender and National Literature: Heian Texts in the Constructions of Japanese Modernity.* Durham, N.C.: Duke University Press, 2004.

Record of Miraculous Events in Japan

Nakamura, Kyoko, trans. *Miraculous Stories from the Japanese Buddhist Tradition.* Cambridge, Mass.: Harvard University Press, 1973.

Philippi, Donald L. "Two Tales from the *Nippon ryōiki.*" *Journal of the Association of Teachers of Japanese* 5 (1960): 53–55.

Ono no Komachi

Fischer, Felice Renee. "Ono no Komachi—A Ninth-Century Poetess of Heian Japan." Ph.D. diss., Columbia University, 1975.

Hirshfield, Jane, and Mariko Aratani, trans. *The Ink Dark Moon: Love Poems by Ono no Komachi and Izumi Shikibu, Women of the Ancient Court of Japan.* New York: Scribner, 1988.

Strong, Sarah M. "The Making of a Femme Fatale: Ono no Komachi in the Early Medieval Commentaries." *Monumenta Nipponica* 49, no. 4 (1994): 391–412.

Teele, Roy E., Nicholas J. Teele, and Rebecca Teele. *Ono no Komachi: Poems, Stories, Nō Plays*. New York: Garland, 1993.

Watson, Burton, trans. "Ono no Komachi." *Montemora* 5 (1979): 128–132.

Sugawara no Michizane

Borgen, Robert. "Ōe no Masafusa and the Spirit of Michizane." *Monumenta Nipponica* 50, no. 3 (1995): 357–384.

Borgen, Robert. *Sugawara no Michizane and the Early Heian Court*. Harvard East Asian Monographs, no. 120. Cambridge, Mass.: Harvard University Press, 1986.

Watson, Burton. *Japanese Literature in Chinese*. Vol. 1, *Poetry and Prose in Chinese by Japanese Writers of the Early Period*. New York: Columbia University Press, 1975.

Watson, Burton. "Michizane and the Plums." *Japan Quarterly* 11 (1964): 217–220.

Classical Poetry

Bownas, Geoffrey, and Anthony Thwaite, trans, and eds. *The Penguin Book of Japanese Verse*. London: Penguin, 1964.

Brower, Robert H., and Earl Miner. "Formative Elements in the Japanese Poetic Tradition." *Journal of Asian Studies* 16 (1957): 503–527.

Brower, Robert H., and Earl Miner. *Japanese Court Poetry*. Stanford, Calif.: Stanford University Press, 1961.

Carter, Steven D., trans, and intro. *Traditional Japanese Poetry: An Anthology*. Stanford, Calif.: Stanford University Press, 1991.

Ceadel, E. B. "The Ōi River Poems and Preface." *Asia Major* 3 (1952): 65–106.

Ceadel, E. B. "Tadamine's Preface to the Ōi River Poems." *Bulletin of the School of Oriental and African Studies* 18 (1956): 331–343.

Cranston, Edwin A. "The Dark Path: Images of Longing in Japanese Poetry." *Harvard Journal of Asiatic Studies* 35 (1975): 60–100.

Cranston, Edwin A. "The Poetry of Izumi Shikibu." *Monumenta Nipponica* 25 (1970): 1–11.

Harries, Phillip T. "Personal Poetry Collections: Their Origin and Development Through the Heian Period." *Monumenta Nipponica* 35, no. 3 (1980): 299–317.

Kamens, Edward. "Dragon-Girl, Maidenflower, Buddha: The Transformation of a Waka Topos, 'The Five Obstructions.'" *Harvard Journal of Asiatic Studies* 53, no. 2 (1993): 389–442.

Kamens, Edward. *Utamakura, Allusion, and Intertextuality in Traditional Japanese Poetry*. New Haven, Conn.: Yale University Press, 1997.

Konishi Jin'ichi. "Association and Progression: Principles of Integration in Anthologies and Sequences of Japanese Court Poetry: A.D. 900–1350." Translated by Robert H. Brower and Earl Miner. *Harvard Journal of Asiatic Studies* 21 (1958): 67–127.

LaMarre, Thomas. "Writing Doubled Over, Broken: Provisional Names, Acrostic Poems, and the Perpetual Contest of Doubles in Heian Japan." *Positions* 2, no. 2 (1994): 250–273.

Miner, Earl. *An Introduction to Japanese Court Poetry*. Stanford, Calif: Stanford University Press, 1968.

Miner, Earl. "Japanese and Western Images of Courtly Love." *Yearbook of Comparative and General Literature* 15 (1966): 174–179.

Miner, Earl. "Waka: Features of Its Constitution and Development." *Harvard Journal of Asiatic Studies* 50, no. 2 (1990): 669–706.

Morrell, Robert E. "The Buddhist Poetry in the *Goshūishū*." *Monumenta Nipponica* 28 (1973): 87–100.

Morris, Mark. "Waka and Form, Waka and History." *Harvard Journal of Asiatic Studies* 46, no. 2 (1986): 551–610.

Ooka Makoto. "Color, Colors, and Colorlessness in Early Japanese Poetry." Translated by Hiroaki Sato. *Chanoyu Quarterly* 41 (1985): 35–49.

Rexroth, Kenneth, trans. *Love Poems from the Japanese*. Edited by Sam Hamill. Boston: Shambhala, 1994.

Rexroth, Kenneth, trans. *One Hundred More Poems from the Japanese*. New York: New Directions, 1976.

Rexroth, Kenneth, trans. *One Hundred Poems from the Japanese*. New York: New Directions, 1964.

Rexroth, Kenneth, and Ikuko Atsumi, trans. *The Burning Heart: Women Poets of Japan*. New York: Seabury Press, 1977.

Smits, Ivo. "The Poem as a Painting: Landscape Poetry in Late Heian Japan." *Transactions of the Asiatic Society of Japan*, 4th ser., 6 (1991): 61–86.

Smits, Ivo. *The Pursuit of Loneliness: Chinese and Japanese Nature Poetry in Medieval Japan, ca.* 1050–1150. Stuttgart: Steiner, 1995.

Smits, Ivo. "Unusual Expressions: Minamoto no Toshiyori and Poetic Innovation in Medieval Japan." *Transactions of the Asiatic Society of Japan*, 4th ser., 8 (1993): 85–106.

Walker, Janet A. "Conventions of Love Poetry in Japan and the West." *Journal of the Association of Teachers of Japanese* 14, no. 1 (1980): 31–65.

Kokinshū

Ceadel, E. B. "The Two Prefaces of the *Kokinshū*." *Asia Major*, n.s., 7, pts. 1–2 (1968): 40–51.

Konishi Jin'ichi. "The Genesis of the *Kokinshū* Style." Translated by Helen Craig McCullough. *Harvard Journal of Asiatic Studies* 38 (1978): 61–170.

McCullough, Helen Craig. *Brocade by Night: Kokin wakashū and the Court Style in Classical Japanese Poetry*. Stanford, Calif.: Stanford University Press, 1985.

McCullough, Helen Craig, trans. *Kokin wakashū: The First Imperial Anthology of Japanese Poetry, with Tosa nikki and Shinsen waka*. Stanford, Calif.: Stanford University Press, 1985.

Rodd, Laura Rasplica, and Mary Catherine Henkenius, trans. *Kokinshū: A Collection of Poems Ancient and Modern*. Princeton, N.J.: Princeton University Press, 1984.

Wixted, John Timothy. "The *Kokinshū* Prefaces: Another Perspective." *Harvard Journal of Asiatic Studies* 43, no. 1 (1983):215–238.

The Tale of the Bamboo Cutter and Other Early Tales

Cranston, Edwin A. "Atemiya, a Translation from the *Utsubo monogatari*." *Monumenta Nipponica* 24, no. 3 (1969): 289–314.

Keene, Donald, trans. "The Tale of the Bamboo Cutter." *Monumenta Nipponica* 11, no. 4 (1956): 1–127.

Kristeva, Tsvetana. "The Pattern of Signification in the *Taketori monogatari*: The 'Ancestor' of All Monogatari." *Japan Forum* 2, no. 2 (1990): 253–260.

Lammers, Wayne P. "'The Succession' (*Kuniyuzuri*): A Translation from *Utsuho monogatari*." *Monumenta Nipponica* 37, no. 2 (1982): 139–178.

Whitehouse, Wilfred, and Eizo Yanagisawa, trans. *The Tale of Lady Ochikubo*. New York: Doubleday Anchor, 1971.

The Tales of Ise and Other Poem Tales

Bowring, Richard. "The *Ise monogatari*: A Short Cultural History." *Harvard Journal of Asiatic Studies* 52 (1992): 401–480.

Harris, H. Jay, trans. *Tales of Ise*. Tokyo: Tuttle, 1972.

Klein, Susan Blakeley. "Allegories of Desire: Poetry and Eroticism in *Ise monogatari zuinō*." *Monumenta Nipponica* 52, no. 4 (1997): 441–465; 53, no. 1 (1998): 13–43.

McCullough, Helen Craig, trans. *Tales of Ise: Lyrical Episodes from 10th-Century Japan*. Stanford, Calif: Stanford University Press, 1968.

Tahara, Mildred. "Heichū, as Seen in *Yamato monogatari*." *Monumenta Nipponica* 26, nos. 1–2 (1971): 17–48.

Tahara, Mildred. "Yamato monogatari." *Monumenta Nipponica* 27, no. 1 (1972): 1–37.

Tahara, Mildred, trans. *Tales of Yamato: A Tenth-Century Poem-Tale*. Honolulu: University of Hawai'i Press, 1980.

Videen, Susan Downing. *Tales of Heichū*. Cambridge, Mass.: Harvard University Press, 1989.

Vos, Frits. *A Study of the Ise-monogatari*. 2 vols. The Hague: Mouton, 1957.

Tosa Diary

McCullough, Helen Craig, trans. *Kokin wakashū: The First Imperial Anthology of Japanese Poetry, with Tosa nikki and Shinsen waka*. Stanford, Calif.: Stanford University Press, 1985.

Viswanathan, Meera. "Poetry, Play, and the Court in the *Tosa nikki*." *Comparative Literature Studies* 28, no. 4 (1991): 416–432.

Kagerō Diary

Arntzen, Sonja, trans. *The Kagero Diary*. Ann Arbor: University of Michigan Press, 1997.

Mostow, Joshua S. "The Amorous Statesman and the Poetess: The Politics of Autobiography and the *Kagerō nikki*." *Japan Forum* 4, no. 2 (1992): 305–315.

Mostow, Joshua S. "Self and Landscape in *Kagerō nikki*." *Review of Japanese Culture and Society* 5 (1993): 8–19.

Seidensticker, Edward G., trans. *The Gossamer Years: The Diary of a Noblewoman of Heian Japan*. Rutland, Vt.: Tuttle, 1964.

Watanabe, Minoru. "Style and Point of View in the *Kagerō nikki*." Translated by Richard Bowring. *Journal of Japanese Studies* 10, no. 2 (1984): 365–384.

The Pillow Book

Morris, Ivan, trans. *The Pillow Book of Sei Shōnagon*. 2 vols. New York: Columbia University Press, 1967, 1991.

Morris, Mark. "Sei Shōnagon's Poetic Catalogues." *Harvard Journal of Asiatic Studies* 40 (1980): 5–54.

Waley, Arthur, trans. *The Pillow-Book of Sei Shōnagon*. London: Allen & Unwin, 1957.

Japanese and Chinese Poems to Sing

Rimer, J. Thomas, and Jonathan Chaves, eds. and trans. *Japanese and Chinese Poems to Sing*. New York: Columbia University Press, 1997.

Smits, Ivo. "Song as Cultural History: Reading *Wakan rōeishū* (Texts)." *Monumenta Nipponica* 55, no. 2 (2000): 225–256.

Smits, Ivo. "Song as Cultural History: Reading *Wakan rōeishū* (Interpretations)." *Monumenta Nipponica* 55, no. 3 (2000): 399–427.

The Tale of Genji

Abe, Akio. "The Contemporary Studies of *Genji monogatari*." *Acta Asiatica* 6 (1964): 41–56.

Abe, Akio. "Murasaki Shikibu's View on the Nature of Monogatari." *Acta Asiatica* 11 (1966): 1–10.

Bargen, Doris G. "The Search for Things Past in the *Genji monogatari*." *Harvard Journal of Asiatic Studies* 51, no. 1 (1991): 199–232.

Bargen, Doris G. *A Woman's Weapon: Spirit Possession in The Tale of Genji*. Honolulu: University of Hawai'i Press, 1997.

Bowring, Richard. *Murasaki Shikibu: The Tale of Genji*. Landmarks of World Literature. Cambridge: Cambridge University Press, 1988.

Cranston, Edwin A. "Aspects of *The Tale of Genji*." *Journal of the Association of Teachers of Japanese* 11 (1976): 183–199.

Dalby, Liza. "The Cultured Nature of Heian Colors." *Transactions of the Asiatic Society of Japan* 3 (1988): 1–19.

De Gruchy, John Walter. *Orienting Arthur Waley: Japonism, Orientalism, and the Creation of Japanese Literature in English*. Honolulu: University of Hawai'i Press, 2003.

Field, Norma. *The Splendor of Longing in the Tale of Genji*. Princeton, N.J.: Princeton University Press, 1987.

Fujii, Sadakazu. "The Relationship Between the Romance and Religious Observances: *Genji monogatari* as Myth." *Japanese Journal of Religious Studies* 9, nos. 2–3 (1982): 127–146.

Gatten, Aileen. "Death and Salvation in *Genji monogatari*." In *New Leaves: Studies and Translations of Japanese Literature in Honor of Edward Seidensticker*, edited by Aileen Gatten and Anthony Hood Chambers, 5–27. Ann Arbor: University of Michigan Press, 1993.

Gatten, Aileen. "Murasaki's Literary Roots." *Journal of the Association of Teachers of Japanese* 17 (1982): 173–191.

Gatten, Aileen. "The Order of the Early Chapters in the *Genji monogatari.*" *Harvard Journal of Asiatic Studies* 41, no. 1 (1981): 5–46.

Gatten, Aileen. "Weird Ladies: Narrative Strategy in the *Genji monogatari.*" *Journal of the Association of Teachers of Japanese* 20, no. 1 (1986): 29–48.

Gatten, Aileen. "A Wisp of Smoke: Scent and Character in the *Tale of Genji.*" *Monumenta Nipponica* 32 (1977): 35–48.

Harper, Thomas J. "Genji Gossip." In *New Leaves: Studies and Translations of Japanese Literature in Honor of Edward Seidensticker*, edited by Aileen Gatten and Anthony Hood Chambers, 29–44. Ann Arbor: University of Michigan Press, 1993.

Harper, Thomas J. "Medieval Interpretations of Murasaki Shikibu's 'Defence of the Art of Fiction.'" In *Studies in Japanese Culture*, edited by Saburo Ota and Rikutaro Fukuda, 1:56–61. Tokyo: Japan P.E.N. Club, 1973.

Harper, Thomas J., trans. "More Genji Gossip." *Journal of the Association of Teachers of Japanese* 28 (1994): 175–182.

Kamens, Edward, ed. *Approaches to Teaching Murasaki Shikibu's The Tale of Genji.* New York: Modern Language Association of America, 1993.

Kobayashi, Yoshiko. "The Function of Music in the *Tale of Genji.*" *Journal of Comparative Literature* 33 (1990): 253–260.

Mills, Douglas E. "Murasaki Shikibu—Saint or Sinner?" *Japan Society of London Bulletin* 90 (1980): 3–14.

Morris, Ivan. *The Tale of Genji Scroll.* Palo Alto, Calif.: Kodansha, 1971.

Morris, Ivan, ed. *Madly Singing in the Mountains.* London: Allen & Unwin, 1970.

Mostow, Joshua S. "*E no gotoshi*: The Picture Simile and the Feminine Re-guard in Japanese Illustrated Romances." *Word & Image* 11, no. 1 (1995): 37–54.

Murase, Miyeko. *Iconography of the Tale of Genji: Genji monogatari ekotoba.* Tokyo: Weatherhill, 1983.

Noguchi, Takehiko. "The Substratum Constituting Monogatari: Prose Structure and Narrative in the *Genji monogatari.*" In *Principles of Classical Japanese Literature*, edited by Earl Miner, 130–150. Princeton, N.J.: Princeton University Press, 1985.

Okada, H. Richard. *Figures of Resistance: Language, Poetry, and Narrating in The Tale of Genji and Other Mid-Heian Texts.* Durham, N.C.: Duke University Press, 1991.

Pekarik, Andrew, ed. *Ukifune: Love in the Tale of Genji.* New York: Columbia University Press, 1982.

Pollack, David. "The Informing Image: 'China' in *Genji monogatari.*" *Monumenta Nipponica* 38, no. 4 (1983): 359–375.

Puette, William J. *Guide to The Tale of Genji.* Rutland, Vt: Tuttle, 1983.

Ramirez-Christensen, Esperanza. "The Operation of the Lyrical Mode in the *Genji monogatari.*" In *Ukifune: Love in the Tale of Genji*, edited by Andrew Pekarik, 21–61. New York: Columbia University Press, 1982.

Rimer, J. Thomas. *Modern Japanese Fiction and Its Traditions: An Introduction.* Princeton, N.J.: Princeton University Press, 1978.

Rowley, G. G. *Yosano Akiko and The Tale of Genji.* Ann Arbor: Center for Japanese Studies, University of Michigan, 2000.

Seidensticker, Edward G. "Chiefly on Translating the *Genji.*" *Journal of Japanese Studies* 6, no. 1 (1980): 16–47.

Seidensticker, Edward G., trans. *The Tale of Genji*. New York: Knopf, 1976, 1981.

Shirane, Haruo. "The Aesthetics of Power: Politics in *The Tale of Genji*." *Harvard Journal of Asiatic Studies* 45, no. 2 (1985): 615–647.

Shirane, Haruo. *The Bridge of Dreams: A Poetics of The Tale of Genji*. Stanford, Calif.: Stanford University Press, 1987.

Shirane, Haruo. "The Uji Chapters and the Denial of the Romance." In *Ukifune: Love in the Tale of Genji*, edited by Andrew Pekarik, 113–138. New York: Columbia University Press, 1982.

Stinchecum, Amanda Mayer. "Who Tells the Tale? 'Ukifune': A Study in Narrative Voice." *Monumenta Nipponica* 35 (1980): 375–403.

Tyler, Royall. "I Am I: Genji and Murasaki." *Monumenta Nipponica* 54, no. 4 (1999): 435–480.

Tyler, Royall. "Lady Murasaki's Erotic Entertainment: The Early Chapters of *The Tale of Genji*." *East Asian History* no. 12 (1996): 65–78.

Tyler, Royall. "Rivalry, Triumph, Folly, Revenge: A Plot Line Through *The Tale of Genji*." *Journal of Japanese Studies* 29, no. 2 (2003): 251–287.

Tyler, Royall, trans. *The Tale of Genji*. New York: Viking, 2001.

Tyler, Royall, and Susan Tyler. "The Possession of Ukifune." *Asiatica Venetiana*, no. 5 (2000): 177–209.

Ueda, Makoto. "Truth and Falsehood in Fiction: Lady Murasaki on the Art of the Novel." In *Literary and Art Theories in Japan*, edited by Makoto Ueda, 25–36. Cleveland: Press of Western Reserve University, 1967.

Ury, Marian. "The Real Murasaki." *Monumenta Nipponica* 38, no. 2 (1983): 175–189.

Ury, Marian. "*The Tale of Genji* in English." *Yearbook of Comparative and General Literature* 31 (1982): 62–67.

Waley, Arthur, trans. *The Tale of Genji*. London: Allen & Unwin, 1957.

Zolbrod, Leon. "The Four-Part Theoretical Structure of *The Tale of Genji*." *Journal of the Association of Teachers of Japanese* 15, no. 1 (1980): 22–31.

Murasaki Shikibu's Diary

Bowring, Richard. *The Diary of Murasaki Shikibu*. London: Penguin, 1996.

Omori, Annie Shepley, and Kōchi Doi. *Diaries of Court Ladies of Old Japan*. Tokyo: Kenkyūsha, 1961.

Sarashina Diary

Morris, Ivan, trans. *As I Crossed a Bridge of Dreams: Recollections of a Woman in Eleventh-Century Japan*. New York: Dial Press, 1971.

Other Literary Diaries

Bowring, Richard. "Japanese Diaries and the Nature of Literature." *Comparative Literature Studies* 18, no. 2 (1981): 167–174.

Brazell, Karen W., trans. *The Confessions of Lady Nijō*. Stanford, Calif.: Stanford University Press, 1976.

Cranston, Edwin A. *The Izumi Shikibu Diary: A Romance of the Heian Court*. Cambridge, Mass: Harvard University Press, 1969.

Kristeva, Tsvetana. "Japanese Lyrical Diaries and the European Autobiographical Tradition." In *Europe Interprets Japan*, edited by Gorden Daniels, 155–162. Tenterden: Norbury, 1984.

Miller, Marilyn Jeanne. *The Poetics of Nikki bungaku*. New York: Garland, 1985.

Miner, Earl, trans. *Japanese Poetic Diaries*. Berkeley: University of California Press, 1969.

Omori, Annie Shepley, and Kōchi Doi. *Diaries of Court Ladies of Old Japan*. Tokyo: Kenkyūsha, 1961.

Sarra, Edith. *Fictions of Femininity: Literary Conventions of Gender in Japanese Court Women's Memoirs*. Stanford, Calif.: Stanford University Press, 1999.

Ury, Marian. "Ōe no Masafusa and the Practice of Heian Autobiography." *Monumenta Nipponica* 51 (1996): 143–152.

Walker, Janet A. "Poetic Ideal and Fictional Reality in the *Izumi Shikibu nikki*." *Harvard Journal of Asiatic Studies* 37, no. 1 (1977): 135–182.

Wallace, John R. "Reading the Rhetoric of Seduction in *Izumi Shikibu nikki*." *Harvard Journal of Asiatic Studies* 58, no. 2 (1998): 481–512.

Literary Essence of Our Country

Watson, Burton. *Japanese Literature in Chinese*. 2 vols. New York: Columbia University Press, 1975, 1976.

The Stories of the Riverside Middle Counselor

Backus, Robert L., trans. *The Riverside Counselor's Stories: Vernacular Fiction of Late Heian Japan*. Stanford, Calif.: Stanford University Press, 1985.

Benl, Oscar. "Tsutsumi chūnagon monogatari." *Monumenta Nipponica* 3, no. 3 (1940): 504–524.

Hirano, Umeyo, trans. *The Tsutsumi chūnagon monogatari: A Collection of 11th-Century Short Stories of Japan*. Tokyo: Hokuseido Press, 1963.

Reischauer, Edwin O., and Joseph K. Yamagiwa. *Translations from Early Japanese Literature*. Cambridge, Mass.: Harvard University Press, 1951.

Waley, Arthur, trans. "The Lady Who Loved Insects." In *Anthology of Japanese Literature: From the Earliest Era to the Mid-Nineteenth Century*, edited by Donald Keene, 170–176. New York: Grove Press, 1955.

The Tale of Sagoromo

D'Etcheverry, Charo B. "Out of the Mouths of Nurses: *The Tale of Sagoromo* and Mid-Rank Romance." *Monumenta Nipponica* 59, no. 2 (2004): 153–177.

Late Heian Tales

Hochstedler, Carol, trans. *The Tale of Nezame: Part Three of "Yowa no Nezame monogatari."* Cornell University East Asia Papers, no. 22. Ithaca, N.Y.: China-Japan Program, Cornell University, 1979.

McCullough, William H., and Helen Craig McCullough, trans. *A Tale of Flowering Fortunes: Annals of Japanese Aristocratic Life in the Heian Period*. 2 vols. Stanford, Calif.: Stanford University Press, 1980.

Pflugfelder, Gregory. "Strange Fates: Sex, Gender, and Sexuality in *Torikaebaya mono-gatari*." *Monumenta Nipponica* 47, no. 3 (1992): 347–368.

Rohlich, Thomas H., trans. *A Tale of Eleventh-Century Japan: Hamamatsu chūnagon monogatari*. Princeton, N.J.: Princeton University Press, 1983.

Willig, Rosette F., trans. *The Changelings: A Classical Japanese Court Tale*. Stanford, Calif.: Stanford University Press, 1983.

The Great Mirror and Other Mirror Histories

McCullough, Helen Craig, trans. *Ōkagami: The Great Mirror; Fujiwara Michinaga (966–1027) and His Times*. Princeton, N.J.: Princeton University Press, 1980.

Perkins, George, trans. *The Clear Mirror: A Chronicle of Japan During the Kamakura Period*. Stanford, Calif.: Stanford University Press, 1998.

Yamagiwa, Joseph K., trans. *The Ōkagami*. London: Allen & Unwin, 1967.

Collection of Tales of Times Now Past

Brower, Robert H. "The *Konjaku monogatarisyū*." Ph.D. diss., University of Michigan, 1952.

Dykstra, Yoshiko Kurata, trans. *The Konjaku Tales: Indian Section: From a Medieval Japanese Collection*. Osaka: Intercultural Research Institute, Kansai University of Foreign Studies, 1986.

Jones, S. W., trans. *Ages Ago: Thirty-seven Tales from the Konjaku monogatari Collection*. Cambridge, Mass: Harvard University Press, 1959.

Kelsey, W. Michael. *Konjaku monogatari shū*. Boston: Twayne, 1982.

Kelsey, W. Michael. "*Konjaku monogatari-shū*: Toward an Understanding of Its Literary Qualities." *Monumenta Nipponica* 30, no. 2 (1975): 121–150.

Ury, Marian, trans. *Tales of Times Now Past: Sixty-two Stories from a Medieval Japanese Collection*. Berkeley: University of California Press, 1979.

Wilson, William Ritchie. "The Way of the Bow and Arrow: The Japanese Warrior in *Konjaku monogatari*." *Monumenta Nipponica* 28 (1973): 177–233.

Treasured Selections of Superb Songs

Kim, Yung-Hee. *Songs to Make the Dust Dance on the Beams: The Ryōjin hishō of Twelfth-Century Japan*. Berkeley: University of California Press, 1994.

Kwon, Yung-Hee. "The Emperor's Songs: Emperor Go-Shirakawa and *Ryōjin hishō kudenshū*." *Monumenta Nipponica* 41, no. 3 (1986): 261–298.

Kwon, Yung-Hee. "Voices from the Periphery: Love Songs in *Ryōjin hishō*." *Monumenta Nipponica* 41, no. 1 (1986): 1–20.

Moriguchi, Yasuhiko, and David Jenkins, trans. *The Dance of the Dust on the Rafters: Selections from Ryōjin-hishō*. Seattle: Broken Moon Press, 1990.

Nakahara, Gladys. *A Translation of Ryōjin-hishō: A Compendium of Japanese Folk Songs (Imayō) of the Heian Period*, 794–1185. Lewiston, N.Y.: Mellen, 2003.

THE KAMAKURA PERIOD

Saigyō

Allen, Laura W. "Images of the Poet Saigyō as Recluse." *Journal of Japanese Studies* 21, no. 1 (1995): 65–102.

Heldt, Gustav. "Saigyō's Traveling Tale: A Translation of *Saigyō monogatari*." *Monumenta Nipponica* 52, no. 4 (1997): 467–521.

LaFleur, William R. "The Death and the 'Lives' of Saigyō: The Genesis of a Buddhist Sacred Bibliography." In *The Biographical Process: Studies in the History and Psychology of Religion*, edited by Frank E. Reynolds and Donald Capps, 343–361. The Hague: Mouton, 1976.

LaFleur, William R., trans. *Mirror for the Moon: A Selection of Poems by Saigyō* (1118–1190). New York: New Directions, 1978.

Takagi, Kiyoko. "Saigyō: A Search for Religion." *Japanese Journal of Religious Studies* 4, no. 1 (1977): 41–74.

Watanabe, Manabu. "Religious Symbolism in Saigyō's Verses: A Contribution to Discussions of His Views on Nature and Religion." *History of Religions* 26, no. 4 (1987): 382–400.

Watson, Burton, trans. *Saigyō: Poems of a Mountain Home*. New York: Columbia University Press, 1991.

Fujiwara no Shunzei

Hisamatsu, Sen'ichi. "Fujiwara Shunzei and Literary Theories of the Middle Ages." *Acta Asiatica* 1 (1960): 29–42.

Royston, Clifton. "The Poetics and Poetry Criticism of Fujiwara Shunzei." Ph.D. diss., University of Michigan, 1974.

Shirane, Haruo. "Lyricism and Intertextuality: An Approach to Shunzei's Poetics." *Harvard Journal of Asiatic Studies* 50 (1990): 71–85.

Poetry Matches

Huey, Robert N. "Fushimi-in Nijūban Uta-awase." *Monumenta Nipponica* 48, no. 2 (1993): 167–203.

Huey, Robert N. "The Kingyoku Poetry Contest." *Monumenta Nipponica* 42, no. 3 (1987): 299–330.

Ito, Setsuko. *An Anthology of Traditional Japanese Poetry Competition, Uta-awase, 913–1815*. Bochum: Brockmeyer, 1991.

Ito, Setsuko. "The Muse in Competition: *Uta-awase* Through the Ages." *Monumenta Nipponica* 37, no. 2 (1982): 201–222.

Royston, Clifton. "Utaawase Judgements as Poetry Criticism." *Journal of Asian Studies* 34 (1974): 99–108.

Fujiwara no Teika

Brower, Robert H. *Fujiwara Teika's Hundred Poem Sequence of the Shōji Era, 1200*. Monumenta Nipponica Monograph, no. 55. Tokyo: Sophia University Press, 1978.

Brower, Robert H. "Fujiwara Teika's *Maigetsushō*." *Monumenta Nipponica* 40, no. 4 (1985): 399–425.

Brower, Robert H., and Earl Miner. *Fujiwara Teika's Superior Poems of Our Time: A Thirteenth-Century Poetic Treatise and Sequence*. Stanford, Calif.: Stanford University Press, 1967.

Bundy, Roselee. "Poetic Apprenticeship: Fujiwara Teika's *Shogaku hyakushu*." *Monumenta Nipponica* 45, no. 2 (1990): 157–188.

Kamens, Edward. "The Past in the Present: Fujiwara Teika and the Traditions of Japanese Poetry." In *Word in Flower: The Visualization of Classical Literature in Seventeenth Century Japan*, edited by Carolyn Wheelwright, 16–28. New Haven, Conn.: Yale University Art Gallery, 1989.

Lammers, Wayne P. *The Tale of Matsura: Fujiwara Teika's Experiment in Fiction*. Michigan Monograph Series in Japanese Studies, no. 9. Ann Arbor: Center for Japanese Studies, University of Michigan, 1992.

Smits, Ivo. "The Poet and the Politician: Teika and the Compilation of the *Shinchokusenshū*." *Monumenta Nipponica* 53, no. 4 (1998): 427–472.

Shinkokinshū

Bialock, David. "Voice, Text, and the Question of Poetic Borrowing in Late Classical Japanese Poetry." *Harvard Journal of Asiatic Studies* 54 (1994): 181–231.

Brower, Robert H. "Ex-Emperor Gotoba's Secret Teachings: *Gotoba no in Gokuden*." *Harvard Journal of Asiatic Studies* 32 (1972): 3–70.

Morrell, Robert E. "The *Shinkokinshū*: 'Poems on Sakyamuni's Teachings (*Shakkyōka*).'" In *The Distant Isle: Studies and Translations in Honor of Robert H. Brower*, edited by Thomas B. Hare, Robert Borgen, and Sharalyn Orbaugh, 281–320. Ann Arbor: Center for Japanese Studies, University of Michigan, 1996.

One Hundred Poems

Carter, Steven D., trans. "One Hundred Poems by One Hundred Poets." In *Traditional Japanese Poetry: An Anthology*, translated, with an introduction, by Steven D. Carter, 206–238. Stanford, Calif: Stanford University Press, 1991.

Galt, Tom, trans. *The Little Treasury of One Hundred People, One Poem Each*. Princeton, N.J.: Princeton University Press, 1982.

Mostow, Joshua S. *Pictures of the Heart: The Hyakunin isshu in Word and Image*. Honolulu: University of Hawai'i Press, 1996.

Other Medieval Poets and Poetry

Brower, Robert H. "The Foremost Style of Poetic Composition: Fujiwara Tameie's *Eiga no Ittei*." *Monumenta Nipponica* 42, no. 4 (1987): 391–429.

Brower, Robert H. "The Reizei Family Documents." *Monumenta Nipponica* 36, no. 4 (1981): 445–461.

Bundy, Roselee. "*Santai waka*: Six Poems in Three Modes." *Monumenta Nipponica* 49, nos. 2–3 (1994): 197–227, 261–286.

Cranston, Edwin A. "'Mystery and Depth' in Japanese Court Poetry." In *The Distant Isle: Studies and Translations in Honor of Robert H. Brower*, edited by Thomas B.

Hare, Robert Borgen, and Sharalyn Orbaugh, 65–104. Ann Arbor: Center for Japanese Studies, University of Michigan, 1996.

Fujiwara, Yoshitsune. *The Complete Poetry Collection of Fujiwara Yoshitsune* (1169–1206). Yokohama: Warm-Soft Village Branch K-L, 1986.

Huey, Robert N. *Kyōgoku Tamekane: Poetry and Politics in Late Kamakura Japan.* Stanford, Calif.: Stanford University Press, 1989.

Huey, Robert N. "The Medievalization of Poetic Practice." *Harvard Journal of Asiatic Studies* 50, no. 2 (1990): 651–668.

Huey, Robert N. "Warrior Control over the Imperial Anthology." In *The Origins of Japan's Medieval World: Courtiers, Clerics, Warriors, and Peasants in the Fourteenth Century,* edited by Jeffrey P. Mass, 170–191. Stanford, Calif: Stanford University Press, 1997.

Huey, Robert N., and Susan Matisoff. *"Tamekanekyō wakashō:* Lord Tamekane's Notes on Poetry." *Monumenta Nipponica* 40, no. 2 (1985): 127–146.

Kubota, Jun. "Allegory and Thought in Medieval *waka*—Concentrating on Jien's Works Prior to the Jōkyū Disturbance." *Acta Asiatica* 37 (1979): 1–28.

Kamo no Chōmei

Gerling, Reuben. "The Fictional Dimension of Chōmei's *Hōjōki.*" *Bulletin of the European Association for Japanese Studies* 23 (1985): 8–16.

Hare, Thomas B. "Reading Kamo no Chōmei." *Harvard Journal of Asiatic Studies* 49, no. 1 (1989): 173–228.

Katō, Hilda. "The *Mumyōshō* of Kamo no Chōmei and Its Significance in Japanese Literature." *Monumenta Nipponica* 23, no. 3 (1968): 321–430.

Keene, Donald, trans. "Hōjōki." In *Anthology of Japanese Literature: From the Earliest Era to the Mid-Nineteenth Century,* edited by Donald Keene, 197–212. New York: Grove Press, 1955.

Marra, Michele. "Semi-Recluses (*tonseisha*) and Impermanence (*mujō*): Kamo no Chōmei and Urabe Kenkō." *Japanese Journal of Religious Studies* 11 (1984): 313–350.

Moriguchi, Yasuhiko, and David Jenkins, trans. *Hōjōki: Visions of a Torn World.* Berkeley, Calif.: Stone Bridge Press, 1996.

Sadler, A. L., trans. *The Ten Foot Square Hut and Tales of the Heike.* Westport, Conn.: Greenwood Press, 1970.

A Collection of Tales from Uji

Foster, John S., trans. *"Uji shūi monogatari:* Selected Translation." *Monumenta Nipponica* 20 (1965): 135–208.

Mills, Douglas E., trans. *A Collection of Tales from Uji: A Study and Translation of Uji shūi monogatari.* Cambridge: Cambridge University Press, 1970.

Other Collections of Anecdotes (*Setsuwa*)

Dykstra, Yoshiko Kurata. "Jizō, the Most Merciful: Tales from *Jizō Bosatsu reigenki.*" *Monumenta Nipponica* 33 (1978): 179–200.

Dykstra, Yoshiko Kurata. "Tales of the Compassionate Kannon: *The Hasedera Kannon genki.*" *Monumenta Nipponica* 31 (1976): 113–143.

Geddes, Ward. *Kara monogatari: Tales of China.* Occasional Paper, no. 16. Tempe: Center for Asian Studies, Arizona State University, 1984.

Kamens, Edward, trans. *The Three Jewels: A Study and Translation of Minamoto Tamenori's Sanbōe.* Ann Arbor: Center for Japanese Studies, University of Michigan, 1988.

Kelsey, W. Michael. "Salvation of the Snake, the Snake of Salvation: Buddhist–Shintō Conflict and Resolution." *Japanese Journal of Religious Studies* 8, no. 1 (1981): 83–113.

Moore, Jean Frances. "*Senjūshō*: Buddhist Tales of Renunciation." *Monumenta Nipponica* 41, no. 2 (1986): 127–143.

Morrell, Robert E. "Mirror for Women: Mujū Ichien's *Tsuma kagami.*" *Monumenta Nipponica* 35 (1980): 45–75.

Morrell, Robert E. "Mujū Ichien's Shinto–Buddhist Syncretism—*Shasekishū*, Book 1." *Monumenta Nipponica* 28 (1973): 447–488.

Morrell, Robert E., trans. *Sand and Pebbles (Shasekishū): The Tales of Mujū Ichien, a Voice for Pluralism in Kamakura Buddhism.* Albany: State University of New York Press, 1985.

Pandey, Rajyashree. "Women, Sexuality, and Enlightenment: *Kankyo no Tomo.*" *Monumenta Nipponica* 50, no. 3 (1995): 325–356.

Rodd, Laurel. "Nichiren and *setsuwa.*" *Japanese Journal of Religious Studies* 5, nos. 2–3 (1978): 159–185.

Tyler, Royall, trans. *Japanese Tales.* New York: Pantheon, 1987.

Ury, Marian. "Recluses and Eccentric Monks: Tales from the *Hosshinshū* by Kamo no Chōmei." *Monumenta Nipponica* 27, no. 2 (1972): 149–173.

The Tales of Hōgen

Kellog, E. R. "Hōgen monogatari." *Transactions of the Asiatic Society of Japan* 45, no. 1 (1917): 25–117.

Wilson, William R., trans. *Hōgen monogatari: Tale of the Disorder in Hōgen.* Monumenta Nipponica Monograph. Tokyo: Sophia University Press, 1971.

The Tale of Heiji

Reischauer, Edwin O., and Joseph K. Yamagiwa. *Translations from Early Japanese Literature.* Cambridge Mass.: Harvard University Press, 1951.

Scull, Penelope Mason. "A Reconstruction of the *Hogen-Heiji monogatari emaki.*" Ph.D. diss., New York University, 1970.

The Tales of the Heike

Bialock, David T. *Eccentric Spaces, Hidden Histories: Narrative, Ritual, and Royal Authority from The Chronicle of Japan to The Tale of the Heike.* Stanford, Calif.: Stanford University Press, 2006.

Brown, Steven T. "From Woman Warrior to Peripatetic Entertainer: The Multiple Histories of Tomoe." *Harvard Journal of Asiatic Studies* 58, no. 1 (1998): 183–200.

Butler, Kenneth Dean, Jr. "The *Heike monogatari* and the Japanese Warrior Ethic." *Harvard Journal of Asiatic Studies* 29 (1969): 93–108.

Butler, Kenneth Dean, Jr. "The *Heike monogatari* and Theories of Oral Epic Literature." *Seikei Daigaku Bulletin of the Faculty of Letters* 2 (1966): 37–54.

Butler, Kenneth Dean, Jr. "The Textual Evolution of the *Heike monogatari*." *Harvard Journal of Asiatic Studies* 26 (1966): 5–51.

Hasegawa, Tadashi. "The Early Stages of the *Heike monogatari*." *Monumenta Nipponica* 22 (1967): 65–81.

Kitagawa, Hiroshi, and Bruce T. Tsuchida, trans. *The Tale of the Heike*. With a foreword by Edward G. Seidensticker. 2 vols. Tokyo: University of Tokyo Press, 1975.

McCullough, Helen Craig, trans. *The Tale of the Heike*. Stanford, Calif.: Stanford University Press, 1988.

Ruch, Barbara. "The Other Side of Culture in Medieval Japan." In *The Cambridge History of Japan*. Vol. 3, *Medieval Japan*, edited by Kozo Yamamura, 500–543. Cambridge: Cambridge University Press, 1988.

Sadler, A. L., trans. "The *Heike monogatari*." *Transactions of the Asiatic Society of Japan* 46, no. 2 (1918): 1–278; 49, no. 1 (1921): 1–354.

Sadler, A. L., trans. *The Ten Foot Square Hut and Tales of the Heike: Being Two Thirteenth-Century Japanese Classics, the "Hojoki" and Selections from "The Heike Monogatari."* 1928. Reprint, Tokyo: Turtle, 1972.

Varley, H. Paul. "Warriors as Courtiers: The Taira in *Heike monogatari*." In *Currents in Japanese Culture: Translations and Transformations*, edited by Amy Vladeck Heinrich, 53–70. New York: Columbia University Press, 1997.

Essays in Idleness

Chance, Linda H. *Formless in Form: Kenkō, Tsurezuregusa, and the Rhetoric of Japanese Fragmentary Prose*. Stanford, Calif.: Stanford University Press, 1997.

Keene, Donald, trans. *Essays in Idleness: The Tsurezuregusa of Kenkō*. New York: Columbia University Press, 1967.

Marra, Michele. *The Aesthetics of Discontent: Politics and Reclusion in Medieval Japanese Literature*. Honolulu: University of Hawai'i Press, 1991.

THE NORTHERN AND SOUTHERN COURTS AND MUROMACHI PERIODS

Marra, Michele. *The Aesthetics of Discontent: Politics and Reclusion in Medieval Japanese Literature*. Honolulu: University of Hawai'i Press, 1991.

Marra, Michele. *Representations of Power: The Literary Politics of Medieval Japan*. Honolulu: University of Hawai'i Press, 1993.

Varley, H. Paul, trans. *A Chronicle of Gods and Sovereigns*. New York: Columbia University Press, 1980.

Warrior Tales

Cogan, Thomas J., trans. *The Tale of the Soga Brothers*. Tokyo: University of Tokyo Press, 1987.

McCullough, Helen Craig, trans. *The Taiheiki: A Chronicle of Medieval Japan*. New York: Columbia University Press, 1959.

McCullough, Helen Craig, trans. *Yoshitsune: A Fifteenth-Century Japanese Chronicle*. Tokyo: University of Tokyo Press, 1966.

Mills, Douglas E. "*Soga monogatari, Shintōshū* and the Taketori Legend." *Monumenta Nipponica* 30, no. 1 (1975): 37–68.

Minobe, Shigekatsu. "The World View of *Genpei jōsuiki.*" *Japanese Journal of Religious Studies* 9, nos. 2–3 (1982): 213–233.

Varley, H. Paul. *The Ōnin War: History of Its Origins and Background with a Selective Translation of the Chronicle of Ōnin.* New York: Columbia University Press, 1967.

Yonekura, Isamu. "The Revenge of the Soga Brothers." *East* 8, no. 5 (1972): 25–33.

Ballad Drama

Araki, James. *The Ballad-Drama of Medieval Japan.* Berkeley: University of California Press, 1964; Rutland, Vt.: Tuttle, 1978.

Nō Drama

Bainbridge, Erika Ohara. "The Madness of Mothers in Japanese Noh Drama." *U.S.-Japan Women's Journal: A Journal for the International Exchange of Gender Studies* 3 (1992): 84–110.

Bender, Ross. "Metamorphosis of a Deity: The Image of Hachiman in *Yumi yawata.*" *Monumenta Nipponica* 33, no. 2 (1978): 165–178.

Bethe, Monica, and Karen W. Brazell. *Dance in the Nō Theater.* 3 vols. Cornell University East Asia Papers, no. 29. Ithaca, N.Y.: China-Japan Program, Cornell University, 1982.

Bethe, Monica, and Karen W. Brazell. *Nō as Performance: An Analysis of the Kuse Scene of Yamamba.* Cornell University East Asia Papers, no. 16. Ithaca, N.Y.: China-Japan Program, Cornell University, 1978.

Brandon, James R., Frank Hoff, and William Packard. "Japanese Noh." In *Traditional Asian Plays,* edited by James R. Brandon, 173–177. New York: Hill & Wang, 1972.

Brazell, Karen W. "Atsumori: The Ghost of a Warrior on Stage." *Par Rapport: A Journal of the Humanities* 5–6 (1982–1983): 13–23.

Brazell, Karen W. "Citations on the Noh Stage." *Extrême-Orient, Extrême-Occident* 17 (1995): 91–110.

Brazell, Karen W. "In Search of *Yamamba:* A Critique of the Nō Play." In *Studies in Japanese Culture,* edited by Saburo Ota and Rikutaro Fukuda, 1:495–498. Tokyo: Japan P.E.N. Club, 1973.

Brazell, Karen W. "Zeami and Women in Love." *Literature East and West* 18, no. 1 (1974): 8–18.

Brazell, Karen W., ed. *Traditional Japanese Theater: An Anthology of Plays.* New York: Columbia University Press, 1998.

Brazell, Karen W., ed. *Twelve Plays of the Nō and Kyōgen Theaters.* Cornell University East Asia Papers, no. 50. Ithaca, N.Y.: East Asia Program, Cornell University, 1990.

Bresler, Laurence, trans. "*Chōbuku soga:* A Noh Play." *Monumenta Nipponica* 29, no. 1 (1974): 69–81.

Brock, Sam Houston, trans. "Sotoba komachi." In *Anthology of Japanese Literature: From the Earliest Era to the Mid-Nineteenth Century,* edited by Donald Keene, 264–270. New York: Grove Press, 1955.

Foard, James H. "Seiganji: The Buddhist Orientation of a Noh Play." *Monumenta Nipponica* 35 (1980): 437–456.

Goff, Janet. "Noh and Its Antecedents: 'Journey to the Western Provinces.'" In *The Distant Isle: Studies and Translations in Honor of Robert H. Brower*, edited by Thomas B. Hare, Robert Borgen, and Sharalyn Orbaugh, 165–181. Ann Arbor: Center for Japanese Studies, University of Michigan, 1996.

Goff, Janet. *Noh Drama and the Tale of Genji: The Art of Allusion in Fifteen Classical Plays*. Princeton, N.J.: Princeton University Press, 1991.

Hare, Thomas B. "A Separate Piece: Proprietary Claims and Intertextuality in the Rokujō Plays." In *The Distant Isle: Studies and Translations in Honor of Robert H. Brower*, edited by Thomas B. Hare, Robert Borgen, and Sharalyn Orbaugh, 183–204. Ann Arbor: Center for Japanese Studies, University of Michigan, 1996.

Hare, Thomas B. *Zeami's Style: The Noh Plays of Zeami Motokiyo*. Stanford, Calif.: Stanford University Press, 1986.

Hayashi, Tetsumaro. "Zeami's Dramatic Time-Structure in *Komachi at Sekidera*." *Literature East and West* 21 (1977): 163–169.

Hoff, Frank. *Song, Dance, Storytelling: Aspects of the Performing Arts in Japan*. Cornell University East Asia Papers, no. 15. Ithaca, N.Y.: China-Japan Program, Cornell University, 1978.

Hoff, Frank, and Willi Flint. "The Life Structure of Noh: An English Version of Yokomichi Mario's *Analyses of the Structure of Noh*." *Concerned Theater Japan* 2, nos. 3–4 (1973): 210–256.

Horiguchi, Yasuo. "Literature and Performing Arts in the Medieval Age—Kan'ami's Dramaturgy." *Acta Asiatica* 33 (1977): 15–31.

Huey, Robert N. "*Sakuragawa*: Cherry River." *Monumenta Nipponica* 38, no. 3 (1983): 295–312.

Inoura, Yoshinobu. *A History of Japanese Theatre I: Noh and Kyōgen*. Tokyo: Kokusai bunka shinkōkai, 1971.

Jones, Stanleigh H., Jr., trans. "The Nō Plays *Obasute* and *Kanehira*." *Monumenta Nipponica* 18 (1963): 261–285.

Katō, Eileen, trans. "*Kinuta*." *Monumenta Nipponica* 32, no. 3 (1977): 332–346.

Keene, Donald. *Nō: The Classical Theatre of Japan*. Tokyo: Kodansha International, 1966.

Keene, Donald, ed. *Twenty Plays of the Nō Theatre*. New York: Columbia University Press, 1970.

Keith, Nobuko T. "Ezra Pound and Japanese Noh Plays: An Examination of Sotoba Komachi and Nishikigi." *Literature East and West* 15–16 (1971–1972): 662–679.

Klein, Susan Blakeley. "When the Moon Strikes the Bell: Desire and Enlightenment in the Noh Play *Dōjōji*." *Journal of Japanese Studies* 17, no. 2 (1991): 291–322.

Kominz, Laurence. "The Noh as Popular Theater: Miyamasu's *Youchi soga*." *Monumenta Nipponica* 33 (1978): 441–459.

Komparu, Kunio. *The Noh Theater: Principles and Perspectives*. Tokyo; Weatherhill, 1983.

Komparu, Zempo Motoyasu. "Ikkaku Sennin." Adapted by William Packard from a translation by Frank Hoff. In *Four Classical Asian Plays in Modern Translation*, edited by Vera R. Irwin, 241–269. Baltimore: Penguin, 1972.

Malm, William P. "The Musical Characteristics and Practice of the Japanese Noh Drama in an East Asian Context." In *Chinese and Japanese Music-Dramas*, edited by J. I. Crump and William P. Malm, 99–142. Michigan Papers in Chinese Studies, no. 19. Ann Arbor: Center for Chinese Studies, University of Michigan, 1975.

Matisoff, Susan. "Images of Exile and Pilgrimage: Zeami's *Kintōsho.*" *Monumenta Nipponica* 34 (1979): 449–465.

Matisoff, Susan. "*Kintōsho:* Zeami's Song of Exile." *Monumenta Nipponica* 32 (1977): 441–458.

Minagawa, Tatsuo. "Japanese Noh Music." *Journal of the American Musicological Society* 10, no. 3 (1957): 183–185.

Morrell, Robert E., trans. "Passage to India Denied: Zeami's *Kasuga ryujin.*" *Monumenta Nipponica* 37, no. 2 (1982): 179–200.

Mueller, Jacqueline. "The Two Shizukas: Zeami's *Futari shizuka.*" *Monumenta Nipponica* 36, no. 3 (1981): 285–298.

Nakamura, Yasuo. *Noh: The Classical Theater.* Translated by Don Kenny, with an introduction by Earle Ernst. Performing Arts of Japan, no. 4. New York: Walker/Weatherhill, 1971.

Nearman, Mark J. "*Kyakuraika:* Zeami's Final Legacy for the Master Actor." *Monumenta Nipponica* 35 (1980): 153–197.

Nearman, Mark J. "The Visions of a Creative Artist: Zenchiku's *Rokurin ichiro* Treatises." *Monumenta Nipponica* 50, nos. 2–4 (1995): 235–261, 281–303, 485–522;.51, no. 1 (1996): 17–52.

Nearman, Mark J. "Zeami's *Kyūi:* A Pedagogical Guide for Teachers of Acting." *Monumenta Nipponica* 33 (1978): 299–332.

Nearman, Mark J., trans. "*Kakyō:* Zeami's Fundamental Principles of Acting." *Monumenta Nipponica* 37, nos. 3–4 (1982): 333–374, 459–496.

Nippon gakujutsu shinkōkai. *Japanese Noh Drama.* 3 vols. Tokyo: Nippon gakujutsu shinkōkai, 1955, 1959, 1960.

Nogami, Toyoichirō. *Japanese Noh Plays: How to See Them.* Tokyo: Nogaku shorin, 1954.

Nogami, Toyoichirō. *Zeami and His Theories on Noh.* Translated by Ryōzō Matsumoto. Tokyo: Hinoki shoten, 1973.

O'Neill, P. G. *Early Nō Drama: Its Background, Character and Development,* 1300–1450. London: Humphries, 1958.

O'Neill, P. G. A *Guide to Nō.* Tokyo: Hinoki shoten, 1954.

Pinnington, Noel. "Crossed Paths: Zeami's Transmission to Zenchiku." *Monumenta Nipponica* 52 (1997): 201–234.

Pound, Ezra, and Ernest Fenollosa, trans. *The Classic Noh Theatre of Japan.* New York: New Directions, 1959.

Quinn, Shelley Fenno. "How to Write a Nō Play: Zeami's *Sandō.*" *Monumenta Nipponica* 48, no. 1 (1993): 53–88.

Raz, Jacob. "The Actor and His Audience: Zeami's Views on the Audience of the Noh." *Monumenta Nipponica* 31, no. 3 (1976): 251–274.

Rimer, J. Thomas, and Yamazaki Masakazu, trans. *On the Art of Nō Drama: The Major Treatises of Zeami.* Princeton, N.J.: Princeton University Press, 1984.

Rubin, Jay. "The Art of the Flower of Mumbo Jumbo." *Harvard Journal of Asiatic Studies* 53, no. 2 (1993): 513–541.

Sata, Megumi. "Aristotle's Poetics and Zeami's Teachings on Style and the Flower." *Asian Theatre Journal* 6, no. 1 (1989): 47–56.

Shidehara, Michitarō, and Wilfrid Whitehouse, trans. "*Seami jūroku bushū*: Seami's Sixteen Treatises." *Monumenta Nipponica* 4, no. 2 (1941): 204–239.

Shimazaki, Chifumi. *Battle Noh: In Parallel Translations with an Introduction and Running Commentaries*. Vol. 2 of *The Noh*. Tokyo: Hinoki shoten, 1987.

Shimazaki, Chifumi. *God Noh*. Vol. 1 of *The Noh*. Tokyo: Hinoki shoten, 1972.

Shimazaki, Chifumi. *Restless Spirits from Japanese Noh Plays of the Fourth Group: Parallel Translations with Running Commentary*. Cornell University East Asia Series, no. 76. Ithaca, N.Y.: East Asia Program, Cornell University, 1995.

Shimazaki, Chifumi. *Troubled Souls from Japanese Noh Plays of the Fourth Group*. Cornell University East Asia Series, no. 95. Ithaca, N.Y.: East Asia Program, Cornell University, 1998.

Shimazaki, Chifumi. *Warrior Ghost Plays from the Japanese Noh Theater: Parallel Translations with Running Commentary*. Cornell University East Asia Series, no. 60. Ithaca, N.Y.: East Asia Program, Cornell University, 1993.

Shimazaki, Chifumi. *Women Noh: In Parallel Translations with an Introduction and Running Commentaries*. Vol. 3 of *The Noh*. Tokyo: Hinoki shoten, 1987.

Shively, Donald H. "Buddhahood for the Nonsentient: A Theme in Nō Plays." *Harvard Journal of Asiatic Studies* 20, no. 1 (1957): 135–161.

Terasaki, Etsuko. "Images and Symbols in *Sotoba Komachi*: A Critical Analysis of a Nō Play." *Harvard Journal of Asiatic Studies* 44, no. 1 (1984): 155–184:

Terasaki, Etsuko. "Is the Courtesan of Eguchi a Buddhist Metaphorical Woman? A Feminist Reading of a Nō Play in the Japanese Medieval Theater." *Women's Studies: An Interdisciplinary Journal* 21, no. 4 (1992): 431–456.

Thornhill, Arthur H., III. "The Goddess Emerges: Shinto Paradigms in the Aesthetics of Zeami and Zenchiku." *Journal of the Association of Teachers of Japanese* 24, no. 1 (1990): 49–59.

Thornhill, Arthur H., III. *Six Circles, One Dewdrop: The Religio-Aesthetic World of Komparu Zenchiku*. Princeton, N.J.: Princeton University Press, 1993.

Tyler, Royall. "Buddhism in Noh." *Japanese Journal of Religious Studies* 14 (1987): 19–52.

Tyler, Royall. "The Nō Play *Matsukaze* as a Transformation of *Genji monogatari*." *Journal of Japanese Studies* 20, no. 2 (1994): 377–422.

Tyler, Royall, trans. *Granny Mountains: A Second Cycle of Nō Plays*. Cornell University East Asia Series, no. 18. Ithaca, N.Y.: East Asia Program, Cornell University, 1978.

Tyler, Royall, trans. and ed. *Japanese Nō Dramas*. London: Penguin, 1992.

Tyler, Royall, trans. *Pining Wind: A Cycle of Nō Plays*. Cornell University East Asia Series, nos. 17–18. Ithaca, N.Y.: East Asia Program, Cornell University, 1978.

Waley, Arthur. *The Nō Plays of Japan*. 1921. Reprint, New York: Grove Press, 1957.

Weatherby, Meredith, and Bruce Rogers, trans. "Birds of Sorrow." In *Anthology of Japanese Literature: From the Earliest Era to the Mid-Nineteenth Century*, edited by Donald Keene, 271–285. New York: Grove Press, 1955.

Yamazaki, Masakazu. "The Aesthetics of Transformation: Zeami's Dramatic Theories." Translated by Susan Matisoff. *Journal of Japanese Studies* 7, no. 2 (1981): 215–257.

Yasuda, Kenneth K. "The Dramatic Structure of *Ataka*, a Noh Play." *Monumenta Nipponica* 27 (1972): 359–398.

Yasuda, Kenneth K. *Masterworks of the Nō Theater.* Bloomington: Indiana University Press, 1989.

Yasuda, Kenneth K. "The Prototypical Nō Wig Play: *Izutsu.*" *Harvard Journal of Asiatic Studies* 40, no. 2 (1980): 399–464.

Yasuda, Kenneth K. "The Structure of *Hagoromo*, a Nō Play." *Harvard Journal of Asiatic Studies* 33 (1973): 5–89.

Comic Theater

Akira Shigeyama International Projects, executive producer, Akira Shigeyama. *Busu* (video recording). New York: Insight Media, 1996.

Brazell, Karen W., ed. *Traditional Japanese Theater: An Anthology of Plays.* New York: Columbia University Press, 1998.

Brazell, Karen W., ed. *Twelve Plays of the Nō and Kyōgen Theaters.* Cornell University East Asia Papers, no. 50. Ithaca, N.Y.: East Asia Program, Cornell University, 1990.

Golay, Jacqueline. "Pathos and Farce: *Zatō* Plays of the *kyōgen* Repertoire." *Monumenta Nipponica* 28, no. 2 (1973): 139–149.

Haynes, Carolyn. "Comic Inversion in Kyōgen: Ghosts and the Nether World." *Journal of the Association of Teachers of Japanese* 22, no. 1 (1988): 29–40.

Haynes, Carolyn. "Parody in Kyōgen: *Makura Monogurui* and *Tako.*" *Monumenta Nipponica* 39, no. 3 (1984): 261–279.

Kenny, Don. *A Guide to Kyōgen.* Tokyo: Hinoki shoten, 1968.

Kenny, Don. *The Kyogen Book: An Anthology of Japanese Classical Comedies.* Tokyo: Japan Times, 1989.

McKinnon, Richard N., trans. *Selected Plays of Kyōgen.* Tokyo: Uniprint, 1968.

McKinnon, Richard N., trans, and intro. "*Thunder:* A Kyōgen Play." *Literature East and West* 11 (1967): 361–372.

Morley, Carolyn A. "The Tender-Hearted Shrews: The Woman Character in Kyōgen." *Journal of the Association of Teachers of Japanese* 22, no. 1 (1988): 41–52.

Morley, Carolyn A. *Transformation, Miracles, and Mischief: The Mountain Priest Plays of Kyōgen.* Cornell University East Asia Series, no. 62. Ithaca, N.Y.: East Asia Program, Cornell University, 1993.

Sakanishi, Shio, trans. *Japanese Folk-Plays: The Ink-Smeared Lady and Other Kyōgen.* Tokyo: Tuttle, 1960.

Ikkyū and Gozan Literature

Arntzen, Sonja. *Ikkyū and the Crazy Cloud Anthology.* Tokyo: University of Tokyo Press, 1986.

Parker, Joseph D. "Attaining Landscapes in the Mind: Nature Poetry and Painting in Gozan Zen." *Monumenta Nipponica* 52 (1997): 235–258.

Pollack, David. *Zen Poems of the Five Mountains.* New York: Crossroad, 1985.

Ury, Marian. *Poems of the Five Mountains: An Introduction to the Literature of the Zen Monasteries.* Tokyo: Mushinsha, 1977.

Watson, Burton, trans. "Poems in Chinese by Buddhist Monks." In *Anthology of Japanese Literature: From the Earliest Era to the Mid-Nineteenth Century*, edited by Donald Keene, 312–313. New York: Grove Press, 1955.

Late Medieval Poetry and Scholarship

Brower, Robert H., and Steven D. Carter, trans. *Conversations with Shōtetsu*. Ann Arbor: Center for Japanese Studies, University of Michigan, 1992.

Carter, Steven D. *Regent Redux: A Life of the Statesman-Scholar Ichijō Kaneyoshi*. Ann Arbor: Center for Japanese Studies, University of Michigan, 1996.

Carter, Steven D. "'Seeking What the Masters Sought': Masters, Disciples, and Poetic Enlightenment in Medieval Japan." In *The Distant Isle: Studies and Translations in Honor of Robert H. Brower*, edited by Thomas B. Hare, Robert Borgen, and Sharalyn Orbaugh, 35–58. Ann Arbor: Center for Japanese Studies, University of Michigan, 1996.

Carter, Steven D. "*Waka* in the Age of *renga*." *Monumenta Nipponica* 36, no. 4 (1981): 425–444.

Carter, Steven D., ed. *Literary Patronage in Late Medieval Japan*. Ann Arbor: Center for Japanese Studies, University of Michigan, 1993.

Carter, Steven D., trans. *Unforgotten Dreams: Poems by the Zen Monk Shōtetsu*. New York: Columbia University Press, 1997.

Carter, Steven D., trans. *Waiting for the Wind: Thirty-six Poets of Japan's Late Medieval Age*. New York: Columbia University Press, 1989.

Isao, Kumakura, and Steven D. Carter, trans. "Sanjonishi Sanetaka, Takeno Joo, and an Early Form of Iemoto Seido." In *Literary Patronage in Late Medieval Japan*, edited by Steven D. Carter, 95–103. Ann Arbor: Center for Japanese Studies, University of Michigan, 1993.

Karaki, Junzo. "Perspectives on the Self: Suki, Susabi, and Sabi in Medieval Japanese Literature." *Chanoyu Quarterly* 35 (1983): 30–51.

Karaki, Junzo. "Wafting Petals and Windblown Leaves: Impermanence in the Aesthetics of Shinkei, Sōgi, and Bashō." *Chanoyu Quarterly* 37 (1984): 7–27.

Linked Verse

Carter, Steven D. "A Lesson in Failure: Linked-Verse Contests in Medieval Japan." *Journal of the American Oriental Society* 104, no. 4 (1984): 727–737.

Carter, Steven D. "Mixing Memories: Linked Verse and the Fragmentation of the Court Heritage." *Harvard Journal of Asiatic Studies* 48, no. 1 (1988): 5–45.

Carter, Steven D. *The Road to Komatsubara: A Classical Reading of the Renga hyakuin*. Cambridge, Mass.: Harvard University Press, 1987.

Carter, Steven D. "Rules, Rules, and More Rules: Shōhaku's *renga* Rulebook of 1501." *Harvard Journal of Asiatic Studies* 43, no. 2 (1983): 581–642.

Carter, Steven D. "Sōgi in the East Country, *Shirakawa kiko*." *Monumenta Nipponica* 42, no. 2 (1987): 167–209.

Carter, Steven D. *Three Poets at Yuyama*. Berkeley, Calif.: Institute of East Asian Studies, 1983.

Carter, Steven D. "Three Poets at Yuyama: Sōgi and *Yuyama sangin hyakuin*, 1491." *Monumenta Nipponica* 33, nos. 2–3 (1978): 119–149, 241–283.

Cranston, Edwin A. "Shinkei's 1467 *Dokugin hyakuin*." *Harvard Journal of Asiatic Studies* 54, no. 2 (1994): 461–507.

Ebersole, Gary L. "The Buddhist Ritual Use of Linked Poetry in Medieval Japan." *Eastern Buddhist* 16, no. 2 (1983): 50–71.

Hare, Thomas B. "Linked Verse at Imashinmei Shrine, *Anegakōji imashinmei hyakuin 1447.*" *Monumenta Nipponica* 34, no. 2 (1979): 169–208.

Hirota, Dennis. "In Practice of the Way: *Sasamegoto*, an Instruction Book in Linked Verse." *Chanoyu Quarterly* 19 (1977): 23–46.

Horton, H. Mack. "Renga Unbound: Performative Aspects of Japanese Linked Verse." *Harvard Journal of Asiatic Studies* 53, no. 2 (1993): 443–512.

Horton, H. Mack. "Saiokuken Sōchō and Imagawa Daimyō Patronage." In *Literary Patronage in Late Medieval Japan*, edited by Steven D. Carter, 105–161. Ann Arbor: Center for Japanese Studies, University of Michigan, 1993.

Horton, H. Mack. "Saiokuken Sōchō and the Linked-Verse Business." *Transactions of the Asiatic Society of Japan* 1 (1986): 45–78.

Horton, H. Mack. *Song in an Age of Discord: The Journal of Sōchō and Poetic Life in Medieval Japan*. Stanford, Calif.: Stanford University Press, 1999.

Horton, H. Mack, trans. *The Journal of Sōchō*. Stanford, Calif.: Stanford University Press, 1999.

Keene, Donald. "Jōha, a Sixteenth-Century Poet of Linked Verse." In *Warlords, Artists, and Commoners: Japan in the Sixteenth Century*, edited by George Elison and Bardwell L. Smith, 113–131. Honolulu: University Press of Hawai'i, 1981.

Kinjiro, Kaneko, and H. Mack Horton, trans. "Sōgi and the Imperial House." In *Literary Patronage in Late Medieval Japan*, edited by Steven D. Carter, 63–93. Ann Arbor: Center for Japanese Studies, University of Michigan, 1993.

Konishi, Jin'ichi. "The Art of Renga." Translated, with an introduction, by Karen W. Brazell and Lewis Cook. *Journal of Japanese Studies* 2, no. 1 (1975): 29–61.

Miner, Earl. *Japanese Linked Poetry: An Account with Translations of Renga and Haikai Sequences*. Princeton, N.J.: Princeton University Press, 1979.

Miner, Earl. "Some Theoretical Implications of Japanese Linked Poetry." *Comparative Literature Studies* 18, no. 3 (1981): 368–378.

Okuda, Isao. "Renga in the Medieval Period." *Acta Asiatica: Bulletin of the Institute of Eastern Culture* 37 (1979): 29–46.

Pollack, David. "Gidō Shūshin and Nijō Yoshimoto: Wakan and Renga Theory in Late Fourteenth Century Japan." *Harvard Journal of Asiatic Studies* 45, no. 1 (1985): 129–156.

Ramirez-Christensen, Esperanza. "The Essential Parameters of Linked Poetry." *Harvard Journal of Asiatic Studies* 41, no. 2 (1981): 555–595.

Ramirez-Christensen, Esperanza. *Heart's Flower: The Life and Poetry of Shinkei*. Stanford, Calif.: Stanford University Press, 1994.

Ueda, Makoto. "Verse-Writing as a Game: Yoshimoto on the Art of Linked Verse." In *Literary and Art Theories in Japan*, edited by Makoto Ueda, 37–54. Cleveland: Press of Western Reserve University, 1967.

Yoshimura, Teiji. "Shinkei's Aesthetics in the Art of Chanoyu." *Chanoyu Quarterly* 1, no. 4 (1970): 16–28.

Muromachi Tales

Araki, James T. "Bunshō sōshi: The Tale of Bunshō, the Saltmaker." *Monumenta Nipponica* 38, no. 3 (1983): 221–249.

Araki, James T. "Otogi-zōshi and Nara-ehon: A Field of Study in Flux." *Monumenta Nipponica* 36 (1981): 1–20.

Childs, Margaret H. *"Chigo monogatari*: Love Stories or Buddhist Sermons?" *Monumenta Nipponica* 35 (1980): 127–151.

Childs, Margaret H. "Didacticism in Medieval Short Stories: *Hatsuse monogatari* and Akimichi." *Monumenta Nipponica* 42, no. 3 (1987): 253–288.

Childs, Margaret H. "The Influence of the Buddhist Practice of *sange* on Literary Form: Revelatory Tales." *Japanese Journal of Religious Studies* 14, no. 1 (1987): 53–66.

Childs, Margaret H. "Kyōgen-kigo: Love Stories as Buddhist Sermons." *Japanese Journal of Religious Studies* 12, no. 1 (1985): 91–104.

Childs, Margaret H. *Rethinking Sorrow: Revelatory Tales of Late Medieval Japan*. Ann Arbor: Center for Japanese Studies, University of Michigan, 1991.

Keene, Donald, trans. "The Three Priests." In *Anthology of Japanese Literature: From the Earliest Era to the Mid-Nineteenth Century*, edited by Donald Keene, 322–331. New York: Grove Press, 1955.

Kimbrough, R. Keller. "*Little Atsumori* and *The Tale of the Heike*: Fiction as Commentary, and the Significance of a Name." *Proceedings of the Association for Japanese Literary Studies* 5 (2004): 325–336.

Mills, Douglas E. "The Tale of the Mouse: Nezumi no sōshi." *Monumenta Nipponica* 34, no. 2 (1979): 155–168.

Mulhern, Chieko Irie. "Cinderella and the Jesuits: An Otogi-zōshi Cycle as Christian Literature." *Monumenta Nipponica* 34, no. 4 (1979): 409–447.

Mulhern, Chieko Irie. "Otogi-zōshi: Short Stories of the Muromachi Period." *Monumenta Nipponica* 29, no. 2 (1974): 181–198.

Putzar, Edward D. "The Tale of Monkey Genji: Sarugenji-zōshi. Translated with an Introduction to Popular Fiction of Medieval Japan." *Monumenta Nipponica* 18 (1963): 286–312.

Ruch, Barbara. "Medieval Jongleurs and the Making of a National Literature." In *Japan in the Muromachi Age*, edited by John W. Hall and Toyoda Takeshi, 279–309. Berkeley: University of California Press, 1977.

Ruch, Barbara. "The Origins of *The Companion Library*: An Anthology of Medieval Japanese Stories." *Journal of Asian Studies* 30, no. 3 (1971): 593–610.

Skord, Virginia. "Monogusa Tarō: From Rags to Riches and Beyond." *Monumenta Nipponica* 44, no. 2 (1989): 171–198.

Skord, Virginia, trans. *Tales of Tears and Laughter: Short Fiction of Medieval Japan*. Honolulu: University of Hawai'i Press, 1991.

Steven, Chigusa. "*Hachikazuki*: A Muromachi Short Story." *Monumenta Nipponica* 32 (1977): 303–331.

Popular Linked Verse

Keene, Donald. "The Comic Tradition in Renga." In *Japan in the Muromachi Age*, edited by John W. Hall and Toyoda Takeshi, 241–277. Berkeley: University of California Press, 1977.

PERMISSIONS

The editor and publisher acknowledge with thanks permission granted to reproduce in his volume the following material. In most cases, revisions were made by the original translator or the editor.

From *The Tale of Genji*, translated by Edward G. Seidensticker. Copyright © 1976 by Alfred A. Knopf. By permission of the publisher.

From *A Collection of Tales from Uji: A Study and Translation of Uji Shūi Monogatari*, translated by D. E. Mills. Copyright © 1970 by Cambridge University Press. Reprinted with the permission of Cambridge University Press.

From *Essays in Idleness: The Tsurezuregusa of Kenkō*, translated by Donald Keene. Copyright © 1967 by Columbia University Press. By permission of the publisher.

From *Japanese Literature in Chinese*, Vol. 1, translated by Burton Watson. Copyright © 1975 by Columbia University Press. By permission of the publisher.

From *The Pillow Book of Sei Shōnagon*, translated by Ivan Morris. Copyright © 1967 by Columbia University Press. By permission of the publisher.

From *The Confessions of Lady Nijō*, translated by Karen Brazell. Copyright © 1973 by Karen Brazell. Used by permission of Doubleday, a division of Random House, Inc.

From *Miraculous Stories from the Japanese Buddhist Tradition*, translated by Kyoko Nakamura. Copyright © 1973 by Harvard-Yenching Institute. By permission of the publisher.

From Donald Keene, "The Tale of the Bamboo Cutter," *Monumenta Nipponica* 11, no. 4 (1956). By permission of Sophia University.

INDEX

TRANSLATIONS FROM THE ASIAN CLASSICS

Essays in Idleness: The Tsurezuregusa of Kenkō, tr. Donald Keene. Also in paperback ed. 1967

The Pillow Book of Sei Shōnagon, tr. Ivan Morris, 2 vols. 1967

Two Plays of Ancient India: The Little Clay Cart and the Minister's Seal, tr. J. A. B. van Buitenen 1968

The Complete Works of Chuang Tzu, tr. Burton Watson 1968

The Romance of the Western Chamber (Hsi Hsiang chi), tr. S. I. Hsiung. Also in paperback ed. 1968

The Manyōshū, Nippon Gakujutsu Shinkōkai edition. Paperback ed. only. 1969

Records of the Historian: Chapters from the Shih chi of Ssu-ma Ch'ien, tr. Burton Watson. Paperback ed. only. 1969

Cold Mountain: 100 Poems by the T'ang Poet Han-shan, tr. Burton Watson. Also in paperback ed. 1970

Twenty Plays of the Nō Theatre, ed. Donald Keene. Also in paperback ed. 1970

Chūshingura: The Treasury of Loyal Retainers, tr. Donald Keene. Also in paperback ed. 1971; rev. ed. 1997

The Zen Master Hakuin: Selected Writings, tr. Philip B. Yampolsky 1971

Chinese Rhyme-Prose: Poems in the Fu Form from the Han and Six Dynasties Periods, tr. Burton Watson. Also in paperback ed. 1971

Kūkai: Major Works, tr. Yoshito S. Hakeda. Also in paperback ed. 1972

The Old Man Who Does as He Pleases: Selections from the Poetry and Prose of Lu Yu, tr. Burton Watson 1973

The Lion's Roar of Queen Śrīmālā, tr. Alex and Hideko Wayman 1974

Courtier and Commoner in Ancient China: Selections from the History of the Former Han by Pan Ku, tr. Burton Watson. Also in paperback ed. 1974

Japanese Literature in Chinese, vol. 1: Poetry and Prose in Chinese by Japanese Writers of the Early Period, tr. Burton Watson 1975

Japanese Literature in Chinese, vol. 2: Poetry and Prose in Chinese by Japanese Writers of the Later Period, tr. Burton Watson 1976

Scripture of the Lotus Blossom of the Fine Dharma, tr. Leon Hurvitz. Also in paperback ed. 1976

Love Song of the Dark Lord: Jayadeva's Gītagovinda, tr. Barbara Staler Miller. Also in paperback ed. Cloth ed. includes critical text of the Sanskrit. 1977; rev. ed. 1997

Ryōkan: Zen Monk-Poet of Japan, tr. Burton Watson 1977

Calming the Mind and Discerning the Real: From the Lam rim chen mo of Tsoṇ-khapa, tr. Alex Wayman 1978

The Hermit and the Love-Thief: Sanskrit Poems of Bhartrihari and Bilhaṇa, tr. Barbara Stoler Miller 1978

The Lute: Kao Ming's P'i-p'a chi, tr. Jean Mulligan. Also in paperback ed. 1980

A Chronicle of Gods and Sovereigns: Jinnō Shōtōki of Kitabatake Chikafusa, tr. H. Paul Varley 1980

Among the Flowers: The Hua-chien chi, tr. Lois Fusek 1982

Grass Hill: Poems and Prose by the Japanese Monk Gensei, tr. Burton Watson 1983

Doctors, Diviners, and Magicians of Ancient China: Biographies of Fang-shih, tr. Kenneth J. DeWoskin. Also in paperback ed. 1983

Theater of Memory: The Plays of Kālidāsa, ed. Barbara Stoler Miller. Also in paperback ed. 1984

The Columbia Book of Chinese Poetry: From Early Times to the Thirteenth Century, ed. and tr. Burton Watson. Also in paperback ed. 1984

Poems of Love and War: From the Eight Anthologies and the Ten Long Poems of Classical Tamil, tr. A. K. Ramanujan. Also in paperback ed. 1985

The Bhagavad Gita: Krishna's Counsel in Time of War, tr. Barbara Stoler Miller 1986

The Columbia Book of Later Chinese Poetry, ed. and tr. Jonathan Chaves. Also in paperback ed. 1986

The Tso Chuan: Selections from China's Oldest Narrative History, tr. Burton Watson 1989

Waiting for the Wind: Thirty-six Poets of Japan's Late Medieval Age, tr. Steven Carter 1989

Selected Writings of Nichiren, ed. Philip B. Yampolsky 1990

Saigyō, Poems of a Mountain Home, tr. Burton Watson 1990

The Book of Lieh Tzu: A Classic of the Tao, tr. A. C. Graham. Morningside ed. 1990

The Tale of an Anklet: An Epic of South India—The Cilappatikāram of Iḷaṅkō Aṭikaḷ, tr. R. Parthasarathy 1993

Waiting for the Dawn: A Plan for the Prince, tr. with introduction by Wm. Theodore de Bary 1993

Yoshitsune and the Thousand Cherry Trees: A Masterpiece of the Eighteenth-Century Japanese Puppet Theater, tr., annotated, and with introduction by Stanleigh H. Jones, Jr. 1993

The Lotus Sutra, tr. Burton Watson. Also in paperback ed. 1993

The Classic of Changes: A New Translation of the I Ching *as Interpreted by Wang Bi,* tr. Richard John Lynn 1994

Beyond Spring: Tz'u Poems of the Sung Dynasty, tr. Julie Landau 1994

The Columbia Anthology of Traditional Chinese Literature, ed. Victor H. Mair 1994

Scenes for Mandarins: The Elite Theater of the Ming, tr. Cyril Birch 1995

Letters of Nichiren, ed. Philip B. Yampolsky; tr. Burton Watson et al. 1996

Unforgotten Dreams: Poems by the Zen Monk Shōtetsu, tr. Steven D. Carter 1997

The Vimalakirti Sutra, tr. Burton Watson 1997

Japanese and Chinese Poems to Sing: The Wakan rōei shū, tr. J. Thomas Rimer and Jonathan Chaves 1997

Breeze Through Bamboo: Kanshi of Ema Saikō, tr. Hiroaki Sato 1998

A Tower for the Summer Heat, by Li Yu, tr. Patrick Hanan 1998

Traditional Japanese Theater: An Anthology of Plays, by Karen Brazell 1998

The Original Analects: Sayings of Confucius and His Successors (0479–0249), by E. Bruce Brooks and A. Taeko Brooks 1998

The Classic of the Way and Virtue: A New Translation of the Tao-te ching *of Laozi as Interpreted by Wang Bi,* tr. Richard John Lynn 1999

The Four Hundred Songs of War and Wisdom: An Anthology of Poems from Classical Tamil, The Puṟanāṉūṟu, ed. and tr. George L. Hart and Hank Heifetz 1999

Original Tao: Inward Training (Nei-yeh) and the Foundations of Taoist Mysticism, by Harold D. Roth 1999

Lao Tzu's Tao Te Ching: *A Translation of the Startling New Documents Found at Guodian,* by Robert G. Henricks 2000

The Shorter Columbia Anthology of Traditional Chinese Literature, ed. Victor H. Mair 2000

Mistress and Maid (Jiaohongji), by Meng Chengshun, tr. Cyril Birch 2001

Chikamatsu: Five Late Plays, tr. and ed. C. Andrew Gerstle 2001

The Essential Lotus: Selections from the Lotus Sutra, tr. Burton Watson 2002

Early Modern Japanese Literature: An Anthology, 1600–1900, ed. Haruo Shirane 2002

The Sound of the Kiss, or The Story That Must Never Be Told: Pingali Suranna's Kala-purnodayamu, tr. Vecheru Narayana Rao and David Shulman 2003

The Selected Poems of Du Fu, tr. Burton Watson 2003

Far Beyond the Field: Haiku by Japanese Women, tr. Makoto Ueda 2003

Just Living: Poems and Prose by the Japanese Monk Tonna, ed. and tr. Steven D. Carter 2003

Han Feizi: Basic Writings, tr. Burton Watson 2003

Mozi: Basic Writings, tr. Burton Watson 2003

Xunzi: Basic Writings, tr. Burton Watson 2003

Zhuangzi: Basic Writings, tr. Burton Watson 2003

The Awakening of Faith, Attributed to Aśvaghosha, tr. Yoshito S. Hakeda, introduction by Ryuichi Abe 2005

The Tales of the Heike, tr. Burton Watson, ed. Haruo Shirane 2006

Tales of Moonlight and Rain, by Ueda Akinari, tr. with introduction by Anthony H. Chambers 2007

Traditional Japanese Literature: An Anthology, Beginnings to 1600, ed. Haruo Shirane 2007

The Philosophy of Qi, by Kaibara Ekken, tr. Mary Evelyn Tucker 2007

The Analects of Confucius, tr. Burton Watson 2007

The Art of War: Sun Zi's Military Methods, tr. Victor Mair 2007

One Hundred Poets, One Poem Each: A Translation of the Ogura Hyakunin Isshu, tr. Peter McMillan 2008

Zeami: Performance Notes, tr. Tom Hare 2008

Zongmi on Chan, tr. Jeffrey Lyle Broughton 2009

Scripture of the Lotus Blossom of the Fine Dharma, rev. ed., tr. Leon Hurvitz, preface and introduction by Stephen R. Teiser 2009

Mencius, tr. Irene Bloom, ed. with an introduction by Philip J. Ivanhoe 2009

Clouds Thick, Whereabouts Unknown: Poems by Zen Monks of China, Charles Egan 2010

The Mozi: A Complete Translation, tr. Ian Johnston 2010

The Huainanzi: A Guide to the Theory and Practice of Government in Early Han China, by Liu An, tr. John S. Major, Sarah A. Queen, Andrew Seth Meyer, and Harold D. Roth, with Michael Puett and Judson Murray 2010

The Demon at Agi Bridge and Other Japanese Tales, tr. Burton Watson, ed. with introduction by Haruo Shirane 2011

Haiku Before Haiku: From the Renga Masters to Bashō, tr. with introduction by Steven D. Carter 2011

The Columbia Anthology of Chinese Folk and Popular Literature, ed. Victor H. Mair and Mark Bender 2011

Tamil Love Poetry: The Five Hundred Short Poems of the Aiṅkuṟunūṟu, tr. and ed. Martha Ann Selby 2011

The Teachings of Master Wuzhu: Zen and Religion of No-Religion, by Wendi L. Adamek 2011

The Essential Huainanzi, by Liu An, tr. John S. Major, Sarah A. Queen, Andrew Seth Meyer, and Harold D. Roth 2012

The Dao of the Military: Liu An's Art of War, tr. Andrew Seth Meyer 2012